THE WORLD'S CLASSICS

# THE DECAMERON

GIOVANNI BOCCACCIO (Certaldo 1313–75) was the illegitimate son of a successful businessman who wanted him to become a banker, sending him to Naples for training. Showing no enthusiasm for commerce, he transferred to legal studies, again reluctantly. His vocation was for literature and, from the moment he was free from paternal constraints, he began one of the most adventurous and prolific writing careers of the Middle Ages. His early work is derivative in content though often technically innovative. Back in Florence after a financial crisis, his work turned to more pathetic themes expressed in allegorical writing, and in an innovatory novel. Witnessing the Black Death (1348–9) in Florence, he used the resultant chaos as the background for his most famous work, the *Decameron* (1351?), in which ten young people, fleeing the city, keep their spirits up, and scandal at bay, by telling stories. A stylistic masterpiece defining Italian prose usage right to the present day, the *Decameron* is also a lesson in how to tell stories. Sex, violence, intrigue; humour, generosity, and compassion—all find a place in a rich, controlled narrative. Boccaccio showed that art resides not in the subject matter, which may be ribald or distressing, but in the manner of expressing it. His ten narrators finish their story-telling as unruffled as when they had started. Boccaccio subsequently turned away from fiction, espousing biography, literary criticism, and mythology, gaining a reputation which lasted till the Renaissance.

GUIDO WALDMAN, a publisher's editor by profession, was born at Lausanne in 1932 and educated at Downside School and Brasenose College, Oxford. He is author of a novel and a children's book, editor and part-translator of *The Penguin Book of Italian Short Stories*, and his translations also include Antonio Fogazzaro's *A House Divided* and Ludovico Ariosto's *Orlando Furioso*.

JONATHAN USHER, head of Italian at Edinburgh University, was born in Bangor, N. Wales in 1948, and studied at Reading and London University. He has written numerous articles on Boccaccio, on Dante and modern Italian literature. He is currently preparing a book on Boccaccio.

OXFORD WORLD'S CLASSICS

# THE DECAMERON

GIOVANNI BOCCACCIO (Certaldo 1313–75) was the illegitimate son of a successful businessman who wanted him to become a banker, sending him to Naples for training. Showing no enthusiasm for commerce, he transferred to legal studies, again reluctantly. His vocation was for literature and, from the moment he was free from paternal constraints, he began one of the most adventurous and prolific writing careers of the Middle Ages. His early work is derivative in content though often technically innovative. Back in Florence after a financial crisis, his work turned to more pathetic themes expressed in allegorical writings, and in an innovatory novel. Witnessing the Black Death (1348) in Florence, he used the resultant chaos as the background for his most famous work, the *Decameron* (1353), in which ten young people, fleeing the city, keep their spirits up, and scandal at bay, by telling stories. A stylistic masterpiece defining Italian prose usage right to the present day, the *Decameron* is also a lesson in how to tell stories. Sex, violence, intrigue, humour, generosity, and compassion all find a place in a rich, controlled narrative. Boccaccio showed that art resides not in the subject matter, which may be ribald or distressing, but in the manner of expressing it. His ten narrators finish their story-telling as unsullied as when they had started. Boccaccio subsequently turned away from fiction, to pursue biography, literary criticism, and mythology, gaining a reputation which lasted till the Renaissance.

GUIDO WALDMAN, a publisher's editor by profession, was born at Lausanne in 1932, and educated at Downside School and Brasenose College, Oxford. He is author of a novel and a children's book, editor and part-translator of *The Penguin Book of Italian Short Stories*, and his translations also include Antonio Fogazzaro's *The Patriot* and Ludovico Ariosto's *Orlando Furioso*.

JONATHAN USHER, head of Italian at Edinburgh University, was born in Hampton, Middlesex in 1948 and studied at Reading and London University. He has written numerous articles on Boccaccio, on Dante and modern Italian literature. He is currently preparing a book on Boccaccio.

THE WORLD'S CLASSICS

GIOVANNI BOCCACCIO

# The Decameron

*Translated by*

GUIDO WALDMAN

*Introduction and Notes*

JONATHAN USHER

Oxford New York

OXFORD UNIVERSITY PRESS

1993

*Oxford University Press, Walton Street, Oxford* OX2 6DP
*Oxford New York Toronto*
*Delhi Bombay Calcutta Madras Karachi*
*Kuala Lumpur Singapore Hong Kong Tokyo*
*Nairobi Dar es Salaam Cape Town*
*Melbourne Auckland*
*and associated companies in*
*Berlin Ibadan*

*Oxford is a trade mark of Oxford University Press*



*First published as a World's Classics paperback 1993*



*British Library Cataloguing in Publication Data*
*Data available*

*Library of Congress Cataloging in Publication Data*
*Boccaccio, Giovanni, 1313–1375.*
*[Decamerone. English]*
*The Decameron/Giovanni Boccaccio; translated by Guido Waldman; introduction and notes by Jonathan Usher.*
*p. cm. — (The World's classics)*
*I. Waldman, Guido. II. Usher, Jonathan. III. Title. IV. Series.*
*PQ4272.E5A38 1993 853'.1—dc20 92-32256*

*ISBN 0-19-282712-X*

1 3 5 7 9 10 8 6 4 2

*Typeset by Pure Tech Corporation, Pondicherry, India*
*Printed in Great Britain by*
*BPCC Paperbacks Ltd*
*Aylesbury, Bucks*

# CONTENTS

SECOND DAY

THIRD DAY

# INTRODUCTION

FROM the moment it began circulating amongst the new reading public of the latter half of the fourteenth century, the *Decameron* was recognized as a masterpiece. A group-portrait of the age, a lesson in how to tell stories, proof that the new vernacular could rival Latin as a prose medium, the work had an enormous influence not only in Italy, where Boccaccio is regarded as one of the 'three crowns' (with Dante and Petrarch), but throughout Europe, where both the *Decameron* model of a community of narrators, and the stories themselves, have spawned countless imitators.

The only coolness came from the early humanists, Petrarch included. The mature Boccaccio too, like Petrarch, affected to despise his own Italian writing, calling it trifling. Despite this, even when engaged on the Latin works of his old age, he lovingly rewrote the *Decameron*, making only the most minor of changes, twenty years after its initial conception and in a very different cultural climate.

This ambivalence tells us about Boccaccio's approach to writing. He was unsure of the place he should occupy in the literary canon, feverishly attempting every genre whilst consistently undervaluing his achievements. Even so, he lavished enormous artistic energy on his projects, as if hoping for classic status.

Petrarch teased him about this insecurity, asking whether Boccaccio was content to be number three in the Italian pantheon (after Dante and himself). Petrarch's own sense of cultural self-confidence, and Boccaccio's lack of it, distorted their relationship into one of master and disciple yet, despite Petrarch's superiority as an organized humanist, it was Boccaccio who first recognized the importance of Greek thought and language for the renewal of culture, and promoted Hellenistic studies in Italy.

The origins of Boccaccio's insecurity have been traced by some to his illegitimacy: others have argued that the age in which Boccaccio lived, the 'autumn of the Middle Ages', was one of multiple crises—in banking and commerce; in agricultural and industrial productivity; in political institutions, communal and regional; in religious expression and ecclesiastic government. Culturally, too, the age was transitional, with the monolingual Latin culture of the West challenged by hesitantly emerging national identities and literatures. New social classes were beginning to participate in literary life, both as readers and writers, radically altering perceptions of traditional canons.

There has been lively debate as to whether Boccaccio was the last brilliant representative of this culture on the wane, or one of the first spokesmen of a more modern age. It is more profitable to examine how such an unstable position contributed to the way Boccaccio wrote, and to understand how his ambitions and abilities, originally ill matched, came together in the *Decameron*.

Boccaccio's output was prodigious, and the *Decameron*, though monumental, represents only a fraction of his total *œuvre*. He was prolific in Latin and the vernacular, fiction and non-fiction, verse and prose. The spontaneity and sure touch we regard as the hallmarks of the *Decameron* are actually the fruits of a tentative process whereby Boccaccio absorbed and gradually learnt to control a sprawling culture.

His extraordinarily indiscriminate reading, and the eclectic way he amassed knowledge, contrast starkly with Petrarch's more programmatic approach, with its clear idea of what was and wasn't worth studying. For Boccaccio, everything was worth reading, and he displays none of the cultural snobbery which constipated the early humanists.

His background was not especially conducive to intellectual pursuits (but then neither was Petrarch's or Dante's). His father sent him to school to gain the rudiments of literacy and numeracy essential for commerce. What exposure there was to the classics came from the usual schoolroom anthologies of 'accessible' authors. Some, like Ovid, were to be lifetime favourites.

Boccaccio's move to Naples, with its mixture of professional constraint (bank traineeship) and casual intellectual exposure (contact with the vigorous Neapolitan intelligentsia and access to the magnificent Royal Library) whetted his appetite for study, but provided no formal mental framework, and it was predictable that his subsequent university course in law would be compromised by the distractions of literature. He was as interested in the classics proper—Virgil, Statius, Lucan, the rhetoricians, the historians—as by rambling scientific compendia and medieval romantic fiction.

Overall, he preferred 'middle-brow' Latin culture, with Ovid and Apuleius firm favourites: even 'highbrow' writers such as Virgil tended to be read episodically for purple passages, and not for continuity.

Vernacular culture was also a distraction. Boccaccio's mother-tongue, Tuscan, gave him an incalculable advantage in appreciating the most accomplished lyric verse of the previous generation, and Naples was host to some of the most prestigious names of the Florentine diaspora, including Dante's 'first friend', Cino da Pistoia.

Foremost amongst vernacular inspirations was Dante. Boccaccio's first Italian work, the *Caccia di Diana* (Diana's Hunt) not only responds to a challenge in Dante's *Vita nuova* (New Life), to name in verse the sixty most beautiful ladies of the city, but bravely uses the same *terza rima* Dante had used for the *Comedy*. Dante quotations abound in Boccaccio's subsequent works, and he would later write an influential Dante biography. The very last project Boccaccio undertook in his lifetime was a lecture series on the *Divine Comedy*.

If Dante was the major vernacular influence, there were a host of minor ones, not all of them Italian. Through the Angevin milieu at court he became familiar with the *fabliau* tradition of bawdy French tales, and with French romances. Through the close links between Naples and the Greek world he had indirect access to the still-vigorous Byzantine heritage. Finally, we must remember that medieval culture was predominantly oral, and what better place to swap yarns than a Mediterranean seaport like Naples?

Boccaccio's middle-brow culture cannot be blamed entirely on limited intellectual opportunities. He was instinctively attracted to material which had a vulgar energy, which revelled in showmanship. His favourite authors all had one thing in common: whatever the scope of their material, its organization tended to be cellular. It was articulated in autonomous sequences which allowed the reader to ignore any overarching synthesis. Ovid's *Metamorphoses* is an obvious example, and Apuleius' *Golden Ass* is another. Even medieval digests of astronomy could be read in this way, and Pliny's *Natural Histories* could easily become a game of 'Trivial Pursuits'.

Phenomenal as Boccaccio's reading must have been, it was matched by his hyperactivity as a writer. At first, he wore his culture rather heavily. The early works imitate conventionally prestigious models—*stilnovo* lyric (the new, psychologically sophisticated love poetry introduced by Guinizelli and Cavalcanti and perfected by Dante), allegorical poetry, the prose romance, the martial epic—and there are signs that he was not always in control of his material. Allegory becomes forced or confused; erudite digressions branch out in all directions. Boccaccio's early characters, too, are prone to quote, when in crisis, long lists of literary figures whose afflictions parallel their own.

In a lesser writer such traits might have ensured deserved anonymity, but Boccaccio always had something special to offer. From the start he displayed a finely tuned ear, incorporating other people's styles and voices into his own work with indecent ease. Whilst this ability first appeared as an imitation of other writers, it was later to stand him in good stead when creating directly from life. He became the most accomplished writer of dialogue in Italian until the playwrights of the Renaissance (who plundered him shamelessly).

Though Boccaccio's early work is derivative, often a mere show-case for newly acquired erudition, it is innovative when it comes to style and genre. In verse, his approach to metre was revolutionary: by using strategic mid-line breaks and exaggerated enjambements, along with a decidedly non-canonical vocabulary, he was able to create a fluid medium which, whilst outwardly respecting traditional prosody, became a free form of prose. Conversely, much of his prose, even in the *Decameron*, is couched in camouflaged poetic metres.

In genre, too, he was adventurous: he explored almost all the genres available to his generation (and invented some, like the psychological novel and the symbolic triumph), but he also experimented with 'genre-bending', composing in one genre what had traditionally been subject-matter for another. The *Teseida*, Boccaccio's response to Dante's comment in the *De vulgari eloquentia* (On Eloquence in the Vulgar Tongue) that no Italian had produced a martial epic, rapidly evolves into unashamedly romantic fiction: even the gory battle scenes are just amplified duels between erotic rivals. The *Comedia delle ninfe fiorentine* (Comedy of the Florentine Nymphs), intended as a complex moral allegory, really takes off when the young ladies symbolizing the virtues start relating their love-lives with scabrous enthusiasm.

Gradually, Boccaccio's exploration of his cultural habitat became more methodical. The last two works to be completed before the *Decameron* show discipline, and offer something new in vernacular literature. The *Elegia di madonna Fiammetta* (Elegy of Lady Fiammetta) tells of a seduction and abandonment, but seen, for the first time since Ovid's *Heroides*, from the woman's point of view. The plot is mechanical, but Boccaccio's intimate portrayal of a woman torn between a decent but dull husband and an unreliable but attractive lover is a masterpiece of psychopathic tension. The *Ninfale fiesolano* (Nymphs of Fiesole) is a pastoral myth explaining the origins of Fiesole and the names of tributaries of the Arno. Such aetiological fables are common in medieval literature, but Boccaccio's shepherd and nymph are depicted with a sympathetic realism far removed from the cursory characterization typical of the genre.

If there is a common trait in Boccaccio's pre-*Decameron* works, it is the same phenomenon we have seen in his reading. He is at his best in episodes, in mini-narrations within narrations. Though many of his works are of vast proportions, Boccaccio's imaginative stamina was more suited to shorter forms of composition. Significantly, many of his earlier writings are themselves developments of limited episodes from other writers' large-scale works. Some of Boccaccio's best writing is to be found in digressions and interludes.

Wavering between ambition and a sense of inadequacy, Boccaccio must have been aware of the mismatch. How to combine his competence in small-scale narration with the artistically irresistible prestige of a grand structure? The obvious avenues, the epic and the allegorical poem, had proved difficult to handle, as Boccaccio's seriousness of purpose was apt to let him down. Similarly, in his hands the novel had degenerated into digression (*Filocolo*) or monomania (*Fiammetta*). What was needed was a momentous structure, itself a short form of narration, which could act as a vehicle for dignifying other short narrations. In the *Decameron*, whether by instinct or design, Boccaccio chanced upon the perfect vehicle.

The *Decameron* is the story of ten young people who leave the physical and moral confusion of Florence during the 1348 plague. Seeking refuge in idyllic retreats, they maintain morale by singing songs and telling each other stories. Whilst readers through the centuries have latched on to the individual stories and have been less interested in the framing narrative, we must still ask why Boccaccio bothers with such an elaborate scenario.

His aim was to elevate the novella (unpretentious in his day) into a serious and respectable genre. Dante had attempted a similar cultural nobilitation for the vernacular lyric by enclosing love-poetry within the commentary of the *Vita nuova*. Petrarch's tinkering with the order of the *Canzoniere* reveals a similar quest for status via portentously structured compilation.

Promotion starts with the title: *Decameron* ('Ten Days', in Boccaccio's approximate Greek), imitates *Hexaemeron*, St Ambrose's commentary on the six days of creation in Genesis. Whilst numerically indicative of the ten days of story-telling, the title's suggestion of the Creation (and attendant Fall) cannot be ignored—a theme of inescapable topicality after the calamity of the plague, and a pointer to fiction's own power of regeneration.

The choice of the plague as occasion for restorative story-telling seems counter-productive, and Boccaccio apologizes in his Introduction, saying it was the only way he could relate a positive aftermath. Whilst this ploy follows the topos of an author's humble subservience to events, it is also a candid admission that Boccaccio could find no better way to grace his narrations with a grandiose, providential context.

Perhaps at the back of his mind was a coincidence of opposites. Dante had set the fictional date of his *Comedy* during the Jubilee of 1300, a year promising salvation to humanity, but which represented for the poet a mid-life crisis (born in 1265, Dante had reached half-way to his biblical three-score years and ten). The plague of 1348 not only promised the apparent perdition of humanity, but was also exactly half-way through Boccaccio's canonical life-span.

The subtitle, 'Prince Galehaut', is an overt Dante reference: in *Inferno* V, Francesca blames her surrender to illicit passion on her reading of the episode in the prose *Lancelot* where Galehaut, Lord of the Far Isles, encourages the first kiss between Guinevere and Lancelot. Our modern reading of the Francesca episode is negative: Galehaut, and by inference literature, is a sordid go-between for forbidden liaisons. For Boccaccio, however, Galehaut, like Pandaro in the *Filostrato*, had been a loyal friend who had taken risks to help lovers. The *Decameron*, too, will take risks to console its readers.

This interpretation is confirmed by the Proem, where Boccaccio, grateful for timely help when he was lovesick, says that he is writing the *Decameron* to help others in the same predicament. Gratitude is best repaid to those who are most in need, and Boccaccio, following Ovid, is quick to point out that in passionate predicaments a woman's chances of relief from suffering are more limited by social pressures than a man's. So the *Decameron* is dedicated to women unhappy in love.

Even this gallantry needs careful interpretation. Boccaccio's admission of infatuation for a lady nobler than himself may be less an erotic confession than an oblique reference to his presumptuous courting of literary fame. Boccaccio had, after all, insisted that Petrarch's Laura was a symbol of poetic ambition rather than a flesh-and-blood mistress. Similarly, the dedication to lovelorn ladies merely inverts the traditional appeal to the Muses, where the poet tends to be in trouble and asks the Muses for help. A further blow to Boccaccio's feminist reputation is that, in later life, he was to beg a friend not to let the *Decameron* anywhere near the women of his household for fear of giving them ideas!

The plague description dominates the Introduction. It is one of the high points of medieval writing, combining sweeping vision with sophisticated rhetorical symmetry. Chronicles of great calamities were a traditional literary exercise, and the model for Boccaccio's plague portrait is thought to be a passage from Paulus Diaconus's *History of the Lombards.* Though the urgency of Boccaccio's account gives the impression of a pen artlessly impelled by the pressure of events, the underlying structure tells another story. Even his apology for distressing the reader reinforces parallels with Dante's *Comedy*: the arduousness of the experience will contribute to the intensity of subsequent pleasure, just as Earthly Paradise follows Hell and Purgatory.

The description moves through a series of carefully graded stages, each with a characteristic stylistic register. The opening sequence grandly places the pestilence in the context of human and sacred history. A medieval reader would expect at this point a homily on divine retribution for man's sins, but Boccaccio refuses to elucidate the plague's cause. Instead, he plunges downward, rehearsing the symptoms and evolution of the epidemic in unvarnished language. A brief indication of the alarming contagiousness of the disease is reinforced by an anecdote about its transmission from man to animals. Whilst the tone of this anecdote is fundamentally *mirabile dictu*, its placing alerts us to a series of comparisons between men and beasts which sets the moral agenda for the *Decameron.*

Human reaction to the pestilence varies: some seek refuge in abstinence; others seek solace in excess; nearly all shun the sick, as if societal bonds had finally snapped. This breakdown is exemplified by the uncaring disposal of the dead, the rich being buried without pomp, the poor being heaped into charnel pits. Urban desolation gives way to rural mortality, where humans, once the higher authority, have abdicated, leaving domestic animals to maintain their former routines as if endowed with human reason.

The plague sequence closes with an impassioned rhetorical flourish: where are the luminaries of a once-flourishing society? The plague has carried them away. In what seemed merely a descriptive chronicle of cataclysm, Boccaccio has cunningly undermined our confidence in the moral basis of human behaviour, and has even insinuated doubts about divine intervention. The world has been emptied: it is time for the ten days of a new Genesis.

In contrast to such degradation, the seven lady story-tellers are models of reason and responsibility: they persist in religious observance; they have not abandoned their kinsfolk; they still care about their reputations. Their age and social class are also calculated to provide an idealistic note, as is their number (seven is the sum of the cardinal and theological virtues, and of the liberal arts). Their assumed names, far from protecting real persons, convey an aura of literary continuity, with references to Virgil (Elissa is Dido's other name), Petrarch (Lauretta), *stilnovismo* (Neifile), and Boccaccio himself (Fiammetta, Pampinea, Philomena, Emilia).

Pampinea's proposal to leave Florence is not an attempt to flee death, but a chance to escape the moral contagion of the plague. By forming a microcosm based on reason, the ladies hope to survive ethically unscathed, whatever the clinical outcome. Philomena counters that an exclusively female society is bound to come to grief, and, after a long argument about the propriety of mixed company, they agree to invite men, trusting once again to the protective power of reason. Allegorically, this is a lesson to the reader that even potentially salacious or disreputable subject-matter can be read quite safely, provided the reader is armed with a proper understanding of the literary process.

Like Virgil's providential appearance in *Inferno* I, three suitable men arrive, each enamoured of one of the seven young ladies and related to the other four. Their names, too, are redolent of Boccaccio's previous literary exercises. Despite this preciosity, it is important to note that Boccaccio constitutes his regenerative microcosm through healthy commerce between the sexes, and not via the dead-end of segregated conventualism.

The ten now head for their rural villa. It is a place of extraordinary refinement, calculated, like the descriptions of the company itself, to instil a sense of order plucked from chaos. Physically, it is hardly a stone's throw from the city, but the distance is essentially imaginative. The refuge is a fictional construct, magically summoned like Dianora's garden (X. 5), in which story-telling can be appreciated freely for what it is. Like the garden in the *Roman de la rose*, Boccaccio's blissful bowers are stocked with flora more familiar to the iconographer than the botanist.

Once there, the party legislate their existence, establishing daily routines, schedules for servants, and, most importantly, a rota of leadership. Each narrator is to rule for one day, and the symbol of their reign is to be a laurel wreath, headgear of Apollo, coveted by poets. By this sequential crowning, Boccaccio is hinting that not only the stories themselves but also their ordering and interrelation are matters of artistic ambition, just as Petrarch's *Canzoniere* was to acquire its meaning not from the individual poems, but from their juxtaposition and patterning.

Though the company has other diversions—music, dancing, chess—Pampinea suggests story-telling as a pastime because its pleasures are mutual. Boccaccio alerts his readers to that ideal community not only between narrator and listener, but also between different listeners.

The first day's story-telling has no special theme: fictionally this is because the narrators have had no time to prepare their topics. Rhetorically, however, the free choice is an astute move, offering a sampler of the variety of selective themes later in the book. After this first day the company opt for fixed topics in subsequent sessions. The thematic organization of the different days, and the sub-themes within days, shows both programmed symmetry (Boccaccio's hankering after the grand dimension) and a shrewd grasp of the universals which are the combinative ingredients of story-telling.

The themes, indicated by the rubrics which precede both the days and the individual novellas, progress by oppositions. After the free choice of day one, the second day, as if in response to the impact of the plague, deals with man as the plaything of belatedly benevolent fate. The next day takes this same ingredient, fate, and shows how man can turn it to advantage. The following days, the fourth and fifth, deal with love, first as an overwhelmingly destructive force, and then as a challenge which can be profitably exploited.

The sixth day deals with the power of language to alter the course of events. Symbolically it advertises the analogous role of the Word in fiction, and it is no coincidence that the first story of the day deals with the problematic business of story-telling itself.

The seventh and eighth days explore still further the way in which the course of events can be altered, but this time the stratagems are not exclusively verbal. The seventh day deals with the tricks played by adulterous wives on their husbands. One would expect the eighth, following the oppositional matrix, to deal with husbands deceiving their wives, but Boccaccio is not averse to trickery either. He alters the theme, widening it to include any deceptions in the war between the sexes. The reason for this pattern-change is that Boccaccio found (like Dante describing fraud in the *Malebolge* of the *Inferno*) that deception is a rich narrative vein requiring extensive exploitation.

Barring the tenth novella of each day, which is a free choice anyway, Boccaccio has now maintained subject-discipline for a total of sixty-three stories. The ninth day, however, sees a return to an open topic. Whilst one can agree with the day's queen that it is time for a change, there may be other motives for this patterning. By rounding off symmetrically at nine days, then appending a tenth, Boccaccio is consciously imitating the '9 + 1 = 10' model which informs so much of the *Divine Comedy*. In addition, had he moved from the vulgar atmosphere of infidelity in Day Eight to the august theme of liberality in Day Ten, the transition might have seemed somewhat abrupt. Actually, despite the freedom of the rubric, the ninth day's stories would almost all have fitted happily into the previous two days' disciplines.

Liberality, the tenth day's topic, restores a virtue which the plague had conspicuously diminished. The magnanimous gesture of *noblesse oblige* may well embody those feudal values which are a nostalgic sub-text to much of the *Decameron*, but Boccaccio is principally attracted by the opportunities that liberality, like love, another irrational impulse, offers to the author in search of narrative surprise.

So the one hundred novellas constitute a typological catalogue of story-patterns, combining in different proportions the standard ingredients of character-motivation—fate, passion, idealism. It all sounds highly organized, but this is an illusion fostered by Boccaccio's framing devices—the division of the stories into set 'days'; the use of rubrics to impose meaning; the critical manipulation by narrators who comment on their own stories. For the truth is that the novellas have a life of their own, and joyousiy resist regimentation.

Few novellas were actually composed to order for the *Decameron*. Many derive from other writers and traditions, and of those apparently written by Boccaccio, a number seem to have circulated before he assembled his masterpiece. The greatest achievement of the *Decameron* lies elsewhere, in the telling of stories rather than in their content. The novella of Madonna Oretta (VI. 1) makes exactly this point, with the knight unable to press home the advantage of a basically good story because his narrative technique is disastrous.

What makes Boccaccio a good story-teller? Some things are obvious, others less so. Language is probably the most important element: Italian prose before Boccaccio was a stilted, apologetic affair, with limited vocabulary, stunted syntax, and clumsy rhetoric. Even Dante's prose shows a mind-set formed by the unequal hierarchy between the prestige and mature expressivity of Latin, and the untried uncouthness of the vernacular. The attempts at fictional narrative, such as the anonymous *Novellino* (1280?) or the prose passages in Francesco da Barberino's *Reggimento e costumi di donna* (Rule and Manners of the Lady, 1318–20), were written more in the manner of prompts rather than finished artistic prose. The one place where there was beginning to be a genuine vernacular tradition of sophisticated public story-telling was in church, where the sermon and the *exemplum* often held congregations spellbound with surprisingly secular narratives.

Boccaccio's facility with Italian comes both from his belonging to the next generation, able to digest the experience of the pioneers, and from the fact that his career through the genres of fiction had been overwhelmingly in the vernacular, even in fields traditionally the domain of Latin. This exploration of the Italian language gave Boccaccio a command of expression which no other writer was to match for centuries. When Pietro Bembo, the great Renaissance grammarian, wanted to define exemplary prose in Italian, he could think of no model more accomplished than Boccaccio's.

The flexibility of Boccaccio's language allowed him to range effortlessly from the rotund periods of the Proem, with their elaborate hypotaxis and use of *cursus*, to the pithy exchanges between a shit-smeared Andreuccio and a terrifying pimp in a Naples back alley (II. 5).

Medieval poetics assumed uniform register within a work according to its genre (the 'three styles'). But Boccaccio's register is never fixed at the outset of a novella: instead it changes, often abruptly, as the story progresses. A typical example occurs in the novella of Simona and Pasquino (IV. 7), where Boccaccio veers from the pseudo-academic in the opening section on the theory of love, through grotesque low-comic in the garden love scene and Pasquino's poisoning, to inflated panegyric in the celebration of Simona's reunification in death, ending with a vulgar fling in the account of the funeral.

The intention of such variation is clearly to delight by showing off, but it is also a constant reminder of the power of the story-teller over the story. Boccaccio's flagrant manipulation of language undermines conventional attitudes towards situations: almost invariably a tragic novella will contain a comically disrespectful quip, just as lighter tales may contain examples of the purplest prose. The result is that it is notoriously difficult to tell whether Boccaccio ever means what he says, or whether all content is merely an excuse for stylistic *tours de force*.

When it comes to Boccaccio's narrative technique, there is no one formula which can adequately describe his approach. It is easier to describe what he does not do, and for this there is again no better checklist than the one in the story of Madonna Oretta (VI. 1). It shows a Boccaccio aware, like Horace before him, of the practical craft of story-telling: an author not in awe of abstract theories of composition.

This practical craft manifests itself both in plot and characterization. Whereas both the *novellino* and *exemplum* traditions tended towards unidirectional structures culminating in a 'punchline', Boccaccio's novellas often work by ironic repetitions: things happen twice—but not quite in the same way.

The stories of Simona and Pasquino (IV. 7) and Nastagio degli Onesti (V. 8) are obvious examples, but even the multiple bedding of Alatiel (II. 7) or the sequential 'murder' of Griselda's children can be seen to follow the same pattern.

Such iterative plots not only increase suspense by gradual realization of foreknowledge, they also allow for stylistic variations on a common theme, an exercise dear to medieval theoreticians of poetics, and one which Boccaccio performs with consummate skill. Giving the illusion of drawing out a story, when the novella still sits comfortably within the confines of short-story length, is a playful process: one can sense Boccaccio's wry grin as he stays the hand of a Tancredi out to avenge his daughter's honour (IV. 1) only to proceed to an even more grisly conclusion later.

Boccaccio's characterization is a strange mixture of the medieval and the modern. At the beginning of his novellas he will use formulaic descriptions: 'a noble lady, graced with both beauty and charm, loftiness of spirit and acuteness of mind . . .'. However, such perfunctory concessions to tradition are soon superseded by a characterization based on speech-patterns and action. The characters of Ser Cepperello (I. 1), Brother Cipolla (VI. 10), and Maso del Saggio (VIII. 3) are constructed almost entirely out of what they say. Similarly, we learn more about Lisabetta (IV. 5) from the spine-chilling detail of her pious but desperately improvised beheading of her lover's corpse than we would from some long psychological portrait or interior monologue.

Characterization is, of course, a matter of technique, but there is also the question of choice of characters. Quite a number of characters, from a wide range of backgrounds, are authentically documented: kings like the Lombard Agilulf (III. 2), Guy de Lusignan of Jerusalem and Cyprus (I. 9), Charles I of Anjou (X. 6) lend an air of historicity to the *Decameron*, however much the episodes described in the novellas may be fictions. Local notables like Guido Cavalcanti (VI. 9) and Giotto (VI. 6) give that sense of civic identity and pride still evident in Tuscany to this day; even highwaymen like Ghino di Tacco (X. 2) or lowly wall-painters like Calandrino (VIII. 3, 6; IX. 6) commemorate people who really existed, and contribute, however humbly, to that sense of almost electoral-roll completeness so striking in the *Decameron*.

But alongside these historical figures Boccaccio places another vast category which one might define as pseudo-historical, combining some genuine elements of identity with something which merely sounds genuine. The Rufolo family really was one of the most prominent in Ravello: none of them went by the name of Landolfo (II. 4), though the name is one you might have expected to come across in Campania at the time. Similarly with Paganino da Mare (II. 10), the family is authentic, but the individual has been made up using a first name appropriately characteristic of the Genoa area.

The settings, social milieu, and moral outlook of the *Decameron* have attracted a good deal of critical attention, usually from those who would like to identify Boccaccio's ideological orientation. The fact that women can give as good as they take, that servants can answer back to their masters, that merchants can undertake odysseys as heroic as those of crusaders or pilgrims, that laymen can take on the Inquisition at its own game, has been interpreted as evidence that Boccaccio was a social and moral reformer. Given his penchant for stylistic manipulation and ironic language, it would be unwise to rely too much on such evidence. After all, from a reading of *stilnovo* poetry one might think women were the dominant power in medieval Italian society. Boccaccio was of course writing fiction, and was attracted to subversive situations precisely because they were out of the ordinary. The female characters of the novellas may indeed be able to answer back, and the servants in the stories may temporarily achieve parity with their masters, but in the frame narrative which surrounds the novellas the ladies have to be extremely vigilant about their reputations, and the servants are brutally silenced if they step out of line.

If there is one area, however, in which the *Decameron* is revolutionary, it is in its noticeably non-spiritual dimension. Boccaccio was no atheist: the climax of the *Filocolo* is an account of religious conversion; the *Amorosa visione* (Vision of Love) is a theological review of history. Indeed, a decade after writing the *Decameron* Boccaccio took holy orders, apparently in all sincerity. Even the story-tellers of the *Decameron* begin and end their adventure in church, and interrupt their narrations to accommodate religious observance.

Non-spirituality has more to do with attitude than belief. Just as the description of the plague avoids conclusions about a divine role, so the same resolutely secular horizon is maintained in the individual novellas. Even when dealing with religious practices, Boccaccio limits his examination to the earthly consequences arising from them. If anything, this is a sign that religious attitudes and customs are so firmly anchored in his world-view that he, like many of his contemporaries, takes them for granted. So, contrary to the opinion of his Counter-Reformation censors, Boccaccio was not being irreligious: he just assumed that faith, by its very existence, was fair game in fiction, just like other 'facts of life' or motivations such as love or fate.

Indeed, love and fate, seen in this secular light, have to be understood in a radically different way. Fate is no longer the instrument of a divine agency, but rather a narrative expedient capable of turning stories in unexpected directions, and providing timely endings to novellas threatening to outgrow their allotted space. Love, too, changes. For writers such as Dante, secular love was a distraction from a greater good, namely God. Attaching excessive importance to earthly passion was a misuse of the intellect whose final cause was to love its Maker. Boccaccio's earthly love not only frees itself from such prejudices, it also elevates itself into a natural law which none can resist, for there is no reason at all to resist it. It goes without saying that the new-found status of fate and love conferred an immense advantage when it came to realizing powerful plot-lines.

Though Boccaccio's secularity and mischievous attitude towards social conventions suggest an author impatient with external disciplines and willing to contravene codes, the *Decameron*'s main achievement is in creating a harmonious sense of order out of a naturally anarchic raw material, human life. Not for nothing does the company end up at the beginning of Day Nine, after days of story-telling under Apollonian laurels, crowning itself with garlands of oak-leaves, attributes of a temperate, balanced Jupiter. For the ten have passed the ultimate test: that of narrating, and listening to, potentially corrupting material whilst yet remaining chaste.

If the story-tellers demonstrate this ability by example, Boccaccio is also at pains to point it out explicitly to his readers. In the Proem, in the Introduction to Day Four, and in the Author's Conclusion, he counters various charges that his material might corrupt or deprave. This spirited self-defence is the first manifesto of artist's freedom in modern European literature and ranks in critical importance alongside Petrarch's famous defence of poetry in his *Invective contra Medicum* (Invectives against a Certain Doctor, *c.*1355).

Boccaccio's is a lesson in how to live vicariously through literature: virtue resides in attitude and not in content. The freedom to write about absolutely anything, which Boccaccio gives himself in the *Decameron*, is bought at the cost of moral control of the process of reception. The frame, with its codified comportment of meals, ablutions, songs, and stories, is the outward manifestation of this compact, but its writ extends to the novellas themselves, for despite all their challenges to moral, social, and literary beliefs, they invariably end up re-establishing an equilibrium, whether a return to the *status quo* or a refinement of existing justice. The narrators prove this by their own example, enjoying the exceptional privilege of their rural sojourn, but returning unchanged to a pestilential Florence at the end. Boccaccio flaunts his power as narrator by taking institutions and characters to the brink, only to retrieve them with an adroit flourish of the pen.

It is this civilized moral separation between content and narrative function which provides the basic unity of the *Decameron*. It is an adult book not because it contains material unfettered by social constraints, but because it is able to address the confusion of the real world from the stable vantage-point of art. The *Decameron* is escapist not because the ten young people head for the hills, ignoring the suffering in Florence below, but because by having them tell stories properly, and listen to them correctly, Boccaccio proves that one can temporarily transcend the contingent. Only temporarily, though: the *Decameron*, by its title, advertises its parallels with the Creation, but if we follow through the biblical account, we see that man's sojourn in the Garden of Eden is followed by the Fall. Boccaccio's ten young narrators, having loitered in the secular Eden of fiction, are obliged to re-descend to Florence and all its attendant travails, just as Boccaccio's reader, running out of stories, reluctantly finds himself obliged to close the book.

So, paradoxically, Boccaccio achieves his grand dimension not through the weighty dignity of his content, like Virgil or Dante, but through a constant writerly respect for form as a creative principle. In this sense he is nearer to a medieval Ovid, except that the *Decameron*'s transformations take place without the helping hand of active divinities. Boccaccio has brought story-telling down to earth, like Prometheus bringing fire to mankind, and it is a sublime and dangerous gift, not to be trifled with. The protean power of the individual novellas makes the interpretative screen of the *Decameron*'s frame essential for the reader. Only through the order of an ideal cultural discipline can one be fully aware of the bewildering chaos of narrative possibilities. Like the institutions and characters he portrays, Boccaccio has taken his readers to the brink, only to retrieve them by an adroit flourish of the pen.

# TRANSLATOR'S NOTE

BOCCACCIO'S avowed purpose in writing these stories was to provide solace and entertainment, and my principal aim in translating them for the English-speaking reader has been to convey the pleasure and the vigour of good story-telling. Many of the stories raised eyebrows at the time they were first published, and in his Afterword (p. 685) the author artlessly advises his modest lady readers to look at the heading that precedes each story: it comprises a detailed synopsis so that they may skip any tale they think liable to make them blush. Readers today, though, whatever their susceptibilities, usually take it amiss if a publisher or reviewer gives away the tale's ending before they have started reading it. I have therefore in certain cases rewritten the story's *heading* to preserve the element of surprise; I believe the general reader will be grateful, but I must crave the indulgence of the student if those headings have not been translated with the rigorous fidelity I have sought to bring to the stories themselves.

G.W.

*June 1992*

# SELECT BIBLIOGRAPHY

The critical edition of the original Italian text, based on the Hamilton 90 MS, established by V. Branca for the Accademia della Crusca (1976), is available in its most convenient form in volume IV of *Tutte le opere di Giovanni Boccaccio*, ed. V. Branca (Milan, Mondadori, 1976).

### *Bibliography*

V. Branca, *Linee di una storia della critica al 'Decameron' con bibliografia boccaccesca completamente aggiornata* (Rome, Dante Alighieri, 1939)—covers material up to the late 1930s; E. Esposito, *Boccacciana: Bibliografia delle edizioni e degli scritti critici (*1939–1974), (Ravenna, Longo, 1976)—continues Branca to the 1970s. The regular 'Bollettino bibliografico' in the journal *Studi sul Boccaccio* 1 (1963– ) is useful because it also covers items whose titles might not always indicate their relevance to Boccaccio. The '*Due-* and *Trecento* II' section of the bibliographical review *The Year's Work in Modern Language Studies* provides brief but pithy coverage of books and articles on Boccaccio, useful in that they are more up to date than the entries in *Studi sul Boccaccio*.

### *Selected Individual Studies in English Covering the* Decameron


Almansi, G., *The Writer as Liar: Narrative Technique in the Decameron* (London and Boston, Routledge & Kegan Paul, 1975)—highly stimulating, if somewhat eccentric reading of key psycho-sexual imagery in the *Decameron*.

Barolini, T., 'Giovanni Boccaccio', in W. T. H. Jackson (ed.) *European Writers: The Middle Ages and the Renaissance*, ii. (New York, Scribners), 509–34—succinct and informative survey of the 'life and works', which nevertheless manages to squeeze in some striking perceptions on the moral ordering of the *Decameron*.

Bergin, T. G., *Boccaccio* (New York, Viking, 1981)—straightforward, dependable introduction to the 'man and works'.

Branca, V., *Boccaccio: The Man and his Works*, trans. Richard Monges (New York, New York University Press, 1976)—translation of parts of Branca's classic *Profilo biografico* and *Boccaccio medievale*.

Cottino Jones, M., *An Anatomy of Boccaccio's Style* (Naples, Cymba, 1968)—jargon-ridden but useful stylistic analysis of Boccaccio's linguistic register in *Decameron* I. 1; II. 2; VI. 4; IV. 2; IV. 9.

—— *Order from Chaos: Social and Aesthetic Harmonies in Boccaccio's Decameron* (Washington, DC, University Press of America, 1982)—looks for 'deep structures' in the *Decameron*: stimulating, but needs to be read with caution.

Hastings, R., *Nature and Reason in the Decameron* (Manchester, Manchester University Press, 1975)—first in a long line of books trying to identify the moral underpinnings of Boccaccio's fiction.

Hollander, R., *Boccaccio's Two Venuses* (New York, Columbia University Press, 1977)—a more sophisticated examination of Boccaccio's bipolar ethics.

Kirkham, V., 'Boccaccio's Dedication to Women in Love', in *Renaissance Studies in Honor of Craig Hugh Smyth*, i. (Florence, Giunti Barbera, 1985), 333–43—short, but central to the understanding of one of the major puzzles of the *Decameron* (see also Smarr, below).

Lee, A. C., *The Decameron: Its Sources and Analogues* (London, 1909)—dated but still useful catalogue both of Boccaccio's sources and of the influences he has had on other authors. More up-to-date information, for Italian readers, can be found in the introductions to each novella in Branca's edition of the Decameron (Turin, Einaudi, 1987).

McWilliam, G. H., Translator's Introduction to Boccaccio, *The Decameron*, (Harmondsworth, Penguin, 1972), 21–43—spirited yet serious examination of the often less-than glorious history of English translations of the *Decameron*.

Marcus, M., *An Allegory of Form: Literary Self-Consciousness in the Decameron* (Saratoga, 1979)—examines Boccaccio's attitudes towards his own text: 'meta-literary' approach now somewhat dated, but worth reading for insights into individual novellas.

Marino, L., *The Decameron Cornice: Allusion, Allegory and Iconology* (Ravenna, Longo, 1979)—good straightforward literary job on the framing narrative, but not so convincing about possible symbolic values enshrined in the frame characters.

Mazzotta, G., *The World at Play in Boccaccio's Decameron* (Princeton, Princeton University Press, 1986)—scintillating, exceptionally well-informed essays showing how Boccaccio ruthlessly subverts social, religious, medical, literary, and legal codes.

O'Cuilleanain, C., *Religion and the Clergy in Boccaccio's Decameron* (Rome, Edizioni di storia e letteratura, 1984)—gives a detailed picture of just how imbued Boccaccio's apparently 'lay' world is with religious imagery and thought-patterns.

Potter, J. H., *Five Frames for the Decameron: Communication and Social Systems in the Cornice* (Princeton, Princeton University Press, 1982)—anthropological examination of the frame characters' ritual, and the way the narratives proper are kept only for the initiates: a good deal more eccentric than Marino.

Scaglione, A. D., *Nature and Love in the Late Middle Ages: An Essay on the Cultural Context of the Decameron* (Berkeley and Los Angeles, University of California Press, 1963)—looks at the inherent struggles between passions and institutions, and at how Boccaccio understood the mediating role of morality as a conciliation between nature and society.

Smarr, J. L., *Boccaccio and Fiammetta: The Narrator as Lover* (Urbana and Chicago, University of Illinois Press, 1986)—serious attempt to look at the way Boccaccio's various addressees, mostly female, as in the *Decameron*, represent a veiled internal debate on the limits of an author's control of his readership: repays close reading.

Wallace, D., *Boccaccio: Decameron* (Cambridge, Cambridge University Press, 1991)—brief introduction aiming to show how Boccaccio can be read as a sign of his times.

# A CHRONOLOGY OF GIOVANNI BOCCACCIO

1313 Born illegitimate in Certaldo: brought up by businessman father who had worked in Paris and was now resident in Florence, where Boccaccio went to school

1327 Joins father in Naples, working in Bardi bank, the main financiers of the Angevin monarchy. Banking apprenticeship gratefully abandoned after three years in favour of university course in law. Father's return to Paris allows Boccaccio to neglect law in favour of literature

1334 Probable date of *Caccia di Diana* (Diana's Hunt), long venatory poem celebrating Neapolitan beauties in a confused but lively allegory

1336–8 Probable date of *Filocolo*, meandering prose romance dealing with pagan Florio's desperate search for his Christian sweetheart Biancifiore. Some aspects will be incorporated later into the *Decameron*

1339 Composition of *Filostrato*, poem in octaves dealing with Trojan hero Troiolo's anguish when his lover Criseida crosses over to the Greek camp during siege of Troy

1339–41 Composition of *Teseida*, supposedly first epic war poem in Italian, but in practice yet another romantic adventure, as Arcita and Palemon, backed by various gods and mortals, compete for the hand of the Amazon princess Emilia

1340–1 Reluctant return to Florence in the wake of banking crisis in Naples. Period of psychological as well as financial depression

1341–2 Composition of *Comedia delle ninfe fiorentine*, allegorical work celebrating the purificatory powers of love via a series of erotic confessions

1342 Composition of *Amorosa visione*, Dantesque vision in which the triumphs of Fame, Wealth, Love, Fate, and Death are depicted. Probable date of *De vita et moribus domini Francisci Petracchi* (On the Life and Habits of . . . Petrarch), written eight years before meeting the poet in the flesh

1343–4 Probable date of *Elegia di madonna Fiammetta* (Elegy of Lady Fiammetta), long first-person prose narrative describing a married woman's torment at being jilted by her lover

1344–6 Composition of *Ninfale fiesolano* (Nymphs of Fiesole), pastoral poem in octaves, relating, through the love of the shepherd Africo for the nymph Mensola and the birth of their soon-to-be orphaned son Pruneo, the origin of the city of Fiesole and the names of tributaries of the Arno

1345–8 Away from Florence, first at Ravenna, then at Forlì. Translates third and fourth Decades of Livy's *History of Rome*, an important milestone in Boccaccio's stylistic development

1348 Witnesses Black Death at first hand in Florence

1349 Father dies. Boccaccio starts work on *Decameron*

1350 Sent to Ravenna to present Florentine pension to Dante's daughter. Meets Petrarch for the first time in Florence

1351 Political and diplomatic duties for Florentine government, including informing Petrarch of the revocation of the confiscation order passed against his father and of the offer of a chair at Florence University. Writes first draft of *Trattatello in laude di Dante* (Little Treatise in Praise of Dante), an influential biography. Finishes first draft of *Decameron*

1352 Ambassador to the court of Ludwig of Bavaria

1353–5 Various journeys (Ravenna; Avignon; Naples, from where he makes important discoveries of classical texts at Monte Cassino). Towards the end of this period (though others place dating around 1365–6), he writes misogynist *Corbaccio* in which a lover is appraised of a widow's faults by the ghost of the husband

1355–7 Begins a series of encyclopaedic works in Latin: *De montibus, silvis, fontibus, lacubus, fluminibus, stagnis seu paludibus et de nominibus maris liber* (Book of Mountains, Woods, Springs, Lakes, Rivers, Bogs or Marshes, and Names of the Sea) is an inventory of classical literary toponymy rather than a geographical treatise

1359 Promotes the founding of the first chair of Greek at Florence University

| | |
|---|---|
| 1360 | Finishes first drafts of two more erudite Latin works: *Genealogia deorum gentilium* (Genealogies of the Pagan Gods) is a comprehensive mythological dictionary in fifteen books laid out according to the family trees of the pagan gods. It was to remain a standard textbook until the nineteenth century. *De casibus virorum illustrium* (On the Misfortunes of Famous Men) is an anti-triumph in which the souls of famous men explain the pitfalls and transience of worldly achievements. Obtains papal dispensation to take holy orders (illegitimacy had been a bar). Suffers from being identified as friendly with the leaders of the failed coup in Florence |
| 1361 | Leaves Florence for Certaldo. Undergoes a religious crisis, and is comforted by Petrarch. Begins *De mulieribus claris* (Of Famous Women), moralistic biographies |
| 1362 | Fails to find employment in Naples |
| 1363 | Stays with Petrarch in Venice |
| 1365 | Political changes in Florence mean that Boccaccio is rehabilitated along with other suspects of the 1360 coup |
| 1370–1 | Revision of the *Decameron* |
| 1373 | Revision of *De casibus* and *Genealogia* |
| 1373–4 | Delivers first ever public lectures on Dante's *Comedy*, but forced by ill health to stop at *Inferno* XVII |
| 1374 | Death of Petrarch |
| 1375 | Boccaccio dies in Certaldo |

# THE DECAMERON

*Here begins the book called* Decameron, *known also as the* Book of Prince Galehaut,* *comprising one hundred stories told in the course of ten days by seven ladies and three young men.*

## AUTHOR'S FOREWORD

It is inherently human to show pity to those who are afflicted; it is a quality that becomes any person, but most particularly is it required of those who have stood in need of consolation and have obtained it from others; now if ever there was a man who craved pity or valued it or rejoiced in it, that man was I. From my tenderest youth until today I have been aflame with love, with the loftiest and most noble love: maybe it has far exceeded anything suited to my inferior condition, speaking for myself, although persons of discretion have commended me for it and formed an undeservedly high opinion of me once they have been apprised of it. This love has, none the less, proved wellnigh unendurable, not because my beloved has rebuffed me—far from it—but because my disordered appetite has ignited in my heart an uncontrollable fire which has refused to leave me satisfied with moderate expectations but has caused me constant and quite needless vexation. In this unhappy state I derived so much refreshment from pleasant conversation with friends and their admirable support, I cannot doubt but that if I'm still alive it is thanks to them. My love, then, was passionate beyond all measure; no amount of good resolutions, wiser counsels, blatant humiliations, no conceivable risks had ever been able to destroy or temper it, until eventually, as it pleased Him who is infinite but has imposed on everything here below the inflexible law of transience, it began to wane of its own accord. Now all that survives of it in my heart is the joy it is inclined to afford to those who do not launch out too far across its dark waters. Thus all the pain of it has now been remitted and I feel that what was once a burden has become a pleasure.

Well, my sorrows may be at an end, but this has not made me forgetful of past favours accorded me by persons who could not bear to see me suffer, such were their kindly feelings towards me: I do believe that nothing short of death will ever erase the memory. And as gratitude is in my view the most commendable of virtues, and its opposite a crying shame, to avoid appearing ungrateful now that I can consider myself a free man again, I have decided to discharge my obligation, within the limits of my competence, by offering some pleasant distraction to those in need of it—even if not to those who came to my support, for conceivably by good management (or good luck) they can do without it. True enough, what I am to provide may be (and surely is) only the tiniest crumb of comfort to those in distress; none the less I feel it should be offered where the need appears the greatest, because that way it will be all the more useful and will prove all the more welcome.

And who is going to deny that this offering, such as it is, should properly be devoted to the fair sex very much in preference to the men? It is women who timorously and bashfully conceal Love's flame within their tender breasts; and those who have had experience of it know well enough how much harder it is to control the suppressed than the open flame. Moreover, circumscribed as women are by whatever it is their fathers and mothers, their brothers, their husbands desire or require of them, they spend most of their time within the narrow confines of their bedchambers; here they sit in relative idleness, torn between yes and no as they brood on all manner of things, not all of which can procure them unalloyed happiness. And if Love's craving leaves their thoughts tinged with sadness, they are condemned to remain gloomy unless such thoughts are driven out by some fresh distraction. Besides which women have anyway far less endurance than men. Now we have only to look to see that men in love meet with nothing of this kind. If a man is down in the dumps or out of sorts, he has any number of ways to banish his cares or make them tolerable: he can go out and about at will, he can hear and see all sorts of things, he can go hawking and hunting, he can fish or ride, gamble or pursue his business interests. The effect of such activities will be to improve his spirits to a greater or lesser degree and stave off depression for a while at any rate, after which somehow or other he obtains comfort or else the problem recedes.

Now since Fortune has tended to be at her most niggardly in that one quarter where strength has proved the most defective, as is evident in the gentle sex, I will to some degree make amends for her sin: to afford assistance and refuge to women in love—the rest have all they want in their needles, their spools and spindles—I propose to tell a hundred tales (or fables or parables or stories or what you will). They were narrated—as will transpire—in the course of ten days by a goodly company of seven ladies and three young men which assembled during the last incidence of the plague. There will also be a few songs which the aforementioned ladies sang for their pleasure. The stories will portray the happy and hapless fortunes of love and other hazards of chance, whether these occurred in our day or in olden times. And the womenfolk to whom I have been alluding will be able, as they read them, to derive entertainment from the amusing events there described and, equally, helpful advice, for they will contrive to grasp what is to be avoided and what to pursue—none of which will take effect (so I believe) without raising their spirits. And if, God willing, spirits *are* raised, let the ladies give thanks to Love: by relieving me of his bonds, he has permitted me to attend to their pleasure.

*Here begins the first day of the* Decameron, *wherein the Author sets forth the occasion that brought together for conversation the persons shortly to be described. Under the reign of Pampinea, the topic for story-telling is at the choice of each person.*

Every time I stop to consider your natural inclination to pity, most gracious ladies, I recognize that you will find the opening of this present work abhorrent and distressing; for so is the painful recapitulation of the recent deadly plague, which occasioned hardship and grief to everyone who witnessed it or had some experience of it, and which marks the introduction of my work. I should be sorry, however, if you let this discourage you from reading on, as if to do so were to condemn you to unremitting sighs and tears. You are to look upon this grim opening as travellers on foot confront a steep, rugged mountain: beyond it lies a most enchanting plain which they appreciate all the more for having toiled up and down the mountain first. And just as sorrow will come to displace the most abundant happiness, so will the arrival of joy put paid to sorrow. This brief affliction (I call it brief for it is contained in not all that many letters) will quickly give place to the sweet relief already promised you: were I not to mention it, you might perhaps never have expected it after an opening such as this. The fact is, had I been able to find some suitable alternative path by which to bring you to where I want, other than along this steep one, I should willingly have done so; but as I could not have explained the reasons underlying what you are about to read unless I broached this matter of the plague, I find myself virtually obliged to write about it.

The era of the fruitful Incarnation of the Son of God had arrived at the year 1348 when the deadly plague reached the noble city of Florence, of all Italian cities the most excellent. Whether it was owing to the action of the heavenly bodies or whether, because of our iniquities, it was visited upon us mortals for our correction by the righteous anger of God, this pestilence, which had started some years earlier in the Orient, where it had robbed countless people of their lives, moved without pause from one region to the next until it spread tragically into the West. It was proof against all human providence and remedies, such as the appointment of officials to the task of ridding the city of much refuse, the banning of sick visitors from outside, and a good number of sanitary ordinances; equally unavailing were the humble petitions offered to the Lord by pious souls not once but countless times, whether in the course of processions or otherwise. As the said year turned to spring, the plague began quite prodigiously to display its harrowing effects. Here it did not develop as it had done in the East, where death was inevitable in anyone whose symptoms were a loss of blood through the nose. Its first sign here in both men and women was a swelling in the groin or beneath the armpit, growing sometimes in the shape of a simple apple, sometimes in that of an egg, more or less: a bubo was the name commonly given to such a swelling. Before long this deadly bubo would begin to spread indifferently from these points to crop up all over; the symptoms would develop then into dark or livid patches that many people found appearing on their arms or thighs or elsewhere; these were large and well separated in some cases, while in others, they were a crowd of tiny spots. And just as the bubo had been, and continued to be, a sure indication of fatal disease, so were these blotches for those on whom they appeared. No physician's prescriptions, no medicine seemed of the slightest benefit as a cure for this disease. In addition to those trained in medicine, the number of men and women who claimed to be physicians without having studied the subject at all grew immensely; however, whether it was that the nature of the malady would not permit it, or because doctors were unable to discover its origins and therefore could not apply the proper remedy, not only did few people recover but indeed nearly all the sick would succumb within three days of the above-mentioned symptoms' first appearance; some died sooner, some later, and the majority with no fever, nothing.

And the plague gathered strength as it was transmitted from the sick to the healthy through normal intercourse, just as fire catches on to any dry or greasy object placed too close to it. Nor did the trouble stop there: not only did the healthy incur the disease and with it the prevailing mortality by talking to or keeping company with the sick—they had only to touch the clothing or anything else that had come into contact with or been used by the sick and the plague evidently was passed to the one who handled those things. You will be quite amazed by what I am about to tell you: were it not that many people witnessed it and I saw it with my own eyes, I would never have dared believe it, still less set it down in writing, even if I had had it on the most reliable authority. So potent was the contagion as it was passed on that it was transmitted not only between one person and the next: many a time it quite clearly went further than that, and if some animal other than a human touched an object belonging to a person who was sick or had died of the plague, the animal was not merely infected with it but fell dead in no time at all. As I have just mentioned, I saw this for myself one day in particular: the rags of a pauper who had died of the plague had been tossed out into the street and two pigs happened upon them; they nosed about them with their snouts, as pigs do, then took them in their jaws and shook them this way and that; it was not long before they fell into convulsions, as if they had swallowed poison, and then dropped dead on top of the rags they had so haplessly snatched up.

This sort of thing, as well as many another that was similar to it if not worse, produced in the survivors all manner of terrors and suspicions all tending to the same solution, and a very heartless one it was: they would keep their distance from the plague-victims, and from their chattels too, thus hoping to preserve their own skins. There were some who inclined to the view that if they followed a temperate life-style and eschewed all extravagance they should be well able to keep such an epidemic at bay. So they would form into a group and withdraw on their own to closet themselves in a house free of all plague-victims; here they would enjoy the good life, partaking of the daintiest fare and the choicest of wines—all in the strictest moderation—and shunning all debauchery; they would refrain from speaking to anyone or from gleaning any news from outside that related to deaths or plague-victims—rather did they bask in music and such other pleasures as were at their disposal. Others found the contrary view more enticing, that the surest remedy to a disease of this order was to drink their fill, have a good time, sing to their hearts' content, live it up, give free rein to their appetites—and make light of all that was going on. This was their message, this their practice so far as they were able; day and night would find them in one tavern or another, soaking up the booze like sponges, and carousing all the more in other people's houses the moment word got out that that's where the fun was to be had. This was easy enough to do because everyone had let his property go, just as he had let himself go, as if there was to be no tomorrow. Most houses therefore lay open to all comers, and people would walk in off the streets and make themselves at home just as if they owned the place. And while they pursued this brutish behaviour they still took every care to avoid all contact with the sick.

Now with our city in such a sorry state, the laws of God and men had lost their authority and fallen into disrespect in the absence of magistrates to see them enforced, for they, like everyone else, had either succumbed to the plague or lay sick, or else had been deprived of their minions to the point where they were powerless. This left everyone free to do precisely as he pleased. There were many others who adhered to a middle way between these two, neither following the frugal regimen of the first group nor letting themselves go in the drunken, dissolute life-style of the second. They partook of their fill but no more and, instead of shutting themselves away, they would go about holding flowers to their noses or fragrant herbs, or spices of various kinds, in the belief that such aromas worked wonders for the brain (the seat of health), for the atmosphere was charged with the stench of corpses, it reeked of sickness and medication. Others there were who were totally ruthless and no doubt chose the safest option: there was in their view no remedy to equal that of giving the plague a very wide berth. On this premise any number of men and women deserted their city and with it their homes and neighbourhoods, their families and possessions, heedless of anything but their own skins, and made for other people's houses or for their country estates at any rate, as though the wrath of God, in visiting the plague on men to punish their iniquity, was never going to reach out to where *they* were; as though it was meant to harry only those remaining within their city walls, as though not a soul was destined to remain alive in the city, as though its last hour had come.

And even if not all of them died who clung to these various persuasions, not all of them lived either; in each of these groups many fell sick, here, there, and everywhere, and mindful of the example these people had given when they were still in good health, those whose health remained sound left them to languish unattended. One citizen avoided the next, there was scarcely a man who would take care of his neighbour, kinsmen would seldom if ever call on each other, and even then would keep their distance—but this was not all: men and women alike were possessed by such a visceral terror of this scourge that a man would desert his own brother, uncle would forsake his nephew, sister her brother, and often a wife her husband. What is more, believe it or not, mothers and fathers would avoid visiting and tending their children, they would virtually disown them. Therefore those who fell sick—and they were a number beyond counting, of either sex—had no recourse beyond the charity of their friends (the few they had) or the cupidity of their servants: these were few and far between, even though they were recruited with absurdly inflated wages, and comprised men and women of the commonest sort, for the most part totally untrained, whose ministrations amounted to little more than handing the patient such objects as he requested or watching him die. Quite often in the course of his duties the servant lost his life along with his wages. Now this desertion of the sick by their neighbours, their families and friends, and the scarcity of servants, led to a practice hitherto unheard of: when a woman fell ill, she could be the neatest, prettiest, most refined of ladies, but she made no bones about being attended by a male, any male, never mind his age, and displaying to him any part of her anatomy quite without embarrassment, just as she would do with another of her sex, if her invalid condition required it. Conceivably this might have occasioned a certain lapse from the path of virtue among those women who subsequently recovered their health. At all events many people succumbed who might have pulled through had they obtained help. In the absence of the sort of ministrations the sick required but could not obtain, and as the pestilence continued unabating, the number of people who died in the city night and day was impossible to credit on hearsay, let alone on witnessing it. Thus the survivors were virtually forced to engage in practices totally at variance with the traditional Florentine way of life.

It had been the custom—as we see it is today—for the female relatives and neighbours to assemble in the house of the deceased and join with his nearest and dearest in mourning over him; outside the house the menfolk would foregather—the dead man's kinsmen and neighbours and a great number of townsmen—while such clergy as suited the man's social standing would arrive; he would be carried on the shoulders of his peers to the church he had chosen before his death, with all the funeral rites of candles and dirges. Most if not all of these practices were suspended as the plague's ravages became more ruthless, only to be superseded by what was hitherto unheard of: not merely did many people die bereft of their attendant feminine company, all too many passed away without so much as a single witness. Barely a handful were accorded the benefit of seeing their dear ones in floods of compassionate tears: far from it, the new order called for quips and jollity more suited to a festive gathering. The womenfolk had largely suppressed their natural pity and become well practised in this new frivolity to assure their own survival. Seldom were there more than ten or a dozen neighbours to escort the body of the deceased to church. Nor would the corpse be borne on the shoulders of prominent and distinguished citizens: the bier would be taken in charge by a tribe of pallbearers, people of the commonest sort who liked to call themselves undertakers and who fulfilled the function against payment in cash. They would bend their hastening steps, not to the church appointed by the deceased before his death, but to the nearest one, more often than not, preceded by maybe a half-dozen clerics holding the odd candle—sometimes with none at all. With the help of the pallbearers they would drop the corpse into the nearest available tomb that had space, without too much effort being wasted on a lengthy or solemn requiem. If you examined the situation of the common people, and even that of much of the middle class, it looked a great deal bleaker still: they stayed at home for the most part, whether it was hope or sheer poverty that kept them there, and caught the plague by the thousand right there in their neighbourhood, day after day; in the absence of any help at all, paid or otherwise, they were virtually all beyond saving. Many there were who passed away in the street, by day as by night, while scores of those who died indoors only made their neighbours aware of their decease by the stench of their decaying corpses; the whole city was full of these and others dying all over the place.

Neighbours tended all to follow the same procedure, motivated as they were by fear of being tainted by the corpses no less than by kindness towards the dead. With the aid of bearers if they could find any, otherwise on their own, they would carry the corpses into the street and lay them down outside the front door; anyone who took a turn in the street, in the morning especially, would have noticed any number of them. Then they would send for coffins (unless these proved unobtainable, in which case planks would have to serve); and on more than one occasion a single bier would be loaded with two or three corpses—it happened frequently, and you could have counted a good number that bore away wife and husband, or two or three brothers, or father and son, and so on. There were countless occasions, too, when a couple of priests would go with a crucifix to fetch somebody only to find that three or four groups of pallbearers had fallen in behind them with their biers, so that whereas the priests were expecting to have one deceased person to bury, they might find themselves with half a dozen or more. Which is not to suggest that these obsequies were attended by any tears, any display or candles, any company: things had reached the point where the dying received no more consideration than the odd goat would today. What was inescapably apparent was that if the occasional minor disaster that occurs in the normal course had failed to teach patience to the wise, the sheer scale of the prevailing evil had taught even the simplest soul a degree of placid resignation.

As there was not sufficient consecrated ground in which to bury the vast number of corpses that arrived at every church day after day and practically hour by hour, least of all while any effort had been made to give each person his own burial plot in accordance with age-old custom, enormous pits were dug in the graveyards, once saturation point had been reached, and the new arrivals were dropped into these by the hundred; here they were packed in layers, the way goods are stowed in a ship's hold, and each layer would get a thin covering of earth until the pit was filled up.

Before I go into yet more detail about the afflictions our city underwent in those days, I should only add that if the townsfolk were having such a ghastly time of it, the neighbouring countryfolk were spared none of the rigours. To say nothing of the market-towns, which were like the city if on a smaller scale, in the remote villages and out in the fields the labourers, poor penniless wretches, and their households died like brute beasts rather than human beings; night and day, with never a doctor to attend them, no sort of domestic help, they would pass away, some indoors, others out on the roads or among their crops. As a result they, like the townsfolk, became feckless in their habits, neglecting their affairs and their possessions; indeed, far from encouraging their animals, their fields, their earlier labours to bear fruit, they all bent their best efforts to dissipating whatever came to hand, as though they were simply awaiting the day on which they could see they were going to die. Which is why the oxen, the donkeys, the sheep and goats, the pigs and hens, even the faithful hounds were driven off and went wandering at leisure through the fields where the harvest stood abandoned, not gleaned, not gathered in. Many of them behaved like perfectly rational beings, browsing to their hearts' content all day and at nightfall returning replete to their quarters without any herdsmen in attendance.

Leaving the countryside and returning to the city, what more is there to say but that, what with the inordinate wrath of Heaven and doubtless also to some extent the cruelty of men, between March and July more than a hundred thousand human beings are in all certainty believed to have lost their lives within the walls of Florence: this as a result partly of the sheer inexorability of the plague, partly of the terror possessing the survivors, which prevented them from attending and ministering to the sick in their need? Before the plague struck, who would have believed the city even numbered that many inhabitants? Oh think of all the great palaces, the fine houses and gorgeous mansions that once boasted full households, now bereft of their masters and mistresses, abandoned by all, down to the humblest menial! Imagine all those memorable family names, those vast estates and egregious fortunes left without a legitimate heir! How many gallant men, how many fair women and bright young people whom anybody would have pronounced among the fittest—even physicians as eminent as Galen, Hippocrates, and Aesculapius* would have—sat down to breakfast with their families and friends only to find themselves dining that night with their forbears in the next world!

It gives me no pleasure to go raking over all these tribulations, and I propose to make no mention of whatever may suitably be passed over in silence. Now I have it on good authority that as our city was in these straits and practically deserted, one Tuesday morning seven young ladies assembled in the hallowed church of Santa Maria Novella.* They were virtually the only people present to hear the Divine Office, and were dressed in mourning as the times required. They were united in a bond of friendship or blood, or else they were neighbours, and the eldest was not past 28, the youngest not less than 18 years of age, and each one of them was gifted with good birth, beauty, charm, sagacity, and a fetching innocence. I should give them their real names if I had not a valid reason to avoid doing so, and this is that I shall be reporting what they said and what they listened to, and should not wish any of them to feel embarrassed on this account in the future: in those days a good deal of licence was accorded not merely to their age-group (for the reasons stated) but even to their elders, whereas today a certain austerity once more prevails. Besides, the vindictive are ready to take issue with the most blameless of lives and I don't want to offer them any grounds to impugn the good ladies' morals with scandalous talk. So, in order to give an account of what each of them said without causing embarrassment, I will provide them with names that to a greater or lesser degree reflect each one's character: the first and eldest we shall call Pampinea, the second Fiammetta, the third Philomena, the fourth one Emilia, the fifth Lauretta, the sixth Neiphile, and the last we shall justifiably call Elissa.*

These ladies assembled, by chance more than by design, in a certain part of the church, drew up their chairs in a circle and, after giving vent to a few sighs, left off telling their beads and began discussing life from various angles. And as after a while they fell silent, Pampinea spoke up and said: 'There is no offence in putting one's brain to a legitimate use—as both you and I will have heard any number of times—and it's only sensible for us, born as we are into this life, to do all we can to foster and protect it. Indeed, this is allowed even to the extent that people have on occasion committed murder without incurring blame, when this has been to protect their own lives. Now if this is permitted by law—and the law is, after all, responsible for the common weal—then we and all others are only the more entitled to take such steps as will harm no one else in order to assure our own survival. The more I ponder what we've been up to this morning, and all these other mornings besides, and think over the discussions we keep having, the more I realize that we're all of us not a little anxious about our safety—you must have realized this too. It's hardly surprising. What *does* surprise me, though, considering that we all share a woman's feelings, is that none of us is taking any precautions against that which we've every reason to be afraid of. Here we carry on, if you ask me, for all the world as if we had an urge or a duty to testify to the number of corpses carried off for burial, or to listen out to ensure that these friars (whose numbers are depleted practically to zero) are singing the office at the proper times, or maybe to display to anyone we meet the variety and depths of our afflictions, as witness our attire. And if we step out of here what do we see? Corpses or invalids being carried about. Or people running about the city with brazen impudence, people whom the Law banished for their misdeeds, but who see now that those who represent the Law are either indisposed or deceased, and treat it with contempt. We see the dregs of the population calling themselves undertakers all in a state of ferment and smelling blood as they go charging about on horseback in all directions, and jeer at our misfortunes with scurrilous songs. All we ever hear is: "The So-and-sos are all dead", or "So-and-so's at his last gasp"; we'd hear weeping on all sides if there were anyone left to weep. And I don't know what it's like for you going home, but in my case I go back to find nobody left but my maid—and we once were such a large household. And I find it terrifying, my hair stands on end—I can feel it—because anywhere I go about the house, anywhere I stop, I fancy I see the ghosts of those who've died, and they don't look the way I've known them, they look utterly ghastly, heaven knows why. So I don't feel the least bit comfortable whether I'm in here or outside or at home, and it's all the worse because we seem to be the only ones who've stayed on—anyone else who has a little money and somewhere to go to, as we have, has made off. As for them, if any of them are still left, how often have I heard and seen them enjoying the time of their lives, day and night, alone or in a crowd, simply catering to their lusts without the smallest concern for moral scruples. And it's not only people free of religious ties I'm talking about; even those in the monastic orders have convinced themselves that what's permissible to everyone else is equally permissible to them too; so they break their vows and surrender to the lusts of the flesh, as though this is a way of escape: they have grown remiss and debauched. Now if this is the situation, and quite clearly it is, what are we doing here? What are we waiting for? What are we hoping for? What's making us so much lazier and more casual than the rest of the city when it comes to taking care of ourselves? Do we set a smaller value on ourselves? Do we imagine that our bodies and souls are more solidly linked together than other people's are, so we don't have to worry about any harm coming to us? Well how very wrong we are, and what an absurd thing to believe!—we have only to stop and think of all those young people of either sex who've succumbed to this cruel plague.

'Well, I don't know if it seems to you the way it seems to me, but what if the worst befalls us simply because we're too supine and lackadaisical to avoid it by looking after ourselves? In my view the best thing we can do in our present situation is to leave the city, as so many have done before us and are still doing, and go to stay on our country estates—each one of us has a good choice of these. We would avoid like grim death the disgraceful example set by other people and live virtuously in the country, having a good time and making merry as best we may without overdoing anything. There we can hear the birds sing, and watch the hills and plains turn green; there are fields like a sea of waving corn, and all sorts of trees, and a nice open sky to look at: the heavens may be scowling at us but they still won't refuse us their glimpse of eternal beauty—and that's a great deal more beauty than we'll ever find staring at the empty buildings in this city! The air is much fresher, there's far more of all the basic necessities of life that one needs at a time like this, and not as many difficulties to contend with. Of course the labourers in the fields are dying just as the townsfolk are; but as there are fewer houses and fewer people about than we have here in town, it's all that much less distressing. Besides, we're not deserting anybody, if I'm not mistaken; it would be far truer to say that it's we who have been deserted—our families have abandoned us alone to all this misery, just as if we didn't belong to them, for they've either died or run away from death. No one will blame us, therefore, if we do as I suggest; if we don't, the likely result will be sheer misery and possibly death. So the best thing we can do, if you agree, is to take our maids and have our things sent after us—whatever we need—and stop here today, there tomorrow, and enjoy ourselves with the best of whatever the times will provide. Let's stay away until we can see what the heavens have in store—unless death catches up with us first. Remember, if we go away to live virtuously we've far less to be ashamed about than those women have who stay behind to lead sordid lives.'

After listening to Pampinea, the other ladies did not simply applaud her proposal but were only too ready to adopt it and immediately began to discuss how to put it into effect, as if the moment they got up from their seats they were to set out on their way. But Philomena, who was nothing if not shrewd, had this to say: 'Pampinea is absolutely right in what she says, but don't let's rush into it the way you all seem about to do.

Bear in mind that we're all women, and none of us is too young to be aware that women on their own have no idea how to go about things sensibly and need a man to guide them. Look how capricious we are, how restive, suspicious, timid, and faint-hearted! So I can't help worrying, if we commit ourselves purely to our own resources, that we'll all be going our several ways a good deal sooner than we'd need to, and looking a bit shabby, what's more. Shouldn't we do well to attend to this matter before we get going?'

'True it is that men are women's leaders', observed Elissa, 'and we seldom have reason to flatter ourselves on our achievements unless men have taken charge. But where are we going to find these men? We all know that most of our menfolk are dead, and those still alive have joined one group or another to escape the same thing we want to escape from. How are we to know where they've got to? Picking up strange men would be not at all suitable. So if we want to look after ourselves we'll have to see to organizing our life in such a way that we enjoy a happy, restful time without giving scandal or offence.'

While the young women were engaged in these discussions, who should come into the church but three young men, of whom the youngest was aged not less than 25. Being in love, nothing could dampen, let alone extinguish, their ardour—not the present adversity, not the loss of their friends and kinsmen, nor even fear for their own safety. The first was called Pamphilo, the second Philostrato, and the last Dioneo,* each one a charming young gentleman, and they had come in search of their loved ones for the consolation of their company in these disastrous times. As it happened, these ladies of theirs were among the seven we have mentioned, while the other four had ties of kinship with some of them.

The women noticed them almost at the same moment that they were spotted by the men, and Pampinea remarked with a smile: 'Look at the good luck attending the start of our venture! Here we are presented with three dashing young men who have their wits about them: they'll be only too glad to be our leaders and servants if we're prepared to engage them.'

At this, Neiphile blushed scarlet, for she was one of those being courted by one of the young men. 'For Heaven's sake,

Pampinea, think what you're saying!' she cried. 'I readily admit that there's not one word of criticism to be said against any of them. I'm sure they're fully up to this task and greater ones besides. And of course they would provide good and wholly unexceptionable company for us and indeed for women a great deal more beautiful and alluring than we are. But it's widely known that they're in love with some of us. I fear that we'd occasion scandal and censure through no fault of theirs or ours if we took them with us.'

'Nonsense!' said Philomena. 'So long as my conduct is above reproach and I have nothing on my conscience, I don't care what anyone says—God and the truth will fight my battle for me. If only they'll be ready to come! As Pampinea remarked, we could honestly say we'd be setting out with luck on our side.'

This argument of hers effectively silenced them and they all spoke in favour of calling the men over: they would tell them of the plan they had formed and invite them to keep them company on this expedition. So without another word, Pampinea, who was related to one of the young men, got up and went over to them as they stood watching; she greeted them cheerfully, apprised them of their proposal, and asked them, speaking for all the others, if they would consent to accompany them in a spirit of pure brotherly affection. The men's first thought was that they were being teased, but when they could see that Pampinea was speaking in earnest they answered that they were most cheerfully at their service. And without wasting a moment, they had, before leaving the church, arranged all that needed preparing prior to their departure. And when everything necessary had been prepared to the last detail and they had sent word ahead to their destination, the ladies left the city the following morning (Wednesday) at crack of dawn, and set out accompanied by a few of their maids and by the young men with three of their manservants. They had to go barely two miles to reach their intended stopping-place.

The place was set back a little from every main road and occupied a knoll; its variegated shrubs and leafy greenery were a pleasure to the eye. Perched atop the knoll was a mansion built round a lovely spacious courtyard; it comprised loggias, public rooms, and bedrooms, each one of which was exquisitely decorated with charming paintings. The house was ringed with splendid gardens and meadows, there were wells of the freshest water and cellars filled with the choicest of wines—not really the thing for sober, self-respecting ladies so much as for the enlightened tippler. On arrival the party was not a little delighted to find the whole place swept, the beds made up, flowers in season everywhere, and the floors strewn with rushes.

They sat down the moment they arrived and were addressed by Dioneo, the most engaging of young men and something of a wit: 'It's your good sense, ladies, rather than our providence that has brought us here. I don't know what you're proposing to do with your cares; mine I left at the city gates as I came out with you a while ago. So either you must be ready to join me in singing and laughing and living it up—without prejudice, of course to your dignity—or else you must give me leave to return to the city of affliction and resume my worries again.'

Pampinea answered cheerfully, as if she too had rid herself of all her cares: 'How right you are, Dioneo: the thing is to have a good time, that's been the whole point of leaving all that misery behind us. But anything that's going to last must have prescribed limits, and it seems to me—and I'm the one who first opened the discussion out of which this nice company has originated—it seems to me that, if we want to prolong our enjoyment, we shall have to appoint one of our number as our leader, someone to honour and obey as our sovereign; that person's entire concern will have to be to assure us of happy days. Now to ensure that each one of us experiences both the cares and the privileges of office, weighing the one against the other and finding therefore no occasion for envy, I suggest that the burden and the honour be bestowed upon each of us for a day. Let all of us choose the first one, and let the subsequent ones be decided each evening at six by whoever has exercised sovereignty for that day. The sovereign shall decide upon the duration of his or her office, and shall establish how and where we are to dispose of our time.'

These words won general approval and Pampinea was unanimously elected queen for the first day; then Philomena ran quickly to a laurel bush, plucked a few sprigs, and turned them into an impressive and dignified garland, for she had often heard people remark on the honour which attached to its leaves and what dignity they conferred on the person who was deservedly garlanded with them. So she placed the garland on Pampinea's head, and for the duration of their companionship this garland remained the outward sign of royal imperium.

Pampinea, now appointed queen, sent for the young men's attendants and for the ladies' maids, who numbered four, and enjoined silence on everybody; when she had obtained it, she spoke as follows: 'I will be the first to set you all an example to ensure that we conduct our affairs in an orderly and agreeable manner, constantly improving our situation and avoiding any taint of scandal, and that we thus continue for as long as we wish. So I will start by appointing Dioneo's man Parmeno* as my major-domo: to him will I commit the entire charge and responsibility for our household, and he shall supervise our table. Pamphilo's man Sirisco shall be our steward and treasurer, and shall answer to Parmeno. Tindaro shall wait upon Philostrato and the other two young men as valet of the bedchamber at such times as the other two servants are prevented from doing so by their own duties. My Misia and Philomena's Licisca shall serve in the kitchens, devoting themselves to the preparation of such dishes as Parmeno commands of them. As for Lauretta's girl Chimera and Fiammetta's Stratilia, we will make them responsible for the ladies' rooms and for the cleanliness of those rooms in which we foregather. Furthermore it is our wish and command that all of you, if you value our favour, shall forbear—wherever you go, whencesoever you come, whatever you see or hear—to bring us back any news from outside unless it be cheerful.'

These orders briefly imparted to everyone's approval, Pampinea stood up and genially observed: 'Here we have gardens, meadows, and other quite enchanting corners: so off you go and amuse yourselves until the clock strikes nine—then be back here and we'll eat while it's still cool.'

Thus dismissed by their new queen, the young men and pretty ladies, a happy band, sauntered off through one of the gardens, discussing pleasant topics, fashioning themselves nice garlands out of various kinds of foliage, and singing amorous snatches. They were occupied in this fashion during the interval proposed by the queen, after which they returned to the house, where they saw that Parmeno had made a diligent start to his duties: entering a ground-floor room, they found the tables laid with snow-white linens and glasses that glistened like silver, and the whole place embellished with sprigs of broom. At the queen's behest, they rinsed their hands and took their places as Parmeno had appointed. They were served the most exquisite fare and the finest of wines, the three men-servants providing discreet attendance. Such things raised everyone's spirits, for they betokened beauty and measure, and they dined to the accompaniment of cheerful banter. When the tables were cleared, as all the ladies, and the young men too, were familiar with round dances, while several of them were excellent singers and musicians, the queen sent for the musical instruments; at her bidding Dioneo took a lute, Fiammetta a viol, and they struck up a mellow dance. The servants were sent off to take their own meal and the queen and her sisters stepped out slowly with the two young men on a round dance. After this they sang charming, gay songs. Thus they employed themselves until the queen felt it was time for them to retire for their siesta; so she dismissed them all and the three men withdrew to their rooms, separate from the women's. These they found with the beds neatly made up and as replete with flowers as the dining-room; the women found the same in their rooms, so they undressed and went to bed.

Not long after three o'clock had struck the queen got up and had the other ladies all awoken, and the men too, for, so she claimed, too much sleep in the daytime is harmful. Off they went into a meadow of tall green grass and out of the sun; here they could feel a gentle breeze, and they all sat down on the grass in a circle, as the queen required. 'As you see', she told them, 'the sun is high, the heat intense; the only sound is that of the crickets in the olive trees. There's certainly no sense in our going off anywhere at present. It's lovely and cool here and there are games tables with chess sets, as you see, and you can all amuse yourselves as the fancy takes you. But with these games, one player's bound to get upset, which is not all that much fun for the other or for the onlookers; so if you follow my advice, we shall spend this sultry part of the day not playing games but telling stories: in this way one narrator entertains the entire company. By the time you've each told a little tale the sun will be on the decline, the heat will have abated, and we can go and enjoy ourselves wherever you feel like. So if you agree with my suggestion, let us do it—I'm perfectly ready to meet your wishes. If this is not what you feel like doing, let's go off until six and all follow our own inclinations.'

They all, men and women alike, spoke in favour of the story-telling.

'Very well', said the queen, 'if that is your wish, I shall on this first day leave you all free to choose whatever topic you prefer.'

She turned to Pamphilo, who was sitting on her right, and kindly invited him to make a start with a story of his own. On hearing the summons, Pamphilo promptly addressed his attentive audience in the words that follow.

I. 1. *Cepperello of Prato, after a lifetime devoted to evil, hoodwinks a holy friar with a deathbed confession and comes to be venerated as Saint Ciappelletto.*

It is right and fitting that everything we do should stem from the hallowed name of the One who created all things. Therefore, as it falls to me to make a start on your story-telling, dear ladies, I'm going to begin with one of the Good Lord's wonders: listening to it will serve to confirm our trust in Him, as in One immutable, and we shall never cease to praise His name.

As the things of this world are subject to transience and death, it is clear that they are wholly oppressive, wearisome, noxious inside and out, and subject to every kind of hazard: how could we endure the situation, bound up in it, nay, steeped in it as we are, or what protection might we have were it not for the strength and wisdom afforded us by God's special dispensation? Now we are not to imagine that God's grace comes down on us and remains in us because of any merit of our own; it derives from His innate goodness and from the prayers of those who were mortals like us and, while they yet lived, sought to do His will, and now live with Him in eternal bliss; to such as these, as to intercessors who from their own experience grasp our frailties, we offer our prayers for the things we take to be necessary, maybe not daring to confront so great a Judge with our petitions. Bounteous as is His mercy towards us, we recognize how much greater it is on those occasions when, unable as we are with our mortal eye to penetrate the secret of His mind, we may be misled by false preconceptions and appoint as our advocate before the face of the Divine Majesty one who has been banished from it to eternal exile. The Lord none the less, from Whom nothing is hidden, will consider the good faith of the petitioner rather than his ignorance or the banishment of the one through whom the prayer is addressed, and will grant the request just as though the intercessor were indeed one of the blessed in the court of heaven. You'll be able to see this clearly enough in the story I'm going to tell—it will show what happens when people follow the judgement of men rather than the wisdom of God.

We're told that a great merchant of enormous wealth, Musciatto Franzesi, received a knighthood in France and was required to go to Tuscany with Charles Sansterre,* brother to the King of France, at the behest of Pope Boniface VIII.* Urged as he was to come, the merchant was conscious that his affairs were in no little disorder (as merchants' affairs tend so often to be), and that it would take time and effort to set them to rights. He decided, therefore, to entrust them to a number of people, and indeed managed to do so in every case save one: he was not sure whom to appoint who would be up to the task of recovering loans he had made to a number of Burgundians. His doubt arose from reports that the Burgundians were a litigious lot of villains and inclined to mischief, and he could think of no one whose cunning he could rely on to get the better of their sharp practices. After giving much thought to the problem, he recalled to mind a certain Cepperello, a man from Prato who used to frequent his house in Paris. He was a little fellow and ever so dapper, which is why the French, not knowing what to make of Cepperello—they took it to be something to do with *chapeau*, their name for a hat—found themselves calling him Ciappelletto in view of his diminutive size. Everyone knew him as Ciappelletto whereas only a handful called him Cepperello.

What sort of a man was this Ciappelletto? Well, he was a notary, and though he issued few instruments, nothing caused him greater shame than when one of them was found to be anything other than fraudulent: he'd never refuse a request for a dud certificate, and he'd sooner hand one of these out for free than issue a genuine one against a hefty payment. He took a particular delight in bearing false witness, whether he was asked to or not, and as in those days the French set the greatest store by statements on oath, his dishonesty won him as many lawsuits as he was called on to defend under oath, for he cared little to be a man of his word. What really made him happy, what he really applied himself to, was to sow discord, enmity, and scandal between friends, kinsmen, and whoever else; the worse the ensuing misery, the happier he was. Ask him along to a murder or any such felony and he'd never say no—he'd be off with you, eager as could be; many's the time he'd step forward himself to deliver the fatal blow. There was no one like him for cursing and swearing and taking the Lord's name in vain—with a temper like his he'd start cussing at the drop of a hat. He never went near a church, but scoffed at the sacraments and disparaged them in the foulest language. The taverns, on the other hand, and other such raffish establishments received his custom regularly. Women? He adored them the way a dog adores a thrashing—there was nobody keener, though, on another sex. He'd put his heart into robbing and stealing the way a good man would into giving alms. He ate enough for six and drank like a fish, so much so that he'd sometimes make a thorough spectacle of himself. At cards and dice he would cheat with single-minded application. I could go on . . . Suffice to say, possibly a worse man was never born. It was this man's craftiness that underpinned the fortune and position of Musciatto Franzesi: many's the time it had rescued him from private individuals who'd suffered all too much at his hands, and from the Law, which he was forever flouting.

So when Musciatto was reminded of this man Cepperello, with whose life-style he was all too well acquainted, he considered that he'd be the very man to put those slippery Burgundians in their place. He sent for him, therefore, and said: 'As you know, Ciappelletto, I'm leaving here for good. As I have unfinished business with certain Burgundians (among others) and they're a crafty lot, I can't think of anyone better suited than you are to collect what they owe me. So, as you're not doing anything for the moment, if you'll take care of this for me I'll see that you obtain some advancement at court. I'll also give you your due share of what you collect.'

Finding himself without employment and in straitened circumstances, and realizing that Musciatto, who had long been his refuge and mainstay, was about to leave, Ciappelletto made up his mind on the spot, as though he had no choice: 'I'll be glad to', he said. So they agreed terms and when Musciatto had left, Ciappelletto, armed with a commission and with royal Letters Patent, departed for Burgundy, where he was virtually a stranger. Here he adopted a wholly uncharacteristic kindliness and gentleness as he set about the debt-collecting that was the object of his mission; it was as if he were holding his wrath in reserve. He took lodgings, as he pursued this task, with two Florentine brothers who were here practising usury, and who were accustomed to offer Ciappelletto a great deal of hospitality for Musciatto's sake. While here, he fell ill, and the brothers promptly sent for doctors and nurses to attend him, and for whatever else was needed to restore him to health. He was beyond help, however, for he was getting on in years and had led a dissolute life; his condition deteriorated from day to day: his was a terminal illness—so said the doctors—and the two brothers were most upset.

One day the brothers held a discussion right outside the sick-room door. 'What shall we do with him?' they asked each other. 'Look what a mess he's landed us in! If we throw him out in his present condition it wouldn't look at all good, in fact people would think we were out of our minds, seeing that we'd taken him in and gone to such trouble to have him looked after and cured, only to throw him out when he's at death's door and there's nothing he can have done to upset us. What's more, a reprobate like him isn't going to make his confession or receive any sacrament of the Church; so he'll die unshriven and no church will want to accept his body so he'll be dumped in a ditch like a dog. Even if he does go to confession, his sins are so many and so ghastly, it will come to the same thing: there won't be a friar or priest willing or able to give him absolution and, without it, he'll still be thrown in a ditch. And if that happens, the folk in these parts, who find our calling iniquitous and are constantly railing against it, and who are always out to rob us, will make no end of a fuss when they see it; "Look at these Italian moneybags!" they'll shout. "They never set foot inside a church. We'll not put up with them a moment longer!" And they'll descend on our houses and plunder our possessions—chances are they'll make away with us altogether. Either way things won't look too bright for us if our chap pegs out.'

Now this conversation took place, as we have said, right next door to where Ciappelletto was lying and, as we so often notice in the sick, his hearing was acute and he picked up all they said about him. So he sent for them and told them: 'You're not to have the least anxiety on my account; you needn't be afraid you'll suffer any harm because of me. I overheard what you were saying about me, and I've no doubt that things would indeed finish up the way you said if matters took the turn you've been predicting—but that's not the way they're going to work out. I've served the Good Lord so many bad turns during my life that if I serve Him one more on my deathbed, it'll make little difference to Him. Just see to fetching me a good holy friar, the best and holiest you can find, if there are any about, then leave it to me—I shall arrange matters for you and me in such a way that, mark my word, all will be well and you shall rest content.'

The two brothers placed little hope in this assertion but none the less off they went to a convent of friars and enquired for a holy and wise man who might hear the confession of an Italian banker lying sick in their house. They were offered an elderly friar whose life was holy and virtuous, well versed in the Scriptures and held in the highest regard—all the local people were utterly devoted to him. So they brought him home, and when he was in the sick-room he sat down beside Ciappelletto's bed and offered him kind words of comfort; after which he asked him how long it was since his last confession.

'Father', replied Ciappelletto, who had never in his life been to confession, 'I normally go to confession at least once a week, quite often more. The fact is, though, that since I fell ill, about a week ago, I've not been to confession at all, for my sickness has proved too much for me.'

'Well done, my son; keep it up! As you go so frequently to confession, I see it won't take much to hear yours or to examine you.'

'Oh don't say such a thing! However many times I've been to confession, there's never been a time I've not wanted to make a general confession of all my sins, every one I could remember, from the day I was born up till my latest confession. I entreat you therefore, good father, question me as closely as if I'd never confessed before. And don't spare me because I am sick: I'd far sooner do injury to my body than pamper it at risk of losing my soul which my Saviour redeemed with His precious blood.'

These words were balm to the holy man; they testified, he thought, to a good frame of mind. He much commended Ciappelletto for this habit of his, then asked him whether he had ever committed sins of the flesh with any woman.

Ciappelletto sighed. 'I'm ashamed to admit the truth about this, father: I'm afraid to sin by vainglory.'

'Don't worry, just tell me: nobody ever sinned by telling the truth, whether in confession or in anything else.'

'Since you reassure me on this point, I'll tell you: I'm a virgin, just as I came out of my mother's womb.'

'Well, God bless you! Well done! This makes you all the more deserving than we are, or anyone else under obedience to a Rule, for you've had that much more freedom to follow your perverse inclinations.'

The friar then asked him whether he had offended God by the sin of gluttony. Ciappelletto heaved a great sigh and said yes, ever so often, because, as he had the habit of fasting on bread and water at least three days a week—in addition to the regular fast-days observed throughout the year by devout people—he had drunk the water with all the relish and greed of the worst wine-bibber, especially when he was exhausted from prayer or in the course of a pilgrimage. And how often had he not craved for one of those green salads women tend to make when they go out into the countryside! Sometimes, too, his meals had seemed to him better than they ought to have done to a man fasting, as he did, out of piety.

'These failings are natural, my son', said the friar; 'they could not be of less importance, and you're not to burden your conscience with them more than you need. However holy he is, every man will find that, eating is a good thing after a long fast, and so is a drink after toiling.'

'Oh you mustn't say such a thing to console me, father! You know as well as I do that whatever is done in the service of God must be done with a heart that is entirely clean and uncontaminated. Whoever does so otherwise is a sinner.'

The friar was delighted. 'Well I'm glad that's how you feel about it; your good, clean conscience in this matter is a joy to me. But tell me now: have you ever sinned by avarice, wanting more than your due, or keeping what you should not have kept?'

'Father', said Ciappelletto, 'I shouldn't want you to take account of the fact that I'm lodging with these usurers. I've nothing to do with them, indeed I came to bring them a warning and a reprimand and turn them away from this wicked kind of profiteering. I do believe, in fact, that I should have succeeded had not the Good Lord visited this sickness upon me. Let me tell you that my father left me a rich man, and when he died I gave most of my inheritance to charity. To earn my living, and to be in a position to help Christ's poor, I went into trade in a small way, and I did aim to make a profit; but I'd always share my earnings equally with the poor, allowing one half to support my own needs and making the other half over to them. And my Creator has so prospered me in this that my business has gone from strength to strength.'

'Very good. But how often have you lost your temper?'

'Well, I'll tell you straight: many times. Who could keep his temper, seeing the foul things people get up to every day, neglecting God's commandments, showing no respect for His judgements? Many's the time I've been ready to die, seeing youngsters pursuing idle pleasures, coming out with curses and oaths, haunting the taverns, avoiding church, choosing the ways of the world in preference to those of God.'

'This is virtuous anger, my son, and far be it from me to take you to task for it. But might it ever have happened that your anger led you to kill someone? Insult someone to his face? Act unjustly?'

'Goodness me!' replied Ciappelletto. 'What kind of man of God are you to suggest such a thing! If it even crossed my mind to do any of the things you mention, d'you imagine I'd believe that God would still have shown me such favour? That's all strictly for brigands and evil men of their sort; whenever I see people like them I always say, "May God change your ways." '

'Then tell me, my son—so may God bless you: Did you ever bear false witness against anyone, or speak evil of another, or take another man's property without his leave?'

'Did I not!' cried Ciappelletto. 'Of course I've spoken ill of another person: I once had a neighbour who without the smallest justification kept beating his wife, so I told her family what I thought of him—I was so sorry for the poor little thing who was left in sad shape (God knows) every time he'd had a glass too many.'

'Very well. You tell me you were a merchant. Did you ever cheat anyone, as merchants do?'

'To be honest, I did. I don't know who he was, but I'd sold him some cloth and he'd brought me the money he owed me; I put it away in a box without counting it and only discovered a month or so later there were four farthings over. I kept them for a good year to give back to him, but as I never saw him, I gave them to charity.'

'That was a trifle, and you did well to dispose of them as you did.'

The holy friar put many other questions to him, all of which he answered in like fashion. When he was about to give him absolution, Ciappelletto said: 'There's still one sin I've not confessed.'

'What sin?' asked the friar, and he said: 'I remember making my servant sweep the house one Saturday afternoon and it was past three o'clock, so I didn't respect the Lord's Day the way I ought to have done.'

'Oh, that's nothing', said the friar.

'Don't say it's nothing! You can never pay enough respect to a Sunday, for that's the day on which Our Lord rose from death to life.'

'Well, is there anything else?'

'Yes. I unthinkingly spat once in God's house.'

'My son', said the confessor with a smile, 'think nothing of it—that's a thing we clergy do every day.'

'Well that's very wrong! Nothing should be kept as spotless as the holy temple in which sacrifice is offered up to the Lord.'

In a word, Ciappelletto had a great deal to say along these lines. Eventually he started to sigh, then burst into tears—which he knew how to turn on and off at will.

'What is the matter, my child?' asked the holy friar.

'Oh dear, sir', replied Ciappelletto. 'I still have one sin left which I've never confessed, I've been too ashamed. Every time I think of it I weep, as you see, for I'm quite certain that the Lord will never show me His mercy because of this sin.'

'Come, child, what are you saying? If every sin ever committed, or destined to be committed by the whole of mankind to the end of time, were all the work of a single man, and he had repented and shown contrition the way I see you have, so great is the Lord's goodness and mercy that, if that man confessed, he'd be freely pardoned. So don't be afraid to tell it.'

Still weeping copiously, Ciappelletto said: 'Oh dear, father, my sin is simply too big; I can scarcely believe I should ever obtain God's forgiveness, unless you pray for me.'

'Tell; don't be afraid—I promise I'll pray for you.'

Ciappelletto kept crying and wouldn't say, while his confessor kept exhorting him to speak out; finally, after keeping the friar on tenterhooks for a good long time with his weeping, he heaved a deep sigh and said: 'Now that you've promised to pray for me, father, I'll tell you: when I was only a tot I once swore at my mamma.' With this, he burst out crying again.

'Come, my child, does this seem to you so grave a sin? People are cursing the Lord all the day long, but He still forgives them freely when they're sorry they've done so. What makes you think He won't forgive *you*? Now stop crying, take heart: if you'd been one of the men who'd put Him on the cross, He'd most certainly pardon you after you showed the contrition you've shown me.'

'Heavens, father, what are you saying! There was my darling mamma, who bore me for nine months in her womb, day and night, and carried me at her breast more than a hundred times! I did a terrible thing when I swore at her, it's too frightful a sin, and if you don't pray for me, God will never pardon me for it.'

When the friar saw that Ciappelletto had said all he had to say, he absolved him and gave him his blessing. He took him to be a thoroughly holy man, fully convinced that Ciappelletto had been telling him the truth—as well he might, seeing that his penitent was coming out with these things on his deathbed. At the end he said to Ciappelletto: 'With God's help you will soon be better. But supposing the Lord summoned your blessed and righteous soul to Himself, would you like your body to receive burial in our convent?'

'Yes', answered Ciappelletto. 'Indeed there is nowhere else I'd wish to be as you've promised to pray for me. Besides, I've always had a special devotion for your Order. So, when you get back, do please see that I'm brought the true Body of Christ that you consecrate each morning at the altar. Though I am not worthy, I mean, by your leave, to receive it. Then I should like to receive the holy Extreme Unction so that, if I've lived a sinner, I may at least die a Christian.'

The holy man said that that was well spoken and he was only too glad to do so: he would have it all brought at once—which he did.

The two brothers, who strongly suspected that Ciappelletto was fooling them, had posted themselves next to a partition wall that divided the sick-room from the room adjacent, and they listened in; they easily overheard and grasped what Ciappelletto was saying to the friar, and on occasion they had such an urge to laugh as they heard the things he confessed to, they were close to bursting. They kept remarking to each other: 'What sort of a man is this? Neither age nor sickness nor fear of death which he sees impending, nor fear of God, before whose judgement seat he expects to appear in a little while, nothing's been able to divert him from his wickedness, or make him think twice about dying as he has lived.' However, seeing that he'd told them he would have his funeral in church, nothing else really mattered to them.

A little after this, Ciappelletto received Holy Communion, and as his condition deteriorated severely, he was given Extreme Unction. Shortly after Vespers, that very day on which he had made his good confession, he died. So the two brothers, drawing on the deceased man's funds, made all the necessary arrangements for him to receive honourable burial: they sent word to the friars to come and hold the customary vigil that evening, and to fetch away the body the following morning. The holy friar who had heard his confession went to see the prior when he learnt that his penitent was dead, and rang the bell to summon the community to the chapter house. He told the assembled friars what a saintly man Ciappelletto was, as he had established from his confession, and, in the hope that the Lord would display many miracles on his account, he persuaded them to welcome his body with the greatest reverence and piety. The prior and community were readily convinced and gave their consent, so that evening they went in a body to where Ciappelletto was laid out and held a great, solemn vigil over his corpse. In the morning they set forth to fetch it, all of them dressed in alb and cope, holding their breviaries and preceded by their processional crosses; they bore it back with utmost pomp and circumstance to their chapel, followed by practically the entire population of the town, men and women alike.

Once they had laid him down in church, the holy friar who had heard his confession went up into the pulpit and preached a sermon about him and his life, coming out with the most wonderful facts about his fasts, his virginity, his simple innocence and holiness; he described, among other things, what

Ciappelletto had tearfully confessed to him as his gravest sin, and how he had scarcely been able to persuade his penitent of God's forgiveness. He went on to upbraid the listening congregation: 'And look at you, accursed of God!' he cried. 'You go swearing at the Good Lord and His Mother and the whole court of Heaven at the drop of a hat!' He said a whole lot else besides about Ciappelletto's integrity and purity, and, in a word, he so affected the minds and hearts of the local people, who were fully convinced by his sermon, that when the service was over the whole crowd surged forward to kiss the dead man's feet and hands and rip the clothes off his body, for anyone who could make off with a stitch of it was in raptures. It was decided to leave his body lying there all day so that everyone would have the chance to come and see it. That night he was given honourable burial in a marble tomb in a side-chapel, and the next day people started to come and light candles and venerate him, putting up waxen votive images in earnest of their good intentions. And such was the spread of his reputation for sanctity, and of the devotion accorded to him, that in whatever adversity people found themselves, there was scarcely a soul who would invoke another saint but him. They called him Saint Ciappelletto; they still do. Many are the miracles, it is said, that God has performed through him and continues to perform for those who devoutly commend themselves to him.

This, then, is how Cepperello of Prato lived and died and became a saint, as you have heard. I don't wish to deny the possibility that he is now enjoying beatitude in the presence of God for, however evil and wicked he was in his life, he may have shown such contrition at the last moment that the Lord had mercy on him and accepted him into His kingdom; as there is no way of knowing this, however, and I'm concerned only with the evidence, I should say that he's more likely to be in the devil's keeping, in hell rather than in heaven. And if that *is* the case, we should recognize the immensity of God's goodness towards us for, regardless of our error, He looks only at the purity of our faith and hears our prayer even when we choose one of His enemies for mediator, mistaking him for a friend of God—so finally it is the same as if we had invoked a true saint as channel for divine grace. In order, then, that we may by His grace be preserved all together in this happy company, safe and sound during our present afflictions, let us praise His name, wherein we first assembled together, and reverently commend ourselves to Him in our need, fully confident that we shall be heard.

With this he fell silent.

I. 2. *Giannotto urges his Jewish friend Abraham to become a Christian. As Abraham insists on first making a visit to Rome, Giannotto fears that his cause is lost.*

Parts of Pamphilo's tale provoked the ladies to mirth; all of it won their approval, and they listened to it closely. When it was finished, Neiphile, who sat next to him, received the queen's command to tell a story that continued the present entertainment. Neiphile, a lady of charming manner as well as a beauty, was glad to accept the summons and this is how she began:

In his story Pamphilo has shown how God in His goodness overlooks our mistakes when they result from ignorance. And in mine I propose to show how far the same divine goodness will go in its patient toleration of the failings in those who ought to be testifying to it in word and deed: even as they do the opposite of what they should, He provides an irrefutable demonstration of His goodness so that we should hold to our convictions with the greater constancy.

In Paris there was once upon a time a great merchant, so I've heard it said. The worthy fellow was called Giannotto de Chauvigny, a thoroughly honest, upright man who carried on a not-inconsiderable trade in cloth. Now he entertained a singular friendship with a very wealthy Jew called Abraham, a merchant like himself, and the soul of probity and honest dealing. In view of his friend's honesty and probity, Giannotto found it all too distressing that the soul of a man as good, wise, and virtuous as he should go to perdition for not possessing the Faith. So he took to urging him in friendly fashion to forsake the errors of the Jewish faith and turn instead to the truth of Christianity—a good, holy Faith which, as he could see, continued to wax and prosper, whereas his own (as he could not fail to observe) was quite dwindling away. The Jew's response was that the only good, holy religion in his view was the Jewish one; he had been born into it and in it he intended to live and die; and there was nothing that would ever make him budge. This did not prevent Giannotto from reverting to the question in similar terms a few days later, demonstrating to his friend, in the blunt language merchants generally adopt, the reasons that made our Faith superior to that of the Jews. Now although Abraham was steeped in the knowledge of the Jewish faith, whether under the impulse of his great friendship with Giannotto, or whether it was the Holy Spirit influencing the words of this unlettered man, the fact is that the Jew acquired a taste for Giannotto's doctrinal exposition. He remained obstinate in his beliefs, though, and was not to be converted.

But however constant Abraham remained, Giannotto would never give up pressing him, until the Jew's resistance was overcome by such unrelenting pertinacity and 'Very well, Giannotto', he said. 'You want me to become a Christian, and I'm ready to do so, but only if I first go to Rome and see the person you call the Vicar of God on earth. I wish to acquaint myself with his style of living and that of his brother cardinals. If it is clear to me from that, as well as from your words, that your Faith is superior to mine, as you've been at pains to demonstrate to me, then I'll do as I have said. Should that not be the case, however, I shall remain a Jew as I am now.'

Giannotto was quite devastated on hearing this. 'All my efforts gone to waste!' he brooded. 'Here was I thinking I'd put them to such good effect and that I'd converted him. If he goes to the court of Rome and observes the impious and disgusting life-style of the clergy, far from turning to Christianity from Judaism, he'd revert to being a Jew if he had already turned Christian.' He turned to Abraham and said: 'Come, my friend, what makes you want to incur all the trouble and expense of getting from here to Rome? For a rich man like you the journey is fraught with dangers both by land and sea. Don't you think you'll find anyone here to baptize you? If you have any perplexities about the Faith I've explained to you, where will you find scholars more learned in Christian doctrine than here in our university? They'll be able to clear up any question you want. Which is why, if you ask me, your journey is quite unnecessary. Bear in mind that over there the prelates are no different from the ones you can see here, indeed they'll be all the holier for being that much closer to the Supreme Pastor. So, if you'll take my advice, you'll leave this outlay of energy for some future occasion when you want to go on a pilgrimage—and maybe then I'll keep you company.'

'I do believe the matter is as you state it, Giannotto, but, to put it in a word, if you really want me to do as you've kept urging me, I've made up my mind to go and if I don't, that's the end of that.'

Seeing him so determined, Giannotto bade him Godspeed and concluded that his friend never would become a Christian once he had taken a look at the court of Rome. He pressed him no further for there was nothing to be gained.

The Jew rode off to the court of Rome, arriving there as soon as he could. Here he received an honourable welcome from his Roman fellow-Jews. During his visit he told nobody what it was that had brought him here, but began a discreet surveillance of the Pope, the cardinals, the other prelates and papal courtiers, to see how they carried on. Being a man whom little escaped, he noticed—and received information from others—that every one of them, from the greatest to the least, was given over to the worst sort of lechery, not merely the kind which accorded with Nature but also that practised by sodomites. They did so, moreover, without a scrap of shame or conscience, and the courtesans and pretty boys could ask the earth in exchange for their favours.

Aside from their lechery, they were one and all gluttons (he discovered), topers forever at the bottle, and like brute beasts, more concerned with stuffing their paunches than with anything else. On further scrutiny he found that they were all so grasping and money-grubbing that they would buy and sell human—nay Christian—blood and, by the same token, sacred objects of whatever sort, be they destined to sacrificial uses or to good works: there was greater traffic in such things and more dealers involved than there were cloth-merchants or what have you in Paris. This blatant simony was termed 'placements', while gluttony was known as 'provisioning', as though the Good Lord failed to understand these miscreants' intentions, never mind the meaning they attached to words; as though He were as prone as men are to be deceived by labels. Now Abraham was a sober and temperate man and all this grieved him not a little, as did many other things to be passed over in silence; when he felt he had seen quite enough, he decided to return to Paris. Giannotto went to call on him when he heard of his return, though his friend's conversion was the last thing he hoped for; they were delighted to see each other again, and after Abraham had rested for a day or two, Giannotto asked him what he thought of the Holy Father, the cardinals, and the rest of the papal court.

'What an unspeakable lot, Heaven rot them all!' the Jew promptly replied. 'Mark my words, if I judged correctly, I was not aware of having seen in a single clergyman there the smallest degree of holiness or piety, nor any work of mercy, or example to follow; only lust, greed, gluttony, deceit, envy, arrogance, that sort of thing and worse if worse there be in a person—all these things held, as I could see, in such high esteem, it was enough to leave me thinking I was in the devil's smithy, not in God's workshop. The way it looks to me, your Sovereign Pastor and, as a result, all the rest of them are devoting all their care, all their intelligence and skill to expunging the Christian religion and ridding the world of it, whereas they are supposed to be its bedrock and mainstay. However, as I can't see that what they're striving for is taking effect, but rather that your religion continues to spread and to acquire ever brighter radiance, I think I'm right to see the Holy Spirit at work in it, acting as bedrock and mainstay of what is in effect a religion of greater truth and holiness than any other. So if I used to be obstinately resistant to your exhortations and refused to become a Christian, I'll tell you now straight out: nothing will stop me from becoming one. Let us therefore go to church, and you, can have me baptized in accordance with the rites of your holy Faith.'

Giannotto had been expecting him to arrive at the very opposite conclusion, and so these words made him as happy as could be. Together they went to Notre Dame, where he asked the priests to baptize Abraham. This they hastened to do when they heard that it was at his own request. Giannotto stood godfather to him and christened him Giovanni, after which he entrusted him to some men of eminence to instruct him fully in the doctrines of our Faith, in which he proved a proficient pupil. Thereafter he remained a man of holy and unexceptionable life.

I. 3. *Saladin sets a trap for the Jew Melchizedek, who circumvents it with a tale of three gold rings.*

Neiphile's tale won general applause and, when it was over, Philomena began hers at the queen's bidding, thus:

Neiphile's story reminds me of the danger once encountered by a Jew. As the truths about our religion and God have already been given a thorough airing, no one should take it amiss if I descend now to the events and activities of us mortals. When you have heard my story, you ladies will perhaps be more circumspect in replying to the questions that may be put to you.

People in the happiest situations will often land themselves in the most dire distress by their own stupidity, as well you know; and, similarly, the wise man will use his head to escape from the gravest peril and achieve security for himself. That prosperous folk come to grief through their own stupidity is demonstrably attested by any number of instances, which it is not our present task to enumerate—we see countless examples every day. What I'm going briefly to demonstrate, however, in a short tale, as I promised, is that a little *nous* can get a man out of trouble.

Saladin* was a man who possessed such qualities that they not only turned him from a nobody into the Sultan of Babylon,* they procured him victory after victory over Saracen and Christian kings. Once he had exhausted his entire treasure in various campaigns, though, and in the most lavish disbursements, he found himself in sudden need of a round sum of money and could not think how to lay his hands on it as fast as the situation required. Then he remembered a rich Jew called Melchizedek, who practised usury in Alexandria, and thought here was the man to help him out at will. The Jew, however, was such a miser that he would never have helped voluntarily, and yet Saladin did not want to use force; his need, though, was pressing, so he pondered how he might obtain the man's assistance and hit upon a reasonable pretext to force his hand.

So he sent for Melchizedek, welcomed him without ceremony, sat him down beside him, and told him: 'I've been hearing from a number of people, my good sir, that you're as wise as can be and extremely well versed in the knowledge of God. So I should be glad if you'd tell me which of the three religions, the Jewish, the Saracen, or the Christian, you consider to be the true one.'

It was all too obvious to the Jew, for the man was no fool, that Saladin was bent upon tripping him up so as to bring the law down upon him. He considered that he could not commend any one of these three religions above the rest without playing into the sultan's hands. As he clearly needed an answer that would avoid the trap, he sharpened up his wits and soon hit upon a suitable one. 'My lord', said he, 'that's a nice question you've put to me and, if you're to know my view of the matter, I shall have to tell you a little story. Here it is: If I remember rightly, I've often heard it said that there once was a rich man of high standing, and among the precious gems in his treasure he owned a ring—the most beautiful and priceless of rings. It was so beautiful and of such value that he wanted it to stand out from the rest and remain in the family as a permanent bequest; so he issued instructions that whichever of his children was found possessed of the ring as part of his inheritance, he was the one to be considered his heir, and was to be treated with honour and respect as head of the family by his other children. Now the son to whom this man left the ring made a similar disposition with regard to his own descendants—he followed his predecessor's example. In short, this ring passed from hand to hand from one heir to the next and eventually came into the possession of a man who had three sons; all three were handsome, good lads and most obedient to their father, so he loved all three of them equally. And the boys, who were familiar with the tradition about the ring, were each one of them longing for the place of honour and each solicited his father as best he could in the hope that the ring would be left to him when the pater died, for he was now an old man. Well, he was a splendid fellow and he loved them all equally and could not for the life of him decide which of them to leave it to; as he had promised it to each one of them, he devised a way to keep all three of them happy: he had a good goldsmith secretly make another two rings identical with the first, so much so that even he, who had had them made, could scarcely tell which was the original. At his death each son was secretly given his own ring. When their father was dead, they each claimed the title of son and heir, and the honours that went with it, and rejected the others' claims; and each one justified his assertion by producing his ring. Now the rings, as they discovered, were to such a degree identical, there was no way of telling which one was the original, and the question of which of the three was the true heir to their father remained unresolved. It still is. And that's what I'm telling you, my lord, concerning the three religions given by the Father to the three nations, which you're asking me about: each one considers his inheritance, his religion and commandments the one to give him title to the truth—but, as in the case of the rings, where the true title lies is still in dispute.'

Saladin recognized that the Jew had contrived a perfect escape from the trap he had set for his feet, and therefore decided to tell him what it was he needed and see whether the man was ready to help him. He disclosed to him, furthermore, what he had been proposing to do if Melchizedek had not given him such a circumspect answer. The Jew placed at Saladin's entire disposal everything he was asked for, and subsequently the sultan paid him back in full, with some lavish gifts on top, and treated him as a friend forever after, maintaining him in a position of great honour at his court.

I. 4. *A monk sins and merits the most dire punishment. To save his skin, he makes the abbot his accomplice.*

When Philomena left off speaking, at the conclusion of her story, Dioneo, who sat beside her and realized from the order that it would be his turn next, spoke up without awaiting a further command from the queen. This is what he said:

If I have correctly understood what it is you fond ladies have all been proposing, what we're here for is to entertain ourselves with stories. Therefore, so long as we do not work against this proposal, I consider that we are each entitled to relate whatever story is deemed most likely to occasion pleasure—precisely what our queen was saying a few moments ago. Very well then, having heard the way Abraham saved his soul through the good advice of Giannotto de Chauvigny, and how Melchizedek used his wits to protect his fortune from the snares of Saladin, I expect to incur no censure if I give you a brief account of the precaution taken by a monk to save his skin from a swingeing punishment.

In the Lunigiana, a place not far from here, there is a monastery which used to enjoy a larger complement of monks—and of piety—than it does today. One of the monks, a fresh, vigorous young man, despite the wasting effect of fasts and vigils, happened to be out and about on his own near the secluded abbey church one day—it was round the middle of the day and the other monks were all having a nap—when he noticed a ravishing girl, possibly the daughter of a local labourer, on her way across the fields picking herbs. The moment he laid eyes on her he started lusting after her desperately. So he went over to her and struck up a conversation, and one thing led to another until she didn't mind if he took her back to his cell, unobserved. Well, he got rather carried away and was enjoying a reckless bout of slap and tickle when who should sneak past his cell but the abbot; he had just got up and he heard the rumpus the two of them were making. He stole up to their door to listen and better identify the voices, and it became clear enough to him that there was a girl in that cell. He was strongly tempted to have them open up, but then on second thoughts he returned to his own room and waited for the monk to emerge. The monk was wholly intent upon the simply marvellous time he was having with this girl, but he still remained a little wary; so when he fancied he heard a shuffle of feet outside the dormitory cells, he put his eye to a small chink and had a clear view of the abbot eavesdropping. It was abundantly obvious that the abbot could have realized there was a girl in his cell and, knowing what a heavy punishment he might incur, he was quite shattered. However, without betraying any of his anxiety to the girl, he quickly turned over in his mind various ideas to see whether he might hit upon some way of escape—and indeed a novel stratagem did occur to him which he put into effect the moment he thought of it.

On the pretence of feeling that she had been there long enough, he told her: 'I'm just going to see about getting you out of here without being spotted. Wait here quietly till I'm back.'

He stepped outside, locked the door, and went straight to the abbot's room. Handing him the key to his cell, as every monk did when he went out, he cheerfully told him: 'This morning I wasn't able to fetch in all the firewood I had cut; so with your leave, father, I should like to go to the woods and have it all brought in.'

This was a happy chance for the abbot, who would be able to discover more about the monk's lapse—he could tell that the lad was unaware it had been noticed. So, with equal readiness, he took his key and gave him leave to go. Once he saw him gone, the abbot turned his mind to the question of which would be preferable: to open the cell door in the presence of the whole community, so they could behold his wickedness with their own eyes, thus depriving them of any excuse to grumble at him when he punished the monk; or to find out first from the girl precisely what had taken place. She could, he mused, be So-and-so herself, or perhaps Mr So-and-so's daughter, and he wouldn't like to have exposed her to the humiliation of giving all the monks a look at her; so he decided he would first discover who she was, then take a decision; and off he went noiselessly to the cell, opened the door, slipped inside, and shut it behind him. The girl was appalled to see the abbot come in and, fearful of being put to shame, burst into tears.

The abbot looked her over and observed that she was a pretty young creature and, elderly man though he was, he felt the same instinct surge through him as had stirred up his young monk. 'Well', said he to himself, 'why don't I take my pleasure when it comes my way? After all, if it's trouble and vexations I want, I can have them any time for the asking. Here's a pretty lass, and there's not a soul knows that she *is* here. If I can persuade her to let me make love to her, I don't see what's to stop me. Who will find out? No one will ever know, and if you hide your sin it's already half-forgiven. I'll scarcely get a chance like this again: it seems to me it's only common sense to grab a good thing when the Good Lord sends it.'

So saying, he sidled up to the girl, for he had something quite different in mind to what had first brought him in here, and gently set about comforting her; he begged her not to cry, and step by step reached the point of acquainting her with his desire. The girl was not one of your snow-maidens and submitted herself to the abbot's good pleasure with alacrity. He hugged and kissed her repeatedly, then got on to the monk's narrow bed where, possibly in deference to the great burden of his dignity and to the lass's tender years, and anxious not to subject her to his excessive avoirdupois, he forebore to climb on top of her but laid her down on his chest and took his pleasure with her for some considerable time.

The monk had only pretended to set out for the woods but had concealed himself in the dormitory; the moment he observed the abbot go alone into his cell he felt immensely relieved and assured of the success of his plan; seeing the abbot lock himself in, he was beyond doubting it. He left his hiding-place and stole off to station himself at a chink through which he could see and hear what the abbot was doing and saying. When the abbot felt he had spent enough time with the girl, he shut her in the cell and returned to his own until, a little while later, hearing the monk and imagining that he was back from the woods, he decided to give him a thorough dressing down and have him locked up—that way he would remain in sole possession of the prize. So he summoned the monk, rebuked him as austerely and solemnly as could be, and condemned him to a prison cell.

'But father', the monk was quick to reply, 'I've not been in the Order of Saint Benedict long enough to have learnt every one of its ins and outs. And you had not yet shown me the way monks need to be crushed under the weight of women as they are under those of fasts and vigils. But now that you have shown me how to do it I promise you, if you'll forgive me this once, never again to fail in this respect, but always do as I have seen you do.'

The abbot, who was no fool, was quick to recognize that the monk had not only outwitted him but even witnessed his activities. Conscience-struck as he was by his own sin, he did not possess the effrontery to visit upon the monk the penalty he had equally incurred, so he pardoned him and swore him to silence over what he had seen. Then they discreetly ushered the girl off the premises—and, as likely as not, fetched her back in again on more than one occasion thereafter.

### I. 5. *With a banquet consisting of chicken, and a touch of wit, the Marchioness of Monferrato checks the French king's improper advances.*

The ladies listened with a tinge of embarrassment as Dioneo told his tale—this was evident from the honest blushes that suffused their cheeks; but as they caught each other's eyes, they could barely repress their giggles and went on listening, all smiles. When he had finished, though, they issued him with a gentle rebuke: such stories, they said, were not the kind to be told in the presence of ladies. Then the queen turned to Fiammetta, who was sitting beside him on the grass, and told her to follow. This Fiammetta cheerfully and indeed playfully did, with her eyes on the queen as she began:

I'm glad that our stories are giving instances of neat, spontaneous rejoinders and the impact these can have. This being the case, and also because a man, if he's wise, will always look to court a woman of higher standing than himself, while a woman, if she has any sense, will take good care not to accept the advances of a man of higher station—for both these reasons I want to show in my story how a noblewoman guarded against this and by her words and actions deterred a suitor.

The Marquis of Monferrato was a man of rare excellence: Gonfalonier* of the Holy Roman Church, and one of the men who crossed the sea in the armed expedition mounted by the Christians. Once, when his virtues were being discussed at the court of Philip Augustus* (the one-eyed), who was making ready to leave France and embark on that same expedition, one knight happened to remark that there was not another couple under heaven to match the marquis and his lady, for just as the marquis was renowned among the entire nobility for every excellence, so was his lady outstanding among all her sex for beauty and spirit. Such was the effect of these words on the King of France that there and then he fell passionately in love with the lady—whom he had never set eyes on—and determined that on his coming venture he would take ship at Genoa and nowhere else: this overland passage would give him a plausible excuse to call on the lady. The marquis being, as he realized, away from home, he should find it possible to compass his desire. This plan he carried into execution, sending his entire contingent on ahead, then setting out with a small band of knights. As he approached the marquis's territory he sent word to the lady with a day's notice to say that she was to expect him for dinner the following day.

The lady was sharp as well as wise, and she was happy to send answer that she took this for an exceptional favour and he was heartily welcome. When she turned to consider what a king such as he might be up to, paying her a visit in her husband's absence, she was not deceived in her conclusion—that he had been drawn by her reputation for beauty. However, being the good woman she was, she determined to serve him well, and summoned her remaining retainers to consult with them about the arrangements; she issued the necessary orders, but reserved to herself the preparation of the dishes to be served at the banquet. She at once assembled every chicken in the neighbourhood and instructed her cooks to prepare a variety of dishes for the royal feast using these alone.

So the king arrived on the appointed day, and the lady gave him a right festive and respectful welcome. Once he had seen her, he found in her even greater beauty and breeding than he had been led to expect from his knight's words; she quite dazzled him and he could not speak highly enough of her; the further she surpassed his expectations, moreover, the more passionate he felt about her. After he had rested a little in a suite furnished with all the magnificence appropriate to such a royal occupant, it was time for dinner, and he sat down at a table with his hostess while the rest were invited to take their places at other tables in order of seniority.

Here the king was served course after course, each accompanied by the choicest vintage wines, and he was really enjoying himself, the more so as he could feast his eyes on the dazzling lady. And yet, as each dish succeeded the last, he could not but be a little surprised that, however varied was the fare set before him, every dish consisted solely of chicken. Now to the king's knowledge this neighbourhood must be teeming with all manner of game, and he had after all given her sufficient warning to enable her to organize a hunt; nevertheless, however puzzled he was, he would make no allusion to the question beyond raising the matter of the chickens. 'My lady', he said, turning agreeably to his hostess, 'do you breed only hens in these parts, without a single cock?'

The lady understood his question perfectly well, and felt that here was the God-sent opportunity she had wanted in order to show her hand; so she turned to the king and replied, quite unabashed: 'Not so, my lord; but, however much they may differ in their apparel and station, women here are made no differently to women the world over.'

These words, and the mettle in them, were not lost on the king, who grasped the significance of this chicken-feast and realized that he would be wasting his breath on a woman of her quality and there would be no forcing her. So, after falling so recklessly in love with the lady, he thought it wise to quench his misconceived passion for his own honour's sake. Therefore he exchanged no further banter with her, fearing her ripostes, but continued the meal bereft of hope; and when the dinner was ended he thanked his hostess for her hospitality and, to acquit himself of the shame of his arrival by a prompt departure, once she had bidden him goodbye, he left for Genoa.

## I. 6. *A friar's hypocrisy is punctured by a plain man's quip.*

They all applauded the forthright but gentle rebuke administered by the marchioness to the King of France. Then at her queen's behest Emilia, who sat next to Fiammetta, launched boldly into her story.

Well, I too shall tell you of a pungent rejoinder: this one was made by an honest burgher to a grasping cleric. His quip is admirable, and amusing as well.

Not long ago in our city there was a friar. He was a Franciscan and his task was to root out heresy. He did his best to exhibit a tender regard for the Christian Faith—as they all do—but he was every bit as good at sniffing out a well-filled purse as a defective appreciation of the Faith. It was this first concern that brought to his attention, by chance, a man blessed with far more money than sense: the fellow happened to be chatting one day with his friends and dropped the remark (oh, there was nothing wrong with his faith but maybe the wine or the company had made him a little too merry and loosened his tongue): 'I've got a wine that's so delicious', he said, 'Christ Himself would drink it.' This remark got back to the inquisitor, who discovered that the man owned a big estate and kept his purse well loaded. So he rushed off 'with swords and staves'* to pin a highly serious charge on him, for he was alert to the prospect of laying his hands on some plentiful coinage, never mind setting the culprit free from the toils of disbelief. He sent for the man and asked him if what was alleged was true.

'Yes', replied the simple fellow, and told him all about it.

So the most reverend and devout disciple of St John Moneypenny* said: 'Are you then making Christ out to be a toper, a vintage bibber like the rest of you inebriated quaffers? And are you now telling me that, to put it mildly, this is a matter of no consequence? Well that's not quite the position! It's the fire for you, my friend, if we take you in hand the way we should.'

With these words and a great deal more he addressed him, a steely look on his face, as though the culprit were Epicurus* in person, denying the after-life. In no time the friar had the poor fellow so terrified he sent emissaries to grease the inquisitorial palm in the hope of obtaining mercy—the ointment employed is a first-class remedy for the disease of avarice which tends to afflict the clergy, not least the friars minor who dare not handle money. The ointment certainly proved so effective (for all that it does not feature in Galen's medical texts) that the threatened fire was mercifully transmuted into a cross—as though he were destined for an expedition beyond the seas, he was bidden to wear a yellow cross* on a black ground for a truly pretty emblem. Moreover, after receiving the money, the friar kept the man at his beck and call for several days, enjoining on him as a penance that he attend daily Mass at Santa Croce,* and report to him every lunchtime, after which the rest of the day would be at his own disposal.

The penitent was diligent in fulfilling this duty. One morning when the Gospel was chanted at Mass, the passage he listened to happened to include the words: 'Ye shall receive a hundredfold and shall inherit everlasting life.'* These words he committed to memory, and went, as ordered, to attend upon the inquisitor as he sat eating lunch.

'Have you', asked the friar, 'been to Mass this morning?'

'Yes', he was quick to reply.

'Was there anything in it that raised doubts in your mind or that you want to ask me about?'

'Oh for sure I didn't have a doubt about a single thing, I believe every bit of it to be true. What I did hear was something that made me feel very sorry for you friars—it still does—when I think of your unhappy plight in the next world.'

'What was it, then, that's made you feel so sorry for us?'

'It was that bit in the Gospel about "ye shall receive a hundredfold".'

'That's true enough', said the inquisitor. 'But why did the passage touch you?'

'Well, it's like this, sir. Since I've been keeping company with you I've noticed every day that a lot of poor people outside here are given a huge big cauldron of soup—sometimes two cauldrons—which you and your convent don't need. So if you are going to receive a hundredfold in the next life for each cauldron of soup, you'll be getting back so much soup you'll all be drowning in it.'

The other people sitting at table all burst out laughing, and the inquisitor was extremely put out that the man had seen through the hypocrisy of their 'charitable works'. And were it not that he had been driven on to the defensive, he would have pinned further charges on the man for having made a fool of him and his fellows. In a fit of pique he told the good man to run along and just stay out of his way in future.

I. 7. *Cangrande della Scala suffers an unexpected attack of stinginess. Bergamino cures him with a little tale about Primasso and an Abbot of Cluny.*

The queen and all the company were greatly amused by Emilia's pleasantry and the whole of her story; and they were much taken with the touch about the crusader's emblem. Once they had stopped laughing and fallen silent, though, Philostrato (whose turn it was) began to speak as follows:

To hit a motionless target is already quite a feat; but if some object shoots up unexpectedly and an archer contrives to bring it down, that is practically miraculous. The profligate and grubby life-style of our clergy in many respects offers a constant target to ribaldry—anybody so inclined may find room to disparage and criticize it. So, however much we may applaud the stout fellow who got in a dig at the inquisitor over the friars' two-faced charity, giving to the poor the trash they'd do better to toss out or feed to the pigs, the man I'm going to tell you about (prompted as I am by the last story), seems to me eminently more commendable. This man took a mighty lord, Cangrande della Scala,* to task on account of a sudden and uncharacteristic attack of meanness. He told him a charming tale, borrowing its characters to stand in for himself and the great lord. Here it is.

Throughout virtually the whole world His Lordship Cangrande della Scala enjoyed the most brilliant reputation: Fortune's favourite as he was, he stood among the most prominent and open-handed princes Italy has ever known since the days of the Emperor Frederick II.* After deciding to give a memorable, a prodigious feast in Verona, so that scores of people had been arriving from all over the place, not least courtiers of every hue, he suddenly changed his mind for Heaven knows what reason; he offered some sop to those who had turned up and sent them on their way. One man, though, remained behind. His name was Bergamino, a man of ready wit and a pretty turn of phrase—you had to hear it to believe it—and as he had received no largess nor been invited to leave, he continued to hope that things would turn out to his advantage. Cangrande had come to the conclusion, however, that every gift he made could just as well have been thrown straight into the fire for all the use it was—not that he'd say so or even hint at it. Now the days passed without Bergamino being summoned or required to offer pertinent services and, what with the bills he was running up for the lodging of his servants and the stabling of his horses, he began to feel depressed. He kept waiting, however, in the conviction that to leave would be the wrong move to make. In order to attend the feast with fitting decorum, Bergamino had brought with him three opulent and beautiful gowns, which had been presented to him by other princes; when his landlord required payment, he made over to him the first of the gowns and later, as his visit continued a great deal longer, he had to present him with the second one if he was to remain here. Then he started taking his meals on the pledge of the third; he was determined to remain and see how long this would serve him, then be on his way.

Now, while he was still subsisting on the third gown, he happened one day to find himself in the prince's presence as he was dining. Bergamino was pulling a very long face and Cangrande said, rather to nettle him than to take pleasure from one of his quips: 'What's the matter, Bergamino? You look a right misery. Tell us about it.'

Bergamino did not stop to think—it was as though he had already given it much thought—but launched straight away into this tale, which related to his own situation: 'I expect, my lord, you have heard of Primasso,* a Latinist of no mean talent, and as a ready rhymester there was no one to touch him; such was the regard, such the fame in which he was held on account of these accomplishments that even if he was not recognized everywhere on sight, there was scarcely a man who did not know Primasso at least by name and reputation. Finding himself once in Paris in straitened circumstances—his usual condition, for those with the power of the purse have little use for men of talent—he chanced to overhear a conversation about a certain abbot of Cluny,* who is considered to be the wealthiest prelate in the whole Church, aside from the Pope, on account of his revenues; he heard wonderful things said of him and his liberality, how he kept open house and when he was at table anyone who called in on him could be sure to be offered food and drink for the asking. Now it did Primasso's heart good to see men of rank who were men of virtue, so on hearing this he determined he would go and sample this abbot's munificence for himself. He asked how far the abbot's residence was from Paris, and was told he was on one of his domains some six miles out. Primasso reckoned he could get there in time for lunch if he made an early start. So, as he could find no one else going there, he obtained directions, but still remained anxious in case he was unlucky enough to lose his way and fetch up at some place where a meal would not be so easy to come by. Against this possibility, therefore, he thought to bring three bread-rolls with him so that he would not go hungry: as for water, he could get a drink of that anywhere, not that it was a beverage to which he was all that partial. So, stuffing the rolls inside his shirt, he set out and made such good progress that he reached the abbot's domain before it was time for lunch. In he went and took a look around, and saw any number of tables set out and things going full swing in the kitchens and every sign of elaborate preparations for lunch. "My heavens", he said to himself, "like they say, here's a man who does nothing by halves." The abbot's steward was generally keeping an eye on things and, as it was now time to eat, he gave the order for hands to be washed; water was provided for this, after which he seated the entire company at table. Now Primasso happened to be assigned a place right opposite the door to the room from which the abbot was to make his entrance into the refectory. It was the custom of the house that no wine or bread, no food or drink of any kind was set out on the tables until the abbot had taken his seat. Once the steward had everyone seated, he sent word to the abbot that dinner awaited his good pleasure.

'The abbot had the door opened to go into the refectory and, looking in as he entered, the first man his eye happened to light upon was Primasso. Now Primasso was far from well turned out and, besides, the abbot did not know him by sight. The first thought that came into the abbot's head after setting eyes on him was a disagreeable one, and one that had never before occurred to him: "Just look", he remarked to himself, "who it is I'm feeding!" He turned on his heel, had the door shut behind him again, and asked his retinue if any of them knew who that tramp was, sitting at table right opposite the door. They all said they did not know. Primasso, who had been on quite a walk and anyway was not accustomed to fasting, was more than ready for a bite to eat; after waiting a while he noticed that the abbot was not coming, so he pulled out of his shirt one of the three rolls he had brought along and set to. The abbot waited awhile, then told one of his servants to look and see if the fellow had gone. "No", was the servant's reply; "in fact he's eating some bread which he's evidently brought with him." "Well", observed the abbot, "let him eat his own stuff if he has any—he'll get nothing of ours to eat today." He would have been glad if Primasso had taken himself off, as he was reluctant to have him removed. Primasso, however, having eaten up his first roll, started in on the second as there was still no sign of the abbot. This, too, was reported to the prelate, who was having a watch kept for the man's departure. Still the abbot did not appear and eventually Primasso, having consumed his second roll, got to work on the third—which was also reported to the abbot, who was now struck by a thought: "Come, what can have got into me today? Is it stinginess? Petulance? But why? All these years I've been providing meals to anyone who wanted; it never made any difference to me whether a person was well born or not, whether he was rich or poor, tradesman or crook; I've seen my provisions squandered on any number of vagrants, and the idea has never crossed my mind that this man has put into my head today. One thing's for sure: if he's brought out the miser in me there must be more to him than meets the eye. He may look like a tramp but there must be something to him, as I feel too cheap to offer him hospitality." Thus he told himself, and wanted to know who the man was; on discovering that it was Primasso, who had heard about the prelate's munificence and had come to attest it for himself, the abbot was mortified—he had long known Primasso by reputation for a man of great ability. Anxious to make amends, he contrived all manner of ways to play host to him. After they had eaten, the abbot had Primasso dressed in courtly attire suitable to his dignity, made him a gift of money and a palfrey, and invited him to be his guest until such time as he felt like leaving. Primasso was well satisfied and thanked the abbot a thousand times, then returned to Paris on horseback, having arrived on foot.'

Now the prince was sharp enough to grasp Bergamino's drift without needing further explanation. 'Well, Bergamino', he told him with a smile, 'that's been a very neat way of showing me your parlous state, your high merits, and my stinginess, as also what it is you want from me. The fact is I've never before been taxed with meanness until you've done so now, and I shall dispose of it with the stick you've fashioned for me.' So he had the account settled with Bergamino's landlord and the three gowns returned to him, dressed him in a most sumptuous new one from his own wardrobe, presented him with money and a palfrey, and invited him to stay or leave at his own good pleasure.

gentlemen, more lavish in his entertainment of natives and strangers than any other Genoese of his day.

I. 9. *A Gascon lady recalls the King of Cyprus to his duty.*

The only person left at the queen's bidding was Elissa, who launched merrily into her story without awaiting the summons.

It's happened time and again: you keep reprimanding and punishing a person and it hasn't the slightest effect; then you drop some casual word by the by, and there—that's done the trick! Lauretta's tale shows this clearly enough, and I propose telling you another very short one to the same effect: a well-turned rebuke can always be beneficial, whoever it is who utters it, and so it should be received with an open mind.

In the days of the first King of Cyprus,* after Godfrey of Bouillon's conquest* of the Holy Land, a lady of gentle birth, from Gascony, went on a pilgrimage to the Holy Sepulchre and stopped in Cyprus on her way home; here some blackguards took the basest advantage of her. Quite prostrate and beyond comforting, she decided to go and lay her complaint before the king. 'A complete waste of time', she was told; 'he's such a wet rag, far from avenging the wrongs done to others and bringing the miscreants to justice, he's too lily-livered even to stand up for *himself*, and anyone who feels disgruntled simply takes out his temper on the king, heaping insults and shame on him.'

Hearing this, the lady gave up hope of obtaining justice, but decided there might be some comfort in speaking her mind to the king on the subject of his flabbiness. She appeared before him in tears and said: 'My lord, if I come into your presence it is not to obtain justice over the injury that has been done to me. But I pray you, grant me satisfaction by teaching me how you endure the outrages committed, so I understand, against your person. If I can only learn from you, I shall patiently endure my own lot—which, God knows, I should willingly lay upon your shoulders if I could, since you are so good at swallowing insults.'

The king, who till then had been so inert and passive, started suddenly out of his slumber, as it were, and meted out harsh justice to the lady's wrongdoers, and this was just the start: he went on to impose the toughest sanctions upon any who thenceforward impugned the dignity of his crown.

### I. 10. *Master Alberto of Bologna, twitted for loving a young woman, deflects the shaft on to his accusers.*

When Elissa finished, it only remained for the queen to tell a tale, and so she embarked in queenly fashion on hers:

As the stars are the ornament of a limpid night sky, and flowers adorn the green meadows in springtime, so it is that good social usage and agreeable conversation are embellished by a nicely turned quip. And inasmuch as its feature is brevity, it is more to be commended in women than in men, for women far more than men are to be discouraged from talking too much and at needless length, though today there are few, if any, women who can come out with a quip, or indeed respond to one: here's a defect that reflects badly on us and on all our sex. You see, whereas a woman used to be judged by her character, today's woman relies entirely on her outward trappings; the woman dressed in the richest medley of flounces and stripes and furbelows is confident of attracting the greatest admiration; little does she realize that if the outward trappings were what counted, a donkey could be dressed up to the point where it would attract more admiration than she. I'm ashamed to say it, for if I speak against my sex I speak against myself; these women all tricked out in their flounces and fripperies and all painted up either pass for statues in their wordless, marble passivity, or, if they do answer when spoken to, they'd have surely done better to keep silent. If they cannot carry on a conversation with an honest man, they like to set this down to their innate purity, whereas it's nothing but stupidity, for all that they prefer to call it virtue, as though the only virtuous woman is the one who confines her conversation to her maid, her laundress, or her baker's wife. Now if that is in accordance with Nature, as they like to believe, then Nature would have found some other way to cut their cackle.

Of course in this, as in everything else, some account must be taken of the time and place and who it is one's talking to, because it can happen to a woman, or man, that they're expecting to embarrass the other party with some offhand remark, but have failed to get the measure of the other party and end up put to the blush themselves. So then, to put you ladies on your guard, and to ensure that you will never be the butt of the proverb which is constantly being trotted out—that it always takes a woman to put her foot in it—I'm going to tell the last of today's stories (since it's my turn), and I'll tell it for your instruction: that way, just as your high-mindedness marks you off from other women, so you'll be clearly set apart by the superiority of your behaviour.

Not many years ago there was a doctor living in Bologna; he was a first-rate physician, with a virtually world-wide reputation, called Master Alberto—conceivably he is still alive. He was close on 70, but his force of character was such that, although life's natural warmth had largely forsaken his body, he remained in spirit as receptive as ever to the flames of love. He had noticed a most beautiful widow, on a social occasion, called (so it's said) Margherita de' Ghisilieri, and found her irresistible; he was as smitten as any young sprout, so much so that, any day during which he had not set eyes on his lovely lady's sweet, ravishing face, he could look forward to a bad night's sleep. So he took to haunting the street in front of the lady's house, sometimes on foot, sometimes mounted, whatever best suited him. She, and several others of her sex, therefore, realized what prompted these perambulations and often had a good giggle together over it—fancy a learned old gent like that being in love! They evidently believed that this most charming of emotions, love, could dwell solely and exclusively in the hearts of callow youths.

Anyway, Master Alberto continued his frequentation of Margherita's street, and one feast-day, as she sat outside her door with a number of her *commères* and spotted the old man in the distance bearing down towards them, they hatched a plot to welcome him among them then tease him over his infatuation. This they did: they all stood up and invited him into a cool inner courtyard where they plied him with the choicest wines and delicacies, after which they put the question to him as prettily as possible: 'How comes it that you're in love with this lovely lady, aware as you must be that she is courted by any number of handsome, attractive young gentlemen?'

Master Alberto, realizing that this question was a delicate barb, genially replied: 'My being in love should occasion no surprise to any reasonable person, my lady, least of all my being in love with you, as you deserve it. While in the natural order old men are deprived of the powers needed for amorous activity, they do not lose the ability to dispose of their hearts nor the sense to discern what is lovable—indeed they naturally have a better grasp of this, for they possess that much more experience than the young. Now here's what gives hope to an old man like me, loving as I do a lady with so many young suitors: many a time have I seen ladies taking their luncheon out in the open, and watched them eating lupins and leeks. While the leek is totally inedible, its head is less noxious and somewhat more savoury than the rest. You ladies, however, generally get it all wrong: you hold the leek by the head and eat the leaves, which possess no nutritional value and, what's more, taste horrible. When you make your choice of lover, my lady, is that how you would proceed? Were you to get it right, I should be the one chosen, the others would be dismissed.'

Margherita and her friends were somewhat mortified by this. 'That, sir, was a most courteous rebuke to our impertinence. Be that as it may, I set great store by your love, as well I might, seeing what a good, wise man you are; I hold myself, therefore, at your entire disposal, so far as my good name permits it.'

Master Alberto and the friends who had come with him got up; he thanked Margherita and took his leave of her in the best of spirits. So the lady, being careless with her banter, missed her mark and got herself spiked. A word to the wise, ladies: watch out!

The sun was beginning to set and the heat had largely abated by the time the young women and the three young men realized that their story-telling was at an end.

Their queen therefore jovially remarked: 'Now, my dear sisters, there's nothing left for me to do today in the exercise of my sovereignty except to provide you with a new queen to make her dispositions for tomorrow as she sees fit, so as to afford herself and us some wholesome entertainment. True it is that today still has some time to run before it turns to night; but in my view it isn't possible to make adequate preparations for the morrow unless one allows oneself sufficient time, so, to give the new queen the chance to make ready whatever it is she decides for tomorrow, I think that the new day ought to begin always at this point. And therefore, out of reverence for Him on whom all that lives depends, and to our own solace, our realm shall for this second day be under the governance of Philomena, a young woman of great wisdom.' This said, she stood up, took the laurel garland off her head, and respectfully placed it on Philomena's; then she was the first to hail her as queen, followed by the other ladies and the three young men, who all paid her agreeable homage.

Seeing herself crowned queen, Philomena blushed a little for shyness, but remembered what Pampinea had been saying a short while before in opening her story; so, to avoid appearing at a loss, she plucked up her courage, confirmed the appointments made by Pampinea, and gave instructions for dinner and for the morrow, remaining where they now were. Then she addressed them as follows: 'Pampinea may have appointed me queen to reign over you all, out of her kindness rather than owing to my qualities; I am none the less disinclined to follow my judgement alone in establishing our style of living, but would invoke your views as well. Now to acquaint you with what I should like to do, thus enabling you to add to or subtract from it at your pleasure, I shall in a few words tell you what I have in mind. If I have rightly observed the methods employed today by Pampinea, they strike me as having been both commendable and agreeable and, so long as they do not become tedious through repetition or otherwise, I am minded to leave them unchanged. After setting further in train what we have already begun, therefore, we shall leave here to attend to our pleasures until sunset, at which point we shall dine out in the cool; then, after a little singing and other such entertainments we'll do well to retire to bed. Tomorrow we shall get up while it is still cool and again go off to take our pleasure in whatever way each of us chooses; then we shall, as we did today, come back to eat at the proper time, and dance; after our siesta we'll return here to tell stories, as we have done today, for in my view this pastime affords us a great deal of pleasure and, likewise, of profit.* In fact I mean to initiate something that Pampinea was unable to do as she was elected queen so late in the day: I'll confine our story-telling to a given theme and give you prior notice of it so that you'll have leisure to think up a nice tale to tell on the theme I shall propose. Here it is, if it's to your liking: from the beginning of time people have been subject to the whims of Fate, and so shall they be till the world ends; and your stories are all to show how a person who has been thwarted by ill fortune comes to a happy ending that defies his expectations.'

They all approved of this suggestion, men and women alike, and promised to observe it, all except for Dioneo who said, once the others had fallen silent: 'Everyone else has told you, my lady, what fun your proposal is and how thoroughly commendable—and I agree with them entirely. Nevertheless I'm going to ask you for a special favour, and I want it to be confirmed for the duration of our assembly. And it is that *I* should not be bound by this rule to speak on the proposed theme if I choose not to, but to tell whatever tale I please. And in case anyone thinks I'm asking this favour because I'm at a loss for stories, I'm ready from this moment always to tell mine last.'

As the queen recognized that Dioneo was the life and soul of the party, and well knew that his request was in order to tickle the company with some merry tale if they grew weary with their story-telling, she was happy to make him this concession, and the others concurred. She stood up and they sauntered off towards a limpid brook that streamed down from a hillside to enter a thickly wooded, shady coomb, as it flowed amid lush grass and lustrous pebbles. Here they waded into the water with bare feet and bare arms and all began to frolic about in it. As supper-time approached, they returned to the villa and enjoyed their meal, after which they sent for their musical instruments and the queen bade Lauretta lead the dance while Emilia was to sing a song, accompanied on the lute by Dioneo. Thus bidden, Lauretta promptly led off with a dance as Emilia sang this soulful ditty:

My beauty, ah my beauty so enthralls me,
The thought of any other love appals me.
  I gaze in the glass and I see
  The source of my honest contentment,
  Which shall never be taken from me
  By fresh sorrow or settled resentment.
What else allures, what different pleasure calls me?
The thought of any other love appals me.

  Its virtue remains in my keeping,
  And affords me a comfort unfailing.
  The mere thought of it sets my heart leaping;
  To describe it at all's unavailing.
Lives there a man who in this realm forestalls me?
The thought of any other love appals me.

  The sight of it sets my heart burning,
  And I offer my total surrender;
  All else is fit only for spurning;
  None but this will my passion engender.
I care not what in this base life befalls me—
The thought of any other love appals me.

When the little ballade was over (everyone having happily joined in the refrains), its words did leave certain persons somewhat pensive. However, a few round dances followed, after which, as the short night had already run a part of its course, the queen decided to bring the first day to an end. Torches were lit and everyone was told to retire to bed until the following morning—so they all withdrew to their rooms and did as bidden.

*Here ends the first day of the* Decameron *and the second day begins; under the reign of Philomena, the stories show how a person who has been thwarted by ill fortune comes to a happy ending that defies his expectations.*

The light of the sun had penetrated everywhere and brought in the new day, to which the birds sonorously bore witness as they trilled and warbled agreeably in the leafy branches, when the ladies and the three young men all arose and went into the gardens. They strolled here and there across the dewy grass, making themselves pretty garlands and enjoying themselves at leisure. And today they did just as they had done on the previous day: they had their alfresco meal followed by a little dancing, then took their siesta until at about three they got up, assembled in the cool meadow and, at the queen's behest, sat round her in a circle. She was indeed a fair lady, Philomena, with a most affable expression, and on her head she wore her laurel garland as a crown. She paused awhile as she looked each of her friends in the face, then commanded Neiphile to open the story-telling with a tale of her own. Neiphile made no excuses but cheerfully began her story as follows:

II. 1. *Martellino pretends to be cured of paralysis by Treviso's Saint Arrigo. When the Trevisans discover his deceit and turn on him, his friends come to his rescue with a plan that drops him out of the frying pan into the fire.*

How often has it happened that those who have set out to make fun of others have been the ones to end up looking silly and indeed have got their fingers burnt—not least where religious susceptibilities have been involved. Now in order to do as the queen has bidden me and initiate our chosen topic with a story of mine, I'm going to tell you what befell one of our fellow-citizens: it started unluckily but turned out fortunate beyond his expectations.

Not very long ago at Treviso there was a man called Arrigo.* He came from Bolzano (where they speak German) and, being of negligible means, hired himself out as a porter to carry loads. At all events he was generally considered a man of virtuous and saintly life, which is why, when he died, the cathedral bells at Treviso were all set a-ringing on their own, without anybody pulling the ropes—maybe it is true, maybe not, but that is what the Trevisans claim. This was taken for a miracle and everyone said that Arrigo was a saint. The whole of Treviso surged into the house in which his body was lying and bore it off to the cathedral as a sacred relic. Hither they brought the lame and the paralytics, the blind and those suffering from whatever sickness or physical disability, as if they were all to recover their health on touching the corpse.

While the Trevisans were all scurrying about in great excitement, who should turn up but three Florentines, called Stecchi, Martellino, and Marchese. They tended to visit princely courts and entertain their public by putting on disguises and mimicking all and sundry quite outrageously. They had never been here before and were surprised to see everybody dashing about; when they discovered the reason they were anxious to go and see for themselves.

They left their things at an inn, and Marchese said: 'We want to go and see this saint. How we'll do it I don't know, because the square, so I'm told, is crowded with his fellow-Teutons and scores of men-at-arms brought in by the local overlord to keep the peace. What's more, it seems the cathedral is so packed it's just about impossible to get in.'

Martellino wanted to go and take a look, though, and he said: 'Don't let that stop us: I'll find some way for us to get up to the saint's body.'

'How?' asked Marchese.

'I'll tell you: I'll pretend I'm a paralytic. You'll support me on one side, Stecchi on the other, as though I can't walk on my own, and you'll pretend you're trying to get me in there so as to be cured by the saint. When they see us they'll make way for us, every one of them, and let us through.'

Marchese and Stecchi thought this an excellent idea, and they wasted no time in leaving the inn and making for a secluded spot; here, Martellino put his hands and fingers, his arms and legs through such contortions, not to mention his mouth and eyes, indeed his entire face, that he looked an utter fright. Anybody setting eyes on him would have sworn that he was a cripple with a vengeance. Marchese and Stecchi now laid hold of him and proceeded to the church, looking as pious as could be and meekly asking any who stood in their way to be kind enough to step aside. Such requests were readily granted and in no time they reached the spot where the saintly Arrigo's body lay, as everyone deferred to them and shouted 'Make way, make way!' Here Martellino was quickly picked up by some gentlemen gathered round the body and laid upon it, so that by its virtue he might recover the blessing of good health. As the whole crowd watched to see what would happen to him, Martellino began after a minute or two—excellent feigner that he was—to straighten one of his fingers, and then a hand, then his arm, and gradually to unknot himself. Seeing this, the crowd burst into such a clamour of praise for Saint Arrigo, the sound of thunder would have been lost in it.

Now a Florentine happened to be on hand who was well acquainted with Martellino, though he had failed to recognize him when he had been brought in so thoroughly seized up. Now that he saw him straightened out he did recognize him, whereupon he burst out laughing.

'Well, I'll be damned!' he cried. 'The way he looked when he came in, you'd have sworn he really was a cripple!'

Some of the Trevisans heard what he said and at once asked him: 'What's that? Wasn't this man a paralytic?'

'Good gracious no!' said the Florentine. 'He's always been as limber as you or me but, as you've seen, he has a gift for play-acting and taking on whatever role he chooses.'

This was all they needed: they surged forward, shouting: 'Grab the scoundrel! Make fun of God and His saints, would he! Coming here to flout us and our saint, pretending to be paralysed! Some cripple!' With this, they seized him and dragged him down, and grabbed him by the hair and tore his clothing to shreds and laid into him with their fists and feet;

Martellino could not see a single person holding back. He yelled for mercy, and defended himself as best he could, but all to no avail—the mob was building up every minute. As they watched, Stecchi and Marchese felt that the situation was looking far from bright; they were worried on their own account and little inclined to lend Martellino a hand—indeed, they joined in with the rest in baying for his blood, even as they mulled over ways to rescue him from the mob, which would assuredly have done him to death had not Marchese hit upon an expedient. The Podestà's* watch had been mustered there in force, and Marchese approached their lieutenant in charge at the first opportunity and cried: 'Help! That's the rascal who's cut my purse; it had a good hundred gold florins in it. Please arrest him, so I can get it all back.'

At this, a dozen constables dashed off to the spot where the unfortunate Martellino was being given a thorough pasting, and it was all they could do to break through the mob and snatch him out of its hands; they hauled him off, all battered and bruised, to the Podestà's palace. When the crowd heard that he had been arrested as a cut-purse, many of those who felt he had insulted them followed him there and put in their own claims to the effect that he had cut their purses, too, for lack of any better excuse to get him into trouble. The Podestà's magistrate was a man of little finesse; when he heard the charge he at once drew him to one side and set about interrogating him. Martellino, however, made light of his arrest and merely twitted the magistrate; the man lost his temper and subjected him to the strappado, giving him several sharp jerks of the rope with a view to making him confess to the charges laid against him, so that he could go ahead and hang him.

Once he had been let down again, he was asked by the magistrate whether there was any truth in the accusations made against him. As nothing was to be gained from denying it, Martellino said: 'I'm ready to admit the truth, sir. But make each one of my accusers state when and where it was that I cut his purse, then I shall tell you what I did and did not do.'

The magistrate consented to call some of them in; one man said that Martellino had cut his purse a week ago, another six days ago, another said four days, while others said it was today.

'They're all lying in their teeth, sir', cried Martellino when he heard this. 'And I have proof for you that I'm telling the truth: I never set foot in this city till a short time ago, and would that I never had done so! When I arrived, I had the misfortune to go and look at this saintly corpse and got myself worked over as you can see. The truth of what I'm saying will be attested by your official in charge of the registration of foreigners—it will be down in his book—and our innkeeper will tell you too. These scoundrels here want you to torture me and put me to death: but if you find that the matter is as I say, pray don't.'

While affairs were at this pitch, Marchese and Stecchi were in a thorough panic, for they had heard that the Podestà's magistrate was taking a tough line with Martellino and indeed had subjected him to the strappado. 'Now we've gone and done it', they brooded. 'We've dropped him out of the frying pan and into the fire.' So, to leave no stone unturned, they went to find their landlord and told him exactly what had happened. This left him grinning, but he took them to see a certain Sandro Agolanti, a Florentine living in Treviso, who had a considerable influence with the local ruler; the whole story was repeated to him, and he was besought by the landlord and the other two to take an interest in Martellino's predicament. Sandro had a good laugh, but went to the ruler with the request that Martellino be sent for. This was done, and those sent to fetch him found him still before the magistrate in nothing but his shirt, terrified and at his wits' end because the magistrate refused to listen to his defence; indeed, as he happened to nurse a grudge against Florentines in general, he had made up his mind to hang him, and was on no account ready to hand him on to his master until he was reluctantly compelled to do so. Once Martellino had been brought before the ruler and the facts had been finally rehearsed, he besought him to be very kind and let him go, for until he was back in Florence he'd constantly feel the noose about his neck. The lord found the misadventure quite hilarious and he presented each of them with a gown; then, after the three of them had practically given up hope of escaping from such grave danger, they all returned home safe and sound.

II. 2. *Rinaldo d'Este, the victim of highwaymen, reaches Castel Guglielmo and finds shelter with a widow—who sends him safely on his way.*

Neiphile's account of the misfortunes that befell Martellino had the ladies in fits of laughter, and the men too, especially Philostrato. As he was sitting next to Neiphile, it was him the queen ordered to speak next, and he began without delay, as follows:

I'm inclined to tell you a story which has to do with sacred matters and with misadventures and with love, all these together, and I dare say it will serve you well enough, my pretty ladies, to have heard it. This applies particularly to those who are engaged on a journey through the hazardous realms of love: here, the traveller who has not made a habit of praying to Venus—I'm sorry, I mean to Saint Julian*—may find a passable bed but will be in for a rough night.

In the days when Ferrara was under the rule of Marquis Azzo,* there was a merchant called Rinaldo d'Este. He had gone on business to Bologna and, when it was done, he turned for home. As he left Ferrara and was riding towards Verona, he fell in with some men who passed for merchants but were in fact brigands, men of evil life and character. He got into conversation with them and imprudently joined their company. Recognizing him for a merchant, and imagining that he must be carrying money on him, these men decided to rob him at the first suitable opportunity. And, to put him off his guard, they behaved towards him as meek, gentle creatures—so far as they knew how to be—and, like respectable, well-bred folk, conversed with him about honest dealing and such virtuous topics. Rinaldo therefore felt he was very lucky to have run into them, for he was riding alone except for a servant. As they rode along, the conversation shifted from one topic to the next, for that is the way with conversation, until they fell to discussing the prayers people make to God.

One of the brigands—there were three in all—said to Rinaldo: 'How about you, good sir? What prayer do you tend to say when you are travelling?'

'Well, the fact is', replied Rinaldo, 'when it comes to this I'm a rough, down-to-earth sort of fellow: I'm not a great one for prayers, in fact I'm an old-fashioned bloke and not given to splitting hairs. This said, it's always been my habit, when I'm on the road, to say an Our Father and a Hail Mary in the morning as I leave my inn, for the souls of Saint Julian's father and mother (whom he killed by accident before he became a Hospitaller) and then I offer him and the Good Lord a prayer requesting good quarters for the coming night. Many a time have I been in great danger on the road, but I've always survived and found a safe refuge and good lodging for the night. So I'm quite convinced that Saint Julian has obtained this favour for me as I've offered a prayer in his honour. And I never expect a day to turn out well for me, nor the coming night, unless I've said the prayer that morning.'

'Did you say it this morning?' his questioner asked him.

'Of course.'

So the other, who knew how matters were expected to proceed, observed to himself: 'Much good may it do you: if our plan doesn't miscarry, I reckon that you'll be poorly lodged.' Then he told him: 'I too have travelled a great deal, and I've never said that prayer—though I've heard many people speak very highly of it—but that hasn't stopped me always fetching up in good accommodation. The chances are that this evening you'll be able to see who gets the better lodging, you who've said it or I who have not. I do, though, say another instead, the *Dirupisti* or the *Intemerata* or else the *De Profundis*,* which carry a lot of weight, so my grandmother used to tell me.'

And, chatting of this and that, they pursued their journey as they awaited the right place and time to effect their evil plan. It was already late and they were beyond Castel Guglielmo* and happened to come to a river-crossing when the three brigands, noticing how late it had grown and how deserted and enclosed the place was, assaulted Rinaldo and robbed him, and left him standing, dismounted, in nothing but his shirt. 'So long!' they said; 'Let's see if your Saint Julian sends you a good lodging tonight—ours will give *us* one all right!' With these parting words they forded the river and went their way.

Seeing his master attacked, Rinaldo's man did nothing to help him but turned his horse, the coward, and never stopped galloping till he reached Castel Guglielmo; in he went, as it was evening, and found lodging without troubling himself further. It was freezing cold and snowing a blizzard. Left out there in only a shirt and stocking-feet, Rinaldo was at his wit's end: night had fallen and, shivering and with chattering teeth, he peered about him in search of some shelter for the night, lest he freeze to death, but there was none to be seen because the region had just been swept by war and everything was burnt to the ground. So, driven by the cold, he set off at a trot towards Castel Guglielmo (with no idea whether or not that's where his servant had escaped to); he thought that if he could get in, God would send him help of some kind. He was a good mile short of the town, though, when night, pitch-black, overtook him, so he got there too late—the gates were shut, the drawbridges raised, and he could not get in. He wept for utter distress and looked about to see where to put himself so that he might at least be out of the falling snow. And he happened to notice that a house was built on top of the town walls and jutted out over the edge a little; he decided, therefore, to take shelter beneath this projection till daybreak. He went over to it and beneath the corbelled house he noticed a door in the wall; it was locked, but there was some chopped straw close at hand, so he raked some together by the door and settled down glumly, addressing many a complaint to Saint Julian: 'A fine way', he said, 'to repay the trust I've placed in you!' Saint Julian, however, was indeed keeping him in mind, and arranged a good billet for him without too much delay.

Now there was a widow living here, a woman of matchless beauty; the Marquis Azzo loved her as much as he cherished his own life, and had installed her here at his disposal. The house in which she lived was the very one beneath which Rinaldo had gone for shelter. Well, the marquis happened to have arrived at Castel Guglielmo that day, meaning to join her in bed that night, and he had quietly ordered a bath to be prepared for himself in her own house, and a sumptuous dinner to follow. When everything was ready and all she was waiting for was the marquis's arrival, a page turned up at the gate with a despatch for the marquis, that resulted in his having to take horse at once. So he sent word to the lady that she was not to expect him and off he went. The lady was somewhat put out and at a loss; however, she decided to take the bath prepared for the marquis, eat the supper, then go to bed. So she got into the bath.

The bath was adjacent to the door by which poor Rinaldo was huddled, outside the walls. As she was in the bath, therefore, the lady heard him weeping and shivering, for all the world like a stork clacking its beak. So she called her maid and told her: 'Go up and look over the wall and see who it is outside this door; find out who he is and what he's up to.' The maid went up and, as it was a clear night, she spotted him sitting there, as we have said, in nothing but his shirt and stocking-feet and shivering like anything. So she asked him who he was. Rinaldo was shaking so hard he could barely get the words out, but he told her as briefly as could be who he was and how he came to be here. And he made a pitiful plea to her: could she possibly not leave him out here in the night to perish with cold? The maid took pity on him and reported everything to her mistress; she, too, felt sorry for him, and remembered that she possessed the key to that door, which the marquis used on occasions for his secret visits. 'Go and let him in quietly', she said. 'Here's this dinner and no one to eat it; and we've more than room enough to accommodate him.'

The maid much applauded her mistress's kindness and went to open the door and bring him inside, whereupon the widow, who saw that he was practically frozen stiff, said to him: 'Quick, my friend, into this bath with you: it's still warm.' This he gladly did without awaiting a further invitation. The warmth quite revived him and he felt he was back among the living. The widow lent him some clothes that had belonged to her husband, recently deceased, and when he put them on, they seemed made to his own measure. As he waited at the lady's further bidding, he offered thanks to the Good Lord and Saint Julian who had delivered him from the ghastly night he was expecting and brought him to a good lodging, from what he could see. The lady paused a moment to rest, then had a blazing fire lit in a room with a fireplace. To that room she repaired and asked her maid how the good fellow was faring.

'He's got dressed, ma'am, and looks a handsome man; has a touch of class, too, I should say.'

'Go and fetch him, then. Tell him to come here by the fire and he'll have supper, for he won't have eaten.'

Rinaldo entered the room with the blazing fire and looked at the lady, who seemed to him a person of consequence; he greeted her respectfully and thanked her to the best of his ability for the kindness she had done to him. From the look of him and the way he spoke the lady decided that she shared her maid's opinion of him; she welcomed him cordially and, forgoing ceremony, made him sit beside her by the fire. She asked him about the mischance that had resulted in his being here, and Rinaldo told her the whole story as it had befallen. She had already heard something of this on the arrival of Rinaldo's manservant, so she quite believed his account; she assured him that he would easily recover his man in the morning and told him what she knew of him. When supper was ready they washed their hands and Rinaldo sat down to table with the lady, as was her wish. Rinaldo was a tall, handsome man in his middle thirties, with a pleasant face and a charming manner. The lady could not take her eyes off her guest—she was far from indifferent to him, the more so as she was sexually aroused, for the marquis was supposed to have come and slept with her tonight. After supper, when the table was cleared, she consulted her maid and asked her whether, as the marquis had trifled with her, there would be any harm in her helping herself to that which Fortune had sent her way.

The maid knew exactly what her mistress wanted and gave her every encouragement to satisfy her craving, so the lady returned to the fire where she had left Rinaldo on his own and began to dart passionate glances at him. 'Come, Rinaldo', she said, 'why are you brooding so? You've lost a horse and a few clothes—d'you think you'll never get over it? Take heart, cheer up, make yourself at home—in fact, shall I tell you something?

Seeing you in these clothes, which used to be my late husband's, I've almost taken you for him, and goodness knows how many times tonight I've felt an urge to throw my arms round your neck and kiss you. In fact I should have done so already were I not afraid you wouldn't like it.'

Noting her words and the gleam in her eye, Rinaldo, who was no dullard, advanced on her with open arms. 'Considering that it's thanks to you, my lady, that I'm still alive', he said, 'and bearing in mind what it is you rescued me from, I should be a proper scoundrel if I didn't do everything in my power to oblige you. Do, therefore, hug and kiss me to your heart's content, and I'll hug and kiss you with the best will in the world.'

Further words were not needed. Aflame with desire, the lady threw herself into his arms, clasped him in a tight embrace and planted a thousand kisses on him. She received as many back, after which they adjourned to the bedroom and were in bed within seconds; before day dawned they had fully and repeatedly assuaged their passion. But at the first sign of dawn the lady chose to get up, so that nobody should suspect a thing, and handed him some rags to dress in; she filled his purse with money, asking him to keep it out of sight, and ushered him out of the door in the wall by which he had come in, after giving him instructions for getting back inside the walls and recovering his manservant.

Once it was broad daylight and the town gates were opened, he went in as though just arrived from some distance, and found his man. He changed into his own clothes which had stayed in his valise, and was about to mount the servant's horse when, almost miraculously, the three brigands who had robbed him the previous night were brought in: they had been taken shortly afterwards committing another felony. As they confessed, Rinaldo recovered his horse, his clothes, and his money—all he lost was a pair of garters which the brigands did not know what they had done with. So Rinaldo offered thanks to the Good Lord and to Saint Julian, mounted his steed, and returned home safe and sound, while the three brigands were all dangling from gibbets the very next day.

II. 3. *Three rich but spendthrift brothers end up in penury. Their nephew restores their fortunes by contracting a good marriage with the King of England's daughter.*

The perils encountered by Rinaldo d'Este left the ladies and the young men full of admiration as they listened, and they spoke well of his devotion; they gave thanks to the Good Lord and to Saint Julian for helping him in his hour of need. Though they did not say it in so many words, they even considered that the woman had acted perfectly sensibly in making the most of the luck God had sent her way. And while they continued joking about the jolly night the lady had spent, Pampinea, who sat next to Philostrato and saw that it was to be her turn next (she was not wrong), turned over in her mind the question of what story she would tell. At the queen's bidding she started off with cheerful assurance:

If you stop to think about it, the more we talk about the doings of Fortune, the more remains still to be said. This is scarcely surprising if you give it more than a moment's thought: everything we're foolish enough to regard as being in our own control is in fact in the lap of Fate and she consequently, in her obscure wisdom, will keep chopping and changing a situation in what seems to us a totally random fashion. I know that this is evident enough day after day and in the most obvious manner, and that it has been demonstrated already in some of the previous stories; nevertheless, this being the topic our queen has been pleased to choose, I'll contribute a tale of my own which I think ought to find favour among my listeners—they may even find it useful.

There was once a knight in our city called Tebaldo. He was, according to some, a Lamberti, while others maintain that he belonged to the Agolanti, possibly arguing from the trade his sons were to follow—a calling traditional among the Agolanti—rather than on any other grounds. But never mind which of the two was the actual case, what I'm saying is that Tebaldo was in his day a knight of enormous wealth, and he had three sons, called Lamberto, Tedaldo, and Agolante, all of them good-looking young gallants, though the eldest was not yet 18 when their wealthy father died. As his lawful heirs he bequeathed to them his entire estate, both the real property and the moveable assets. So they found themselves rolling in wealth, in cash, and in kind, and embarked on a life-style of unbridled extravagance, heedless of any rule but that of their own pleasure: servants galore, thoroughbreds by the dozen, hawks and hounds. They kept open house, lavishing presents on everyone, holding tournaments, in a word, behaving like the nobility, nay, more: indulging any and every one of their youthful whims. They had not long been living in that style before the inheritance left them by their father ran out. As they could not meet their commitments by exploiting their income, they started to mortgage and sell off their properties, one today, the next tomorrow, barely noticing that they had come virtually to the end of their resources. Wealth had made them blind; it was poverty that opened their eyes.

So one day Lamberto called the other two. He pointed out to them what their father's standing had been in the community and what theirs was; how rich they had been, and how poor they had become thanks to their careless extravagance. And he encouraged them as best he could to join him in selling off what little they were left with and going away, before their poverty became even more evident. So that's what they did. They left Florence without ceremony or leave-taking and never stopped until they had arrived in England. Here they took a small house in London, pared their expenses to the bone, and set themselves up as grasping money-lenders—wherein Luck so smiled on them that in a few years they had accumulated a fortune. One after the other of them, therefore, took his money and returned to Florence, where they bought back most of their former possessions together with a whole lot more. They also married. They continued their money-lending activities in England, sending out a young nephew called Alessandro to keep an eye on things. The three brothers, meanwhile, quite forgetting to what they had earlier been reduced by their immoderate spending, went back to lavishing money hand over fist, even worse than before—never mind that now they all had families to support—and there was no limit to their credit-worthiness in the eyes of the business community. Their outlays were covered for some years by the funds sent them by Alessandro, who was making loans to the barons on the security of their castles and other revenues—these gave him an excellent return.

And while the three brothers thus continued their lavish disbursements, borrowing whenever the funds ran out, their hopes forever pinned on England, a war happened to erupt, contrary to the general expectation, between the king and his son;* this war split the island, some siding with the one, some with the other. As a result, Alessandro was deprived of all his baronial castles and his other sources of income stopped yielding. Alessandro kept hoping that from one day to the next father and son would come to terms and he would recover all his assets, both principal and interest, so he remained in the island. The three brothers in Florence, meanwhile, did not trim their huge expenses in the slightest and fell each day more deeply into debt. But as the years passed and Alessandro saw his hopes were not to be realized, the three brothers found all their credit withdrawn, worse—their creditors had them all arrested, and as their remaining assets were insufficient to cover their debts, they were committed to prison in default of payment. As for their wives and young children, some left for the country, one here another there, in a beggarly condition, with no idea what lay in store for them other than to finish their days in penury.

Alessandro remained in England several years, waiting for the return of peace. As he saw no sign of it, however, and felt that his continued residence there was not only fruitless but actually placed his life at risk, he decided to return to Italy and set out all on his own. As he was leaving Bruges, he chanced to see an abbot in his white Benedictine* habit also leaving, accompanied by several monks and a big retinue and baggage-train. Two elderly knights were also of the party; they were related to the king, and as Alessandro knew them he went over to join them and they welcomed his company. As they pursued their journey together, Alessandro quietly asked them who were the monks riding on ahead in such a big company and where were they bound for. One of the knights told him: 'That's a young relative of ours riding ahead of us. He has just been elected abbot of one of England's greatest monasteries. But as he is too young for such a dignity according to canon law, we are escorting him to Rome to seek a dispensation from the Holy Father and have him confirmed in office despite his being under age. However, you must keep all this to yourself.'

As the newly fledged abbot rode with his retinue, sometimes at the front, other times at the rear, the way gentlefolk tend to when they're on the road, he found himself beside Alessandro, a very personable, good-looking young lad, and as charming, attractive, and well brought-up as could be. The abbot was quite exceptionally drawn to him on the instant; he called the boy over and engaged him in a pleasant conversation, asking him who he was, where he had come from and whither he was bound. Alessandro told him everything and answered all his questions; he offered to be of service to him in whatever modest way he could. The abbot delighted in the charm and simplicity of Alessandro's words, and after reflecting on his whole manner, he concluded that the lad must be well born even if he followed a humble calling, and he felt all the more drawn to him. He felt enormous pity for the boy's afflictions and responded to him with the friendliest encouragements, telling him to be of good cheer because, if he conducted himself well, the Good Lord would more than make good his lost fortunes. 'Since you're on your way to Tuscany', he said, 'do please keep me company, as that's where I'm going too.' Alessandro thanked him for his kind words. 'I am', he added, 'at your entire disposal.'

From the moment he had set eyes on Alessandro, the abbot's spirit was in quite unusual turmoil. However, they continued on their way for some days, until they came to a village where there was a distinct shortage of inns. As this is where the abbot wanted to stop for the night, Alessandro had him dismount at the house of an old friend of his, a publican; here he saw to it that a room be got ready for the guest in the least uncomfortable part of the house. He had more or less become the abbot's bailiff, being of a practical bent, and he found lodging for the whole party all round the village as best he could. When the abbot had had supper and the evening was fairly well advanced, Alessandro asked his host where he might bed down for the night, everyone else having by now retired to sleep.

'Oh dear', said his host. 'I don't know. We're quite full up, as you see; you'll find my family and me sleeping on benches. In the abbot's room, though, there are some grain-chests: I could take you in there and make you up a bed in one of those, and you can get a little sleep that way tonight if you like.'

'How am I to sleep in the abbot's room?' asked Alessandro. 'You know how small it is. That's why none of his monks could sleep in it. Had I known about it, I'd have had the monks sleeping in the grain-chests after the abbot's bed-curtains were drawn, and I'd have slept where the monks are sleeping.'

'Well, this is how things are', said his host. 'You can be ever so comfortable there if you want. The abbot's asleep and his curtains are drawn. I'll be very quiet and bring you a mattress, and you can bed down.'

Seeing that this could be done without disturbing the abbot, Alessandro consented and settled down as quietly as possible to sleep. The abbot was not asleep; his mind was churning with his unusual desire. He overheard Alessandro's discussion with their host and could hear where the boy had lain down. He was delighted and said to himself: 'Here's a God-sent opportunity to answer my desire; if I don't grasp it now, it could be ages before I'll have another chance.' And fully determined to seize it, all now appearing to be quiet in the inn, he softly called Alessandro and told him to come and lie down beside him. Alessandro made various excuses, but finally got undressed and into the abbot's bed.

The abbot laid a hand on Alessandro's chest and started to fondle him the way a girl in love would fondle her lover; this left the boy not a little surprised, and wondering whether the abbot's urge to touch him the way he was doing betokened a perverted love. The abbot was quick to grasp what was going through Alessandro's mind—maybe he guessed, maybe the boy gave himself away. At all events, he smiled, promptly pulled off the shirt he was wearing, took hold of Alessandro's hand, and placed it on his own chest, saying: 'Get rid of your silly idea, Alessandro, and feel here and realize what it is I'm hiding.'

The lad rested his hand on the abbot's chest and discovered two dainty little breasts, round and firm—they might have been made of ivory. Recognizing from this that his bed-mate was a female, he awaited no further invitation to take her in his arms, and he was about to kiss her when she said: 'Before you come any closer, wait while I tell you something. As you've noticed, I'm a woman, not a man. I left my home, a virgin, and have been on my way to the Pope so he could marry me off. Call it your good luck or my bad luck, when I set eyes on you the other day I fell madly in love with you—no woman's ever loved a man so much. So I've decided you're the man I want above all to marry. If you don't want me for wife, out you get and go back to your own bed.'

For all that his acquaintance with her was slight, Alessandro took account of her retinue, from which he judged that she must be rich and nobly born; that she was exceedingly beautiful he could see for himself. So without too much reflection he replied that he was more than delighted if this was what she wanted. Whereupon she sat up in bed, put a ring on his finger before a holy picture of Our Lord, and betrothed him, after which she took him in her arms and they spent what remained of the night affording each other much pleasure. When it was morning and Alessandro got up, they had decided how to give effect to their proposals. He left the bedroom as he had entered it, with no one knowing where he had slept. Beside himself with happiness, he resumed his journey with the abbot and their company, and reached Rome several days later.

When they had been there a few days the abbot took the two knights and Alessandro, but nobody else, to an audience with the Pope. He made the customary genuflection, then said: 'As Your Holiness must know better than anyone, whoever proposes to lead a good, upright existence must do his best to avoid every occasion that would induce him to do otherwise. A life of virtue is what I aspire to, and the better to be able to achieve this I donned this habit in which Your Holiness sees me and fled away in secret with a very substantial part of my father's treasure—he is King of England and proposed to give me as bride to the King of Scotland,* a very elderly gentleman, whereas I, as Your Holiness can see, am a young woman in my first youth. I set out, therefore, to come here so that Your Holiness might marry me off. What made me escape was not the age of the Scottish king so much as the fear, were I married to him, lest the frailty of my youth led me to do something contrary to the law of God and the honour of my father's royal blood. Now finding me thus disposed, the Almighty, who alone knows best what are each person's needs, set before my eyes (in His mercy, I believe) the man He would give me for husband. It was this young man'—she indicated Alessandro—'standing here beside me as Your Holiness sees; he behaves with a gallantry that makes him worthy of any great lady, for all that he may be of less exalted birth than a person of royal blood. Him therefore have I taken, him I want, nor will I ever accept another, whatever my father or anyone else thinks about it. The chief purpose of my departure is thus removed. I wished none the less to undertake the journey both to visit the holy places in which this city abounds, and Your Holiness himself; and also in order that the marriage contracted between myself and Alessandro simply in the presence of God might be made public in Your Holiness's presence and thus to the world at large. Therefore I humbly beg Your Holiness, that what has been pleasing to God and to me might be agreeable also to you; and I crave Your Holiness's blessing upon it, so that we might together live and eventually die to the glory of God and of Your Holiness, with greater certainty of enjoying His favour whose Vicar you are.'

Alessandro was amazed to hear that his bride was daughter of the King of England—the news filled him with a wonderful secret joy. The two knights, however, were even more surprised and so outraged that if they had been anywhere else than in the papal presence, they would have laid rough hands on Alessandro and possibly on the lady as well. The Pope was not a little surprised himself, both at the lady's attire and at her choice; he recognized, however, that there could be no turning back, so he agreed to fulfil her wish. First of all he spoke words of encouragement to the knights, knowing how angered they were, and effected a reconciliation between them and the two spouses. Then he made the necessary arrangements. On the appointed day, the Pope had the lady brought to him in the presence of all the cardinals and of many other leading citizens invited to a most sumptuous feast he had prepared. The lady was dressed as a princess and deservedly won everyone's praise for her beauty and charm; Alessandro arrived in similarly gorgeous attire, looking and behaving quite like a prince and not at all like a lad who had made his living as a money-lender; the two knights treated him with great respect. Here the couple's betrothal was solemnly re-enacted, the wedding followed, a beautiful, splendid ceremony, and then His Holiness dismissed the bride and groom with his blessing.

From Rome, Alessandro and his bride chose to travel to Florence, where news of them had already arrived. Here they were welcomed with every possible honour, and the princess arranged for the three brothers, Alessandro's uncles, to be released from prison, their every debt to be settled, and all three, together with their wives, to be restored to their former possessions. So Alessandro and his lady, who had secured everyone's goodwill, left Florence, taking Agolante with them, and continued to Paris, where the king gave them an honourable welcome too.

From here the two knights returned to England and prevailed on the king to pardon his daughter and receive her back, together with his son-in-law, in the most festive of spirits. It was not long before he conferred a knighthood on Alessandro and made him Earl of Cornwall. Now Alessandro possessed the qualities and shrewdness needed to restore peace between the king and his son; this brought great blessings to the whole island and Alessandro secured to himself the love and goodwill of the entire nation. Agolante recovered in full all that was owing to him, and returned to Florence richer than ever, but not before the Earl of Cornwall had obtained him a knighthood. The earl lived gloriously with his lady ever after, and, according to one account, he turned his intelligence and courage to such good effect that, with his father-in-law's help, he went on to conquer Scotland and was there crowned king.

II. 4. *Landolfo Rufolo, a rich merchant, loses everything but his shirt, suffers shipwreck, but is taken in hand by Fortune.*

When Pampinea's story reached its triumphant conclusion, Lauretta, who sat beside her, embarked on her own story without awaiting the command:

It seems to me that Fortune never worked to better effect than it did in Pampinea's story about Alessandro, raising him from the most abject condition to that of a prince. Now any story told within our brief for today must fall short of Pampinea's conclusion, so I'll make no apologies for telling you a tale which touches on even worse misadventures but does not end quite so magnificently. Of course I know that after listening to her story you may not devote all that much attention to mine—but there's nothing I can do about that so you'll have to forgive me.

The coast between Reggio and Gaeta is generally considered to be the pleasantest part of Italy. There is a stretch here close to Salerno known locally as the Amalfi coast, with plenty of little towns, gardens, and fountains, and teeming with rich men who engage in commerce with quite singular zeal. One such town, called Ravello, which even today boasts some extremely rich men, was once upon a time the home of Landolfo Rufolo, a man of exceptional wealth. Not content, though, with what he possessed, he wanted twice as much, and in the attempt to get it he came close to losing the lot—and his life along with it.

Anyway, after working out his costs the way merchants do, he bought a large ship and loaded it with all kinds of merchandise at his own expense, and sailed for Cyprus. Here he found that all too many other vessels had arrived carrying precisely the same range of goods, and he had to sell his off at bargain prices, indeed he practically had to give them away. So he was just about ruined. Of course he was not a little dejected by this turn of affairs; he couldn't think what to do and saw himself reduced in no time to virtual penury after being so immensely rich. Determined not to return home a pauper after setting out a wealthy man, he decided to restore his fortunes by brigandage or die in the attempt. So he found a buyer for his great hulk and used the proceeds, in addition to what he raised from the sale of his wares, to buy the slender galley he needed for buccaneering. This he fitted out with the best of everything for his purpose, and set about seizing other men's goods—he preyed mostly on the Turks.

In this calling he fared considerably better than he had done as a trader: within a year he had taken and stripped so many Turkish ships that he had not merely recovered all he had lost in trade, he had more than doubled his assets. And so, chastened by the loss he had first incurred, but sure in the knowledge that he had all he needed to avoid any further loss, he persuaded himself to rest content with what he now possessed and leave it at that. He therefore decided to return home with his winnings. These he did not invest in anything, for he was wary of any form of merchandise; he simply set off under oars in the little craft in which he had recovered his wealth and made for home.

He had reached the Aegean when at nightfall a sirocco blew up, a contrary wind that raised a great sea, more than his little craft could contend with; so he took refuge in a bay sheltered from the wind by a little island; here he proposed to ride out the storm. He had not been long in the bay when two stout Genoese merchantmen struggled in: they had come from Constantinople and were seeking shelter likewise. On sight of the little galley, the Genoese blocked its line of escape, for they had discovered whose ship it was and what a wealthy man owned it; with their usual propensity to greed and love of gain, they made ready to capture him. They landed a strongly armed body of crossbowmen and deployed their forces in such a way as to prevent any crew leaving the galley unless they wanted to be shot to pieces with arrows. Then the Genoese were taken in tow by their longboats and, aided by the current, closed in upon Landolfo's galley and had little trouble in effecting a quick capture of the vessel and its crew, sustaining no loss themselves. Landolfo was taken on board one of the two stout merchantmen, while his vessel was stripped bare then scuttled, leaving the prisoner in nothing but his shirt.

The next day the wind shifted and the merchantmen set sail westwards. They made good progress all that day, but at nightfall a storm blew up, raising a huge sea, and the two vessels became separated. Now it happened that the vessel carrying poor Landolfo was thrown on to a reef with a mighty thud and splintered into smithereens, like a glass smashed against a wall. This was on the island of Cephalonia. With the sea full of floating merchandise, crates, and planks, as usually happens in these circumstances, a night black as pitch and a high sea running, the unfortunate seamen—those of them who could swim—grabbed hold of whatever happened to float within reach. The day before, poor Landolfo had several times prayed for death, for even death was better, he thought, than returning home in his present abject state; but seeing death now close at hand he shrank from it in fear and, like the others, he grabbed hold of a plank as it floated within reach, hoping that if he staved off drowning, God would see to keeping him alive. Astride his plank, pushed this way and that by the wind and waves, he kept afloat as best he could till daybreak.

When it was day he looked about him and saw nothing but clouds and sea, and a chest floating in the waves, which caused him no little anxiety whenever it came close, in case it crashed into him and did him an injury. Each time it floated close he did his best to ward it off with his hands, though he had little strength left. It so happened, though, that a sudden squall ripped across the sea and carried the chest hard against Landolfo's plank; the plank was tipped on end, Landolfo was shaken off and sank beneath the waves; he swam to the surface, helped more by fear than by strength, but the plank, he saw, had drifted quite out of reach and he was afraid he would never get to it. So he made for the chest which floated close by and heaved himself up to lie across its lid as best he could, using his arms to keep it upright. Tossed this way and that by the waves, fasting (for he had nothing to eat) but drinking more than his fill, with no idea of where he was and nothing to look at but the sea—this is how he endured all that day and the following night.

The next day Landolfo, now a veritable sponge as he clung tightly with both hands to the edges of the chest, as a drowning man clutches at straws, found himself driven ashore, whether by God's providence or the wind's. He was driven ashore on the island of Corfu, where a poor woman chanced to be washing her pots and pans, scouring them shiny with sand and salt-water. She drew back in alarm and cried out when she first saw him, for she did not recognize in him any human form. Landolfo was unable to speak and could scarcely see, and so said nothing to her; but as the sea washed him ashore, the woman recognized the chest for a chest, and on a closer look she perceived that there were arms clamped over the chest, and a face above it, and she realized what it was. Pitying him, she waded a little into the sea, which had now subsided, grasped him by the hair, and pulled him and the chest ashore. Here she had some trouble unfastening his fingers from the chest, then carried him like a child up on to dry land, while she got one of her little daughters to carry up the chest on her head. She put him in a tub and scrubbed him and washed him with hot water until the lost warmth returned into his body together with some fresh vigour. When she thought he was ready she took him out of the tub and gave him a little wine and something to eat to fortify him, and sheltered him as best she could for a few days, until he had gathered his strength and could take in where he was. Then the kind woman thought it was time to give him back his chest which she had rescued, and leave him to continue on his way—which she did.

Landolfo had forgotten all about the chest, but took it when the kind soul returned it to him, reckoning that it must at least be worth enough to see to his expenses for a day or two—though he couldn't expect much for it, weighing as little as it did. Still, when the woman was out, he forced it open to see just what it contained; what he found was a whole mass of precious stones, some loose, others strung together, and he knew a precious stone when he saw one. They were worth a fortune, he realized, so he praised God for not deserting him yet, and quite recovered his spirits. However, as Fate had already twice shot him through with arrows and he did not want a third peppering, he decided to take all possible care to convey these little objects home with him. So he bundled them up hastily in some rags and told his kind woman that he had no further use for the chest: could she let him have a sack? As for the chest, she was welcome to keep it.

This she gladly did; and, after thanking her with all his heart for her kindness to him, Landolfo shouldered his sack, bade her farewell, and boarded a ship for Brindisi. Thence he travelled from port to port until he came to Trani, where he found some compatriots who were drapers. He told them of all the misfortunes he had suffered (saving any mention of the chest), and they, more or less out of holy charity, reclothed him and lent him a horse and sent him, with an escort, on to Ravello where he said he was bent on returning.

Once home, he felt safe at last, and thanked God for bringing him back. Then he unfastened his sack and looked through the contents more thoroughly than he had done the first time. What he had, he realized, were gems in such profusion and of such quality that if they fetched their proper price, or even less, he would be twice as rich as when he first set out. Well, he did succeed in selling the jewels; he sent a good sum of money to the kind soul who had pulled him out of the sea in Corfu, to thank her for her help, and he did the same for the men in Trani who had reclothed him. The rest he kept for himself and, with no desire to engage any further in commerce, he lived out the rest of his days in becoming dignity.

II. 5. *Andreuccio of Perugia goes to Naples to buy horses. He suffers three misadventures in one night, but it is not a wasted journey.*

The gems found by Landolfo [Fiammetta began, for it was now her turn] remind me of a story just about as venturesome as Lauretta's; the difference is that whereas hers took place over maybe a number of years, this one happened all in a single night, as you shall hear.

Once upon a time in Perugia there lived, so I've heard, a young man called Andreuccio di Pietro. He was a horse-dealer by trade, and when he heard that there was a good horse fair* at Naples, he put five hundred gold florins into his purse and off he went there with some other merchants, though he had never before set foot outside his own city. He arrived on a

Sunday evening, obtained some advice from his innkeeper, and the following morning went to the market. Here he looked at dozens of horses, and as there were plenty that he liked, he entered into negotiations over a great number, but not once was he able to strike a bargain. However, to show that he was a serious buyer he kept pulling out his purse full of florins—incautious young bumpkin that he was—to flaunt in the presence of the passers-by.

Engaged as he was in haggling, and flashing his purse around, he failed to notice a young Sicilian beauty (one of those ready to gratify any man for a modest fee), as she brushed past him and spotted his purse. 'Who'd be sitting prettier than I', she mused, 'if that money were mine?' And she continued on her way. Now she was in the company of an old woman, also from Sicily, and when this woman noticed Andreuccio, she let the girl go on ahead and ran to give him an affectionate embrace, while the girl quietly stood to one side and observed them both. Andreuccio turned round and recognized the old woman and was delighted to see her; she promised to come and look him up at his inn, but she didn't keep him there talking all that long—she went her way, while Andreuccio returned to his horse-trading, though he bought nothing that morning. The young woman, meanwhile, who had first taken note of Andreuccio's purse and then of the old woman's intimacy with him, began guardedly questioning her to see if there were any way of laying hands on the money or some part of it: Who was the fellow? she asked. Where was he from? What was he doing here? How did she come to know him? The old woman gave her an answer in the greatest detail, much as if Andreuccio were answering for himself, for she had long known his father in Sicily and later at Perugia. She told the girl, too, where he would be returning to and what he had come for.

Once she was fully apprised of the names and relationships of all his kith and kin, the young woman built her scheme on this knowledge, resorting to a little guile to gain her ends. She returned home and kept the old woman busy all day to prevent her going back to Andreuccio. Then she sent for her maid, who was well trained to run such errands, and despatched her to Andreuccio's inn at nightfall. When she got there, she chanced to run into him all by himself in the entrance, so she enquired for Andreuccio from the very man. 'That's me', he said, so she drew him to one side and told him: 'There's a gentlewoman who lives here, sir, who'd be glad of a word with you, if you don't mind.'

As he listened to her he took a good look at himself and decided that, yes, he wasn't all that bad-looking a fellow, and the lady must have fallen for him, as if there were no other good-looking youngsters then in Naples. 'I'm ready', said he promptly. 'Where is she? When does she want to see me?'

'She is waiting for you at home, any time it suits you.'

'Fine. Lead on and I'll follow', said the lad hastily, without leaving word at his inn.

So the maid led him to the young woman's house. The district she lived in was called Malpertugio, and the place really was a hole as its name implied,* but Andreuccio had no inkling of suspicion as to how insalubrious the place was; he thought he was calling on a respectable lady in the best part of town, and followed the maid into the house without a qualm. He climbed the stairs after the maid had called her mistress and told her 'Andreuccio's here', and there at the top of the stairs he found her waiting for him.

The girl was not all that old herself; she was tall and had the prettiest face, while her dress and jewellery were thoroughly decorous. As Andreuccio was on the point of reaching her, she spread out her arms and came down the top three steps to meet him; she threw her arms round his neck and stopped thus awhile, as though too moved for words. Then she tearfully kissed him on the forehead and brokenly uttered: 'O Andreuccio mine! How welcome you are!'

Such tenderness left him not a little surprised. 'Well it's my pleasure, madam', he said.

She took him by the hand and led him up into her sitting-room and on, without a word, through into her bedroom. This room was fragrant with roses and orange-blossom and all manner of scents, and had a most beautiful four-poster bed, the bedposts draped with any number of dresses, as the local fashion was; seeing these and noting the splendour and magnificence of her wardrobe, he took her to be a lady of the first rank—wordly-wise he was not. They sat down side by side on a chest at the foot of the bed and she addressed him in these words:

'Andreuccio, I'm sure that all this affection and emotion of mine will come as a great surprise to you, for you don't know me and, as it happens, have never heard any mention of me. What you're to hear, though, will maybe surprise you even more: I am your sister. Believe me, now that the Good Lord has done me the favour of letting me set eyes on one of my brothers before I die, much though I should like to see all of you, when I do die I shall die happy. Now if this is the first you've heard of it, let me tell you the story.

'Pietro, my father and yours, spent many years in Palermo, as I'm sure you know, and everyone who knew him found him the nicest, most agreeable man and were devoted to him—they still are. But no one loved him more than my mother, a gentlewoman who was a widow at the time; she got the better of her fear of her father and brothers and her concern for her reputation and became so intimate with him that I was the result—and here I am as you find me! After this, Pietro had to quit Palermo and return to Perugia, leaving me with my mother—I was still a little mite—and, from what I've heard, he never gave Mother or me another thought. Were he not my father, I'd find him very much to blame for this—what rank ingratitude towards my mother, never mind me, whom he ought to have loved as his daughter: after all, I wasn't born of a chambermaid or a harlot! Such was her love and her devotion, Mother put herself and all that she owned into his hands, without knowing a great deal about him. Still, when a person has behaved badly, and it's all very much in the past, it's so much easier to point the finger than to put matters right. That's how it was.

'I was a little girl when he left me in Palermo, where I grew up till I was more or less as I am now. Then Mother, who was well-to-do, married me off to a man from Girgenti, a good man and well born, and he came to settle in Palermo for my sake and Mother's. He was a dyed-in-the-wool Guelph,* though, and was in secret touch with our King Charles.* King

Frederick,* though, got wind of the plot before it was ready to hatch, so we had to flee from Sicily just when I was expecting to become a baroness to outrank all the nobility the island had ever known. So we snatched up what little we could carry (little in comparison to all our wealth), forsook our palaces and estates and took refuge here, where King Charles showed himself so obliged to us, he made up to us a good part of what we had lost for his sake: he gave us houses and lands and provides my husband (your brother-in-law) with a handsome allowance, as you shall see. And that's how I come to be here, and it's thanks to the Good Lord rather than to you, my dear brother, if I've at last set eyes on you.' This said, she embraced him again and, weeping, kissed him tenderly on the forehead.

Andreuccio listened to this tale of hers, which she so embellished with detail in the telling, never for a moment faltering or running out of inspiration, that he took her words to be Gospel truth: it was true, he remembered, that his father had lived in Palermo, and he knew from his own experience how readily young people fall in love; besides, there were all those soft tears, those hugs and chaste kisses. When she had finished, he said: 'You'll be scarcely surprised at my amazement. The fact is, whatever he did with your mother, my father never dropped a word about you or her, or if he did, I never got to hear of it, and I never knew about you—it was just as though you didn't exist. So I'm all the gladder to have found my sister here as I'm all on my own and such a hope never entered my head. What's more, I don't know of any man, however highly placed, who wouldn't cherish you, to say nothing of a little trader like me. But do tell me one thing: how did you know I was here?'

'I was told this morning by a poor woman who's with me quite a bit; she spent a good deal of time with our father, so she tells me, both in Palermo and Perugia. If it hadn't seemed to me more proper to welcome you here where you're at home rather than call on you under someone else's roof, I'd have paid you a visit long ago.'

This said, she began enquiring after each of his relatives in turn, mentioning them individually by name, and Andreuccio gave her news of them all—and found the young woman all the more believable though he'd have done better to be sceptical.

As it was very hot and they had been talking for a long time, she sent for wine (white *Greco*) and refreshments and had Andreuccio served with a drink. After this, he wanted to take his leave as it was supper-time, but she would not hear of it and looked thoroughly put out. She threw her arms round him and said: 'Oh dear, it's obvious how little you care for me! To think that you're here with your sister you've never met before, here in her own home, where you should have put up when you arrived in Naples, and now you want to leave and go back to your inn for supper! You must have supper with me. I know my husband isn't here, which is a great pity, but I'm still quite capable of playing hostess in my womanly way.'

Not knowing what to say to this, Andreuccio replied: 'I'm as fond of you as ever one should be of a sister, but if I don't go, they'll be expecting me all evening for supper, and that would be bad manners on my part.'

'Well, thank God, I do have people I can send with a message to say not to expect you—though you'd be doing me a big favour, as well as your duty, if you sent for your companions to join you here for supper; afterwards, if you still wanted to go back, you could all go together.'

Andreuccio answered that he could do without his companions this evening, and if this is what she wanted, why, he was at her disposal. So she pretended to send a message to the inn not to expect him for supper, then, after a good deal more chat, they sat down to their meal and were served quite a number of courses, an opulent affair. The young woman took care to draw the meal out till well into the night, and when they left the table and Andreuccio made to leave, she told him that this was quite out of the question—Naples was no place to be wandering about in at night, least of all if you were a stranger. Moreover when she had sent to the inn to say he would not be in for supper, she had also left word that he'd not be there for the night either. He took her word for it and stayed on, for he did enjoy her company, misguided man that he was. After supper they chatted on—for good reason—

well into the night, then she left Andreuccio to sleep in her bedroom, with a little lad to see that he had whatever he needed, while she retired to bed in another room with her maids.

It was very hot, so as soon as Andreuccio saw he was alone he stripped off his doublet and hose and laid them at the head of the bed. Then, feeling the urge to relieve his bowels, he asked the lad where this might be done. 'In there', said the lad, pointing to a door in a corner of the room. So in he went with assured step, but he trod by chance on a plank whose other end was not secured to the joist beneath, with the result that the plank tipped up and down it fell, taking Andreuccio with it. At least God loved him well enough to prevent his being injured in his fall, though it was a considerable drop. However he found himself plastered with the excrement that lay thick on the ground. To clarify what I've just said and what follows I'll describe the place to you: there was a narrow alley such as one often sees between two houses, bridged by a pair of joists, and across these joists were laid a number of planks together with something to sit on. It was one of these planks that fell through with him.

Finding himself down in the alley, then, and feeling none too happy, Andreuccio shouted for the boy, but the boy ran to tell the young woman the moment he heard him fall, and she hurried into her bedroom and quickly looked to see if his clothes were there. She found his clothes and the money with them, for he took no chances but foolishly carried it all on his person. Once she had secured that which she had laid her trap for, making herself out to be sister to a Perugian when in fact she came from Palermo, she didn't give him another thought but went quickly to shut the door through which he had stepped when he fell.

Getting no answer from the lad, Andreuccio shouted all the louder, but it was no use. His suspicions aroused, and coming finally to realize that he had been tricked, he climbed on to a low wall that closed off the alley, jumped down into the street, and went to the front door which he recognized readily enough; here he kept vainly calling out, and thumped and shook the door like anything. Then he burst into tears as he realized the extent of his disaster. 'Oh dear', he said, 'how little time it's taken me to lose five hundred florins and a sister!'

And he ranted and raved and went back to thumping the door and shouting and carrying on until several of the neighbours got up, roused from their slumbers and unable to endure the racket. One of the woman's maids, too, came to the window, pretending to be barely awake, and tartly said: 'Who's that knocking down there?'

'Oh', said Andreuccio, 'don't you recognize me? I'm Andreuccio, I'm your mistress Fiordaliso's brother.'

'Go and sleep it off, my good man', she said, 'if you've drunk too much, and you can come back in the morning. I don't know of any Andreuccio, I don't know what you're talking about. Now run along and let us get some sleep, there's a good chap.'

'What? You don't know what I'm talking about? Of course you do! But if this is the way of kinships in Sicily, that they are so soon forgotten, at least let me have my clothes back which I left with you, and I'll gladly be on my way.'

'My good man', she replied with a touch of mockery, 'you've got to be dreaming', and as she said this she drew in her head and slammed the window shut.

This made Andreuccio quite convinced of his loss, and if he was pained and angry before, he now quite lost his temper and proposed to use force to gain his ends where words had failed; so he picked up a large stone and went back to hammering on the door far more savagely than before. Many of the neighbours were now awake and out of their beds; they took him for a simple nuisance who was making this scene quite gratuitously just to annoy the lady, so they were incensed by his knocking and shouted at him from their windows, just the way all the dogs in a neighbourhood will bark at a stray from outside. 'Now this just won't do', they said, 'coming here at this hour to talk a lot of rubbish outside a lady's house! Please now, be off with you like a good fellow and let us get some sleep. If you have business with the lady, call again in the morning and stop bothering us at this time of night.'

Maybe encouraged by these words, a man Andreuccio had never seen or heard before came to a window of the lady's house; he was a pimp of hers, and he boomed out savagely: 'Who's that down there?'

Andreuccio looked up at the sound of that voice, and saw a man who, from what he could tell, had all the appearance of being a big shot, with a bushy black beard on his face—and all the appearance of having been got out of bed or woken from a deep sleep as he yawned and rubbed his eyes. In some trepidation Andreuccio told him: 'I'm a brother of the lady in there.'

The man, however, did not wait for Andreuccio to finish but snarled at him worse than before: 'Just you wait till I get down and thrash you to within an inch of your life—you tiresome drunken oaf! Can't you let anyone sleep tonight?' And he pulled his head in and slammed the window shut.

Some neighbours, who knew what sort of a man he was, gently advised Andreuccio: 'Be on your way for heaven's sake, man, unless you want to be done in. Clear off for your own good.'

Terrified as he was by Bushy-beard's voice and look, and prompted by those who had just spoken to him evidently out of the goodness of their hearts, Andreuccio left; as heartsore as could be and in despair of recovering his money, he made off back to his inn, taking the direction from which he had followed the maid the previous day, though he had no idea where he was going. But as he didn't care for the smell he was giving off, and wanted to get to the sea to wash himself, he took a turning to the left, called Ruga Catalana. On his way up into the city he chanced to see two men coming towards him carrying a lantern; he feared they might be the king's men or else other people up to no good, so he slipped into a hut he saw close by in order to escape them. But they went into the very same hut, as though it had in fact been their destination; here one of them dropped a number of tools he had been carrying round his neck, and they both set about examining them with a good deal of discussion.

They talked on, then one of them said: 'What's this I smell? It's the worst stench I've ever come across.' And he raised the lantern a little and spotted poor Andreuccio. 'Who are you?' they asked in astonishment.

Andreuccio kept mum, but they went closer to him with the lantern and asked him what he was doing here so filthy. So Andreuccio told them the whole story. They could imagine where such a thing might have befallen him and remarked to each other: 'It must have been at the gang-boss Buttafuoco's place.'

One of the men turned to him and said: 'All right, so you've lost your money, but thank your stars you fell and couldn't get back into the house: without that fall, mark my words, you'd have been murdered the moment you fell asleep; that way you'd have lost your life as well as your cash. Well, no use crying over spilt milk—that won't get you back a penny, you may as well cry for the moon. You know you can still end up dead if that one gets to hear you've been blabbing.'

After conferring together awhile they turned to him again: 'Look, we feel sorry for you', they said. 'If you feel like joining us in what we're going to do, we're quite sure your share will come to a great deal more than what you've lost.'

Things were so hopeless for Andreuccio that he said he was willing.

That day Filippo Minutolo,* Archbishop of Naples, had been buried; they'd interred him sumptuously in full canonicals and with a ruby ring on his finger worth over five hundred gold florins; these men were on their way to rob him of this. They acquainted Andreuccio with their purpose, and he, proving more greedy than judicious, went along with them.

On their way to the cathedral, as Andreuccio was reeking, one of the men said: 'Can't we find some way for him to wash a bit somewhere, so he doesn't stink so horribly?'

'Yes', said the other, 'there's a well nearby and it always has its pulley and a great big bucket. Let's go and give him a quick wash.'

When they got to the well, they found that the rope was in place but the bucket was missing; so they decided to tie him to the rope and lower him into the well; he could wash down there, and once he was clean he'd give the rope a tug and they'd pull him out.

After they had lowered him into the well, though, who should turn up but some of the sheriff's men, who had come to the well for a drink, on account of the heat and because they had just been involved in a chase. On sight of them the pair took to their heels without being spotted. When Andreuccio, down in the well, had finished washing, he gave the rope a tug. The thirsty men, who had laid aside their bucklers and weapons and stripped off their tunics, drew on the rope in the expectation of finding the bucket brim-full of water on the end of it. As Andreuccio saw the edge of the well close to hand he let go of the rope, reached out, and flung himself over the edge. At this the sheriff's men took fright, released hold of the rope, and fled without a word, much to Andreuccio's surprise—and had he not held on tightly he would have fallen to the bottom of the well with dire and possibly fatal consequences.

However, out he climbed and he found these weapons, which astonished him all the more, for he knew they did not belong to his companions. Quite perplexed, and bewailing his luck, he left everything alone and decided to make off, though not knowing whither. Thus it was that he ran into his two companions, who were on their way back to pull him out of the well. They were very surprised to see him and asked him who had drawn him out. Andreuccio told them he had no idea, and described just what had happened and what he had found by the well.

Realizing what had occurred, the two burst out laughing and told him why they had fled and who it was who had drawn him up out of the well. It was now dead of night and so they stopped talking and off they went to the cathedral, which they entered without difficulty, and made for the tomb, a huge one in marble. With their tools they prised up the enormously heavy lid enough to let a man get in, and they propped it open.

This done, one of them asked: 'Who'll step inside?'

'Not me', said the other.

'Me neither', said the first. 'Andreuccio can go.'

'No I won't', said Andreuccio.

'What d'you mean, you won't?' said the other two, rounding on him. 'Get in there or, by heaven, we'll give you such a pasting round your head with one of these crowbars, you'll just drop dead.'

Andreuccio stepped inside, quaking, and as he did so he thought: 'They've got me in here to pull a fast one on me: once I've handed everything out to them they'll skip off while I'm still struggling to get out of the tomb, and I'll be left empty-handed.' So he decided to help himself as a first step, and, remembering the precious ring he'd heard them mention, he slipped it off the archbishop's finger the moment he was inside and put it on his own, after which he passed out the crozier, the mitre, and the gloves and stripped him down to his shirt; he handed everything to them and that, he said, was all there was. The robbers insisted that the ring must be there, and told him to look all over, but he answered that he couldn't find it and kept them waiting as he pretended to go on searching. They, however, were no less crafty than he was. 'Keep looking', they urged him and, choosing their moment, they tugged out the prop holding up the lid and made off, leaving him shut up inside the tomb. How Andreuccio felt when he realized this, I leave you to imagine.

He tried several times, with his head and with his shoulders, to see if he could shift the lid, but all in vain. Feeling quite overcome, he fell down in a dead faint over the archbishop's corpse—and anyone who had seen them then would have been hard put to tell which of the two was the deader, the archbishop or Andreuccio. When he came round, he wept most bitterly, for he could see only two possible endings to his story: either no one else would come to open the tomb, and he would die in it from hunger and the stench amid the worms from the dead body; or someone would come and find him in there, in which case he'd be hanged as a robber. While he was thus brooding and grieving, he heard the sound of many people walking and talking in the church; it occurred to him that they were about to do the very thing he had just done with his companions—and this scared him all the more. But when these people had got the tomb open and propped the lid, they started quarrelling over who was to go inside, as none of them wanted to. After much argument, however, a priest said: 'What are you afraid of? D'you think he'll eat you? The dead don't eat people. I'll get in myself.' With this, he laid his chest on the rim of the tomb, and swivelled round, with his head outside and his legs within, so he could drop down inside. Seeing this, Andreuccio stood up, grabbed the priest by one leg and made as if to pull him in. When he felt this, the priest let out a yell and dived out of the tomb—which so terrified all the others that they left the tomb open and fled, for all the world as if they had a hundred thousand devils at their heels.

Such a sight made Andreuccio happy beyond his wildest hopes. He leapt out of the tomb and left the cathedral by the route he'd used to get in. It was close to daybreak, and he set off at a venture, with the ring on his finger, until he came to the sea-front and found his way back to the inn, where, he discovered, his companions and the innkeeper had been up all night worrying about him. Andreuccio told them all his adventures, and on their host's advice they decided he ought to leave Naples at once. So he returned promptly to Perugia, having invested his money in a ring, though it was horses that he had set out to buy.

II. 6. *Fortune deprives Beritola of her husband and children, scattering them to the four winds and leaving her marooned on an island with three deer for company. Little by little, however, her lot improves.*

Fiammetta's account of Andreuccio's adventures had provoked great mirth among the lads and equally among the lasses. Then, on hearing the end of it, Emilia began her story at the queen's bidding.

The random developments of Fortune are no easy thing to bear, indeed they are an affliction. But as our minds tend to drift off in happy fancies, the more we air this question the more alert they become, so I consider we should never be reluctant to listen to accounts of Fortune, whether her strokes are lucky or not: we can learn from the lucky strokes, while we take comfort from the unlucky ones. So although a great deal of weighty things have already been said on this topic, I propose to tell you a story about Fortune that is as true as it is heart-breaking: although the story had a happy ending, it involved such a burden of hardship over so long a period, I could scarcely believe it would ever relent and conclude happily.

You must know that on the death of Emperor Frederick II, Manfred* was crowned King of Sicily. In his suite there was a gentleman from Naples called Arrighetto Capece, who lived in considerable state, and was married to a beautiful woman, like himself a Neapolitan of gentle birth, whose name was Beritola Caracciola. The government of the island was in Arrighetto's hands, but when he heard the news that Manfred had been defeated and slain at Benevento* by King Charles I of Anjou, to whom the entire realm was now turning in allegiance, Arrighetto made ready to escape—he had little faith in the fleeting loyalty of the Sicilians and no wish to become liegeman to his master's enemy. When the Sicilians discovered this they seized him and several others among King Manfred's retainers and friends and handed them over as prisoners to King Charles, along with possession of the island. With such a reversal of fortune Beritola, who did not know what had become of Arrighetto, was in a state of constant apprehension. Fearing that she might be violated, she abandoned everything and, pregnant and penniless as she was, took her son Giusfredi, then about 8 years old, and escaped to Lipari in a small vessel. Here she gave birth to another boy, whom she called the Outcast. She engaged a nurse and they all boarded a little boat to return to her family in Naples.

But things did not go as planned: although the vessel was bound for Naples, a strong wind carried it to the island of Ponza, where they entered a little cove and awaited conditions more favourable to their voyage. Beritola landed with the others and found herself a secluded and solitary spot in which to withdraw on her own and weep for her Arrighetto—this became her daily practice. Now as she was thus absorbed in her grieving, a pirate galley chanced to arrive without anyone—sailors or passengers—noticing; the pirates made a clean sweep of the entire company and cleared off. When she had finished her day's lamenting, Beritola returned to the seashore as she always did to be with her children, and found nobody there.

This surprised her but, at once suspecting what had happened, she looked out to sea and saw the galley, not yet all that far out, with her little craft in tow. This brought home to her all too clearly that she had lost her children as she had lost her husband. Realizing that here she was, poor, alone, and deserted, with no idea how she might ever find any of them again, she cried out for her husband and children, then fainted away on the beach. There was nobody on hand to restore her to her senses with the help of cold water or whatever else, so these were free to wander at leisure where their fancy took them. But when the strength that had deserted her returned to her poor body, together with her sighs and tears, she spent ages calling her children and searching for them in every cave until eventually she realized that her efforts were wasted, and, conscious that night was falling, as she kept hoping without knowing quite what for, she took stock of her own needs and left the shore to return to the cave in which she was accustomed to give vent to her misery.

The night passed in an agony of terror and grief, and the new day dawned; she had eaten nothing the previous evening and by mid-morning she was ravenous, so she found sustenance in wild herbs. After her meal she wept as she brooded over her future. While she was thus absorbed, she saw a doe approaching; it went into a cave close by, only to re-emerge a moment later and disappear into the woods. So Beritola got up and went into the cave which the doe had just left, and there she saw two little fawns, born probably this very day, the sweetest and most darling little things she'd ever seen. As her own milk had not yet dried up after her recent parturition, she tenderly gathered up the little fawns and suckled them. The fawns did not reject what she offered them, but fed at her breast as they would have fed at their mother's teats; after that, they would make no distinction between Beritola and their dam. Now as the lady felt she had found a little companionship in this desert place, she settled down to live and die here, with herbs to eat and water to drink, and weeping for her husband and children and her old life as often as she was reminded of them. She became as friendly with the doe as with her two fawns.

Several months passed, during which the lady reverted to living in a state of nature, until a small Pisan ship happened to put in here, where she had arrived earlier, driven, as she had been, by a storm-wind. It stopped here for a number of days. On board was a gentleman called Currado de' Marchesi Malespini with his wife, an excellent, saintly woman; they were on their way home from a pilgrimage to all the shrines in the Kingdom of Naples. One day, to keep his spirits up, Currado made an excursion across the island with his wife, a few of his servants, and his hounds; not far from where Beritola had taken up residence the hounds picked up the trail of the two baby roebucks who were browsing—they had now grown a little. Pursued by the hounds, where did the creatures flee to if not to Beritola in her cave? She stood up when she saw this, grasped a stick, and drove off the dogs. Currado and his wife, who had been following them, now appeared, and were amazed to see her, all swarthy, lean, and hairy as she had become. She, however, was even more surprised to see them. At her request Currado called off his dogs, after which, by dint of much pressing, she was prevailed upon to tell them who she was and what she was doing here; she gave them a full account of her situation, her misadventures, and the hard resolution she had taken. Now Currado was well acquainted with Arrighetto Capece, and he wept for pity at her tale; he spoke to her at length in an effort to dissuade her from so relentless a decision, and offered to escort her back to her family home or else to accord her hospitality as though she were his sister—she could stay until such time as the Good Lord sent her happier fortune. Beritola was not to be persuaded, so Currado left her with his wife, instructing her to have food sent up, and to clothe her, dressed as she was in rags, in some dress of her own, and to do all she could to bring her away with them. So the lady stayed with Beritola, and shed many tears with her over her misfortunes; then she had food and clothing fetched in, though it required endless trouble before she could prevail on her to accept the clothes and to eat. In the end, after many entreaties, during which Beritola insisted that she would never go anywhere where she might be recognized, she persuaded her to accompany them to their home in the Lunigiana, together with the two young roebucks and the doe, which had returned in the meantime and fawned all over her—which left the good Pisan lady not a little surprised.

When the weather improved, Beritola embarked with Currado and his wife, and with the doe and her young—as her name was not generally known, Beritola came to be nicknamed the Doe. With a favourable wind they made a fast passage to the mouth of the Magra, where they landed and continued up to their estate. Here Beritola, dressed in widow's weeds, pursued a virtuous, humble, obedient existence in the suite of Currado's lady. Meanwhile she continued to look after her deer, to whom she was devoted.

The pirates who had captured the boat on which Beritola had arrived at Ponza, after leaving her behind inadvertently, proceeded to Genoa with everyone else. Here the booty was shared out among the galley's owners, and among the part that fell to one Guasparrino d'Oria were Beritola's two children along with their nurse. He sent nurse and children to his residence, to be employed as household serfs. Heartsick at the loss of her mistress and the wretched fate to which she saw herself and the two children consigned, the nurse wept for a long time. Seeing, though, that there was nothing to be gained by tears, and that she was in the same bondage as the children were, the nurse pulled herself together as best she could—though a poor woman, she had her share of common sense and prudence: she noted where it was that they had fetched up, and realized that if the two boys were recognized they could easily fall victim to further mischief, given that the Genoese were allied to Charles of Anjou. Besides, she hoped that all in good time their luck would change and, if they stayed alive, they might be able to recover their lost estate; so it occurred to her not to reveal their identity to a soul until she saw occasion to do so: her answer to whoever asked was that the boys were hers. The elder child she called Giannotto of Procida rather than Giusfredi, while she did not trouble to alter the younger one's name. And she took endless pains to show Giusfredi why she had changed his name and what danger he ran if he were recognized; this she told him not once but again and again, and the boy, who was a bright child, played his part admirably in accordance with the prudent nurse's instructions. Thus did the two boys and the nurse patiently endure many years in Guasparrino's household, ill clad and worse shod, employed in the most menial duties.

Now when Giannotto was 16, possessed as he was of greater spirit than befitted a slave, he spurned the degradation of his bondage and quit Guasparrino's service, boarding a galley in a fleet bound for Alexandria. He knocked about the world but could never improve his situation. Eventually, some three or four years after leaving Guasparrino, in despair of any change of luck, Giannotto arrived, in the course of his wanderings, in the Lunigiana, where, so it happened, he took service with Currado de' Malespini: he served him most punctiliously and gave entire satisfaction. He was now a tall, handsome young man. He had had news of his father to the effect that he was still alive—not dead, as he had supposed—but kept prisoner by King Charles. And though from time to time he saw his mother, who was attached to Currado's wife, not once did he recognize her, nor she him: both had been so transformed by age from the way they used to look when they had last seen each other.

While Giannotto was in Currado's service, a daughter of Currado's called Spina, married to one Niccolò da Grignano, was widowed and returned to her father's house. She was a most beautiful and enchanting girl, little more than 16 years old, and she happened to cast an eye on Giannotto and he upon her; they fell passionately in love, and it was not long before they carried this love to its consummation. Months went by and nobody noticed, so they became somewhat over-confident and behaved with less prudence than the affair required. One day, as Spina was walking with Giannotto through a pretty, closely planted wood, they left the rest of their company and pressed on until, imagining that they had stolen a good march on the others, they turned off into a pleasant spot, all grassy and flower-strewn and hemmed in by trees; here they began to make love. And though they had been at it for a good while, the sheer pleasure of it made them imagine that but a moment had elapsed, and they were caught in the act, first by the girl's mother, then by Currado. The sight cut him to the heart and, without offering an explanation, he had three of his attendants truss the pair up and take them away to a castle of his. He was boiling with rage and indignation and disposed to put them to a shameful death. The girl's mother had grasped from a stray word of Currado's what he proposed to do with the culprits, and though she too was beside herself with rage and considered that her daughter's offence deserved all manner of cruel punishment, she could not suffer what her husband envisaged; so she hastened to catch up with the angry man and begged him not to rush headlong into procuring his own daughter's death in his old age and soiling his hands with a page's blood: let him devise some other way, she said, to satisfy his wrath, like incarceration—let them languish in prison and rue their sin. The saintly woman told him this and much else besides, until she made him reconsider his decision to kill them. He gave orders that each of them was to be confined in a different place, they were to be closely guarded and kept on short rations and in minimal comfort until such time as he thought of something else for them—all of which was carried out.

I leave you to imagine the life they led in captivity, the ceaseless tears, and those fasts which continued far longer than their health required. So Giannotto and Spina thus languished and a whole year passed without Currado giving a thought to them. Now it happened that King Pietro of Aragon* made a pact with Gian di Procida and fomented a rebellion in Sicily and wrested the kingdom from Charles—much to Currado's delight, for he was a Ghibelline.*

Hearing of this from one of his gaolers, Giannotto sighed deeply. 'Oh what a pity!' he remarked. 'Here I've been wandering from pillar to post for fourteen years and barely subsisting as I've waited for nothing else but this: and, now that it's happened, it's just my luck to be in prison with no hope of getting out till I'm dead—I wasn't to be given a chance!'

'What?' said the gaoler. 'What does it matter to you what royalty gets up to? What did you ever have to do with Sicily?'

'It breaks my heart', said Giannotto, 'to think what my father had to do with it: I was only a little lad when I escaped, but I remember observing it was my father who governed the island, in King Manfred's day.'

'Your father? Who was he?'

'My father? Well, there's no harm telling you now—I can see I'm no longer threatened by the danger I ran before if I'd let out the secret. His name was Arrighetto Capece—it still is, if he's alive—and my name is not Giannotto but Giusfredi. One thing I'm sure about: if I were out of here and back in Sicily, I'd be a man of great importance.'

The worthy gaoler sought no further but told the whole story to Currado at the first opportunity. Currado listened to the gaoler and appeared to shrug off his story; but he went to Beritola and amiably enquired whether she'd had a son by Arrighetto called Giusfredi. She wept as she answered that if the elder of her two sons were still alive, that's what he'd be called, and he would be 22 years old.

From this Currado recognized that he must be the lad, and it occurred to him, if this was the case, that he might at one stroke perform a great kindness and obliterate the stain on his daughter's honour and his own by marrying her off to him. So he sent for Giannotto in secret and questioned him closely on his previous life. Finding clear enough evidence that he must indeed be Giusfredi, son of Arrighetto Capece, he said to him: 'You know well enough, Giannotto, the nature and the degree of your offence, the injury you have done to me through my own daughter. I had treated you well and kindly, so it was your duty as my attendant to make my honour, my possessions the object of your unfailing care and concern. Many there are who would have put you to an ignominious death, had you treated them the way you treated me. I, however, could not bring myself to such a step. Now, as it appears from your account that you are the son of a gentleman and lady of good birth, I mean to bring your sufferings to an end, if that is your own wish, and release you from your dreary imprisonment and redress at once your honour and my own. Now Spina, whose lover you were, though this ill became the pair of you, is (as you know) a widow, and possesses a good, ample dowry. Her character is known to you, as are her father and mother. I'll say nothing of your own present situation. If, then, you are agreeable, I am ready to make her your virtuous wife whereas she has been your disreputable mistress; and you may take up your residence here as my son, with Spina and me, for as long as you please.'

Incarceration had macerated the young man's flesh but failed to reduce the noble spirit that derived from his breeding, or to diminish the total love he bore his lady. And however passionately he longed for that which Currado was offering him—an offer capable, as he knew, of fulfilment—he did not flinch from replying as his lofty spirit prompted him: 'Currado', he said, 'never did I resort to treachery, laying snares against your person or your property, never was I driven by lust for power, or greed for gain, or any other urging. I loved your daughter, I love her, I will always love her, because I consider her worthy of my love. And if I consorted with her in a manner that vulgar opinion considers improper, I committed a sin that has forever formed a bond among young people; to do away with the sin, it would be necessary to do away with young people; and were the elderly prepared to recall that they were young once, and to measure others' failings against their own and their own against others', then this sin would not carry the weight of gravity with which you and many others endow it. It was as a friend, not an enemy, that I committed it. What you are offering to do is a thing I have always wanted, and had I believed it would ever be vouchsafed to me, I should have requested it long ago. Now it will be the more precious to me as I entertained so little hope of it. If it is not really your intention to do as you say, don't feed me with empty hopes; return me to prison and afflict me to your heart's content, for I shall always love Spina, and equally shall I love you for her sake, whatever you do to me, and I shall continue to respect you.'

Currado heard him out in some astonishment; impressed by his lofty sentiments, and convinced of the fervour of his love, he felt all the more kindly disposed to the lad. He stood up, gave him a hug and a kiss, then wasted no more time but ordered Spina brought to him in secret. In prison she had grown thin, pale, and feeble; she looked practically a changed woman, just as Giannotto looked like a different man. In Currado's presence they were betrothed, by mutual consent, according to the custom we follow.

Several days later, having had the pair supplied with all that they needed to afford them satisfaction, all without a word of it getting out, Currado felt it was time to impart to the mothers this occasion for rejoicing, so he summoned his wife and the Doe and thus addressed them: 'What would you say, madam, if I restored your elder son to you as the husband of one of my daughters?'

'There's nothing I could say', replied the Doe, 'but this: if I could be more beholden to you than I am already, I should be only the more so inasmuch as you would be restoring to me something I value more than my own self. And, restoring it to me in the way you say, you would somewhat rekindle in me my lost hopes.' Thus saying, she wept.

Currado then turned to his wife: 'And you, wife, what would you think if I presented you with such a son-in-law?'

'Never mind one of those gentlemen—if you were content with a tramp, then so would I be.'

'Then I hope in a day or two to make you ladies happy.' And when he saw that the two young people had been restored to their original constitutions, he had them dressed in accordance with their enhanced station and asked Giusfredi: 'Would you appreciate it, beyond the happiness you're now enjoying, if you found your mother here?'

'I can scarcely believe that she would have survived her misfortunes and the sorrow inflicted upon her. But if she were still alive, nothing would make me happier, and with her advice I should feel confident of going a long way towards retrieving my situation in Sicily.'

Then Currado sent for the two ladies, who both offered the warmest congratulations to the bride, though they were not a little perplexed to imagine what on earth could have put Currado into such a kindly frame of mind as to give his daughter away in marriage to Giannotto. What Currado had said made Beritola give the boy a closer look; some hidden force stirred her to a recollection of her son's features as a child and, without waiting for further demonstration, she opened her arms and fell about his neck; overcome by maternal love and happiness, she could not utter a word—indeed the shock to her senses made her drop half-dead in his arms. He was very much surprised: he did recollect having seen her many a time before in this very household without once having recognized her, but he knew intuitively now that she was his mother and cursed himself for having been so unobservant, as he folded her with tears into his arms and kissed her tenderly. Currado's wife and daughter pitifully came to Beritola's assistance and brought her round with cold water and other ministrations, after which she hugged her son yet again, with many tears and many tender words; brimming with motherly love, she could not stop kissing him, and he responded with great filial respect.

Three or four times they demonstrated their simple pleasure, much to the delight of the onlookers, and each gave the other a full account of their adventures. Currado had already rejoiced all his friends with his announcement of the new alliance he had contracted and made arrangements for a fine, splendid celebration, whereupon Giusfredi said to him: 'You have contributed so much, Currado, to my happiness, and you have long afforded your hospitality to my mother. Now, to leave nothing undone that lies in your power to do for us, I would ask you to complete my happiness and my mother's, and that of my wedding, with the presence here of my brother: he is being detained as a serf in the household of Guasparrino d'Oria who, as I told you, secured the two of us in a pirate raid. Could you also send someone to Sicily to obtain full information about conditions there and seek out news of Arrighetto, my father, and discover whether he is alive or dead and, if alive, what are his circumstances? When he has found out everything, could he return to us?'

Currado approved of Giusfredi's request and lost no time in sending persons of the highest discretion to Genoa and to Sicily. The envoy to Genoa sought out Guasparrino and earnestly conveyed Currado's request for the return of the Outcast and the nurse; he described to him precisely what Currado had done for Giusfredi and his mother.

The news came as a great surprise to Guasparrino, who said: 'Believe me, I'd do anything in my power to please Currado. And I have indeed kept the lad you're asking for in my household these last fourteen years, along with his mother; I'll gladly send them to him. But tell him from me not to set too much store by anything Giannotto may tell him (or Giusfredi, as you say he now calls himself)—the boy's a good deal more devious than he thinks.'

This said, he made the worthy fellow welcome, and secretly sent for the nurse, whom he cautiously questioned on the subject. Now as she had heard about the uprising in Sicily and was told that Arrighetto was still alive, she overcame her erstwhile fear and told him exactly how matters stood, explaining the reasons that had induced her to follow the course she had. Seeing that the nurse's account tallied perfectly with that of Currado's envoy, Guasparrino was ready to believe what he was told; he was the sharpest of men, though, and looked into the matter from all angles in order to establish additional facts to confirm his belief. This done, he felt ashamed of the disgusting way he had treated the boy, recognizing who his father Arrighetto was, and to make amends he bestowed upon him the hand of a pretty 11-year-old daughter of his, together with a handsome dowry. This betrothal was duly celebrated, after which he boarded a well-found galliot in the company of his daughter and the lad, the envoy of Currado and the nurse, and sailed for Lerici. Here he was met by Currado, and the whole party proceeded to a castle of his in the vicinity where the festivities had been lavishly set in train.

Never could I find words to describe the welcome given by the mother on seeing her son again, and the welcome the two brothers gave each other, and that which the three of them lavished on the faithful nurse; nor the welcome they all extended to Guasparrino and his daughter, which he reciprocated; nor the joy that possessed them all—Currado, his wife, his children, and friends: I leave it, ladies, to your imagination. And in order that their joy might be perfect, the Good Lord, the most bounteous of givers once He starts, chose to throw in happy tidings of Arrighetto Capece, that he was alive and well. For who should arrive, as the festivities were at their height and the guests, men and women, were still seated at table for the first course, but the envoy who had been despatched to Sicily? Included with the news he brought of Arrighetto was this, that he had been held prisoner at Catania by King Charles when the country rose in rebellion against the monarch, and the populace had stormed into the prison, butchered the guard, and hauled him out to make him their own leader—for he was the king's principal opponent—and to follow him in the slaughter and expulsion of the French.* As a result, he had found the highest favour with King Pietro, who had seen to his recovering all his rank and possessions, so he was once more in excellent fettle. Arrighetto, he added, had given him a most flattering reception and rejoiced beyond telling at the news of his wife and son, of whom he had heard not a word since his capture. He was sending some gentlemen in a galliot to fetch them—they were following behind.

The messenger received a hearty welcome and a delighted audience. Currado then hastened off with some friends to meet the gentlemen who had come to fetch Beritola and Giusfredi and welcomed them gladly, and brought them in to the banquet, which was not yet half-way through. Here Beritola and Giusfredi and all the rest showed such happiness at seeing them, the like of which had never been known; and they, before sitting down to eat, conveyed greetings from Arrighetto, and on his behalf thanked Currado and his wife to the best of their powers for the hospitality extended to his wife and son; through his messengers Arrighetto placed himself and all that lay in his power at their entire disposal. Then they addressed Guasparrino, of whose contribution to the general happiness they had been unaware, and said that once Arrighetto came to hear of what he had done in the Outcast's favour, he would show himself equally grateful, if not more so. Then, in the happiest frame of mind, they joined the two brides and bridegrooms at table.

Currado's celebration for his son-in-law and the rest of his family and friends lasted not only today but many more days; when it ended, and Beritola, Giusfredi and the others felt it was time to leave, they boarded the galliot, taking Spina with them, and with many tears took their leave of Currado, his wife, and Guasparrino. With a favourable wind they soon reached Sicily, and there's no way of describing the joy with which Arrighetto welcomed them all at Palermo, his sons and the ladies equally. And it is believed that they all lived happily ever after, thankful for all that had been bestowed upon them, in the friendship of the Good Lord.

## II. 7. *The Sultan of Babylon sends his beautiful virgin daughter as bride to the King of Africa; she takes four years to reach him, passing from hand to hand, and when she does, is no longer a virgin.*

Had Emilia's story gone on any longer, Beritola's misfortunes might well have reduced the pitiful ladies to tears. But she finished her tale, and the queen was pleased to have Pamphilo go next; and he, obedient fellow, began as follows:

It is not easy to know what's best for us. I mean, how often has one seen it happen?—people think that if only they were rich they could live a safe, trouble-free life, so they'd pray God to make them wealthy, they'd move heaven and earth, they'd spare themselves no danger, no exertion to acquire a fortune. And once they'd achieved their object, they'd find someone coming along and murdering them for the sake of their ample possessions—someone who in the days before they made their fortune would have striven to keep them alive! Others there are of humble stock who would fight a thousand desperate battles to rise, through the blood of their own brothers and friends, to the heights of royal dominion, imagining that here they should find the ultimate happiness—only to discover the countless anxieties and fears to be seen lurking there, and to meet their deaths in the realization that what is drunk in the golden goblets at the king's table is poison. Many have there been who above all things longed for physical strength and beauty, or for outward trappings; but scarcely had they realized how misplaced were their ambitions than those very objects became the cause of their death or of enduring misfortune. Rather than go minutely into each one of our human desires, let me state that there's not a single one that a living person might choose deliberately as guaranteeing a happy outcome. If we wanted to go about these things the right way, we should dispose ourselves to accept and cherish whatever He bestows on us Who alone understands our needs and is able to satisfy them. Now, just as we men go variously astray in our desires, you sweet ladies incur one particular fault in that you needs must be beautiful: not content with the beauty afforded you by Nature, you seek with consummate artistry to improve on it. I should like, therefore, to tell you of the misfortunes that accrued to a Saracen lady on account of her beauty, which brought her nine times to the marriage-bed in the course of some four years.

A long time ago there was a Sultan of Babylon* called Beminadab, a man for whom things generally turned out the way he wanted. He had a large number of sons and daughters, including a girl called Alatiel, who was then, in the opinion of everyone who had set eyes on her, the fairest woman on earth. Now the King of Africa had rendered the sultan exceptional service when he was attacked by a horde of Arabs and roundly defeated them; so when the king sought Alatiel's hand in marriage as a special favour, the sultan conceded his request: he had a ship soundly fitted out and copiously provisioned and sent his daughter on board accompanied by a right honourable retinue of ladies and gentlemen, and with a splendid, lavish equipage. Then away to the King of Africa he sent her, bidding her Godspeed.

Seeing the weather set fair, the seamen hoisted sail, put out from the harbour of Alexandria, and enjoyed several days' fair sailing. But once past Sardinia and with the end of their journey in sight, so they thought, the day suddenly brought savage squalls gusting in from all directions, and the ship was so buffeted that Alatiel and the sailors on more than one occasion gave themselves up for lost. And yet for all that they were harassed by enormous seas, they devoted all their strength and skill for the next two days, veteran sailors that they were, to keeping the vessel afloat; but with the third night since the beginning of the storm, which continued only to gather strength, the men no longer had any idea of their position, unable as they were to obtain a fix either by sight or by dead reckoning, for the night was black with cloud. They were not far off Majorca when they felt the ship breaking up. As they did not know what more they could do to remedy the situation, it became a matter of 'each man for himself' as they dropped a longboat over the side and the ship's officers all determined to look to it for their safety rather than remaining with the vessel as it foundered. Little by little all the men on board followed them, everyone jumping down into the ship's boat in spite of being stood off at knife-point by the first men in; they imagined they were going to escape with their lives but they stumbled straight to their deaths, for, with the seas in such turmoil, the little boat could not support so great a mob, and it sank and all aboard perished.

The ship, meanwhile, was driven onwards by the mighty gale, splitting though it was at the seams and quite waterlogged, with no one left on board save the princess and her ladies (who all lay prostrate and half-dead from fear and the sea-storm). Carried at enormous speed, the vessel was flung ashore on a beach in the isle of Majorca. Such was the impetus with which it ran aground, it became wellnigh totally embedded in the sand, maybe a stone's throw from the shore. Here it remained stuck fast all night, pounded by the waves, for the wind could shift it no further.

When it was broad daylight and the storm had somewhat abated, the princess raised her head: she was more dead than alive and quite unstrung as she set to calling her menservants, first one, then another, but to no effect—those summoned were at no mean distance from her. Obtaining no reply and seeing no sign of any of them, she was quite bewildered and a great fear stole over her. She staggered to her feet and saw her ladies and maidservants lying prostrate every one of them; so she fell to calling and shaking them, one after another, but found that only a few showed signs of life, many having expired, whether from acute indisposition of the stomach or from sheer terror. This only increased the lady's alarm but, finding herself all alone and in urgent need of advice, for she had no idea where she was, she kept prodding those women who were still alive till she had got them on to their feet. The women could not tell her where the menfolk had got to, and she could see that the ship was aground and full of water, so she and they all fell to weeping most disconsolately. It was mid-afternoon before they spotted anyone on the beach, or anywhere else, on whose pity and assistance they might call.

Now towards three o'clock a gentleman called Pericone da Visalgo happened to be riding past with his suite as he returned from one of his estates. When he noticed the vessel he at once imagined what had happened, and told one of his men to try in all haste to climb aboard and bring him word of what he discovered. The man contrived with difficulty to get aboard and found the young lady with her few companions hiding timorously in the forepeak. When they saw him, they repeatedly begged for mercy with tears in their eyes, but then realized that he did not understand them nor they him; so they tried with gestures to convey their plight. Pericone's servant took it all in to the best of his ability and reported back to his master, who promptly had the women brought ashore, together with the most precious objects on board that might be retrieved. Then he left with them for his domain, where he revived them with food and rest. From the sumptuous baggage he realized that the lady he had chanced upon must indeed be a lady of rank and the owner of these objects, and he readily identified her by the singular respect with which the other ladies treated her. And although the storm had reduced her to a very sorry sight and left her quite ashen faced, Pericone none the less found that she was remarkably shapely, so much so that he decided on the spot that he would marry her if she were not already married—and if he could not marry her, well then, he'd like her for his mistress.

Pericone, a sturdy man of commanding appearance, had the lady waited on hand and foot for several days, with the result that she quite recovered from her ordeal. Now he saw that she was indeed beautiful beyond belief, and nothing vexed him more than his inability to understand her speech, nor she his, which left him unable to discover who she was. However, he was immoderately taken with her beauty and, by making himself agreeable, indeed lovable in her eyes, he strove to overcome her resistance and bend her to his pleasure. But this was not to be: she remained wholly unresponsive to his overtures, while he became only the more passionate. Alatiel noticed this and, after she'd been here a few days and had realized, from the local customs, that she was among Christians and in a place where to reveal her identity, even had she been able to do so, would have profited her little, she loftily determined she would not submit to the wretchedness of her fate, even though she recognized that sooner or later Pericone would have his way with her whether by brute force or by enticement. She ordered her ladies—the three remaining to her—never to tell a soul who they were, until such time as they found themselves in a place where they could count on receiving assistance towards the recovery of their freedom. She went on forcibly to urge them to maintain their chastity, asserting her own intention that nobody other than her husband would ever take his pleasure with her. Her ladies approved of her words and told her they would at all costs do her bidding.

Pericone, however, grew more impassioned by the day, and all the more so seeing the object of his desire so close to hand and yet so remote; but while he realized how fruitless was his coaxing, he still relied on the schemes of his brain, leaving mere brawn as a last resort. Now he'd noticed once or twice that the lady enjoyed a spot of wine, a drink to which she was unaccustomed as her law forbade it, so it occurred to him that he might seduce her with this, employing it as an accomplice to Venus. Therefore if she avoided him he pretended indifference, and one evening he laid on a fine dinner under guise of a great celebration, and the lady was among the guests. The dinner had everything to make it a festive event, and Pericone told the manservant attending upon the lady to serve her a good variety of wines blended together—an order the man fulfilled admirably. So Alatiel, all unwary, was indeed seduced by so agreeable a beverage and partook more liberally than her virtue should have permitted. She dismissed all thought of her past afflictions and grew exceedingly merry; when she saw some women performing a Majorcan dance, she set about dancing one of her Alexandrian dances. Pericone felt within reach of his goal when he saw this; he kept the banquet going well into the night, plying the guests with ever-more food and drink. Eventually the other guests departed and Pericone went into the bedroom alone with Alatiel who, flushed as she was with wine rather than tempered by sober rectitude, undressed in his presence without a trace of bashfulness, as though he were one of her ladies, and got into bed. Pericone was not slow to follow her; he put out all the lights, promptly climbed in from the other side, and lay down next to her; he took her in his arms and began to make love—to which she offered no resistance. Once she had experienced this (for she'd previously had no idea what tool men used for breaking and entering) she was close to regretting that she'd never responded to Pericone's approaches; without awaiting a further invitation to such a night-time's pleasure, she would now often invite herself, not in words, which would not interpret her meaning, but in action.

Now Fortune, not content with having turned a king's bride into a squire's paramour, set before Alatiel a new love-bond that was barely endurable after the pleasure she and Pericone had been taking in each other. Pericone had a brother aged 25, a handsome, fresh-faced lad called Marato. He had taken a great fancy to the girl on sight, and imagined, to judge by her comportment, that she was by no means indifferent to him; nothing prevented his having his way with her, he reckoned, save the close guard kept on her by Pericone. His thoughts turned, therefore, to a desperate remedy—which he straight away put into dastardly effect. A ship happened then to be lying in the harbour, laden with merchandise and bound for the port of Chiarenza in the Peloponnese; it was under the command of two young Genoese brothers, and its sails were hoisted, ready to leave the moment the wind served. Marato struck a bargain with the two whereby they were to receive him on board that night with the lady. This done, and having determined how to proceed, as night fell he went undetected to Pericone's house with a number of trustworthy friends he had asked to join him in the enterprise; Pericone was not expecting any threat from such a quarter, so Marato hid inside the house in accordance with his plan. When the night was well advanced, Marato let his companions in; they proceeded to the room in which Pericone was sleeping with Alatiel, opened the door, killed the man as he slept, and took away the woman, who wept as she awoke—they threatened to kill her if she made a sound. Nobody heard them as they left for the harbour, having helped themselves to a good share of Pericone's valuables. Marato and Alatiel boarded the ship without delay, his friends went home, and the sailors set sail to a fresh, favourable breeze.

The princess bitterly lamented her earlier misfortune and now this new one; Marato, however, brought her such consolation with the serviceable talisman the Good Lord had supplied to him that she'd soon made her peace with him and quite forgotten Pericone. Indeed, she had quite recovered her spirits when Fate dealt her another blow, not satisfied with the previous ones. She was, as we have several times observed, a ravishing beauty, and of unimpeachable deportment, and the two young shipmasters fell so madly in love with her they could think of nothing else; they devoted themselves exclusively to serving her, to acquiring her good graces, while taking care that Marato should never penetrate their motives. Once each brother realized that the other was smitten, they discussed the matter in secret and agreed to gain her love in partnership, as though love might be subject to a shareholding, like merchandise or the profits from trade. Marato, however, kept a close watch on her, which inhibited their pursuing their proposal; so one day, when the vessel was flying along under sail and Marato, all unsuspecting, was standing at the poop gazing out over the water, they stepped up as one man, grabbed him from behind, and pitched him into the sea—and they had continued on course for a further mile and more before anybody noticed that Marato had fallen overboard. When Alatiel heard about it, seeing no possibility of his being rescued, she relapsed into her bitter lament on shipboard. The two lovers hastened to comfort her and did contrive to soothe her with tender words and lavish promises, not that she understood very much of it: her tears arose more out of self-pity than out of regret for the lost Marato.

After the two had taken turns entertaining her with endless speeches, they believed they had finally restored her good humour, so they withdrew to discuss the question of which of them was to be the first to take her off to bed. Each insisted on going first; no composition was possible; they resorted to insults, the quarrel flared, and in their rage they pulled out their daggers and hurled themselves at each other. The rest of the crew were unable to separate them before they had slashed each other several times; one of them dropped dead on the spot while the other, though badly wounded all over, escaped with his life. The princess was most upset: here she was, all alone (as she saw), with no one to turn to for help or advice, and she was terrified lest the friends and relatives of the two shipmasters made her the scapegoat. What saved her from the threat of death were the entreaties of the wounded survivor, and their prompt arrival at Chiarenza. Here she disembarked with the wounded man, with whom she lodged at an inn. The rumour of her exceptional beauty was all over town in a trice, and it came to the ears of the Prince of Morea, who was there in residence. So he wanted to see her and, when he had done so, she struck him as being even more beautiful than the reports suggested, and he fell so passionately in love with her that he could think of nothing else. On learning the circumstances of her arrival here, he concluded that he should be able to gain possession of her. When the relatives of the wounded man discovered that the prince was scheming to lay hands on the lady, they lost no time in sending her to him, which gladdened the prince's heart—and the lady's, too, for this appeared to deliver her from a great danger.

The prince noticed that she was not only beautiful to behold but also that she betrayed princely manners; unable to discover anything further about her identity, however, he decided that she must be a lady of rank, which served only to redouble his ardour; he showed her every courtesy and treated her not as a mistress but as if she were his spouse. Alatiel, therefore, felt she was now in clover, especially by comparison with her previous disasters, and she quite recovered her assurance and high spirits, which added a fresh bloom to her beauty; as a result she became the talk of the Peloponnese, and the Duke of Athens discovered in himself a wish to see her. The duke was a handsome young gallant, a friend and kinsman of the prince. On the pretext of paying his relative a visit—as he did at intervals—he travelled to Chiarenza with a fine, noble retinue, and was welcomed with becoming dignity and high festivity. A few days later, as the conversation turned to the lady's beauty, the duke asked the prince whether she really was as remarkable as people said.

'Far more', said the prince. 'Don't take my word for it, though: trust the witness of your own eyes.'

The duke held him to his promise and together they went to call on her. Forewarned of their visit, Alatiel offered them a cheerful and most civil welcome. They had her sit between them but could derive no pleasure from conversing with her, for she could understand scarcely a word of their language. So they both just stared at her as at some apparition, not least the duke, who could scarcely persuade himself that she was a mortal; as he gazed at her he failed to notice that his eyes were drinking in Love's venom—he thought he was simply taking pleasure in looking at her, but he fell passionately in love and unfortunately remained caught in her toils. After he and the prince had taken their leave of her, and he had had leisure to brood a little, it struck him that the prince must be the happiest man in the world to have so gorgeous a creature at his beck and call. And, turning over various ideas in his mind, he let his ardent love gain the better of his sense of honour, and determined, come what may, to rob the prince of his joy and take her for his own pleasure. Setting aside every consideration of reason and justice, he decided to strike while the iron was hot, and devoted his thoughts to treachery. So one day, in accordance with his evil scheme, he had all his baggage and horses made ready in the greatest secrecy for departure; in this he was aided by a highly trusted valet of the prince, Ciuriaci by name.

That night he had himself secretly introduced into the prince's bedroom by the same Ciuriaci, together with a companion, both of them armed; the lady was asleep and the prince, he noticed, was standing naked at a window—it was a hot night—facing the sea, to enjoy a little breeze blowing off it. He had already instructed his companion in what he was to do, and he himself now moved stealthily across the room to the window, drove a knife into the prince's back so that the blade emerged the other side, grabbed him, and heaved him out of the window. The palace stood on a cliff high above the sea, and the window at which the prince had been standing looked on to some houses fallen to ruin by the sea's action, so that seldom if ever did anyone go near them—a factor on which the duke had been counting. The prince's fall, therefore, escaped notice, for nobody could have heard it. Seeing the matter despatched, the duke's companion pretended to offer a caress to Ciuriaci but quickly slipped a cord round his neck—he had brought the cord for this very purpose—and drew it tight so that the man could not make a sound; the duke stepped up, they strangled Ciuriaci, and tossed him out of the window after the prince. It was clear to the duke, when they had done this, that neither Alatiel nor anyone else had heard a thing; so he took up a lamp, carried it over to the bed, and quietly exposed all of the girl, who was sound asleep; he looked her over carefully, with the greatest admiration: if he'd been attracted to her when she was dressed, how much more so was he now that she had nothing on. Inflamed with lust and undisturbed by the crime he had just committed, he lay down beside her, his hands still bloody, and possessed her—in her drowsy state she thought it was the prince.

But after he had spent some moments with her, procuring himself an immense degree of pleasure, he got up, called in some of his men, had the girl seized in such a way that she could not make any noise, and took her out by a secret door through which he had first entered; he set her on horseback and left as silently as possible with his full retinue, to make his return to Athens. As the duke had a wife, however, he installed Alatiel not in Athens but on a beautiful estate he owned a little outside the city, overlooking the sea; the girl was as heart-sore as could be, but the duke had her treated with deference and saw that all her needs were attended to as he kept her in seclusion.

The prince's courtiers, meanwhile, had waited till mid-afternoon the next day for their master to get up; in the absence of any sound from his quarters they pushed open the doors, which were closed but not locked, and found nobody within, which led them to assume that he had gone off somewhere on the sly with his beautiful lady to enjoy a few days' dalliance. They did not, therefore, trouble themselves further. This was how matters stood when the next day a lunatic wandered into the ruins where the bodies of the prince and Ciuriaci lay, and came out hauling the servant's body by the halter round its neck. As he dragged the corpse along he occasioned no little wonder among the many who observed this; they succeeded in coaxing the fellow to lead them to where he'd found the body. Here they discovered the prince's corpse and the whole city, with great mourning, gave it a solemn burial. When they made to discover who had perpetrated this heinous crime, they noticed that the Duke of Athens was no longer about but had made a furtive departure, so they concluded, quite rightly, that he must be the culprit and that he had taken the lady off with him. The citizens promptly replaced the dead prince by one of his brothers and urged him with all their might to wreak vengeance. The new prince discovered from various other indications that their suspicions were correct, and called upon friends, kinsfolk, and henchmen from far and wide; soon he had mustered a very considerable army in great array, with which he set forth to make war on the Duke of Athens.

Getting wind of this, the duke similarly marshalled his forces to defend himself; many lords came to his assistance, including two despatched by the Emperor of Constantinople: his son Constanzio and his nephew Manovello, with a fine great host. The duke gave them a princely welcome, and the duchess even more so, for she was their sister and cousin. As war grew daily more imminent, the duchess chose her moment to have the two sent along to her chamber, where she told them the entire story in a great many words and with copious tears. She explained the reasons for the war and the slight done to her by the duke on account of that other woman, whom he imagined he was keeping in secret. As she grieved bitterly over this, she begged them to do whatever they could to set this matter to rights for the sake of the duke's good name and her own peace of mind. The young men knew exactly how it had all come to pass, so they did not question the duchess much further but comforted her to the best of their ability and left her feeling more hopeful; they discovered from her where the lady was living, then went on their way.

Now as they had frequently heard the praise lavished on the lady for her exceptional beauty, they were anxious to set eyes on her and asked the duke for a sight of her, which he promised to afford them, quite forgetting what had befallen the prince as a result of showing the lady off to *him*. He had a splendid banquet prepared in a beautiful garden on the estate where Alatiel was residing, and the next morning he took them, with just a few friends, to dine with her. As he sat with her, Constanzio looked at her in awe, for assuredly he had never set eyes on anything so exquisite. Obviously (he mused) the duke was to be forgiven, as indeed was any other man, if he had stooped to treachery or other wickedness for the sake of possessing so fair an object. The more he looked at her the greater grew his admiration, until the same thing happened to him as had befallen the duke: he was besotted with her when he left, and, abandoning all thought of the war, he bent his mind to considering how he might wrest her from the duke. Meanwhile he most effectively disguised his love from everybody.

But while he was being consumed by this fire, the time came to take the field against the prince, who was advancing upon the duke's dominions; so the duke and Constanzio and their entire host sallied forth from Athens, according to plan, to engage the prince at certain frontier points and impede his advance. Here they stopped for several days, and Constanzio, whose thoughts, whose heart was still in the lap of his lady, considered that, with the duke no longer in the vicinity, he had a golden opportunity to give effect to his desire; as an excuse to return to Athens, he pleaded a serious indisposition. The duke gave him leave, so he turned over his command to Manovello and returned to his sister's in Athens. Here, after a couple of days, he brought the conversation round to the insult she felt she was suffering from the duke's conduct on account of that kept woman of his. 'Just say the word', he told her, 'and I can certainly be of assistance—I'll have the woman removed.' The duchess assumed that he would be doing this for her sake and not out of love for Alatiel, and told him she'd be only too delighted, always provided that he did it in such a way that the duke never came to know that she had put him up to it. Constanzio gave his word and the duchess agreed to his going ahead as he thought best. Constanzio secretly had a slender craft fitted out and sent away that evening to take its station off the garden to the lady's house. He issued instructions to his band of stalwarts on board, then set out with further men for the lady's residence. Here he was given a cheerful welcome by her servants, as also by the lady herself; in the company of her retinue and Constanzio's she went out with him (for such was his wish) into the garden.

Now, making as if to impart to her a message from the duke, he walked with her, alone, towards a gate giving on to the sea. This had been opened by one of his men, and on reaching it he gave the agreed signal to hail the boat. In a trice he had her taken and carried on board, while he turned to her retinue and said: 'Don't any of you make a move or utter a word, unless he wants to die: my purpose is not to steal the duke's lady from him but to repair the injury he is doing to my sister.'

This silenced them all, so Constanzio went on board with his henchmen, took his station beside the weeping Alatiel, commanded the oarsmen to set to, and away they went. Skimming, indeed flying, through the water, they reached Aegina at dawn the next day. Here they went ashore to rest and Constanzio took his pleasure with the lady, who kept ruing her ill-fated beauty. After this they returned on board and in a few days arrived at Chios, where Constanzio chose to stop, for he feared his father's reproof and the danger of the ravished lady being taken from him, so this seemed a safe haven. The fair Alatiel lamented her unhappy lot for many a day, but eventually Constanzio succeeded in comforting her and, as on previous occasions, she began to derive some pleasure from that which Fate had kept in store for her.

This was the situation when Osbec, King of the Turks at the time, and continually at war with the emperor, chanced to arrive at Smyrna. Here he heard that Constanzio was living in dalliance with a woman he had abducted; that he was settled, moreover, on Chios with no thought to his protection. So he left by night with a few small fighting ships, made a secret landing with his men, and caught many of Constanzio's household in bed before they even realized that the enemy had landed; a few who, startled out of their sleep, ran to their weapons, ended up slaughtered; the place was turned over to arson and pillage, the booty and prisoners taken on board, and the ships sailed back to Smyrna. Osbec was a young man, and he was only too delighted to see the fair creature when he was back in Smyrna and inspected the prisoners; he knew her for the one caught in bed asleep with Constanzio. He lost no time in making her his wife; the wedding was celebrated and he slept with her most contentedly for many months.

Now before these events took place, the emperor had been in negotiation with Basano, King of Cappadocia, whereby the king was to descend upon Osbec with his troops while the emperor himself attacked him from the other side. Before the treaty had been concluded, however—for he had been unwilling to fulfil certain provisions required by Basano, finding them unacceptable—the emperor learnt of what had befallen his son and, cut to the quick, wasted no time in fulfilling the king's conditions; then he pressed him for all he was worth to take the field against Osbec, while making his own preparations to attack. On receiving news of this, Osbec marshalled his forces and, leaving his beautiful wife behind at Smyrna in the charge of a trusty friend and servant, he sallied forth against the King of Cappadocia before he could be trapped between two such powerful monarchs. Shortly afterwards he engaged the King of Cappadocia in battle and was killed, and his army was defeated and scattered. The victorious King Basano was free to advance upon Smyrna, and everyone on his path submitted to him as the victor.

Osbec's retainer, Antioco by name, in whose custody the fair lady had been left, was well advanced in years; none the less, he found her quite ravishing and fell in love with her, disregarding the duty of fidelity he owed his lord and friend. He was familiar with her language, which was a great boon to her after years of having to live as though practically deaf and dumb because she had understood no one, nor had anyone understood her; so, under Love's prompting he grew most intimate with her in only a few days, and it was not long before their relationship moved from friendship to that of lovers; heedless of their lord, who was away campaigning under arms, the pair afforded each other admirable pleasure between the sheets. When they learnt of Osbec's defeat and death, and that Basano was helping himself to everything in his path, they both agreed not to tarry here for him, but left together in secret for

Rhodes, taking with them the bulk of Osbec's most precious possessions. They had not been long, though, in Rhodes before Antioco fell mortally sick. Now there happened to be lodging with him a Cypriot merchant, a close friend whom he loved dearly; as he felt his end draw near, he decided to bequeath to him his most cherished possessions, including his beloved mistress.

When he was at death's door, Antioco summoned the two of them and said: 'I can tell without a doubt I'm not long for this world—which I find a great pity, for I've never enjoyed life so much as I have lately. One thing there is, though, which assuredly makes me die happy, and that is that, while I'm fated to die, I can see myself expiring in the arms of the two people I love more than any in this world: you, dearest friend, and this lady whom, ever since I came to know her, I've loved more than my own self. What does cause me serious concern, though, is thinking that when I die she will be left here, a stranger with no one to turn to for help and advice; how much worse would it be if I didn't feel that you were here to look after her for my sake as well as you would look after me. So I do most earnestly beg you, allow me to commend to you my property and this lady, if I die, to do with the one and the other as you deem would most gladden my heart. And you, dearest love, pray don't forget me after I'm dead, but let it be my boast in the next life that I was loved in this one by the most beautiful woman ever fashioned by Nature. If you leave me a good hope of both these things, I shall without a doubt depart in peace.'

His friend the merchant, and equally the lady, wept as they listened; and when he had finished they comforted him and promised faithfully to do as he asked, if he were to die. This he did shortly afterwards, and they had him given an honourable burial.

A few days later the Cypriot merchant had concluded his business in Rhodes and proposed returning to Cyprus on board a Catalan vessel then in port; so he asked Alatiel what she wished to do, as he had to go back to Cyprus. Her answer was that she would gladly accompany him, if he didn't mind, for she hoped that he would treat her with respect and like a sister for Antioco's sake. The merchant replied that her satisfaction was his pleasure, and, the better to protect her from anything untoward that might threaten her on the way to Cyprus, he put it about that she was his wife. They went aboard and were assigned a cabin in the stern; to avoid his behaviour being at variance with his word, the merchant slept with her in the narrowest of bunks. That which ensued as a result was something neither of them had intended as they left Rhodes: what with the dark and the warmth and snugness of their bed, none of which factors is to be underestimated, they forgot the duty of love and friendship to the deceased Antioco, and under the same impulse began to arouse each other, so that by the time they reached Paphos, whence the merchant hailed, they had become quite well acquainted. At Paphos Alatiel stayed a good while with the merchant.

Now a gentleman called Antigono happened to arrive in Paphos on business; he was of a great age and of greater wisdom but of only modest wealth, for he had acted in a number of transactions as factor to the King of Cyprus but luck had gone against him. As one day he was passing the house in which Alatiel resided, the Cypriot merchant being then on a trading mission to Armenia, he chanced to notice the lady at her window; and he fell to staring at her, beautiful as she was, and recollected having seen her on some previous occasion, though he could not for the life of him remember where. Now Alatiel, so long the plaything of Fortune, was coming to the appointed end of her troubles: the moment she espied Antigono she remembered having seen him at Alexandria in a position of no mean authority at her father's court. Hope, therefore, suddenly dawned in her that she might yet be able to return to her royal estate with the help of his counsel. Knowing that her merchant was away, she sent for Antigono there and then. When he arrived she bashfully asked him whether she was right in thinking that he was Antigono of Famagusta.

'Yes', said Antigono, and went on: 'I fancy I recognize you, my lady, though I can't begin to remember where I saw you; would you do me a favour, if you don't object, and remind me who you are?'

Once she had heard that it really was he, Alatiel burst into tears and threw her arms round his neck; he was not a little surprised, and after a while she asked him whether he hadn't ever seen her in Alexandria. Hearing this question, Antigono recognized her at once for Alatiel, the sultan's daughter, whom everyone thought had been lost at sea. He made to pay her his respects but she would not permit him—she requested that he sit with her awhile. With this he complied, and respectfully asked her how she came to be here, when had she arrived, and where from, because it was generally supposed in Egypt that she had drowned at sea many a year ago.

'Would that that had happened', she said, 'instead of my leading the life I've led—and I do believe my father would wish the same thing, if he ever learnt of it.' With these words she relapsed into unaccountable tears, which led Antigono to say: 'Do not lose heart, madam, before you must. Please tell me of your adventures, tell me what sort of life you have been leading: the chances are matters have not yet reached such a pitch that they may not be mended, God willing.'

'When I saw you, Antigono', she said, 'it was as if I'd seen my own father and, though I might have remained hidden, I revealed myself to you in an impulse of love and tenderness such as I am bound to feel for him. And of all the people I might have chanced to see there are few whom I'd have been so happy to find as you—whom I saw and recognized before anyone else. So while I've always made a secret of the facts of my unhappy fate, to you I shall disclose them, as to a father. When you've heard my story, if you can see any way of restoring me to my former position, I beg you to put it in hand; if you can see no way, please never tell a soul that you saw me or that you ever heard news of me.'

This said, she tearfully described to him everything that had befallen her from the day of her shipwreck on Majorca up to this moment. Antigono himself wept for pity, but after musing for a while he said: 'As your identity remained concealed, madam, throughout all your misadventures, I shall not fail to restore you to your father, and he will cherish you more than ever; after which you shall be married to the King of Africa.'

She asked him how, and he described to her precisely what they were to do. Furthermore, to avoid anything else cropping up in the interval, Antigono returned at once to see the king at Famagusta. 'If it please your highness', he said to him, 'you may advance your own honour immeasurably and at the same stroke do me a great favour, impoverished as I am in your service—and all at little cost to yourself.'

Invited to explain himself, Antigono continued: 'The fair young daughter of the sultan has arrived at Paphos, the one who has long been assumed to have drowned. She has endured endless misfortunes in order to preserve her chastity, and now she finds herself in much reduced circumstances and longing to return to her father. If you were pleased to send her back to him in my charge, great honour would accrue to you, and great good to me. It is my belief that the sultan would never forget this service.'

The king assented at once with right royal magnanimity and, sending for Alatiel, had her conducted in style to Famagusta, where he and the queen welcomed her most cordially and with every honour. Questioned about her misadventures by the king and queen, the girl gave them a full account in accordance with Antigono's instructions. A few days later, at her request, the king sent her back to the sultan, in the charge of Antigono and with a fine, noble escort of ladies and gentlemen-in-waiting. There's no need to ask whether the sultan welcomed her with joy, as he also welcomed Antigono and the whole company. When she had rested a little, the sultan wished to discover how she came to be alive and where she had been all this time without sending him any news of herself.

Excellently rehearsed by Antigono, the young woman answered her father as follows: 'About twenty days after I left you our ship sprang a leak in a violent storm, and one night was cast ashore away in the West, near a place called Aigues Mortes. What became of the men on board I didn't know and never discovered. All I remember is that, when morning came and I more or less returned from death to life, the wrecked ship was spotted by the local people, who came running from every quarter, intent on plundering it. Scarcely had I been taken ashore with two of my handmaidens than some young men made off with us, each in a different direction. What became of them I never discovered; but, in spite of my resistance, two young men laid hold of me and tugged me by the hair, while I cried like anything; and while they pulled me along a road to get into a huge great wood, four horsemen happened at that moment to ride by, and when the youths saw them they let me go and took to their heels. The four horsemen who, to all appearances, were men of highest authority, noticed this and came galloping over to where I was standing and plied me with questions and I prattled away to them but they didn't understand a word I was saying, nor I them. They held a long discussion, then sat me on one of their horses and took me to a monastery for women according to their religion. I don't know what they said, but I was kindly received here by all the women and treated the whole time with great respect, and so joined them in the most devout service to Saint Augmenta in the Hollow, for whom the local women all had a soft spot.

'But after I had stayed with them for some while, and had learnt a smattering of their language, they asked me who I was and where from; knowing where I was and fearing, therefore, if I told them the truth, that they would drive me out as an enemy of their religion, I told them that I was the daughter of one of Cyprus's leading citizens, and he had sent me away as bride to a Cretan husband, but we had been driven here and wrecked by a storm. And all too often in all manner of ways I observed their Rule for fear of worse. Then the women's superior, whom they call abbess, asked if I wanted to go back to Cyprus, and I said there was nothing I should like more. She, however, was concerned for my virtue, and would never entrust me to anyone bound for Cyprus until, about two months ago, some honest Frenchmen arrived with their wives. One of them was related to the abbess, and when she discovered that they were on their way to Jerusalem to visit the Holy Sepulchre, where they buried the One Whom they regard as God, after the Jews killed Him, she entrusted me to them and asked them to restore me to my father in Cyprus. It would take too long to tell you how kindly treated I was by those gentlemen, how warmly I was welcomed by them and their wives.

'So we took ship and after some days reached Paphos. Seeing that I was now landed there, a total stranger, and not knowing what to say to the gentlemen who were going to hand me over to my father in compliance with the venerable abbess's instructions . . . maybe God felt sorry for me, because He had Antigono waiting on the quayside at Paphos just as we came ashore. I quickly called him and, speaking in our own tongue so as not to be understood by the gentlemen and their ladies, I told him to welcome me as his daughter. He caught my meaning at once and gave me the most joyful welcome, and entertained the gentlemen and their wives to the best of his scanty means. He brought me to the King of Cyprus, and I could never tell you all he did to make me welcome and how he sent me back here to you. If there's anything left to add, let Antigono say it, for he has heard this story of my adventures many a time.'

Antigono then turned to the sultan and said: 'What she has told you, my lord, is a meticulous account, just as she has several times told it to me and as the gentlefolk with whom she came described it all. There's just one thing she neglected to mention, and I think that's because it was not for her to do so: I mean everything those gentlefolk with whom she travelled had to say about the exemplary life she had led with the pious women, her virtue, her commendable behaviour—how those ladies and gentlemen wept when they took leave of Alatiel after entrusting her to me! If I were to give you a full account of everything they told me, I should need not only the rest of today but the entire night as well. Suffice to say, considering the evidence of their words and of my own eyes, you can boast of possessing the most beautiful daughter, and the most virtuous and stalwart of any monarch who today wears a crown.'

This left the sultan in raptures, and he repeatedly prayed the Lord to second his efforts in bestowing suitable thanks on anyone who had shown hospitality to his daughter, not least on the King of Cyprus, who had sent her back to him in such pomp. After a few days, he had the most lavish presents made ready for Antigono, and gave him leave to return to Cyprus; he sent letters and special envoys to the king, thanking him most profusely for all he had done on his daughter's behalf.

After this, hoping to bring to fruition what he had once started, that is, to make his daughter wife to the King of Africa, he wrote a letter to the king with a full account of what had happened, adding that, if he still desired her, he was to send for her. The King of Africa rejoiced at this; he sent an honourable escort to fetch her and welcomed her delightedly. So the girl, who had slept with eight men a good ten thousand times, lay down beside him as a virgin, and got him to believe it. She went on to live a long and happy life as his queen. Whence the saying:

There's no misfortune in a mouth well kissed:
It prospers, rather, like the waxing moon.

II. 8. *Because of calumny, the Count of Antwerp, from the first man in the kingdom, becomes the last, and seeks refuge in England; but Fortune never wholly abandons him nor his children.*

The various misadventures that befell the beautiful woman had the ladies all sighing—though who knows whether they were moved to pity or merely a little wistful at so much wedding and bedding? But, leaving this aside for the present, the queen realized that Pamphilo's last words, which made them all laugh, brought his story to an end, and so she turned to Elissa, bidding her follow. This Elissa was glad to do.

What a vast field it is (she began) that today we are venturing into! Any one of us could as easily attempt a dozen forays into it as a single one, so frequently has Fortune intervened in her strange and hapless ways. Let me, therefore, pick one instance out of the hundreds.

The transfer of the Roman Empire from French to German hands* occasioned the bitterest enmity between the two nations, attended by continual hostilities. In order to defend their own country and attack the enemy, the King of France and his son strained every sinew to recruit from their own resources and from those of their relatives and allies a mighty army with which to march upon the Germans. Not wishing to leave the country without a government, however, before setting out they appointed Walter, Count of Antwerp, to the sole charge of the Kingdom of France, to act as their lieutenant-governor and regent. They had been advised that he was a wise and upright man, totally loyal to them, and, however well versed he was in the arts of war, they considered him better suited to the council-chamber than to the battlefield. This appointment made, they set forth. So Walter entered upon his duties in a sensible, orderly fashion, and always shared his counsels with the queen and her daughter-in-law—true, both ladies were committed to his care and authority, but he always strove to treat them with the deference he owed his sovereigns. The count was a remarkably handsome man of about 40; he was truly a man of honour and quite the most prepossessing character, besides which he was the very paragon of refinement, and in dress and appearance as neat as a new pin.

The count's wife had died, leaving him with two small children, a boy and a girl. Now it happened that while the King of France and his son were away at the wars and the count was at court, frequenting the queen and princess and discussing with them the business of the state, the princess took a fancy to him: she was strongly attracted by both his good looks and his charm, and secretly fell in love with him. Conscious that she herself was a young lass and fresh as a daisy, while he was without a woman, she considered that she would have no trouble working her way with him; the only obstacle, she thought, could be a sense of shame, but this could be disposed of, she decided, by putting her cards on the table. She chose a moment one day when she was on her own, and sent for him on the pretext of wanting to discuss quite other matters. The count went to her on the instant, with nothing in his mind akin to her thoughts. She was in her bedroom, and made him sit down beside her on a divan, just the two of them; twice the count asked her why she had sent for him, and received no reply, but eventually, under Love's impulse, she blushed crimson and in a tremulous voice she stammered out her avowal, and as she spoke she wept:

'My lord and dearest, dearest friend! Wise man that you are, you can readily understand what fragile creatures men and women are—and circumstances can make one woman more fragile than the next. This is why a just judge will do well not to award the same penalty to different people convicted of the same offence. Who will deny that it is far more reprehensible in a pauper, who needs must toil incessantly for his or her subsistence, if he or she respond to Love's enticements than it is for a lady of wealth and leisure, who lacks for nothing in the fulfilment of her desires? I believe no one would deny it. This is why I think that a woman is very largely absolved if perchance she has been swept off her feet but can offer such an excuse in her favour; for the rest, if she has elected to love a man of wisdom and true worth, that will complete her absolution. Now I am sure that both these factors are present in my case, to impel me to love, along with the added factors of my youth and of my husband's being far away; if I'm passionately in love with you, these should serve in my defence. If such excuses carry the weight one might expect them to carry in a judicious mind, I beg you to afford me your help and advice in what I shall ask of you. With my husband away, I cannot hold out against the urges of the flesh and the power of love—strong men, to say nothing of frail women, are overwhelmed by such forces day in day out; and I have to admit that, basking in the lap of luxury and idleness as you see me, I've let myself be carried away in a surge of amorous passion. And though if this got out, I'd have to concede that it's disgraceful, while it remains under cover you're not to regard it as in any real sense a bad thing: Love, you see, has served me so well, not simply by guarding me from an indiscriminate choice of lover, but by pointing you out to me as a worthy object of love to a woman such as I am. For my choice rests, if I am not mistaken, on the most gallant, the most handsome, attractive, and intelligent knight in the entire kingdom. Moreover, as I can claim to be without a husband, so are you equally without a wife. And so I beseech you, by the great love I bear you, do not withhold your love from me but take pity on my youth—it is being consumed for you as ice melting by the fire.'

The princess had intended to continue her entreaties but she was interrupted at this point by such a flood of tears that she could not utter another word; quite overcome, she bowed her face and collapsed so that her head came to rest against the count's bosom. Being a man of outstanding integrity, the count rebuked her most solemnly for her ill-considered passion and thrust her away from him as she was on the point of throwing her arms about his neck. 'On my honour', he said, 'I should sooner be disembowelled than consent to such a stroke (whether I or another undertook it) against the honour of my lord.'

Hearing these words, the princess forgot all about love and was stung to fury. 'Am I then, you despicable knight, to be thus spurned in my desire? Since you mean to drive me to my death, please God I shall first drive you out and see *you* dead!' This said, she thrust her hands into her hair and tore at it and dishevelled it, then ripped open her dress at her breast and shrieked out: 'Help! Help! The count is raping me!'

As Walter could reckon more surely with the courtiers' envy than upon the purity of his conscience, and feared therefore that the lady's spite would carry more conviction than his own innocence, he leapt up when he saw this and fled from the room and from the palace. Back home, without a second thought, he mounted horse with his two children and made all haste towards Calais.

Everyone came running at the princess's shrieks. When they caught sight of the lady and heard the reason for her cries, they believed her on this evidence, but also accepted that the count's habitual gallantry and polished manners were a long-cultivated stratagem towards achieving his goal. So they all ran, seething, to the count's domain to arrest him; not finding him there, they ransacked the place, then razed every building to the ground. Word was brought to the king and his son in the field, portraying the count in the worst light. They were thoroughly angered by this and condemned the count and his descendants to permanent exile, with a great price on his head if he was brought in, dead or alive.

The unhappy count, who realized he had compromised his innocence by his flight, reached Calais without making himself known to a soul and, unrecognized, crossed to England. Dressed as a pauper he travelled towards London, but before arriving there he instructed his children in a number of things, but principally in two: the first was to endure patiently their condition of poverty to which he and they were now fated through no fault of theirs; and the second, to take the greatest care never to tell a soul where they were from or whose children they were, if they valued their lives. The boy, called Luigi, was about 9, while the girl, Violante, was about 7. So far as they could grasp it at their tender age, they understood their father's lesson perfectly and were to follow it to the letter. To facilitate this, he decided to change their names: the boy he rechristened Perotto, the girl, Giannetta. They arrived in London poorly dressed and went around begging, the way French vagabonds always do.

One morning when they had taken up their station outside a church, a great lady happened to come out; she was the wife of one of the King of England's field marshals. She saw the count and his two children begging and she stopped to ask him where he was from and whether the children were his. He told her that he was from Picardy, and that owing to a crime committed by his reprobate elder son, he had had to leave with these other two children of his. She was a compassionate lady and very much took to the little girl on sight, for she was a pretty and engaging child with a hint of breeding. 'My good man', she said, 'if you don't mind leaving your little girl in my care, I'll be glad to take her in, for I like the look of her; if she turns out well, I'll make a suitable match for her at the proper time.'

This request delighted the count, who readily agreed; he handed her over with tears in his eyes and entrusted her warmly to the lady's care. Now that his daughter was settled with a person he could vouch for, he decided to remain in London no longer, and set off across the island with Perotto, begging from place to place, till they reached Wales—a most fatiguing journey, for he was unused to travelling on foot. Here dwelt another of His Majesty's field marshals, who kept a great estate and a numerous retinue; the count and his son were frequent visitors to this court in search of a meal. Here Perotto came to join in the games of the field marshal's sons and the children of the court gentlemen; they would vie with each other in running and jumping, and Perotto proved himself their equal—indeed, often he came first. The field marshal would sometimes watch the children at play, and he took a fancy to Perotto, a well-mannered, agreeable child. On enquiring about him, he was told that the boy was son of a pauper who sometimes came in to beg for alms. So the field marshal sent for him, and the count, who could have asked for nothing better, freely handed the boy over, though he was sorry to lose him. With both his children thus settled, the count decided against remaining any longer in England, but made his way across to Ireland as best he could. When he reached Strangford he entered into the service of a local earl's vassal, and was employed in the normal duties of a house-servant or stable-boy. Here for a long, long time he lived a life of endless toil and privation, but he preserved his incognito.

Violante, now known as Giannetta, grew up in London in the household of the noble lady and increased in years, in stature, and in beauty; she gained so much in the good graces of the lady and her husband, indeed of the entire household and of all who knew her, it was quite wonderful to behold. Anyone taking note of her deportment and conduct was bound to admit that she deserved to go far. So the lady concluded that she ought now to marry the girl off, making an honourable match in accordance with what she imagined to be her station—having acquired the lass from her father, she had never been able to establish who he was, other than from his own account of himself. But God, who sets a just value upon a person's merits, recognized in her a blameless noblewoman who suffered for another's fault, and appointed otherwise. What now came to pass, which prevented her being allotted to a man of humble birth, was undoubtedly the work of benign Providence.

The lady and her husband, to whose household Giannetta belonged, had an only son, the apple of his parents' eyes because he was their son and also because he deserved their love, being every inch a gentleman—handsome, brave, and gifted. He was some six years older than Giannetta. She was so sweet and beautiful in his eyes that he fell deeply in love with her, and he had eyes for her alone. As he took her to be a woman of the lowest class, he did not dare ask his parents for her hand in marriage, indeed he did his very best to conceal his love for fear that he would be rebuked for setting his cap at too humble an object. Keeping his love suppressed in this way made it only the more painful, and as a result of such a heartache he came down with a serious illness. Several doctors were called to his sick-bed; they took note of the various symptoms but failed to determine the cause of his ailment and each one of them washed his hands of him. Never were a mother and father so heart-broken. They kept pitifully asking him what was the matter, but his only answer was to sigh, or to say he felt he was wasting away.

One day a very young but thoroughly proficient doctor was sitting beside the patient, holding his wrist so as to feel his pulse, when Giannetta, who out of duty to the mother waited solicitously on her son, came into the sick-room for some reason. The lad made no move and said not a word, but on sight of her he felt love's fire flare up within him, and his pulse therefore started to beat faster; this took the doctor by surprise—he waited in silence to see how long this higher pulse-rate lasted. When Giannetta left the room, the pulse went back to normal. The doctor felt he was now on the way towards discovering the cause of the boy's illness. After an interval, on the pretext of wanting to ask Giannetta something, he sent for her but kept hold of the patient's pulse. She came at once to his summons, and scarcely was she in the room than the boy's pulse-beat quickened, to slow down again the moment she left.

The doctor needed no further convincing; he stood up and took the boy's father and mother aside: 'Your son's recovery', he told them, 'is beyond the help of doctors. It lies in the hands of Giannetta. I've recognized the signs very clearly—he is passionately in love with her, though my impression is that she's unaware of it. So if you value his life, you know what you have to do.'

The parents rejoiced at this news as it offered some means to obtain the boy's recovery. It was, none the less, a cruel blow that the way to do so was, they feared, that of making Giannetta his wife.

When the doctor left, the parents went to their patient and the mother said: 'My son, I should never have imagined that you'd conceal from me any wish of yours, especially as I see you wasting away for want of obtaining your heart's desire. You should have known that there's nothing I would not do for you if I could to make you happy, even if it were something that did you less than full credit—I'd do it for you as though it were for my own self. But if you've kept your secret, the Good Lord has been kinder to you, as it happens, than you have been to yourself and has revealed to me the cause of your illness, lest you should die of it; what you have is simply an excessive love for a certain young woman—such as we find her. Truly, you should not have been ashamed to confess it: at your age you *ought* to be in love—if you were not, I'd think the less of you. So don't hold back from me, son, but tell me quite freely what it is you want. Be rid of the brooding melancholy that has given rise to your illness, and take heart: rest assured, there's nothing I would not do for your satisfaction if you asked me and it lay within my power, for I love you more than my own life. Don't be frightened, don't be ashamed, just tell me if there's anything I can do to serve your love, and see if I don't move heaven and earth on your behalf—if I fail to, then consider me the cruellest mother who ever brought forth a child.'

His mother's words made the boy feel bashful at first, but on reflection he realized that no one could more effectively satisfy his wish than she could, so he took courage and said: 'If there's one thing, mother, that's forced me to conceal my love, it's seeing the way older people generally refuse to remember that they were young once. But as I see that you at any rate are understanding, I shan't deny that you're right about what you say you've noticed; I shall even tell you who the person is, provided that you keep your promise so far as it lies in your power. That way you'll have me cured.'

His mother, who was now quite confident she would not have to fulfil her pledge along the lines she originally had feared, readily invited him to speak his mind and she would lose no time in procuring him the gratification he sought.

'Mother', said the boy, 'our Giannetta is so beautiful, so utterly enchanting, and yet I could not make my feelings known to her, let alone invite her compassion; I never dared let a soul into my secret. This is what has brought me to the present pitch, and if you do not fulfil your promise to me in one way or another, you can be sure I'm not long for this world.'

His mother smiled; this was not the time for remonstrations, she felt, but for consolation. 'Why, son, is that what has brought you to this pass?' she exclaimed. 'Take heart, leave it to me, you're going to get well again.'

The young man was greatly encouraged and very quickly showed signs of a marked recovery. His mother was delighted, and was ready to see what she could do to honour her promise. She sent for Giannetta one day and put the question to her in a gently bantering tone: 'Is your heart bespoken?'

'I'm a poor little maid, my lady, driven from home', replied Giannetta, blushing. 'I live here as your servant. It would be quite inappropriate for me even to think of giving my heart.'

'Well, if you have no lover, we intend to give you one. He'll make you happy, and you'll take all the more pleasure in your beauty; it's not right that a creature as pretty as you are should never have a lover.'

'My lady', said Giannetta, 'you took me, a pauper, off my father's hands and brought me up as your own daughter, so it is right that I should do everything you ask of me. But this once I shall not fall in with your wish, however well-meaning you find it. If you are pleased to give me a husband, him I shall love, but none other. I have inherited nothing from my own family save this one thing: my honour. This I mean to defend as long as I live.'

This response totally confounded the plan devised by the lady to keep her word to her son, though she was a sensible enough woman to approve Giannetta's stand completely. 'What, Giannetta', she cried, 'if a gallant young man like His Majesty the King wanted a little dalliance with a beautiful young lady like you, would you refuse him?'

'He might force me, but he would never have my free consent to anything that was dishonourable.'

Knowing now what she was made of, the mother wasted no more words but decided to test her out. She told her son to get her alone in his room once he had recovered and try to seduce her, because she found it distasteful to play the procuress and press the girl on his behalf. The boy did not care for this plan one jot, and his health took a rapid turn for the worse. So the mother reopened the question with Giannetta, but, finding her still adamant, told her husband where matters stood. And though they hated the thought of it, they both agreed she would have to be their son's bride—they'd sooner have a son alive and married below his station than dead and a bachelor. And, after further discussion, that is what they did. Giannetta was over the moon, and devoutly thanked God for not forsaking her. Never, in all this time, did she admit to being anything but the daughter of a man from Picardy. The young man recovered, they got happily married, and he settled down to enjoy his wife.

Perotto, meanwhile, had grown up in Wales in the household of the King of England's field marshal, and he earned his lord's favour; he grew into a very handsome lad, as valiant as any man on the island, and there was no one to match him in jousts and tournaments and other feats of arms. Perotto of Picardy he was called—he was known far and wide. And just as God had not forsaken his sister, so He showed He was watching over the boy: a mortal plague ravaged the neighbourhood and carried off nearly half the population, while the majority of the survivors fled in terror from the scene and left the region seemingly deserted. Among those who died were the field marshal, his lady, and their son and heir, along with several other sons, nephews, and kinsmen; the only ones to survive were a daughter of marriageable age and a handful of retainers, including Perotto. When the plague had somewhat abated, the daughter took Perotto for her husband—he was, after all, a gallant and worthy man, and the few surviving neighbours all heartily approved her choice. Thus she made him master of all that came to her by inheritance. Before long the king heard of his field marshal's death; Perotto of Picardy's virtues were known to him and he appointed him to the deceased field marshal's position. And that, briefly, is the story of the two innocent children whom the Count of Antwerp had given up for lost.

It was eighteen years since the Count of Antwerp had fled from Paris. In Ireland he had been eking out a wretched existence and suffered all manner of hardships, and he realized how he had aged. Now the urge came to him to see if he could discover what had become of his children. His appearance had changed out of all recognition, and it was plain to him that the robust physique that had characterized him as a young man of the leisured classes had not survived his years of menial labour. Penniless and dressed like a tramp, he left the man he had stayed with all this time, crossed over to England, and went to the place where he had left Perotto. He discovered that his son was a great lord, the king's field marshal, a good-looking, well set up young man, he could see. Immensely pleased though he was to see this, he would not reveal his own identity to him until he had learnt what had become of Giannetta. He continued on his way, therefore, until he reached London, where he made cautious enquiries about the lady to whom he had entrusted his daughter, to learn how she was faring. Giannetta was married to the son of the house, he discovered, and he was so delighted that all the evil he had suffered hitherto was of little consequence to him, now that he had found his children alive and prospering. Anxious to set eyes on her, he took up his station as a beggar close to her house, until one day Giannetta's husband (Giachetto Lamiens was his name) noticed and took pity on him, for he looked a poor old man. He bade one of his servants fetch him in and give him a meal for the love of God, which the servant was glad to do.

Giannetta had given Giachetto several children, the eldest not above 8 years old; they were the prettiest, sweetest children imaginable. Seeing the count sitting down to his meal they all crowded round him in a happy throng, as if some occult power had taught them that this man was their grandfather. For his part, he knew them for his grandchildren, and straight away made a big fuss of them, so the children would not leave him, never mind that their tutor kept calling them. Giannetta overheard it all, left her room, came into the room where the count was and threatened to give them all a good hiding if they didn't do as their tutor bade them. The children set up a howl and said they wanted to stay with the nice man who was much kinder to them than their tutor was. Their mother and the count laughed. The count had stood up, not at all in the role of her father but as a pauper, out of courtesy to his daughter who was also the lady of the house. The sight of her was balm to his soul. She, however, failed to recognize him either now or later, so radically had he altered in appearance: he was a bearded old man with grey hair, a gaunt, swarthy man, and he didn't remotely tally with her recollection of her father. Seeing that her children wouldn't be parted from him and cried when she made to send them out, she told their tutor to leave them a little longer.

So the children stayed on with the nice man. Then in came Giachetto's father and learned from the tutor what was going on. As he did not care for Giannetta, he said: 'Let them be, curse them! They take after their mother—she comes from a line of tramps, so it's not surprising if her children like to consort with tramps.' These words did not escape the count's ears, and they made him smart; but he'd suffered all too many slights and shrugged this one off with the rest. Giachetto himself heard what a merry time the children were having with their nice man (the count, in other words), and he was none too pleased with their behaviour; but he did dote on them and hated to see them cry, so he gave instructions that the man was to remain in the household if he was ready to enter his service in some capacity. 'Willingly', said the count, 'but all I can do is look after the horses—that's what I've been doing all my life.' So a horse was assigned to him and, after grooming it, he returned to playing with the children.

While Fortune conducted the Count of Antwerp and his children in the manner thus determined, the King of France, who had made a series of truces with the Germans, died. The crown passed to his son—it was his spouse who had contrived the count's banishment. The latest truce expiring, he returned to war against the Germans as savagely as ever. The King of

England, who had recently taken a French royal bride, sent ample reinforcements under the command of his field marshal Perotto and of Giachetto Lamiens, son of his other field marshal. The nice man (in other words, the count) went with him, and remained all the while in the army, employed as a groom and escaping recognition. Here he performed sterling service; his advice and exertions went far beyond what was required of him.

During the war the Queen of France fell gravely ill and, realizing she was at death's door, repented all her sins and made a devout confession to the Archbishop of Rouen, a man generally esteemed as a model of sanctity. Among her sins she confessed the grave wrong she had done to the Count of Antwerp. She did not rest content with this confession, but gave a detailed account of the affair to an assembly of good men. 'Prevail upon His Majesty', she implored them, 'to restore the count to his estates if he is still alive; if not, then to restore his children.' Shortly afterwards she departed this life and received a dignified burial.

The queen's confession was transmitted to the king, whose heart ached for the worthy count so unjustly persecuted. He was moved to issue a proclamation throughout the army and elsewhere, far and wide: whoever succeeded in tracing the Count of Antwerp or any child of his (it ran) would be handsomely rewarded by His Majesty in respect of each one discovered, inasmuch as His Majesty held the count to be innocent of the charges for which he had been banished, as was proved by Her Late Majesty's confession; His Majesty proposed to restore the count to his former estates and yet greater ones.

The count, in the guise of a groom, heard the proclamation and understood that it was authentic, so he went straight to Giachetto with the request that they both call at once on Perotto, because he wished to reveal to them the object of the king's quest. When the three were together, the count said to Perotto, who was already in two minds whether to identify himself: 'Perotto, Giachetto is married to your sister, but received her without a dowry. Your sister is not to go without a dowry, and therefore I propose that Giachetto and none other is to earn the handsome reward promised by His Majesty in your regard. Disclose yourself as the Count of Antwerp's son, and Violante as your sister and Giachetto's wife—and report me for the Count of Antwerp, your father.'

Perotto looked keenly at the count when he heard this, and instantly recognized him. He threw himself weeping at his feet, and embraced him and said: 'Oh welcome, father, a thousand times welcome!'

Hearing the count's words and then seeing how Perotto reacted to them, Giachetto was struck with amazement and at the same time quite overjoyed—he was completely lost for words. However, he took what they said to be true, and was thoroughly ashamed of the insults he had now and then hurled at his stable-boy; he, too, fell weeping at the count's feet and humbly sought pardon for his every discourtesy. The count drew him to his feet and cheerfully forgave him. Then they narrated what had befallen each of them—an occasion for both merriment and tears—after which Perotto and Giachetto made to put the count into new attire. He would not hear of it, however: he had promised the king's reward without fail to Giachetto, and he meant to be presented to His Majesty just as he was, dressed as a groom, to make him feel all the more ashamed of himself.

So Giachetto appeared before the king with the count and Perotto, and offered to present the count and his children to him if he received the reward in accordance with the proclamation. The king promptly had the reward prepared in respect of all three of them—Giachetto found the prize quite dazzling—and bade him take it if he really could identify the count and his children as he was promising to do. Giachetto turned, then, and thrust his groom and Perotto in front of him, saying: 'Your Majesty, here is the father and the son. The daughter is my wife; she is not here but pray God you shall see her shortly.' At these words the king looked at the count and, although he had changed a great deal, after scrutinizing him a while he recognized him, and with tears in his eyes he lifted him up off his knees and kissed and embraced him. He gave Perotto a hearty welcome, and gave orders for the count to be supplied that instant with clothing, servants, horses, and all the trappings due to his rank. And this was done. The king gave a royal welcome also to Giachetto and wished to have a full report from him of all that had occurred.

When Giachetto received the magnificent reward for tracing the count and his children, the count said to him: 'Take these gifts from the bounty of His Majesty; they will remind you to tell your father that your children—his grandchildren and mine—are not descended from tramps on their mother's side.' Giachetto took the gifts and sent for his wife and his mother. Perotto's wife also came to Paris, where they had a grand festive reunion with the count, restored now by the king to all his former estate and raised to even greater heights than before. Then they were given leave each to return home while the count remained in Paris, dwelling in greater splendour than ever until his dying day.

II. 9. *Bernabò worships his wife Ginevra but is hoodwinked by Ambrogiuolo into believing her an adulteress, and has her put to death. She survives, however, and succeeds in bringing her husband's deceiver to justice.*

After Elissa had served her turn with the moving tale she told, Queen Philomena (a tall beauty with the nicest face and a twinkling eye) collected her thoughts and observed: 'We must keep our bargain with Dioneo, and therefore, as he and I are the only two left to tell a story, I shall tell mine first and he, at his request, will provide the last.' This said, she thus began:

There's a proverb that folk are forever coming out with: 'He who laughs last laughs best.' Don't ask me to prove it to you—you've only got to look around you. So, sticking to our proposal, what I want to do is to show you how true this saying is, my dearest ladies. What's more, it's a story you'll be glad to hear: it will teach you how to take care of tricksters.

A number of leading Italian merchants were assembled in a hotel in Paris, each one there in pursuit of his business, as was their habit. And one evening in particular, after they had all enjoyed a festive supper, they settled down to discussing one thing and another, and the conversation eventually came round to the topic of their wives, whom they had left at home.

And one of them jovially remarked: 'I've no idea how mine gets by; what I do know is that if I get my hands on a wench who takes my fancy, why, I don't let my love for my wife stand in the way—I have my fill of the girl in hand.'

'That's just what I do', said another. 'Suppose I believe my wife makes hay while the sun shines: so she does. And what if I don't believe it? She'll do it just the same! What's sauce for the goose is sauce for the gander; as a man sows, so does he reap.'

The third man said more or less the same thing and, in short, they all appeared to be agreed on this point, that if you leave a woman alone, she won't let the grass grow under her feet.

There was only one dissenter, a Genoese called Bernabò Lomellin. He asserted that, by the Good Lord's special providence, he had a wife who was replete with every quality that befitted a lady or indeed, to a great extent, a knight or squire, and her like probably did not exist in Italy: she was a ravishing beauty, she was youthful, clever, robust, and there was not a woman to match her in those accomplishments that fell within a lady's competence, like working in silk and so forth. What is more, he said, there was not a gentleman's attendant or page who could wait on a great man's table with half the aplomb she exhibited, for she was a model of grace, competence, and discretion. He commended her, too, for sitting a horse, handling a falcon, reading, writing, and keeping the accounts better than any merchant. This, after much additional praise, brought him to their present topic, when he affirmed on oath that you would never find a woman as virtuous and chaste as she was: if he stayed away from home for ten years or for ever and a day, he was quite convinced that she would never get up to any of those little games with another man. Now one of those merchants taking part in the conversation was a young man from Piacenza called Ambrogiuolo and, when Bernabò praised his wife on this last account, he burst into fits of laughter and enquired in bantering tone whether this was a privilege the emperor had conferred on him in preference to all other men. Bernabò replied a little tetchily that it was not the emperor but God Himself, whose powers extended somewhat beyond those of the emperor, who had granted him this favour.

So Ambrogiuolo said: 'I'm sure you're convinced of the truth of what you're saying, Bernabò, but it does seem to me you're failing to see things as they really are: if you take a good look, you strike me as sharp enough to have noticed things about our nature that would make you speak of such matters with a little less assurance. The rest of us have been making free with our wives' reputations, and I wouldn't want you to be thinking that we see our wives in a different light than you, merely that we're talking on the basis of simple experience of life; so I should like to go into this matter with you a little. Among all the living creatures God created, the noblest animal, so I've always heard, is the human male; then comes the female; the male, however, has the greater perfection, it is generally believed, and furthermore it's clear from the way he acts. Now as he is the more perfect, he must necessarily be the more constant, as indeed he is, because women everywhere are more flighty, and the reason for this could be adduced from any number of arguments from nature, not that I propose to go into them now. If men are the more steadfast sex and yet cannot stop themselves wanting a woman who takes their fancy, to say nothing of a woman who makes eyes at them; and not merely wanting, but stopping at nothing in order to possess the woman—not simply once a month, moreover, but at all hours of the day and night: how do you expect a woman is going to cope, susceptible creature that she is, with all the supplications, attentions, presents, and the thousand other tactics employed by a clever man who is courting her? Do you honestly believe she can hold aloof? I don't care how much you insist, I just don't believe you can really think that. You yourself admit that your wife is a woman, made of flesh and blood like all the others. Now, that being the case, she must have the same urges as other women, and but the same powers of resistance to these natural appetites. She may be the soul of virtue, but the possibility does exist that she will do as her sisters do, and nothing within the bounds of possibility should be denied as vehemently as you are doing, nor should you be so insistent on the opposite.'

'I'm a merchant, not a philosopher', said Bernabò in reply, 'and I'll answer as a merchant. I grant that what you say can indeed happen to your flutterheads who are without shame. But a sensible woman is so careful of her honour—something men don't trouble themselves about—she becomes stronger than any man in order to protect it. That's how my wife is.'

'The fact is', said Ambrogiuolo, 'if each time they got involved in such pursuits they sprang a horn on their forehead as evidence of what they'd been up to, I suspect that not many of them would get involved in this sort of behaviour. But, far from growing horns, the woman who goes about it the right way doesn't leave a trace, not the smallest footprint, behind her—and if things don't come to light, why, there's no question of shame, honour remains unblemished. So a woman who can do it on the quiet does it; and if she doesn't, more fool her. Mark my words: the only chaste woman is the one who's never been chased, or who did the chasing and got turned down. I know I'm right: it stands to reason, I'm simply arguing from nature; even so, I shouldn't talk so downright if I hadn't tested out what I'm saying, any number of times on scores of women. Let me tell you, if I were anywhere near this paragon wife of yours, I'd be sure to get her exactly where I wanted her in no time at all, just as I've done with her sisters.'

'We could go on arguing all night', snapped Bernabò. 'You'd say your piece, I'd say mine, and we'd just go round in circles. But as you insist that they're all so readily available and you can twist them round your little finger, just to prove to you that *my* wife is above reproach I'm ready to have my head cut off if you ever succeed in seducing her; if you fail, I'll be satisfied with taking a thousand gold florins off you.'

Ambrogiuolo was thoroughly roused. 'I shouldn't know what to do with your blood if I won, Bernabò', he replied. 'But if you want proof of what I've been saying, stake five thousand gold florins, which you can better spare than your head, against a thousand of mine. And if you set no time-limit, I shall undertake to go to Genoa and have my way with your wife not later than three months from the day I set out from here; as proof, I shall bring back some of her most cherished possessions, with such other elements of proof as will make you admit I told you the truth, provided that you promise me on your honour not to go to Genoa during this period, and not to write to her anything about this.'

'Perfect!' cried Bernabò. And though the other merchants involved tried their best to put a stop to the wager, for they realized that no good could come of it, the two contenders were so carried away that, regardless of anyone else's wishes, they confirmed their compact in a neat holograph document.

Thus committed, Bernabò stayed in Paris while Ambrogiuolo wasted no time in travelling to Genoa. After he had spent a day or two there, making cautious enquiries to establish the name of the lady's street and discover what sort of person she was, his information bore out all that Bernabò had told him, and more so. What madness, he concluded, to have taken up this challenge! Nevertheless, he scraped acquaintance with an impoverished woman who had regular access to the lady's residence and was treated by her as a good friend; unable to obtain any other concessions from the woman, he did manage, by dint of bribery, to have her smuggle him not merely into the house but into the lady's very bedroom, concealed in a chest specially made for the purpose. In accordance with Ambrogiuolo's instructions, the worthy woman entrusted the chest to the lady for a day or two on the pretext of needing to absent herself for a while. Here was the chest in the bedroom, then; and when it was night and Ambrogiuolo reckoned that the lady was asleep, he opened the chest with his keys and quietly emerged into the room, which was lit by a lamp. Thus he could take in the layout of the room, the paintings, and anything else of note, and commit everything to memory. Then he approached the bed and could hear that she was sound asleep, as also was a little girl in bed with her, so he slowly laid her bare. She was, he saw, as exquisite naked as clothed, but could observe no particular feature on which to remark, unless it were a mole beneath her left breast, surrounded by a few light golden hairs. After noticing this, he quietly covered her up again, even though, finding her so beautiful, he was strongly tempted to lie with her, at risk of his life. However, in view of her reputation for craggy untouchability when it came to dalliance, he did not risk it, but merely lingered in the bedroom for most of the night; he went to her chest and abstracted a purse, a tunic, a ring or two, and the odd belt,* laid them all in his own chest, then climbed back inside and locked himself in as before. He spent two nights in this fashion without the lady noticing a thing. On the third day the excellent crone came back, as instructed, to reclaim her chest and had it removed to whence it came. Ambrogiuolo emerged, paid off the woman as promised, and returned to Paris as fast as he could with the purloined objects, before the time-limit expired.

Here he assembled the merchants who had been present when the discussion had taken place and the wager had been set and, in Bernabò's presence, claimed that he had won their bet because he had accomplished what he had boasted he would do. In proof of this, he sketched out the plan of the bedroom and described the paintings in it, after which he displayed the objects he had brought back from her, asserting that she had given them to him. Bernabò conceded that the room was as he described it and that the objects had indeed belonged to his wife; he observed, however, that some household servant could very well have described the room to him and equally have given him these things; therefore, if that was all he had to say, it did not strike him as enough to make him the winner.

'Well that *ought* to be enough', retorted Ambrogiuolo, 'but if you insist I go on, so I will: your lady Ginevra has a fair-sized mole beneath her left breast, with a good six fine hairs round it, light as gold.'

Bernabò looked as if he had been stabbed through the heart when he heard this; the pain was so great, his face was transformed—he need not have said a word, he made it all too obvious that Ambrogiuolo had spoken true. After a pause he said: 'Gentlemen, what Ambrogiuolo says is true. So he has won; let him come whenever he chooses and he shall be paid.' And the next day Ambrogiuolo was paid off in full.

Bernabò left Paris and set off for Genoa, nursing venomous thoughts against his wife. When he was close to the city he chose not to enter it but stopped some twenty miles short, at a villa of his. He sent a servant on to Genoa, a man he trusted well, with two horses and with his letters: he wrote informing his wife that he was back and she was to come and join him under the man's escort. To his man he gave secret orders that, on reaching a spot that seemed to him suitable, he was to despatch the woman quite mercilessly then return to him. So the servant arrived in Genoa, handed over the letters, and passed on the message, while the wife welcomed him with open arms. The next morning she took horse with the attendant and set out for the villa.

They rode along, chatting of this and that, until they came to a deep ravine, utterly secluded and hemmed in with towering crags and trees. This seemed to the man just the place to execute his master's order safely, so he drew his dagger, seized the lady by the arm, and said: 'Commend your soul to God, madam, for you are to die before you go any further.'

Seeing the dagger and hearing what the man was saying, Ginevra cried in terror: 'Mercy for God's sake! Before you kill me, tell me what I've done to you, that you have to kill me.'

'You haven't done anything to *me*, madam. And I've no idea what you've done to your husband, but he did instruct me to kill you quite mercilessly as we made this journey. If I failed to do so, he threatened to have me hanged. You know how much I'm obliged to him and that I can't refuse him anything he bids me do. God knows, I'm sorry for you, but what else am I to do?'

'Oh for Goodness' sake have pity', cried Ginevra in tears. 'Don't turn your hand against a person who never did you any harm, just to do another man's bidding. God, who knows everything, knows I never did anything that deserved such a reward from my husband. But never mind that. If you're willing, you can do a favour to the Good Lord, to your master, and to me all at once. This is how: give me just your jerkin and hood, take my clothes, and bring them to your master and mine and tell him you've killed me. And I swear to you by the reprieve you will have given me, I'll vanish and disappear to some place from which neither you nor he nor anyone in these parts will ever hear of me again.'

Reluctant as he was anyway to kill her, the man was quick to show mercy; he took her clothes, gave her a great big jerkin and hood of his, left her with the money she had on her, entreated her to vanish and, leaving her dismounted in the ravine, went on to his master. 'I've done your bidding', he told him, 'and what's more, I've left her body to some wolves.' Bernabò returned to Genoa a little later, where he was roundly censured once the affair became known.

Dejected and forsaken, Ginevra disguised herself so far as she could and, when night fell, approached a cottage in the vicinity and obtained from an old woman the things she needed: she altered and shortened the jerkin for a better fit, turned her chemise into a pair of hose, cut her hair short, and transformed herself into a seaman. Then she left for the sea and happened upon a Catalan gentleman—his name in Catalan was Segner En Cararch—who had come ashore at Albenga to freshen up at a fountain while his vessel lay a little way off. She got into conversation with him and he engaged her as his personal attendant, so she embarked under the assumed name of Sicurano, from Finale. Fitted out in better attire, Sicurano proved himself such an excellent, discreet attendant that the Catalan was delighted with him.

Not long after this, the Catalan chanced to set sail with a cargo for Alexandria, including some peregrine falcons he was bringing as a gift to the sultan. The sultan occasionally entertained him to a meal and noticed Sicurano, who was in constant attendance on his master; he was much taken with the servant's manner and asked the Catalan to let him have the man. So the Catalan left Sicurano with the sultan, although it was quite a sacrifice. Nor was it long before Sicurano's attentive service had earned him the sultan's grace and favour to no lesser extent than the Catalan's.

Now at a certain time of year there was a large gathering of Christian and Saracen merchants at Acre for a fair; Acre was a fiefdom of the sultan, who made a practice of sending officers of the crown, together with palace dignitaries with their retinues, in order to provide a guard to protect the merchants and their wares. As the time for this arrived, he decided to send Sicurano on this mission, for he already spoke the language fluently. So Sicurano arrived in Acre as captain of the guard protecting the merchants and their wares; he attended to his duties competently and with all due diligence and, as he circulated among all those merchants—Sicilians, Pisans, Genoese, Venetians, and others from Italy—he readily consorted with them out of nostalgia for his own part of the world.

Now on one occasion when Sicurano had stopped at a warehouse of some Venetian merchants, he spotted, among assorted jewellery, a purse and a belt he promptly recognized for ones he used to own. This surprised him, but he concealed his feelings and blithely enquired whose they were and whether they were for sale.

Ambrogiuolo had come here from Piacenza with a large quantity of merchandise on board a Venetian vessel. Hearing that the captain of the guard was asking whose they were, he stepped forward and said with a chuckle: 'They're mine, sir, and I'm not selling them. If you like them, I'll gladly make you a present of them.'

Seeing the man grinning, Sicurano wondered whether he might not have betrayed his own identity to him by some gesture. However, without turning a hair he pursued: 'Would you be laughing because a military man like me is asking about these womanly objects?'

'It's not that, sir', replied Ambrogiuolo; 'I was laughing over how I came to acquire them.'

'Go on, then, let's hear how you came by them, if the tale's repeatable—so may God prosper you!'

'A Genoese lady gave me these things, along with various other objects, one night when I slept with her. She was the wife of Bernabò Lomellin, Ginevra was her name, and she asked me to take them as a keepsake. What made me laugh was remembering what an idiot Bernabò was, laying five thousand gold florins against a thousand of mine that I'd never succeed in seducing his wife. Well, seduce her I did, and won the bet. He left Paris and went back to Genoa where, from what I've heard since, he had the woman murdered—mind you, rather than punishing her for doing what all women do, it's himself he ought to have punished for being such an ass!'

From this, Sicurano (that is, Ginevra) readily grasped the reason for Bernabò's bitterness against her; it was all too clear that this man was the author of all her troubles, and she made up her mind that he would not be allowed to escape punishment. Sicurano therefore pretended to relish this story and artfully contrived a close friendship with Ambrogiuolo. When the fair was over he coaxed the merchant to bring all his merchandise and go with him back to Alexandria, where Sicurano had a warehouse established for him and placed a handsome sum of money in his hands. Ambrogiuolo consequently saw great advantage in remaining there, which he did willingly. Anxious to convince Bernabò of his wife's innocence, Sicurano never rested until, with the help of certain leading Genoese merchants then in Alexandria, he invented a pretext for fetching him thither. Bernabò was in the most straitened circumstances, so Sicurano quietly arranged for a friend to give him hospitality until the moment seemed right to carry out his intention.

Sicurano had already made Ambrogiuolo tell his story to the sultan, procuring a chuckle from the potentate; but seeing that Bernabò was now here, he decided there was no point in delaying matters, so at an opportune moment he sought leave of the sultan to summon Ambrogiuolo and Bernabò to an audience: then, in Bernabò's presence, he would pry out of Ambrogiuolo—using pressure if he proved at all recalcitrant—the truth behind his boast regarding Bernabò's wife. So when Ambrogiuolo and Bernabò appeared, the sultan, an austere look on his face, publicly summoned Ambrogiuolo to confess how he had won five thousand gold florins off Bernabò. Sicurano, in whom Ambrogiuolo reposed the greatest trust, was on hand, but looking black as thunder and uttering threats of dire tortures if he didn't come clean. So Ambrogiuolo, hard pressed and seeing cause for fear whichever way he turned, described in Bernabò's presence and that of many others precisely what had happened; the worst he expected by way of punishment was to have to hand back the five thousand gold florins and the other objects.

When Ambrogiuolo had finished, Sicurano, as though deputizing for the sultan, turned on Bernabò and asked: 'And you, what did you do to your wife on account of this lie?'

'I was beside myself with fury, what with losing my money and with the disgrace I thought my wife had brought upon me, so I had my servant put her to death. From what he told me, a pack of wolves made a meal of her in no time.'

All this was propounded in the presence of the sultan, who took it all in without yet understanding what had induced Sicurano to request and arrange this meeting. Sicurano turned to him: 'My lord', he said, 'you may judge for yourself whether the good woman had any cause to congratulate herself on her lover and her husband. Her lover at one stroke robs her of her good name and ruins her husband; while her husband sets greater store by another man's lies than by the truth with which he might have been acquainted from long experience, and has her killed and devoured by wolves. So great, indeed, is the love and devotion her friend and her husband feel for her that they live with her for ages and quite fail to recognize her. To ensure, however, that you may recognize beyond a shadow of doubt what each one of them has deserved, if, as a special favour to me, you punish the deceiver and absolve his dupe, I shall summon the wife into your presence and theirs.'

Disposed as he was to do whatever Sicurano wanted in this matter, the sultan gave his approval and requested that the wife be sent for. Bernabò was astounded, so convinced was he that his wife was dead. As for Ambrogiuolo, he already had an inkling of what lay in store for him and feared that paying out money was not to be the end of the matter; he did not know what to hope, nor what in particular to fear if the wife made her appearance, but he was above all in a state of bewilderment as he awaited her arrival.

Once the sultan had granted his request, Sicurano fell on his knees before his master; disinclined to continue playing a man's role, and discarding her man's voice, Ginevra burst into tears and cried: 'My lord, I am the poor, unfortunate Ginevra. For six years I've roamed about the world in a man's disguise, deceitfully slandered by this miscreant Ambrogiuolo and handed over by this merciless villain to be slain by his servant and fed to the wolves!' And she ripped open her bodice to expose her bosom and apprise the sultan and everyone else of the fact that she was a woman. Then she turned upon Ambrogiuolo and scathingly asked him when it was that, as he had been boasting, he had been to bed with her. Ambrogiuolo recognized her instantly and was so ashamed he was lost for words and made no answer.

The sultan had always taken her for a man and was so astonished by what he was seeing and hearing that he could only wonder whether he wasn't dreaming. However, once he got over his shock and realized the truth of the matter, he spoke most highly of Ginevra (lately Sicurano)—the way she had lived, her constancy, her character and virtues. He sent for attire suitable for a lady of the highest standing, and for maids of honour to attend upon her; then he absolved Bernabò, in accordance with her request, from the sentence of death he merited. And Bernabò, who recognized her, threw himself, sobbing, at her feet begging her pardon, and she graciously extended it to him, little though he deserved it, and raised him to his feet and embraced him in a tender, wifely embrace.

Next, the sultan gave orders for Ambrogiuolo to be seized at once and bound to a stake in the sun, up on the city heights, and smeared with honey and simply left there until he dropped; after which he commanded that everything belonging to Ambrogiuolo be handed over to the lady—a fortune amounting to more than ten thousand doubloons. Then he prepared a splendid feast at which he entertained Bernabò as the husband of Ginevra, and the lady as a most excellent woman, and presented her with jewellery and tableware in gold and silver, and with money, all amounting to the value of a further ten thousand doubloons. He had a ship made ready and, once the feast he had offered them was ended, gave them leave to depart for Genoa whenever they wished. So they returned, enormously rich and radiantly happy, to the most flattering welcome, especially for Ginevra, whom everybody had thought was dead. And for the rest of her days she was held in high esteem as a lady of formidable gifts. As for Ambrogiuolo, the very day on which he was bound to the stake and smeared with honey, which left him in agony from the horse-flies, wasps, and bluebottles in which the place abounded, he was left not merely dead but eaten down to the bone. Indeed, his bones were allowed to remain there for ages untouched, all bleached and held together by the sinews, as a testimony to his wickedness for whoever set eyes on them.

'He who laughs last laughs best.' So it proved.

II. 10. *In his old age Ricciardo marries a pretty young wife, but loses her to Paganino, the pirate. When he goes to Monaco to pay her ransom, it is clear he has not brought the right money.*

The story told by their queen was roundly applauded by the excellent company, and most of all by Dioneo, the only one left today still to narrate. After praising the queen's story, he said:

I had a story I was going to tell you, but something in the queen's has made me change my mind and turn to a different one. I mean Bernabò's stupidity (however harmless it proved to him in the end) and the absurdity of all those men who are ready to believe what he evidently did, that as they go roaming about and enjoy a romp with one woman after the next as occasion serves, their wives just sit at home with their thumbs tucked into their belts: we men are born and raised among women, we live in their company—how could we ever fail to recognize what it is they hanker for? My tale will serve to show you ladies what imbeciles they are—the Bernabòs of this world—and furthermore to demonstrate how those men are all the sillier who think they can hold back Nature and achieve by far-fetched demonstrations what is actually beyond their powers: to force others into their own mould, whereas in fact there's no arguing with Nature's mould.

Once upon a time in Pisa there was a judge called Ricciardo di Chinzica, not the brawniest of men but a great intellect. It is possible he considered that the faculties he brought to his legal studies would prove more than sufficient to satisfy a wife, so, being a wealthy man, he devoted no little care to obtaining a bride: a pretty young bride—though had he been as capable of benefiting from his own advice as he was of imparting it to others, those are the two qualities he'd have done well to avoid. Success came his way when Lotto Gualandi bestowed on him a daughter of his called Bartolomea, one of the prettiest and most enchanting young women in the city—where admittedly there are few who would avoid being mistaken for lizards.*

The judge brought her home amid great celebrations and laid on the most magnificent wedding. On the wedding night, however, when it came to consummating the nuptials, he managed only once to mount a chance attack on her queen, after which he had to settle for a stalemate. Next morning, being the scrawny, wizened little runt he was, he could only return among the living by fortifying himself with a drop of *Vernaccia** and dainty morsels of food and suchlike restoratives. Now this judge, who had become a better judge of his own capabilities than he had been, set about teaching the calendar to his wife: he used a calendar from which children were taught their alphabet. This calendar may well have originated in Ravenna (whose religious year featured a unique abundance of holy days), because—as he pointed out to her—there was not a day but celebrated a saint, sometimes several saints, and on such holy days it was for various reasons only respectful (as he pointed out) for men and women to abstain from couplings of this kind. What is more, they were also to be eschewed on fast days, during the Ember weeks, on the vigils of apostles' feast days, not to mention scores of other saints' days, together with Fridays and Saturdays and the Lord's Day and the whole of Lent, as well as during certain phases of the moon, and on many another exceptional occasion. It was no doubt his view that, just as he took holidays from the lawcourts, so he should take holidays from his wife's bed. This, then, became the pattern of his life, which irked his lady not a little, for it was barely once a month that he'd make love to her. He kept a close eye on her, though, in case somebody else came along to teach her how to observe the ferias as he had the feast days.

Well, it so happened once, during the dog days, that Ricciardo conceived the wish to go for a little relaxation to a delightful place he had out near Monte Nero; he'd enjoy a few days with a change of air, and he'd bring his comely lady with him. To provide her with a little entertainment in the course of this visit he arranged one day for them to go fishing. Two boats were used: he went in one with the fishermen while Bartolomea joined some ladies in the other, and off they went to watch. They were enjoying the excursion so much, they continued several miles out to sea, more or less without noticing, and while their attention was wholly taken up a galliot suddenly hove in sight, spotted the fishing boats, and bore down on them. The galliot belonged to Paganino da Mare, a notorious pirate in those days, and he caught up with the women's boat before they could make their escape. Seeing the pretty lady in the boat, he took her on board—that was all the prey he wanted—and made off while Ricciardo looked on from the shore. No need to ask whether the judge was agonized on seeing this—he was so jealous he kept the very air under suspicion. He went off to Pisa and elsewhere to complain of the pirates' malfeasance, to little purpose: he did not know who it was who had made off with his wife, nor whither he had taken her.

Paganino, for his part, felt rather pleased when he saw what a beauty she was. Being single, he decided to keep her and therefore set to work gently comforting her as she sobbed her heart out. When it was night, as he had somehow mislaid his calendar and could no longer tell feast day from work day, he turned to comforting her in more practical ways, feeling that words had been of small effect in the daylight hours. And such was the method he employed in consoling her that by the time they fetched Monaco she had quite lost sight of the judge and his regulations and was enjoying the time of her life with Paganino. Once he had brought her home he continued to afford her his consolation day and night, and kept her in all the dignity he would have accorded a wife.

In the course of time Ricciardo came to hear of his wife's present location. Realizing that nobody knew exactly how to set about doing what had to be done, he himself took ship and sailed to Monaco; so passionate was his wish to recover her, he was prepared to ransom her regardless of cost. In Monaco he caught sight of her and she of him—a fact she mentioned that evening to Paganino, acquainting him with her own intention in the matter. Next morning Ricciardo spotted Paganino and engaged him in conversation; it took him little time to strike up quite an intimate friendship with him, as Paganino made a pretence of knowing him and waited to see what he was leading up to. So at what he took to be an opportune moment Ricciardo did his best to apprise him, in the most agreeable manner, of the object of his visit, and requested him to accept whatever ransom he pleased, but to let him have his wife back.

Paganino answered with a smile: 'Sir', he said, 'you are most welcome! Let me answer you in a few words: it is true that I have a young woman in my house, though whether she's your wife or another's I wouldn't know. After all, I'm not well acquainted with you, nor indeed with her, beyond the little time she has been staying with me. If you are her husband, as you say you are, I shall bring you to her, seeing that I find you an agreeable gentleman, and I'm sure she'll recognize you. If she admits that it is as you say, and wants to leave with you, for the sake of your good nature I'll settle for whatever ransom you yourself are willing to give me. Should it prove otherwise, you would be quite despicable to try taking her from me: I'm a young man and why should I not keep a woman just as others do—especially this one, the most delightful woman I ever came across?'

'Of course she's my wife. Take me to her and you'll soon see: she'll throw her arms round my neck at once. So I ask nothing better than to do as you propose.'

'Very well', said Paganino. 'Let's go.'

So they went home to Paganino's and he sent for Ricciardo's wife to join them in the parlour; in she came from her bedroom, dressed for company, but such words as she addressed to Ricciardo were no different to those she might have addressed to any stranger Paganino had brought home. The judge was most surprised to see this, for he had expected her to welcome him with open arms. 'Could it be', he brooded, 'that my features have been so altered by my dejection and by the endless misery I've endured since I lost her that she does not recognize me?'

So he said: 'Taking you out fishing cost me dear, my dear: there's nothing to equal the agony I've been through since I lost you; and you speak to me so primly anyone would think you didn't recognize me. Can't you see I'm your Ricciardo? I came here to pay this good gentleman in whose house we are to have you back and take you away. I was going to pay him whatever he asked but he's been kind enough to say I can have you for whatever price I choose to pay.'

Bartolomea turned to him with a fleeting smile: 'Is it me you are addressing, sir? Might you have mistaken me for another person? Speaking for myself, I cannot recall ever having set eyes on you before.'

'Think what you're saying. Take a good look at me: jog your memory and you'll see that I'm your own Ricciardo di Chinzica.'

'Sir, you'll have to forgive me', she said. 'To keep staring at you is not, you can imagine, all that seemly on my part, but still I've looked at you hard enough to know that I've never before laid eyes on you.'

It occurred to Ricciardo that she was behaving this way out of fear of Paganino and reluctance to admit in the pirate's presence that she knew him. So after a while he asked Paganino if he would be kind enough to let him have a word with her in the privacy of her bedroom. Paganino made no objection, provided that he did not snatch a kiss against her will; and he told Bartolomea to go with him into the bedroom, listen to what he had to say, and answer in whatever way she chose.

So Bartolomea and Ricciardo adjourned to the bedroom and sat down, whereupon Ricciardo began: 'Ah, heart of my heart, light of my eyes, ah my treasure, don't you recognize your Ricciardo, who loves you beyond all telling? How can it be so? Am I so changed? Come, my sweet, take another look at me.'

Bartolomea burst out laughing and broke in: 'Of course I know you're Ricciardo di Chinzica my husband—I'm not *that* big a flutterhead! But when I was living with you, it was pathetic how little you knew me, so it seemed: if you'd had any sense, or have any now—and you like to pass for a clever fellow—you ought to have been awake enough to notice that I'm a hale and hearty young woman, and to realize what it is that young women need beyond feeding and clothing, even if it's a thing they're too modest to give a name to. Well, you know well enough how you coped with *that*! And if you were happier with your law-books than with your wife, you should never have taken a wife. In fact you never looked much of a judge to me—you always struck me more as a proclaimer of holy days and fast days and vigils, so well acquainted were you with them all. My word! If you'd imposed as many feast days on the labourers tilling your acres as you did on yourself working my little plot, you'd never have gleaned so much as a single grain of wheat. Now I've fallen in with this man, by the grace of the Good Lord who has mercifully taken account of my girlhood; and this is the room we share, and in this room we're oblivious of feast days—I mean the feast days you keep celebrating as you're so much more devoted to the service of God than to a woman's needs. None of your Fridays or Saturdays ever crossed *this* threshold, none of your vigils or Ember weeks or Lents—and goodness, how Lent drags on! Far from it, work continues here day and night, and the card's never out of the wool. If we did it once we did it a dozen times—don't I know it?—before Matins rang out the night. So while I'm young I mean to stay with him and stay at work; the holy days and pardons and fasts can keep for when I'm an old woman. As for you, be off with you as fast as you can, and the best of luck to you: keep every feast day you like, only without me.'

These words were more than Ricciardo could bear, and when he saw she had finished, he said: 'Come, darling heart, what is it you're saying? Have you no thought for your family honour and your own? Would you live here as this man's concubine, and in a state of mortal sin, rather than as my wife in Pisa? When *he* tires of you he'll throw you out, and what a humiliation for you that will be. Me, I'll always cherish you and you'll always, willy-nilly, be mistress in my house. Are you going to forsake your honour and desert me, who love you more than my own life, all on account of this dissolute and disgraceful appetite of yours? Come, my beloved, don't say such things, do come away with me. Now that I know what it is you want, I'll make a real effort, so change your mind, dearest, and come with me—I've known nothing but misery since you were taken from me.'

'I'm not going to have anyone show greater concern for my honour than I do', she replied, 'now that it's too late. Would to God my family had been more considerate of it when they allotted me to you! If they gave no thought then to my honour, why should I bother about theirs now? And since I'm anyway living in sin, who cares what name you give it? Call it mortal when he comes through my portal—that's my problem, not yours! Let me tell you, here I feel like Paganino's wife: in Pisa I felt like your strumpet, to think that we depended on phases of the moon and geometrical calculations for the conjunction of *our* planets. Here Paganino clasps me all night long in his arms and cuddles me and nibbles me; his particular attentions I'll leave to the Good Lord to describe. You say you're going to make a real effort. What with? A third throw of the dice? A third cast of the line, then pull it up to see if you've hooked anything? Of course since I last saw you you've turned into a sturdy rider! Go on, try living in the real world, you scrawny, stunted little thing—the way you look to me you've one foot in the grave. And another thing: should Paganino turn me out, though I doubt he'd want to so long as I'm ready to stay, I still wouldn't go back to you: why, if you were stuck in a press you wouldn't yield a spoonful of fluid—*that* I know to my cost, for I tried! I'd look elsewhere for my percentage. So I tell you again, we keep no feasts or vigils here, and here's where I intend to stay. Be off with you, then, and the sooner the better, otherwise I'll shout that you're trying to violate me.'

Seeing that he had the worst of the argument, and realizing at last how stupid he had been to have married a young wife in his state of impotence, Ricciardo left the room in a sorry frame of mind; he had a good deal more to say to Paganino but he might have saved his breath. Finally he left Bartolomea, having achieved nothing at all, and returned to Pisa. Here, driven out of his mind by sorrow, he had only one observation to make to anyone who stopped him in the street to greet him or ask him anything: 'Can't stand feast days, can't it?—the rotten hole!' He died soon after, and when Paganino heard of it he married her as his lawful wedded wife, knowing how much she loved him. And they enjoyed themselves without sparing a thought for feast days or vigils or Lenten observance, tilling their plot so long as their legs held up.

Which is why it seems to me, my dear ladies, that when Bernabò was arguing with Ambrogiuolo, he didn't know his arse from his elbow.

This story had them all in such fits of laughter, there was not one whose jaw did not ache. The women were all agreed that Dioneo was quite right and Bernabò had been a complete ninny.

Now that the story was finished, and the laughter was done, the queen noticed that it was growing late and everyone had told their tale, so her reign was at an end. She therefore followed the established procedure and removed her garland and placed it on Neiphile's head, observing with a smile: 'Now, dear friend, let this little realm be in your charge.' Then she resumed her seat, and Neiphile blushed a little on account of the honour conferred on her. Indeed her face took on the colour of a fresh rose at the dawn of an April day: her lovely eyes sparkled beneath lowered lids—not unlike the morning star. However, when the cheerful hubbub subsided, which had betokened a ready acceptance of her queenship, she recovered her composure and, sitting up a little straighter than usual, she said:

'Since I am your queen, I shall state my views in few words and these we will follow if they earn your approval—I shall not depart from the procedures adopted by my predecessors, whose rule you sanctioned by your obedience. Tomorrow, as you know, is Friday, and the day after is Saturday, both days that most people find somewhat dreary on account of the meagre fare. Friday merits respect, furthermore, as being the day on which the One who died for our salvation underwent His passion; it would therefore seem to me right and proper to honour the Lord on this day by attending to prayer rather than to story-telling. And the next day, Saturday, women as a rule wash their hair and scrub away all the dust and dirt that will have accumulated in the course of the week's activities; they also make it a custom to fast in honour of the Virgin

Mother of God's only Son, and to rest from all labours as a tribute to the ensuing Sunday. So, as we cannot on that day pursue our normal round to the full, I should deem it suitable once more to abstain from our story-telling. Another thing: we shall have been here four days, and if we want to avoid strangers calling on us, I think we might do well to change our residence: and I've already thought where that might be and made arrangements. When we foregather there next Sunday after our siesta, as we've been given plenty of scope today in choosing a story to tell, and you'll have ample time to think up the next one, and as, besides, somewhat restricting the limits of choice can only be to the good, here's what I propose: the topic will be a single aspect of the hand of Fate and, specifically, about the way a person uses his wits to acquire something greatly prized, or to recover something lost. So let everyone think of a story that will conduce to the profit, or at any rate to the pleasure, of the company, always excepting Dioneo's privilege.'

The queen's proposal won universal approval and so it was decided. This done, she summoned her major-domo and gave him full instructions on where to lay the tables this evening and whatever else needed attending to for the duration of her reign. Then she stood up, together with her company, and dismissed them to pursue their various pleasures.

So then they all, men and women, made their way to a little garden for an enjoyable interval until it was time for supper, which proved to be a most festive occasion. When they left the table, Emilia led the dance—for so it pleased the queen—while Pampinea sang this song, the other ladies joining in the refrain:

Hear me sing my happy song
Now that I've that for which I long.

Come, add your voice to mine, sweet Love,
  The cause of all my joy;
We'll sigh no more for grief, sweet Love,
  We'll shun what doth annoy.
For bliss reigns in my heart, sweet Love,
  And brightly burns my flame;
My spirit leaps, I come, sweet Love,
  To bless your holy name.

You set before my eyes, sweet Love,
  The day my heart took fire,
A boy whose every look, sweet Love,
  Enkindled my desire.
O brave and gallant lad, sweet Love,
  The best of all his race!
To him my heart's gone out, sweet Love,
  Rejoicing in your grace.

And if I shout for joy, sweet Love,
  Here's cause to be enraptured:
For, thanks be to your grace, sweet Love,
  His own heart have I captured.
My cup of life is full, sweet Love,
  And since my troth is plighted,
In paradise to come, sweet Love,
  My faith shall be requited.

They sang a number of other songs after this, and danced many a dance and played all manner of tunes, until the queen thought it was time they went to bed; so off they went to their rooms, preceded by torches. The next two days they devoted to the activities of which the queen had earlier spoken, as they eagerly looked forward to Sunday.

*Here ends the second day of the* Decameron *and the third day begins; under the reign of Neiphile, the stories show how a person uses his wits to acquire something greatly prized, or to recover something lost.*

As the sun rose that Sunday and the dawn sky turned gradually from vermilion to saffron, the queen left her bed and roused her companions. The major-domo had long since sent ahead to their new destination a fair part of what they would be needing, together with those who were to make things ready; now on seeing the queen set forth, he promptly had everything else loaded up, struck camp, and followed the ladies and gentlemen with the rest of their personal household and the remaining chattels. The queen, then, wended her way westwards at a gentle pace, accompanied by her suite of ladies and the three young men; guided by the song of a good score of nightingales and sundry other birds, they proceeded along a fairly unfrequented grassy path strewn with flowers that were all opening their petals to the rising sun. After not more than a couple of miles' walk, laughing and jesting with her friends all the while, she brought them, well before mid-morning, to a most splendid and sumptuous mansion overlooking the plain from a slight eminence. In they went and explored the entire house; the spacious public rooms, the clean, dainty, beautifully appointed bedrooms won their complete approval, and they imagined that the owner of such a house must indeed be a lavish patron. Downstairs they took in the vast and cheery courtyard, the cellars stocked with the best of wines, the abundant spring of ice-cold water, and their praise knew no bounds. Now ready as they were for a rest, they sat down in a loggia that overlooked the courtyard and was replete with every flower the season could provide and with leafy branches; here the provident major-domo came to offer them a welcome and restore them with the most delicate of snacks and the choicest of wines.

After this, they had a garden opened to them which lay adjacent to the house; it was a walled garden and as they went in, they were struck by its sheer beauty even before they inspected it in any detail. The garden was surrounded and intersected by a great many broad paths, each one straight as an arrow and covered over by trellised vines that gave every promise of producing grapes in abundance that year; they were all in flower and so imbued the garden with their fragrance that, added to all manner of other scents wafting about, they conveyed a sensation of concentrating here every aromatic plant to which the East ever gave birth. The sides of these paths were virtually hemmed in by bushes of red and white roses and jasmine, so that one could walk along any of them in the delicious fragrant shade and be protected from the sun not only in the morning but even when it was at its zenith. As for the species of plants in the garden, it would take too long to list or enumerate them, or describe how they were arranged; there was not a single good plant that did not proliferate here provided that it was suited to our climate. By no means one of the least attractive features of the garden was a lawn in the middle of it, a lawn of close-cropped grass that was dark, dark green and dotted with all kinds of flowers; it was surrounded by orange and other citrus trees of the most luscious green foliage, which kept their old fruit along with the new, and remained in blossom, providing not only a pleasant shade for the eyes but also a delight to the nostrils.

At the centre of the lawn there was a fountain of gleaming white marble with superbly sculpted reliefs; and in the middle there stood a pillar surmounted by a statue through which a jet of water (whether naturally or artificially induced) sufficient to turn a mill-wheel shot up high into the air to drop most musically into the limpid pool. The surplus water in the fountain was drawn off by a conduit concealed beneath the lawn, to re-emerge in the most beautiful and ingenious water-courses that encircled it; thence the water criss-crossed the garden in a network of similar channels and ultimately was collected at a point where it flowed out to descend to the plain in a crystal stream; before it reached the plain, however, it applied its immense power to turning a pair of mill-wheels—to the not inconsiderable profit of the landowner.

The sight of this garden, so beautifully laid out, with its plants and the fountain and the watercourse fed by it, so enchanted the ladies and the three young men, they all insisted that, were it possible to build a heaven on earth, they would be at a loss to know how else to embody it but as this garden, nor could they imagine a single thing that might enhance its splendour. As they wandered blissfully about the garden and made themselves lovely garlands out of foliage of various kinds, they could listen to the birds vying with each other in a dozen different strains of song. Absorbed as they were with these delights, they failed at first to observe yet another: the garden, they noticed, was inhabited by a good hundred varieties of attractive wild creatures, and now they pointed them out to each other—rabbits hopping out here, over there a scurrying of hares, roebucks resting somewhere else, and young fawns browsing, all manner of harmless animals going about their business for all the world as if they were tame. All of this added immeasurably to their pleasure.

But once they had looked around to their hearts' content, they had the tables set beside the pretty fountain and here, at the queen's wish, they assembled for lunch, after singing a half-dozen songs and dancing a few dances. The meal was served as decorously as could be, the fare was exquisite, and they left the tables in an even more buoyant mood, to launch into another round of music and dancing. Eventually, as the day became more sultry, the queen thought it was time for those who felt like it to retire for a nap. Some of them did so, while the rest found the place too enchanting and preferred not to: they stayed where they were and read romances or played chess or backgammon while the others were resting.

When it had gone three, however, everybody got up, splashed their faces with cold water, and crossed the lawn to the fountain as the queen required; here they sat down the way they usually did and waited to tell their stories on the topic she had proposed. The first person charged with this task was Philostrato, and this is how he began:

III. I. *Masetto becomes a deaf-mute in order to be engaged as gardener in a nunnery. How the sisters encourage him to be a zealous husbandman.*

There are scores of men, and women too, who entertain the foolish notion that the moment a girl has the white veil placed on her head and the black cowl over her shoulders she ceases to be a woman, she no longer feels the sexual urge as other women do—in short, she turns to stone when she enters a convent. Such people are infuriated if they hear a word spoken against this conviction of theirs, as if some hideous and heinous crime had been committed against Nature. They don't stop to think, or consider their own situation: they're perfectly free to do precisely as they please, but does that leave *their* appetite assuaged? Do they reflect at all upon the incalculable effects of solitude and inactivity? Similarly there are many people all too ready to believe that those who till the soil are brainless oafs who don't know what it is to feel lust—the result (they imagine) of the most basic of diets and of hard toil with mattock and spade. How wrong they all are! As the queen bids me narrate, and I mean to remain within the scope she has given us, here is a little story with which I should like to elucidate this question.

There was once upon a time in these parts a convent with a great name for holiness—it still exists and I shall not identify it so as not to detract in the slightest measure from its reputation. Not long ago the community comprised only eight nuns and their abbess, all of them young. They kept a little fellow to tend their most beautiful kitchen garden, but as he was dissatisfied with his wages, he settled accounts with the convent bursar and returned to his own village, Lamporecchio. The villagers welcomed him back cheerfully, and one of their number was a tough, brawny labourer called Masetto, not a bad-looking young man for a peasant and with the most attractive face. Masetto asked the little fellow—his name was Nuto—where he had been all this time, and Nuto told him.

'What work did you do in the convent?' asked Masetto.

'They had this great big garden, beautiful it was, and I worked in it, and I went to the wood to cut firewood and

I went to fetch water and I did a bit of this and that, but those women, they gave me so little pay, I hadn't enough, hardly, to buy meself a pair o' drawers. And another thing, they're all young girls and it seems to me they keep playing merry devil and whatever I do is wrong. Here I be, a-working in the garden, and one of 'em comes along and says "Put this here" and the next comes and says "No, put *this* here" and another comes along and takes the mattock out of my hands and says "You're doing it *all* wrong." Such right nuisances they were, I'd just drop everything and go out of the garden and what with one thing and another I didn't care to stay on and I quit. And their bursar, he comes up to me as I'm a-quitting and he says: "If you know of anyone who can do this work", he says, "you just send him along to me", and I says "All right", but if he thinks I'm going to go a-rummaging around and send him somebody, he's got another think coming.'

Nuto's words filled Masetto with such a craving for those nuns, he could not wait to be with them: it was perfectly clear to him from what the old fellow said that he ought to be able to have his way with them. He realized, however, that he would get nowhere if he said anything about it to Nuto, so all he said was: 'Well, my goodness, you're well out of it! Look what happens to a man stuck among women. He's better off with devils for company—more often than not women have no idea themselves what it is they want.'

After their conversation, Masetto applied his brain to the problem of how to get in with the nuns. He knew he could perform the tasks Nuto had described, so that would be no problem—his worry was that he would be rejected for being so youthful and good-looking. He turned over a number of possibilities then decided: 'The place is a good distance from here and nobody there knows me. If I can just pretend to be a deaf-mute they're sure to take me on.'

He looked no further than this, but set off for the convent without telling anyone where he was going; he dressed like a pauper and carried an axe over his shoulder. On arrival, in he went and in the courtyard happened upon the bursar, whom he addressed by gestures as deaf-mutes do, and asked him for food, out of love of God; he was ready to split logs, he added, if need be. The bursar readily gave him a meal, then confronted him with some logs that Nuto had been unable to split; Masetto, who was strong as an ox, made short work of them. After this, the bursar, needing to go into the woods, brought Masetto with him and set him to work chopping timber. Then he led up the donkey and signed to Masetto to load the wood and carry it back to the convent. He acquitted himself so well that the bursar retained him for several days to do a number of jobs that needed attending to. Thus it happened that one day the abbess noticed him and asked the bursar who the man was.

'He's a poor man, he's deaf and dumb, and came here a day or two ago begging for alms. I gave him some and set him to work doing various jobs that needed doing. If he could work in the garden and wanted to stay, I do believe we'd get good service out of him: we could certainly do with him, in fact he could be put to practically any task one chose, a man of his muscle. What's more, you wouldn't have to worry about him chatting up your young ladies.'

'By heaven you're right', said the abbess. 'Find out if he knows about husbandry and do your best to keep him. Give him the odd pair of shoes and some old cape and flatter him, wheedle him, feed him up.'

The bursar promised and Masetto, who was close by, pretending to sweep the courtyard, heard every word and exulted to himself: 'You take me in, and I'll till your patch for you as it was never tilled before!'

Seeing that Masetto knew exactly how to handle a spade, the bursar used signs to ask him whether he would like to stay on, and Masetto signalled that he was at his entire disposal; so he engaged him and set him to work in the kitchen garden, showing him all that needed doing. Then he left him in order to attend to other convent business. As he worked his plot day after day, the nuns began to make a nuisance of themselves and tease him—which is often the lot of deaf-mutes—and they called him every name under the sun, assuming that he couldn't hear. The abbess paid little or no attention, doubtless reckoning that a man who had no tongue would also lack another appendage.

Now one day when he had been hard at work in the garden and was taking a rest, two of the nuns—mere youngsters—who were walking in the garden came over to him as he feigned sleep and took a good look at him. Then one of them, who was somewhat more forward than the other, observed to her companion: 'If I felt you could keep a secret, I'd share a thought with you, one I've had from time to time—maybe it would appeal to you too.'

'Carry on: I shan't tell a soul.'

'Well, I don't know if you've ever stopped to think how our wings are clipped in this place—there's not a man who dares set foot in here, except for the bursar, who's a bit past it, and this deaf-mute. And how many times have I heard any number of women who've visited us saying that every pleasure the world has to offer is utter moonshine compared with what a woman gets going to bed with a man. So it's often crossed my mind to try it out for myself with this dumb fellow, for lack of anyone else. Anyway, he's just what's needed when you consider that he couldn't tell on us even if he wanted to. Just look at him, the great dumb hulk with a brain the size of a pea! Come on, what d'you think of it?'

'Heaven help us!' cried the other. 'What is it you're saying? Don't you realize we've vowed our virginity to the Lord?'

'Oh, He's promised so many things all day long, but what does He actually receive? Maybe we've made our promise, but let Him find some other women to deliver.'

'What if we got pregnant? What then?'

'There you are already worrying about something that may never happen. Let's cross our bridges when we come to them. There's no end of ways to keep it a secret, so long as we don't blurt it out ourselves.'

The other nun, who was even keener than her friend to find out what manner of beast a man was, said: 'Very well, how do we go about it?'

'Look, it's getting on for mid-afternoon, and I expect all the nuns are having their siesta, apart from us two. Let's take a look round the garden to see nobody's about, and if the coast is clear, all we have to do is take him by the hand and lead him into this hut, where he shelters from the rain. One of us goes in with him while the other keeps a look-out. He's such an oaf, he'll do whatever he's told.'

Masetto overheard every bit of this discussion and was perfectly ready to oblige; all he was waiting for was to be taken in hand by one of these two. They had a good look round and established that they could not be observed from anywhere; then the nun who had instigated the proceedings approached Masetto and woke him. Up he got at once, and she took him by the hand and with coaxing gestures led him off into the hut, while he smirked idiotically. In the hut he awaited no second invitation to do as she had in mind. When she had had her fill she dutifully made way for her friend, and Masetto, while continuing to play the half-wit, once more performed as required. By the time they adjourned, they had each repeated the experiment of being mounted by the deaf-mute. Thereafter they often reverted to the subject, maintaining that the activity was every bit as delightful as they had been told, indeed more so. They would choose their moment and go off regularly to take their pleasure with Masetto.

One day another of the sisters happened to glance out of her cell window and see what was going on; she pointed it out to two others and, after they had considered going to the abbess and informing on them, they changed their minds and came to an agreement with them whereby they acquired an interest in Masetto's garden-plot. In the course of time the remaining three nuns somehow or other joined the scheme. Last of all the abbess, who had remained unaware of what was going on, happened upon Masetto as she was walking by herself through the garden one very sultry day; he was stretched out, fast asleep, in the shade of an almond tree, for after a hard night in the saddle the smallest exertion by day was enough to lay him out. Now a puff of wind happened to have plucked up the front of his smock, leaving him totally exposed. The lady stopped to take in the sight and, seeing that she was alone, found herself possessed by the same appetite that had taken hold of her younger sisters. So she woke Masetto, led him into her cell, and kept him there for several days, much to the indignation of the nuns—why was the gardener not tilling his plot? The abbess, however, experienced time and again the bliss she had been in the habit of castigating for the benefit of her charges.

Eventually the abbess sent him off to his own room, but she would keep summoning him back to her cell—indeed, she was inclined to give him full-time employment. As Masetto was unable to satisfy so many demands, he realized that being deaf and dumb could prove a positive disadvantage if he stayed here much longer. So when he was with the abbess one night the string of his tongue was loosed, and he spoke as follows: 'People tell me, ma'am, that one cock is all it takes to satisfy ten hens, but ten men have the devil of a job satisfying one woman. Well I'm serving nine of you and I can't go on like this, I simply can't—after what I've been put through, I'm so wrung out I'm not fit for anything. So either you'll have to let me go or you're going to have to sort this out some other how.'

Hearing the deaf-mute (as she supposed) speaking, the abbess was quite bowled over. 'What's all this?' she cried. 'I thought you were deaf and dumb!'

'So I was, but I wasn't born this way, it was an illness that made me dumb. Tonight's the first time I've got my speech back, and I thank God for it from the bottom of my heart.'

She took his word for it and asked him what he meant about having nine to satisfy. Masetto told the abbess how matters stood, from which she concluded that there was not a sister in the convent but was cannier than she was. However, being nothing if not discreet, she refused to leave him go but sought to come to an arrangement with her nuns so that Masetto should not bring disgrace on the convent. Now as their bursar had lately died, once the sisters had admitted to what had been going on, they all agreed, with Masetto's consent, to put it about that he had recovered the use of his tongue, after being so long a deaf-mute, as a result of their prayers and the merits of the saint to whom the convent was dedicated. They appointed him bursar and parcelled out his duties in such a way that they did not prove too burdensome to him. In the fulfilment of these duties he begot a large number of baby monks and nuns, but all was done with such discretion that it was only after the death of the abbess that any word of it got out. Masetto was now on the threshold of old age and anxious to return home, a prosperous man. His wish was granted readily once it was known.

So, thanks to the cunning he had employed in his youth, Masetto became a father and a wealthy man without having, in his old age, to toil for the support of his children, and without having to pay for their upkeep. As he returned whence he had set out with an axe across his shoulder: 'This', he asserted, 'is the way Christ treats the man who makes a cuckold of Him by making free with His brides.'

## III. 2. *How a groom lies with King Agilulf's wife, and what the king does about it.*

Philostrato's story made the ladies laugh, though on occasion it brought a blush to their cheeks; when it was over, the queen was pleased to have Pampinea follow, which she did merrily enough:

There are people who show little sense, the way they insist on ferreting out the truth of matters they would do better to ignore, and letting everyone know they've done so; as they reprove the hidden faults in others they may think they're erasing their own shame but sometimes all they do is make it worse. I shall prove this to you ladies with an instance of the opposite case, in this story of a fellow (maybe not quite on a par with Masetto) who pitted his wits against those of a noble king.

Like his predecessors before him, Agilulf, King of the Lombards, established his capital in the city of Pavia. He had married Teudelinga,* the widow of the old Lombard king Autari; she was the wisest, most virtuous of women and exceedingly beautiful, but unlucky in love. Thanks to the wisdom and might of this King Agilulf, however, the Lombard realm was enjoying peace and prosperity.

Now it happened that one of the queen's grooms fell passionately in love with her majesty. He was a man of the lowest social condition but of quite princely good looks and regal build that set him far above his station. The groom knew his place well enough, though, and realized how inappropriate his love was, so he had the wit to keep it to himself and not let the queen read it in his eyes. And for all that he entertained no hope of ever winning her love, he did congratulate himself on having aimed so high in his affections. Aflame as he was, he strove far harder than any of his fellows to anticipate the queen's every pleasure—which is why, when the queen went out riding, she would choose the horse tended by this groom in preference to any other. On these occasions he considered himself the most highly privileged of men, and never left his place beside her stirrup, deeming it a great happiness if he could but touch her garments.

But we see it happen all too often: the more futile a person's hope, the more urgent his love—and the poor groom, too, found it wellnigh impossible to conceal his passion as he continued to do, without a shred of hope. As he could not cure himself of his love, he turned repeatedly to thoughts of suicide. But how? In such a way, he decided, that it would be clear that he had died for love of the queen. Moreover, he proposed to make an end to himself in a gamble to achieve his desire, or at any rate some part of it. He did not risk breathing a word to the queen or betraying his love by writing to her, for he knew that he would speak or write in vain. If he was to go to bed with her, he would have to see how far his native wit might serve him. The only stratagem that came to mind was to impersonate the king and gain access to her room that way—he knew that the king did not regularly sleep with her. Now in order to observe how the king went in to her bedroom on those occasions he did, and what he wore, the groom slipped into the great chamber that separated the king's bedroom from the queen's, and hid for several nights—until one night he saw the king emerge from his room wrapped in an ample cloak, and carrying a little torch in one hand and a rod in the other. He advanced to the queen's room and, without a word, struck the door a couple of times with the rod. The door was opened and the torch taken from his hand.

He watched this, and similarly watched the king's return. 'I shall do likewise', he thought, so he contrived to lay hands on a cloak like the one he had seen wrapped round the king, and a small torch and a rod. But first of all he gave himself a thorough wash in a tub, lest his stench of manure from the stables should disgust the queen or alert her to the deception.

This done, he hid as before in the great chamber. When it sounded as though the entire household was asleep and he felt that the time had come to give rein to his desire—or to go to embrace death in such a noble cause—he kindled a flame and lit the torch with the flint and steel he had brought with him. Then, wrapped in his cloak, he advanced to the queen's door and gave it two taps with the rod. The door was opened by a sleepy maidservant, who took his torch and put it out, whereupon, without a word spoken, he slipped through the bed-curtains, laid aside his cloak, and slid into bed beside the queen. He took her passionately in his arms and pretended to be in a bad temper, for he knew that as a rule when the king was cross he didn't want to hear a word; so without hearing a word nor uttering one, he took his pleasure with her time and time again. He could scarcely bring himself to leave her, but he feared that if he lingered too long his joy would be turned to tears, so he got up, took his cloak and torch, and left, still without a word, to return to his own bed as fast as he could.

Hardly was the groom back in bed than the king got up and went in to the queen, which surprised her not a little. He got into bed with her and greeted her cheerily. She took courage from his genial mood and said: 'What's come over you tonight all of a sudden, my lord? You've only just left after taking more pleasure with me than usual, and here you are already back for more! What are you up to?'

From these words the king instantly grasped that the queen had been taken in by somebody of similar build to himself and with similar mannerisms; but he was canny enough to keep it all to himself, seeing that the queen was all unsuspecting and no one else knew. Most fools would have reacted differently: 'It wasn't me', they would have said, 'so who was it? What happened? Who could it have been?' This would have given rise to all manner of consequences: he would have needlessly hurt his wife—and put into her head the desire for a further dose of the same medicine. Keeping quiet, he could save his reputation; speaking out, he could ruin it.

If he seethed inwardly, then, neither his face nor his voice betrayed it as he answered her: 'Don't you see me as a man to come back for more though I've just been in?'

'Certainly, my lord', she replied. 'But do think about your health.'

To which the king replied: 'Well, I don't mind taking your advice. I shall leave you this time without putting you to further trouble.' And in a fury at what had been done to him, he gathered up his cloak and left the room.

As he went, he considered how he might surreptitiously discover the culprit: the man must, he thought, be of his household and, whoever he was, he must still be inside the building. So he took the feeblest little rushlight and made for the long loft built over the palace stables, where most of the household servants slept. He was going on the assumption that whoever it was who had done as his wife described would not yet have recovered from the strain of the protracted exercise, and his pulse and heartbeat would betray him. So the king started at one end of the loft and quietly worked his way along, feeling each person's heart for a quickened beat. They were all sleeping soundly—all but the groom who had slept with the queen: he was not yet asleep. As he saw the king coming and what it was he was looking for, the groom was terrified; if his heart beat fast from his recent efforts, it beat even faster now for sheer terror: if the king noticed, he realized, he would put him to death at once. He turned over in his mind the various courses of action open to him, but as the king, he could see, was carrying no weapon, he decided to pretend to be asleep and see what happened. So when the king had felt one sleeper after another without finding any who might be the culprit, he came to the groom and felt his heart really thumping. 'Here's the one', he remarked to himself.

Wishing to keep his plan to himself, however, he confined himself to cutting off a lock of the groom's hair—in those days people wore their hair long—with a pair of scissors he had brought with him. That way he should be able to recognize him in the morning. This done, he returned to his own room. The groom, of course, had missed none of this; and being no fool himself, he knew well enough why he had been marked out in this way. So without wasting a minute he got up, found a pair of scissors ready to hand—one of the pairs used on the horses—and stole down the loft clipping off an identical lock over each sleeper's ear. This he did without being noticed, then went back to bed.

In the morning the king got up and gave orders that before the palace gates were opened his entire household was to turn out before him. This was done: they all stood before him bare-headed and he scrutinized them each in turn to pick out the one he had shorn of a lock. When he saw that most of them had the same lock missing he was most surprised and said to himself: 'The man I'm looking for may be the basest varlet, but clearly he's no simpleton.' Realizing that he could not achieve his aim without creating a fuss, he decided against risking his reputation for the sake of a small revenge, and contented himself with a simple word of admonishment, from which the culprit would know that he had been seen through, whoever he was. So without singling anyone out, he said: 'Whoever did it, let him never do it again. Now go about your business.'

Another man would have put them all on the rack, tortured them, subjected them to close interrogation and, by so doing, would have brought into the open what was better left concealed. Once the story was out and vengeance had been exacted in full, far from satisfying the man's honour it would have made the stain all the worse, and his lady's good name would also have been compromised. Those who heard the king's little speech were much perplexed, and spent a long time sifting it to find out what he had meant. But no one could make it out apart from the man for whom it was intended. And as long as the king lived, the groom had the sense never to explain the utterance—and never again to stake his life in such a venture.

III. 3. *A married lady sets her heart on a stranger. To procure his love she has recourse to a holy friar, who abets what he believes he is preventing.*

When Pampinea finished speaking, the groom won general applause for being so bold and canny, as did also the king for his good sense. Then the queen turned to Philomena, bidding her to go next, which Philomena gracefully did, in these words:

What I'm going to tell you is a true story, about a trick played by a pretty woman on a stuffy old cleric. The clergy are complete nitwits for the most part and they do have the most peculiar habits; so we layfolk will enjoy my story all the more, considering that they have such a high opinion of themselves and think they know everything whereas in fact they're worthless compared with us: after all, they're so pathetic and incapable of making their way in the world as other men do, they have to take refuge in a place that will feed them, like pigs. So I'll tell you about this trick not only to do as I am bidden, but also to wake you up to the fact that even monks and friars (whom we women tend to trust too blindly, gullible creatures that we are), can be and occasionally will be slyly hoodwinked, and not only by men but by one of our own sex.

Our city is a place for knavery rather than for love and trust. This is where, not so many years ago, there lived a lady of beauty and breeding; she possessed an innate nobility of spirit and a sharpness of wit to match that of any woman, and her name—that I shan't tell you (any more than the names of anyone else who comes into this story, for all that I know what they are) because it would give offence to certain people who are still alive, whereas it ought to be shrugged off with a smile. Conscious as the lady was of her family pride, but being married to a wool manufacturer on account of his ample wealth, she could never overcome the sense of injury arising out of her conviction that a man from the lower orders, never mind how rich he was, could never deserve the hand of a real lady. He might be as rich as rich could be, but the fact was that his capabilities did not extend beyond creating a textile pattern or setting up a loom or arguing with a spinning-woman about her yarn; she concluded, therefore, that his embraces were something she could very well do without, so far as it lay in her power to deny him access, but that she would obtain her satisfaction from some man whom she felt was a more deserving case than her wool-maker was. So she set her heart upon a man of true quality, no longer in his first youth; if a day passed in which she did not set eyes on him, she was tossing and turning all that night. The worthy fellow was quite unaware of her passion, though, so it left him utterly indifferent, while the lady, who was the soul of prudence, dared not apprise him of her feelings by sending a woman with a message or writing him a *billet-doux*, for fear that this might store up danger for the future.

Now she had noticed that this man spent a great deal of his time in the company of a friar: a fat fellow and thick as two planks, but who led the most saintly life and consequently enjoyed an almost universal reputation for holiness. Here, she thought, was the ideal procurer between herself and her beloved. After considering how to go about it, she went at a suitable hour to his church, sent for him, and told him that, if he had no objection, she would like him to hear her confession. The friar could tell at a glance that she was a well-bred lady and heard it willingly. Now when she had finished she said: 'Father, I'm going to need your help and advice over a problem of mine. You of course know my family and my husband—I've told you about them. My husband absolutely dotes on me and he gives me whatever I want, straight away, for he is rolling in money and can easily satisfy my wish. That's reason enough for me to love him with all my heart, and if I were ever to entertain the thought of doing, let alone actually do, anything contrary to his honour or good pleasure, I'd deserve to go to the stake more than any trollop ever did. Well, there's a man—I don't actually know his name but he looks respectable enough to me and, if I'm not mistaken, he's a friend of yours. He's a tall, good-looking man who dresses with becoming sobriety, but evidently he doesn't appreciate what my feelings are, for he seems to have laid siege to me: I can't show myself at a door or window or leave the house without his cropping up in front of me—it's surprising he's not here right now. I find this an almighty nuisance because this sort of behaviour can get an honest woman a bad name even if she's totally blameless. I've once or twice made up my mind to get my brothers to have a word with him about it, but on second thoughts it has occurred to me that men have a way of delivering messages in a manner to provoke an unpleasant response; angry words are exchanged and then they're at each others' throats. So I've kept quiet to avoid creating a scandal, and decided to tell you instead, rather than anyone else: you seem to be a friend of his and, besides, taking a friend or indeed a stranger to task over such a matter would come better from you. So I ask you in God's name to reprimand him and ask him to stop it. There'll be plenty of other women ripe and ready for such dalliance; they'll not mind a bit if he ogles them and pursues them. *I* find it a beastly nuisance—it's something for which I don't have the slightest inclination.' This said, she bowed her head as though ready to weep.

The holy friar realized at once whom it was she was talking about. He much applauded her excellent dispositions and, not for a moment doubting the truth of her statement, assured her that he would see to it that the individual in question would vex her no further. Realizing, moreover, that she was not short of money, he reminded her that virtue resided in almsgiving and the exercise of charity—and advised her of his needs.

'I do beg you in the name of God', the lady said to him. 'And should he deny it, be sure to tell him that it was I who told this to you and complained to you about him.'

So she concluded her confession, was given her sacramental penance and, bearing in mind the friar's exhortation to almsgiving, furtively dropped a fistful of money into his palms with the request that he offer Masses for her dear departed. Then she stood up and returned home.

It was not long before the gentleman paid the good friar one of his customary visits and, after they had chatted a while about this and that, the friar drew him aside and very tactfully admonished him for paying his addresses (so he believed) and ogling the lady, as she had given him to understand. This perplexed the worthy fellow, for never had he clapped eyes on her, indeed he only very seldom passed her house. He made, therefore, to exculpate himself, but the friar interrupted him, saying: 'Now then! Don't pretend to be surprised; don't waste your breath denying it, for you can't; what I have is not simply neighbourhood gossip—she told me about it her very self, and was extremely bitter about you. This kind of nonsense does you no credit and, let me tell you, what's more, if ever I met a woman who had no time for this sort of thing, she is the one. So for the sake of your reputation and her peace of mind, do please give over and leave her alone.'

The stalwart fellow, who was sharper than the friar, did not take long to tumble to the lady's stratagem; he feigned embarrassment and undertook to pay her no further attention. On leaving the friar, he went to the lady's house. She, meanwhile, stood watching at a little window to catch sight of him if he passed this way. As she saw him approach she gave him such a delighted and affable welcome, he could only conclude that he had put the right interpretation on the friar's words. From that day on he would regularly pass along that street, taking every precaution, and making it look as if he were pursuing some other objective; thus he afforded the lady (and himself too) no end of gratification and solace.

After a while, once it was clear to her that he was as taken with her as she with him, anxious as she was to fire up his love and convince him of hers, she found occasion to return to the friar. She sat down at his feet in church and burst into tears. The good friar tenderly asked her what was the matter.

'The matter, father, is that wretched friend of yours, whom I complained to you about the other day. I do believe that he was born to be a thorn in my flesh, and he could make me do something I'm bound to regret—and then I'll never dare sit at your feet any more.'

'What? Has he not stopped molesting you?'

'Far from it', cried she. 'Ever since I complained to you, he must have taken umbrage at my going to you about it because, if he used to pass my door once, I'm sure he now passes it seven times, as though out of spite. Well, would to God he had confined himself to passing my door and staring up at me; but he's grown so brazen and barefaced, why, only yesterday he sent me a woman with some inane message and, as if purses and girdles were a thing I'm short of, he sent me a purse and a girdle. This upset me so much, if I had not considered the scandal, and my devotion to you, I do believe I'd have raised merry hell. Anyway, I managed to control myself, and I've not wanted to do or say a thing without first telling you about it. So I handed the purse and girdle back to the little woman who had brought them, so she could take them back to him, and I told her to go to the devil; but then I was afraid she might keep them for herself and tell him I'd accepted them—I'm told this is what they sometimes do—so I called her back and snatched them angrily out of her hands, and I've brought them along to you: will you please return them to him and tell him I don't need anything of his because, thanks to the Good Lord and my husband, I've got purses and girdles coming out of my ears. Now I must ask your fatherly pardon but, if this man does not leave off, I shall tell my husband and my brothers and let the chips fall where they may: I'd far sooner see him taken down a peg if that has to be than see myself pilloried on his account. That, father, is what the matter is!'

This said, she drew out from beneath her long cloak the most beautiful and expensive purse and the dearest, daintiest little girdle and, sobbing her eyes out, threw them into the friar's lap. He believed every word she said and took them both. Seething with indignation, he said: 'I'm not surprised if this has made you angry, my daughter, and I cannot blame you—indeed, you've done very well to follow my advice. I told him off the other day, but he has not been faithful in observing the promise he gave me. So, what with that and now with this latest thing he's been up to, I'm sure I'm going to give him such a dressing down, he won't give you another moment's bother. Now God bless you and don't let your anger get the better of you and prompt you to mention the matter to any of your relatives: that could lead to a very ugly situation. And you're not to worry about this hurting your reputation, for I shall always be the staunchest witness to your virtue before God and men.'

The lady pretended to take a little comfort from his words and, changing the subject (aware as she was of the cupidity endemic in this friar and his kind): 'Father,' she observed, 'these last nights several of my departed relations have appeared to me, and they seem to me to be greatly tormented; they keep asking for alms, especially my mamma—she looks so wretched and woebegone it quite breaks my heart to see her. I think she's finding it very hard to take the sight of me so harassed by this spawn of the devil. So I'd be glad if you'd say the thirty Masses of Saint Gregory—better make that forty—for the repose of their souls, and your other prayers, that God might rescue them from the penal fire.' With this, she placed a florin in his hand.

The holy friar accepted it gladly; he strengthened her good resolution with improving words and many edifying stories, then sent her on her way with his blessing. After she had gone he sent for his friend, little realizing that the lady had been pulling the wool over his eyes. His friend came and noticed that he was frowning, from which he was quick to conclude that the woman had had words with the friar, and waited to hear what he would say. The friar reminded him of what he had told him before, and spoke to him again very sharply; he denounced him for what the lady accused him of. The excellent fellow, not entirely clear yet about the friar's drift, made only the feeblest denial that he had sent her the purse and girdle, for if the woman had left these items with the friar, he did not want to allay the cleric's suspicions.

This infuriated the friar. 'How can you deny it, miscreant! Look, here they are: she brought them to me herself, weeping. Don't you recognize them?'

The man feigned the deepest embarrassment and said: 'I do indeed recognize them. I confess I did wrong. But since I see she has made up her mind, I promise you'll not hear another word about this.'

A great deal of discussion took place, none the less, but eventually the blockhead friar passed the girdle and purse to his friend and sent him on his way, although not before reading him a lesson and urging him to forbear from such activities in future, which his friend promised to do. Exulting in the evident assurance of possessing the lady's heart as well as the lovely present, the gentleman left the friar and repaired at once to his lady's. Here, he furtively exhibited both items to her; she was delighted to see them, the more so because of this evidence that her plan was going from strength to strength. To bring it to fruition all she had to wait for was her husband's absence somewhere, and it was not long before he had reason to make a visit to Genoa.

The morning that he climbed into the saddle and rode off, she went to the worthy friar, full of complaints, and sobbed: 'I tell you, father, I can't take any more of it. But I did promise you the other day I wouldn't do anything without telling you first; so I've come now to explain. You won't believe that I've every reason to cry and complain unless I tell you what this friend of yours—devil, more like—did to me this morning just before daybreak. It was just my luck that he should get wind of my husband's leaving for Genoa yesterday morning; anyway, this morning—I've just told you when—he came into my garden and climbed up a tree to my bedroom window (it gives on to the garden). He had the window open and was about to step into my room when I woke up and jumped out of bed, and was all set to shriek, had he not pleaded with me not to—he wasn't yet in the room—for the love of God and for your sake, and he told me who he was. When I heard this I kept silent for your sake, and ran, mother-naked, to shut the window in his face. I think he must have left, and good riddance—at all events, that's the last I heard of him. Judge for yourself if this is any way to behave or if I should stand for it. I for one am not going to put up with it another day; as it is, I've endured more than enough out of consideration for you.'

This story put the friar into a towering rage, and he was at a loss for words. He kept asking her whether it couldn't just possibly have been someone else.

'Would to God I were still unable to tell him apart from someone else! I tell you it was he, and if he denies it, don't believe him.'

'Well then, there's nothing to be said but that this time he's gone too far, what he's done is inexcusable, and you did the right and proper thing in driving him away as you did. But, as God has protected your virtue, I should like to beg of you, as you twice before took my advice, please do so again this time: don't go and complain to your family but leave it to me—let's see what I can do to curb this unbridled devil—and I thought he was a saint! If I succeed in curing him of this licentiousness of his, so much the better. If I don't, you have my word right now, you may do with him just as you please, and my blessing on it.'

'Very well', said she. 'Just this once I won't cross or disobey you; but take care that he doesn't bother me any more for, upon my word, I'm not going to come back to *you* about this business.' That is all she would say as she flounced off in a pretended huff.

Scarcely had she left the church when the gentleman appeared and the friar called him over, drew him to one side, and gave him the wigging of a lifetime, calling him a man of straw, a backslider, a blackguard. On two previous occasions the good fellow had worked out what lay behind the friar's admonishments, and he remained alert and endeavoured to draw him out with a bewildered response. 'Why so cross, my friend?' he asked. 'Have I crucified Christ?'

'Why, the barefaced impudence of the man! Just listen to him! The way he talks, it's as if a year, two years, had passed and after such a long time he'd clean forgotten about his iniquitous conduct! Might it have slipped your mind between this morning and now that you behaved offensively to a certain person? Where were you this morning just before daybreak?'

'I've no idea where I was. Word of it reached *you* soon enough, though.'

'How right you are, it did reach me soon enough! It seems you expected, as the husband was away, that the lady would welcome you at once with open arms. And calls himself a man of honour, by heaven! He's turned into a night-time prowler, breaking into people's gardens, climbing their trees! Do you think your importunity will get the better of this lady's virtue, that you climb up trees at dead of night to reach her window? There's nothing she loathes more than what you're doing, but you keep doing it. Quite apart from the fact that she's made her feelings known in any number of ways, look what profit you've derived from *my* words of warning! Now mark my words: she's so far told nobody what you've been up to, not out of any love for you but only because I've begged her not to. But she'll keep silent no longer: I've given her leave to do just as she pleases if you cause her the slightest vexation again. What will you do if she tells her brothers?'

Clearly grasping what was required, the stalwart fellow pacified the friar to the best of his ability with a host of resounding promises, then off he went, and next morning in the small hours he went into the garden, climbed the tree, found the window open, stepped into the bedroom, and fell into his pretty mistress's arms without losing a moment. She had been expecting him most eagerly and gave him a rapturous welcome. 'A thousand thanks to his reverence', she cried, 'for giving you such clear instructions on how to get here.' Then they made love, affording each other boundless pleasure, chatting all the time and having a good giggle at that gullible oaf of a friar, and passing rude comments on such objects and utensils of the wool trade as slubs,* combs, and cards. Thereafter they contrived so to organize matters that they could be together and share their pleasure many another night, with no need for further visits to the friar. And I pray the Lord in His mercy that He might soon bring me and all other Christian souls that way inclined to enjoy nights such as those.

III. 4. *Don Felice, a friar, teaches the pious layman Puccio an arduous short-cut to heaven, and helps his wife to get there by a different path.*

When Philomena fell silent on finishing her tale, Dioneo, in honeyed words, much commended the woman's wit, as also Philomena's closing prayer. After which the queen laughed and looked at Pamphilo to say: 'It's your turn, Pamphilo, to entertain us with some trifle.' Pamphilo promptly assented and began:

How many people there are, my lady, who struggle to get to heaven without noticing that it's somebody else they're sending that way. This is what happened not all that long ago to one of our Florentine ladies, as you shall hear.

Next door to San Pancrazio, so I've been told, there once lived an honest, well-to-do burgher called Puccio di Rinieri. He turned very devout and became a Franciscan tertiary* under the name of Brother Puccio. His household consisting of a wife and a maidservant, he had no need to pursue any trade, so he could spend a great deal of time in church to indulge his spiritual life. Being of obtuse and plodding disposition, he would recite his Our Fathers, attend sermons, go to Mass, never miss the layfolks' hymn sessions, observe the fasts, and mortify his flesh—indeed rumour had it that he was a flagellant. His wife, Isabetta, was still a pretty young woman of but 28 or 30, fresh as a daisy, plump as an orchard-grown apple, but all too often she was kept on a diet far longer than she would have wished, thanks to her husband's piety, and maybe also to his age; and when she was ready for sleep, or maybe for a little frolic with him, he would be reciting her the life of Christ or the sermons of Brother Nastagio,* or Mary Magdalen's lament or suchlike.

Now about this time a friar of the community of San Pancrazio returned from Paris and his name was Don Felice; he was a handsome youth with a sharp intelligence and a considerable learning, and he became a close friend of Brother Puccio. This friar was very good at resolving Brother Puccio's perplexities, and Brother Puccio determined, on closer acquaintance, that he was of pre-eminent holiness, so he took to bringing him home occasionally for lunch or dinner as the case might be. Isabetta also became friendly with the friar for her husband's sake, and welcomed him with open arms. As a regular visitor to Brother Puccio's, the friar noticed how fresh and chubby the young lady was, and understood what it was she'd be most starved of; he decided, therefore, to save his friend the trouble and see what he could do to fulfil her need. With a clever play of meaningful glances one time and another the friar kindled within her the same desire he was nurturing in himself; once he had recognized this, he took the first occasion to speak to her of what he had in mind. But however willing he found her to play along with him, they could find no way for her to do so because the one and only place she would trust herself with the friar was in her own home—and this was out of the question because Brother Puccio was forever hanging round the place. This made the friar not a little glum until, after a good while, he hit upon a way to be with Isabetta in her house and not have to worry even though Brother Puccio were on hand.

So one day when Brother Puccio was paying him a visit, he told him: 'It's abundantly clear to me, Brother Puccio, that your one desire is to become a saint. Well, you seem to me to be going about it the long way round whereas there *is* a short-cut: it's a method known to the Pope and his highest prelates, and they follow it but don't want anyone else to hear of it. This is because the clergy depend largely on charity, and they would go out of business at once if the laity stopped supporting them with their offerings and the like. But as you are my friend and have been very hospitable to me, if I were sure you wouldn't reveal it to a soul but were ready to follow it yourself, I'd teach it to you.'

Brother Puccio longed to know about it and begged and entreated the friar to teach him; he swore never to breathe a word to anyone except to the extent he was given leave to do so, and assured him that he would certainly embark on this method if he could.

'As I have your promise', said the friar, 'I shall teach it to you. Bear in mind that the holy Doctors of the Church maintain that anyone wishing to become a saint must carry out the penance you shall hear about. Now listen carefully: I'm not saying that after the penance you won't be the sinner you are now. Here's what will happen: all the sins you committed up to the time of the penance will be purged away and forgiven because of it; and the sins you commit subsequently will not be charged to your perdition but will be washed away with a little holy water, as venial sins are now. Very well, when the penitent starts his penance he must first of all confess his sins with the utmost diligence; then he must undertake an enormous fast and abstinence lasting forty days; during this time you're to abstain from touching your wife, to say nothing of other women. In addition to that, you need to have some place in your house from which you may look at the heavens at night, and at the hour of Compline* this is where you have to go. In this place you must have a very broad plank set up in such a way that you can rest your back against it as you're standing up; you're to stand on the floor and spread your arms in the attitude of one crucified. If you want to support your arms on pegs, you may do so. Standing thus, you're to gaze at the heavens, without moving an inch, until morning. If you had some education you'd have to recite certain prayers, at this time, that I would give you; but as you're unlettered, you'll have to say three hundred Our Fathers and three hundred Hail Marys in honour of the Holy Trinity. As you look at the heavens you're constantly to think of God, the creator of heaven and earth, and of the passion of Christ, as you hold the position He was in as He hung on the cross. When the bell rings for Matins you may, if you wish, go and drop, fully clothed, into bed and get some sleep. In the morning you're to go to church and attend not less than three Masses and say fifty Our Fathers and as many Hail Marys. After that you may attend to a few simple duties if you have any, then have lunch, and be back in church for Vespers, when you're to say certain prayers I'll write out for you—and these you cannot manage without. Then, at Compline, you go on to do as I've already described. If you do this—as I did once—I hope that before you've come to the end of your penance you'll be filled with a marvellous sense of eternal beatitude, provided you carried it out with devotion.'

'This isn't all that much of a burden', said Brother Puccio; 'it doesn't take all that long, in fact it's easy enough to do. So I'm going to start on Sunday, in the name of the Lord.'

He left and returned home and told his wife all about it—with the friar's leave. The bit about standing all in one position till morning gave her the clearest indication of what the friar had in mind, and it seemed to her an excellent solution. So she told Brother Puccio that she was all in favour of it and indeed of whatever else he did for the good of his soul; and that she would join him in fasting, that the Lord might all the more prosper his penance, but she would not join him in the rest.

Thus agreed, when Sunday came Brother Puccio began his penance, and the friar arranged with Isabetta to turn up at a time when he would not be noticed; he would have supper with her most evenings, always arriving with some choice delicacy or beverage for the table. Then he would join her in bed till Matins, when he would get up and leave, and Brother Puccio would retire to sleep.

Now the room in which Brother Puccio had chosen to perform his penance was next door to Isabetta's bedroom, from which it was separated by nothing but the thinnest partition. So as the friar and the lady urged each other on in their amorous rough-and-tumble, Brother Puccio thought he felt the whole floor shake. So he called a halt after reciting a hundred of his Our Fathers and, without budging, called to his wife and asked her what she was up to. Isabetta was in playful spirits and replied, no doubt as she was busy keeping her seat on her prancing mount: 'Well bless you, husband! What's wrong with stretching a leg?'

'Stretching a leg? What *are* you on about?'

High-spirited woman that she was, and nobody's fool, Isabetta burst out laughing—maybe she was being tickled—and said: 'Well *you* ought to know! . . . The amount of times I've heard you say, "Supperless to bed, up all night".'

She had been making a pretence of fasting, and Brother Puccio thought this fast of hers must be the reason why she could not sleep but kept tossing and turning. So he said to her in all innocence: 'Well I did tell you *not* to fast, but since you've insisted, just stop thinking about it, think instead about getting some sleep. You're turning in bed so violently, the whole room keeps shaking.'

'Come, don't give it another thought', said his wife. 'I know what I'm about. You mind what you're doing and I'll take care of what I'm doing, if I can.'

So without another word Brother Puccio returned to his Our Fathers. Isabetta and the friar, however, made themselves up a bed in another part of the house from this night on, and here, for the duration of Brother Puccio's penance, they cavorted to their heart's content. The moment the friar left, Isabetta would return to her own bed where, shortly afterwards, she would be joined by Brother Puccio, straight from his penance.

The pious tertiary, then, kept on with his penance in this way, while his wife pursued her amours with the friar. Frequently she would joke with him: 'You've imposed a penance on Brother Puccio which has sent the two of us straight to heaven!' Isabetta took to this new routine like a duck to water, and grew so accustomed to enjoying the fare provided by the friar that even after her husband had completed his penance, the lady, who had regularly been kept by him on short rations, found a way to have her fill elsewhere with the friar, and long continued to take her pleasure with him on the sly. Thus it came about that Brother Puccio—if we are to come back to our starting-point—imagined he was gaining his place in heaven by his penance, whereas what he did was to send thither the friar, who had shown him the short-cut, and his wife, who had been living in constant want of that which the compassionate friar afforded her in such profusion.

III. 5. *Ricciardo, generally known as 'Sunday-best', trades a thoroughbred for a few words with Francesco Vergellesi's wife. Francesco believes he has the best of the bargain, but he has not been dealing with a fool.*

Pamphilo concluded his tale of Brother Puccio—the ladies, be it said, found it quite amusing. Thereupon the queen turned a regal gaze upon Elissa, summoning her to follow. Elissa broached her tale somewhat tartly, not because she was a cross-patch but because of an innate urge to castigate where necessary.

The trouble with your know-alls, and there are plenty of them, is that they imagine that everyone else is pig-ignorant; how often do they lay a trap for another party only to discover that it is they themselves who have fallen into it! I take the man to be an uncommon fool who clashes wits with his fellows for no good reason. Of course, not everyone may agree with me, which is why, as it is my turn to speak, I'm going to tell you the story of a knight from Pistoia.

There was once in Pistoia a knight called Francesco, of the Vergellesi family. He was very rich and, moreover, clever and wise, but he was the world's worst miser. When he had to leave for Milan to take up his duties as Podestà, he assembled everything he would require to maintain the dignity of his office, all except for a suitably splendid mount: he couldn't find a single one he was really happy with, and this was a worry.

Now there was a young man in Pistoia called Ricciardo; he was of humble birth but very well off, and as he was always so dapper and neatly turned out, everyone called him 'Sunday-best'. For ages Sunday-best had been pining and moping for Francesco's wife, a great beauty, and virtuous with it. Now Sunday-best was owner of one of the finest thoroughbreds in Tuscany, the apple of his eye. As it was an open secret that Sunday-best was smitten with Francesco's wife, somebody suggested to her husband: 'Why don't you ask Sunday-best for his horse? He'll let you have it out of love for your wife.' Francesco, mean as ever, sent for Sunday-best and asked if he could buy his horse, the idea being that the animal would then be offered to him as a gift.

The proposal appealed to Sunday-best, and he replied: 'If you gave me everything you possessed, sir, you couldn't buy my horse off me. However, you can have it as a free gift any time you say, on one condition: before you take possession of it, I am to have—with your free consent and in your presence—a few words with your lady wife, she and I just so far removed from anyone else that we're out of earshot.'

With avarice as a spur, the knight told Sunday-best that he had no objection, let him talk as long as he wished. Then, with a mind to cheating the suitor, he left him waiting in the hall while he went up to the bedroom and explained to his wife that he could win the horse as easy as blinking, all she had to do was go down and listen to Sunday-best, but just to take care not to utter so much as a word in reply. His wife spoke very ill of this proposal, but was bound to do as her husband required, so she consented and followed him into the hall to hear what Sunday-best had to say to her.

The bargain duly ratified, Sunday-best sat down with the lady at one end of the hall, well away from everyone else, and thus he addressed her: 'Excellent lady, I'm sure you're shrewd enough to have realized long ago that I am hugely in love with you, compelled as I am by your beauty, which far surpasses any I ever laid eyes on; then there's your sheer goodness, your unique virtue which cannot but force the admiration of any self-respecting man. So I don't need words to show you that my love is the biggest, the most passionate that any man ever felt for any woman. And so it shall continue to be, while wretched life still inhabits this frame of mine; indeed, if loving goes on beyond the grave as it does here, thus shall I love you for all eternity. And so you can be sure that there is not a thing you own, whether it be precious or common, that is so firmly in your possession and at your disposal as I am, for all I'm worth, and with all that I possess. Make no mistake about it, I assure you that I should feel myself far more blessed if you bade me do anything, no matter what, for your pleasure than if I could give orders and see the whole world obey me on the instant. So if I am yours as you have heard me say, I may justly make my prayer to your ladyship, in whose hands alone and in none other's are my peace, my every good, my salvation. And I beg you as your most humble servant, you dearest and only hope of mine, that as this my hope is nourished in Love's fire, you will be good to me, you will so far relax your past severity towards your slave that I may draw comfort from your mercy and rightly say that your beauty has not only inflamed my love but also restored my life. If your proud spirit does not bend to my prayer, this life of mine will surely fail and I shall die, and it may be said that I died at your hand. And never mind that my death will do you little credit; even so, I believe your conscience will sometimes nag you, and you will be sorry you let it happen, and, in a better frame of mind, you'll find yourself saying: "Oh dear, how wrong I was not to have been kinder to my Ricciardo!" But, alas, you will have repented too late and you'll only rue it the worse. So take care now, while you can still prevent it, to ensure it doesn't happen; be moved to pity for me ere I die, for it rests only with you to make me the happiest or the most wretched man alive. I hope you will be truly gracious to me and not suffer me to incur death as the reward for so great a love; I hope you will raise my spirits with a merciful response to cheer me, for now in your presence I am full of fear and trembling.'

He fell silent, shed a few tears, fetched up some ample sighs, then waited to hear what her answer would be.

For love of her Sunday-best had courted her patiently, had worn her colours in the lists, had serenaded beneath her balcony, and heaven knows what besides, but all to no avail. These loving words spoken with such fervour did, however, succeed in moving the lady; she began to experience what she had not felt for him before—love. And though she held her tongue, in obedience to her husband's command, she could not quite suppress the odd little sigh, which would have been allowed free expression had she been able to reply.

Sunday-best waited a while and saw that she was not answering, which puzzled him, until it dawned on him that her husband had put her up to it. However, as he watched her face he noticed that she shot him some meaning glances, besides which her sighs did not escape him—they reached him in attenuated form, but they reached him—so he was somewhat encouraged; whereupon he hit upon a new plan and made answer for her, in her hearing, as follows: 'My own Ricciardo, of course I've known for ages what a tremendous, what a perfect love you bear towards me, and now your words have made this even clearer to me, and I'm so pleased, as why should I not be? I may have seemed to you cruel and hard-hearted, but you're not to imagine my face ever reflected my true feelings. Far from it—I have always doted on you and loved you more than any other man, but I had to act the way I did out of circumspection and to protect my good name. But now the time has come for me to show you clearly that I love you; now I can repay you for the love you have borne me. So take heart and keep up your spirits, for Francesco is about to leave for Milan, as you know, to be Podestà—indeed it is for love of me that you have presented him with that fine horse of yours. Once he's gone you can be quite sure, you have my word for it as a woman who loves you dearly, you'll be with me in a matter of days and then we'll make love to our heart's content. Rather than speaking again on this subject, I'll tell you right now that the day you see a pair of towels hanging from my bedroom window, which overlooks our garden, come to me that same evening through the garden gate, but take care not to be seen; I'll be waiting for you and we'll enjoy our long-awaited night's pleasure.'

Having thus spoken on the lady's behalf, he replied in his own name: 'My beloved, your gracious response leaves me quite stunned with happiness, I scarcely can find words to thank you with. And if I could speak as freely as I wished, eternity would not be long enough to thank you as I'd like to and ought to. May I leave it to your imagination to take in what I cannot put into words? All I shall say is, I shall certainly do as you have asked; once I've drawn strength from the gift you have promised me, I shall do my utmost to convey my thanks unstintingly. Well, there's nothing more to add for the moment, so, my beloved, God grant you your heart's desire and every happiness.'

All this while, Francesco's wife spoke not a word. Sunday-best got up and went across to the husband, who met him half-way. 'Well, what d'you say?' asked the knight with a grin. 'Have I been as good as my word?'

'No sir', replied Sunday-best. 'You promised to let me have a word with your wife, but all I spoke with was a marble statue.'

Francesco was very pleased with this; his high regard for his wife now knew no bounds. 'That steed of yours, then, is clearly mine', he said.

'You're right, sir', answered Sunday-best. 'But if I had expected that this favour of yours would yield me the profit it *has* done, I should have given you the horse without requesting the favour. Indeed, would that I had done so, for you have bought the horse but I never made a sale.' Francesco laughed.

A few days after this, equipped with a mount, he left for Milan to assume his office of Podestà. His wife stayed behind, a free woman in her own home. She thought over what Sunday-best had said to her, and how much he loved her—why, he had given away his horse for love of her—and as she saw him pass her house the whole time, she said to herself; 'What am I doing? Why am I wasting my youth? My man's gone to Milan and won't be back for six months. When will he make them up to me—when I'm an old woman? Anyway, when should I ever find another suitor like Sunday-best? I'm on my own, I've no one to be afraid of. Why shouldn't I make hay while the sun shines? I'll never have another chance like this one, and no one's ever to know. Besides, what if anyone did? I'd sooner do it and then repent than kick myself for not having done it.' After thus musing, the day came when she hung out two towels from the window giving on to the garden, as Sunday-best had said. Sunday-best was delighted to see them; that night he made his furtive way on his own to the garden gate, which he found open. He passed through to a door leading into the house, where the lady was waiting for him. She stood up and went to him as soon as she saw him come in, and welcomed him with open arms—they couldn't stop hugging and kissing. Then he followed her upstairs, and a moment later they were lying in each other's arms and indulging. This was the first occasion but by no means the last—while the husband was in Milan, and after his return home as well, Sunday-best was a frequent visitor and never ceased to give, and obtain, satisfaction.

III. 6. *Catella dotes on her husband Filippello Sighinolfo, and consequently finds herself in a dark room at the public baths. Here she addresses herself to the wrong party, one Ricciardo Minutolo with unpredicted results.*

Elissa had nothing left to say, so the queen commended Sunday-best for his sagacity then told Fiammetta to carry on. 'Gladly, ma'am', said she with a twinkle, and thus began:

Our city is rich in examples on any and every subject, just as it is rich in all else; however, we must leave it awhile and talk about what has happened elsewhere in the world, just as Elissa has done. So we're going to Naples for my story about one of your prim and proper ladies who always shy away from sex, and how a crafty suitor induced her to taste the forbidden fruit before she'd so much as sniffed the blossom. It's a story which will be an object lesson to you for the future as well as affording you a little entertainment over what is now in the past.

In Naples, a very ancient city and as pleasant as any city in Italy, maybe more so, there was once a young man called Ricciardo Minutolo;* he came from one of the best families, and his wealth was simply dazzling. His wife was a woman of the greatest beauty and charm, but he none the less fell in love with another lady who was generally considered to be the city's paramount beauty; her name was Catella* and she was married to another well-born young man, Filippello Sighinolfo, whom she doted on, being a thoroughly virtuous wife. So here was Ricciardo in love with this Catella, and he did all the things a man has to do to earn the love and favours of a woman, but none of this brought him any closer to his goal, and he was practically at his wit's end; he could not or would not conquer his passion and he could neither bring himself to die nor find any taste for living. This being his situation, he was strongly urged one day by some ladies who were relatives of his to desist from his amorous quest: he was wasting his efforts, they said, in as much as Catella had eyes only for Filippello, indeed she was so possessive about him, she was convinced that every bird that flew through the air was going to snatch him from her. When he heard about Catella's possessiveness, Ricciardo instantly considered how this might be turned to his own ends. He pretended to have given up hope of securing Catella's affections and therefore to have transferred his own to another lady,* for love of whom he now began to enter the lists as her champion and to do all the things he had hitherto been doing for Catella's sake. He had not long been acting this way before virtually the whole of Naples, not excluding Catella herself, was of the opinion that it was no longer she for whom Ricciardo pined but this new lady; and he so persevered in this course that everyone's opinion hardened into a firm conviction, so much so that even Catella herself relaxed the austerity with which she had been wont to discourage his advances, and she would now greet him as cheerily as she did any other friend or neighbour.

Now as the weather was hot, it happened that great numbers of ladies and gentlemen would make up parties in the Neapolitan fashion to have lunch or supper by the seashore. Ricciardo knew that Catella was to be on such an outing, and joined a party of his own going to the same spot, where he was welcomed by the ladies in Catella's party—but only after they had had to press him a great deal, for he displayed a considerable reluctance to join them. Here all the ladies, and Catella with them, started teasing him about his new infatuation, and he played up to them, giving them all the more scope for gossip. By and by the ladies went their various ways, as happens on such occasions, one by one, till Ricciardo was left with Catella and one or two of her woman-friends, and he made a casual quip about her husband Filippello being himself a gallant. This remark stung her to jealousy and she secretly burned to discover what Ricciardo meant. For a little while she held herself in check but eventually she succumbed and begged him, for the sake of his own lady-love, to explain what he meant by his remark.

'As you've asked me for the sake of a person on whose account I should never dare to deny you any request you made of me', said Ricciardo, 'I'm willing to tell you. Only you have to promise me not to breathe a word about it to him or to anyone else until you've seen for yourself the truth of what I shall tell you—I can show you, whenever you wish, how to see it for yourself.'

Catella did not object to his request; what's more, she believed him, and promised not to say a word. So he took her to one side, out of earshot, and told her: 'If I still loved you the way I used to, I shouldn't dare tell you anything which I thought might hurt you. But as that love is in the past, I won't be so chary about telling you how matters stand. I don't know whether Filippello ever took it amiss that I was in love with you, or whether he was ever persuaded that you returned my love; in any event, he never showed the least concern with regard to me. Maybe he's been waiting to catch me off my guard, because now he seems disposed to do to me what I've no doubt he's been worried I might do to him, that is, take his pleasure with my wife. From what I've discovered, he's taken fairly recently to pestering her in secret, but she has told me all about it, and I've had her reply to him according to my own instructions. Now this very morning before I came here I found my wife deep in conversation with a woman who had stopped by; I recognized immediately where she was from, so I called my wife and asked her what the woman wanted. And she told me: "It's that pest Filippello—answering him and fanning his hopes the way you make me, you've got me well and truly stuck with him now. He says he's got to know what my intentions are. He says that if I'm willing, he'll arrange for us to meet in secret at some public baths in the town. He's urging me and pressing me to such a meeting, and were it not for all these discussions you've made me keep going with him, God knows why, *I*'d have sent him about his business and cured him of any interest in my doings." At this point I felt things had gone far enough and could no longer be endured, and I decided to let you know, so that you'd realize what thanks you were getting for your perfect fidelity which brought me close to my grave a little while ago. As I don't want you to go thinking I'm making this up, you can, if you like, see it all with your own eyes: I had my wife tell the woman that she was prepared to come to the baths tomorrow mid-afternoon, when people are having their siesta. The woman was delighted with this answer and left. Of course I don't imagine you'll be expecting me actually to send her along. If I were you, I'd arrange for him to find me there instead of the lady he's expecting, and when I've spent a few moments with him, I'd have him discover just who it was he's been consorting with, and I'd give him a piece of my mind. That way, I think, you'd leave him so utterly mortified you'd get your revenge for the shabby trick he wants to play on you and me.'

Catella took his word without a moment's hesitation, quite regardless of who this man was, telling her these things, or whether it mightn't be a little fishy—that's always the way with your jealous types. Moreover she could make certain past events fit into this new picture. 'That's just what I shall do', she said angrily; 'it won't take much effort, and believe me, if he turns up I'll make him look such a fool, he'll never look at another woman without remembering what's happened.'

Ricciardo found this most satisfactory; he felt he was on the right track and everything was going according to plan. Still, he told her a whole lot more which served to confirm her belief, and asked her none the less not to tell a soul she'd ever learnt it from him—which she promised him on her honour.

Next morning Ricciardo went to see a woman of easy virtue who was in charge of the public bath-house he'd mentioned to Catella. He told her what he proposed to do and asked her to do all she could to facilitate his scheme. As she had a soft spot for him she said of course she would, and worked out with him what she was to do and say. In the bath-house there was a room with no window to admit any light, so it was in almost total darkness. As agreed, she got it ready and made up a bed in it as comfortably as possible. After lunch Ricciardo got into this bed and waited for Catella.

Having given Ricciardo's words more credence than they deserved, Catella was in a black mood when she returned home that evening, and when Filippello got home he happened to be preoccupied with matters of his own, so perhaps he didn't greet her with his usual affability. This served only to enhance her suspicions, and she brooded: 'It's obvious the man's thinking about the woman he's expecting to make love to tomorrow—but that is simply not going to happen.' Such reflections, and a rehearsal of what she was going to say to him when they were together the next day, kept her busy most of the night. Come mid-afternoon Catella left, attended by a woman, and went of set purpose to the public baths specified by Ricciardo. Here she asked the woman in charge whether Filippello had been in today.

'Are you the lady', she asked, as instructed by Ricciardo, 'who was to come and have a word with him here?'

'That's me.'

'Good. You'll find him in there.'

Catella, seeking for what she shouldn't have cared to find, had herself shown to the room where Ricciardo was waiting; she covered her head, went in, and locked the door. Pleased to see her come in, Ricciardo stood up, folded her in his arms, and softly bade her welcome. Catella, to ensure she should not give herself away, hugged and kissed him and showed herself most affectionate, though she said not a word for fear that she might be recognized by her voice. The room was in almost total darkness, which suited both of them very well—nor was there any question of their eyes growing accustomed to the dark. Ricciardo got her into bed and here, without exchanging a word lest their voices betrayed them, they took their time giving each other a great deal of pleasure.

But when Catella felt the time had come to give vent to her indignation she'd been nursing, she burst out angrily in these words: 'Oh how wretched is the lot of us women! How ill-conceived is the love of so many wives for their husbands! For eight years I've loved you more than my life—worse luck!—and now I hear you've been itching and pining for another woman, you filthy beast! So who d'you think you've been living with all this time? You've been living with a woman who's slept beside you for eight years; with a woman you've been deceiving for ever so long with honeyed words, pretending to love her while your heart has been elsewhere. I am Catella. I am not Ricciardo's wife, you faithless wretch. Listen: don't you recognize my voice? It's me all right. I can't wait for us to be back in the light so I can really make you blush for shame as you deserve, disgusting pig that you are! O poor me! To think of all the love I've lavished on you all these years! All for this two-faced brute—there he goes, thinking he's got another woman in his arms, and he's fawned over me and fondled me more these last few minutes I've been with him than in all the time we've been married. You've been lusty enough today, you dog—at home you're always so washed out and flabby! But thank God it's your own field you've been ploughing, not someone else's, as you've been thinking. No wonder you kept your distance from me last night! You were waiting to discharge your burden elsewhere, and you wanted to arrive in the lists an energetic rider. But God be praised—and my own sharpness—the water has flowed in its proper channel as it was meant to do. Well? Why don't you answer, wretch? Why don't you say something? Have you lost your tongue? I don't know what's holding me from sticking my fingers in your eyes and plucking them out! You thought you could betray me on the sly, but you were too clever by half! You didn't get away with it: you never expected me to catch you out so fast, did you now?'

These words were music to Ricciardo's ears. He made no answer but kept hugging and kissing her and fondled her more than ever, so she burst out again: 'No use thinking you're going to win me over and soothe my feelings with all this empty fawning, you cur. I shan't be happy till I've shown you up for what you are to every one of your relations, to all our friends and neighbours. Tell me, aren't I as beautiful as Ricciardo Minutolo's wife? Aren't I as well born as she? Well, answer, damn you! What has she got that I haven't? Get away from me, don't touch me—you've made enough passes for one day. I'm well aware that now you've discovered who I am, you're laying it on especially thick. But if God does me a favour, I'm going to keep you with your tongue hanging out. I don't know what's to stop me from sending for Ricciardo; he's been in love with me more than with anything in the world, and he couldn't ever boast that I gave him so much as a glance. I can't see what harm there'd have been in my doing so. You thought you had his wife here with you, and it's just as though you did—it's no thanks to you if she never came. Right, so if I sent for him you'd have no just cause to hold it against me.'

Catella, then, had a great deal to say and much to lament, until eventually Ricciardo decided that he should reveal himself and undeceive her, otherwise, if she continued in her present conviction, things might turn out very badly. So he drew her into his arms and pinioned her so that she could not escape, then said: 'Don't be angry, my darling. What I could not obtain simply by loving you, I've obtained by a trick taught me by Love. I am your own Ricciardo.'

Catella recognized his voice and instantly tried to throw herself out of bed, but she could not. She tried to cry out, but Ricciardo laid a hand across her mouth and said: 'Look, what's done cannot be undone, not if you kept shouting for the rest of your life. If you do shout or indeed make this known to anyone outside in any manner, two things will follow: first, your honour and reputation will be tarnished, which must be of some concern to you, because while you may claim that I tricked you into coming here, I shall say that this is not true, but rather that I got you here with a promise of money and presents, and that as I did not fulfil my promise as well as you hoped, you lost your temper and created this rumpus; and you know people's propensity to believe the worst—they'll be as likely to believe my account as yours. Add to that, your husband and I will become sworn enemies, and at the end of the day things could reach the pitch where I'm as likely to kill him as he is to kill me; and that will spell the end of your happiness. So take care, my honey, not to bring shame on yourself and put your husband and me at what could turn out to be fatal odds. You are not the first woman, nor will you be the last to be deceived, and I never deceived you to steal what is yours, but out of the abundant love I feel and will always feel for you—I wish to remain your humblest servant. And while I and what is mine, my abilities and talents, have long been at your entire disposal, so do I intend they should continue to be, only more so. In all other things you are a wise woman: I know that in this you will be so too.'

As Ricciardo was thus speaking, Catella was weeping buckets. And yet, however furious and aggrieved she felt, she paid enough attention to his plain words to recognize that he could be right in his predictions, so 'Ricciardo', she said, 'God knows how I'm going to stomach the wrong, the fraud you've practised on me. I won't cry out here, where I've been brought by my naïvety and my exaggerated jealousy; but you can be quite sure I shan't be happy until I've got my revenge on you, one way or another, for what you've done to me. So let go of me, stop holding me. You've had what you wanted, you've mocked me to your heart's content. It's time to let go of me. Now please let me go.'

Ricciardo realized that she was still extremely upset, but he was determined not to leave her until he had obtained her forgiveness. So he set about soothing her feelings with gentle words, and ultimately said enough and made enough impassioned entreaties to overcome her resistance and make up their quarrel. Indeed, by common consent they remained together most blissfully for a good long while after this. As for Catella, now that she could see how much more relish there was in her lover's caresses than in her husband's, her previous austerity melted into tender feelings for Ricciardo, and she loved him most dearly from that day forth; frequently they contrived to enjoy their love by devious means. God grant we too may enjoy our loves.

III. 7. *Tedaldo, turned out of the house by his mistress, goes away and returns years later disguised as a pilgrim, though everyone believes he has been killed. How he recaptures his lady's good graces and restores harmony all round.*

Fiammetta fell silent amid a chorus of praise, after which the queen, with no time to waste, promptly bade Emilia speak next. And thus she began:

I should like to return to our own city, as the last two narrators chose to desert it; and I shall tell you how one of our Florentines recovered his lady after losing her.

Once upon a time in Florence there was a youth of noble birth called Tedaldo degli Elisei, who was passionately in love with a lady, whom he found thoroughly commendable, the wife of Aldobrandino Palermini, and her name was Ermellina; and he was deemed worthy to enjoy his heart's desire. Fortune, however, who is no friend of the happy, took against him: after granting her favours to Tedaldo for a time, the lady, for whatever reason, suddenly ceased to accommodate him—she wouldn't listen to any message from him, she would not so much as set eyes on him. This made him quite sick at heart, though he had so well concealed his love that no one imagined this to be the cause of his gloom. He tried one thing and another in a resolute attempt to regain her love, which he felt he had lost through no fault of his own, but after finding his efforts all to no avail, he determined to quit the social scene in order not to afford her (the author of his sorrows) the pleasure of seeing him waste away. Taking such cash as he could assemble, he slipped away without a word to friend or kinsman (other than to one friend who was in the secret) and arrived in Ancona under the pseudonym of Filippo di San Lodeccio. Here he made the acquaintance of a rich merchant and entered his service, and travelled with him to Cyprus aboard one of his ships.

The merchant was so taken with his charm and character that not only did he assign him a good salary but he took him into partnership and put him in charge of a good proportion of his business. This he attended to so well and so scrupulously that in a very few years he became a solid, rich, and well-considered merchant in his own right. Although he often thought of his hard-hearted lady and remained deeply in love with her and longed to see her again, he devoted himself so single-mindedly to his business affairs that he won this battle for fully seven years. But it happened in Cyprus one day that he heard someone singing a song that he used to sing, a song about the love he bore his lady and she him, and the pleasure he took with her. 'It's not possible', he told himself, 'that she can have forgotten me'; and he was so fired with the urge to see her again that, unable to endure it any longer, he decided he must return to Florence.

So, putting his affairs in order, he left for Ancona with only a servant for company. When his possessions caught up with him here, he forwarded them all to Florence, to the keeping of a friend of his Ancona partner, then followed secretly with his attendant, dressed as a pilgrim back from the Holy Sepulchre. On reaching Florence he put up at a small inn, close to where his lady lived, which was owned by two brothers. He had but one first destination and that was his beloved's house, with a view to seeing her if he could; but he noticed that the doors and windows were all shut, which left him with a strong suspicion that she was dead or had moved away. Considerably disturbed, he made his way to his brothers' house and found four of them out in front of it, all dressed in black, which greatly surprised him; but, realizing that he was so changed, both in dress and in looks, from what he was when he had left that he would not readily be recognized, he confidently went up to a cobbler and asked him why those four were dressed in black.

'They're dressed in black', replied the cobbler, 'because their brother was killed not two weeks ago—his name was Tedaldo and he had not been here for a long time. I gather they've proved in court that he was murdered by a man called Aldobrandino Palermini, who has been arrested—Tedaldo was in love with his wife and had returned incognito to be with her.'

Tedaldo was astonished that anyone could so closely resemble him as to be mistaken for him, and he was sorry for the disaster that had overtaken Aldobrandino. The wife was alive and well, he learned. As night had fallen he returned to the inn, his mind crowded with thoughts, and after dining with his servant he was shown up to bed right at the top of the house. Here, agitated by his teeming thoughts, and owing to the discomfort of his bed and maybe to the meagreness of his supper, Tedaldo had still not been able to get to sleep when the night was half over. He was awake, therefore, when, in the middle of the night, he thought he heard people climbing off the roof into the house; after which, through the cracks in his bedroom door, he saw a light coming up the stairs. So he quietly approached a chink and peeped through to see what this was all about. He saw a most beautiful girl holding the lamp, while three men who had climbed in off the roof met her and there was a general exchange of greetings, after which one of the men told the girl: 'We can breathe easy now, thank God. We know for a fact that the brothers have pinned Tedaldo Elisei's death on to Aldobrandino Palermini—he's confessed, and the verdict has been entered. Even so, we'd better keep our mouths shut—if it ever got out that we were the ones who did it, we'd be in the same pickle he's in.' After telling her this, which caused her the greatest satisfaction, they went downstairs to bed.

These words left Tedaldo musing at the manifold errors into which the human mind could stumble. He thought of his brothers: first, they had wept over a stranger and buried the man in place of himself, and then they had accused an innocent fellow on false suspicions and, with the support of mendacious witnesses, had brought a sentence of death upon him. He brooded also upon the blind severity of the law and its practitioners, who all too often applied torture in order to prove a lie, under guise of a scrupulous search for the truth. They call themselves the Lord's appointed ministers of justice when they are nothing but instruments of the devil in compassing evil. Then he addressed his thoughts to rescuing Aldobrandino and determined how to proceed.

In the morning he got up and, leaving his servant behind, chose his moment to proceed on his own to his beloved's house. He chanced to find the door open and went in, and saw his lady in a little ground-floor room, seated on the floor (as befits a mourner), and swollen with tears and bitter thoughts. The pity of it almost brought tears to his own eyes; he approached her and said: 'Don't be distressed, madam. Your peace is near at hand.'

Ermellina looked up when she heard him and said, as she wept: 'You look to me, good sir, like a pilgrim from foreign parts: what do you know about peace or my troubles?'

'I'm from Constantinople. I've just arrived. God has sent me here to change your tears into laughter and to deliver your husband from death.'

'If you're from Constantinople and have only just arrived, how do you know who my husband is, or who I am?'

The pilgrim rehearsed the entire tale of Aldobrandino's tribulations; he told her who she was, how long she had been married, and any number of other things about herself with which he was perfectly well acquainted. Ermellina was absolutely astonished and took him for a prophet; she knelt at his feet and begged him for God's sake to hurry, if he had come to save Aldobrandino, because time was short.

Said the pilgrim, affecting to be an eminently holy man: 'Get up, madam, and don't cry; listen carefully to what I'm going to say to you, and take good care not to breathe a word of it to a soul. From what the Lord has revealed to me, your present tribulation has beset you on account of an offence you committed in the past; with this trial God has wanted to purge you somewhat of your sin, and He wants you to make full reparation, otherwise you would land in even worse trouble.'

'My sins are countless, sir. I don't know which one in particular the Lord wants me to make amends for. So, if you know, tell me and I'll do my best to set it to rights.'

'I know perfectly well which sin it is, and if I put the question to you it is not to find out more, but to give you the greater remorse by confessing it yourself. Now here's the point: do you recall ever having had a lover?'

Ermellina heaved a great sigh when she heard this, and was much surprised, for she had assumed that the affair had never become known, for all that, at about the time the man mistaken for Tedaldo had been murdered and buried, a rumour had gone the rounds on the strength of one or two ill-considered words dropped by Tedaldo's friend, who had been in the secret. 'I see', she said, 'that God reveals everyone's secrets to you, so I'm not inclined to conceal mine from you. It is true that when I was young I was deeply in love with the unfortunate young man whose death has been laid at my husband's door. If I've cried so much over his death, if it has grieved me the way it has, that is because, however hard and inflexible I showed myself before his departure, nothing has ever been able to oust him from my heart—not his departure, not his long absence, nor his wretched death.'

'You never loved the poor lad who was killed; it was Tedaldo Elisei you loved. Tell me, though: what turned you against him? Did he ever hurt you?'

'Not at all. The reason for my turning against him lay in the words of a damnable friar who once heard my confession. When I told him about my love for Tedaldo and the intimacy we shared, he browbeat me so mercilessly I still tremble at the very thought of it: if I didn't give it up, he said, I'd fetch up in the devil's maw, in the very depths of hell, and I'd be consigned to the tormenting flames. This left me so terrified I decided to have nothing more to do with him—and to avoid all occasion to do so I refused his letters and messages. I expect, though, that if he had persevered, instead of going off in despair because (so I imagine) I was watching him waste away like snow in the sun, I would have been persuaded out of my determination, for there was nothing in the world I wanted more than him.'

Then the pilgrim told her: 'This now is the only sin to cause you trouble. I know perfectly well that Tedaldo did not force you in any way: when you fell in love with him, you did so of your own free will as you were attracted to him, and he came to you in accordance with your own wishes and became intimate with you; in this, you showed him such kindness in word and deed that, if he was already in love with you before, you increased his love for you a thousandfold. Now if that was the case, as I know it was, what could have induced you to deny yourself to him so inflexibly? These are things you should have thought about right at the start, and if you considered that you ought to have thought better of it, that it was wrong, then you shouldn't have done it in the first place. Just as he became yours, you became his. Whether or not he became yours was entirely up to you, it was your decision; but snatching yourself away from him, to whom you belonged, that was less than honest, it was theft so long as he had not consented.

'Now I'll have you know that I am a friar, which means I know what they are all made of. So if I handle them without kid gloves in your own interest—well, I have a better title than others to do so. And I want to talk about them so that you'll know them better in future than you seem to have done up till now. Once upon a time the friars used to be the best and holiest of men, but the people who call themselves friars nowadays and like to be considered as such have nothing in common with those friars apart from their cowls; not that even these have much to do with the Orders because, while their founders prescribed mean, unassuming habits of coarse weave, in keeping with a spirit that had spurned the things of this world on clothing itself in such beggarly attire, it is not so with today's friars: their cowls are amply cut in the finest and glossiest material, and with a lining; they make them at once seductive and pompous and are not in the least embarrassed to go strutting about the churches and squares in them, just as the laity do in *their* finery. They're just like those fishermen who scoop up a single great mass of fish out of the river in their weighted nets—only these friars make a great sweep of their cowls to gather up any number of sanctimonious old maids, scores of widows, and other silly females, and men too, and that's really all they think about. If you want to know the truth, those people don't wear friars' cowls, only clothes of the same dye. And while the friars of old sought the salvation of mankind, those of today only want to chase skirts and line their own pockets. Their one concern is to upset feeble minds with their thunders, their garish imagery; their concern is to prove that almsgiving and Mass-offerings make satisfaction for sin: that way, those who find refuge in the mendicant orders not out of pious conviction but as the line of least resistance, the easy option, enjoy the advantage of this man's offering of bread, that one's tribute of wine, another one's providing them with their dinner for the sake of his dear departed. I'm not denying that prayer and almsgiving make reparation for sin; but if those who gave alms just saw whom they were giving them to, if they had any idea, they'd sooner keep them for themselves or else cast them before swine.* And, recognizing as they do that the fewer there are to share an ample fortune, the better off each participant is, they'll all try deploying scare-tactics to clear others off the pitch they want for themselves. They rail against men's lechery so that, with those thus chided out of the way, the women remain at the disposal of the denouncers. They castigate usury and dishonest gain so that, when restitution is made, they can take the very substance which would, they allege, lead its owner to perdition, and use it to procure themselves more ample cowls—or bishoprics and other canonical advancement. And when they are taken to task for these and other such reprehensible activities, their rejoinder is, "Do as we say, not as we do": this they take to be a suitable discharge of their every fault, as if constancy and iron rectitude came more easily to the flock than to the shepherds. And most of them in fact realize how many there are who are requited with this answer but don't grasp its meaning. Friars today would have you do as they say: fill their purses with money, let them into your secrets, stay chaste, be patient, forgive wrongs, avoid slander—all good, upright, holy things, but why do they ask this? Why, so that they can do what otherwise they could not do, if layfolk were all doing it. I don't have to tell you that it takes money to support an idle life-style: if you lavish your money on your pleasures, the friar won't be able to take it easy in his Order. If you layfolk go chasing after skirts, then there'll be none for the friars to chase after. If you don't practise patience and forgiveness, the friars won't risk dropping in on you to debauch your household. I don't need to spell it all out. They show themselves up every time they trot out this justification for the benefit of people who see through it. If they can't trust themselves to be chaste and holy, why don't they just keep to their own quarters? While if they do want to be chaste and holy, why don't they stick to that other Gospel passage, "Christ began to do and to teach"?* Let them practise first and preach afterwards. I've seen thousands of them in my day, flirting, courting, philandering—and they include some of the biggest pulpit-thumpers. Moreover it's not only women in the world they go after, it's the nuns as well.

'Are these, then, the sort of people we're going to follow? Those who do so are doing as they want, but God knows if they're acting wisely. Still, even supposing that the friar's rebuke cannot be gainsaid and that it is very wrong to violate your marital fidelity, is it not far worse to steal from a man? Is it not far worse to murder him, or to make him an outcast, a penniless vagrant? There's no denying it. A woman who has intimate relations with a man sins after nature; when she robs him or kills him or drives him out, she's acting with malice aforethought. I've already shown that you robbed Tedaldo, when you deprived him of yourself, whom you had given to him of your own free will. What's more, seeing that he was a part of you, you were the one to kill him, for it was no thanks to you, the way you treated him ever more harshly, if he didn't take his own life. And the law states that the person who is the occasion of an offence remains an accessory to the one who perpetrates it. And there's no denying that you were the cause of his banishment and of his seven years of vagrancy. You, therefore, committed a far graver sin under these three heads than ever you did by your intercourse with him. But stay: perhaps Tedaldo deserved these things? Absolutely not: you've admitted as much yourself and, besides, I know for a fact that he loves you more than his own self. No woman was ever more acclaimed, applauded, extolled above all other women than you were by him, if ever he was in a position to speak of you freely and candidly. Into your hands he committed all his well-being, all his honour, all his freedom. Was he not a young man of noble birth? Was he not among the most handsome men in town? Was he not accomplished in those skills that pertain to young men? Was he not popular, a favourite with one and all? You shan't deny it. So how could you harden your heart towards him all because of what some envious little ass of a friar had to say? I simply don't understand those women who are so wrong-headed they spurn the menfolk and fail to appreciate them, whereas, if they stop to think what sort of people they are and what nobility the Lord vested in men above all other beasts, they ought to take a pride in being loved by a man, they ought to cherish him above all else and devote all their thoughts to pleasing him so that he will never falter in his love for them. Well, you know well enough what *you* did under the impulse of a friar who will undoubtedly have been one of your fatties who stuff their faces with cream-buns—I expect he was aiming to step into the shoes of the man he was set on ousting. This, then, is the sin that Divine Justice was not going to leave unpunished, for it ever performs its task with even-handedness: just as you strove to detach yourself from Tedaldo without cause, so has your husband been needlessly plunged into danger and you into affliction on account of Tedaldo. And if you want to be delivered from it, here is what you must promise to do, and above all, do it: should Tedaldo ever happen to return here from his long exile, restore him to your favour, your love and affection, your intimacy, restore him to the position he occupied before you were silly enough to listen to that idiot friar.'

When the pilgrim ended his speech Ermellina, who had hung upon his every word, for they seemed to her as true as could be, was left convinced that her troubles stemmed from the offence she had heard him describe. 'Friend of God', she said, 'I see all too plainly how true are the things you've been saying, and, largely thanks to your pointing it out, I can see the friars for what they really are, though up till now I've always taken them for holy men. And assuredly I acknowledge how very wrong I was in the way I treated Tedaldo; and if I could, how gladly would I make amends in the manner you say—but how is this to be done? Tedaldo can't come back: he's dead, so I can't see the point of promising you something that cannot be fulfilled.'

'No, from what the Lord has revealed to me, Tedaldo is not dead. He's alive and in fine fettle, provided he's restored to your favour.'

'Now mind what you're saying: I saw him right outside my door and he was dead with any number of stab-wounds. I held him in these very arms and bathed his dead face with so many tears, which was maybe why some fellow started that shabby rumour.'

'Say what you will, I assure you that Tedaldo is alive; and if you want to have him back by making that promise, I trust you'll soon be seeing him.'

'Of course I will', said she. 'Nothing could make me happier than to see my husband freed without harm, and Tedaldo alive.'

Now Tedaldo felt the time had come to make himself known and to encourage Ermellina with more definite hopes for her husband. 'Listen', he said, 'I'm going to give you some comfort regarding your husband, but it means letting you into a great secret—you must guard it with your life and never betray it.'

They were all alone in an isolated spot, the lady feeling quite at ease with the pilgrim, who looked such a holy man. Tedaldo therefore pulled out a ring* given him by Ermellina the last night they were together, which he had kept with all possible care. 'Tell me, madam', he said as he showed it to her, 'do you recognize it?'

She recognized the ring on sight. 'Yes. I gave it to Tedaldo.'

The pilgrim stood up and promptly shook off his long, loose-fitting pilgrim's smock and plucked his hat off his head. 'How about me', he said in Florentine, 'do you recognize me?'

She recognized him for Tedaldo when she saw him, and was petrified with fear, as one is on sight of a dead man's ghost walking about. She did not fling herself at a Tedaldo returned to her from Cyprus, but made to flee from a Tedaldo come back from the dead.

'Come', he said, 'don't be alarmed! I am your Tedaldo, I'm alive and well, I never did die, I wasn't killed, whatever you and my brothers may think.'

This somewhat reassured her. She recognized his voice, and the more she looked at him the surer she was it must be he. So she burst into tears, threw her arms round his neck, kissed him, and cried: 'Tedaldo my darling, oh how welcome you are!'

Tedaldo hugged and kissed her, then said: 'We don't have time yet for a more intimate welcome. I've got to go and see to your getting Aldobrandino back safe and sound; I hope that before tomorrow is done you'll receive news to make you happy. If I have good news of his safety, as I think I'll have,

I'll want to come back to you tonight and tell you all about it at greater leisure than I can at this minute.'

He put on his hat and pilgrim's smock again, gave Ermellina another kiss and further words of comfort, then left. He went to the prison in which Aldobrandino was brooding on his imminent death rather than entertaining hopes for his release. Pretending to be a prison-visitor, the pilgrim was allowed in by the warders and he sat down beside Aldobrandino and said: 'I'm a friend, Aldobrandino. I'm sent to you by God in order to save you, for your innocence has stirred Him to compassion. So if you're willing to afford me a little present I shall ask of you out of reverence for Him, before tomorrow evening you shall without fail hear yourself pronounced free of guilt, whereas here you are expecting a sentence of death.'

'Since you are concerned for my safety, kind sir, you must indeed be a friend, even though I do not know you and cannot recall ever having seen you before. The truth is that I never did commit the crime for which people say I ought to be sentenced to death. I have done a great deal of other bad things, and perhaps they are what has brought me to this pass. But let me tell you this with due respect to the Lord: if He is now having mercy on me, there's nothing, however big, never mind small things, that I should not readily promise to do and, what's more, go ahead and do it. So ask whatever you will: if I survive, I'll do it absolutely without fail.'

'All I want of you is this', replied the pilgrim. 'Forgive Tedaldo's four brothers for bringing you to this pass in the belief that you were guilty of their brother's murder. Treat them as your friends and brothers if they come and ask your pardon for this.'

'No one but the victim knows the sweet taste of vengeance and how passionate is the craving for it', replied Aldobrandino. 'Still, if God is going to rescue me I shall willingly pardon them, I do so right now. If I get out of here alive, I'll arrange matters in a way you'll find wholly satisfactory.'

This gratified the pilgrim, who had nothing more he wished to add but earnestly entreated him to be of good heart, for by the end of the next day he would assuredly receive definite notice of his reprieve.

After leaving him he went to the Signoria* and had a private word with the gentleman entrusted with that office. 'We should eagerly strive, sir, each one of us, to bring the truth to light, and nobody more so than a man in your position: that way no sentence will fall upon people who have committed no offence, while the guilty will be punished. That's why I'm here, to see that things work out to your honour and the detriment of those who deserve to be punished. You have, as you know, taken harsh measures against Aldobrandino Palermini, imagining you've established for a fact that it was he who murdered Tedaldo Elisei; and you're on the point of condemning him to death. However, the allegation is false beyond a shadow of doubt, and I'm confident of proving this to you before this night is half done, and of delivering the young man's killers into your hands.'

The excellent fellow gave a willing ear to what the pilgrim was telling him, for he felt sorry for Aldobrandino. Tedaldo went into the question at some length, and later conducted him to the inn where the two innkeeper brothers and their maid were arrested without a blow struck, not long after they had gone to bed. To get at the truth of what had happened the authorities were minded to apply torture, but the prisoners would not let it come to that: they each singly and then all together confessed that they had been the ones to kill Tedaldo Elisei, whom they did not know. When asked their reason, they said that he had been bothering the wife of one of them while they were away from the inn, and had sought to violate her.

Being apprised of this, the pilgrim took his leave of the gentleman from the Signoria and made his way in secret to Ermellina's; he found her on her own waiting up for him, the rest of the household having retired to bed; she was equally anxious to hear glad tidings of her husband and to be fully reconciled with her Tedaldo. When he came in he smiled and told her: 'Cheer up my darling—you'll have your Aldobrandino back here safe and sound tomorrow, that is certain.' He gave her a full account of all he had done, the better to confirm her belief. Ermellina was as overjoyed as any woman ever was, meeting so suddenly with two such strokes of luck—getting Tedaldo back alive when she was convinced she had wept over his corpse, and seeing Aldobrandino out of danger when she was sure she would be grieving over his death only a few days hence. Affectionately she hugged and kissed her Tedaldo, and off they went to bed together, where they happily made peace with an abundance of good feelings and most satisfactorily took their pleasure with each other. As day dawned Tedaldo got up, after explaining to Ermellina what he proposed to do and urging her once again to keep it all to herself; still in his pilgrim dress, he left her house to attend to Aldobrandino at the proper time.

That morning the Signoria hastened to release Aldobrandino, feeling that all the facts were now in their possession; and a few days later the delinquents were beheaded on a conviction for homicide. So Aldobrandino was free again, much to his joy and that of his wife and all his friends and relations. Recognizing that it was all thanks to the pilgrim, they kept him as guest in their house for as long as he felt like staying in Florence, and here they could not do enough to entertain him—not least, Aldobrandino's wife, who knew the identity of their guest. After a few days, however, Tedaldo felt it was time to reconcile his brothers with Aldobrandino—he realized that not only did his reprieve expose their guilt, but also that they were frightened and went about armed; so he reminded Aldobrandino of his promise, and was told that he would readily honour it any time. The pilgrim, therefore, had a fine banquet made ready for the following day, at which Aldobrandino, his kinsmen, and their wives were to welcome the four brothers and their wives; Tedaldo himself would, he added, go straight round and invite them on his behalf to his banquet and reconciliation. Aldobrandino was quite happy with the pilgrim's proposals, so the pilgrim left there and then to find the four brothers. After exchanging such courtesies as the occasion required, he went on to persuade them easily enough, with irrefutable arguments, that they ought to ask Aldobrandino's pardon and win back his friendship. This done, he invited them and their wives to lunch with Aldobrandino the next day; on the security of his word, they did not hesitate to accept the invitation.

So the next morning Aldobrandino awaited Tedaldo's four brothers, who arrived in time for lunch dressed in black, together with some of their friends. Here, in the presence of everyone he had invited to share the occasion, they threw down their weapons and entrusted themselves to Aldobrandino, craving his pardon for the wrong they had done him. Aldobrandino, in tears, received them with compassion, giving them each a kiss on the lips and with a few hasty words forgiving them for every offence. Then their sisters and wives came up, all dressed in mourning, and were welcomed kindly by Ermellina and the other ladies.

They had all, the women no less than the men, been given the best of everything at the banquet, which could not be faulted in any particular save one: the reticence of Tedaldo's family, who were but recently plunged into mourning, as their dark attire bore witness; (in fact some of them had criticized the pilgrim's initiative and the invitation, as he was aware). However, when the time came to be done with this taciturnity, Tedaldo stood up, just as he had planned, while the guests were still at the fruit course, and said: 'There's only one thing missing to make this meal a really happy event and that is Tedaldo. As he has been here with you all the time and you have not recognized him, I'm going to reveal him to you.'

He threw off his pilgrim's attire, smock and all, and stood in a gorgeous green silk costume,* while they all gazed at him in amazement before any of them would risk identifying him as Tedaldo. Seeing this, Tedaldo spoke to them at length about their degrees of kindred, family matters, and his own adventures, until his brothers and the other men, all weeping for joy, ran to embrace him, and so did the womenfolk, whether they were relatives or not, all except for Ermellina.

'What?' cried Aldobrandino when he noticed this. 'Ermellina, why aren't you greeting Tedaldo as the other ladies are doing?'

Everybody listened as she answered: 'There's not a woman who would welcome him with better will than I, for none of them are as greatly beholden to him, considering that it's thanks to him that I have you back. What's stopping me are the scurrilous things that were being said at the time when we were still grieving over the man we took to be Tedaldo.'

'Fiddlesticks!' cried Aldobrandino. 'Do you think I believe those gossips? Tedaldo saved me and so proved well enough what rubbish they were talking, not that I ever swallowed it. Come on, go and give him a hug.'

Ermellina, who had no other wish, was not slow in obeying this instruction from her husband; up she got and went, as the other women had done, to greet him with her happiest embrace. Tedaldo's brothers and everyone else who was present, man and woman, were delighted with Aldobrandino's magnanimity; it served to dispel the last trace of ill feeling to which the rumour had given rise in some people's minds. When they had all given a welcome to Tedaldo, he himself ripped his brothers' black attire and their wives' and his sisters' brown dresses, and insisted on sending for other garments. When they had put these on, the place was given over to singing and dancing and all manner of entertainments, so that if the banquet had started on a quiet note, it ended fortissimo. Then off they all went in the best of spirits, just as they were, to Tedaldo's house for supper. Indeed they prolonged the celebrations for several days more in the same strain.

For many a day the Florentines stared at Tedaldo as at some sort of prodigy, a man back from the dead. A little lingering doubt remained in many people's minds, not excluding his brothers', as to whether it really was he; they still were not wholly convinced, and perhaps they would not have been for ages, were it not for something that happened which cleared up the question of the dead man's identity. Here is what occurred:

One day some soldiers from the Lunigiana passed in front of their house; noticing Tedaldo with his brothers, they went up to him and said: 'Why hallo there, Faziuolo!'

'You've got the wrong man', returned Tedaldo, in his brothers' presence.

Hearing him speak, the soldiers were mortified. 'Begging your pardon', they said. 'The fact is, we've never seen a fellow look so much like another as you look like our mate Faziuolo. He's from Pontremoli and came here, oh, about a couple of weeks ago. Never caught hide nor hair of him since. We *were* a bit startled by your costume, of course—he was only a plain soldier like us.'

At this Tedaldo's eldest brother stepped forward and asked what this Faziuolo had been wearing. They told him, and what they said accorded perfectly with the facts; from this and other indications it was clear that the murdered man must have been Faziuolo and not Tedaldo, who thereupon excited no further suspicions in his brothers or in anyone else. Tedaldo, who had returned to Florence a very rich man, persevered in his love for Ermellina, who never again took against him; by operating with stealth they enjoyed their love for a long time. God grant we may enjoy ours.

III. 8. *As a cure for jealousy Ferondo is sent for a spell in Purgatory, while his wife obtains consolation from a holy abbot.*

Emilia's story reached its conclusion. For all its length, none of them found it wearisome, indeed, they felt that it had gone at a swinging pace, so many different things happened in it. Then the queen gave the nod to Lauretta, who took her cue and began:

It looks to me as if I'll have to tell you a true story that has every appearance of being utter moonshine. I was put in mind of it after hearing the story of a man buried and lamented in the mistaken belief that he was somebody else. This one is about a living man who was buried for dead and then resurrected; many people, himself included, took him for a man back from the dead—and the man who wrought this wonder, far from getting any blame, was worshipped thereafter as a saint.

There was once an abbey in Tuscany (it's still there), located, as they tend to be, in quite an unfrequented spot. The monk elected abbot was of supreme holiness in all matters save one—women; these he pursued so furtively, however, that practically no one ever found out or even suspected him. He was deemed irreproachable on every score.

Now there was a very wealthy rustic who had struck up a friendship with the abbot; his name was Ferondo and he was a man of quite exceptional stupidity; the only reason the abbot endured his friendship was that he derived a certain simple pleasure out of occasionally pulling his leg. What their friendship did bring to the abbot's notice, however, was that the bumpkin had a most gorgeous wife—he fell head over heels in love with her and could think of nothing else, day or night. Ferondo, however, might be a total fool in all else, but when it came to taking care of his wife he was as shrewd as could be; when the abbot realized this, he was wellnigh driven to despair. But he still had the wit to persuade Ferondo to bring his wife from time to time to enjoy the delights of the monastery garden; here he would converse with them very simply on such topics as the bliss of life eternal, and the holy deeds of so many men and women of old, until eventually the wife conceived the wish to go to the abbot for confession; she sought her husband's leave and received it.

So she went to make her confession to the abbot, much to his delight, sat down at his feet, and said, by way of preamble: 'Father, if God had given me a proper husband or none at all, maybe I'd find some way to follow your teaching and take the path you speak of, that leads to eternal life. But when you think what sort of a man Ferondo is, and that he's as stupid as they come, you could say that I'm really a widow, even if I'm married—while he's around I can't take another husband. As well as being plain stupid, he's so madly jealous without the slightest cause, I tell you, living with him is a constant trial. So before I start my confession I beg you as humbly as I can please to give me your advice on this question; because if I can't make a start here to finding some answer to my problem, going to confession won't do me much good, nor will any other good deed.'

The abbot was delighted to hear this, and felt that Fortune had opened the way for him to achieve his greatest wish. 'My daughter', he said, 'it must indeed be a veritable nuisance for a beautiful and refined lady like you to be saddled with an oaf of a husband, and it must be ten times worse if he's jealous. As he is both, I can well believe what you say about your problem. I can't really see any solution to this, save one, and that is, in a word, to cure Ferondo of his jealousy. Now I know perfectly well how to effect the cure, but only if you can find it in yourself to keep quiet about what I am going to say to you.'

'Don't worry about that, father. I'd sooner die than say anything you told me to keep to myself. So how is this going to be done?'

'If we want him to be cured', said the abbot, 'he's going to have to go to Purgatory.'

'How can he do that if he's alive?'

'He's going to have to die and go to Purgatory. And when he's suffered a sufficient penalty to purge him of his jealousy, we'll ask the Lord—there are certain prayers for this—to bring him back to life, and He will do so.'

'You mean, I'll be widowed?'

'That's right', said the abbot. 'For a little while: and during this time you must take good care not to remarry, or the Good Lord won't like it, and when Ferondo returns you'll have to go back to him, and he'll be more jealous than ever.'

'If only he's cured of this rotten habit of his, and I don't go on having to live like a prisoner, I don't mind. Do carry on.'

'All right then', said the abbot. 'But what will my reward be for this service?'

'Whatever you suggest, father, so long as it's possible. But what suitable gift can a woman like me give to a man in your position?'

'You can do no less for me than I'm going to do for you: what I'm about to do for you will be conducive to your satisfaction—similarly you can do something for me that will afford *me* satisfaction.'

'In that case', said the woman, 'I'm at your service.'

'Good', said the abbot. 'Give me your love, make me happy: I feel quite passionate about you.'

The woman was dumbfounded. 'Good heavens, father, what's that you said? Here was I thinking you were a saint! How comes it that a holy man makes that kind of proposition to a lady who goes to him for advice?'

'Well don't be so surprised, sweetheart', cried the abbot. 'This won't make me one jot less holy; holiness resides in the spirit, you see, while what I'm after is a sin of the flesh. At all events, Love leaves me no choice, I'm so smitten with your beauty. Nay you, more than any other woman, should take pride in your beauty, considering that holy men take pleasure in it—after all, they are used to contemplating the beauties of heaven. Besides, I may be an abbot but I'm still a man like any other and, as you see, not all that old. So you won't find it burdensome, I assure you, in fact it should be just what you're wanting; while Ferondo is in Purgatory I'll keep you company at night and give you the sort of comforts he would have given you. No one will ever find out, either, as they all take me for the sort of person you did till just now. Don't reject the gift God is sending you; scores of women would love to have what's being offered to you, and which will be yours if you're sensible and take my word for it. Added to that, I have some lovely gems, very valuable ones, and I don't propose to give them to anyone but you. So, my pet, do for me what I'm ready enough to do for you.'

The woman would not meet his eyes, and did not know how to refuse him, even though to concede must, she felt, be wrong. The abbot, however, noticed that she had listened to him closely and was hesitant in replying, so he reckoned that she was already half convinced; he kept on talking, therefore, until she was quite persuaded that what he was asking was maybe all right. So she answered, somewhat bashfully, that she would do whatever he asked, although she could not until Ferondo had gone to Purgatory.

'We'll see to it at once', said the abbot gleefully. 'Send him over to me tomorrow or the day after.' He furtively slipped a pretty ring into her hand and bade her goodbye. The woman was charmed with the gift, and with the prospect of more to come; she rejoined her companions and on their way home told them marvellous things about the abbot's holiness.

A day or two later Ferondo went to the abbey; when the abbot caught sight of him he set about sending him to Purgatory. A great prince, somewhere out in the Levant, had once given him a powder which the Old Man of the Mountain,* he assured him, was in the habit of using when he wanted to send someone to his Paradise, or recall him from it: the powder sent the recipient to sleep—a lighter or heavier sleep according to dosage—without the least ill effect, and the sleeper looked to all appearances dead while the effect lasted. The abbot now went for this powder and took as much as he needed to assure him of three days' sleep; then he took some wine that had not yet settled clear, and poured out a glassful with the powder in it and gave it to the unsuspecting Ferondo to drink, in his cell. After this he took him out into the cloisters, and, in the company of other monks, started teasing him.

It wasn't long before the powder took effect and Ferondo was stricken with a sudden torpor: he fell asleep on his feet and collapsed. The abbot made a show of alarm; he had Ferondo's clothes loosened and sent for cold water to throw in his face and issued a whole string of further orders, as though he were trying to revive him after an attack of the vapours. However, none of these measures brought the man round, as the abbot and monks could see; they felt for a pulse-beat but there was none—so they had to conclude that he was dead. Then they sent for his wife and relatives, who soon arrived and wept over him a little, after which the abbot laid him, dressed as he was, in a tomb.

The wife returned home and announced that she did not propose to be parted from the little boy she had had by Ferondo. So she settled down to look after her home, her child, and her property, which had been Ferondo's.

In the night the abbot got up quietly and went to lift Ferondo out of his tomb with the help of a monk he trusted, a Bolognese who had just this day arrived from Bologna; they put him in a cellar that never saw the light of day—it had been built as a punishment cell for monks. They undressed him and clothed him in a monk's habit; then they laid him on a straw pallet and left him to recover consciousness. Meanwhile the Bolognese monk, who had his orders from the abbot, waited for Ferondo to come round. No one else knew a thing about it.

The next day the abbot went with some of his monks to the woman's home on the pretext of a courtesy call; he found her dressed in black and grieving, so he offered some words of consolation, then quietly reminded her of her promise. Realizing that she was no longer tied down by Ferondo or anyone else, and spotting another nice ring on his finger, she told him she was ready and they arranged to meet that night.

So when night came the abbot, disguised in Ferondo's clothes and accompanied by his monk, went and shared her bed—a delicious experience—then returned to the abbey. This journey was to become all too frequent. Occasionally he would run into someone, coming or going, and the word soon did the rounds of the village rustics to the effect that Ferondo was roaming about the neighbourhood as a penance; his wife got to hear the rumour more than once, though of course she knew where matters stood.

When Ferondo came to his senses he had no idea where he was. Then in came the Bolognese monk, speaking in a terrible voice and brandishing a bundle of rods with which he gave him a thorough thrashing.

All Ferondo could do was to weep and yell and keep asking: 'Where am I?'

'You're in Purgatory', answered the monk.

'What? Am I dead, then?'

'Of course!'

Ferondo burst again into tears for himself, his wife, and child, and came out with the oddest babblings.

Then the monk brought him something to eat and drink. 'What, do the dead eat?' exclaimed Ferondo.

'Yes. And what I am bringing you comes from the wife you used to have: she brought it to church this morning as a Mass-offering for the repose of your soul and the Good Lord wills that it be set before you.'

'Well, God bless her! I loved her very dearly before I died; I'd hold her in my arms all night long and would never stop kissing her—and something else besides, when I felt the urge.' This said, he fell to his food and drink with a will. The wine, however, seemed to him none too good. 'God damn her—she didn't give the priest the wine from the cask by the wall!'

When he had finished eating, the monk took up the rods again and gave him another thrashing.

'Hey, why are you doing this to me?' cried Ferondo, after much bawling.

'You're to get this twice a day; the Lord said so.'

'Why?'

'Because you were jealous, though you had the best wife in the neighbourhood.'

'How right you are', sighed Ferondo; 'the sweetest, too; she was a real honey-bun. But I never knew that the Lord didn't care for jealous men or I wouldn't have been one.'

'You should have realized this and mended your ways when you were still on earth. If you ever get back there, take care to remember what I'm doing to you now, and don't be jealous ever again.'

'Do the dead ever go back?'

'Yes, if God wills.'

'Oh', said Ferondo, 'if ever I get back there, I'll be the best husband in the world; I'll never beat her, I'll never speak to her unkindly—except about the wine she's just sent me. And she never sent me a candle either: how am I supposed to eat in the dark?'

'She did send some, but they were burned at Mass.'

'Well, I expect you're right. If I go back, I'll certainly let her do as she likes. But tell me, who are you, carrying on this way?'

'I'm dead too', said the monk. 'I'm from Sardinia. My master was a jealous man, and as I encouraged him in this, God has doomed me to this punishment—to furnish you with food and drink and thrashings until He makes some other provision for the two of us.'

'Is it just the two of us?'

'There are thousands of us, but you can't see or hear the rest, nor they you.'

'How far are we from home?'

'How far? It's twice there and four times back and then some.'

'Phew! That's a long way! Seems to me that where we are now must be quite out of this world!'

Discussions like this, mealtimes, thrashings marked the passage of ten months during which Ferondo was held prisoner—and during which the abbot ventured forth on frequent visits to the pretty lady and enjoyed her favours most delectably. But all good things come to an end: the lady got pregnant, and told the abbot the moment she knew. It struck both of them that they had to release Ferondo from Purgatory and restore him to life (and to her) at once, so she could say she was pregnant by him.

So that night the abbot went to Ferondo's prison and called out to him, disguising his voice: 'Ferondo, be of good cheer.

It is God's will that you return to the world. There, you will have a child by your wife, and you shall call him Benedict,* because it is through the prayers of your holy abbot and of your wife, and for love of Saint Benedict, that this favour is being granted you.'

Ferondo was delighted to hear this. 'How splendid', he said. 'God bless the Good Lord and the abbot and Saint Benedict and my little wife, that yummy-scrummy little sugar-plum.'

The abbot sent him some wine mixed with sufficient of the powder to put him to sleep for a good four hours. He dressed him once more in his own attire and with his monk's help secretly returned him to the tomb in which he had been laid. Ferondo came to at daybreak; in his tomb he saw a chink of light, the first he had seen in some ten months. He felt he was alive and started to yell 'Let me out! Let me out!' and shoved so hard against the tomb's lid with his head that little by little he shifted it off (the lid was not immovable). The monks were just out from Matins; they ran to the tomb, and as they recognized Ferondo's voice and saw him stepping forth they were terrified—they had never seen such a thing—and dashed off to the abbot.

The abbot, pretending to rise from his prayers, said: 'Never fear, my children. Take the crucifix and the holy water and follow me. Let us see what God in His might wishes to show us.'

Hidden from the daylight for so long, Ferondo was all pale when he came out of the tomb. On seeing the abbot he ran to throw himself at his feet and said: 'Father, your prayers and those of Saint Benedict and my wife, so I've been told, have freed me from the pains of Purgatory and brought me back to life. And I pray God send you a good year today and yesterday and so on.'

'Praise be to God in His power', said the abbot. 'Go, my son, since the Lord has restored you to us, and comfort your wife, who has been in tears ever since you departed this life; and from henceforth be a friend and servant of the Most High.'

'Well put, father', exclaimed Ferondo. 'Just leave it to me: I'll be kissing her the moment I get to her, I love her so much.'

Left with his monks, the abbot feigned no little astonishment at what had happened and had a devout Miserere intoned.

Ferondo returned home. Everyone who saw him fled as from some horrid sight, but he would call them back and insist that he had come back from the dead. His wife too was afraid of him.

Eventually the people accepted his assurances, seeing that he really was a living person; they put all manner of questions to him, as if he'd come back less addled than before, and he brought them all news of their dear departed, inventing the most remarkable stories about Purgatory, and announcing to all the revelation made to him by the Archangel Gabigrael before he resurrected. So he returned home to his wife, resumed possession of his worldly goods, got her pregnant—or so he imagined—and after a suitable interval (the prevailing opinion of the simple-minded accords a woman precisely nine months' gestation) his wife gave birth to a boy, christened Benedict Ferondi.

In view of Ferondo's return and his testimony, nearly everyone believed that he had risen from the dead, which greatly enhanced the abbot's reputation for sanctity. As for Ferondo, who had received such a drubbing on account of his jealousy, he was cured of it and was never jealous again, thus fulfilling the abbot's promise to his wife. She was happy enough to live with him virtuously as before—and indeed, when the occasion offered, she would willingly consort with the holy abbot, who had served her so faithfully and well in her greatest need.

III. 9. *Giletta marries a very reluctant husband, Beltram, who escapes to Florence without consummating the marriage. To keep her away he imposes two conditions for his return that she could never (he believes) fulfil. But Giletta is nothing if not resourceful.*

If she was not to infringe Dioneo's privilege, no one was left to speak apart from the queen, now that Lauretta had finished her tale. So she awaited no prompting from her subjects but began pleasantly enough:

Who will come out with a really satisfying story after hearing Lauretta's? Certainly it has been all to the good that she was not the first to speak, for not many of the subsequent ones would have found favour, and indeed I fear that the rest of the stories to be told today will fail in this. At all events, I'll tell you the story, such as it is, that comes to mind on today's theme.

In the Kingdom of France there was once a gentleman called Isnard, Count of Roussillon. As his health was poor, he was constantly accompanied by a physician called Gerard of Narbonne. The count had an only son called Beltram, a very handsome and agreeable lad who was brought up with other children of his age; among these was a daughter of the physician, called Giletta, who fell in love with Beltram to a degree scarcely suitable to one of her tender years. Now when the count died, the boy was made a ward of the Crown and had to move to Paris, which left the girl not a little distressed. Her own father died not long after, and she would willingly have gone to Paris to see Beltram, had she found some unexceptionable excuse for the visit. She could not determine any, however, for she had been left a solitary rich girl and was therefore closely guarded. She was now of marriageable age but, as she had never been able to put Beltram out of her mind, she had rejected many men to whom her family had wanted to marry her, without giving the reason.

Now as she continued to burn more than ever for love of Beltram, who had grown (she heard) into a quite dazzling young man, news reached her about the King of France: a growth on his chest which had been badly tended had left him with a fistula that caused him no end of pain and misery. And although numerous doctors had exercised their skills on him, one had yet to be found who could effect a cure. Indeed, they had all contrived to make matters worse. As a result the king had quite lost hope, and was now rejecting all medical treatment and advice. This news left Giletta absolutely delighted: not only did it give her, she felt, a legitimate excuse to go to Paris but, if the disease was what she believed it was, she would obtain Beltram for her spouse without the slightest difficulty. She had learnt a great deal from her father, so she made up a powder from certain herbs that were beneficial to what she took to be the affection in question, and travelled to Paris on horseback. The first thing she did on arrival was to endeavour to set eyes on Beltram; then she came into the king's presence and asked him to favour her with sight of his infirmity. Seeing that she was a pretty and attractive young woman, the king could not refuse, and showed it to her.

The moment she examined it she was confident that she could cure it. 'My liege', she said, 'if it is your pleasure, I place my hope in God to be able to cure you of this disease within a week, all without afflicting or wearying you.'

These words left the king snorting to himself: 'The world's greatest physicians have been powerless against this disease—what can a young woman know about it?' So he thanked her for her kind thought but advised her that he had decided to follow no further doctors' prescriptions.

'You despise my skills because I am young and a woman, my liege', she said. 'But I should have you know that my treatments are not based on my own medical knowledge but on the help of the Good Lord and on the skills Gerard of Narbonne, who was my father and a famous physician in his day.'

Then, 'Perhaps she has been sent to me by God', the king mused. 'Why don't I find out what she can do, as she says she can cure me in a short while without putting me to any discomfort?' So he decided to give it a try and said: 'Tell me, young lady, if you make us reverse our decision but you fail to cure us, what would you like to result from that?'

'Keep me under guard, my liege. And if I haven't cured you within a week, have me burnt at the stake. But if I do heal you, what reward will come my way?'

'You appear to have no husband. If you do that, we will bestow you right nobly and well.'

'How glad I should be, my liege, if you marry me off; but the husband I want is none other than the one I shall request from you. I shall not be asking you for any son of yours, nor for any member of the royal house.'

This the king promised there and then, and the girl began her treatment. Briefly, she restored him to health ahead of the appointed time and, finding himself cured, he assured her that she had certainly earned herself a husband.

'In that case, my liege', said she, 'I have earned Beltram of Roussillon. I fell in love with him as a little girl and have been deeply in love with him ever since.'

This struck the king as a great deal to ask, but as he had given his word he was not going to repudiate it. He sent for Beltram and said to him: 'You're a grown man now, Beltram, and we want you to return to govern your province. You're to take with you a young woman we have bestowed upon you as your wife.'

'Who is the young woman, my liege?'

'She is the one who has restored me to health with her medicine.'

Beltram knew her and had seen her before; beautiful though he found her, he was aware that she did not come from a class that assorted well with his own rank, and he petulantly replied: 'What, my liege? Do you want to give me a woman who practises medicine as my wife? God forbid that I should ever bestow myself upon a woman of that sort!'

'Is it your wish, then, that we should fail to honour our word? You it was whom the young woman requested for husband, as the reward for restoring us to health, and this was our promise to her.'

'My liege', said Beltram, 'you may take from me all that I possess; you may bestow me upon whom you please, for I am your man. But take my word for it: never shall I be happy with a match such as this.'

'Of course you will! She is a beautiful young lady, she is clever, and she loves you very much. Therefore we hope that you will enjoy a far more blissful life with her than you would do with a lady of higher rank.'

Beltram held his peace, and the king set in hand great preparations to solemnize the betrothal. When the appointed day arrived, Beltram, in the presence of the king, with the greatest reluctance pledged his troth to Giletta, who so adored him. This accomplished, he took his leave of the king, saying that he wished to return to his own province and there to consummate his marriage. In fact he had already decided what he was going to do: he took horse and rode away, not to his own land but to Tuscany. The Florentines were at war with the Sienese, as he discovered, and he chose to take their side: so he was welcomed gladly and with every honour by the Florentines who put him in command of a band of men and paid him a handsome salary. He spent a considerable time in their service.

This turn of affairs afforded little joy to the bride, but she hoped that if she behaved well enough she might recall her husband to his estates; so she proceeded to Roussillon, where everybody welcomed her as their liege-lady. Here she found that in the prolonged absence of any count everything had gone to rack and ruin, so she applied her wisdom, her every care and solicitude to restoring order. This was eminently to the satisfaction of her subjects, who responded to her with the greatest love and devotion, while they thought very ill of the count for failing to be content with her. After Giletta had set the whole province to rights, she sent two knights to advise the count of this, and to ask him to tell her if he was keeping away from his estates on her account, in which case she would satisfy him by taking herself off. His reply was as dour as could be: 'She may do whatever she pleases', he told them. 'As for me, I'll go back to her when she wears this ring on her finger and carries in her arms a child conceived of me.' The ring was one he prized beyond all telling and never took off, for it possessed some particular virtue—so he had been given to understand. The knights grasped the difficulty of the condition underlying these two virtually impossible requirements; seeing that he was not to be budged from his position by any word of theirs, they returned to their lady and reported his answer. She was greatly distressed but, after much consideration, determined to find out whether these two things might be accomplished and, if so, where, in order to recover her husband. Once she had seen how she was to proceed, she called together some of the best and most prominent men in the land and set before them most precisely, and indeed movingly, everything that she had done for love of the count, and what had been the result; she concluded by telling them that she had no intention of keeping the count in perpetual exile because of her residence here: rather, she proposed to devote the rest of her days to pilgrimages and to works of mercy for the salvation of her soul. She besought them to undertake the government and safe-keeping of the province and to advise the count that she had left the state to him free and unencumbered, and had gone away resolved never more to set foot in Roussillon. As she spoke, the good folk shed many a tear and begged her please to change her mind and stay; but it was all to no avail.

She bade them goodbye and set out on her journey, with a male cousin and a maidservant for company, dressed as pilgrims, and well supplied with money and expensive jewellery. Nobody knew whither she was bound, and she did not pause to rest until she had arrived in Florence. Here she happened to stop at a small inn kept by a good widow, and here she remained discreetly, in the guise of a poor pilgrim, as she hankered for news of her lord and master. Well, the next day she happened to see Beltram ride past the inn with his squadron. Although she recognized him perfectly well, she asked her hostess who the man was.

'He is a foreign gentleman', her hostess said; 'his name is Count Beltram and he is a charming, gallant man whom everyone is fond of. He's head over heels in love with a neighbour of ours, a woman of gentle birth but no means. A thoroughly upright young lady she is, who has not yet got married on account of being so poor; she lives with her mother, a really good, wise woman. Were it not for her, it's possible that she would by now have fallen in with the count's wishes.'

The countess paid close attention to these words and pondered over them in detail; and once they were absolutely clear in her mind she made a decision. She discovered the names of the lady and her daughter, the count's beloved, and the house in which they lived, and paid them a discreet visit one day, dressed as a pilgrim. She found mother and daughter in very straitened circumstances and, after greeting them, told the mother that, if she did not mind, she would be glad of a word with her.

The mother stood up and said she was ready to listen to her, so they went, just the two of them, into her bedroom and sat themselves down. 'It looks to me', the countess began, 'that

Fortune is proving as hostile to you as she is to me. If you're willing, though, you may well be able to do yourselves and me a good turn.'

'There's nothing I should like better than to mend my fortune by any honest means.'

'Then I'm going to need your word', pursued the countess; 'if I take you into my confidence and you betray me, you'll spoil things for yourself as well as for me.'

'Tell me anything you like. I'll never be the one to betray you.'

Then the countess told her who she was and all that had happened to her, starting with her first falling in love and carrying her story up to this day; and the mother fully believed her, for she had already heard parts of it from other sources, and the way she was told it left her feeling quite sorry for her. After explaining her situation the countess went on: 'Now, along with all my troubles you've heard what the two things are that I need to obtain if I am to recover my husband. And there's only one person I know who might help me obtain them and that is you, if there's any truth in what I'm told, that my husband is passionately in love with your daughter.'

'Whether the count loves my daughter I really don't know; he makes a great show of doing so. But what is it that you would like me to do about it?'

'I will tell you. But first I'll have you know what I propose should be the result of your assisting me: I notice that your daughter is a pretty girl, and old enough to be married; and from what I've heard and believe I've understood, you're keeping her at home for lack of a dowry to give her away with. The reward I propose for the service you are going to do me is to give her at once, out of my own funds, such a dowry as you yourself would consider suitable in order to find her an honourable match.'

Needy as the mother was, she was attracted by the offer; however, given her rectitude, she replied: 'Just tell me, madam, how I may be of service to you and, if it be consistent with my virtue, I will readily do it. For the rest, you're to do as you think fit.'

'What I need', said the countess, 'is for you to send word to my husband the count, by some person on whom you can rely, to say that your daughter is ready to do his every pleasure provided she can be assured that he loves her as much as he claims to do. The only thing that will convince her of this is if he sends her the ring he wears on his finger, which she has heard he is so attached to. If he does send it to you, you're to pass it to me. After that, you'll send word to him to say that your daughter is ready to do his pleasure, and you'll arrange for him to come here in secret and for me to take your daughter's place beside him. Perhaps God will grant me the favour of conceiving so that, with his ring on my finger and his baby in my arms, I shall recover him and live with him as a wife ought to live with her husband—and it will all have been thanks to you.'

To the good lady this seemed no trifling matter, for she was troubled at the idea of compromising her daughter. She concluded, however, that it was perfectly fair to arrange for the countess to win back her spouse, and that the countess was venturing upon this step for a perfectly valid purpose so, relying upon the purity of her intention, she gave the countess her word. Furthermore, she discreetly obtained the ring within a few days, in accordance with the countess's instructions—not that the count was all that eager to part with it—and she cleverly contrived for the lady to take the girl's place in bed with the count. Now during those first couplings that the count sought with such ardour, it pleased the Good Lord to leave the countess pregnant with twin boys—as became evident in due course when she gave birth. Though it was not once but several times that the kind lady gave the countess the satisfaction of making love with her husband, she contrived everything in such secrecy that not a word of it ever got out and the count went on believing that he had been to bed with his beloved, not with his wife. Indeed, when he came to leave her in the morning he would make her a present of many fine, expensive jewels which the countess carefully treasured.

Finding herself pregnant, Giletta had no desire to put the lady to further trouble, so she told her: 'Thanks to the Good Lord and to you, I have what I wanted, and therefore the time has come for me to fulfil your wishes, after which I can leave.'

The lady replied that she was only too pleased if the countess had received something that was to her liking; but she had not done anything in anticipation of a reward, she was merely doing a good deed to which she felt in duty bound.

'How very kind', said the countess. 'And for my part, I'm not proposing to give you what you ask of me simply as a reward but because it is right and proper and seems to me the correct thing to do.'

Constrained as she was by penury, the lady made a very bashful request for a hundred lire with which to marry her daughter. Noticing her embarrassment as she listened to her polite request, the countess presented her with five hundred lire together with fine, costly jewellery to most likely the same value. The lady was overjoyed and thanked the countess as best she could. The countess took her leave and returned to the inn. Now to deprive Beltram of any further excuse to send word to her or to make his visits, the lady left with her daughter for the country to stay with relatives. A little while later Beltram received a summons from his folk in Roussillon and, on hearing that the countess had vanished, he returned home.

When she heard that Beltram had left Florence and returned to his own estates the countess was very pleased. She stayed in Florence until her time came to give birth: she produced twin boys, the spitting image of their father, and took care to put them out to nurse. When the time seemed ripe she set out with them on her journey and reached Montpellier without being recognized by anybody. Here she rested for several days, while she made discreet enquiries after the count and his present whereabouts. She discovered that he was to play host to a great gathering of knights and ladies in Roussillon on the Feast of All Saints, so that is where she went, still dressed in her customary pilgrim's attire.

Once she saw that the knights and ladies had assembled in the count's palace to go in to dine, she climbed the stairs, with her babies in her arms and still in the same pilgrim dress, picked her way among the menfolk to where she saw the count, and threw herself, weeping, at his feet. 'My lord', she cried, 'I am your unhappy wife. I've been roaming about the world for ages in order to leave you free to return home. Now I'm asking you in God's name to abide by the conditions you imposed upon me when you saw the two knights I sent to you. Look, here in my arms are not one but two sons of yours; and here is your ring. It is time, therefore, that you accept me for your wife, according to your promise.'

The count was utterly staggered at this, recognizing the ring as he did, and the children too, for they looked like him. 'What on earth's been going on?' he asked.

The countess described everything that had happened, from beginning to end, leaving the count and all the rest of the assembly quite amazed. As for the count, he recognized the truth of what she had described and noted how artful and tenacious she had been; he looked at the two children—such a pretty pair—and, in order to adhere to his promise and to satisfy his ladies and gentlemen, who were pressing him to accept her with honour as his lawful wedded wife, he overcame his stubborn hostility and drew her to her feet. He gave her a hug and kiss and acknowledged her as his true wife and the babies as his own. He had her dressed in becoming attire and continued the celebrations most festively, not only for the rest of the day but for several days beyond, to the huge delight of all those present and indeed of all his other vassals who came to hear of it. And from that day forth he treated her with the respect due to a wife and consort, and loved and cherished her above all things.

III. 10. *Young Alibek joins a desert hermit in the service of the Lord; she willingly helps him to put the devil back into hell.*

Dioneo had closely followed the queen's narrative. When he heard her finish, as his was the only story waiting to be told, without awaiting the command, he smiled and began:

I don't suppose you charming ladies ever heard how the devil is to be consigned to hell, so I shall scarcely be departing from the topic you have been concentrating on the whole day if I tell you. Conceivably when you've learnt how it's done it will help you save your souls. And for all that Love prefers to reside in prosperous palaces and cosy bedrooms than in pauper's shacks, you'll discover that he does, none the less, occasionally make himself felt in the depths of the forest, among the stark mountains and in desert caves—which goes to show that all things are subject to Love's power.

Well, then, in a city of the Barbary coast, Gafsa by name, there once lived an extremely rich man. One of his children was a pretty girl of charming manners, called Alibek. She was not a Christian, but had heard many of her Christian neighbours speak highly of their own faith and the service of God; so one day she asked one of them how this service of God was performed, what was the simplest way to go about it. He told her that those people best served God who most avoided the things of this world, like those who had sought the solitude of the Egyptian desert round Thebes. So Alibek, who was a very naïve 14-year-old (or thereabouts), didn't breathe a word to a soul but slipped away all on her own the next morning in the direction of the Theban desert, motivated by a childish enthusiasm rather than by any well-considered inclination. It was an exhausting journey but, buoyed up by her enthusiasm, she reached those lonely parts a few days later. Seeing a hut in the distance, she turned her steps towards it and found a holy man standing at the door; he was surprised to find her here and asked her what it was she was looking for. She told him that God had inspired her to seek to enter His service, and also to seek for one to teach her the best way she might serve Him.

Seeing how young and comely she was, the good man was afraid the devil would ensnare him, should he keep her; so, after praising her virtuous disposition and feeding her on root vegetables, wild apples, and dates, with water to drink, he told her: 'My daughter, not far from here there's a holy man who'll instruct you far better than I can in the thing you are seeking for. Go to him.' And he sent her on her way.

She went to him, therefore, and he addressed her in the selfsame words, so on she continued till she reached the cell of a young hermit called Rustico, who was as good and pious as could be, and she made the same request of him as she had of the others. Now he, anxious to put his constancy to the test, did not send her away or pass her on as the others had done, but kept her in his cell. And when it was night, he prepared for her a bed of palm-fronds in one corner and told her to lie down there to rest.

This done, it took no time at all for his resistance to come under attack from Temptation, which easily got the upper hand, so he turned tail after rather few assaults and conceded victory. Leaving to one side all pious thoughts and devotions and holy disciplines, he indulged himself in dwelling upon her youth and beauty, and in considering ways and means to persuade her towards his goal without leaving her to think that he was a dissolute man. First he tentatively questioned her and established that she had no previous carnal knowledge of men and was every whit as simple as she appeared to be—which indicated to him the way to bend her to his pleasure under guise of serving the Lord. First he devoted many words to explaining to her what an enemy to God the devil was; then he gave her to understand that the service the Good Lord found the most pleasing was to put the devil back into hell, to which the Lord had condemned him.

How, the girl asked him, was this done. 'That you'll know in a moment', said Rustico. 'Just watch what I do and copy me.' He stripped off the few garments he was wearing and was left naked; the girl did likewise. Then he kneeled down as if to pray and made her kneel facing him.

In this posture, as Rustico's appetite was stoked up at the sight of such a beauty, he experienced the resurrection of the flesh, and Alibek looked on in amazement. 'Rustico', she said, 'what's that thing you've got there sticking out that way? I don't have one.'

'Oh my daughter', said Rustico. 'This is the devil I've been telling you about. Look, he's making such a nuisance of himself I can hardly bear it.'

'Well God be praised!' cried the girl. 'I see that I'm better off than you, for *I* don't have this devil.'

'You're right. But you have something else I don't have; that's what you have instead of this.'

'Oh? What?'

'What you have is hell. Mark my word, I do believe that God has sent you here for the salvation of my soul: if this devil goes on molesting me and if you're willing to show me this much mercy, you'll let me put him back into hell. This way you'll give me the most enormous comfort and do God the greatest and most welcome service, if you really have come to these parts to serve Him, as you say you have.'

'Oh my father', she innocently replied, 'since I've got hell, let it be just as you wish.'

'Well God bless you, my daughter! Let's go and put him back so he'll leave me in peace.'

This said, he laid Alibek down on one of their beds and taught her the right posture in order to imprison that creature accursed of God.

The girl, who had never yet put any devil into hell, found it a little painful the first time, and said to Rustico: 'What a horrid thing this devil must be, father! What a real enemy of God, for when he is put back inside he hurts the very hell itself and not just other people.'

'It won't always feel that way', said Rustico. And just to make sure, they put him back in six times before they got up from the bed, and left him for the moment so deflated that he was quite willing to subside.

But as the devil raised his head many a time thereafter and Alibek was always there at his call, ready to deflate him, she started to acquire a taste for the exercise and would say to Rustico: 'I can see how right they were, those good men at Gafsa who kept telling me what a pleasure it was to serve the Lord. I'm sure I can't remember ever doing anything I found so enjoyable as putting the devil back into hell. So it seems to me, anyone who bothers about anything else than serving the Lord is an ass.' Which is why she was going the whole time to Rustico and saying: 'I've come here to serve the Lord, father, not just to hang about. Let's go and put the devil into hell.'

And she would sometimes remark, as they were doing it: 'I don't know why the devil escapes from hell: if he stayed in it as happily as hell welcomes him and keeps hold of him, he'd simply never leave.'

So Alibek kept after Rustico, urging him to the service of the Lord until she had worn him threadbare and left him feeling chilly when he should have been at boiling point. He explained to her, therefore, that the devil was to be punished and put back into hell only when he got above himself. 'Now by God's favour we've left him so prostrate, all he can do is beg the Lord for a little peace.' Thus he contrived more or less to suppress her.

Noticing that Rustico was no longer inviting her to help put the devil back into hell, she one day said to him: 'Your devil may be whipped and giving you no more trouble—but my hell is giving me no peace at all. So the least you can do is let your devil soothe the itch in my hell, just as I helped you take your devil down a peg with my hell.'

Rustico, on his diet of root vegetables and plain water, was unable to measure up. It would take all too many devils, he told her, to assuage her hell, but he would do his best. So he satisfied her now and again, but so seldom that it was no better than throwing a bean into the lion's maw. The girl felt she was not giving God all the service she might, and was inclined to grumble.

But while Alibek's hell and Rustico's devil remained at loggerheads owing to the voracity of the one and the limpness of the other, it so happened that Gafsa was ravaged by a fire, and Alibek's father was burnt to death in his house, together with the entire household and all the rest of his children. Alibek consequently inherited all that he possessed, whereupon a young man called Neherbal, who had squandered his own fortune in high living, set out in search of her, understanding that she was alive, and found her before her father's estate passed to the Crown owing to intestacy. The young man took her off to Gafsa as his bride, much to Rustico's relief and to her immense reluctance. Here he became the joint-inheritor of the family fortune. But when she was questioned by the womenfolk as to how she had served God in the desert—this was before Neherbal had taken her to bed—she told them that her service consisted in putting the devil back into hell, and that Neherbal had done very wrong in taking her away from such service.

'How', the women asked, 'is the devil put back into hell?' The girl explained how, with the aid of words and gestures, and this provoked them to such gales of laughter, they haven't stopped yet. They told her: 'Don't be upset, my child, we do it here too, and Neherbal will serve the Lord with you perfectly well.'

The good women passed the word round the city until it became a proverb that the most agreeable service one could render to God was to put the devil back into hell. This proverb has crossed the water and remains current here too. Learn, therefore, young ladies, as you stand in need of God's favour, to put the devil back into hell: the exercise affords great pleasure to Him as also to the parties involved—and much good can spring from it.

Time and again the good ladies had been sent into fits of laughter by Dioneo's tale, so tickled were they by his words. But when he reached the end, the queen realized that her reign too had reached its term, so she removed her laurel crown and placed it very sweetly on Philostrato's head. 'Now we shall see', she remarked, 'whether the wolf can lead the sheep any better than the sheep have led the wolves.'

Philostrato laughed at this. 'Mark my words', said he, 'the wolves might have taught the sheep how to put the devil back into hell just as capably as Rustico taught Alibek: so don't call us wolves when you've not exactly been lambs. Anyway, as the crown has passed to me I shall govern the realm committed to me.'

'Listen, Philostrato', rebutted Neiphile. 'If you'd wanted to teach us that, the chances are we'd have taught you a little sense the way the nuns taught Masetto to recover the use of his tongue—only you'd not have learnt the lesson before you'd run yourselves ragged with the effort.'

Aware that his own cut and thrust might be parried with a nasty slice, Philostrato left off jesting and turned his attention to his kingly duties. He sent for the major-domo to discover how matters stood, then issued a few sensible instructions for what he judged to be the greater satisfaction of his charges during his tenure of office. This done, he turned to the ladies and said: 'Ever since I've been able to tell good from evil, I've suffered the misfortune of being constantly at Love's beck and call, thanks to the beauty of one of you fond ladies. Little has it profited me to be meek and obedient or to conform to all Love's ways as I've understood them—I've still found myself dropped in favour of another suitor, since when things have only deteriorated. I do believe this is going to be the death of me. So there's only one topic I'd like us to talk about tomorrow, the one that comes closest to my own experience: we'll talk about people whose love has ended in tears, for I cannot see mine ending any way but tragically, and whoever it was who gave me the wretched lovesick name by which you call me knew exactly what he was doing.' With these words he stood up and dismissed the company until suppertime.

The garden offered so much beauty and enchantment that none of them chose to leave it in search of greater pleasure elsewhere; indeed, the sun's heat had abated to the point where they might indulge in a little coursing without discomfort, and some of the ladies started pursuing the deer and rabbits and other creatures in the garden, who had come and disturbed their session time and again by hopping in among them. Dioneo and Fiammetta embarked upon the song about Maistre Guillaume and the Chastelaine de Vergi,* while Philomena and Pamphilo played a game of chess; and thus, as they were all engrossed in their occupations, the time flew and it was supper before they knew it. The tables were laid round the fountain and here they had a most enjoyable meal that evening.

To keep to the path traced out by those who had reigned before him, the moment they left the table Philostrato bade Lauretta initiate a dance and accompany it with a song. 'My lord', said she, 'I have no songs by anyone else, and I can't think of one of my own that would suit the high spirits of our party. But if you'd like one of those I have ready to hand, I'll gladly sing it.'

'If it's yours it's bound to be beautiful and a pleasure to listen to; so go ahead and sing the song you have in mind.'

So Lauretta began to sing gently, with mournful gestures, and the other ladies joined in the refrain:

Is there a sadder maid than I
Who love in vain and needs must sigh?

You made me fair, Creator Lord,
  Such was your pleasure.
You made me a sign, O loving Word,
  That your beauty's to treasure.
But man is wayward, man is blind,
  And I was spurned;
Your radiance that in me shined
  Never discerned.

There was a man who held me dear,
  I ruled his heart,
And prayed he all the live long year
  We'd never part.
My love he won for he was true,
  Aye, he deserved me.
Alas, he's gone: I'm left to rue
  What Fate's reserved me.

Then forward stepped a paltry youth
  And overbearing;
Forced my consent albeit in truth
  He's not endearing.
Shackled he keeps me, jealous swine—
  Weep, Love, for rage
That I, Man's joy, be left to pine
  Within a cage!

Alas for my consent—it leads
  To second wedding.
How false to think my widow's weeds
  Were e'er for shedding!
Oh happier far when, dressed in black,
  I lived respected.
Accursed the day when I, alack!
  New spouse elected.

So, dearest love in whom I placed
  My heart's sweet passion,

Since now your soul's with Him embraced
  Who us did fashion,
Beg Him to call me. Thus may we
  Be reunited,
That I may know 'tis yet to me
  Your heart is plighted.

Lauretta ended her song; everyone had followed it closely, but not all had understood it the same way. Some were inclined to a rather down-to-earth interpretation, that the bird in hand is (for all its faults) worth two in the bush; others took a more uplifting view, which was closer to the truth—but this is not the place to discuss it. Then the king had plenty of good-sized candles lit, out there on the grass dotted with flowers, and called for many another song until the stars had reached their zenith and were beginning to sink, at which point he felt it was time for bed and gave the order for everyone to retire to their rooms, wishing them all a good night.

*Here ends the third day of the* Decameron *and the fourth day begins; under the reign of Philostrato, the stories are about people whose love has ended in tears.*

I always assumed that it was only the high towers, the loftiest tree-tops that bore the brunt of the searing blasts of envy; this is what I have read and myself observed, and what I have heard from the lips of wise men. But I find myself gravely deceived. I avoid, and have indeed always striven to avoid, the fierce onslaught of this rabid spirit of envy: to do so I've made a point of sticking to the low ground, of stealing in furtive silence along the valley floor. This will seem obvious enough to anyone who considers these little tales of mine—not only are they written in the vulgar tongue and in prose (rather than in high-flown Latin verse), not only do they lack even a title,* but they're couched in as humble, unassuming a style as could be. None of this has saved me, however, from being savagely buffeted by this storm-wind, nay, I've been practically torn up by the roots, I'm totally lacerated by it, and it seems to me that those sages came all too close to the truth when they said that in this world nothing is beyond the reach of envy save poverty.

People who have read these stories have been saying that I'm overfond of you bright young ladies and that it's scarcely proper for me to take so much delight in bringing you pleasure and comfort; others have gone further and taxed me even for speaking well of you as I do. Others pretend to be even more judicious when they observe that it's quite unsuitable for a man of my age to be engaged in such matters, talking about women, that is, and currying favour with them. Others there are, many of them, who evince a tender concern for my reputation and insist that I should be wiser to consort with the Muses on Parnassus than to involve myself in all this triviality with *you*. Still others betray more spite than maturity when they say that if I had any sense I'd see to earning my crust instead of tightening my belt as I attend to so much nonsense. Others, again, go out of their way to put a false construction on my tales, to the prejudice of all the care I've taken in writing them for you.

Such are the insinuations, such the taunts and pinpricks with which I am assailed, harassed, pierced to the quick, as I persevere, excellent ladies, in your service—and if I listen to them, God knows I shrug them off lightly enough. Well, maybe it is up to you to rally to my defence, but I'm not proposing to lie back and leave it all to you; rather, what I shall do is not make a great issue out of it but to shake them off with a nonchalant reply—this I'll do straight away. For if before I've completed even one-third of my labour they're already such a swarm and lay such claims upon me, I suspect that before I reach the end, if they're not stopped in their tracks, they will have increased and multiplied to a point where they could trample on me without the smallest effort—and there is nothing you ladies would be able to do about it, for all your considerable powers. But before I make my rejoinder to any one of them, I should like to tell a story in my defence: it won't be a complete story—far be it from me to presume to incorporate any story of mine into those of a company as excellent as the one I have described to you—but it will be part of a story, and its very incompleteness will bear sufficient witness that it has nothing to do with theirs. So, addressing myself to my attackers, I say:

Long ago in our city there lived a man called Filippo Balducci, a person of no great account but prosperous enough and quite proficient in his walk of life. He had a wife he loved dearly, and she him; they lived in untroubled domesticity, their chief concern being each other's well-being. Now it happened that his good wife passed away—the fate of all mortals—and all she had to bequeath him was a son conceived by him, a child of about 2. Filippo was so prostrated by the death of his wife, no man was ever worse afflicted by the loss of a loved one; and, finding himself bereaved of her dear company, he decided to withdraw from the world and devote himself to God's service, and likewise to dedicate his little son. So he distributed all that he possessed among God's poor and left at once for Mount Asinaio, where he established himself with his son in a small cell. They lived a life of prayer and fasting, supported by alms, and he took elaborate care to avoid ever discussing any temporal matter in his son's presence or giving him sight of any temporal objects, lest these might tempt him away from the service of the Lord; all he ever spoke to him about was the glory of life eternal, the glory of God and His saints, and all he ever taught him were holy prayers. He held his child to this life for many a year, never letting him out of the cell, never permitting him the sight of any but himself.

Occasionally the good man would go in to Florence, where charitable souls would offer him such assistance as he needed; then he would return to his cell.

One day when the boy, who had turned 18, asked his now elderly father where he was off to, and was told, 'Father', said the lad, 'you're an old man now and find everything more of an effort. Why don't you take me with you to Florence some time and introduce me to the kind souls who are God's friends and yours? As I am young and have more endurance than you, that would enable me to go to Florence for our purposes whenever you chose, and you could stay here.'

Bearing in mind that this son of his was now grown up and that the service of God was second nature to him, so much so that worldly things would stand little chance of attracting him, 'Well', he said to himself, 'that's true enough.' So as he had to make the journey, he brought the boy along.

Seeing the houses and palaces in Florence, the churches and everything else to be found in the city, the boy was quite bowled over—he had no recollection of ever having laid eyes on sights of this kind. He kept questioning his father about them: what were they? What were they called? And as his father told him, he would be satisfied and question him about the next sight. So they continued, the son questioning, the father replying, until eventually they chanced to meet a group of beautiful young women dressed to the nines—they were on their way home from a wedding. 'What are those?' asked the lad the moment he set eyes on them.

'Eyes down, my boy', said his father, 'don't look at them—they're no good at all.'

'What are they called?'

Anxious to avoid stirring up any counter-productive notion of lechery in the young man, his father would not give the women their proper name but told him they were known as 'geese'.

Well, believe it or not, this boy, who had never before set eyes on such a creature, forgot all about palaces, oxen, horses, donkeys, money, whatever else he had seen, and exclaimed: 'Oh please, dad, let me have one of those geese!'

'Quiet, boy. I tell you they're no good.'

'Is that what they're like, then, no-good things?'

'Yes.'

'Well I don't understand', said the lad. 'I'm not clear what's wrong with them. So far as I am concerned, nothing I've seen is half as pretty and nice as they are. They're much prettier than the painted lambs you've often shown me. Come on, dad! If you care about me at all, do let's bring one of these geese back with us, and I'll see to feeding it grain.'

'Absolutely not!' said his father. 'You don't know which end to feed it.' And it dawned on him then that his providence was no match for Mother Nature, and he wished he'd never brought the boy in to Florence.

But that's as far as I want to take this story; now for a word with those for whom I told it. Some of my critics find it quite reprehensible that I go to such lengths to earn you young ladies' favour; in their view I'm all too fond of you. That I delight in you and court you to the best of my powers I shall not for a minute deny. 'Does this surprise you', I would ask them, 'if you've made a point of observing these young ladies, the sheer grace of their manners, their alluring beauty, their easy charm, the sheer probity of their sex—to say nothing of the delicious hugs and kisses, the sheer bliss of making love to these ineffably sweet creatures? When a boy raised in solitude on a rocky mountain', I'd continue, 'restricted to the tiny confines of a cell and with no company but his father's, as we have seen, when, the moment he first set eyes on you, he had but one wish, made but one request, lost his heart to but one object—you ladies!' Will those people rebuke me, will they censure and chastise me if I, ever since I was a youngster and first was endowed by Heaven with a body suited to love-making, if I have had a weakness for your sex—if I have doted on you, have striven to win your hearts? For how was I to resist the gleam in your eyes, the sweetness of your words and the passion of your sighs? After all, here was a little hermit, a boy totally devoid of finer feelings, indeed little more than a brute beast—and his heart went straight out to you! Of course those who don't care for you ladies and set no store by your love, those who are quite insensible to and ignorant of the pleasures and urges of natural affection, they're welcome to criticize me—their opinion leaves me cold.

Those who criticize me on account of my age have clearly never studied the leek: they will see that whereas it may have a white head, it keeps its tail green. Joking aside, I would say to them that I shall never blush to pay my attentions, even to the limits of old age, to those who were an object of devotion for Guido Cavalcanti and Dante Alighieri in their advanced years, and for Cino da Pistoia when he was a very old man—these men took pride in paying court to the ladies and appreciated the affection they evoked in them. And, were it not that I should be taking liberties with my text, I'd adduce historical instances and cite any number of excellent men from the past who, for all their ripe old age, spared no pains in courting the ladies. If my critics are unaware of this, let them go and learn all about it.

I ought, they say, to stick to the Muses in Parnassus: good advice, I agree, though we cannot dwell permanently with the Muses nor they with us. If a man occasionally forsakes their company to take pleasure in looking upon an object that closely resembles them, why, there's nothing reprehensible in that! The Muses are women, and even if women as a whole do not belong to the same order of being as the Muses, the fact is they look remarkably alike at first glance: so if I had no other reason for admiring the fair sex, here alone would be reason enough. Besides, women have inspired me to write copiously, whereas I never penned a single verse at the Muses' behest. All right, the Muses did lend me a hand and showed me how to go about writing all that I did; and possibly they paid me frequent visits when I was engaged on these admittedly modest little writings of mine—maybe out of deference to women as kindred spirits. So as I work at this loom I'm not straying from Parnassus or the Muses nearly as much as many people may think.

But what shall we say to those who, in their concern lest I go hungry, advise me to take thought for my bread? Well, I don't know, except that if I stop to think what their answer would be to my request for bread in an hour of need, I believe they'd say: 'Go root for it among your fables.' There's many a poet who's found more sustenance among his fables than have a good many rich men among their treasures; and many are the poets who, by attending to their poetry, quickened the age in which they lived, whereas all too many of those who amassed bread beyond their proper needs came to an untimely end. Enough said! Let them drive me away if I come to them begging, not that I yet need to (thank God!); and if I ever did need to, I do know how to abound and to suffer need, in the Apostle's words*—so let no one be more concerned about my welfare than I am.

As for those who deny the truth of what I assert, I should be only too obliged if they would furnish proof to support their own contentions: if it contradicts what I have here set forth, I'd acknowledge the justice of their accusations and would do my best to turn over a new leaf. But so long as they rely exclusively on words, I'll leave them to their opinions and cleave to my own, and will say of them precisely what they are saying about me.

Now, having made sufficient reply for the present, I'll simply say that I will carry on, placing my hope in the protection afforded me by God's help and yours, kindest ladies, and armed, too, with saintly patience. I shall turn my back to this squall and leave it to rage, for I can't see myself faring any worse than a handful of dust: when the wind blows, either the dust remains undisturbed or else it's caught up into the air and deposited, more often than not, on people's heads, on the crowns of kings and emperors, on the roofs of lofty palaces and high towers; and if it is dislodged from these places it cannot fall lower than whence it was scooped up. And if ever I went out of my way to satisfy you ladies in anything, I'm all the readier to do so now, aware as I am that all anyone is entitled to say is that I and others who love you are acting in accordance with Nature; to defy the laws of Nature requires no little strength and those who try will often do so not merely to no purpose but even to their own severe detriment. Let me confess, I possess no such strength myself, and have no ambition to possess it; if I did have it, I'd sooner lend it to others than employ it for my own purposes. Silence, therefore, my critics! If you're insensitive to warmth, very well—stay chilled: you're welcome to your pleasures, your perverse appetites, but leave me to such joy as this brief life affords.

But we must return, my fair ladies, to resume our narrative where we left it, for we have wandered all too far.

When the sun had driven every star from the sky and banished the damp shades of night from the earth, Philostrato got up and had all his company awoken; they went into the lovely garden and here enjoyed themselves until it was time to eat, which they did precisely where they had done so the previous night. Once the sun had reached its zenith they rose from their siesta and took their seats by the fountain in the usual manner; here Philostrato bade Fiammetta tell the first story, and she, awaiting no further summons, made a graceful opening in these words:

### IV. 1. *Tancredi, Prince of Salerno, slays his daughter's lover and sends the young man's heart to her in a golden chalice. The tale has a tragic ending.*

He's certainly given us a sad topic for today's story-telling, has our king, when you think that we have to speak of tears though we've come here to cheer ourselves up; how can we describe such things without the narrator and the listeners being moved to pity? Perhaps he's done this to temper our high spirits of these last few days a little. Anyway, whatever his reason, it's not for me to alter his command, so I shall tell you a pitiable tale of disaster that well deserves our tears.

Tancredi, Prince of Salerno, was a thoroughly humane, well-disposed ruler, except that in his old age he did sully his hands in the blood of two lovers. In all his life he had but a single daughter, and he would have been happier if he had not produced even her. He loved her as dearly as a father ever loved a daughter, which is why, long after she had reached marriageable age, he would not marry her off as he could not bear to part with her. Eventually he bestowed her on a son of the Duke of Capua, but she was widowed shortly afterwards and returned to her father. In face and frame she was as beautiful as any woman before or since; she was youthful, full-blooded, and possessed greater wit than one would look for in her sex. She lived, then, with her doting father in the lap of luxury, as befits a great lady, and she could see that he was too besotted with her to give much thought to finding her another husband. As she felt it would be improper to ask him for one, she decided to find herself, if she could, a sturdy lover on the sly. Her father's court was frequented by many men of high and low degree, as is customary, and she looked them over and considered the comportment of several of them, until she found one she particularly liked. He was a young page of her father's, called Guiscardo, a lad of humblest birth but stamped with nobility in his character and manner. She saw him very often and developed a secret passion for him, finding ever more to praise in him. The page was sharp-witted and her feelings did not escape his notice; he responded to them so heartily that loving her became practically his sole preoccupation.

So they pined for each other in secret, and the princess wished for nothing better than to be alone with him; there was not a soul in whom she would confide, but she thought up a novel ruse to get word to him of how they might proceed. She wrote a letter telling him what he was to do to be with her the next day; this letter she concealed inside a length of cane, between two knots, and handed it playfully to Guiscardo saying: 'It can serve for bellows—give it to your maid tonight to rekindle the fire with.'

As he took it, Guiscardo realized that she had her reason for giving it to him and speaking as she did, so he took it home with him; here he noticed that the wood was split, opened it up, found her letter, read it, and grasped what he had to do. This made him the happiest man in the world, and he saw to carrying out the instructions whereby he was to gain access to her. Next to the prince's palace there was a cave, cut into the hillside in times long past; this cave was lit by an opening let into the rock-wall, but in the abandoned state of the cave it had become overgrown with weeds and brambles. A secret stairway leading from one of the ground-floor rooms in the princess's quarters gave access to the cave; it was closed off, though, with a very massive door. No one recollected this stairway's existence as it was years since anyone had used it; but Love, whose eye searches out even the most secret things, brought it to the attention of the lovesick princess. To be sure that nobody would get wind of it, she pitted her wits against that door day after day before she succeeded in getting it open. Once opened, she descended alone into the cave, noticed the embrasure, and sent word to Guiscardo that he must try to climb in that way—she indicated its height above ground. To achieve his purpose Guiscardo at once made ready a rope, complete with knots and loops for ease of climbing up and down, dressed himself in a leather jerkin as protection from the brambles and, without telling a soul, went to the cave opening that night, secured one end of the rope tightly to a stout shrub rooted in the opening and used it to slide down into the cave and await his lady. In the morning she pretended she meant to stay in bed and sent her ladies out. When she was alone she locked her door, opened the door into the cave, and went down to fetch Guiscardo. They fell into each other's arms, then went up to her bedroom and spent the greater part of the day together most delightfully. After organizing their trysts to ensure total secrecy, Guiscardo returned to the cave and she shut the door after him, then went out to join her ladies. When night fell, Guiscardo climbed up his rope, got out by the cleft he'd come in by, and returned home. With this route mastered, he used it frequently thereafter.

But Fate, grown envious of such great and lasting happiness, turned the two lovers' joy into sadness and tears by means of a tragic accident. Tancredi had the habit of occasionally visiting his daughter in her room, all on his own, and having a chat with her, then leaving. Now one day he went down to her after lunch to find Ghismonda (as the princess was called) out in the garden with all her ladies. He went into her room unheard and unobserved, and as he did not want to intrude on her pastime in the garden, he sat down in a corner on a stool at the foot of the bed. The windows, he found, were shut and the curtains pulled round the bed; he rested his head on the bed, drew a bed-curtain over himself, as if it was his intention to hide, then fell asleep. Unfortunately this was a day when she had sent for Guiscardo; while Tancredi slept, she left her ladies in the garden, stole into her bedroom, locked the door, and let in her lover without noticing that there was anyone else in the room. They got into bed as usual, and while they were playing their lovers' games Tancredi woke and heard and saw what Guiscardo and his daughter were up to. Sick at heart, his first thought was to haul them over the coals, but then he decided to stay mum and remain hidden if possible, so that he could proceed more cautiously to do what he now proposed to do—and incur less shame in the process. The two lovers spent a long time together, as they always did, quite oblivious of Tancredi; and when they felt it was time, they got out of bed, Guiscardo returned to the cave, and she left the room. Tancredi left too, climbing through a window into the garden, though he was an elderly man, and returned unseen to his room, feeling utterly wretched.

On his orders Guiscardo was captured by two men that night, at the time people retire to bed, as he emerged from the window in the cave-wall, hampered as he was by his leather jerkin. He was brought in secret to Tancredi, who was almost in tears as he said: 'Guiscardo, the kindness I have shown you never deserved the insulting, the shameful use to which you have put what is mine—as I witnessed today with my own eyes.'

To this Guiscardo had nothing to say beyond remarking that against the power of Love, he and the prince were equally helpless. So Tancredi had his page quietly confined to a room under guard.

Next day, while Ghismonda remained quite unaware of what had happened, Tancredi turned over a number of proposals in his mind and, after lunch, following his usual habit, he went to his daughter's room. He sent for her, shut the door, and started weeping as he said: 'I thought, Ghismonda, that I was well acquainted with your goodness, your probity. I should never have dreamed, whatever anyone said, that you'd so much as consider yielding yourself to any man who was not your husband, let alone that you would actually do so, had I not seen you with my very eyes. The thought of it will sadden me for the little space of life still left to my old age. Since you had to sink to such shameless conduct, would to God you had at least chosen a man more suitable to your own rank. Instead, of all the people who frequent my court you had to choose Guiscardo, a boy of the most abject condition, raised in our court as a foundling, out of charity, to this very day. Now you've left me utterly prostrate—and I've no idea what to do with you. Guiscardo I had seized last night as he came out of the cave; he's in prison, and I know what I'm going to do with him. But you—God only knows what I am to do with you. I'm tugged one way by the love I've always borne you, a greater love than any father ever felt for a daughter; but I'm pulled the other way by my righteous anger at your unspeakable folly. My love seeks to forgive you, my anger seeks to contradict my nature and punish you. But before I reach a decision I want to hear what you've got to say on the matter.' With these words he bowed his head and cried like a child who's been well spanked.

As she listened to her father and realized not only that their secret was out but also that Guiscardo had been caught, her heart missed a beat and she was many times very close to bursting into tears, as most women do; but she was too proud to give in to emotion and with remarkable self-control her face betrayed nothing of her feelings. Sooner than make any plea on her own account she was resolved to die, imagining that her Guiscardo was already dead.

So there was nothing of the broken-hearted maiden, no hangdog expression in Ghismonda, indeed she looked unconcerned and indomitable, dry-eyed, straightforward, totally in control as she replied to her father: 'I am not disposed either to deny or to beseech, Tancredi; the first would do me no good, and I have no use for the second. Furthermore, I don't propose to take the smallest step to conciliate your love and goodwill; rather shall I admit the truth and defend my reputation with valid reasons. Then I shall conduct myself as befits a woman of courage. I do indeed love Guiscardo and so long as I live—which will not be long—I shall go on loving him; and if love continues after death, I shall never stop loving him. It was not my feminine weakness that induced me to this so much as your negligence in finding me a husband, and his qualities. You're made of flesh, Tancredi, and it should be clear enough to you that you begot a daughter of flesh and blood, not of stone or iron. You should bear in mind, too, for all your present age, what the laws are that apply to young people, and how binding they are. Although you are a man and you spent some of your best years under arms, you should none the less understand what a life of leisure and luxury does for young and old alike. I'm made of flesh and blood, then, as you begot me, and I've lived only a little, I'm still young. For both these reasons I do have a sexual appetite, and it has only been sharpened by having been married and having experienced the pleasure that comes from assuaging it. I, at any rate, couldn't resist the urge, being young and a woman, so I let myself be drawn and followed my inclination to fall in love. And I certainly did my utmost to avoid bringing shame on myself or on you as I yielded to my sinful but natural appetite. Love was kind and Fortune smiled on me, for they showed me a secret way to compass my desire without anyone knowing. I've no idea who pointed it out to you or how you came to discover, but I don't deny it. I didn't make a haphazard choice, as many women do, when I chose Guiscardo. I chose him before all others quite deliberately; our liaison was the result of a careful plan, and I long enjoyed my pleasure with him because he and I both acted with level-headed tenacity. Now evidently you've preferred common prejudice to objective truth, for if you reproach me with having loved sinfully, you reproach me far more bitterly with having taken for lover a man of humble birth, as though you'd not have minded if I'd chosen a lover from the nobility. So you've failed to notice that it's not my fault but that of Fate you're rebuking, as Fate often raises the worthless to eminence and leaves men of real merit at the bottom of the heap.

'Anyway, let's leave this and take a look at principles: we all of us, you see, draw our bodies from a common stock, and our souls, created with equal powers, equal potentialities, equal qualities, all derive from the same Creator. We were all born equal, and what in the first place set us apart from each other was merit: those who were given and displayed the larger share of merit were accounted noble, while the rest were not. And although this law has subsequently come to be honoured in the breach, neither nature nor good usage has yet abrogated or defaced it. Therefore if a man is virtuous in his actions and shows himself to be well-bred, but is addressed as though he were otherwise, it is not the man so addressed who is at fault but the one who addresses him. Take a look at all your nobles, scrutinize their lives, their conduct, and then consider Guiscardo's: if you're going to judge dispassionately, you'll say that he is a man of singular nobility while your nobles are louts every one of them. Where Guiscardo's qualities and merits are concerned I was not swayed by anyone else's opinion, only by the witness of your words and my own eyes. Who ever spoke as highly of him as you did, commending him for all that deserves praise? And how right you were! Unless my eyes deceived me, there was nothing for which you praised him that I did not see borne out in his own actions, and even more remarkably than your words could suggest. Had I been deceived, it would have been because you deceived me. Are you going to maintain, then, that I have cast my lot with a man of base condition? Then you'll simply be wrong. Tell me I've cast my lot with a penniless man, and I'd agree with you, to your shame, for that's the state in which you have left a good man who is in your service. It's not poverty, however, that degrades a person, it is wealth. Many kings, many great princes started off poor, while many a man who digs the earth and tends the sheep started off extremely rich; such people still exist.

'As for the last question you raised, what to do with me, don't give it another thought: if you are disposed to resort to barbarity in your old age, which you never did when you were younger, go ahead and vent your cruelty on me. I'm the instigator of this sin—if sin it is—and I'm not proposing to plead on my own behalf. Indeed I give you notice that if you don't deal with me precisely as you have dealt with (or will deal with) Guiscardo, I will see to it by my own hand. Now be off with you, go and cry your heart out among the women. If it's harsh measures you want, and you think we've deserved them, kill me and him at one stroke.'

The prince was well acquainted with his daughter's spirit, but even so he did not believe she would prove as resolute as her words suggested. When he left her, therefore, he put aside any notion of laying a finger on her, but decided to cool her passion by taking care of her lover. He sent word to the two men guarding Guiscardo that they were to strangle him that night without commotion, cut out his heart, and bring it to him. This order was duly carried out.

The following day the prince had a beautiful big golden chalice brought to him. He placed Guiscardo's heart in it and sent it by a trusted servant to his daughter, bidding him tell her as he handed it to her: 'Your father sends you this to make up to you for what you've treasured most, to match the solace you have afforded him over that which *he* has most treasured.'

As for Ghismonda, she was not to be deterred from her brutal resolution and, as soon as her father had left her, she had sent for poisonous plants and roots, which she had distilled into a liquid, to have it ready to hand if her fears turned out to be justified. So when the prince's attendant arrived with the gift and the message, she took the chalice, stony-faced, lifted off the lid, looked at the heart as she listened to the message, and was in no doubt that this was Guiscardo's heart. She looked up at the attendant and said: 'A heart such as this one deserved nothing less than gold for its burial: my father has acted wisely.' She brought it to her lips and kissed it, and went on: 'My father's love for me has always and in every way been exceptionally tender, I can tell you, but never more so than at this final moment; so you will convey to him the last thanks I shall ever render to him, for so great a gift.'

This said, she turned back to the chalice she was clutching tightly and spoke to the heart: 'Alas, sweetest refuge of all my delight, accursed be the cruelty of the man who would have me see you thus with my own eyes! It was enough for me to keep you in my mind's eye from moment to moment. You have run your course, the one allotted you by Fate. You're free of it. You've come to the end for which all of us are making; you've left behind the woes and toils of the world, you've been given a worthy burial by your enemy himself. Indeed your obsequies have been worthily fulfilled in all points save one: the tears of the woman whom you so loved when you were still living. To give you my tears, God inspired my pitiless father to send you to me; and give them to you I shall, for all that I had proposed to meet my end dry-eyed and impassive. And when I have shed them, I shall without delay see to it that my spirit goes to join the one which you so cherished when it dwelt within you. And in whose company could I travel more happily and with better assurance to the unknown world beyond this one? I know that his soul still resides here in you and is looking at the place where he and I knew happiness; I know his soul loves mine, which so loves his, and that it is there waiting for me.'

This said, she looked down into the chalice and, without the usual sound of sobbing, she began to shed so many tears she might have had a spring of water in her head—it was marvellous to behold; and she kissed the dead heart time and again. Her waiting-ladies, who were standing round her, did not know what this heart was or what she meant by her words, but they were all moved to tears and in their pity vainly asked her what it was that made her weep, and they did all they could to try and comfort her.

When Ghismonda had wept her fill, she raised her head, dried her eyes, and said: 'O beloved heart, all I was to do for you I have now done, and nothing remains but to come and unite my spirit with yours.' Then she asked for the little cruet containing the distillation she had prepared the previous day, and poured it into the chalice that held the heart now so abundantly bathed with her tears. Without flinching she put the chalice to her lips and drank it off, then got on to her bed, still holding the chalice, and composed herself into a becomingly chaste posture, held her dead lover's heart close to her own, and without another word waited for death.

The princess's ladies were watching and listening but did not know what liquor it was that she had drunk; they sent word of it all, however, to Tancredi who, fearing what must have happened, rushed to his daughter's room and arrived just as she was settling herself on the bed. And too late he began to speak soothing words to her, for he could see the straits she had now come to, and he wept most miserably.

'Save your tears, Tancredi', his daughter told him; 'keep them, don't give them to me, I don't want them; keep them for those who find Fortune's last gift less welcome than I do. Who ever saw anyone but you weep over the thing he sought for? But if anything remains of the love you used to feel for me, make me one last gift: as you could not brook my living secretly with Guiscardo, let my body lie next to his, wherever you've had it thrown, for everyone to see.'

The prince could not speak for tears, so Ghismonda, feeling that her end was near, pressed the dead heart to her breast and murmured: 'Farewell, I'm going.' Her eyes dimmed, her senses were all numbed, and she quit this sorry life.

This was the sad end of Guiscardo's and Ghismonda's love, as you have heard. Tancredi wept and wept, too late regretting his cruelty. Mourned by the whole of Salerno, the couple were, on the prince's orders, given honourable burial in a single tomb.

### IV. 2. *Brother Alberto gains access to a young woman's bed in the guise of the angel Gabriel. He ends up with rather too many feathers.*

Fiammetta's story had several times brought tears to the ladies' eyes, but when it was finished the king remarked, stony-faced: 'If I had to give my life for only half the pleasure that Ghismonda enjoyed with Guiscardo, that would seem to me a small price to pay, and this should come as no surprise to you ladies, inasmuch as I die a thousand deaths every hour of my life and don't derive the smallest particle of happiness for all that. But leaving my own concerns to one side for the moment,

I want Pampinea to speak next on this passionate topic, taking some account at any rate of my own situation; if she follows where Fiammetta has led, I've no doubt I shall begin to feel the effects of a little dew upon my fire.'

Hearing herself thus bidden, Pampinea was more swayed by her sense of what prevailed in the ladies' minds than she was by the king's spoken command; consequently she was more inclined to solace her sisters than to satisfy the king simply out of obedience, so she chose to tell a comic tale, which still remained within the day's brief, and thus she began:

Folk have a saying: 'The villain who passes for saint | Can do ill and incur ne'er a taint' (or, otherwise, 'The plausible villain can get away with murder'). This gives me ample scope to talk on the subject proposed to me. It also enables me to demonstrate the lengths to which the religious orders go in their hypocrisy. There they are in their great flowing habits with their artificially pallid faces; humble and meekly spoken as anything when they're out begging, they rant and roar when they're castigating others for the vices they practise themselves; and they proclaim that *they* achieve their salvation by receiving, others by giving. Furthermore, they behave not like the rest of us who have to strive for our place in heaven, but as if they owned heaven and lorded it up there, assigning to each departing soul a better or worse place according to the amount of money left to them. In this way they try to deceive themselves first of all, if they believe what they say, and then those who lend credence to their words. Were I permitted to make known as much as I might, I'd soon show all those simple souls just what the religious keep hidden inside their capacious cloaks. I only wish to God that they would all be paid off for their lies the way one of them was—a friar minor (of a certain age) whose convent was in Venice though the mother-house was at Assisi. I'm only too glad to tell you his story so as to cheer you up with a little laughter, as you've been so affected by the death of Ghismonda.

In Imola there was once a man called Berto della Massa. He lived a wicked, corrupt life and the Imolese were so well acquainted with his despicable conduct that eventually not a soul believed a word he said, even when he was telling the truth. Realizing that he couldn't get away with his mischief here any longer, he was driven to move to Venice, sink of all iniquity,* as he expected that there he should be able to pursue his nefarious activities along fresh lines. Now apparently smitten with guilt over the deplorable life he had been leading hitherto, and possessed (it seemed) by a surge of humility, he became more pious than any man alive, and went off and joined the Friars Minor and took the name Brother Alberto of Imola; in this attire he made pretence of leading an ascetic life, much recommending penance and abstinence, and eschewing all meat and wine that happened not to be to his taste. Before anyone knew it this thief, pimp, forger, and murderer had suddenly become a great preacher, not that he gave up the above-mentioned practices if he could pursue them undetected. He went on to become a priest and every time he was celebrant at the altar he would weep over the passion of Our Saviour—if he had a big enough audience—for tears cost him little when they served his purposes. In a word, what with his homilies and his tears, he so hoodwinked the Venetians that he was appointed the faithful executor and repository of virtually everyone's will and trustee of many a man's money; he became confessor and spiritual adviser to nearly every man and woman, effectively changing from wolf into shepherd of the flock; and his reputation for sanctity in those parts was far greater than Saint Francis's had ever been in Assisi.

Now it happened that a feather-brained young woman called Lisetta da ca' Quirino, the wife of an important merchant who had left with the galleys for Flanders, went with some other women to confess to this holy friar. As she knelt at his feet, and had got some way into her confession, Brother Alberto asked her whether she had a lover.

Now Lisetta was a Venetian (and the Venetians are a conceited lot), so she replied with a scowl:

'Oh come, Brother! Haven't you got eyes? Is my beauty no different from these other women's? If I wanted lovers, I'd have them by the dozen, but beauty like mine is not for just any old Tom, Dick, or Harry! How many women have you ever seen whose beauty can touch mine? Mine would shine out in heaven.' And on and on she went about her beauty—it was painful to listen to her.

Brother Alberto realized at once that he was dealing with an idiot and fell in love with her on the spot, for here was fertile soil, he reckoned, for the digging. Reserving his blandishments, however, for a more convenient occasion, he now rebuked her, in order to exhibit his sanctity; he told her she was indulging in vainglory and so on and so forth, which resulted in Lisetta calling him an ass who couldn't appreciate true beauty when he saw it. As Brother Alberto did not want to make her too upset, he gave her absolution and let her go with her women-friends.

A few days later he went to Lisetta's house with a trusted companion, took her aside in a room where they could not be observed, threw himself down on his knees before her, and said: 'For God's sake forgive me, madam, for what I said to you on Sunday when you spoke to me about your beauty; that night I was so viciously punished for it, it wasn't till today I could leave my bed.'

Said Feather-brain: 'Who punished you?'

'I'll tell you. I was praying in my cell that night, as I always do, and suddenly I saw it brilliantly lit up and, before I could turn round to see what the light came from, I saw a young man of radiant beauty standing over me with a big stick in his hand; he pulled me up by my hood and gave me such a beating he left me all in pieces. I asked him why he had done this and he said: "Because you had the nerve to rebuke my lady Lisetta today on account of her heavenly beauty; I love her more than anything, God alone excepted." "Who are you?" I asked. He told me he was the angel Gabriel. "O my Lord", said I, "I do beg you to forgive me." "I'll forgive you", he said, "on this condition: that you go to her as soon as you can and obtain her pardon; if she won't forgive you I'll come back and give you another thrashing that you won't forget as long as you live." What he went on to tell me I shouldn't dare to make known to you unless you first pardon me.'

Mrs Head-in-air, who was passably rattle-brained, lapped this all up and took it for Gospel-truth. After a moment she said: 'Well I did tell you, Brother Alberto, that my beauty was made in heaven. Still, so help me God, I feel sorry for you, so I'll forgive you right now; that way you'll suffer no further harm, and you can tell me what the angel went on to say to you.'

'Since you've forgiven me', said the friar, 'I'll gladly tell you. But one thing I must warn you: take care not to mention what I'm going to say to a living soul, otherwise you'll wreck your chances, for you are the luckiest woman alive. The angel Gabriel told me to tell you that he was so smitten with you that he would often have come to spend the night with you, were it not for fear of startling you. Now the message I'm to bring you from him is that he wants to pay you a little visit one night. But as he is an angel and you couldn't touch him if he came in an angel's form, he says he wants to come in human shape so as to enjoy you, so you're to let him know when you'd like him to come and which man's body he's to use, and he'll come. There now: consider yourself a woman blessed above all others.'

Mrs Muggins said she was delighted that the angel Gabriel was in love with her, for she loved him too, indeed she was constantly lighting penny candles before any image she saw of him. He'd be welcome, she said, any time he cared to call; he'd find her all alone in her bedroom. One thing, however: he was not to ditch her in favour of the Virgin Mary. It was common knowledge how he doted on her, and indeed it was all too evident—wherever she saw him, he was always kneeling before the Virgin. Aside from that, she didn't mind whose form he borrowed provided that he didn't scare her.

'Spoken like a wise woman, madam. I'll settle it all with him as you say. You can do me a mighty favour, though, and it won't cost you a thing: desire him to come to you in this body of mine. Why is it a favour? Because he'll fetch my soul out of my body and lodge it in paradise, then he'll come into my body; and so long as he's enjoying your company, I'll be in my seventh heaven.'

'Well, why not?' said Mrs Addle-pate. 'I don't mind if you have this solace instead of the beating he gave you because of me.'

'Tonight, then, see to leaving your front door so that he can get in: as he's coming in human form, he could only get in by the door.'

Lisetta said she would see to this. Once Brother Alberto left, she jumped clean out of her drawers with excitement, she couldn't wait for the angel Gabriel to come to her. As for Brother Alberto, reckoning that he would be spending the night in equestrian rather than angelic pursuits, he set to stuffing himself with all manner of victuals lest he be thrown from the saddle for lack of muscle. He obtained leave from his convent and went at nightfall with a companion to the house of a woman-friend which had served as his base on previous occasions when he had gone to corral a filly. From here he went on, disguised, to Lisetta's house when the time seemed ripe, walked in, used the gear he'd brought to change into an angel, climbed the stairs, and went into her room.

Seeing this thing that looked so white, she knelt down before it, and the angel blessed her and drew her to her feet and gestured to her to get into bed, which she did without further prompting; then the angel laid down beside his devotee. Brother Alberto was a well-built, good-looking man and he applied himself vigorously to his equitation; with Lisetta's soft, fresh body offering him a response quite different to what she gave her husband, he took flight several times that night without the aid of wings—and she pronounced herself more than satisfied. He also told her a number of things concerning the glory of heaven. As dawn approached, he arranged to return, then left with his impedimenta and returned to his companion, who was spared the fear of sleeping alone—the lady of the house was friendly enough to keep him company.

After lunch Lisetta, with a companion, called on Brother Alberto and told him all about the angel Gabriel and what she'd heard him say about the glory of life everlasting, and what he looked like, and a whole lot of mind-boggling information besides.

'Well', said Brother Alberto, 'I don't know how things went with you, but what I do know is that last night, when he came to me and I gave him your message, he straight away carried my spirit off to where there were so many flowers, so many roses, you never in your life saw so many, and till this morning I passed the time in the most delightful place imaginable. As for my body, I've no idea what happened to it.'

'Didn't I tell you?' said Lisetta. 'Your body spent the night in my arms with the angel Gabriel. If you don't believe me, take a look under your left nipple: I gave the angel such a tremendous love-bite the mark will remain for days.'

'Very well, today I shall do something I've not done for ages: I'll get undressed to see if you're telling the truth.' And after a great deal more talk, Lisetta returned home; and Brother Alberto paid her several further visits in the guise of an angel without let or hindrance.

However, one day Lisetta happened to be discussing the question of beauty with a girl-friend of hers, and needs must give her own beauty pride of place. Brains were not her strong point, so she remarked: 'If you knew who *my* beauty appeals to, you'd pipe down about anyone else's.'

Her friend was longing to hear: she knew Lisetta all too well. 'You may be right', she said, 'but as I don't know who this person is, I'm not going to change my opinion just like that.'

So Lisetta, who was bursting with the news, told her: 'Don't tell a soul, but the person I mean is the angel Gabriel. He loves me more than his own self because I—this is what he's told me—am the most beautiful lady in all five corners of the world.'

Her friend was ready to burst out laughing but held it in so as to keep her talking. 'Well my goodness, Lisetta', she remarked, 'if it's the angel Gabriel you're talking about and that's what he said to you, then that's that. I never thought, though, that angels went in for that sort of thing.'

'How wrong you are, my friend! Why, God's teeth! My husband's not a patch on him in bed, and the angel tells me they do it up there too. Anyway, he finds me more beautiful than any woman in heaven, which is why he's fallen in love with me and pays me any number of visits. Now do you get the picture?'

When Lisetta's friend left, she couldn't wait to pass the story on, which she did in the greatest detail when she was invited to a party with a whole crowd of other women. These in turn told their husbands, as well as friends of their own sex, who passed it on so that in less than two days the story was all over Venice. But among those who came to hear about it were

Lisetta's husband's family; they said not a word to her but determined to find this angel and see if he knew how to fly. So they kept watch for several nights.

Some whisper of this chanced to reach Brother Alberto's ears, and he went to Lisetta one night to give her a good talking to. He was scarcely undressed before her husband's family, who had seen him arrive, were at the bedroom door and about to open it. As soon as he heard them, Brother Alberto realized what had happened and jumped out of bed; he could see no way out but to open the window, which overlooked the Grand Canal, and take a flying leap. There was sufficient depth of water and he could swim well, so he did himself no injury. He swam across the canal and slipped inside a house that stood open, begging its worthy occupant to save his life for the love of God, and spun him some cock-and-bull story to explain how he came to be there at such an hour with nothing on. The honest burgher, who was about to go out on some errand, took pity on him, put him to bed in his own bed, and told him to stay there till he got back. Locking him in, he went off about his business.

When the husband's family got into Lisetta's room, they found that the bird had flown, leaving his wings behind. Feeling balked, they gave the young woman a piece of their mind, then went home carrying the angel's trappings, and leaving her behind to mope. By now it was broad daylight and while the worthy burgher was on the Rialto, he heard about the angel Gabriel going last night to sleep with Lisetta, and how her husband's family caught him there but he'd leapt, terrified, into the canal and no one knew where he'd vanished to. So the good fellow at once concluded that the man he had left at home must be the fugitive. Back at home, he recognized the man and had a long talk with him, the upshot of which was that Brother Alberto was to see that he received fifty ducats if he did not want to be handed over to Lisetta's husband's family. So they concluded their agreement.

Now as Brother Alberto wanted to leave, his host said to him: 'It can't be done. Or rather, it can, but only if you're amenable. We're having a celebration today: we all go to Piazza San Marco, one of us leading a man dressed up as a bear, another leading a man dressed as a savage,* and so on; when we're all there we enact a hunt in masquerade, which brings the celebration to a close, after which leaders and led go their various ways. If you'd like, I could lead you wherever you want to go, disguised in one of these ways—before anyone gets wind of your being here. Otherwise I don't see how you can leave here without being spotted, for the lady's husband's family know you're somewhere hereabouts and have posted look-outs everywhere to catch you.'

Reluctant though he was to go in such a disguise he braced himself to do so, for he feared Lisetta's relatives; he told his host where he wanted to be led—he did not mind how. So the man spread honey all over him then covered him in downy feathers, secured a chain round his neck, drew a mask down over his head, stuck a big staff in one hand and gave into his other hand a pair of great hounds for him to lead—he had got them off the butcher's. Then he sent word to the Rialto that anyone wishing to see the angel Gabriel should go to Piazza San Marco. That was being truthful after the Venetian fashion. This done, he led him out after a little, Brother Alberto preceding, the man following and holding him by the chain. It was a rowdy progress—'What what what?' cried the Venetians in Venetian—that brought them to the Piazza; here, what with those who arrived in their train and those who had heard the invitation and come directly from the Rialto, there was a vast crowd. Once arrived, he got his savage up on to a high platform and tied him to a pillar, as though waiting for the hunt to start. As the savage was covered all over in honey, the horse-flies, and bluebottles made themselves a thorough nuisance.

Seeing that the Piazza was now quite full, the man pretended he meant to unchain his savage, and pulled the mask off Brother Alberto. 'Gentlemen', he said, 'since the boar has not turned up and there's to be no hunt, I wouldn't have you turning out for nothing. I should like you, therefore, to take a look at the angel Gabriel, who comes down from heaven to earth to bring solace to Venetian women.' When the mask was off everyone recognized Brother Alberto at once. A great roar went up, and the vilest insults imaginable were flung at him—

no scoundrel had ever heard worse—and all manner of garbage was flung at his face. They kept after him this way for a good length of time, until word chanced to reach his convent and six friars arrived to throw a cloak over him, unchain him, and fetch him home, pursued by a great rumpus. They locked him in a cell, and it is believed that he died after a wretched existence.

Here was a man, then, who was considered virtuous but practised evil, lost his credibility, but had the nerve to pass himself off as the angel Gabriel, turned into a savage, was suitably reviled, and was ultimately brought to weep for his sins, though much good did that do him. Would to God the same thing might happen to the whole lot of them!

IV. 3. *Three young lovers take their ladies to enjoy a life of bliss on Crete; but Jealousy comes to spoil the party.*

Hearing the end of Pampinea's story, Philostrato mused for a while, then said to her: 'The end of your story was not bad, but earlier on it was a good deal too jokey—I didn't care for that.' This said, he turned to Lauretta and bade her try to come up with something better.

'You're too hard on lovers', remarked Lauretta with a grin, 'if you want them to come to a sorry end. However, to obey you I shall tell one about three lovers who were equally unfortunate and got little joy from their love.' So she began:

It is no secret that any vice can injure the person who indulges it, and often other people besides; and it seems to me that if there's one vice that can sweep us off our feet and carry us into danger, that vice is anger. Anger is quite simply a sudden, ill-considered surge of emotion; it is spurred by some resentment and drives us into a passionate rage, blinding us to reason.

While men are prone to it, some more than others, in women it wreaks greater havoc because they take fire more readily and give freer rein to it. No wonder, if you consider that soft, light materials ignite more easily than hard, heavy ones. And we are—begging your pardon, gentlemen—tenderer than you, and much, much lighter. Bearing in mind, then, our natural propensity to anger, and considering what horrid mischief it can wreak, let us also remember the great joy and serenity we afford to our chosen menfolk by our gentleness and kindness. And so, the better to arm ourselves against wrath, I shall tell you a story about three young men and as many young ladies whose love (as I mentioned earlier) went badly sour thanks to a fit of feminine pique.

Marseilles is, as you know, an ancient and noble city by the sea in Provence. It used to teem with rich men and great merchants, far more than it does today. One of these was a man called Arnald Civada; he was of humble birth but a man of honour and integrity in his merchant's calling—and of enormous wealth. His wife had given him several children, including three girls who were a good deal older than their brothers. Two of the girls were twins aged 15, while the third was 14; and as soon as Arnald was back from a trading trip to Spain, the family expected to marry them off. The elder girls were called Ninetta and Maddalena, the youngest, Bertella. A young man of good birth but no means, called Restagnone, fell in love with Ninetta and she with him; and they had contrived to take their pleasure together without a soul finding out. After this had gone on for some time, a pair of friends, Folco and Ughetto, fell in love with Maddalena and Bertella respectively. Their father had died leaving them extremely well off.

Ninetta pointed out to Restagnone how matters stood, and he considered how he might profit from her sisters' lovers in order to improve his own financial prospects. So he befriended them and would often accompany the one or the other, or both together, on their visits to the sisters; and once he felt that a good rapport had been established, he invited them home one day and spoke to them as follows: 'The way we've been hobnobbing together lately must leave you in no doubt, my friends, how well disposed I am to both of you. Whatever I did for my own good I should willingly do for yours too. Given my warm regard for you, therefore, I'm going to tell you what's in the back of my mind, and then we'll consider together what is the best way to proceed. From what you keep saying, and from the way you've been carrying on, day and night, I gather that you are head over heels in love with the two sisters, as I am with the third. Now if you really want to slake your thirst in the most agreeable fashion, I have an idea of what we ought to do. You're very rich young men, which I'm not. Suppose you pool your resources so that I get a share, and suppose we consider in what part of the world we'd like to go and settle happily with our ladies, I've no doubt at all that I can persuade them to come with us wherever we choose to go, and to bring a good share of their father's wealth with them. When we're there we'll be able to live like a happy band of brothers, each with his own beloved; it will be sheer heaven. Now make up your mind—take it or leave it.'

The two lads, who were as lovesick as could be, took note that this way they would possess their love-partners and scarcely hesitated before saying that if this was really to be the result, they would most certainly do as proposed. A few days later Restagnone had a tryst with Ninetta (no easy matter to arrange); he had the boys' answer, and after a little dalliance he spoke to her of the proposal they had discussed, and argued his case to her most eloquently. He found her readily persuadable, however, for she was even more anxious than he was to be able to meet without running risks. So she told him straight out that she liked the idea, and her sisters would take her lead, in this most of all. 'Make all the arrangements as soon as ever possible', she said. So Restagnone went back to the two lads, who had been badgering him ever since, and told them that the wheels were already set in motion where the ladies were concerned.

Crete was the place they decided upon. They sold a few possessions under guise of using the proceeds to set up in trade; their remaining assets they turned into cash; then they bought a trim galliot, fitted it out lavishly (and in secret), then awaited the appointed day. For her part, Ninetta, who was well acquainted with her sisters' wishes, fanned the flames with enticing words so they couldn't wait for the day to come.

The night they were to board ship the three sisters opened a large chest of their father's and took out a fortune in jewels and cash, before secretly leaving the house and going to meet their lovers as arranged. Together, they hastened aboard their galliot, had the oars dipped, and away they went. The following evening the young lovers reached Genoa, with no intermediate stops, and there enjoyed the first fruits of their attachment. With their stores replenished they continued on their way, from port to port until, a week later, they arrived without hindrance in Crete. Here they bought enormous estates near Candia on which they built themselves delightful, handsome villas. They engaged large retinues, purchased hawks and hounds and horses, and began to live like lords—it was one round after another of feasting and balls. Never did men live more contentedly with their womenfolk.

What will keep happening, though, as we see, is that there can be too much of a good thing and surfeit ensues. Restagnone had been passionately in love with Ninetta, but now that he could have his fill of her at any time without any impediment, she began to bore him and his love grew lukewarm. So he fell for a local beauty he met at some festivity and started paying court to her and lavishing magnificent parties and presents on her. This did not escape Ninetta's notice, and she grew so fiercely jealous that he could not move a step but she knew of it, and would cause herself and him considerable grief with the scenes she made.

But just as surfeit breeds tedium so does frustrated desire sharpen the appetite, and Ninetta's scenes only made Restagnone the keener on his new love. Before long, moreover, Ninetta became firmly convinced, whatever anyone told her, that the other woman reciprocated Restagnone's love. This made her so upset she became possessed by a cold fury that turned her love for Restagnone into bitter loathing; in a blind rage she decided she must avenge his imagined rebuff by killing him. So she called in an old Greek woman with a gift for concocting poisons, and induced her with promises and gifts to make up a lethal draught; this, without a moment's further reflection, she gave to the unsuspecting Restagnone one evening when he was already in his cups; such was its power, he was dead before morning.

When Folco, Ughetto, and their mistresses came to hear of it, they shed bitter tears over him, as did Ninetta, and had him buried with dignity, quite unaware that he had been poisoned. Not many days later, however, the old woman who had furnished Ninetta with the poisonous draught was caught as a result of another offence; under torture she confessed to her wicked deeds, not excluding this one, nay, spelling out precisely what had occurred. So one night the Duke of Crete threw a cordon round Folco's villa without a word to anyone and arrested Ninetta without noise or opposition. There was no need to torture her—she told him at once all he wanted to hear about Restagnone's death.

Folco and Ughetto had been told by the duke in private—and had informed their ladies—why Ninetta had been arrested. They were appalled, and did their utmost to save Ninetta from being burnt at the stake, for they realized that such a fate was reserved for her and she richly deserved it. However, all was in vain, for the duke had made up his mind to mete out justice. Now Maddalena, a young beauty after whom the duke had long been sighing, but to little purpose, took it into her head to accept his advances in order to save her sister from the stake. She therefore put out feelers, intimating to him in her message that she was at his entire disposal on two conditions: that she retrieve her sister unharmed, and that not a word should leak out. The duke welcomed the approach and, after some consideration, replied that he accepted. With her connivance he had Folco and Ughetto arrested one night, under pretence of wanting to question them about the business; then he went to his secret tryst with Maddalena. With him he brought her sister, whom he had pretended to place in a sack with a view to dropping her into the sea that very night; he gave her back, therefore, as the price of their night together, and when he left in the morning he requested that this, the first night of their love, should not be the last. He further bade her send the guilty sister away before he was obliged to institute further proceedings against her in order to save his own face.

Next morning Folco and Ughetto were set at liberty, after hearing that Ninetta had that night been executed by drowning. This they believed, and returned home to comfort their partners in the loss of their sister. Maddalena did her best to conceal Ninetta's presence, but Folco got wind of it none the less. He was most surprised and at once suspected what had happened, for he had heard of the duke's weakness for his young woman. How come, he asked, that Ninetta was back?

Maddalena spun a long tale, but he was astute enough to disbelieve her and eventually she was forced to confess the truth. Grief turned to fury: Folco drew his sword and killed her as she vainly begged for mercy. Then, fearing the duke's wrath and justice, he left Maddalena lying dead in the room and went to find Ninetta. 'We're off now', he told her with false jollity, 'where your sister has arranged for me to take you, to keep you out of the duke's clutches.'

Ninetta believed him; she was frightened and anxious to be gone; night had fallen, so she set out with him, neglecting to take leave of her sister. They collected together such cash as Folco could lay his hands on—not a great deal—went down to the coast, found a ship, and sailed off Goodness knows where.

The next day Maddalena's corpse was discovered and word was at once brought to the duke—certain people nurtured jealousy and hatred for Ughetto. The duke was in love with Maddalena, and therefore stormed into Ughetto's house and placed him and his Bertella under arrest. Though they were still quite unaware of Folco's flight with Ninetta or anything else, he forced them to confess that they and Folco were guilty of Maddalena's death. Having confessed, they rightly feared the death penalty, so they had the wit to bribe their guards with money they kept hidden at home against such eventualities. Never stopping to pick up any of their possessions, they and their guards slipped aboard a ship and fled by night to Rhodes, where they lived out the last of their short lives in poverty. This was the end result of Restagnone's folly in love and Ninetta's anger.

IV. 4. *Gerbino, the King of Sicily's grandson, falls in love with a princess he has never seen. To obtain her he breaches his royal grandfather's trust and suffers for it.*

Lauretta concluded her story and fell silent, whereupon her listeners turned to each other to shake their heads mournfully over the lovers' sad lot; some of them said it was all Ninetta's fault for losing her temper, others propounded different views, while the king seemed quite abstracted. Eventually he roused himself and gave the nod to Elissa, who began meekly as follows:

There are enough people who imagine that Love's darts proceed solely from the eyes, and pour scorn on anyone who asserts that a person may fall in love on the basis of what he has heard with his ears. How wrong such people are will be clear enough from the story I shall tell: love will be engendered by reputation, the lovers never having laid eyes on each other, and furthermore they will come to a miserable end.

Guglielmo II,* King of Sicily, produced two children, as the Sicilians require, a boy called Ruggieri and a girl called Costanza. Ruggieri predeceased his father, leaving a boy called Gerbino. The lad was carefully raised by his grandfather and turned out a very good-looking youth with a name for gallantry and chivalry. His reputation was not confined to Sicily but travelled abroad and was voiced loud and clear in Barbary,* a nation which in those days was a fiefdom of the Sicilian kings. Now this reputation Gerbino enjoyed as a man of parts and a true knight came to many ears, not excluding those of a princess, daughter of the King of Tunis; all who laid eyes on this lady described her as one of the most beautiful creatures ever formed by Nature, a maiden of impeccable virtue and sublime nobility. She loved to hear tell of gallant men and was all ears whenever the conversation turned to Gerbino and his prowess, and she lapped it all up; musing about him and trying to picture him, she fell deeply in love with him—there was no topic on which she would more happily dwell or hear others discuss.

Equally the princess's peerless renown for beauty and excellence had travelled widely and reached Sicily, where it had come to the ears of Gerbino. The tale did not leave him indifferent, rather it kindled his love for her as powerfully as hers was inflamed for him. Until such time as he could hit upon a good reason to seek his grandfather's leave to go to Tunis—for he was dying to see the princess—each time a friend of his went there he bade him do his best to impart to her the secret of his powerful love in whatever way proved most suitable, and to bring him back news of her. One of them found a very clever way to perform the errand: he brought her some jewellery to look over, as merchants will, and informed her of Gerbino's passion, adding that the prince placed himself and all he possessed at her entire disposal. The princess gave the warmest welcome to the messenger and to the message. 'I burn for him with no less a love', she replied, in token of which she gave the messenger one of her most precious jewels to take back to the prince. No gift could have made Gerbino happier. He wrote to her several times by the same messenger and sent her costly presents; they pledged to take the first opportunity chance afforded them to see and touch each other.

This is how matters stood for all too long; but while the two lovers smouldered, the King of Tunis married off his daughter to the King of Granada.* This vexed the princess not a little: not only would she be separated from her lover by an even greater distance, she was for all practical purposes severed from him. Had she seen a way to do it, she would willingly have eluded her fate by escaping from her father and going to join her lover. Similarly, when Gerbino heard about the marriage he was unspeakably distressed and racked his brains for some way to snatch her by force in the event that she was sent to her husband by sea.

Now the King of Tunis had got wind of the affair and of Gerbino's intention. As the prince was no weakling nor lacking in courage, the king was in some trepidation and, when the time came to send his daughter to Granada, he first despatched a message to the King of Sicily advising him of what he planned to do; he would give effect to his proposal, he said, once he had the king's assurance that he would not be obstructed by Gerbino nor by anyone acting on his instructions. Now King Guglielmo was an old man and had no inkling of Gerbino's love for the princess, so it never crossed his mind that this lay behind the Tunisian request for guarantees; he readily granted the request, in token of which he sent the king his gauntlet.* Furnished with this guarantee, the king had a fine big ship made ready in the port of Carthage, provisioned it with everything necessary to those who were to take passage in it, and embellished it suitably for a vessel carrying his daughter to the King of Granada. Then he awaited the day.

None of this was hidden from the princess, who sent a page in secret to Palermo with instructions to greet the handsome Gerbino on her behalf and advise him that in a few days she would be setting out for Granada. If Gerbino was the man he was reputed to be, and if he loved her as much as he kept insisting, now was the time to show what he was made of. The page fulfilled his mission excellently and returned to Tunis. Gerbino received the message but, knowing that his grandfather had issued a guarantee of safe passage to the King of Tunis, he was in a quandary. However, he was in love, and he could not pass for a coward after receiving his beloved's summons, so he went to Messina and lost no time in fitting out two slender galleys for combat; he recruited a gallant crew and set sail for Sardinia, knowing that his lady's vessel was to pass that way.

Events now followed practically as he had forecast: he had been here only a few days when the princess's ship hove in sight fairly close to where he lay in wait—and it had little wind in its sails. On sight of it Gerbino addressed his crew: 'Gentlemen, if you're as good as I take you to be, there'll be not one of you who has not been in love—and it's my belief that a man's not worth his salt till he *has* been. Now you lovers will grasp readily enough what I'm after. I'm in love, which is why I've brought you here to lend a hand: my beloved is on board that ship you see. It holds my heart's desire—it is also heap-full of treasure, and this shall be ours with little effort if you fight like stalwarts. The only share I want from the victory is a woman, the one I've taken up arms for; the rest is all yours. Let's get after them, then, and may luck be with us—God is on our side: they're wallowing for lack of wind.'

Gerbino the Handsome could have spared his breath—his Messinese were already keyed up to do what he was inciting them to: plunder was their pleasure. When he finished his address they sent up a great roar of assent, sounded the trumpets, seized their weapons, manned the oars, and closed the Saracen ship. The Tunisians saw the galleys advancing upon them from a distance and, as they were unable to make sail, they prepared to ward them off. Once within hailing distance, Gerbino gave orders for the Saracen shipmasters to be transferred to the galleys if they wished to avoid a battle. When the Saracens had established who their assailants were and what they wanted, they claimed that the attack was a breach of King Guglielmo's trust, and they flourished the royal gauntlet to prove it; they asserted, furthermore, that they would never surrender nor cede them anything from their ship unless they were defeated in battle. Gerbino, however, had caught sight of his lady on the vessel's poop-deck and found her even more beautiful than he could ever have imagined, and this only inflamed him the more. When he was shown the gauntlet he remarked that in the absence of falcons he could see no use for a glove. If they were not going to hand over the lady, he said, they had better prepare for a fight. Without further ado the contenders let fly with stones and arrows, and this savage affray continued for a while, with casualties on both sides, until Gerbino, seeing that he was making little headway, set fire to a skiff he had towed out from Sardinia and pushed it against the enemy ship with the aid of his two galleys.

The Saracens now accepted that their only choice was to surrender or die. They therefore brought the princess out on deck—she had been down below, weeping—took her up to the prow of the ship, called across to Gerbino and, as she cried for help and mercy, butchered her in front of his eyes. Then they tossed her overboard, saying: 'Take her! We hand her to you as our situation requires, and your perfidy demands.' The sight of such cruelty left Gerbino feeling positively eager to die. Heedless of stones and arrows, he ordered his galley alongside and plunged into the thick of the enemy, like a hungry lion amidst a herd of bullocks, rending one after the next with his teeth and claws, sating his wrath even before his hunger: thus did Gerbino, cutting down one Saracen after the next with his sword and leaving a pile of savaged corpses. As the fire took hold of the Saracen ship, he bade his seamen help themselves to as much plunder as they could, then disembarked—victorious, but scarcely the happier for that. He had the beautiful princess's body pulled out of the sea, and bitterly wept over her for a long time. On their return to Sicily he gave her a dignified burial in Ustica, a little island that lay off Trapani. This done, he returned home, the saddest man in the world.

When the King of Tunis heard the news he sent ambassadors to King Guglielmo, all dressed in black, to complain of his breach of trust—and they reported what had happened. The king was profoundly shocked. The Tunisian ambassadors demanded justice, and King Guglielmo could see no way to deny their request. He had Gerbino arrested and, turning a deaf ear to his barons' entreaties, condemned him to be beheaded, which sentence was executed in his presence: he would sooner carry on without his grandson than be reputed a king who broke his word.

So the two lovers died a wretched death within days of each other, as I have described, without enjoying any of the fruits of their love.

IV. 5. *Lisabetta's brothers kill her lover. She plants his head in a large pot of basil and waters it with her tears.*

Elissa finished her tale. The king quite liked it, and told Philomena to go next. Philomena, who was feeling ever so sorry for poor Gerbino and his beloved, fetched a great sigh before she began:

My story won't be about anyone as highly placed as those in Elissa's, but I dare say it will be just as sad; I've been reminded of it by the mention just now of Messina, which is where it all happened.

In Messina there once were three young brothers; they were merchants, who had been left extremely well off on the death of their father, a man from San Gimignano, and they had a sister, a very pretty girl of gentle manners called Lisabetta whom, for whatever reason, they had not yet married off. Now in one of their warehouses the three brothers employed a young Pisan who was effectively in charge of their business and his name was Lorenzo; he was a handsome fellow, neatly turned out, and he began to exercise a remarkable attraction on Lisabetta, who saw quite a little of him. Lorenzo gradually became aware of this and began to make room for her in his heart, to the neglect of his other amours. Then one thing led to another and, finding each other equally congenial, it was not long before they made bold to give in to their mutual craving.

They carried on in this way for a while, deriving a great deal of enjoyment from their intimacy, until one night they were not quite furtive enough and, when Lisabetta went to the place where Lorenzo slept, her eldest brother spotted her without her ever realizing it. This brother, though, was no fool, and however upset he was by the discovery, he made the prudent decision to keep it to himself and bided his time until the following morning, as he turned over various considerations in his mind. In the morning he told his brothers what he had seen Lisabetta getting up to last night with Lorenzo. They discussed the question at some length and resolved to avoid any taint of dishonour attaching to them or to their sister by maintaining a discreet silence, and to pretend not to have seen a thing or to have acquired the slightest inkling of it until such time as they might set the matter to rights, without damaging their reputation, before it went any further.

Thus settled in their minds, they continued to joke and banter with Lorenzo in the same old way, and the time came when the three of them made a show of going for a day's outing in the country and invited Lorenzo along. They came to a very remote, isolated spot which they recognized as just what they were looking for; here they murdered Lorenzo, who was totally unsuspecting, and buried him so as to avoid attracting attention. In Messina they put it about that they had sent him away on business; this was perfectly credible for they were constantly sending him about the place on errands. As Lorenzo did not return, Lisabetta would be forever badgering her brothers for news of him, for his long absence weighed on her heart. One day, in view of her persistent questioning, one of her brothers said: 'What are you going on about? What is it to you where Lorenzo is? Why d'you keep asking? If you carry on like this, we'll give you the answer you've got coming to you.' So the unhappy girl, possessed by a nameless fear, gave up asking after him, and many a night she would call him so sadly and beg him to come; sometimes she would sob and weep over his long absence, and she just kept waiting for him, as doleful as could be.

One night, when she had wept for ages over Lorenzo who was still not back, and had eventually cried herself to sleep, he appeared to her in a dream.* He was pale and dishevelled and his clothes were in tatters, a horrible mess, and she dreamed that he said to her: 'O Lisabetta, you do nothing but call me and bewail my long absence and take me cruelly to task with your tears. Understand that I cannot return to you: the last day you saw me, your brothers murdered me.' He described the spot where they had buried him, then told her not to call out for him, not to expect him any more. With this he vanished.

Lisabetta awoke and wept bitterly, for she believed her dream. Getting up in the morning, she dared not say anything to her brothers, but determined to go to the spot shown to her and see if there was any truth in what her dream had indicated. She obtained permission to go on a little trip to the country with a maid who had been their companion in the old days and was acquainted with her secrets. So she went to the spot just as soon as she could and, after removing the dead leaves lying about, felt where the ground was the least hard, and there she dug; nor had she been digging for long before she came upon the corpse of her unfortunate lover, still quite preserved from corruption; so it was clear to her that what she had dreamed was true. Though she was as heartsick as could be, she realized that this was not the place to start crying and, though she would readily have taken away the entire body to give it a more suitable burial, she saw how impossible this was. So she took a knife and, as best she might, severed the head from the trunk and wrapped it in a towel; she shovelled earth back over the rest of the corpse, put the head in the maid's lap, and made her way home unobserved.

Here, she shut herself into her room with the head and shed bitter tears over it for a long time until she had washed it completely, and she planted a thousand kisses all over it. Then she took a beautiful earthenware pot, a great big one, the kind in which marjoram or basil tends to be grown, and in it she put the head, wrapped in a fine cloth; she filled the pot up with earth, planted a number of those lovely basil plants in it, the sort that come from Salerno, and these she would water only with rose-water, orange-flower water, or her tears. She acquired the habit of sitting next to this pot, making it the fondest object of her desires, as it was the repository of her Lorenzo. After gazing at it longingly, she would spend ages shedding tears over it until the basil was all well watered.

What with all the extended care she lavished on the basil and with the richness of the soil on account of the head rotting within it, the plants grew as fragrant and beautiful as could be. And as Lisabetta continued in this practice, her neighbours frequently observed it, and so they told her brothers: 'We've noticed that this is what she does every day.' The brothers had been perplexed at the way she was losing her looks and her eyes had become sunken in her cheeks. Hearing what the neighbours reported, and noticing it now for themselves, they chided her once or twice over this practice, but to no avail; therefore they had this pot secretly removed from her room. When she could not find it she persisted in asking for it back, but it was not returned to her; so there was no end to her tears and she fell ill; from her sick-bed all she would ask for was the return of her pot. The brothers were most surprised at her persistent request and wanted, therefore, to discover what was in this pot; they tipped out the earth, saw the cloth and, wrapped inside it, the head. This was not yet so decomposed that they could fail to identify it as Lorenzo's from the curly hair. Astonished as they were, they took fright at the possibility that news of it might get out. So they buried the head and, without another word, furtively slipped out of Messina and moved to Naples, arranging to have all their possessions shipped after them.

The girl never stopped crying and begging for her earthenware pot; she died weeping, and thus her ill-fated love had an end. Eventually news of it did get out, which was when someone wrote the song we still sing today,* that goes:

Who was he, the wicked thief
That stole my pot from me? . . .

IV. 6. *Andreuola and Gabriotto, secretly married, both have a dream of disaster. Their dreams are fulfilled all too soon.*

The ladies found Philomena's tale enormously satisfying, for they had heard this song countless times but never, however much they asked, had they been able to discover how it came to be composed. But when the king had heard the story to the end, he told Pamphilo to go next, so Pamphilo said:

The dream related in the last story is my cue for telling you a tale that makes mention of two, both of them prophetic, whereas the other was about something that had already happened. No sooner had the dreamers finished describing their dream than both dreams came true. Of course you realize there's nobody living who does not experience a glimpse of all manner of things in his sleep; and however true they appear to the dreamer as he sleeps, when he wakes up he'll decide that in some cases the dream might be true, in others it's plausible, and in others totally unreal; at all events, many a dream does turn out to be prophetic. There are many people who'll believe every dream as implicitly as anything they see in their waking hours, and their dreams fill them with gloom or elation depending on whether they're suggestive of fear or hope. Then there are the opposite, who will never pay the slightest attention to a dream until they've found themselves landed in the very peril it warned them of. I shouldn't commend either, for dreams are neither invariably true nor always untrue. That they don't always turn out to be true we all know from frequent experience; that they're not false every time Philomena has already shown in her story and, as I said, I shall show you in mine. You see, it's my view that one should never be discouraged or deterred from pursuing a life of virtue by any dream that points the opposite way; nor should anyone believe a dream that appears to encourage him toward some evil course. In the first case, however, the dream ought to be entirely believed. But now to my tale.

In Brescia there once lived a gentleman called Negro da Ponte Carraro. He had several children, including a very pretty young daughter called Andreuola, who was unmarried, but happened to be in love with another Brescian, called Gabriotto, a handsome, charming man of humble station but of impeccable conduct. With the active assistance of her maid, Andreuola contrived not only to convey to Gabriotto that she loved him, but even arranged his access to a lovely garden belonging to her father, where many a time they consorted together to their mutual satisfaction. And to avert the possibility that anything other than death might ever sunder this sweet love of theirs, they secretly became man and wife.

As they thus pursued their furtive couplings, one night the girl happened to dream a dream: she was in her garden with Gabriotto, holding him in her arms to the intense pleasure of both of them; as they were thus engaged, she saw a dreadful dark something, quite unlike anything she could recognize, come out of his body; it seized hold of Gabriotto and, despite her efforts, tore him out of her arms with astonishing force and vanished with him beneath the ground; that was the last she was to see of either of them. Her anguish was beyond description and it woke her out of her sleep. Though she was glad, once awake, to realize that it had not happened in reality but only in a dream, she still found the dream alarming. So, as Gabriotto wanted to come to her the following night, she did all she could to dissuade him; in view of his determination, however, she did receive him in her garden that night to avoid arousing his suspicions. She picked a great many roses, white and red,* for this was the season, and went to join him by a beautiful clear fountain in the garden. Here, after devoting themselves to many caresses, Gabriotto asked her why she had earlier told him not to come. She explained her reason by describing to him the dream she had had the previous night and the fear it had left in her.

Gabriotto scoffed when he heard it, and told her how very silly it was to take any notice of dreams; they only happened because one had overeaten or not eaten enough, and there was absolutely nothing to them, it was obvious any day. 'If I were minded to pay attention to dreams', he added, 'it's not your dream but one that I myself had last night that would have kept me away. In mine, I'd gone hunting in a lovely wood, and I'd captured the most beautiful, darling hind you ever saw.

She was whiter than snow, and in no time she was so tame she'd never leave my side. I so treasured her that, to avoid her ever leaving me I put a golden collar round her neck and secured her by a golden chain* I held in my hand. And as this hind was resting with her head in my lap, a greyhound appeared out of nowhere; she was black as coal, ravenous and simply terrifying to look at; she made for me and I was powerless to resist her. She forced her muzzle into my left side and gnawed her way through to my heart; she tore it out and carried it off. The pain I felt startled me out of my sleep: wide awake, I quickly felt my left side to see what had happened but, not finding anything amiss, I called myself a fool for my instinctive action. So where does that leave us? I've had such dreams and far more terrifying ones in my time, and they've never made the slightest difference to what's actually happened to me—so just take no notice of them and let's enjoy ourselves.'

If Andreuola was already badly frightened by her own dream, she was far more terrified when she heard what he said, but she concealed her fear as well as she could in order to avoid distress to Gabriotto. And though she took her pleasure with him, giving him hugs and kisses from time to time and receiving his, she remained on the alert without knowing quite what for: she kept looking into his face, far more than she usually did, and cast an occasional glance round the garden to see if any black thing were approaching from anywhere.

This was the situation when Gabriotto heaved a great sigh and clung to her, saying: 'Oh help, my love, I'm dying!' This said, he fell back on to the meadow grass.

Andreuola drew him onto her lap when she saw this. 'My darling', she almost sobbed, 'what's the matter?'

Gabriotto made no reply but broke out in a sweat and fought for breath; after a moment he had quit the present life.

You can imagine the girl's pain and distress, for she loved him more than her own self. How she wept over him, how many times did she call his name, to no avail! When she finally realized that he was absolutely dead, after she had felt him all over and found him stone cold, she was at a loss what to do or say; heart-broken, she went in tears to find her maid, who was privy to her love, and told her of the disaster over which she was grieving.

After they had both shed bitter tears for a while over the face of the dead youth, Andreuola said to her maid: 'As the Lord has taken him from me, I don't intend to go on living. But before I kill myself, we must find some proper way to protect my good name and the secret of our love, and we must see his body buried, now that it has been forsaken by his gallant soul.'

'O my child, don't speak of taking your life', said her maid. 'You've lost him in this world, and if you kill yourself, you'll lose him also in the next, for you would go to hell, and I'm sure that's not where *his* soul has gone—he was a good lad. You'd do far better to take courage and devote yourself to helping his soul with your prayers and other good works, in case he needs them on account of some sin of his. He could be buried soon enough right here in this garden: no one will ever know, for no one knows he ever came here. If you don't like that, let's just leave him outside the garden—he'll be found in the morning and taken back home and buried by his family.'

However wrought up she was, the sobbing girl did listen to her maid's advice and, while she would not consent to her first suggestion, she answered the second, saying: 'He was such a darling boy, I so loved him—and he was my husband: God forbid that I should ever let him be buried like a dog, or left lying out in the road! I've wept over him and I'll do all I can to see that his family does so too; I think I know what we're going to have to do.'

She sent her maid straight off to fetch a length of silk she kept in a chest. Her maid returned with it, they spread it out on the ground, laid Gabriotto's body on it, rested his head on a cushion, and closed his eyes and lips with many tears. Then they made a garland of roses and scattered round him many more they had picked, after which she said to her maid: 'It's not far from here to the door of his house. So you and I will take him the way we now have him, and set him down outside it. It won't be long till daybreak, when he'll be brought in. And though this won't be much consolation to his family, it will still make me happy, in whose arms he died.'

With these words she fell on his face in a renewed fit of weeping and cried for ages until, at her maid's urgent prompting—as day was now close—she stood up, drew off her finger the ring with which Gabriotto had betrothed her, and slipped it on to his finger, tearfully saying: 'My darling, if your spirit sees my tears, and no sensation or awareness remains in your body now your soul has left it, receive with kindness this last gift from the one whom as you lived you so cherished.' Thus saying, she fell upon him in a swoon.

In a little while she recovered her senses and stood up; she and her maid grasped the silk cloth on which the body lay and left the garden with it, to make their way to Gabriotto's house. On their way, they were caught in possession of the corpse by men from the Podestà's guard, who happened to be out at that moment to attend to some incident. Andreuola recognized the men for who they were but, having more taste for death than for going on with her life, she told them quite openly: 'I know who you are. I know I'd gain nothing by trying to run away. I'm ready to come with you to the Podestà's palace and explain myself to him. But if I obey you, don't any of you dare touch me, or take anything from this corpse, or I'll lay an accusation against you.' So she went to the Podestà's palace with Gabriotto's body, and no one laid a finger on her.

On hearing about it, the Podestà rose up and, as he kept Andreuola there in the room, established for himself just what had happened. Moreover he had some doctors in to ascertain whether the good fellow had been killed by poisoning or some other way, but they all said no, a cyst had ruptured close to his heart and he had suffocated. When he heard this and realized that she could be taxed with only the most trivial offence, he tried making a show of giving her that which he was in no position to sell her: if she was ready to satisfy his desire, he said, he would set her at liberty. As such words proved unavailing, however, he resorted to a quite unseemly use of force, but Andreuola, fired by outrage and therefore endowed with exceptional strength, bravely held him off and forced him back with scornful insults.

When it was fully daylight and the news was brought to Andreuola's father, he was quite sick at heart and went to the

Podestà's palace with several of his friends. Here the Podestà told him the whole story, and he bitterly requested the return of his daughter. The Podestà, who was anxious to meet the accusation of having tried to violate Andreuola before she herself levelled the charge, spoke warmly of the girl and her constancy and said he had treated her the way he had done in order to test her out. And seeing how resolute she was, he had quite fallen in love with her; if he was agreeable, as her father, and she was willing, he would gladly take her for his wife despite the fact that she had been married to a man of no consequence.

While these two were thus conversing, Andreuola came into her father's presence, threw herself down, weeping, before him, and said: 'Father, I don't think I need tell you about how brazen I was, nor what a blow I have received, for I'm sure you know it all from others. So I humbly beg you with all my heart to forgive me for my offence, I mean for having without your knowledge taken for my husband the man I loved best. And if I ask your pardon it is not that my life might be spared, but that I may die still your daughter, not your enemy.' With these words she fell sobbing at his feet.

Her father was an old man by this time, a man of intrinsic kindness, and these words moved him to tears; as he wept he tenderly drew the girl to her feet and said: 'It would have been my dearest wish that you would marry a man who seemed to me suitable for you, and if you had chosen the man you loved, that would have rejoiced my heart. Keeping it a secret as you have done saddens me because of your lack of trust, and all the more so seeing that you have lost him even before I knew anything about it. But this is how things are, and so let me do for him now he is dead what I should willingly have done for your sake while he was yet alive, that is, give him the respect due to my son-in-law.' He now turned to his other children and family and bade them to prepare for Gabriotto's funeral, and it was to be sumptuous and honourable.

Meanwhile the young man's relatives, both men and women, had all arrived on hearing the news—virtually the entire city foregathered. Gabriotto's corpse was laid out in the middle of the palace courtyard on Andreuola's silk cloth with all her roses, and here he was mourned not only by the girl and by all Gabriotto's womenfolk, but nearly all the townswomen wept for him in public, and many of the men, too. Then he was carried out of the courtyard, not as a commoner but as a man of high birth; he was lifted on to the shoulders of the noblest men in the city and borne with greatest pomp to his burial.

A few days later the Podestà pursued his request for Andreuola's hand. Her father spoke to her about it, but she would not hear of it, and her father was willing to accommodate her wishes. So Andreuola and her maid entered a convent renowned for its holiness; here they took the veil and lived virtuous lives for many a year.

IV. 7. *When Pasquino dies from plucking a sage-leaf and rubbing his teeth with it, his beloved Simona is accused of poisoning him. In proving her innocence she goes to join her lover.*

When Pamphilo had delivered himself of his story, the king, evidently quite unmoved by Andreuola's fate, looked at Emilia to indicate his pleasure that she should take up where the others had left off. She began without wasting time:

Pamphilo's tale induces me to tell you one that is quite different to his except in one particular: Andreuola lost her beloved in a garden, and so did the girl in my story. She too was arrested, as Andreuola was, but she escaped the Law's clutches not by force nor by any merit but by dying unexpectedly. As some of us have already observed, however ready Love is to make himself at home in the households of the nobility, that does not stop him exercising his authority in the homes of the poor; indeed, he sometimes displays his power here to such effect that he instils fear into the wealthiest men. This will, to a considerable extent at any rate, be apparent in my tale, with which I should like to return to our own city, as our stories today have followed one thread and another, taking us all over the place, and rather getting us away from home.

There lived in Florence not so long ago a very pretty young wench called Simona; she was graceful in her humble way, her father being a poor man. She had to earn her bread by the labour of her hands, and pursued her trade at the spinning-wheel, which is not to say she lacked spirit or would cringe from the prospect of Love. And Love had shown an interest in gaining admittance for some time now, in the agreeable speech and conduct of a lad who occupied no higher a place in the world than she did—his task was to deliver the wool for spinning on behalf of his master, a wool-merchant. So she welcomed Love in the pleasing features of the youth who courted her—his name was Pasquino—but, however much she yearned for him, she dared not take the necessary steps; as she spun, she would mark each length of yarn wound off the spindle with a thousand burning sighs as she thought of the lad who had brought her the wool. For his part, Pasquino pressed her insistantly to ensure that she spun his master's wool to perfection, as though it was only Simona's yarn and nobody else's that was to be used in the cloth, and hers, therefore, that was his chief concern. So as the boy pressed and the girl relished being pressed, the former grew uncharacteristically bold while the latter overcame a good deal of her customary diffidence and shyness, with the result that they ended up making love, and this was something they both found so much to their taste that, far from waiting to be invited, they vied with each other to be the first to suggest it.

So they pursued their mutual pleasure from day to day, growing the more impassioned all the time, until Pasquino told Simona that she really had to find some way to join him in a garden he wanted to visit with her, as that way they could be together at greater leisure and less risk. Simona was pleased to accept and, one Sunday after lunch, she informed her father that she wished to attend the Indulgence at the church of San Gallo,* and off she went with her friend Lagina to the garden in accordance with Pasquino's directions. Here she found him, accompanied by his mate Puccino, nicknamed Crackpot, who was soon exchanging melting looks with Lagina. Pasquino and

Simona then withdrew to enjoy themselves in one part of the garden, leaving Lagina and the Crackpot to their own devices in another.

In the corner of the garden to which Pasquino and Simona had retired there grew an enormous, splendid sage-bush beside which they sat down and spent a long time in each other's arms; after this they chatted for a good while about a leisurely picnic they proposed to enjoy in this garden. Then Pasquino turned round and plucked a leaf from the great sage-bush and started rubbing it on his teeth and gums: a leaf of sage, he said, was just the thing to clean them of any deposits after eating. He went on rubbing them for a little, then reverted to discussing the picnic, but he had been talking for only a few moments when his face was quite transformed; the next thing was, he lost his sight and the power of speech and, shortly after, he was dead. Simona set up a howl when she saw it and yelled for Crackpot and Lagina, who came running. When Crackpot saw Pasquino not merely dead but all bloated, his face and body marked with livid patches, he burst out: 'You witch, you've poisoned him!' What with the great rumpus, many of the neighbours whose dwellings overlooked the garden rushed in and found the boy quite dead and all bloated; they listened to Crackpot's recriminations and heard him accuse Simona of having cunningly poisoned him, while she, quite beside herself with grief at the unexpected accident that had cost her her lover, couldn't find words to exculpate herself, so that they all accepted Crackpot's account as the true one.

So they seized her as she stayed there weeping and marched her off to the Podestà's palace. Here Crackpot pressed his charges, abetted by two friends who had now appeared on the scene, Apeman and Clumsy Oaf, and a magistrate lost no time in cross-examining her. However, as he failed to understand how she could have acted with malice aforethought or incurred any guilt, he determined to bring her along and take a look at the corpse *in situ* and see how it all fitted her description, for he couldn't make head nor tale of her testimony. So without more ado he had her led off to where Pasquino's body still lay, tubby as a barrel and, after stepping up and viewing it in astonishment, he asked her how it had happened. Simona went up to the sage-bush and, after telling him everything that had led up to the incident, to make it all absolutely clear to him, she imitated Pasquino, rubbing one of those sage-leaves on her teeth. Crackpot, Apeman, and Pasquino's other cronies jeered at this as idle chatter to present a judge with; they pressed their criminal charges all the more assiduously—they would be satisfied with nothing less than the stake as punishment for wickedness such as hers. Now poor Simona, crazed with grief as she was over her lost beloved and with terror at the penalty that Crackpot was demanding, fell victim to the same accident that had overtaken Pasquino from rubbing his teeth with the sage-leaf. All those present were not a little surprised.

O happy souls, one and the same day set a term to your fervent love and your mortal lives! O happier, if together you departed for the same destination! And happier still, if there is loving in the next life, and you love each other there as you did in this! But far and away the happiest of all was Simona's spirit—if you ask us, who have remained behind—as her innocence eluded the fate of succumbing beneath the testimony of Crackpot, Apeman, and Clumsy Oaf, fellows who were probably nothing better than wool-carders, perhaps not even that! Committed to sharing her lover's death, she was afforded a more honourable path by which to escape from their obloquy and follow the soul of her Pasquino whom she loved so dearly.

The magistrate was utterly dumbfounded, and so was everyone else; at a loss for words, he brooded for a while until he recovered his composure. 'Evidently', he observed, 'this sage-bush is poisonous, which sage-bushes generally are not. However, to ensure that it cannot do further injury, have it cut down, root and branch, and thrown on the fire.'

The custodian of the garden carried out this order in the magistrate's presence, and the big bush was no sooner cut down than the cause of the two unfortunate lovers' deaths came to light. Beneath the bush a toad of quite remarkable size was discovered, and the bush had, they realized, become infected with its poisonous exhalations. No one dared approach the creature, so they surrounded it with a huge pyre and burnt it along with the bush. So ended the magistrate's inquest on the death of poor Pasquino, who was buried together with his

Simona, all bloated as they were, in the church of San Paolo by Crackpot, Apeman, Mucky Pup, and Clumsy Oaf, all of whom happened to belong to this parish.

IV. 8. *While the young boy Girolamo is sent away to Paris, his beloved Salvestra is given a husband. The boy returns to find his beloved has forgotten him. What happens when he decides to die.*

Emilia's story reached its conclusion, whereupon Neiphile, at the king's bidding, began hers thus:

There are certain people, to my mind, who believe they have all the answers but the fact is they don't. And that's why they presume to back their own judgement not only against that of other people but even against things as they are. This sort of presumption has always led to the worst outcome—no good has ever been known to come of it. Now of all the things that are in our nature the one that is least receptive to advice or contradiction is love; the nature of love is such that it may more readily burn out of its own accord than be rooted out by anybody's influence. So it has occurred to me to tell you the story of a woman who was not all that clever (nor had she any business to be) but still tried to be; she could not tolerate the situation in which she sought to interfere, and she believed she could extirpate love from a love-struck heart—though possibly it had been planted there by the stars. The result was that in rooting out love from her son's heart she also put an end to his life.

Well, once upon a time there lived in our city, so tradition has it, a very important and wealthy merchant called Leonardo Sighieri. His wife gave him a son called Girolamo, but soon after he was born Leonardo set his affairs in order and passed away. The boy's mother and guardians took good charge of his affairs, conducting them with integrity, and the child grew up with the neighbours' children. Now of all the children along the street the one who became his closest friend was a little girl of his age, a tailor's daughter. As they grew up their friendship turned to love, a love so passionate that Girolamo was happy only in her company; she too, moreover, was every whit as much in love with him.

Noticing this, the boy's mother took him to task several times and chided him but, as Girolamo could not give up the girl, the lady went and complained to his guardians, for in her view the boy's considerable fortune earned him a place with the peacocks, not the sparrows. 'This lad of ours', she told them, 'who's barely turned 14 is so smitten with the daughter of our local tailor—her name's Salvestra—if we don't take him away, the chances are he'll go ahead and marry her one day without anybody knowing, and I'll never smile again. Or else he'll pine away for love of her if he sees her married to someone else. So it seems to me, if we want to avoid this, you ought to send him to some distant spot in connection with the business: once she's far from his sight she'll go out of his thoughts; then we'll be able to marry him to some girl of gentle birth.'

What the mother said was, the guardians agreed, well spoken and they told her they would do their best. They summoned the lad into the office and one of them spoke to him most affectionately: 'Well, my boy, you really are growing up now, and it will be no bad thing if you start to take a hand in the business. We should be only too pleased if you went to live in Paris for a while, as that's where you'll see how a good part of your fortune's being turned to account. Besides, up there you'll develop far better and pick up more polish than you would do staying here, for you'll be learning how to behave as you observe all those gentlemen of high birth and good breeding. Then you may come home.'

The boy listened attentively but replied, in short, that he didn't want to go: as a place to live he found Florence as congenial to him as it was to the next man. The good fellows tried again with an abundance of words, but as they could elicit no different answer from him they applied to his mother. At this she flew into a rage—not because he refused to go to Paris but because he was lovesick—and she gave him a piece of her mind. Later, however, she turned to coaxing and wheedling him with honeyed words, begging him to be a dear and do as his guardians were asking. She so far succeeded that he agreed to go there for one year, and no longer. And off he went.

If Girolamo went to Paris a lovesick swain, after being kept there for two years ('Only another week . . .' 'Just a fortnight more . . .') he returned home more lovesick than ever. Here he found his Salvestra married to a good lad, a tent-maker by trade. So he could not have felt more wretched. However, seeing that it could not be helped, he tried to reconcile himself. He looked to see where it was that she lived and took to passing back and forth in front of her house, as young lovers do, for he imagined that she had not forgotten him any more than he her. This, though, was far from being the case: for all she remembered of him she might never have set eyes on him—and if she did retain any faint recollection, she certainly showed no sign of it. Well, it didn't take the boy two minutes to realize this, and it upset him not a little. He did everything within his power to remind her of himself, and as it all seemed to prove unavailing, he decided he had to speak to her in person, even if that was the last thing he did.

From a neighbour he discovered the plan of her house and one evening, which Salvestra and her husband were spending with neighbours, he crept in by stealth, entered her bedroom, and hid behind some strips of tent-canvas hanging up there. He waited until they came back and retired to bed and he heard the husband go off to sleep; then he moved across to where he had seen her lying, pressed his hand on her breast, and whispered: 'Darling, you're not yet asleep are you?'

Salvestra was indeed awake and made to scream, but the lad quickly blurted out: 'For heaven's sake don't scream: I'm your own Girolamo.'

She was quaking as she said in reply: 'Please, Girolamo, for Goodness' sake go! Being in love with each other was all right when we were children but those days are long past. Now I'm a married woman as you see, and it is no longer right for me to pay attention to any man but my husband. So I beg you in God's name to be gone: if my husband heard you, even if nothing worse happened to me, it could still mean the end of my living with him in peace, whereas he still loves me and we lead a good, peaceful life together.'

Girolamo found this all very painful to hear; he reminded her of old times and of his love which no degree of distance had diminished; he begged and entreated and made her the most lavish promises, but he obtained nothing for his pains. So, wishing now only to die, he made a last prayer that, as a reward for so great a love, she might let him lie down beside her just long enough to warm himself up a little, for he had become frozen as he waited up for her; he promised he would not say a word to her nor touch her, and when he had got back a little warmth he would leave her. Feeling a bit sorry for him, Salvestra granted his wish on the conditions he had proposed, so Girolamo lay down beside her without touching her; and as he considered his long-nurtured love for her and how hard she was now being on him and the loss of his hopes, he made up his mind to live no longer: he concentrated all his faculties, clenched his fists, and without uttering a sound, expired beside her.

In a little while Salvestra started puzzling over the look on his face and, anxious in case her husband woke up, she said: 'Come, Girolamo, why aren't you going?' As she got no answer out of him she assumed he had fallen asleep, so she put out a hand to prod him awake, but found him ice-cold to the touch. Quite bewildered at this, she prodded him the harder and realized that he was not stirring at all; after feeling him all over she knew that he was dead. This caused her the greatest distress and she just lay there for ages, utterly nonplussed. Eventually she had the idea of seeing what her husband's advice would be if the thing had happened at one remove, so she woke him up and told him what had just actually happened to her but recounted it as though it had befallen someone else. 'Supposing that had happened to me', she asked; 'what would you have suggested I do?' The good fellow replied that he thought the dead man should have been carried back quietly to his own house and left there, without thinking any the worse of the wife, for he didn't think she'd done anything wrong.

'Right', said Salvestra. 'That's what we must do.' She took his hand and made him feel the dead youth's corpse. Utterly flabbergasted, he got up, lit a lamp and, without further discussion, put the corpse back into its clothes and hastily lifted it on to his shoulders. Protected by his innocence, he carried the dead boy to his own front door and there he set him down and left him.

When it was day and the boy was discovered lying dead outside his front door, everybody made a great commotion, not least the boy's mother. The doctors examined him all over and, finding no trace of any injury or bruising, they all concluded that he had died of sheer sorrow, as was the case. So the body was borne off to a church, and here the grieving mother came with several other women—neighbours and relatives—to mourn and weep over him copiously, after our traditional fashion.

While all this weeping and wailing was in progress, Salvestra's husband, in whose home the boy had died, said to her: 'Throw a veil over your head and go to the church where Girolamo has been taken, and join the other women; keep an ear open for what they're saying about this, and I'll do the same among the men. That way we'll be able to hear if they're saying anything bad about us.' Salvestra agreed, for she had melted at the last moment and wanted to see the boy now he was dead, though when he was alive she would not requite him with so much as a single kiss. And off she went.

How hard it is to penetrate the power of Love!—it's amazingly difficult, when you think of it. Here was a heart which Girolamo had been unable to touch when Fortune smiled on him, but to which he gained access in adversity: the former passion was rekindled and transformed into a sudden surge of pity. When Salvestra caught sight of the dead boy's face she slipped through the throng of women, wrapped in her cloak, till she arrived at the corpse, whereupon she uttered a piercing cry and flung herself face-down upon the dead youth; if she bathed him in only a few tears, that was because she had scarcely touched him when her life, as that of Girolamo, was forfeit to grief. The women, not recognizing yet who she was, sought to console her and coax her to her feet; as she would not stand up, they tried to lift her but found her quite inert; so then they did raise her up, at which point they discovered that she was Salvestra and that she was dead. On this account all the women present were overcome with a double burden of pity and broke out into even greater fits of weeping.

Word of this spilled out of the church and among the menfolk; so it came to the ears of Salvestra's husband, who was in their company. He wept for ages, deaf to all words of comfort. Then he told a great many of the men there assembled the story of what had taken place in the night between his wife and this young man, so it became clear to everyone what it was that had caused their deaths, much to everybody's distress. Then they took the dead girl and laid her out, dressed for burial, on the same bier beside the youth. They wept over her for a long time, after which the two of them were buried in one tomb. And the pair, whom Love had been unable to unite when they were among the living, were joined in an inseparable bond by Death.

IV. 9. *Guillaume de Cabestaing becomes the lover of Guillaume de Roussillon's wife. Roussillon invites Cabestaing to dinner, with tragic consequences.*

So ended Neiphile's story, leaving the ladies by no means unmoved. Then the king, who was not disposed to infringe Dioneo's privilege, began his tale, there being no one else left to speak.

As lovers' misfortunes occasion you such sadness, you soft-hearted ladies, a story has occurred to me that should appeal to your compassion no less than the last, for the persons involved in the tale I shall tell were of greater consequence, and what befell them was more brutal than in the previous instance.

Be it known, then, that in Provence, as local tradition relates, there were once upon a time two noble knights, each with his own castles and vassals; one of them was called Guillaume de Roussillon, the other, Guillaume de Cabestaing.* As they were both champion warriors they were the closest of friends and habitually attended every tournament, joust, and suchlike armed encounter sporting the identical blazon. Now Guillaume de Roussillon was married to a most beautiful and attractive woman, and although each knight lived in his own castle, some ten miles apart, Guillaume de Cabestaing happened to fall head over heels in love with her regardless of the bond of friendship between the two men, and contrived in one way and another to acquaint the lady with his sentiments. She recognized him for the most gallant of knights and was not indifferent to him; indeed, she began to reciprocate his feelings to the point that he became the exclusive object of her love and desire, and all she awaited was his summons. This was not too long in coming, and they held one tryst after another when they made passionate love.

As they grew a little careless together, her husband found them out and was quite enraged: his devotion to Cabestaing turned into deadly hate, though he was more successful in concealing this than the two lovers had been in their own concealment. He firmly made up his mind to murder the man. Now, with Roussillon thus decided, a great tournament was announced in France, and he at once imparted the news to Cabestaing, sending him an invitation, if he wished, to come and discuss whether they would go and, if so, how. Cabestaing was delighted to send answer that he would come without fail the next day to have supper with him.

From this reply Roussillon concluded that the time had come to kill him, so the next day he set out on horseback, armed, with a small retinue to lay an ambush about a mile from the castle in a wood through which Cabestaing would be passing. After waiting for some time he saw Cabestaing arrive with a couple of pages, none of them carrying weapons, for he expected no danger from this quarter. Once Roussillon saw the visitor reach the spot he had chosen, he leapt out at him, brandishing his lance, with murder in his heart, and cried: 'Traitor, you're a dead man!' As he spoke, he drove the lance through his chest. Transfixed by the lance, Cabestaing fell and soon died without having been able to defend himself or utter a word. His pages turned their horses' heads without discovering who it was who had done this deed, and fled for all they were worth back to their lord's castle. Roussillon dismounted, drew a dagger, opened Cabestaing's breast, and with his own hands plucked out his heart; he had it wrapped in a lance pennoncel and bade one of his men carry it; then he mounted again and, after giving orders that no one was to dare say a word about it, he returned to his castle, night having now fallen.

His wife had heard that Cabestaing was expected for dinner this evening and was eagerly waiting for him; as she did not see him arrive she was not a little perplexed and asked her husband: 'How comes it that Cabestaing is not here?'

'He's sent word to say he cannot come till tomorrow.' This news left the lady somewhat disgruntled.

Roussillon dismounted, sent for his cook, and told him: 'Here's a boar's heart: take it and turn it into the most delectable and savoury dish you can. When I'm at table, serve it up to me in a silver bowl.' The cook bore it off, sliced it thinly, added the choicest spices in good measure, and devoted all his pains and skill to turning it into the most exquisite dainty.

At the appointed time, Roussillon sat down to dinner with his wife. The food arrived, but he ate little, for he was too preoccupied with the crime he had committed. The cook sent in the delicacy and Roussillon had it set in front of his wife; for her benefit he lavished praise on it but claimed to have little appetite this evening. His wife had not lost *her* appetite, however, and tried a little of it; she found it delicious and cleaned up the entire dish.

When he observed that she had finished it: 'Well', he asked. 'How did you like it?'

'Absolutely delicious', she replied.

'Heaven help me, I do believe you: it's hardly surprising that what you so craved for as it lived you should find to your taste now it's dead.'

This remark gave her pause. 'What d'you mean?' she asked. 'What is it you've served up to me?'

'Actually what you've just eaten was the heart of Guillaume de Cabestaing, whom you were so in love with, being the unfaithful wife you are. You can be sure that's what it was because I tore it out of his breast with these very hands, shortly before I came back.'

There is no need to ask whether the lady was distressed when she heard this about the man she loved above all things. After a while she said: 'You behaved as one would expect of a devious and mean-spirited knight: if I gave him my heart when he placed me under no obligation to do so, and in this way affronted you, it was I rather than he who should have been punished. But God forbid that any other food should follow after a morsel as noble as the heart of a brave and gallant knight, for such was Guillaume de Cabestaing!'

There was a window behind her; she stood up and without a second thought dropped backwards out of it. The window was high above the ground, so not only did she fall to her death, she was dashed to pieces. Roussillon was stunned by the sight and felt he had done wrong. As he was afraid of the local people and of the Count of Provence, he had his horses saddled and rode away.

The following morning the entire neighbourhood learned what had happened. The two corpses were gathered up by Guillaume de Cabestaing's retainers and by those from the lady's domain, and were placed in one tomb together, amid bitter weeping and wailing, in the chapel of the lady's castle. On the tomb were inscribed some lines to identify the couple here buried and the manner and occasion of their deaths.

IV. 10. *Two young men steal a chest out in the street, not realizing that inside it is a man sound asleep, and they bring it home. The man wakes up and is arrested as a burglar. Only the quick wit of a maid and a mistress save him from the gallows.*

As the king had completed his tale, the task now confronted only Dioneo. Realizing this, and anyway so instructed by the king, he began:

Those woeful tales told of unhappy love have brought tears to my eyes and sadness to my heart as well as to yours, my ladies; so I could not wait for them to be over and done with. Now that they're finished, thank heavens (unless I took it into my head to make my own sorry contribution to this joyless topic, which God forbid!), I shall make a start upon something better and altogether happier, instead of pursuing such a painful theme, and perhaps give a good indication of what is in store for tomorrow's story-telling.

What you have to know is that not all that long ago in Salerno there lived a surgeon, Mazzeo della Montagna, a man at the top of his profession. He was well advanced in years when he married a wife; a well-born beauty from the same city, and he kept her well supplied with gorgeous and expensive clothing, with jewellery and whatever else is surest to please a lady. In this respect she was better treated than any other woman of Salerno,* though she did, truth to tell, suffer from an almost permanent chill, for her husband neglected to cover her adequately in bed. And just as Ricciardo di Chinzica,* whom we mentioned earlier, taught his wife all about holy days, so did this man demonstrate to his spouse that a man had to sleep with a woman only once to need several days to recover his strength, and nonsense of that kind. This sort of life suited her not one jot. Being a sensible woman, though, and spirited as well, she determined to spare the man of the house and look out in the street for another male whose strength she might sap instead. She passed a good number of young men under review and eventually settled for one on whom she would bestow herself, heart and soul. The young man was delighted when he woke up to this and in his turn fell irrevocably in love with her. His name was Ruggieri d'Ajeroli, a man of high birth but of a reprehensible and pernicious style of living: he no longer possessed a friend or relative who had a good word for him or was willing to see him, and throughout Salerno he enjoyed the most dismal reputation on account of his thieving and similar execrable behaviour. None of this greatly troubled the lady, who found in him other attractions, and with her maid's help she arranged to meet him. Once they had taken their pleasure together a little, the lady chided him over his past life and asked him for her sake to turn over a new leaf, to which end she started supporting him with the occasional sum of money.

As they continued together in this way with every possible precaution, the surgeon happened to be given charge of a patient with a diseased leg. After examining the problem, he told the sick man's family he would have to remove a gangrenous bone from the leg, otherwise there would be nothing for it but to amputate the entire limb or to let him die. He might succeed in curing him, he said, by excising the bone, but he would only accept the patient at their own risk, even if the man were to die. Those responsible for the patient agreed among themselves and entrusted him to the surgeon on his terms. Realizing that the patient would find the pain unbearable and would not let himself be operated on unless he were drugged with an opiate, the surgeon prepared a distillation in the morning, made to his own recipe: once taken, it would put the patient to sleep for as long as he expected to be inflicting pain on him in the course of the operation, which he was going to perform in the evening. He fetched in some of this potion and placed it in a window of his bedroom without telling anyone what it was. That evening, though, as the surgeon was about to attend his patient, he received a message from some close friends of his at Amalfi, saying that he must come straight away without fail: there had been a terrible fight leaving a great many wounded. The surgeon therefore postponed the operation on the leg until the next morning and set out in a skiff for Amalfi. On discovering that he would not be at home that night, as he usually was, his wife sent for Ruggieri in secret and left him in the bedroom, locking him in until certain other members of the household had retired to bed.

Now as Ruggieri waited in the room for his lady, he noticed in the window this phial containing the liquid that the surgeon had prepared for his patient; and, whether he had had a hard day or he'd eaten something salty or whether he simply had a tendency to thirst, as he was dying for a drink he assumed that the liquid was plain water and, setting the phial to his lips, tossed it back to the last drop. A moment later he was overcome with drowsiness and fell asleep. The wife came into the bedroom as soon as she could and found Ruggieri asleep, so she poked him and whispered: 'Come on, wake up!' but all to no purpose—he made no answer and did not stir. So, with a touch of exasperation, she gave him a harder shake and said: 'Wake up, you lazybones! If it's sleep you wanted, you'd have done better to go home and not come here.' Ruggieri had lain down on a chest and her shove landed him on the floor; he showed no more sign of life than you would find in a corpse. Somewhat alarmed now, she tried to pull him up; she shook him more vigorously, grabbed him by the nose, tweaked his beard, but it was all no use—a log never slept more soundly. By now she was very much afraid that he was dead, though she kept on pinching him and searing him with a candle-flame, but to no effect. Her husband might be a physician but she was not, so she was now convinced that he was dead. Desperately in love with him as she was, there's no need to ask whether she felt upset. Without daring to utter a sound, she quietly wept over him and grieved over this disastrous turn of affairs.

After a while, fearing that her loss would be compounded by exposure, it occurred to her that she should not waste a minute in finding some way to get the corpse out of the house. Quite at a loss for ideas, she quietly called her maid, showed her the problem, and asked what she advised. The maid could not believe her eyes, but plucked and pinched him as well until she could see how inanimate he was and concurred with her mistress's opinion that he was unmistakably dead. He must, she advised, be got out of the house.

'Where can we put him, though', the wife asked her, 'so as not to attract suspicion, when he's found in the morning, that he came out of this house?'

'Late this evening, ma'am, I noticed a chest of medium size across the street from the shop of our neighbour the cabinet-maker; if he hasn't brought it in, it will be the very thing: we can pop him inside and stab him a couple of times and leave him there. I can't see why anyone finding him inside it's going to think he came out of here sooner than anywhere else. In fact, as he was such a bad lot they'll think he was up to no good and got done in by some enemy and put inside the chest.'

The maid's advice appealed to her mistress, apart from the bit about stabbing him, for she couldn't for the world find it in herself, she said, to do such a thing. She sent her maid to see if the chest was still where she had noticed it, and she came back to say it was. So the maid, who was young and robust, heaved Ruggieri across her shoulder, with her mistress's help, and off they went, the lady going ahead to see that the coast was clear; they came to the chest, put Ruggieri inside, shut the lid, and left him there.

Around that time a couple of young men had taken up residence in a house a little further on; they were usurers by trade, and inclined towards handsome profits and small outlays. As they were short of furniture and had spotted the chest the previous day, they agreed to fetch it in if it were still there after dark. When the night was well advanced, they stepped outside, located the chest and, without giving it a closer scrutiny, carried it swiftly indoors—though it did strike them as rather heavy—and set it down outside a bedroom in which their womenfolk were sleeping. Without bothering to fix upon a final position for it there and then, they just left it and went to bed.

Ruggieri had had a long sleep, but once the beverage had been absorbed into his system and lost its effect he woke up. It was almost day. But for all that his sleep was ended and he had recovered his senses, he was still utterly dazed, and was to remain fuzzy in the head not only that night but for many days to come. He opened his eyes, saw nothing, felt about him with his hands, and discovered that he was in this chest; then he began to ramble, saying: 'What's this? Where am I? Am I asleep or awake? I remember coming into my lady's bedroom tonight, and now I seem to be inside a chest. What can it mean? Can it be that the doctor returned, or did something else happen which made my beloved hide me in here while I was asleep? I do believe it, that's sure to be the answer.'

So he kept very quiet and strained his ears to see if he could hear anything. He stayed a long time in this posture, and felt thoroughly uncomfortable in the chest, which was far from roomy; as the side he was lying on was hurting him, he tried to turn on to the other, but the only result of his efforts was to force his back against one side of the chest and make the whole thing overbalance and tip over, for it had not been set down on an even base. It made a huge noise in falling, which awoke the women sleeping next door, and they were alarmed—too terrified, indeed, to utter a sound. Ruggieri was greatly alarmed too when the chest fell over, but as he felt it open in the process, he decided he would sooner be out of it than still inside for whatever next ensued. And what with not knowing where he was and one thing and another, he set off groping about the house to see if he couldn't find some stairway or door by which to leave. The women, who were wide awake, heard all this groping and cried: 'Who's there?' But Ruggieri did not recognize their voices and made no answer, so the women called out to the two young men; these were sound asleep, though, and did not hear a thing, for they had stayed up late. So the women were only the more frightened; they got up, went to the window, and shrieked out: 'Help! Thieves!' This brought several of their neighbours running to the house from all over the place, some over the roof-tops, others by one route or another, and the young men got up too, finally awoken by the din.

They caught Ruggieri, who was utterly startled to find himself here and had no idea which way to make his escape. He was handed over to the watch, which had hurried along at the outcry, and brought before the Podestà, who at once submitted him to torture, for Ruggieri had a most villainous reputation. He confessed, therefore, that he entered the usurers' house in order to commit burglary, whereupon the Podestà decided the sooner he hanged the man the better.

In the morning the story was all over Salerno that Ruggieri had been arrested while robbing the usurers' house. When the surgeon's wife and her maid heard it, they were so surprised and bewildered, they were almost ready to persuade themselves they had never actually done what they did in the night, but had only dreamt it. Besides which, the lady was in such agony over Ruggieri's plight, she was driven almost out of her mind.

About half-way through the morning the surgeon was back from Amalfi and asked for his distillation because he was about to operate on his patient; but when he found that the phial was empty he raised a storm: why could people in his house not just leave things where he put them!

His wife, who had other problems to nag her, made an angry rejoinder: 'What', she asked, 'would you have to say about something important when you make such a fuss over a cruet of water spilt? Was that the last drop in the world gone to waste?'

'You think that was plain water but it was not—it was a special distillation to induce sleep.' And he told her why he had prepared it.

This was enough to explain to her that Ruggieri must have drunk it, which was why he had looked to them quite dead. 'That we never realized', she said; 'you'll have to make up some more.' And the surgeon saw there was indeed nothing for it but to make it all over again.

Shortly afterwards the maid, who had been told by her mistress to go and find out what people were saying about Ruggieri, came back and reported to her: 'No one has a good word to say for him, ma'am. From what I gather, not a single friend or relation has come forward or shows any wish to. It's generally assumed that the prosecutor will send him tomorrow to the gallows. What's more, there's something funny I must tell you about: I think I know how he came to be in the money-lenders' house. Listen. You know the cabinet-maker across the way from where the chest was, the one we put him in? He's just had a flaming row with the man who apparently owned the chest, because the man wanted the price the cabinet-maker got for it, but he kept saying he hadn't sold the thing, it had been stolen in the night. And the owner said: "That's not true; you went and sold it to the two usurers; that's what they told me last night when I saw it in their house at the time Ruggieri was caught." Then the cabinet-maker said: "They're lying, I never did sell it to them; they'll have stolen it from me in the night. Let's go and see them." So they agreed to go together to the money-lenders', and I came home. See for yourself, then: I can understand that this is how Ruggieri was taken to where he was found. Though how he came back to life I've simply no idea.'

Now the lady could see exactly what had happened. She told her maid what she'd learnt from the surgeon, and asked for her help in saving Ruggieri. 'If you want to, you can at a stroke save Ruggieri and protect my own good name.'

'Tell me what I'm to do, ma'am, and I'll gladly do it.'

The lady, who felt the devil at her heels, lost no time in hitting upon a plan and gave her maid all the necessary instructions.

First of all the maid went in tears to the surgeon and told him: 'I have to ask your pardon, sir, for a very naughty thing I've done to you.'

'What was that?'

'Sir', she said, still weeping copiously, 'you know the sort of young man Ruggieri d'Ajeroli is. Well, he's fallen for me, and I've lately had to become his mistress—I'm afraid of him and I love him. As he knew you weren't at home last night he wheedled me to bring him here to your house to sleep with me in my room. And as he was thirsty and there was no quick way to fetch him any water or wine, as your wife was in the parlour and I didn't want her to see me, I remembered I'd seen a cruet of water in your room so I dashed off to get it and gave it him to drink, then put the cruet back where I'd found it. And now it seems you've made a great to-do about it. And of course I admit I did a bad thing; but who is there who never ever does anything wrong? I'm ever so sorry I did it. But anyway, what with that and with what happened after, Ruggieri's life's in danger, so I do beg you to forgive me and allow me to go and help him in any way I can.'

Cross though he was, the surgeon answered her in a bantering tone: 'Well, you yourself have earned your pardon! You were expecting to enjoy a night with a frisky lad who'd give you a good run for your money, but you went and picked a dormouse. Off with you, then; go and try to save your lover—and next time, mind you don't bring him back here, or I'll square the accounts and collect the arrears.'

The maid, who felt she had won sufficient ground in this first encounter, hurried off as fast as she could to Ruggieri's prison and coaxed the guard into letting her have a word with the prisoner. She told him what he was to answer the prosecutor if he wanted to escape with his life, then off she went and managed to obtain an audience with the prosecutor himself.

Finding her a seductive little creature, the prosecutor would not lend an ear until he had put his grapnel aboard her, while she for her part was nothing loath if it meant securing his attention. But when he finally cast off, she said: 'Sir, you're holding Ruggieri d'Ajeroli here as a thief, but it's not true he's one.' And beginning at the beginning, she told him the story right to the end: how she was his girl-friend and had brought him into the surgeon's house, and had given him the opiate to drink thinking it was plain water, and how she'd put him into the chest, thinking he was dead. And then she told him about the argument she'd overheard between the cabinet-maker and the man who owned the chest, and thus explained how Ruggieri came to be in the usurers' house.

Seeing how easy it would be to verify her story, the magistrate asked the surgeon about the liquid and established that she had spoken the truth. Then he sent for the cabinet-maker, the owner of the chest, and the money-lenders, and after much beating about the bush it turned out that the money-lenders had stolen the chest in the night and brought it into their house. Last of all he sent for Ruggieri and asked him where he had spent the night. He said he had no idea; all he could remember was that he had gone to spend the night with the maid of Mazzeo the surgeon, and in her bedroom he'd drunk some water because he was very thirsty. But what happened to him after that he didn't know: all he did know was that when he woke up in the usurers' house he found himself inside a chest. The prosecutor derived considerable pleasure from these recitals, and made them all go over their testimony several times—the maid, Ruggieri, the cabinet-maker, and the money-lenders.

Eventually acknowledging Ruggieri's innocence, he fined the money-lenders ten gold florins for stealing the chest, and discharged Ruggieri—and no one need ask how pleased he was; as for his beloved, shc was in raptures. Many a time thereafter she had a good laugh over it with Ruggieri and her precious maid (who was all set to plunge daggers into him), and their pleasure in love increased all the time. If this happened to me I wouldn't mind—though I'd not care to be shoved inside a chest.

If the earlier stories had weighed heavily on the dear ladies' hearts, this last one of Dioneo's left them so merry—especially the bit about the prosecutor and his grapnel—that they quite recovered their high spirits. Noticing that the sun was assuming an orange tinge and his reign had drawn to a close, the king made a very graceful apology to the fair ladies for his misconduct in making them tell stories on such an unfortunate topic as that of unhappy lovers. Once he had made his excuses he stood up, removed the laurel crown from his head, and, as the ladies watched expectantly to see on whom he would confer it, he genially placed it on the flaxen-blonde head of Fiammetta. 'I'm passing this crown to you', he said, 'for you will be the most adept at cheering up your sisters and ensuring that tomorrow makes up for the gloom of today.'

Now Fiammetta had long, wavy, blonde hair touched with gold that fell to her dainty white shoulders; she had a little round face, rose-red cheeks on a lily-white complexion—quite radiant it was—and a pair of eyes bright as a peregrine falcon's, and the most darling little mouth with a pair of ruby lips. She answered with a smile: 'I'm quite happy to accept it, Philostrato. And just to bring home to you what it is you've done, it is my wish and command that all of you here and now prepare to speak tomorrow on the topic of lovers who have suffered the most grievous misfortunes but achieve happiness in the end.' Her proposal won general favour and, after summoning the major-domo to make such arrangements as were needed, she stood up with her company and merrily dismissed them until suppertime.

So until then, off they all went to indulge their various fancies: some stayed in the garden, whose enchantment was unlikely to weary them for quite some time yet; others made for the water-mills outside, and others to yet other destinations. Then they all assembled as usual by the fountain for a most elegantly served dinner of which they partook with enormous pleasure. After this they followed their custom, on leaving the table, of engaging in song and dance. It was Philomena who led the dance, and the queen addressed Philostrato, saying: 'I don't intend to depart from precedent: as my predecessors called for a song, so do I. But as I'm convinced that your songs will be no different from your tales, and we don't want you blighting any more days with your despondencies, let's have you now sing a song of your choice.'

'At your service', replied Philostrato, who straight away began his song:

Have I not reason, Love, for tears,
Now that my heart has been deceived,
Pledges regardless? For thus it appears.

Was she not radiant in my sight
When first my heart, Love, she ensnared?
Open to her my soul lay bared.
Gladly I held my sufferings light.
Love, to what purpose am I aching,
What do I gain as my heart is breaking?
See me, a victim of your spite.

Soon, Love, was I constrained to behold
Sundered the bond of her promise given,
Confidence lost and my spirit riven.
Counting her warm, I found her cold:
Welcomed she now a different swain,
His was the fortune her hand to obtain,
Mine but to grieve with my sorrow untold.

Finding myself from her love excluded,
Sadness and tears my soul oppressed.
Cursed be the day that my eyes were blessed
With the vision that, alas, my peace concluded:
Passion shone out in her radiant face
All vanished and left not the smallest trace.
Would that her love had ne'er intruded.

Love, you can see I'm beyond all caring,
None of your gifts do I seek or crave;
Leave me to rest in a tranquil grave.
Life, wretched life, which is past all bearing,
Wrest it away, for 'tis harsh and vile:
Ransomed at last and freed from bile
Never again shall I risk ensnaring.

Comfortless, joyless in my grieving,
All that remains to me is death.
Take, Love, oh take my dying breath:
Happy, at length, my pain thus relieving.
Bring her, Lord, tidings of my decease—

Thus will her joy in her new love increase.
Once I am gone there's an end to deceiving.

What, little ballad, if all should spurn you?
What if they do? Nay, I should not care!
I am the best one to sing your air.
One task remains, though, to which I must turn you.
Bring Love this message, convey my plea:
'Save me from torment, help me to flee—
Kindness indeed, Love, my thanks shall earn you.'

The words of this song betrayed Philostrato's feelings clearly enough, and what lay behind them. And conceivably the expression on the face of a certain lady engaged in the dance would have thrown further light on the matter were it not that the onset of darkness concealed her blushes. When he was finished, they sang many more songs until it was time to go to bed whereupon, at the queen's bidding, they all retired to their rooms.

*Here ends the fourth day of the* Decameron *and the fifth day begins; under the reign of Fiammetta, the stories are about lovers who have suffered the most grievous misfortunes but achieve happiness in the end.*

The heavens were already bright to the east and our entire hemisphere was flooded with the light of the rising sun when Fiammetta rose from her bed; she was roused also by the birds' sweet singing in the trees, as they merrily chirruped their welcome to the dawning day. She had the other ladies and the three young men called, and then led her friends out into the fields and through the dewy grass of the broad plain for a pleasant stroll as they chatted of one thing and another, waiting for the sun to gain height. Once they felt greater warmth in the sun's rays she turned their steps to their usual haunt, where they were regaled with good wine and tasty snacks to restore them from their little exercise. Then they took their ease in their garden of delight until it was time for lunch. The ever-provident major-domo had the meal ready to serve and, at the queen's pleasure, they were all glad to sit down to it—after they had sung and danced one or two *estampidas** and other such dancing songs. Lunch was a cheerful and decorous occasion, and it was followed, in the prescribed manner, by a few more little dances to the accompaniment of singers and instrumentalists. Then the queen gave them leave to retire for a nap, though, while some of them did retire to rest, others chose to dally in the garden. A little after three, however, they all foregathered by the fountain in their usual manner at the queen's behest. The queen took her seat *pro tribunali** and turned with a smile to Pamphilo, bidding him open the round of stories with happy endings. He raised no objection and thus began:

V. I. *Cimone, a simpleton whose wits are restored by Love, seeks to ravish Iphigeneia, whose hand is denied him. Fate thwarts his plans and he ends up in prison. Here, though, Fate brings him an ally.*

There are any number of stories I might tell, to make a start to a day as enjoyable as this one is going to be. There's one, though, that appeals to me especially, because it will help you delightful ladies understand the happy purpose of the narrations on which we are embarking; it will, moreover, give you an idea of how divine, how potent and wholesome is the power of Love. Many people, speaking in ignorance, quite unjustly condemn and revile Love, so my tale should enchant you—assuming I am right in thinking that all of you are in love.

Well then, once upon a time—as we've read in the old legends of the Cypriot people—there lived in Cyprus a highly eminent gentleman called Aristippus. His worldly possessions made him far and away the richest man on the island, and he would have counted himself as excellently favoured by Fortune were it not for one thing that rankled him: one of his sons was such a tall, handsome lad there was not another boy to touch him—but he was quite hopelessly half-witted. No amount of tutoring, no amount of wheedling or thrashings from his father, nothing anyone had been able to dream up had ever succeeded in instilling into him the smallest fund of learning or of social grace. His actual name was Galeso,* but his hoarse, guttural speech and his behaviour that partook of the animal kingdom more than of human kind had earned him the scornful nickname of Cimone—a name whose equivalent in our own tongue would be Nincompoop. His father could barely endure the thought of such a waste of a good life and, as he had now given up all hope for his son's improvement, he made him go to live among the yokels on his country estate, not wanting to see the occasion of his distress constantly before his eyes. Cimone did not mind in the least: he felt far more at home among the rustics than he'd ever done among the city gentry.

So off went Cimone to the country estate, where he lent a hand with whatever work needed doing. Thus he happened one day, shortly after midday, to be crossing from one sector of the property to another, with his staff over his shoulder, and there was a lovely little wood hereabouts through which his path led; it was in the month of May and the trees were all in leaf. As he walked through it, Fate directed his steps into a clearing hemmed in by tall trees, with a beautiful cool spring in one corner of it; fast asleep beside it on the green meadow grass he saw the most gorgeous young woman; she was wearing such a sheer dress, it barely concealed her milk-white flesh, with just a thin snow-white quilt to cover her from the waist down. At her feet lay her attendants, two women and a man, also sleeping. When Cimone saw her he stopped, propped himself on his staff and, without uttering a word, gazed at her, spellbound with admiration, as though he had never before set eyes on a feminine form. And he could feel an idea stirring in his brutish soul which had remained impervious to the smallest taste of refinement despite a thousand lessons: the idea which now gained a hearing in his dense and simple mind was that here was the most beautiful creature ever beheld by mortal eye. He went on to take her in a bit at a time, admiring her hair, which looked to him like gold, her forehead, nose and mouth, her neck and arms, and above all her bosom, still not fully developed. From a labourer he had turned judge of beauty, and now he wanted above all to see her eyes, which she kept shut, for she was in a deep sleep. Many a time he would have liked to wake her in order to see them but, as he found her so incomparably more beautiful than any other woman he had ever seen, he suspected she must be some goddess, and he had just enough wit to realize that the divinities merit greater respect than the creatures of this world, so he held back and waited for her to awaken of her own accord. The delay taxed his patience but, wrapped up as he was in this unwonted pleasure, he could not tear himself away.

After a long while the girl, whose name was Iphigeneia, woke up before any of her attendants; she raised her head, opened her eyes, and was quite startled to see Cimone standing in front of her, leaning on his staff. 'Why Cimone', she said, 'what brings you into these woods at this time of day?'

Everybody hereabouts knew Cimone, because of his size, his gaucheness, and his father's wealth and station. He answered Iphigeneia not a word but, when he saw that her eyes were open, he gazed into them entranced—it seemed to him a sweetness emanated from them that filled him with a sense of well-being he had never before experienced.

Seeing this, the girl became worried lest this fixed stare of his were a signal for the simpleton to treat her in a manner to bring a blush to her cheeks. So she called her maids, stood up, and said: 'Farewell, Cimone.'

'I'll come with you', he replied.

Refuse his company as she might, for she was wary of him, she was quite unable to shake him off until he had escorted her back to her house. From there he went on to his father's and told him that on no account would he return to the country. His father and the rest of the family were much disturbed by this, but they let him be, and waited to see what it was that had made him change his mind.

Now that Love, thanks to Iphigeneia's beauty, had shot an arrow into the young man's heart, which had been closed to any form of learning, his mind underwent such a swift development that his father, his family, and all who knew him were quite astounded. He first of all asked his father to send him forth as well dressed and well turned out as were all his brothers—which his father was only too pleased to do. After which, he began frequenting the right sort of young men to absorb the forms of behaviour suited to men of breeding, and especially to lovers; and to everyone's total amazement he had in no time mastered the rudiments of reading and writing and gone on to become a man of quite exceptional erudition. Furthermore, as it was his love for Iphigeneia that lay behind all of this, he not only got rid of his uncouth yokel's speech in favour of a refined utterance, but he became a skilled musician, both singing and playing, and he became a past master in the techniques of horsemanship and the use of arms, an expert in the arts of war by land and sea. In fact, to be brief and not list his every accomplishment, not even a quarter of a year had elapsed from the day he fell in love before he had turned into the most polished, the most attractive and accomplished young man in the whole island of Cyprus.

So what, dear ladies, are we to say about Cimone? There's only one thing to say and that is that the sublime gifts with which his valiant spirit were infused had been trussed up with the toughest bonds and shut away by envious Fortune in the tightest corner of his heart, but that Love, who is so much the stronger, shattered and severed them all. Love it is that awakens slumbering spirits; he forcibly thrusts out into the light of day those heaven-sent virtues hitherto confined to the cruel shadows, and manifestly reveals whence it is that he draws out the hearts subject to his influence, and whither he leads them in the beams of his radiance.

In his love for Iphigeneia, Cimone tended to extravagance, as is the way with young men in love; his father, none the less, conscious that it was Love that had turned him from an ape back into a man, took it all in good part and actively seconded him in his pursuit. Cimone, however—he refused to be called Galeso, for he recollected that Cimone was the name by which Iphigeneia had called him—Cimone sought an honourable outcome for his passion, and made several approaches to his beloved's father, Cipseus, to have her to wife; but Cipseus's answer was always the same—the girl was promised to a young nobleman from Rhodes called Pasimundas and he, Cipseus was not going to go back on his word.

When the time came for the arranged marriage to take place and Iphigeneia's intended sent for her, Cimone remarked to himself: 'Now is the time for me to show you, Iphigeneia, how dear you are to me. It's you who restored me to manhood, and if I can make you mine I'm certain I should outdo any god in glory. One thing's for sure: I'll have you or I'll die.' This said, he secretly recruited a few young friends from among the nobility, brought a vessel into commission, fully equipped to fight a naval battle, and put to sea to lay in wait for the ship carrying Iphigeneia to her affianced in Rhodes. Once her father had offered suitable entertainment to the bridegroom's friends, she went on board and they shaped their course for that island. Cimone, who was not asleep, caught up with them the next day and, taking his station in the bows, shouted across to the people on Iphigeneia's ship: 'Heave-to and strike your sails, unless you want to be overpowered and sent to the bottom.' The enemy had fetched their weapons up from below deck and prepared to defend themselves; so Cimone, who had said enough, seized a grapnel and heaved it over the stern of the Rhodian ship as it hastened off, and made the other end fast to the prow of his own. Then, fierce as a lion, without waiting for any support he leapt aboard the other vessel as though deeming his opponents quite negligible; incited by Love, he plunged into the midst of the foe and lay about him, dagger in hand, with phenomenal strength, stabbing them one after the next and striking them down like so many sheep, so that the Rhodians threw down their weapons and cried for quarter almost in unison.

Cimone said to them: 'It's not any thirst for plunder, nor is it any hatred I feel against you that urged me to leave Cyprus and attack you in the open sea. What has pressed me into this venture is the supreme object I could ever acquire, while for you it is but the lightest loss to give her up to me in peace—I mean Iphigeneia, whom I love above all else. As I could not obtain her from her father in peace and friendship, I have been forced by Love to obtain her from you in battle and as your adversary. And I mean to be to her that which your Pasimundas was intended to be. Give her to me, therefore, and be on your way with God's blessing.'

More under the prompting of force than of generosity, the young men handed over the weeping lady to Cimone who, seeing her in tears, said: 'Don't be sad, noble lady. I am your Cimone. I have a far better claim to you by my long-matured love than has Pasimundas on the strength of a promise.'

So Cimone returned to his shipmates, having had the girl transferred to his vessel, but leaving everything else belonging to the Rhodians undisturbed; after which he left them free to go. He was the happiest man in the world now that he had acquired so precious a booty; after devoting some time to comforting the weeping girl, he decided with his companions not to go straight back to Cyprus. They therefore, by common accord, shaped their course for Crete, where nearly all of them, and not least Cimone, felt they would be safe with Iphigeneia thanks to old family ties, or more recent ones, and to a wide circle of friends.

Fate, however, who had positively smiled on Cimone's gaining possession of the lady, now proved fickle, for she on the instant turned the matchless joy of the love-struck young man into bitter sorrow. Not four hours had elapsed since Cimone had left the Rhodians when, at nightfall—and Cimone was expecting that night to be the happiest he had ever experienced—a most violent storm got up; it covered the sky in cloud and the sea with savage squalls. Without visibility it was impossible to take any action or lay a course, indeed the conditions made it impossible to work the ship. No need to ask how much this upset Cimone. It seemed to him that the gods had granted him his wish only so that he should be the sorrier to die, whereas before, death would have made little difference to him. His companions were equally miserable, but most wretched of all was Iphigeneia, who wept bitterly and dreaded each crash of the waves. As she wept, she harshly disparaged Cimone's love and reproached him for his rash deed: the only reason this storm-wind had got up, she said, was because the gods would not abide his enjoying the fulfilment of his presumptuous ambition to make her his bride against their wishes; he would watch her die, and then himself die a wretched death. Amid such grieving, and worse, the sailors had no idea what to do and the wind kept increasing in strength; they could not establish or recognize what heading they were on, and when they arrived off the island of Rhodes they failed to recognize it for what it was and directed all their seamanship in an effort to save their lives by making land there. In this, Fortune abetted them, conducting them into a little cove into which the Rhodians released by Cimone had sailed their vessel only a little ahead of them. No sooner had they awoken to the fact that they had reached Rhodes than dawn broke and, with a somewhat clearer sky, they saw that they lay scarcely an arrow's flight from the ship they had let go the previous day.

Cimone was aghast—and his fears were to prove justified. He ordered his shipmates to strain every sinew to break out from here; after that, let Fate carry them where she would—no place would be worse than where they were at present. So they put their backs into the effort to make their escape, but it was no use: far from being able to draw clear of the little cove, they were so driven by the contrary wind—it was exceedingly strong—that willy-nilly they ended up beached. Thus high and dry, they were recognized by the Rhodian seamen who had disembarked from their own vessel; one of them promptly ran to a nearby house to which the young noblemen had repaired and told them that Cimone had been driven here with Iphigeneia by the same gale. They were enchanted with the news, and hastened down to the seashore after mustering many hands on the estate. Cimone had left the ship with his companions and decided to escape into a wood close by, but they were all caught, including Iphigeneia, and led off to the house. Thence Cimone and his companions were taken off to prison when Lysimachus, who that year held the office of chief magistrate in Rhodes, arrived from the city with a large company of men-at-arms. This fulfilled the bidding of Pasimundas, who had been in the Rhodian senate lamenting his fate when the news reached him.

So it was that, no sooner had the unfortunate Cimone gained possession of his beloved than he lost her, without having stolen anything from her but the odd kiss. Iphigeneia was welcomed by several of the island's gentlewomen, who helped her to recover from the shock of her capture and from the effects of the storm. She was their guest until the day appointed for her wedding. And as Cimone had, on the previous day, given the young Rhodians their freedom, he and his companions were spared their lives—Pasimundas had pressed hard for the death penalty—but were condemned to life imprisonment. So in prison they remained all forlorn, as may be imagined, and with no hope of experiencing any further happiness. Pasimundas, meanwhile, urged on the wedding preparations for all he was worth.

Now Fate, as though regretting the sudden wrong she had done to Cimone, came to his rescue with a fresh twist. Pasimundas had a brother called Hormisdas, who was his junior but otherwise in no way inferior to him. He had long been negotiating for a beautiful young gentlewoman of the city, called Cassandra; Lysimachus, however, was deeply in love with her, and meanwhile the girl's wedding had for one reason and another been postponed a number of times. Now Pasimundas, finding himself on the point of organizing a lavish wedding celebration, thought it would be no bad thing if he could get Hormisdas to the altar on the same occasion, to avoid a duplication of festivity and expenditure. So he resumed negotiations with Cassandra's family and this time reached an agreement; he and his brother arranged with them that they would marry Iphigeneia and Cassandra respectively on the same day. Lysimachus was quite heartsick at the news, for it deprived him of his lingering hope that if Hormisdas did not marry her, then he himself assuredly would. He was wise enough, however, to keep his dismay to himself and turn his mind to considering how to make the plan miscarry; the only possibility he could see was to make off with the girl. The plan was feasible enough, he recognized, because of the office he held, though if he had not held the office at all he could have more easily squared the proposal with his honour. But in short, after much deliberation, Honour gave way to Love and he decided, come what may, to make off with Cassandra. And as he considered what accomplices he would need and how to go about it, Cimone came to mind, whom he had under lock and key with his companions; it occurred to him that in such a venture he could not have a better or more reliable companion.

He had Cimone secretly brought to his room that night and spoke to him as follows: 'Cimone', he said, 'the gods make splendid gifts to men with a free hand. Similarly, they are very shrewd at testing out a person's strengths, and those whom they find steady and constant in meeting any situation they consider to be the most valiant and deserving of the highest rewards. They've wanted to make a surer test of your mettle than could be made within the confines of your father's house, for he is, I know, an extremely wealthy man. So first of all they converted you, so I've been told, from a brute beast to a human being under the stimulus and aspirations of love; subsequently they have wanted to see whether, after your ill luck and your present intolerable confinement, you remain of the same mind as when you enjoyed your brief moment of happiness in possession of your prize. If you are indeed of the same mind, then the gods never offered you anything as conducive to your happiness as that which they're now on the point of presenting to you—and the better to recover your old vigour and spirit, I shall tell you what it is. Pasimundas, who is delighted at your discomfiture and has been only too anxious to see you dead, is pressing ahead as fast as he can with his wedding to your Iphigeneia: that way he will enjoy the prize that Fortune allotted to you when she was well disposed and at once snatched away in anger. How much this must sicken you, if you're as deeply in love as I believe you are, I know well from my own experience: his brother Hormisdas is preparing to do as great an injury to me on the very same day, in respect of Cassandra, whom I love above all else. To avoid such a painful blow of Fate the only path she has left open to us, so far as I can see, is to deploy a brave spirit and a right hand grasping a sword: thus you shall force through your second abduction and I my first. Well then, if you're inclined to recover—I won't say your freedom, for I doubt you set much store by it in the absence of your beloved—but your lady, the gods have set her within your grasp provided that you're willing to join me in this enterprise.'

These words quite put new heart into Cimone, and it took him little time to reply: 'Lysimachus, you won't find a stouter or more reliable comrade than me in such an undertaking, if what you speak of really is to come my way. So tell me what you want me to do and you'll see it carried out with remarkable vigour.'

'The day after tomorrow the brides will first set foot in their husbands' quarters. We shall enter them too, at dusk, you armed and with your companions, and I with a number of mine in whom I have complete confidence. We shall seize the brides from among the guests, take them down to a ship that I've had secretly made ready, and kill whoever presumes to bar our passage.'

Cimone approved the plan and quietly endured his captivity until the appointed time.

Came the day of the wedding, and there was the most splendid array: the brothers' entire house overflowed with joy and festivity. Lysimachus had made all his preparations and, after pronouncing a harangue to kindle the ardour of Cimone and his friends, as also of his own company—all with weapons concealed beneath their clothes—he divided them, when the moment seemed ripe, into three groups: one he prudently sent down to the harbour to ensure there should be no opposition to their boarding ship when the need arose. With the other two he proceeded to Pasimundas's house; here he left one group at the door to prevent the other being locked in or its escape being cut off; with Cimone and the third group he climbed the stairs. When they reached the room in which the brides were sitting down with a great number of other ladies to eat at their allotted places at table, in they strode, overturned the tables, and each seized his own beloved; these they handed to their followers, bidding them fetch the girls away at once to the waiting ship. The brides shrieked and burst into tears, and so did the other women and the domestics; from one moment to the next the whole place was loud with cries and wailing. Cimone, Lysimachus, and their party, however, drew their swords and made for the stairs, and nobody attempted to bar their way. As they went down Pasimundas appeared, drawn hither by the rumpus; he held a stout staff in his hand, but Cimone attacked him vigorously and sliced half his head off—the man dropped dead at his feet. Hormisdas came running to his assistance but the poor fellow was slain by another blow from Cimone; similarly others who tried to close with them were sent reeling back, wounded, by the followers of Lysimachus and Cimone. Leaving the house filled with gore and tumult, with tears and sorrow, they made for their vessel in a tight group, bringing their prizes with them and encountering no opposition. The whole company followed the ladies on board, then manned the oars and cheerfully took their departure, while the shore filled up with men-at-arms come to rescue the captives.

Arriving in Crete, they were given a joyous welcome by a large number of friends and relations. They married their brides amid great celebrations and took pleasure in their plunder. Great was the turmoil and outrage in Cyprus and Rhodes on account of what they'd done, and it would not abate until eventually, thanks to the mediation of friends and kinsmen in both places, a way was found for Cimone, after a long period of banishment, to return happily to Cyprus with Iphigeneia, and similarly for Lysimachus to return with Cassandra to Rhodes. And each of them went on to live for ages happily in his own country with his beloved.

V. 2. *Martuccio, denied the hand of his beloved Costanza for lack of fortune, goes to Barbary where, after setbacks, he becomes the king's favourite. Costanza, seeking her own death, ends up in Barbary too, where Fortune smiles on them both.*

The queen spoke highly of Pamphilo's story when she had heard it to the end; then she told Emilia to follow with one, which she started thus:

We quite rightly rejoice when something we do attracts the reward we are looking for. And as in the long run we deserve to be happy rather than miserable when we are in love, I shall obey the queen far more cheerfully, as I discuss our present topic, than I obeyed the king in talking about his.

Well, you must know that there is a little island off Sicily called Lipari. Here there lived not long ago a most beautiful young woman called Costanza, scion of one of the island's leading families. Now an islander called Martuccio Gomito fell in love with her, a well-bred young man of impeccable manners and a master of his craft. She, moreover, reciprocated his passion to such an extent that she measured her happiness entirely by the amount she saw of him. Martuccio wanted her for his wife, and requested her hand from her father, whose answer was that as the lad was a pauper he wasn't going to give her to him. Martuccio was indignant at being rejected for lack of means; with some friends and relatives he equipped a little vessel and swore he would return to Lipari only as a rich man. Off he sailed and set about scouring the Barbary coast as a corsair, despoiling anyone who could not fight him off. Fortune favoured him in this enterprise, except that he could not leave well alone: not satisfied with having made himself and his companions enormously rich in no time at all, he and they were in the process of piling up ever greater wealth when they were invested by Saracen ships and, after standing them off for a good while, they were all captured and stripped of their goods; most of his company were thrown overboard in weighted sacks, but Martuccio was taken off, his ship being scuttled, and thrown into prison in Tunis, where for ages he was kept on the barest subsistence.

News got back to Lipari, not merely by word of one or two people but from a wide variety of sources, that Martuccio and his entire crew had been drowned. Costanza, already afflicted beyond measure by Martuccio's departure, wept and wept on hearing that he was among the dead, and decided she had no wish to go on living. As she could not bring herself to take her own life by violent means, she hit upon a novel method to put an end to herself. Slipping furtively out of her father's house one night, she went down to the harbour and was lucky enough to find a little fishing boat somewhat remote from the other craft; its owners had only just disembarked, so she found it equipped with oars, mast, and sail. She quickly stepped into it, rowed a little way out to sea, then set the sail—for, like just about every woman on the island, she had some training in seamanship. This done, she threw away the oars and rudder and left herself at the wind's mercy, reckoning that the wind was bound to capsize an unladen boat that was not under helm, or else would drive the craft on to a rock and break it up, with the result that she would drown, being unable to escape even if she wanted to. She wrapped a cloak round her head and lay down, weeping, in the bottom of the boat.

Things, however, turned out quite differently to what she had envisaged: a northerly was blowing, and a mild one at that; the sea was calm, the boat looked after itself, and the following evening she fetched up on a beach close to a town called Sousa, some hundred miles beyond Tunis. Costanza was quite unconscious of being aground, for she had remained in her recumbent position without once on any account raising her head, nor did she intend to. Now as the boat ran aground, a little pauper woman happened to be on the beach, gathering up the nets of her fisherfolk out of the sun. Noticing the boat, she was puzzled that it should have been allowed to run ashore full tilt, all sail set. She assumed that the fishermen on board were asleep, and approached, but all she saw in it was this young woman, sound asleep. She called her again and again and eventually woke her up; recognizing her for a Christian by her attire, she asked her in Italian how she came to have landed here all on her own in this boat. Hearing herself addressed in Italian, Costanza suspected that a different wind must have borne her back to Lipari; she jumped up and looked about, but, seeing herself ashore and not recognizing the landscape, she asked the woman where she was.

'You're in Barbary, my child, close to Sousa.'

Disappointed that God had been unwilling to send death her way, Costanza feared for her virtue when she heard this and, quite at a loss, sat down beside her boat and burst into tears. The sight of this moved the kind woman to pity and she prevailed on the girl to come with her to her little hut, where she eventually coaxed out of her the story of how she came to be here. Realizing that Costanza had not eaten, she set before her some hard bread, a bit of fish, and some water and persuaded her to eat a little. Costanza asked the kind woman who she was, as she spoke Italian, and she learnt that she came from Trapani, her name was Carapresa,* and she looked after some Christian fishermen. However heartsick the girl was feeling, when she heard this name it struck her as a good omen, though she would have been quite unable to say why; new hope sprang up in her, though she had no idea what for, and her death-wish somewhat abated. Without divulging who she was or where she came from, she warmly entreated the kind woman for the love of God to take pity on her tender years and advise her what to do in order to protect her chastity.

At this, Carapresa, good-hearted woman that she was, left the girl in her hut, quickly collected up her nets, then returned and took her off to Sousa, wrapped up in her cloak. When they got there she told her: 'I'm going to take you to a Saracen woman—she's as kind as could be, an elderly woman with a heart of gold, whom I often help around the house. I'll commend you to her as warmly as I can, and I've absolutely no doubt that she will give you a ready welcome and treat you as a daughter. You must do all you can, while you're staying with her, to be of service to her and earn her favour until such time as God sends you better fortune.' And she was as good as her word.

The woman, who was well on in years, looked in the girl's face after listening to Carapresa and was moved to tears; she took Costanza and kissed her on the forehead, then took her hand and led her indoors. She lived here in the company of some other women, but no men, and they all busied themselves with their hands, making all sorts of things out of silk, palm, and leather. Within a few days Costanza had learnt to make some of these things and joined them in their handicrafts; and it was marvellous the way the old lady and her companions took her to their hearts—nor was it long before, under their instruction, she learnt to speak their language.

Thus did Costanza live at Sousa, while at home they had long been mourning her for lost and perished. Meanwhile the throne of Tunis was occupied by one Muli Abd Allah;* but there lived in Granada a highly powerful and well-connected young man who made a claim to the Tunisian crown and, recruiting an enormous host, marched against the King of Tunis to drive him out.

News of this reached Martuccio Gomito's ears in prison. He had an excellent grasp of the Barbary tongue, and when he heard that the King of Tunis was straining every sinew to organize his defence, he told one of the warders guarding him and his companions: 'If I could have a word with the king, I dare say I could give him a piece of advice that would win him his war.'

The warder passed this message to his governor, who at once reported it to the king, and the king sent for Martuccio. 'What', he asked him, 'is your proposal?'

'My lord', said he, 'in the days when I used to pursue my activities in your part of the world, if I looked closely at the way you conducted your battles it struck me that you employed archers in preference to other means. So if there were some way to deprive your enemy of arrows while your men were abundantly supplied, I expect you would win your battle.'

'No doubt, if that were possible, I could count on victory.'

'If you so desire, my lord, it is perfectly possible; I'll tell you how. What you must do is have your archers' bows fitted with much thinner strings than are normally used. Then you must have arrows made with notches that will fit only these thin strings. This must all be done in great secrecy, for if your enemy gets wind of it he'll find a way round. Now here's the reason why I'm suggesting this to you: when your enemy's archers have shot off all their arrows and your own archers have shot theirs, your enemy will need to continue the battle using the arrows shot by your troops, and our men will have to collect up the enemy's arrows. But the enemy will not be able to make use of the arrows shot by your men, as they'll not be able to fit their thick bowstrings to the thin notches, whereas your men will find the opposite with the enemy's arrows, for their thin strings will easily fit arrows with the broader notch. This means that your archers will have a plentiful supply of arrows while the enemy's will run out.'

The king, who was no fool, readily adopted Martuccio's suggestion and, by putting it wholeheartedly into effect, emerged from the war victorious, in consequence of which Martuccio became a favourite and therefore a man of wealth and high station.

News of this travelled far and wide and came to the ears of Costanza: Martuccio was alive, she learned, though she had long imagined he was dead. So her love for him, that had lost its earlier warmth, now flared up again within her, hotter than before, and quickened her dead hopes. She therefore made a clean breast of everything to the lady with whom she was living, and told her of her wish to visit Tunis in order to feast her eyes on that which she hankered for on the evidence of hearsay. The lady fully approved her wish and embarked with her for Tunis, as though she were the girl's mother; here they received a gracious welcome in the home of a relative of hers. Carapresa had come too, and she was sent out to see what she could discover about Martuccio. She brought back a report that he was indeed alive and prospering, so the lady decided that she would be the one to bring Martuccio the news that his Costanza had come here to find him.

So she sought him out one day and told him: 'Martuccio, a servant of yours has arrived in my house from Lipari. He'd like a word with you in secret. Not wanting to entrust the message to anyone else, I've brought it to you myself, as he wanted me to.' Martuccio thanked her and accompanied her home.

When she saw him, Costanza came close to dying for bliss. She could not stop herself running and flinging her arms round his neck and kissing him; then the thought of her past sorrows and present joy proved too much for her and, without being able to utter a word, she wept tears of tenderness. Martuccio was brought up short on seeing the girl, he was quite amazed, but then he said with a sigh: 'O Costanza mine, are you really alive? How long ago I heard that you had perished, and in these parts nobody had any news of you.' This said, he hugged and kissed her, shedding gentle tears. Costanza told him all her adventures, and about the hospitality she had received from the lady with whom she was staying.

They talked for some while, after which Martuccio left her and went to see the king, his master, and told him the whole story—his own and Costanza's. 'By your leave', he added, 'I propose to marry her according to our law.' All this took the king by surprise; he sent for the girl and, on hearing from her own lips that the case was as Martuccio had recited, he said: 'My word, you've certainly deserved him for your husband!' He sent for the most opulent and noble gifts and shared them out between Costanza and Martuccio; furthermore he gave them leave to decide between themselves just what they wished to do. After offering the most lavish hospitality to the lady with whom Costanza had been living, and thanking her for all she had done for the girl and giving her presents suitable to her station, Martuccio bade her goodbye and departed, a tearful occasion for Costanza. Then, with the king's leave, they boarded a little vessel, taking Carapresa with them, and returned with a favourable wind to Lipari. Here their welcome was quite beyond description. Martuccio married her, the wedding was sumptuous, and they lived in the enjoyment of their love in peace and quiet for many a day.

V. 3. *Pietro Boccamazza and Agnolella escape from their families to get married. On their journey they become separated and meet with terrifying adventures; but all is not lost.*

Emilia's story was unanimously approved. Recognizing that it was ended, the queen turned to Elissa, bidding her to go next, which she obediently did, as follows:

I have in mind a story about a dreadful night spent by two foolish young people; as the night in question was followed by many a happy day, my tale does adhere to our plan, and so I'm going to tell it to you.

In Rome, once upon a time—the city used to be the world's head even if now it is only the rump*—in Rome there dwelt a young man called Pietro Boccamazza. He came from one of the leading families, and he fell in love with a very beautiful and charming young woman called Agnolella; she was daughter of one Gigliozzo Saullo, a man of the people but a very popular fellow. Now Pietro so worked on her affections that she came to love him with equal devotion, and so desperate was his love, so unbearable the frustration he suffered because of it, that he asked for her hand in marriage. When his family heard about this, they all turned up on the doorstep and told him in no uncertain terms what they thought of the idea; moreover, they sent to Gigliozzo to say that Pietro's proposal was not even to be entertained: if it was, he would be no friend of theirs and he'd not be considered a relative. Seeing the one door closed to him through which he imagined he might have achieved his desire, Pietro was ready to die of chagrin. Had Gigliozzo consented, he would have taken his daughter to wife no matter what his own family said. Still, he set his heart on achieving his desire, provided that his beloved consented; so, once he knew she was willing, through the good offices of a go-between he arranged for her to elope with him. One morning, according to plan, Pietro got up at crack of dawn and they both took horse and set off for Anagni,* where he had trustworthy friends. In fear of pursuit, they could not give themselves leisure to consummate their wedding but rode along talking about love and occasionally giving each other a kiss.

Now Pietro was none too sure of the way and, some eight miles out of Rome, they happened to branch off to the left when they should have kept to the right. Scarcely two miles on they rode into sight of a small fortress, from which they were spotted and at once a dozen armed men emerged. When these had almost come up with the couple Agnolella noticed them and shouted: 'Pietro, let us flee, we're being attacked!' She set spurs to her pony, clung hard to the saddle, and raced off into a forest.

Pietro had his eyes on her face rather than on the road, and took longer to wake up to the presence of the armed men; he was still looking the wrong way when they caught up with him. They seized him, made him dismount, then asked him who he was. He told them, and they debated what to do with him. 'He belongs with the enemy', they said. 'There's nothing for it but to strip him of his clothes, take his nag, and hang him from one of these oaks—that'll teach the Orsinis.' With one accord they told Pietro to undress. As he did so, he could not but dwell on what lay in store for him, but who should burst in on them but two dozen soldiers, who had been lying in ambush. 'Get them! Kill them!' they yelled—and Pietro's surprised captors forgot about their victim in their haste to defend themselves. They could see that they were outnumbered, however, so they broke and fled, pursued by their assailants. Pietro seized his clothes, leapt on to his mount, and fled for dear life in the direction he had seen his beloved take.

In the forest he could see no trace of a path, nor any hoof-prints. Therefore, when he felt safe from his captors and from the men who had attacked them, he was quite broken-hearted at not finding his Agnolella; he broke down and cried as he rode this way and that through the woods shouting her name. No one replied, and he dared not retrace his steps, nor did he know where he would fetch up if he continued as he was going. Besides, he was worried about the wild beasts that inhabit the forest, both on his own account and on Agnolella's—he could already see her lacerated by a bear or wolf. So poor Pietro rode all day long through the forest, calling her name; occasionally when he thought he was pressing on he was in fact retracing his steps. What with shouting and weeping, what with fear and his long fast, he became so exhausted he couldn't go another step. Seeing that night had fallen, he could think of no better plan than to dismount, tie his beast to a stout oak, and climb up into it to avoid being eaten by wild animals in the night. The moon rose shortly afterwards, casting a bright light everywhere. Pietro dared not fall asleep lest he fall out of the tree—and even if this were not a danger, he would have been prevented from sleeping by his heartsore brooding over his beloved. So he remained wakeful, sighing and weeping and cursing his ill luck.

Agnolella fled (as we have described) with no idea of where to go, leaving her pony to carry her wherever it suited him; he carried her ever deeper into the forest till she could no longer see where it was she'd entered it. So, just like Pietro, she went round in circles, pausing then pressing on through these wilds, weeping and calling and lamenting her misfortune. Eventually evening came with still no sign of Pietro. The maiden happened upon a little track along which her steed took her for a couple of miles; it brought her in sight of a cottage, which she made for as fast as she could. Here she found a kindly man, well advanced in years, and his no less elderly wife.

When they saw her all on her own, 'My goodness!' they said, 'What are you doing out and about on your own in these parts at such an hour?'

Tearfully she told them that she had been parted from her company in the forest, and asked them how far it was to Anagni.

'You won't get to Anagni along this way, my girl', the old man replied. 'It's over twelve miles from here.'

'Are there any houses around here', she asked, 'where I might obtain a lodging?'

'There's none you could get to while it's still daylight.'

'If there's nowhere else for me to go', she asked, 'would you be willing to take me in tonight for the love of God?'

The kind old man answered: 'How glad we shall be to give you lodging tonight, young lady. But you must be warned: the countryside round about is rife with brigands, night and day, some of them friendly to us, others not; they do all manner of harm, and if any of them came here by mischance while you're around, they'd see what a fresh young beauty you are and would subject you to the vilest treatment. And there's nothing we could do to help you. It's as well you should know, for if it happened, we shouldn't want you to hold us to blame.'

Agnolella was quite alarmed by the old man's words, but, seeing how late it was, she said: 'Please God He'll protect you and me from such evil. Even if it happened to me, it's not nearly so bad to suffer at the hands of men as to be torn to pieces by wild beasts in the woods.'

So she dismounted and entered the cottage and sat down with the old man and his wife to such meagre fare as they could provide; then she lay down fully dressed to share their narrow bed. All night long she did not stop sighing and weeping over her sad lot and Pietro's—she had no idea what could have become of him but feared the worst.

A little before daybreak she heard the tramp of a band of men on the march. Up she got, therefore, and slipped out into a big yard at the back of the cottage, where she spotted at one side of it a great heap of hay; in this she hid herself, so that if the men came to the cottage they would not find her straight away. Barely had she finished concealing herself when a mob of evil brigands was at the cottage door. They demanded admittance, went in, found the girl's horse still saddled, and asked whose it was.

'There's nobody here but us', said the kindly old man, noticing the girl's absence. 'Whoever his owner is, this animal must have run away from him; he turned up here last night, and we brought him in or the wolves might have eaten him.'

'Right', said the brigands' chief, 'he'll do for us, as he has no other master.'

So they spread themselves out in the cottage, and some went out into the yard at the back and threw down their spears and bucklers; one of them absently tossed his spear into the pile of hay and came close to killing the hidden maiden—and she to revealing her presence—for its tip glanced by her left breast and tore her dress. She was all set to let out a shriek, fearing she was wounded, but got a grip on herself, remembering where she was, and kept silent. The brigands overran the whole place while they roasted their sucking kids and other meat, ate their dinner, and drank. Then they were off and away, taking Agnolella's pony with them.

When they were well and truly gone, the old man asked his wife: 'What's become of our young lady from last night? I've not seen her since we got up.'

'I don't know', said his wife, and went to take a look around.

Hearing that the men had left, Agnolella came out of the hay; her host was delighted to see that she had not fallen into their clutches. Dawn had now broken, and he said to her: 'Now that it's day, we shall, if you like, accompany you to a castle five miles from here where you'll be safe. You'll have to go on foot, though, for those evil men who've just left took away your mount.' Agnolella did not greatly fret over this, but begged them to take her to the castle. So off they went, and got there toward mid-morning.

The castle belonged to an Orsini,* Liello di Campo di Fiore, and his wife happened to be in residence, a really good soul she was. She recognized Agnolella at once and gave her a hearty welcome. She wanted to hear all about how she came to be there. The girl told her the whole story. The wife knew Pietro as well, for he was a friend of her husband. She was very sad to hear what had happened, and when she heard precisely where he had been captured she felt sure he must have been killed. She said, therefore: 'As you don't know what's become of Pietro, you must stay with me until I can get you safely back to Rome.'

As Pietro was up in the oak-tree in the saddest frame of mind, about the time sleep first comes he saw a good twenty wolves arrive, and they surrounded his horse the moment they saw him. Getting wind of them, the horse jerked his head and snapped the reins by which he was tethered, and tried to escape, but, being surrounded, he could only defend himself for some time with his teeth and hooves. Eventually, however, the wolves brought him down and tore him to pieces from throat to belly and made a meal of him, leaving nothing but the bones. Then they went their way. Pietro had been used to looking to his nag for company and support in his troubles, so he was utterly dismayed at this and felt he was never going to find his way out of the forest. Soon it would be dawn, but up the tree he was dying of cold. As he gazed about him he noticed a great fire lit, maybe a mile off. When it was fully day, therefore, he climbed down from the oak, not without misgivings, and made towards it and kept going till he reached it. He found shepherds gathered round the fire, having their meal and enjoying a little relaxation together; mercifully they made him welcome. He had something to eat and warmed himself, then told them of his misadventures and how he came to be here on his own; he asked them if there was any castle or house in the neighbourhood he might make for. The shepherds told him that they were about three miles from a castle belonging to Liello di Campo di Fiore, and his wife was living there at the moment. Pietro was very pleased to hear this and asked if any of them might show him the way, which two of them were glad to do. On reaching the castle, Pietro happened upon some people he knew, and tried to see if a search of the forest might be mounted to find his beloved. The lady of the house sent for him, however, and he went straight away; imagine his joy when he found Agnolella in her company. He was dying to go and embrace her, but forbore to, feeling a little bashful in his hostess's presence. Now if he was in raptures, his beloved was no less blissful on sight of him.

The lady welcomed him with open arms. She listened to his account of his adventures, and rebuked him quite bluntly for going against his family's wishes. Seeing, however, that his mind was made up, and that the girl was of one mind with him: 'Well', she remarked, 'why should I worry? These two are in love, they know each other well enough, they're both of them friends of my husband, their wish is perfectly honourable, and I think God must have willed them to marry: after all, He's saved one of them from being hanged, the other from being run through, and both of them from the wild beasts. Therefore so be it! If your hearts are set on being husband and wife', she told them, 'then I am content too. Let the wedding proceed right here, at Liello's expense. I'm sure I can make peace between you and your families afterwards.'

So here they got married. Pietro was jubilant, Agnolella even more so. Their hostess carried it off in style, so far as she could in these rustic surroundings. Here the couple plucked the first fruits of their love. Some days later they took horse and, strongly escorted, they returned to Rome, accompanied by their hostess, who found Pietro's family in a towering rage over the young man's escapade, but happily effected a reconciliation. Pietro lived in serene contentment with his Agnolella until their old age.

V. 4. *Lizio's daughter Caterina sleeps out on the balcony in the fresh air and listens to the nightingale; how she catches one and what results.*

Elissa finished her tale and listened as the ladies expressed their approval. Then the queen bade Philostrato tell a story and he chuckled as he began:

Several of you ladies have kept taking me to task for reducing you to tears with the tales of cruelty I inflicted on you; so now I feel obliged to make amends by telling a story that will occasion you a little amusement. What I propose to relate, therefore, is quite a short love story: the only touch of misadventure in it consists of a few sighs and a moment's panic tinged with shame, but it has a happy ending.

In Romagna not long ago there lived a knight called Lizio da Valbona. He was an excellent fellow and a thorough gentleman, and he had a wife called Giacomina who happened to present him with a daughter when he was on the threshold of old age. This daughter grew up to become the fairest and most engaging young lady in the neighbourhood. Being an only child, she was the apple of her parents' eye: her father and mother spared no efforts in bringing her up, with a view to making a splendid match for her. Now there was a handsome, fresh-faced youngster called Ricciardo—he was one of the Manardis from Brettinoro—who was a frequent visitor to their house, and Lizio enjoyed his companionship. The couple felt as much at ease with him as if he had been their own son. Ricciardo had cast an eye more than once upon the girl and found her graceful, pretty, engaging in her manner, and definitely nubile; so he fell madly in love with her, but took pains not to divulge this. His sentiments did not, however, escape the notice of the young lady who made no attempt at evasion but fell in love with him instead—much to Ricciardo's gratification.

Many a time would he have addressed a word to her but he never plucked up the courage until on one occasion he braced himself and said to her: 'Caterina, I beg you, don't make me die of love.'

'God grant that you don't make *me* die of love', was her instant reply.

Such an answer left Ricciardo feeling a great deal happier, and braver too. 'Me, there's nothing I won't do to please you', he said; 'but it's up to you to find some way out for us, if we're to save your life and mine.'

'Ricciardo, look at the way they keep their eye on me; I really can't see how you can do it, but if you can see a way for us to be together without my being compromised, tell me what to do and I'll do it.'

After some consideration Ricciardo said all of a sudden: 'Caterina, my sweet, there's only one solution I can see, and that is if you can sleep out on the balcony overlooking your father's garden, or at least gain access to it. If I knew you were there during the night, you can be sure I'd do my utmost to come to you there, even though it's quite a climb.'

'If you have courage enough for that, I think I can arrange to sleep out there.'

'Yes I do', said Ricciardo, whereupon they stole one hurried kiss and separated.

It was now towards the end of May and the next day Caterina went and complained to her mother that she'd not been able to sleep last night because of the heat.

'The heat, my child? But it wasn't at all hot!'

'Listen, mother, if you'd added "in my opinion" you might be telling the truth: what you must bear in mind, though, is that girls get much hotter than older women.'

'How right you are, child. But I can't make it warm or cool at will as you seem to want. You have to put up with the weather as the seasons dictate. Maybe tonight will be cooler and you'll sleep better.'

'Please God!—though it is rather unusual for the nights to get cooler as we get further into the summer.'

'Well', said her mother, 'what d'you expect anyone to *do* about it?'

'If you and Father don't mind, I'd love to put a cot out on the balcony outside his room, overlooking the garden, and sleep there. Listening to the nightingale* and being in a cooler place, I'd be much better off than I am in your bedroom.'

'Cheer up, then. I'll have a word with your father and we'll do as he says.'

Hearing what his wife had to say, Lizio, maybe a little crabby in his old age, replied: 'What's all this about nightingales to send her to sleep? I'll have her sleeping in broad daylight by the chirp of the crickets!'

When the word got back to Caterina she was so cross that this, rather than the temperature, kept her awake that night—and furthermore she also kept her mother awake listening to her complaints about the heat. In the morning the lady went to Lizio and said: 'You don't seem to care all that much for the girl: what difference does it make to you if she sleeps out on the balcony? She had no relief from the heat all night long. Anyway, what's so surprising about her wish to hear the nightingale sing?—she's only a little girl. Those are the sort of things that give pleasure to youngsters.'

'Very well', said Lizio, 'let her have a bed made up out there that will fit the space, and tuck it up with a cretonne bedspread; let her sleep there and listen to the nightingale to her heart's content.'

Told of this, Caterina hastened to have a bed made up there and, as she would be sleeping in it that night, she waited to catch Ricciardo and passed him the agreed signal to apprise him of what he had to do. When Lizio heard that the girl had retired to bed, he closed the shutters giving on to the balcony from his bedroom and went to bed too. As for Ricciardo, once he could hear that all was quiet, he climbed on to a wall with the aid of a ladder, and from atop that wall he clawed his way up another wall, using certain protruding stones in it, and managed, by dint of great exertion and at no small risk of falling, to reach the balcony. Here he was welcomed with great joy but no noise by Caterina. After a great deal of kissing they lay down together and spent almost the entire night deriving great pleasure and satisfaction from each other—and they set the nightingale a-trilling a great many times. The pleasure was of long duration, not so the night, and day broke upon them before they thought it possible; flushed with the heat and their amorous exertions, they fell asleep without a stitch of clothing on, Caterina lying with her right arm slipped under Ricciardo's neck and her left hand grasping an organ of his that you ladies are too demure to mention in mixed company.

Thus they slept, and the new day did not awaken them. Lizio, however, got up and, remembering that his daughter was sleeping out on the balcony, silenly opened the shutters, saying: 'Let's take a look and see how the nightingale's lulled our Caterina to sleep.' He stepped outside and quietly lifted up the cretonne coverlet thrown over the bed and exposed her and Ricciardo with nothing on, fast asleep in each others' arms in the posture already described. Having clearly identified Ricciardo, he slipped away to his wife's room and called her. 'Quick, woman, up you get!' he said. 'Come and look: your daughter's had such a craving for nightingales, she kept watch and managed to grab one—she's still holding it in her hand.'

'How can this be?'

'Come quickly and you'll see.'

His wife hastened to get dressed and quietly followed him. Together they came to the bed and, lifting the coverlet, Giacomina could see very plainly how her daughter had caught and was still holding the nightingale whose song she had so longed to hear.

Feeling herself very much deceived in Ricciardo, Giacomina was about to yell at him and give him a piece of her mind when her husband told her: 'Wait! Don't say a word if you value my love: let me tell you—now that she's got her hand on it, it'll have to be hers. Ricciardo is a rich young man and of good family; he cannot but be a good match for us. If he and I are to part as friends, the first thing he'll have to do is marry her, that way he'll have stuck his nightingale in a cage of his own and not in someone else's.' Giacomina cheered up at this and held her peace: her husband, she could see, was taking it quite jovially, and her daughter had, after all, enjoyed a good, restful night and had caught her nightingale.

Hardly were these words spoken than Ricciardo woke up. Seeing that it was broad daylight he felt he was as good as dead. 'Good heavens, my love!' he cried out to Caterina. 'What shall we do? The day has come and found me still here.'

Lizio approached at these words, pulled back the coverlet, and remarked: 'You'll do all right!'

On sight of him Ricciardo's heart froze. He sat up in bed and cried: 'Have mercy on me, sir, for God's sake. I recognize that I'm a bad and treacherous man and deserve to die, so do with me as you will. But I do beseech you, if it be possible, show your clemency and spare me my life.'

To whom Lizio replied: 'This has been a poor reward, Ricciardo, for the love I have borne you and the trust I have placed in you. But what's done is done; this is the kind of mistake you're driven to when you're young. Now if you're to avert the death-penalty from yourself and spare me from suffering shame, you must plight your troth to Caterina as your lawful bride before you make another move; that way, as you possessed her this night, so may she be for the rest of her days. This is the way to earn my pardon and your safety. Should you not be prepared to do this, commend your soul to God.'

While these words were being spoken, Caterina released the nightingale, covered herself up, and burst into floods of tears; she begged her father to forgive Ricciardo, and begged Ricciardo to do as her father wished—that way they could be sure to enjoy such nights together for a long time to come. Ricciardo, however, needed little pressing: for one thing, he was ashamed of what he had done and was anxious to make amends; for another, he was scared to death and had a strong urge to escape with his life. Moreover, he was passionately in love and craving to possess the object of his passion; therefore he lost no time in freely consenting to what was proposed. So Lizio borrowed a ring off his wife and Ricciardo, there in their presence, without moving from where he was, plighted his troth to Caterina. This done, Lizio and his wife left; their parting words were: 'Now take your rest—that's probably what you need more than getting up.' When they were gone, the young couple embraced once more and, as they had ridden but six miles in the night, they rode on another two before they got out of bed, and so brought the first day to a close. Eventually they got up and Ricciardo had a more considered discussion with Lizio. A few days later he and Caterina were betrothed once more, as was fitting, in the presence of their friends and relations; he brought her home amid great celebrations and they had a lovely, dignified wedding, after which in all peace and comfort he had every leisure to go after nightingales with her night and day to his heart's content.

V. 5. *Two young men, Giannole and Minghino, fight over a girl and are thrown into prison. Fate intervenes to resolve the quarrel and give the prize to one of the rivals.*

The story of the nightingale had sent all the ladies into such fits of laughter as they listened that even after Philostrato was finished they could not stop laughing. But after they had been chortling away for a good while, the queen said: 'Believe me, if you depressed us all yesterday, today you've so tickled our ribs, none of us ladies has any right to complain of you.' Then she turned to Neiphile and bade her tell a story, which she began cheerfully enough as follows:

Philostrato stepped into Romagna with his story; and that is where I too should like to perambulate a little as I unfold my own.

Two Lombards lived in the city of Fano; one was called Guidotto of Cremona, the other, Giacomino of Pavia. They were now well on in years but in their prime they had been soldiers most of the time and involved in combat. Now Guidotto had no son or other kinsman or friend in whom he confided more than in Giacomino, and on his deathbed he bequeathed to him a daughter aged about 10 and all his wordly goods; after discussing his estate with him at some length, he died. This was around the time when Faenza recovered some measure of stability after a long period of strife and disaster; anyone who wished to return there was left free to do so, and Giacomino, who used to reside there and found it a pleasant place to live in, moved back there bag and baggage; he took with him the little girl entrusted to him by Guidotto, whom he cherished and raised as his own daughter. She grew into a young woman whose beauty was the equal of any woman's in the city. Moreover, she was as virtuous and well-mannered as she was beautiful, so she began to be courted by several men, but by two in particular, both of them well-favoured and respectable young men who doted on her and incurred each other's loathing as a result of mutual jealousy. One was called Giannole di Severino, the other, Minghino di Mingole. She was now 15 years old and either of the youths would gladly have offered her marriage if her family had been willing to countenance it; but as a virtuous union was denied them, they each set about trying to obtain her favours by whatever means they could.

In his household Giacomino kept an elderly maid and a manservant, a jovial and amiable type called Crivello. Giannole and he became the best of friends and, at an opportune moment, he disclosed to the man his passion for the girl and besought him to aid and abet him in obtaining what he was after; he promised him lavish rewards for doing so. 'Well', said Crivello, 'there's only one thing I could do for you and that is to fetch you in to be with her when Giacomino happens to go out to dinner. If I were to speak to her on your behalf, she'd never stop to listen to me. But that much I'll certainly do for you if you like, then it will be up to you to do as you think fit.'

'That will do very nicely', said Giannole, and on this plan they both settled.

As for Minghino, he had made friends with the maid, and to such good effect that she had carried several of his messages to the girl and more or less kindled in her the flame of love. The maid had, furthermore, promised to introduce him into her presence the next time Giacomino happened to leave the house in the evening for whatever reason.

So it happened, not long after these discussions, that Giacomino went out to dine with a friend—Crivello had a hand in it. The manservant then apprised Giannole of this and arranged with him to turn up on a given signal and he would find the front door open. The maid, for her part, quite unaware as she was of all this, informed Minghino that Giacomino was out for supper; he was to stay close by so that, when he saw her make a sign, he could come and slip in. The two suitors had no knowledge of each others' plans, though they were each mistrustful of the other; as night fell, they both set out with a few friends, armed, in order to obtain possession. Minghino took his band to lie up in the house of a friend who was a neighbour of the girl's, as he awaited the signal, while Giannole loitered with his friends at some little distance from her house.

With Giacomino out of the way, Crivello and the maid each tried to get rid of the other. 'Why don't you go to bed?' said Crivello to the maid. 'What's keeping you so busy round the house?'

'Why haven't you gone to attend your master?' she asked him. 'What are you waiting for? You've had your supper.'

Well, neither of them could get the other out of the way, and Crivello, realizing that the moment agreed with Giannole had arrived, muttered to himself: 'Why do I bother with her? If she doesn't keep it to herself, I'll settle her hash.' So he made the pre-arranged signal and went to open the door; Giannole turned up in a trice with his two comrades, went in, found the girl in the parlour, and laid hold of her to lead her away. The girl put up a resistance and made a great hullabaloo, and so did the maid. This came to the ears of Minghino, who dashed up with his friends to find the girl already being dragged through the front door. They drew their swords and 'Why, you blackguards!' they yelled. 'Now you're for it! What's all this rough stuff anyway? You'll never get away with it!' This said, they laid into them. The rumpus brought all the neighbours out into the street with lanterns and weapons; they expressed their disgust at the scene and took Minghino's side; after quite a struggle Minghino wrested the girl from Giannole and returned her to Giacomino's house, but not before the Podestà's watch turned up and started arresting people right and left, including Minghino, Giannole, and Crivello, who were led off to prison. Eventually order was restored and Giacomino returned home; he was thoroughly vexed by the incident, but after looking into it and finding that the girl was in no way to blame, he recovered his composure. He did conclude, however, that he must find her a husband without delay if such a thing was not to happen again.

The next morning the families of the two youths got to hear precisely what had taken place; realizing what a pickle the two prisoners could be in if Giacomino chose to press charges, as he was perfectly entitled to do, they went to find him and with winning words begged him not to consider the wrong he had suffered from the boys' idiotic behaviour, but to consider rather the goodwill that, so they believed, he entertained for his supplicants. On their own behalf and on that of the boys who had done the damage, they offered to make whatever restitution he saw fit to ask.

Giacomino, who was not a bad sort and who anyway had seen it all before, answered briefly: 'If I were back at home, gentlemen, instead of being your guest, I'd still regard myself as being on such friendly terms with you that I would take no step over this or over anything else unless it accorded with your own good pleasure. Indeed I'm all the more obliged to fall in with your wishes inasmuch as it is you who have done yourselves an injury: the point is, this girl is not a native of Cremona or of Pavia, as perhaps many of you think, but she comes from Faenza, though neither I nor she nor the man by whom I was entrusted with her ever did know whose daughter she was. As to what you are requesting of me, I shall do whatever you propose.'

The good folk were quite surprised to hear that the girl came from Faenza; they thanked Giacomino for his obliging attitude and asked him to explain to them how she had come into his keeping, and what made him certain she was a Faentine.

'Guidotto of Cremona was my friend and comrade', said Giacomino. 'He told me on his deathbed that when this city was captured by the Emperor Frederick* and the whole place was sacked, he and his band went into a house which they found crammed with goods and chattels. It had been abandoned by its occupants, all except for this child, who was 2 years old or thereabouts at the time, and as he came up the stairs she called him 'Daddy!' So he took pity on her and when he cleaned out the contents of the house he took her and them with him to Fano. Here he died, and bequeathed her to me together with all his worldly goods. When the time came for me to marry her off, he required me to settle upon her everything that had belonged to her, as a dowry. Now that she has come to marriageable age I've not yet found anybody on whom I would wish to bestow her, though I shall willingly do so before anything like last night's fracas happens again.'

Among the people present was a certain Guglielmino da Medicina. He had been associated with Guidotto on that occasion and knew precisely which house it was that Guidotto had ransacked. 'Bernabuccio', he said as he went up to a man he spotted among those present, 'are you listening to what Giacomino's saying?'

'Yes indeed. And I've been thinking about it, because I remember that in all the confusion I lost a little girl the same age as the one Giacomino has mentioned.'

'Well, she has to be the one, then', put in Giacomino, 'because once I happened to overhear Guidotto pondering where it was that he had ransacked a house, and I recognized it must have been yours. So think back: do you think you could identify her by any mark? If so, take a look for it and you're sure to find that she's your daughter.'

After some thought, Bernabuccio recollected that the girl would have had a scar* in the shape of a cross above her left ear, the result of a cyst being excised shortly before these events. So, without losing a moment, he approached Giacomino, who had not yet left, and asked if he might go with him back to his house and take a look at the girl. Giacomino willingly brought him home and sent for her. Bernabuccio thought he recognized her mother's face in hers—the woman was a beauty even today—but, not to leave it at this, he sought Giacomino's leave to pull back her hair a little from her left ear. Giacomino had no objection. Bernabuccio approached her as she stood there bashfully, and lifted her hair with his right hand and saw the cross. Recognizing her to be in truth his daughter, the tears came to his eyes and he hugged her, while she tried to pull away.

He turned to Giacomino and said: 'This, my friend, is indeed my daughter. It was my house that Guidotto plundered and in the heat of the moment her mother (my wife) overlooked this child; she was left inside and, till this moment we have always thought she was caught in the flames when the house was burnt down that day.'

The girl listened to this and observed that the man was elderly; she believed what she heard and, touched by some unseen force, submitted to his embraces and shed tears of tenderness. Bernabuccio sent straightaway for her mother and the other women of the family, as also for her brothers and sisters; he displayed her to all of them and described what had happened. After any amount of hugs all round, he took her off home amid great rejoicings, in which Giacomino joined.

Now the Podestà was a good sort, and when this development came to his notice, realizing that Giannole, who was being held in detention, was Bernabuccio's son and thus the girl's brother, he decided to take a lenient view of his offence. He took a hand with Bernabuccio and Giacomino in restoring harmony between Giannole and Minghino. To Minghino he accorded the hand of the young lady, whose name was Agnesa, much to the delight of his family, and set him and Giannole free along with Crivello and all the rest who had been caught up in the affair. Then Minghino, in the best of spirits, went on to wed her amid the greatest festivities and brought her home and lived with her for many years in peace and joy.

## V. 6. *Gianni di Procida and his beloved insult the King of Sicily and are condemned to the stake. Gianni's last request, however, is answered beyond his hopes.*

The ladies much enjoyed Neiphile's story. When it was finished, the queen told Pampinea to tell one. She looked up placidly and at once began:

The power of love is tremendous. Lovers undertake prodigious labours and confront dangers you'd never imagine, as you will have gathered from so many stories told today and on other occasions. Even so, I should like to give a further instance, this one about the courage of a young lover.

Ischia is an island very close to Naples. A beautiful, sprightly young lady once lived there, called Restituta, the daughter of an Ischian gentleman called Marin Bolgaro.* On a neighbouring island, Procida, there lived a young man called Gianni, who loved her more than his own life, a love she returned. Gianni would often come from Procida to spend the day on Ischia in order to see her; not only this, he had often come at night too, and if he could not find a boat he would swim across, were it only to be able, for lack of anything better, to set eyes on the walls of her house. While this passionate affair was in progress, Restituta happened one summer's day to be all on her own down by the seashore, prising shellfish off the rocks with a little knife. As she went from rock to rock, she came to a secluded cove where some Sicilian youths had put in from Naples with their cutter—the place was shady and had the added attraction of a cold freshwater spring. Seeing what a beautiful young woman she was, and all on her own, and that she had not yet noticed their presence, they decided to seize her and abduct her. She shrieked and yelled but seize her they did, got her on board, and made off. When they reached Calabria they quarrelled over her, for each of them wanted her, but as they could reach no agreement and feared that she'd prove to be more trouble than she was worth, they all decided to make a present of her to Federigo, King of Sicily;* he was still a young man then, and took pleasure in such things. So on they went to Palermo and that's what they did. The king was delighted with her, seeing how pretty she was; but as he was not in the best of health he had her lodged, until he was back on form, in a beautiful pavilion in his gardens—it was called La Cuba*—and there given every attention. And so it was done.

The young lady's abduction caused a terrible rumpus in Ischia, and the worst of it was that nobody could discover who it was who had made off with her. Gianni, however, was more concerned about it than anyone else and did not wait to receive news of her in Ischia. He knew which direction the cutter had taken, so he had a cutter of his own made ready for the sea, boarded it, and set off as soon as possible to scour the entire coast between the Gulf of Salerno and the Gulf of Policastro, enquiring everywhere for the girl. At Scalea in Calabria he was told that Sicilian sailors had taken her to Palermo. Gianni sailed thither as fast as he could, and, after a great deal of searching, he discovered that she had been given to the king as a present, and he was holding her in La Cuba. This news upset him deeply and left him practically without further hope of ever seeing her again, let alone of getting her back.

Nevertheless, Love kept him there; he sent away the cutter and remained in Palermo, seeing that here nobody knew him. Often he would pass by La Cuba, and one day he happened to catch a glimpse of her at her window, and she of him. Both were delighted. Noticing how secluded the house was, Gianni got as close as he could and spoke with her, and she told him what to do if he wanted to converse with her more intimately. After giving a careful scrutiny to the way the grounds were laid out, he left her, and waited until the night was quite far advanced. Then he returned and entered the garden, climbing over at a point that would not have offered a purchase even to a woodpecker. In the garden he found a pole which he set up against the window she had indicated to him, and up it he nimbly climbed. Now it seemed to Restituta that her honour was practically lost, in defence of which she had hitherto kept Gianni at arm's length; however she felt now that there was no one to whom she could more suitably surrender herself than to him, besides which, she might induce him to escape with her, so she decided to fall in with his every wish. The window, therefore, she had left open, so that he might quickly step inside. Finding the window open, Gianni quietly went in and lay down beside her; she was not asleep. Before they did anything else, Restituta told him what she had in mind, and begged him above all to rescue her and take her away. Nothing would give him greater pleasure, said Gianni, and when he left her he would without fail make his preparations with a view to fetching her away the next time he came. After this they embraced rapturously and took their pleasure—Love offers none greater—time and time again until, before they knew it, they were fast asleep in each other's arms.

The king had been greatly taken with Restituta the first time he laid eyes on her. Feeling that he was now in better shape, he remembered her and, though the night was almost over, he decided to pay her a little visit. So he quietly went to La Cuba with a few of his pages, entered the house, had the door softly opened to the room in which he knew she slept, and in he went, preceded by a great flaming sconce. Looking at the bed, what did he see but the maiden asleep in the arms of Gianni, both of them in the nude. This drove him at once into such a towering rage he was quite speechless, and it was touch and go whether he killed the pair on the spot with the dagger at his waist. But he concluded that it would be quite abject for any man, never mind for a king, to slay two naked sleepers, so he checked himself and determined that they should burn to death in public. He turned to a companion and said: 'What d'you think of this evil woman, in whom I had placed my hope?' Then he asked him if he recognized the youth who had been so rash as to come into his house and flout him with such effrontery.

The man to whom this question was addressed answered that he could not recall ever having seen him.

So the king swept out of the room in a fury, leaving orders that the two lovers were to be taken and bound, naked as they were; when it was fully daylight, they were to be taken to Palermo and tied back to back to a stake in the piazza. Thus were they to be held until nine in the morning, so that everyone could have a look at them; then they were to be burnt, as they deserved. This said, he returned, fuming, to his room in Palermo.

The moment the king had left, many hands seized the two lovers, not only awakening them but promptly trussing them up without mercy. If the youngsters were unhappy at this and feared for their lives, and wept and grieved, I leave you to imagine. They were taken to Palermo, as the king had commanded, and tied to a stake in the piazza, and they watched as the wood was piled up and the fire made ready for their burning at the king's appointed time. Immediately all the citizens, of either sex, crowded along to see the two lovers, and while the men came to look at the girl and spoke highly of her beauty and shapeliness, the women all gathered to look at the boy and praised him for his comeliness and fine physique. But the two unfortunate lovers stood hanging their heads, as embarrassed as could be, and bewailed their unhappy fate as they awaited their cruel death by fire from one hour to the next.

As they were kept here in this way until the appointed hour, and their crime was broadcast all about, word of it came to the ears of Ruggero di Lauria,* a man of inestimable valour and at that time the king's admiral. He went to where they were tied in order to take a look at them and, when he got there, he first inspected the girl and took a highly favourable view of her beauty; after which he went to examine the boy and had little difficulty in recognizing him. He drew closer and asked him, might he be Gianni di Procida?

Gianni looked up and recognized the admiral. 'I certainly was the man you spoke of, sir', he said, 'but I'm on the point of no longer being so.'

The admiral then asked him what had brought him to this pass, and Gianni said: 'Love, and the king's wrath.'

The admiral asked him to elucidate, and when he had the whole story from Gianni and was making to leave, the youth called him back and said: 'Please, sir, could you possibly ask a favour from the person who is thus holding me here?'

'What favour?' Ruggero asked him.

'I see that I am to die, and soon at that', Gianni replied. 'The favour I seek is this: as I am placed with my back to this young woman, whom I've loved more than my life and she me, and her back is to me, might we be turned to face each other, so that, seeing her face as I die, I may go comforted.'

'But of course,' said Ruggero with a laugh. 'I'll see to it that you get to look at her until you've had more than your fill!'

The admiral left him and told the men charged with executing the royal command that they were to proceed no further without fresh instructions from the king. Then without delay he went to the king and, though he found him out of temper, he still told him precisely what he thought. 'Your majesty', he said, 'what have those two youngsters done to offend you, whom you've ordered to be burnt to death down there in the piazza?'

The king told him, and Ruggero pursued: 'Such an offence certainly deserves punishment, but not at your hands. And just as offences deserve punishment, so do good services deserve a reward, beyond pardon and mercy. Those two you mean to burn at the stake, do you know who they are?'

'No', said the king.

'Well', said Ruggero, 'I want you to know; that way you'll realize just how temperate you are, letting your anger get the better of you. The young man is son of Landolfo di Procida; if you are sovereign and lord of this island, it is thanks to the efforts of his brother, Gian di Procida. The young woman is daughter of Marin Bolgaro, and if you continue to hold sway in Ischia, that is by virtue of his power. Furthermore, these are two young people who have long been in love with each other; it has been the force of love, and not any wish to insult your majesty, that has brought them to commit this offence, if that's the right name for what young people do when they're in love. Why, then, do you condemn them to die, when you ought to be entertaining them lavishly and offering them the best of gifts?'

When the king heard this and had ascertained that what Ruggero said was true, he was sorry that he had been on the point of proceeding so harshly against the pair, and indeed sorry for what he had already inflicted on them. So he straight away commanded that they be untied from the stake and brought before him—which was done. He heard from them precisely how matters stood, and decided that in compensation for the injury he had done them he should raise them up and lavish presents on them. He had them dressed again in becoming dignity, and, after establishing their mutual consent, he married off the young lady to Gianni and sent them both happily home, laden with magnificent gifts. They were welcomed with the grandest celebrations, and lived a long life together in joy and contentment.

V. 7. *Teodoro, a freed slave, gets his master's daughter Violante pregnant. The gallows loom, but rescue comes from an unexpected source.*

The ladies were all on tenterhooks until they heard whether the two lovers were to be burnt at the stake or not; hearing that they avoided this fate, 'Thank Goodness!' they sighed and cheered up at once. The queen heard out the tale, then bade Lauretta follow on, which she did happily enough, as follows:

In the days when good King William* ruled in Sicily there was a gentleman called Amerigo Abbate, from Trapani; he was blessed with the goods of this world and with not a few children. As he needed more servants, he bought some youngsters off Genoese slaving galleys which had put in from the Levant after picking up several children off the Armenian coast.* Amerigo took the lads for Turks—most of them looked like shepherds, though there was one who seemed to have a certain breeding and his name was Teodoro. Though his condition in the household was that of a slave, Teodoro was brought up with Amerigo's children; and as he was influenced more by his heredity than by the accident of his present station, he grew up to be a well-bred young gentleman and recommended himself highly to his master, so much so that his master gave him his freedom, had him baptized (taking him for a Turk) with the name of Pietro, and promoted him to the status of chief associate and confidant.

Along with his sons Amerigo raised a daughter called Violante, a pretty and dainty creature waiting to be married off. In the meantime she chanced to fall in love with Pietro, attracted as she was by his manner and behaviour, though she was embarrassed to betray her feelings to him. Love, however, saved her the trouble, for Pietro caught secret glimpses of her and fell in love with her too, indeed he measured his happiness by how much he saw of her. He realized that he was terribly astray in this, and was terrified lest anyone discover his feelings. Now Violante, who set eyes on him all too gladly, remarked his agitation and to reassure him made it plain that his love was indeed utterly welcome to her. This situation persisted for quite a while, neither daring to address a word to the other however much they both wanted to. But while each was equally smitten with the other, Fate evidently decided to smooth their path and found a means to drive off the fear that inhibited them.

About a mile outside Trapani Amerigo owned a delightful property, where his wife and daughter would often bring their women-friends and servants for a pleasant day out. One very hot day they all went there, bringing Pietro with them but, as sometimes happens in the summer, the heavens suddenly clouded over and the party set off hastily back to Trapani to avoid being caught by the storm.* Now Pietro, youthful as he was, outstripped the women in the party and, accompanied by Violante, left them far behind: maybe love as much as fear of the storm lent them wings. When the pair were so far ahead as to be almost out of sight there were several claps of thunder, then it started to hail with a vengeance; the mother and her party took refuge in a workman's cottage. The nearest refuge that Pietro and Violante could find was an abandoned ruin of a shack which still had a bit of its roof left; here they could shelter, though the shelter was so minimal they had, of necessity, to remain cheek by jowl—clinging together like this gave them a little reassurance, and also offered scope to amorous urges.

'Would to God', ventured Pietro, 'that this hailstorm never stopped if I could just stay this way!'

'I wouldn't mind either', said the girl.

This said, they grasped each other's hands, then they hugged each other, and the next thing was they were kissing, with the hail falling all around; and to cut a long story short, by the time the weather cleared they had contrived to go all the way in their love-making. With the storm over, they waited for the mother's party a little further on at the edge of the town, and returned home with her. At home the pair occasionally met in utter secrecy and took their pleasure together, so much so that Violante became pregnant, an eventuality that distressed them both; she tried one thing after another to evade the course of Nature and miscarry, but all to no avail.

Pietro feared for his life and decided to run away, but when he told her this she said: 'If you go, I'll kill myself and that's that.'

'How is it you want me to stay?' he asked his beloved. 'Your pregnancy will betray our sin. They'll forgive *you* readily enough and *I*'ll be the one who'll have to suffer the penalty for both of us.'

'They'll find me out soon enough', she said. 'But you can be sure they'll never learn about you unless you blurt it out.'

'All right', said Pietro. 'If you promise not to tell on me, I'll stay; but you must keep your promise.'

Violante had concealed her pregnancy for as long as she could, but the day she saw that her body would no longer keep her secret she went in floods of tears and told her mother. 'Help me!' she said.

Her mother was thoroughly distraught and scolded her roundly. 'How did this happen?' she asked. The daughter came out with her tale, rearranging the facts to protect Pietro. Her mother believed her, and sent her away to a villa of theirs so as to hide the girl's sorry condition.

When her time came to give birth, Violante cried out as women do in labour. What her mother had not reckoned with, however, was that Amerigo might turn up here, for this was a place he virtually never visited. It so happened, though, that on his way back from snaring birds he stopped by and, as he passed the room from which his daughter's cries were coming, he burst in, perplexed, to enquire what was going on. When she saw her husband arrive, the mother stood up and ruefully acquainted him with what had befallen their daughter. Amerigo, however, was less ready to accept the girl's version of events than her mother was, and said it could not be true that she did not know who had gotten her with child: he absolutely meant to find out, and if she told him, she might earn his forgiveness—otherwise she'd have to make up her mind to die without mercy. Her mother did her best to persuade Amerigo to accept the same version she had, but this was not to be. In a towering rage he drew his sword and advanced upon his daughter saying: 'Either you confess who the father is or you die this instant.' The girl, in the mean time, while her mother talked to distract her father, produced a baby boy.

In fear for her life, she now broke her promise to Pietro and told the whole story. This sent her father into a paroxysm of rage and he barely restrained himself from killing her; but when he had given vent to his wrath with a tongue-lashing, he mounted his horse again and returned to Trapani to seek out the king's lieutenant, whose name was Currado, to report the injury Pietro had done to him. Pietro was arrested before he knew himself even at risk, and, under torture, made a full confession. A few days later he was condemned by the king's lieutenant to be hanged, after first being lashed all the way to the gibbet.

Amerigo, however, whose anger was not assuaged by Pietro's condemnation to death, was determined to be rid of the two lovers and their baby all at once; so he prepared a poisoned chalice of wine and a naked blade, gave both to a retainer of his, and told him: 'Take these two things to Violante and tell her from me she's to choose the one or the other, the poison or the knife; and if she's not quick about it, I'll see her burnt at the stake in the presence of the whole town, as she has deserved. Then take the baby she's just given birth to, knock his brains out against the wall, and feed him to the dogs.' This was the cruel sentence the outraged father issued against his daughter and grandson, and the servant left in not the happiest frame of mind to see it carried out.

The route chosen for Pietro's passage under the lash to the gallows happened to lead past an inn where three noblemen from Armenia were staying. They were on an embassy from the King of Armenia to negotiate with the Pope in Rome on important matters concerned with an impending visit, and they had stopped here in Trapani a few days for rest and recreation; here they had been accorded the honours of the city, and by no one more assiduously than by the nobleman Amerigo. As the ambassadors heard the crowd hustling Pietro on his way, they came to the window to watch. Pietro was naked to the waist, his hands tied behind his back. One of the three ambassadors, a venerable elder of great authority called Fineo, noticed a big red patch on the boy's chest—not in any way daubed on but formed in the skin, like the mark women here call a strawberry-mark. The sight instantly reminded him of a son who had been snatched by corsairs from the beach at Laiazzo fifteen years ago, and whom he had never heard of since. As he considered the age of the poor wretch being flogged along, it occurred to him that if his son were still alive he would be of the same age as this lad appeared to be, and the suspicion dawned on him, because of the birthmark, that this might be his son. If he were my son, he thought, he must still remember his name and his father's and the Armenian tongue.

So when the lad was close by he called out: 'O Teodoro!'

Hearing this voice, Pietro looked up sharply.

'Where are you from?' asked Fineo, speaking in Armenian. 'And whose son are you?'

The guards in charge of Pietro halted him now, out of respect for the gentleman, and Pietro replied: 'I came from Armenia; my father was called Fineo, and I was brought here by strangers as a little boy.'

On hearing this, Fineo was left in no doubt that this must be the son he had lost; so he came down with his companions and passed, weeping, through the guards to embrace him; he threw round his shoulders the very costly cloak he was wearing, and asked the guard sergeant if he would wait here a moment until he received further orders—which the sergeant willingly agreed to do.

Fineo already knew why the lad was being led to his death, for it was by now common knowledge. So he went at once with his colleagues and their retinues to find Currado, the king's lieutenant.

'The man you are sending to his death as a slave, sir', he told him, 'is a free man and my son. He is ready to marry the woman whose virginity he is said to have impaired. Be good enough, therefore, to defer the execution until it may be established whether she will be his wife, so that you do not act in defiance of the law, should she so consent.'

Currado was amazed to learn that the boy was Fineo's son, and quite abashed at the shabby way Fate had treated him. Pietro corroborated Fineo's words, whereupon the lieutenant sent him straight home and summoned Amerigo to tell him how matters stood. Amerigo assumed that his daughter and grandson were by now dead, and he bitterly rued what he had done, knowing that everything could have been put to rights were she still alive; nevertheless he sent a runner after his daughter to annul his order if it had not already been carried out. The new messenger arrived to find the earlier one still berating Violante because she was taking her time over the choice between poison and knife; he was trying to force a decision on her. But on hearing his master's new command, he left her and returned to render his account.

Amerigo, therefore, was a happy man when he went to Fineo and made his apologies with tears in his eyes for what had occurred; he would be delighted, he said, to give away his daughter if Teodoro wished to make her his wife.

Fineo readily accepted his apologies. 'It is my wish', he said, 'that my son take your daughter to wife. Should he not consent, then let the sentence be carried out.' With harmony thus established between the two men they went to find Teodoro, who was still in fear for his life even while he was glad to have found his father again, and they asked him what were his intentions. Told that Violante would marry him if he so wished, he was so ecstatic he felt he'd leapt from hell to heaven in one bound. 'That would be the greatest gift', he said, 'if you are willing to grant it.' So they sent to know the girl's wishes. When she was told what Teodoro had been through and what still awaited him her spirits picked up a little, once she was ready to lend some credence to the message—for she had been expecting to die in the most agonizing of circumstances. 'If I follow my own inclination', she said, 'nothing would please me more than to be Teodoro's wife; but I'll do whatever my father commands.' So friendship prevailed, the young woman was betrothed, and the city joined in general rejoicings.

Violante made a good recovery and nursed her little son, nor was it long before she had quite recovered her radiance. Rising from childbed, she was presented to Fineo once he returned from Rome, and accorded him the respect due to a father. He was delighted to have such a beautiful daughter-in-law and welcomed her as a daughter, so treating her ever after. He arranged a sumptuous marriage, a joyful feast, and after a few days took ship and left for Laiazzo with his son, his new daughter, and grandson. There the two lovers lived out the rest of their days in serene contentment.

V. 8. *A rejected suitor, Nastagio degli Onesti, meets a vengeful horseman and a distressed damsel in a pine-wood and learns their story; it gives him just what he needs to convert the heart of his cruel lady.*

As Lauretta finished, Philomena, at the queen's bidding, thus began:

Just as the quality of mercy is thought to sit well with us, my charming ladies, so is our cruelty rigorously punished by divine justice. I feel, therefore, like telling you a story to demonstrate this and offer you reason to forswear cruelty—besides, it's a most compassionate and delightful tale.

There used to be plenty of rich noblemen in Ravenna, the ancient city in Romagna, and one of these was a young man called Nastagio degli Onesti, who had been left with a fortune beyond all telling on the deaths of his father and uncle. He was unmarried and, as tends to happen to young men, he fell in love: he fell in love with a daughter of Paolo Traversaro, but she was a noblewoman of far higher rank than he. It was his hope, nevertheless, that he might win her love by the way he treated her. But however lavish, stylish, and commendable were the forms his courtship took, far from doing him any good they appeared to have the very opposite effect on her: the beloved damsel responded to him with the coldest of cold shoulders. Maybe it was her exceptional beauty, or perhaps her lofty origins, that had made her so haughty and contemptuous, but she could only find fault with him and with whatever he chose to do for her. This was more than Nastagio could bear and there were several occasions when he was so aggrieved, he was ready to put an end to himself. And though he held back from this, he did, time and again, conclude that he must break off with her completely and, if at all possible, view her with a loathing to match her own. That was all very well, but in fact the more forlorn were his hopes, the more he seemed to dote on her. Nastagio, therefore, persevered in his courtship and the excessive expenditure this entailed. Now a number of his friends and relatives formed the opinion that he was well set to burn himself up and his patrimony to boot, so they kept urging and entreating him to leave Ravenna and settle somewhere else for a while: this way he would reduce both his love and his disbursements. Nastagio would scorn this advice, but they would not let up and he could not hold out for ever. So eventually he consented. He made the most elaborate preparations, as if he were moving to France or Spain or some other such remote destination, then mounted his horse and left Ravenna, accompanied by a host of friends. He rode to a place called Classe, some three miles outside Ravenna and, once here, he sent for tents and marquees and told his friends that this is where he was stopping and they were all to return to the city. Here, then, he pitched his tented camp and embarked on as sumptuous and delectable a style of living as anyone ever did, entertaining one group after another to luncheon or dinner, just as he used to do.

Well, one Friday towards the beginning of May,* it being a beautiful day, he was brooding over his hard-hearted lady and told all his household to leave him alone, the better to give himself up to his brooding; then off he went in a reverie, setting foot before foot, until he found himself inside the pine-forest. It was a little after eleven in the morning, and he had penetrated a good half-mile into the woods, quite oblivious of food or anything else, when all of a sudden he thought he heard great cries and shrieks—a woman's voice. This broke into his gentle meditation and, looking up to see what it was about, he was surprised to find himself inside the pine-wood. As he gazed, he saw the most beautiful girl running towards where he was standing, through a thicket choked with undergrowth and brambles; she was naked, dishevelled, and scratched all over by twigs and thorns, and she was shrieking for mercy. He saw two ferocious great mastiffs* at her heels and flanks, who kept snapping savagely at her wherever they could. Behind her he saw a dark rider on a black horse; he looked wrathful and was threatening to kill her, as he showered on her the most dreadful insults; in his hand he held a dagger. Filled with amazement and alarm, Nastagio's thoughts turned to pity for the unfortunate girl, and he conceived a wish to rescue her, if he could, from this torment and save her life. In the absence of any weapon, he seized a tree-branch to serve as a stick, and strode forth to face the dogs and the rider.

The rider, still some way off when he saw this, shouted at him: 'Nastagio, keep out of this, leave me and the dogs to serve this fiendish woman as she deserves.'

As he said this, the dogs lunged at the girl's hips and brought her to a stop. The rider caught up and dismounted, and Nastagio went to him, saying: 'I don't know who you are though you evidently know me. But let me tell you, it's the basest cowardice when an armed horseman tries to kill a naked woman and sets his dogs on her as if she were a wild animal. Believe me, I'll defend her to the limit.'

'Nastagio', replied the horseman, 'I used to be from your city and was called Guido degli Anastagi. You were still but a little boy when I was in love with this woman, far more so than you are now with the Traversari girl. But such was her arrogance and cruelty towards me, I was driven to despair and one day I killed myself with this dagger you see in my hand, so now I am condemned to eternal torments. How this woman rejoiced at my death! Not long afterwards, though, she herself died, and for her sin of cruelty, for the pleasure she took in my anguish, she too was condemned to hell-fire, because, far from being sorry for what she had done, she was convinced she had behaved irreproachably. Once she was in hell, we were each given our punishment: hers is to flee from me, mine, to pursue her as mortal enemy, not as a woman beloved, though I did love her so. And as often as I catch her I have to kill her with this dagger, with which I took my own life, and open up her back and rip out her heart—her cold, hard heart never penetrated by love or pity—together with her entrails, as you'll see in a moment, and feed them to these dogs. Then God's power and justice require that, shortly afterwards, she gets up again as if she had never been killed, and the painful chase resumes as I pursue her with the dogs. Now every Friday at this time here is where I catch her and carve her up as you'll presently see. Don't imagine, of course, that we take the other days off—I catch up with her in different places where she once was cruel to me or entertained cruel thoughts. As you see, now that from being her lover I've become her enemy, I'm obliged to pursue her this way, one year for each month of her hardness towards me. So leave me to execute divine justice and don't try to prevent what lies outside your power.'

Nastagio became decidedly timid when he heard this, indeed it quite made his hair stand on end. He stepped back, his eyes on the unfortunate girl, as he waited in trepidation to see what the rider would do. The moment he stopped speaking he brandished his dagger and hurled himself at the maiden like a savage hound; she was kneeling down in the grip of the two mastiffs, and shrieked for mercy, but he thrust at her with all of his might, running his blade into the middle of her breast and out through her back. Thus transfixed, the girl fell prone, still crying and yelling, while the horseman reached for a knife, slit open her back, and ripped out her heart with all the adjacent organs and tossed them to the two mastiffs, who devoured them on the spot, for they were ravenous. A moment later the girl leapt up as though none of this had happened, and raced off in the direction of the sea with the dogs snapping at her heels; the rider resumed his mount, clutched his dagger once more, and galloped after her; they vanished in a trice and Nastagio could no longer descry them.

He stood for a long time, torn between pity and terror at what he had witnessed, but after a while it occurred to him that all this might serve his own ends admirably, as it took place every Friday. So he marked the spot, returned to his household and chose his moment to send for several of his friends and relatives and thus address them. 'For ages you've been urging me to give up my love for this girl, this enemy of mine, and to stop being such a spendthrift; now I'm ready to do this if you can obtain a favour for me: see to it that Paolo Traversari comes here to dine with me on Friday next, bringing his wife and daughter and all their relations on the distaff side and any other ladies he chooses. Why I make this request you'll discover then.'

This seemed a small enough favour to ask and they gave him their promise. They returned to Ravenna and at a suitable moment invited the people Nastagio wanted; it was no easy task to bring the girl he was in love with, but she did go along with the rest. Nastagio laid on a veritable banquet and had the tables set out beneath the pine-trees, round the spot where he had seen the hard-hearted woman torn apart. He had the ladies and gentlemen seated at table and saw to it that his beloved was given a place exactly opposite the spot where the action was to take place. As they reached the last course, the desperate shrieks of the hunted girl first came to their ears. They were all quite bewildered and asked each other what was going on, but none of them knew the answer, so they stood up to look and saw the afflicted maiden and the horseman and the dogs. The next moment these had all arrived in their midst, and a mighty roar went up in protest against the dogs and the horseman, and a crowd of people surged forward to help the girl. The horseman, however, spoke to them as he had spoken to Nastagio, and made them all withdraw—indeed he left them cowed and terrified. A great number of the women present were related to the frantic maiden and the rider, and had not forgotten about his love, nor his death; so as he did what he had done the previous time, there was not one of them who did not break down sobbing, as if each one saw herself the victim of his onslaught. With the conclusion of the action the girl and the horseman went their way, leaving those who had witnessed it to comment on it in any number of ways. But among those who had received the worst shock was the heartless girl Nastagio was in love with; nothing had escaped her ear nor her eye and, as she reflected on the cruelty she had ever shown Nastagio, she realized that she was affected more than any other person present. She could already see herself fleeing before his wrath, with the two mastiffs snapping at her sides. This gave her such a scare that, to ensure it never happened to her, she seized the first opportunity, which was afforded her that very evening, to send a trustworthy maid of hers in secret to Nastagio—she'd meanwhile transmuted her loathing into love. The maid brought a message asking him please to call on her, for she was ready to do his good pleasure in all things. Nastagio sent answer to the effect that this was most gratifying but that, if she did not mind, he was not inclined to take his pleasure to the detriment of her honour, and therefore it was to be as his wedded wife. Well aware as she was that if she was not yet Nastagio's wife, this was solely her own decision, the girl conveyed her assent. Indeed she carried the proposal herself to her father and mother, saying that she was happy to be Nastagio's bride; her parents were delighted. Nastagio's betrothal took place the following Sunday; he married her and lived with her happily ever after.

Nor was this happy result the only outcome of that moment of terror: it instilled a lively fear into every woman in Ravenna, and from that moment on they showed far greater compliance to their menfolk's wishes than they ever had done before.

V. 9. *Federigho degli Alberighi ruins himself in his vain courtship of a lady; but Fortune begins to smile on him the day the lady's son covets his prize falcon.*

When Philomena finished speaking, the queen, who saw that no one else was left to speak save the privileged Dioneo, cheerfully began as follows:

It is now my turn, and I should like to tell a story that to some extent resembles the last one, not only to show you, my dearest ladies, what impact your charm has on men of gentle disposition, but also to teach you to distribute your rewards yourselves, as the occasion arises, rather than always leaving it up to Chance. For Chance is an indiscriminate giver—and she usually overdoes it.

Coppo di Borghese Domenichi was in our day, as you must know, a man of eminent authority and held in high esteem in our city—perhaps he is still living; his style and behaviour more even than his high birth contributed to his enduring reputation for excellence. In his old age he often enjoyed reminiscing with his neighbours and others about things gone by—with his orderly mind, his remarkable memory, and his elegant turn of phrase he had a quite singular facility in this sphere. One of his nicest tales was about a Florentine lad called Federigo degli Alberighi; he was without a peer in the whole of Tuscany as a chivalrous young gallant who shone in the lists. Now he fell in love, as do most young men of gentle nurture, and his beloved was called Giovanna, a married woman whose grace and beauty gave her a name with the best of Florentine women in her day. In order to win her love he would joust and tourney, give banquets and make lavish presents, running through his fortune without restraint. She, however, whose beauty was matched by her chastity, paid no attention to all these activities undertaken on her behalf, nor to the one who performed them. So Federigo kept spending and spending far beyond his means, and obtaining nothing in exchange, until he'd no money left (it happens all too easily), and he found himself a pauper. All he was left with was a tiny piece of land, affording him the most frugal living, and a prize falcon. His love for Giovanna was not a whit abated, but he felt that he could no longer maintain his desired life-style in the city so he moved to his country patch at Campi, where he patiently endured his poverty, hunting with his falcon and being beholden to nobody.

While Federigo was thus reduced to these straitened circumstances, Giovanna's husband chanced one day to fall ill; seeing that he was close to death he made a will, leaving all his considerable wealth to his son, a growing boy, but providing that, should the boy die without legitimate issue, then his dearly beloved wife Giovanna was to inherit. Then he died. Now in the summer, following the custom of our ladies, the widow moved with her son to a country property of hers, very close to Federigo's. The boy made friends with Federigo and took pleasure in hawks and hounds; he had often seen Federigo's falcon on the wing and took a strong fancy to it, but however much he yearned, he wouldn't hazard to ask for it, seeing how much the bird meant to Federigo. This was how matters stood when the little boy fell ill. His mother was quite distraught, for he was her only child and she was as devoted to him as could be. She spent the whole day at his bedside, giving him comfort and constantly asking him if there were anything he craved; if there was, she begged him to tell her, for she would see to obtaining it for him if remotely possible.

After he had heard her several times make this offer, he said: 'If you can get me Federigo's falcon, mother, I'm sure I'll get better quickly.'

His mother pondered this awhile and started to consider what she would have to do. She knew that Federigo had long been in love with her and had never obtained so much as a glance, and she mused: 'How am I to send for this falcon, or go myself to ask for it? From what I hear, it's the best falcon that ever flew, and besides, it's the one thing that keeps him going. How could I be so insensitive as to think of depriving such a gentle soul of this, his one remaining pleasure?' She was not a little embarrassed by such considerations, and though she had no doubt the falcon would be hers for the asking, she did not know what to say and put off giving her son an answer.

Eventually, however, her mother's love prevailed and she screwed herself up, come what may, to go herself, rather than sending for it, and to bring it back to him. 'My child', she said, 'take heart and see to somehow getting better, for I promise you, first thing tomorrow morning I'll go and get the bird for you.' At this the child perked up and showed some improvement that very day.

In the morning Giovanna went out for a walk, taking a woman-companion, and called at Federigo's cottage and asked for him. As it was not then the season for hawking, Federigo was out in his kitchen garden where there was some work that needed overseeing. When he heard that Giovanna was at the door asking for him he could scarcely believe it, and ran happily to meet her.

She got up and flashed a winning smile at him as she saw him approach. He greeted her respectfully and she said: 'A good day to you, Federigo. I've come to make amends for the injury you've suffered on my account, because you loved me more than you ought to have done. The way I'm going to make amends is I'm bringing this friend of mine with me to join you for a bite of lunch today, nothing grand, mind you.'

'I can't remember ever receiving any injury from you', was Federigo's meek reply; 'you've done me nothing but good, and if ever I had any merit, that was due to your goodness and to the love I nurtured for you. This gracious visit of yours assuredly means all the more to me than it would if I were still in a position to match the whole sum of my past extravagance, though in fact you have come to a host of slender means.' With these words, he ushered her with some embarrassment through his house and out into the garden, where he had nobody in whose company to leave her, so he said: 'Seeing that there's no one else, this woman will keep you company—she's the wife of my labourer here—just while I go in to set the table.'

Although he was desperately poor, he had still never taken in (though Lord knows he needed to) just how immoderately he had squandered his fortune. This morning, however, as he couldn't find a thing to set before the lady for love of whom he had entertained guests in their thousands, his situation finally came home to him. He dashed back and forth frantically, at his wits' end, and cursed his luck, but he could find neither money nor anything on which to raise some; the morning was well advanced and he was ever so anxious to put on a bit of a spread for the lady, but he refused to turn to anyone for help, least of all to his labourer. Then it was that his eye fell on his fine falcon sitting on its perch in his little parlour. With nothing else to serve, he picked it up, found it plump enough, and decided that this was fare fit for such a lady. Without a second thought he wrung its neck and handed it to his maid to pluck and clean it quickly, put on a spit, and roast to a turn. When the table was set with snowy white table-linen (he still possessed a little), he went out cheerfully to the lady in the garden and told her that lunch was ready, such as it was. So Giovanna and her companion went in and sat down to lunch, where they all unwittingly dined off the prize falcon, served most devotedly by Federigo.

When they left the table, the ladies continued their agreeable conversation with Federigo awhile, then Giovanna felt the time had come to broach the object of her visit and she observed amiably to him: 'If you recollect your old life and my own integrity, which you'll happen to have interpreted as hard-heartedness, I've no doubt that you'll be amazed at my presumption when you hear the main reason that brought me here. However, if you'd had children and knew the bond of love a parent feels, I'm sure you'd more or less forgive me. And though you have no children, I do have one, and cannot escape the constraints of mother-love: they oblige me, whatever my own feelings or common decency say about it, they oblige me to ask you for a present of something I know you particularly treasure—as well you might, for in your wretched circumstances it's all you have left for your pleasure and pastime and consolation. The present is your falcon, which my little boy wants so badly that if I don't bring it back for him I'm afraid his illness will take such a turn for the worse, it will end with my losing him altogether. So I'm asking you, not for the sake of your love for me, which places you under no sort of obligation, but in your generosity—and there never was a man as open-handed as you—please let me have it. Then I shall be able to claim I've saved my son's life by this gift, and I'll be eternally indebted to you on his account.'

Federigo listened to her request and realized that he would be unable to fulfil it, because he had served the bird up to her for lunch; so he burst into tears in front of her, unable to utter a word. Giovanna was inclined to attribute this to his grief at having to part with his prize falcon, rather than to anything else, and she was on the point of saying that she didn't really want it; however, she held back and waited for Federigo to take a hold on himself and answer her, which he did in these terms: 'Ever since it was God's pleasure that I should lose my heart to you, I've reckoned that Fortune has mistreated me in all too many ways and I've complained of her; but all her wrongs were trifling compared with the trick she has now played on me, and I'll never forgive her for it when I think that you, my lady, came to my humble home where you'd never deign to set foot when it was a sumptuous mansion; and you've wanted a little present from me, but she has seen to it that I cannot give it you. Why I can't I'll tell you in a word. When I heard that you were to do me the favour of dining with me, it seemed to me right and proper, considering your high station and your merits, to set before you the choicest fare at my disposal, and not what one might serve to just any guest. So

I thought of the falcon, which you have asked me for, and what a special bird it was, and it occurred to me that it would be a suitable morsel for you, and you've just eaten it, roasted and served on a platter—and I consider it could not have made a better end. But now I see that's not the way you wanted it, I'm so upset I can't give it to you, I don't think I'll ever forgive myself.'

This said, he brought the feathers and feet and beak and tossed them down before her as evidence. Giovanna reproached him for killing a falcon such as this to feed a woman, but thought only the more highly of him for his nobility of spirit, which had remained untouched by his poverty. However, with no further hope of obtaining the falcon and therefore apprehensive of her child's health, she thanked Federigo for his hospitality and goodwill and left glumly to return to her son. Now whether it was for disappointment that he could not have the falcon, or whether his sickness was anyway without remedy, not many days elapsed before he passed away, much to his mother's grief.

Bitter tears were her lot for quite a long time; but she had been left extremely well off and was still young, and her brothers kept pressing her to remarry. She would have preferred not to, but as she was given no peace, she called to mind Federigo and his goodness and his last sublime act, killing his falcon in her honour, and she told her brothers: 'If you don't mind, I'd sooner stay single. But if you insist on my remarrying, upon my word, I'll marry only one man, and that is Federigo degli Alberighi.'

Her brothers thought this was a great joke. 'What's all this, you silly thing?' they said. 'How can you want him? He doesn't have a bean!'

'You're absolutely right, of course', she replied. 'But I'd rather have a man who's in need of money than money lacking a man.'*

Seeing how her mind was settled, and having a high regard for Federigo, for all his indigence, her brothers did as she wished and bestowed her on him with all her fortune. And Federigo, finding himself married to such a lady, whom he had so passionately courted, and finding himself a rich man to boot, learnt to be more provident and finished his days with her in happiness.

V. 10. *A frustrated wife rails against adulterous women while concealing her lover from Pietro, her husband. Unfortunately she is found out—but this tale has a happy ending.*

The queen concluded her tale and everyone praised God for giving Federigo his due reward. Then Dioneo, who never awaited the summons, spoke up:

Don't ask me what the explanation is, whether it is some random blemish in our character or some evil nurture in humankind, or whether Nature herself is to blame: the fact is we are prone to rejoice at what is despicable rather than at the good that people do, and particularly when the matter in question is not our affair. Now the exercise on which I've embarked before and which I'm about to undertake once again has but one end in view, and that is to dispel your gloom and offer you, my love-struck young ladies, a little merriment and good cheer. And although there's something in the story I'm about to relate that is not entirely wholesome, it *can* afford you amusement so I'm going to tell it anyway. As you listen to it, you're to do what you do when you go out into the garden: you stretch out a dainty hand and pluck a rose, avoiding the thorns. That's what you must do, leaving the wretched man to his ill-starred, shabby propensity and enjoying a good laugh at his wife's amorous deceit; show compassion for others' misfortunes when the occasion requires it.

Not all that long ago in Perugia there was a rich man called Pietro di Vinciolo, who married a wife, possibly more with a view to throwing dust in people's eyes and attenuating the general consensus of his fellow-citizens in his regard than out of any tenderness for the lady. Fortune approved of his propensity in this one respect, that the wife he chose was a sturdy young woman, a redhead with the complexion to match, who could readily have accommodated two husbands instead of only one, whereas she was bestowed upon a man whose heart reached out far more willingly to his fellows than ever it did to her. In the course of time she came to recognize this; and aware as she was of her own attractions and her strong disposition towards love-making, she was at first extremely angry and occasionally called her husband some quite unrepeatable names, for he led her a dog's life. Seeing, however, that her recriminations failed to procure any change of heart in her husband but only left her the more frayed in temper, she said to herself: 'If this pervert's going to desert me in order to share a stable with his geldings, I'll find another man to mount me. Moreover, if I took him for my husband and brought him a sizeable dowry, it was because I knew he was a man and believed that he wanted what other men want, quite rightly. And if I hadn't taken him to be a man, I'd never have accepted him. He knew I was a woman: if he didn't care for our sex, why did he marry me? It's not to be endured. Had I wanted to turn my back on the world, I'd have become a nun, but I didn't want to. I want to be in the world and so I am—but if I were to look to this fellow for my pleasure, I'd wait for nothing and just grow old in the process. And when I'm an old crone, how I'll kick myself and regret my wasted girlhood, and to so little purpose, whereas he could be such a good tutor and model to show me how to get the best out of those lusty objects of *his* love. It would be a perfectly commendable thing for me to take such pleasure, whereas for him it's utterly disgraceful. All I would sin against is the law, whereas he sins against both Law and Nature.'

This was the thought that ran through her mind—indeed perhaps it kept recurring to her—and, to put it discreetly into effect, she struck up a friendship with an old woman. On the face of it this woman could have been Saint Verdiana* (the one who fed the serpents); she was never without the rosary in her fingers and she never missed a Pardon; all her talk was about the lives of the Holy Fathers and the stigmata of Saint Francis—she was considered a saint by almost everyone. At a moment she thought opportune the young wife disclosed her purpose in full, and the old woman said to her: 'My daughter', said she, 'God knows (and He knows all things) how very right you are. Though you do this for no other reason, you are bound to do it (and so is every girl bound to) if you're not to fritter away your girlhood. There's nothing more wretched for anyone in their right mind than to have let their time go to waste. Once we are old hags, what in Heaven's name are we fit for except to sit beside the fire and gaze at the embers? If any woman knows it and can bear witness, I am she: now that I'm old, I'm conscious of my lost opportunities, now that it's too late, and how it wrenches my heart to think of it! I won't say I let them *all* go by—you're not to think I was *that* stupid—but I didn't do half of what I might have done, and the thought of it is painful enough, God knows! I mean, just look at me now: there's not a man would stop to give me the time of day! That's not the way it is for men: they're born with a thousand different aptitudes apart from this one, and most of them are a long way from their first youth. We women, though, what are we born for if it isn't just to do this and produce babies?—That's what they love us for. And if nothing else made this clear to you, it would be clear enough from the fact that we women are perpetually ready for it while men are not; what's more, one woman would exhaust a dozen men while no amount of men could ever wear out one woman. This, I say, is what we're born for and I tell you again, the best thing you can do is give your man tit for tat—that way your heart won't be reproaching your body when it's gone to seed. All you get in this world is what you reach out for and grab, and that goes especially for us women, who have to put our time to far better use than men do, while it's still on our side. See for yourself: when we're old, our husbands won't spare us a glance, nor will any other man; they push us out into the kitchen to hobnob with the cat and count up the pots and pans. Worse still, they make us the butt of their jokes when they sing:

Lasses in heat
Get lean meat,
Leaving the bones
To the crones

and a whole lot else beside. Anyway, enough said; just let me add that you couldn't have taken a better person into your confidence than me for I really can help—there's not a man so refined but I'm quite up to the task of telling him what needs to be said, nor any man so rude and boorish but I can butter him up and bring him round to do as I want. So show me the man you're after, then leave the rest to me. There's only one thing else, my daughter: keep me in your mind, for I'm a poor woman, and I'd like you to have a share from now on in all my indulgenced prayers and in every rosary I say, with the prayer that God might turn them into lighted candles for the souls of your dear departed ones.' She said no more.

The young wife, therefore, reached an agreement with the old woman so that if she came upon a certain young man who was often passing that way (and she gave her a description of him), she would know what to do. Then she gave her a joint of salt meat and bade her goodbye. Not many days elapsed before the old woman secretly introduced the man she had described into her bedroom; and a little while later he was followed by another chosen according to the young lady's fancy, for she was not a lass to neglect her opportunities when she was in a position to profit from them, while keeping a wary eye open for her husband. One evening her husband was to dine out with a friend of his called Ercolano, and the wife told the old woman to procure for her a boy who was among the most handsome and attractive in Perugia. The old woman was quick to oblige. But scarcely had she sat down to supper with the lad than who should be at the front door shouting to be let in but her husband Pietro. Hearing this, the wife felt her last hour had come. Still, she wanted to hide the boy if she could, and as she couldn't think how to get him out of the house or find any other place of concealment, she made him hide underneath a hamper of chickens out on a little terrace that gave off the room in which they were dining; she draped over it the rough sacking of a straw mattress she had had emptied earlier that day. This done, she promptly had the door opened to her husband.

Once he had stepped inside she remarked: 'My, you must have bolted your supper!'

'We didn't so much as taste it.'

'How come?'

'I'll tell you', said Pietro. 'We'd just sat down to table, Ercolano, his wife, and I, when we heard a sneeze close by; we took no notice of it, even when it was followed by a second one. But then there came a third sneeze and a fourth, and a fifth, and a whole lot more, which we found rather puzzling. So Ercolano, who was already a little cross with his wife because she'd kept us waiting so long before opening the door to us, he burst out: "What's the meaning of this? Who's the fellow sneezing away like that?" He jumped up from the table and made for the stairs which were right beside us. Beneath the staircase was a cubby-hole, the kind used for storing odds and ends—you see the area at the foot of the stairs used this way in houses all over the place. This, it seemed to him, is where the sneezes were coming from, so he opened the small cupboard door and the moment he opened it, out came the most horrible stench of sulphur. They had both smelt it earlier, in fact, and grumbled about it, though the wife had merely remarked that she'd been using sulphur to bleach her veils, and had put away in that stair-cupboard the copper bowl into which she had poured the sulphur for the fumigation, and the smell was still coming through. Once Ercolano had opened the door and let the fumes disperse a little, he looked inside and saw the man who'd been sneezing—indeed the sulphur was still keeping him at it. A little more of this and the fumes would have so choked him that he'd not have produced another sneeze—nor drawn another breath. "Ah!" cried Ercolano as he spotted him, "now I see why we were kept waiting so long at the door when we arrived a moment ago, woman. But I'm going to pay you back if it's the last thing I do!" Seeing that she'd been caught red-handed, the wife offered no excuses but leapt up from the table and made off Goodness knows where. Ercolano never noticed that his wife had slipped away, as he kept telling the sneezer to come out, but nothing he said would make the man budge—he was too far gone. So Ercolano caught hold of one foot and dragged him out, and he was running to fetch a dagger to finish him off when I stood up and prevented him killing or maiming the lad, for I was worried on my own account in case the Podestà arrived. In fact I shouted so loud as I was protecting the boy that the neighbours came rushing in and hustled him out of the house and away God knows where—he had no fight left in him. That's why our dinner was interrupted and, far from having bolted it, I didn't so much as taste it, which is what I told you.'

Hearing this made his wife realize that there were other women as cute as she was, though occasionally some of them came to grief; she would willingly have sprung to the other woman's defence, but she felt she'd give herself more latitude to pursue her own peccadilloes if she censured those of other people, so she observed: 'Well, I never! What a saintly specimen *she* must be *I*'ll say! *There*'s loyalty in an honest woman! Why, I'd have made my confession to her she seemed to me such a saint! For a woman who's getting on in years, she's setting a fine example to the girls! Accursed be the hour of her coming into the world, and accursed be she for presuming to go on living, faithless and wicked woman that she must be! She's a disgrace to all her sex. Has she not cast her virtue to the winds along with the loyalty promised to her husband and her good name in the eyes of the world? Has she not shamelessly dragged her husband through the mud, a man of his attainments and a respectable citizen, who's taken such good care of her? She disgraced him for the sake of another man—and brought shame on herself as well as on him. As I hope to be saved, I think women of her sort should be given no quarter: they ought to be slaughtered, they ought to be burnt alive and reduced to ashes!'

Then, as she remembered the friend she had stowed beneath the hamper of chickens close by, she tried wheedling Pietro into going to bed, for it was bedtime. He was more interested in food than in sleep, however, and asked her if there was anything for supper. 'So it's supper now is it?' she cried. 'Of course we're *quite* accustomed to having supper when you're not here! We, indeed, are Ercolano's wife! Go on, run along to bed now, why don't you? That's the best thing you can do.'

Now it so happened that some of Pietro's labourers had that evening brought some things from the farm and left their donkeys in a little stable adjacent to the terrace. They had neglected to water the beasts and one of them, who was dying of thirst, slipped his halter and got out of his stall; he was sniffing about here and there in the hope of finding some water to drink, and happened to bump into the hamper underneath which the boy was hiding. The boy was of necessity on his hands and knees, and the fingers of one hand were protruding a little beyond the hamper; so it was just his luck, that's to say his misfortune, that this donkey trod on them and he let out a yell of pain. Pietro was surprised to hear it and noticed that it came from about the house. So he left the room and ran towards the hamper, for he could still hear the boy yelling, as the donkey was still standing on his fingers and bearing down on them hard. 'Who's there?' Pietro asked, and lifted up the hamper to see the lad, who was quaking not only from the pain in his fingers where the donkey had stepped on them, but also for fear of what damage Pietro might inflict on him. Pietro in fact recognized him, for he had long been pursuing him on account of his sexual proclivity; but when he asked the lad what he was doing here, he had nothing to say beyond entreating him for the love of God not to hurt him.

'Get up', said Pietro. 'Don't worry: I'm not going to hurt you, but tell me what brings you here.'

The boy made a clean breast of it, whereupon Pietro took him by the hand and led him into the bedroom where his wife was awaiting him in fear and trembling. Pietro, however, was as overjoyed to have caught him as his wife was heartsick. He sat down opposite her and said: 'A moment ago you were decrying Ercolano's wife and saying she ought to be burnt at the stake, that she was a disgrace to her sex. How is it you never said the same about yourself? If you weren't ready to say the same about yourself, how could you bring yourself to say such things about her, aware as you were that you'd done precisely as she had? There's only one thing that could have prompted you and that is that you women are all the same, and you each try to shelter behind the other's sins. Would to God fire came down from heaven to burn the lot of you, loathsome tribe that you are!'

Seeing that her husband's first response went no further than to give her the edge of his tongue, and realizing well enough that he was cock-a-hoop now that he was holding hands with such a pretty boy, she took heart and said: 'Of course you'd like fire to come down from heaven and consume us all: you have as much appetite for us women as a dog has for a thrashing. But, Heaven knows, you'll not have it your way. I'd be glad enough to get to the bottom of what it is you're complaining about. The fact is, I shouldn't be doing too badly if you were ready to put me on the same footing as Ercolano's wife: *there*'s a pious old humbug for you, and she gets what she wants out of him—he's as fond of her as a man should be of his wife, which is not *my* situation. All right, so you do keep me in clothes and shoes, but you know how well you provide for me in another respect, or how long it is since you last slept with me. I'd sooner go barefoot and in rags but have you look after me well in bed, than own all these possessions and suffer the treatment you give me. Let's be clear about this, Pietro: I'm a woman like the rest of them, and I want the things they want. So if I go and get what you're not giving me, you've no call to criticize me. At least I don't disgrace you by taking stable-boys or tramps to bed.'

Pietro could see that she was set to keep at it all night but, as he did not give a fig for her, he said: 'All right, woman, that's enough. Let's leave it at that. Now, if you'll be so kind, you'll see to producing a little supper for us—I expect this young man will not yet have eaten, any more than I have.'

'Of course he's not yet eaten: we were just sitting down to supper when you turned up, worse luck!'

'Very well, see that we get fed, then I'll sort out this business so you'll have nothing to complain of.'

Seeing that her husband was not upset, she stood up and quickly had the table laid again and the supper brought in that she'd earlier prepared. Then she enjoyed her meal in the company of her reprobate husband and the young lad. How Pietro 'sorted out this business' after supper so that all three were left satisfied I can no longer recall—what I do know is that, in the morning, as the lad was escorted back to the piazza, he was still not entirely sure whether last night he'd served more in the role of wife or husband. So take it from me, my dear ladies, offer tit for tat, and if you can't at that moment, bear it in mind for the next occasion. In this way you should give as good as you get.

Amused though they were by Dioneo's tale, when it was ended the ladies' laughter was tempered by their sense of delicacy. Realizing that her reign was now at an end, the queen stood up, removed her laurel crown, and jovially placed it on Elissa's head, saying: 'Now, madam, you must rule.'

On accepting the honour, Elissa followed precedent by first settling the arrangements with the major-domo that were to be in force during her reign; then the company was pleased to hear her say: 'We have heard many instances of quick-witted people resorting to a happy quip or nice repartee to slap down another person or avert some impending disaster. Now there's a jolly topic and a useful one, furthermore, so what I'd like us to talk about tomorrow, God willing, is this: about people who, on being teased, give as good as they get, or who avoid danger, embarrassment, or loss by dint of a prompt rejoinder.'

This proposal won general approval, so the queen stood up and dismissed the company until suppertime. Seeing the queen on her feet, the excellent company stood up too and, as previously, all went their various ways as the fancy took them. When the crickets had fallen silent the queen assembled her friends for supper, which was a festive occasion and, once it was finished, they devoted themselves to music and singing. At the queen's command, Emilia led the dance while Dioneo was required to sing a song.* Promptly he began with 'Glad tidings I bring you, Dame Aldruda, so . . . tail up!' This set all the ladies shrieking with laughter, not least the queen, who told him to drop that one and try another.

'Well', said Dioneo, 'if I had a tambourine I'd sing: "Lift up your skirts, little lady", or "Here's grass beneath the olive-tree", unless you'd rather I sang "The waves of the sea are making me sick". But I have no tambourine, so you'll have to tell me what to sing. How about "Hey for a turn round the maypole"?'

'No. Try again.'

'Very well', said Dioneo. 'I'll give you "Come, let's fill it up, my Simona".'

'Oh, you're impossible!' cried the queen in her merriment. 'Sing us a nice one if you please—that one won't do.'

'Come, don't take on so. Just tell me which one you'd like. I know thousands of songs. How about "I have this little shell, and ring it like a bell"; or "Gently does it, husband o' mine", or "For a hundred pennies I bought myself a cock"?'

The ladies were all laughing, except for the queen, who was running out of patience. 'Now that's enough, Dioneo', she said. 'Sing us a decent song, or else just watch me lose my temper.'

So Dioneo stopped teasing and launched straight away into this song:

See me ensnared, Love, by her fond bright eyes.
In her grace and in yours my freedom lies.
The splendour, nay, the passion of her glance
Transfixed mine eyes and did my soul entrance.
Her beauty taught me, Love, to hold you dear,
So must I to my love this tribute bear:
Yours is the virtue man should truly prize,
Hers the occasion for my heartfelt sighs.

So find me, Love, new bondsman at your feet.
I come, poor suppliant, to your mercy seat.
Doubt grips my mind and holds my heart perplexed:
In truth my fealty's to her love annexed,
But would that I were able to surmise
That she my humble troth doth recognize.

Go then, sweet Love, go fire up her heart
And bring my message to her and impart
My deep devotion and the bitter pain
Of doubting if her love I'll ever gain.
Your face, dear Love, she readily descries:
Pray lend it me ere Fate this chance denies.

Dioneo fell silent, from which it was plain that his song was ended. The queen then called upon others to sing, not that she stinted her praise for Dioneo's. When the night was somewhat advanced, however, and the queen felt that its freshness had mitigated the daytime heat, she invited the company to retire to bed until the following day.

*Here ends the fifth day of the* Decameron *and the sixth day begins; under the reign of Elissa, the stories are about people who, on being teased, give as good as they get, or who avoid danger, embarrassment, or loss by dint of a prompt rejoinder.*

The moon had completed half her course and was losing her sheen as daylight once more brightened the sky, when the queen rose up and had everybody awoken. Then they left the handsome villa to saunter across the dewy ground, chatting of one thing and another; they discussed the relative merits of the different tales they had heard, and laughed as they recollected incidents in them. Eventually, as the sun gained height and strength, they all felt it was time to return to the house, so they retraced their steps. Now at the queen's bidding they sat down to eat, before the day became too hot; the tables were ready laid and all embellished with sweet-scented verdure and pretty flowers. After their festive meal and before they did anything else they sang a few nice happy songs, then some of them left to have a siesta while others settled down to play chess or backgammon. Dioneo and Lauretta sang duets all about Troilus and Cressida.* When it was time for them to reassemble, the queen had everybody summoned and they took their seats round the fountain as usual. But as the queen was about to command the first story, something happened which had never happened previously: the queen and the rest of them all heard the maids and valets kicking up a dreadful rumpus in the kitchen. The queen sent for the major-domo and asked him who was shouting and what it was all about. The major-domo replied that Licisca and Tindaro were quarrelling but he had no idea why this was, for he had only just come in to silence them when he had been sent for by the queen. So she told him to send Licisca and Tindaro to her at once, and when they arrived, she asked them the reason for their quarrel.

Tindaro was on the point of answering when Licisca, who was no longer a spring chicken and anyway did not number meekness among her virtues, rounded upon him with a scowl, for her blood was up, and said: 'Listen, you moron—don't you dare put your oar in before *I* have spoken! Leave the talking to *me*. This fellow, ma'am', she pursued, turning to the queen, 'thinks he has something to teach me about Sycophant's wife. He's been trying to tell me—as if I don't know the woman inside out—he's been trying to tell me that the first night he slept with her, he had to use his stick to batter down her door and when he pulled out there was blood all over the place. Well it's not true, says I, he stole in like a lamb and he was made very welcome. Look at the idiot!—who but him'd believe that girls are such dumb bunnies they waste their time saying "Yes sir, no sir" to their fathers and brothers who nine times out of ten don't get around to marrying them off till it's a good four years too late. Listen to me, young man: those girls would be in a fine state if they hung about that long! I swear by Christ—and *I* should know what I'm talking about—there's not a girl in my neighbourhood who's gone to the altar a virgin. As for your married women, *they* get up to a trick or two behind their husbands' backs, don't I know it! And here's this oaf thinks he's got something to teach me about my sex, as if I was born yesterday!'

While Licisca was talking the women were all laughing fit to crack their jaws, and though the queen tried to silence her a good half-dozen times, it was useless—there was no stopping her till she had said her piece.

Once Licisca had made an end of it the queen turned to Dioneo with a grin: 'This', she said, 'falls to your competence: when we've told our stories, you're to give your verdict on this matter.'

'My lady', he promptly replied, 'we have our verdict and need no other: Licisca is right, the matter stands, I believe, as she reports it, and Tindaro is an ass.'

On hearing this, Licisca burst out laughing and turned to Tindaro: 'So there, I told you so! Now run along . . . Look at him, still wet behind the ears and thinks he knows more than I do! God willing, I for one shan't have lived for nothing . . .' But the queen now silenced her with a glare and told her to put a lid on it and pipe down if she didn't want a good hiding, then dismissed the pair of them. Had she not done so, Licisca would have been bending their ears for the rest of the day. Once they were out of the way, the queen told Philomena to start the story-telling, and so she cheerfully began:

### VI. 1. *Oretta, obliged to listen to an incompetent story-teller, tactfully persuades him to leave his tale unfinished.*

On clear evenings the sky is adorned with stars; in the spring-time the fields are adorned with flowers and the hills with trees newly in leaf. In just the same way, commendable social behaviour and good conversation have their ornament: the quip. Given its brevity, it suits women even better than men inasmuch as verbosity is less forgiveable in a woman than in a man. And, truth to tell—don't ask me why, it could be defective mental equipment or maybe heaven is proving singularly unkind to our era—today there are few women left, if any, who can come out with a quip on cue, or even catch on if they hear one. Be this said, ladies, to our shame. Still, Pampinea has already been into this question at some length, and I don't propose to take it any further; instead, to demonstrate the beauty of a well-timed quip, I should like to tell you how a gentleman was tactfully silenced by a lady.

As many of you ladies will know, whether from their own observation or from hearsay, there was a lady living in our city not so long ago whose manner and conversation were exquisite, indeed a lady of *her* quality cries out to be named: she was Oretta, wife of Geri Spina.* She was out in the country, as we are, and on her way somewhere in pursuit of pleasure with a group of ladies and gentlemen who had been her guests for lunch that day. The road that took them to their proposed destination may perhaps have been a little long for people travelling on foot, for one of the gentlemen in the company said to her: 'If you like, I'll give you a ride a good stretch of the way—I'll carry you along on a story, one of the jolliest in the world.'

'Oh please do', she said, 'there's nothing I'd like better.'

So our gentleman, whose tongue was all too ill-equipped for story-telling—though perhaps he wielded the sword at his belt no better—embarked upon his tale. It was indeed a very fine tale, but he kept going back over the same word half a dozen times; he repeated himself and would say, every now and then, 'No, that's not it!'; he got names mixed up and would come out with the wrong one—in fact he made a thorough mess of it. What's more, his delivery was hopeless, quite out of keeping with the characters or actions in question.

As Oretta listened to him, she broke out into a sweat, felt herself flagging, indeed, practically at death's door; eventually she could not stand another minute of it. Conscious, however, that the gentleman was up to his knees in the bog and was never going to find his way out, she sweetly remarked: 'I find this horse of yours has too hard a trot; do be good enough to set me down.'

The gentleman, luckily, was a good listener if a bad narrator so he caught her meaning at once, and took her jest in good part. He left his tale unfinished, which he had started only to develop so abysmally, and found another topic of conversation.

VI. 2. *A word to the wise is sufficient. Cisti the baker reminds a gentleman of his manners.*

Everybody, men and women alike, commended Oretta for the way she had spoken, after which the queen told Pampinea to follow on. So Pampinea began:

I cannot for the life of me tell who has made the worse mistake, whether it's Nature conferring a puny body on a noble spirit, or Fate bestowing a humble trade on a body endowed with a noble spirit—as was the case with our fellow-Florentine Cisti and many others who come to mind. Cisti, the very soul of refinement, was, Fate decreed, a baker. I'd be inclined to wish a plague on the pair of them equally, were it not that I knew how exceptionally shrewd Nature can be, and that Fate has a thousand eyes—never mind that idiots depict her as blind. It seems to me they're quite clever enough to do what humans often do: given life's uncertainties, they make provision for their needs by taking their most precious possessions and concealing them in the most unassuming parts of the house, where they're the least likely to be sought for, and it is from here that they fetch them out when the need arises, for they have been better safeguarded in these humble bolt-holes than they would have been in the master bedroom. Similarly these two ministers to the world often hide their most precious possessions in the shadow of reputedly humble trades to ensure that they shine the more brightly when they bring them out from here at the opportune moment. Cisti the baker furnished an instance of this, albeit a modest one, the time he gave Geri Spina something to think about; I should like to tell you about it, in a very short tale, because I was reminded of it by the story we've just heard of Oretta, who was Geri Spina's wife.

Now Geri Spina was held in the utmost consideration by Pope Boniface,* who had sent certain noblemen on an embassy to Florence to treat for him on certain important matters.* These ambassadors stayed at Geri's and in the course of his negotiations with them on the Pope's business, he and they for some reason or other acquired the habit, almost each morning, of passing on foot by Santa Maria Ughi, where Cisti's bakery was located—and where Cisti in person exercised his craft. Although Fate had given Cisti the humblest of callings, she had none the less so smiled upon him that it had made him into a very rich man, and while he had no wish to change it for another, he lived on the grandest scale, enjoying a quantity of good things including the best white wines and red wines to be found in or around Florence. Seeing Master Geri and the papal ambassadors pass his door every morning, it occurred to him that it would be no little kindness on his part if he offered them a glass of his good white wine, given the summer heat. Conscious as he was, though, of his own station compared with that of Master Geri, he felt it would not do to invite him just like that; so he hit upon a way to induce Master Geri to make the proposal himself. He always wore a spotless white doublet and a freshly laundered apron, which made him look more like a miller than a baker; and every morning, at the time he expected to see Master Geri pass by with the ambassadors, he would have a bright new tin bucket of fresh water set outside his door and a little new Bolognese jug of his good white wine and two glasses so crystal clear they had a silver sheen to them. He would sit down, and as they passed he would hawk and spit a couple of times, then start to sip his wine with such a smacking of lips he would have brought on a thirst among the dead.

Two mornings running Geri noticed this. On the third morning he said: 'How is it, Cisti? Good?'

Cisti promptly stood up and said: 'Indeed, Your Honour, but just how good it is I can't tell you, unless you try it yourself.'

Whether it was the weather, or because he was feeling inordinately fatigued, or maybe it was the sight of Cisti drinking with such relish, Geri developed a thirst there and then; he turned with a smile to the ambassadors and said: 'Gentlemen, we should do well to sample this good fellow's wine. It may be of such quality we shan't regret it.' And he ushered them towards Cisti, who had an elegant bench brought out from the bakery and invited them all to be seated. He told their servants, who were stepping forward to wash the glasses: 'Stand back, my friends, and leave this to me. I'm as good at pouring as I am at baking. Don't you expect to taste a drop!' With this, he washed four brand-new glasses, sent for a little jug of his good wine, and attentively poured for Master Geri and his companions, who found the wine the best they had tasted for ages. So Master Geri spoke highly of it, and so long as the ambassadors remained in Florence he brought them practically every morning for a drop of wine.

When the ambassadors had concluded their business and were about to leave, Geri gave them a magnificent banquet, to which he invited some of Florence's most distinguished citizens; Cisti also was invited but on no account would he accept. Geri told one of his servants, therefore, to go to Cisti for a flask of that wine of his, and pour each man a half-glass with the first course. The servant may have been cross that he had never had a chance to taste the wine, for he took along a large flask.

When Cisti saw this he said: 'It's not to me that Master Geri is sending you, my lad.'

The servant repeatedly assured him that it was, but could never obtain any different answer, so he returned to his master and told him. 'Go back to him', said Geri, 'and tell him that it is indeed to him; and if he still gives you the same answer, ask him who it is I'm sending you to.'

So back went the servant. 'Cisti', he said, 'Master Geri is certainly sending me to you.'

'Assuredly he is not.'

'Tell me then—who is he sending me to?'

'To the Arno', said Cisti.

The servant reported this to his master, who understood at once. 'Let me see the flask you've taken', he told his servant. On seeing it he added: 'Cisti's quite right', and he told him off roundly and had him go with a suitable flask.

On sight of it Cisti remarked: 'Now I know well enough that it's me he has sent you to', and he cheerfully filled his flask.

That same day he had a small cask filled with a similar wine and discreetly conveyed to Master Geri's house, whereupon he called on him in person and told him: 'I should not wish you to think, Your Honour, that I was bothered by this morning's big flask. But I thought maybe you had forgotten what I've been showing you these last days with those little jugs of mine, that this is not a wine for the servants' hall. I wanted to remind you of it this morning. Still, as I don't mean to stand guard over it any longer, I've had all of it sent to you: do with it as you please.'

Geri certainly treasured Cisti's present, and thanked him effusively, as he felt he should; ever afterwards he held him in great esteem and regarded him as a friend.

## VI. 3. *Nonna de' Pulci silences the scurrilous Bishop of Florence with a quip.*

When Pampinea finished her tale, everyone applauded Cisti's answer and his generosity. As the queen desired Lauretta to speak next, she brightly began:

Pampinea and Philomena have both hit upon the truth about our deficiencies and the merit of witticisms, and there is no more to be said on that score; what I should like to add, while we're on the subject, is that a quip should of its nature nibble like a sheep, not bite like a dog—a remark with a dog's bite to it is not witty but offensive. Oretta's sally and Cisti's riposte most excellently achieved their effect. Bear in mind, however, that you might be excused if you utter a biting rejoinder after being bitten, but not otherwise. Take care, then, whom you bandy words with, and when and how. We once had a prelate who overlooked this rule and so he received tit for tat—as I shall tell you in this little story.

When Antonio d'Orso, a worthy and sagacious prelate, was Bishop of Florence, a Catalan gentleman arrived in the city as vicegerent for King Robert; his name was Dego della Ratta.* He was a good-looking man and a bit of a rake, and his eye fell on one Florentine beauty in particular, who happened to be the bishop's great-niece. Learning that the lady's husband, for all his high birth, was devoid of scruples and an impenitent skinflint, he agreed to give him fifty gold florins for a night in his wife's arms. So he spent his night with the lady, much against her will, and paid him off in the current small change: silver coinage that he had had gilded. The story got out and the miser became a laughing-stock besides losing financially. The bishop, wise man, pretended he hadn't heard.

Now on St John's Day the bishop and the Catalan, who were close friends, were riding side by side down the street along which the Palio* is run, and admiring the women, when the bishop spotted a young lady called Nonna de' Pulci, Alesso Rinucci's cousin—I expect you all know who I mean—she died, an old woman, in the present plague. In those days she was fresh as a daisy, with a ready wit and few inhibitions; she had recently married in Porta San Pietro. Anyway, the bishop pointed her out to his friend and when they were close enough to her, he clapped his hand on the Catalan's shoulder and cried, 'Nonna, how does this one strike you? D'you think you could manage him?'

It seemed to Nonna that these words somewhat impugned her good name or could raise doubts about it in the minds of the bystanders (there was a milling crowd); not intending to take it lying down but to give as good as she got, she promptly replied: 'The question is, could he manage me—dud coinage wouldn't do.'

Vicegerent and Bishop felt themselves equally punctured by this rejoinder, the former for his dishonest dealing over the bishop's great-niece, the latter as accessory after the fact; so they rode off, silent and shamefaced, and did not look at each other, nor address another word to her for the rest of the day. And so the young woman who was made their mark did not scruple to retaliate with a shaft of her own.

## VI. 4. *Chichibio, a cook, gives his true love a roast leg of crane, but averts the wrath of his master, Currado Gianfigliazzi, with an inspired excuse.*

When Lauretta was finished and everyone had spoken highly of Nonna, the queen told Neiphile to go next.

A ready wit (she said) will often put words into a person's mouth which prove to be fair, pertinent, and lightning-quick as the occasion requires. Sheer luck, too, however, will sometimes come to the aid of the timid and prompt them to speech that would never have crossed their mind in their quieter moments. This is what my tale is going to demonstrate.

As all you ladies are bound to have heard, and noticed for yourselves, Currado Gianfigliazzi has always been an excellent fellow-citizen of ours, a generous, open-handed man, a paragon of chivalry, and a man who has taken a constant delight in his hawks and hounds—his more important activities need not concern us for the present. One day near Peretola his falcon killed a crane. As he found it was a plump young bird, he sent it to his cook, a competent fellow from Venice called Chichibio, with instructions to roast it and serve it up nicely for dinner. Chichibio had all the appearances of a flutter-head, and that is precisely what he was; anyway, he prepared the bird, spitted it, and carefully set it a-roasting. When it was practically cooked and giving off the most fragrant aroma, who should come into the kitchen but Brunetta. Now Brunetta lived up the street, and she was a young woman on whom Chichibio doted passionately. When she saw the crane and smelt the fragrance she wheedled Chichibio to give her one of its thighs.

'Not from me you won't have it, not from me!' sang he teasingly.

'Just you mark my word', said Brunetta a wee bit crossly; 'if you won't give it me, you've had the last favour you'll ever get out of *me*!' Well, they argued back and forth and in the end, to avoid upsetting his beloved, Chichibio cut off a thigh and handed it to her.

So the crane, lacking one thigh, was set before Currado and some guests of his; Currado was quite perplexed at this and sent for Chichibio, to ask him what had become of the bird's other thigh. 'But sir, cranes only have one leg and one thigh', promptly retorted the two-faced Venetian.

'What the devil do you mean, one leg and one thigh?' Currado burst out. 'Have I never seen a crane before?'

'It's like I say, sir. If you want, I'll show you with some live ones.'

For the sake of his guests, Currado forbore to pursue the argument but said: 'As you say you can show me with live ones, though it's something I've never seen before nor even heard of, I don't mind your showing me tomorrow and that will be that. But I swear by all that's holy, if it's not as you say I'll teach you such a lesson—if you live to remember me, it will not be a happy memory.'

No more was said on the subject this evening, but at daybreak the following day Currado, who had not slept off his anger, was still in a thorough temper as he got up and ordered the horses brought round. He had Chichibio ride a hack and led him off towards a river on whose banks cranes were always to be seen at sunrise. 'We'll soon see who was telling a fib last night, you or me', he remarked.

Seeing that Currado's anger had not abated one jot and that he was going to have to make good his lie, Chichibio rode beside him in utter terror, quite at a loss to think how he could do it; he would gladly have made off had this been possible but, as it was not, he looked ahead and behind him and to either side but the only sight that met his eyes seemed to be cranes standing on two legs.

But when they were almost at the river the first cranes he saw on the bank were some dozen birds, all standing on one leg, as they do while they're sleeping. So he hastened to point them out to Currado, saying: 'There you are, sir, you can see I was telling the truth last night when I said that cranes have only one thigh and one leg—just look at those standing over there!'

Currado looked at them and said: 'Wait, I'll show you that they have two.' And, moving a little closer to them, he shouted 'Ho-ho!' At this, the cranes all put down their second foot, ran a few paces, and flew off. Thereupon Currado turned to Chichibio: 'Well, what d'you think, you rascal? Have they two legs or haven't they?'

Not knowing himself where he got the inspiration from, Chichibio blurted out in terror: 'They have, sir. But you never shouted "Ho-ho!" at the one last night. Had you done so, it would have put out its second thigh and leg as these have done.'

Currado was so delighted with this rejoinder that his anger all melted into laughter and good humour. 'You're quite right, Chichibio', he said. 'That's what I ought to have done.'

In this way Chichibio, by his prompt and witty repartee, averted disaster and recovered his master's good graces.

VI. 5. *Forese da Rabatta, the eminent lawyer, and Giotto, the great painter, are caught in a rain-shower; the occasion prompts the one to a sally, the other to a tart riposte.*

Neiphile finished and the ladies were much amused by Chichibio's rejoinder. Then, at the queen's behest, Pamphilo spoke up:

It often happens that Fortune conceals a most abundant spiritual treasure within the breast of one exercising the most trivial calling, as Pampinea has just shown us; similarly, Nature will often lodge the most remarkable intellects in men of the most repulsive appearance. This was strikingly evident in two Florentines about whom I'll tell you a little tale. One of them, Forese da Rabatta, was a misshapen little runt of a man with a moon-face and a squashed nose, compared with whom even the least favoured of the Baronci* would have looked an angel; but he was such an expert in jurisprudence that, in the eyes of many people who counted, he was a veritable encyclopaedia of civil law. The other, whose name was Giotto,* was a genius so sublime that there was nothing produced by Nature, mother and mover of all things in the course of the seasons, that he could not depict to the life, whether his implement was a stylus, a pen, or a paintbrush: his depiction looked not like a copy but like the very thing, so that more often than not the viewer's eye was deceived, convinced that it was looking at the real object and not at his depiction of it. He it was who restored to the light an art which had lain buried for many a century under the distortions of painters more concerned to dazzle the frivolous than to satisfy the *cognoscenti*; he may, therefore, deservedly be called one of the glories of Florence, and all the more so inasmuch as he was a master who earned his reputation but was quite without pretensions and never let himself be lionized. The title of Master, which he rejected, acquired in him all the greater splendour, the more it was coveted by artists of inferior talent or indeed by his pupils. Still, supreme artist though he was, this did not make him one jot more shapely or handsome than Forese. Which brings me to our story.

Forese and Giotto both owned land in the Mugello.* One summer's day when the courts were in recess Forese was returning home from a visit to his estate, mounted on a sorry hack he'd taken on hire, when he ran into Giotto, who was also on his way back to Florence after visiting his own. The painter was no better mounted or turned out than the lawyer. Being old men, they set an ambling pace and fell into step with each other. Now they happened to be caught in a shower—in summer they're frequent enough as we know—and they took shelter from it as quickly as they could in the house of a workman with whom they were both on friendly terms. But after a while, as the rain showed no sign of letting up and they wanted to be back in town before nightfall, they borrowed off the labourer a pair of hideous cloaks that had seen better days and a pair of hats falling to pieces with age—that was the best they could do for themselves—and continued on their way.

After they'd been going along in silence for a while and saw how they were soaked through and thoroughly splattered from the mud thrown up by the horses' hooves, none of which does a great deal for a person's appearance, the weather brightened a little and they struck up a conversation. And as Forese rode along listening to Giotto, who certainly had a way with words, he began to scrutinize him—in profile, full-face, from every angle—and noticed what a scarecrow he looked and, quite oblivious of the sight he himself offered, he burst out laughing. 'Giotto', he said, 'if some stranger happened to come towards us and he'd never set eyes on you before, what makes you think he'd take you for the world's best painter, as you are?'

To which Giotto promptly replied: 'I think he'd believe it, Forese, if he could look at you and imagine that you knew your ABC.' Hearing this, Forese realized his gaffe and found himself paid off in his own coinage.

VI. 6. *Michele Scalza proves that the Baronci are the world's noblest and most ancient family, and wins himself a dinner.*

The ladies were still chuckling over Giotto's pretty repartee when the queen told Fiammetta to follow, which she did in these words:

Pamphilo's mention of the Baronci, whom he is likely to know better than you ladies do, reminds me of a story touching on the strength of their nobility; as it doesn't take us away from our present purpose, I'd like to tell it to you.

Not long ago there lived in our city a young man called Michele Scalza. He was the most engaging and entertaining fellow in the world, and he had any number of juicy stories up his sleeve; so he was very popular with the youth of

Florence, and no party was complete without him. One day he was with a group of friends up on Montughi when they all started arguing about which Florentine family was the most ancient and noble; some claimed it was the Uberti, others spoke for the Lamberti, and they every one had their piece to say.

Scalza listened to them and remarked with a grin: 'Oh, get along with you, you blockheads, you're talking through your hats! The noblest and most ancient house in Florence—come again—in the whole world is that of the Baronci: everyone who knows them as well as I do is agreed on that and so are the what d'you call 'em—schoolmen. And when I say the Baronci let's be clear, I mean the ones next door to you at Santa Maria Maggiore.'

The boys were expecting him to take a different line and they all ribbed him at this: 'Who d'you take us for?' they cried. 'We know the Baronci as well as you do!'

'I'm not teasing', he replied, 'it's the honest truth. Tell you what: I'm willing to bet you a supper, winner to bring six guests of his choice. What's more, I'll accept the verdict of any person you name.'

One of the party, called Neri Mannini, said he wouldn't mind winning this supper, and they agreed to appoint Piero di Fiorentino as judge—it's his house they were in. So they both went off to find him, with the others all tagging along to watch Scalza lose his bet and tell him 'yah sucks boo!', and they put Piero in the picture.

There were no flies on young Piero: he listened while Neri made his case, then turned to Scalza and asked: 'Well? How are you going to prove your assertion?'

'How? With an argument that will convince not only you but even this fellow who's contradicting me. As you know, the more ancient a family, the nobler it is—which is what we were all saying a moment ago. The Baronci are a more ancient family than any other, so they must be the noblest. So once I've proved that they're the most ancient, I'm bound to win the argument. What you have to know is that the Good Lord made the Baronci at the time He was learning to paint, while everyone else was made once He actually knew how. You'll see the truth of this if you consider the Baronci and the others.

All the others, as you'll have noticed, have well made, suitably proportioned features, but take a look at the Baronci faces: some have long thin ones, others have impossibly fat ones; some have long noses, others stubby ones; some have chins that jut out to meet their noses, some have jaws the size of donkeys'; you'll find some with one eye bigger than the other, some with one eye lower than the other—just like the faces children make when they're first learning to draw. Therefore, as I said, it's obvious that the Good Lord made them when He was learning to paint, which makes them more ancient than any, and consequently more noble.'

Piero the judge, and Neri, who had joined in staking the supper, and the others all remembered that this was so, and after listening to Scalza's amusing argument they merrily conceded that he was quite right and that he had won the supper, for the Baronci had to be the noblest and most ancient family not merely in Florence but in the whole wide world this side of the marshes and beyond.

So when Pamphilo wanted to give an idea of how ugly Forese's face was, he was surely entitled to say that it would have looked hideous even in a Baronci.

### VI. 7. *Caught with her lover by her husband, a lady called Philippa is summoned to judgement, and deflects its course with a clever defence.*

Fiammetta fell silent and everyone was still laughing over the novel argument deployed by Scalza in favour of the Baronci family's pre-eminence, when the queen required Philostrato to tell a story. Thus he began:

A ready tongue is a fine thing in any circumstance, but, in my opinion, it is never better than when it answers an immediate need. The story I intend to tell you concerns a gentlewoman who possessed this ability: the result was that not only did she rejoice her listeners but—as you shall hear—she eluded a humiliating death-sentence that lay in store for her.

They used to have a law in Prato, and a harsh, objectionable law it was, that required all women indiscriminately to be burnt at the stake if caught by their husbands in adultery, just as though they had been found consorting with another man for payment. Now it happened, while this statute was in force, that a beautiful and exceptionally love-struck lady called Philippa was discovered in her room one night by her husband, Rinaldo de' Pugliesi, in the arms of Lazzarino de' Guazzagliotri; he was a handsome young nobleman of Prato who doted upon her as she did upon him. Rinaldo was beside himself with rage when he saw this, and he was on the point of flinging himself at them and murdering the pair of them; indeed, all that restrained him was his fear of the consequences if he gave free rein to his anger. But if he restrained himself, it was only to fall back on the provisions of the law which could take his spouse's life, a course not legally open to himself. So, having obtained amply satisfactory witnesses to his wife's misdemeanour, without further reflection he brought charges against her the very next day and had a summons issued. Like most women who are deeply in love, Philippa possessed great courage and, ignoring the advice of many of her friends and relations, made up her mind to answer the summons, confess to the truth, and die without flinching rather than slink off like a coward and, by default, to have to live in exile, proving herself unworthy of a lover such as the one in whose arms she had spent the previous night. And so she appeared before the Podestà, accompanied by an impressive crowd of men and women who all pressed her to deny everything. Looking resolute, she calmly asked him why he had sent for her. The Podestà noticed that she was quite ravishing and carried herself impeccably. It seemed to him clear enough from her words that she was totally undaunted and, though he felt inclined towards leniency, he feared that she would confess to a crime which he should be required to punish with death if he was to be true to his office.

However, he could not avoid questioning her about the accusation made against her. 'As you see, madam', he said, 'here is your husband Rinaldo who has laid a complaint to the effect that he discovered you in adultery with another man. He therefore requires me to condemn you to death in accordance with the law. I cannot do so, however, unless you confess. Take care, therefore, how you answer, and tell me whether your husband's accusation is truthful.'

Losing none of her composure, the lady mellifluously replied: 'It is true, sir, that Rinaldo is my husband, and that last night he found me in the arms of Lazzarino; I have been many times in his arms because I love him with a fine, perfect love. This let me never deny. But, as I am sure you recognize, the laws ought to be even-handed in their application, and framed with the approval of those whom they affect. This has not been the case with this law: it threatens only us poor women—and we are far better able to satisfy several men than they are to satisfy several women. Furthermore, when this law was enacted not a single woman consented to it—indeed not a single woman was even consulted about it. Hence this law may fairly be characterized as iniquitous. Well, if you insist on putting this law into execution, prejudicial though it is to my physical and to your spiritual health, that is your privilege. Before you proceed to judgement, however, I would request a small favour of you: please ask my husband whether or not I conceded myself to him unstintingly every time he wished, and never once refused him.' Without waiting for the Podestà to put the question to him, Rinaldo promptly replied that assuredly his wife had ministered to his every pleasure for the asking. 'In that case', pursued his wife, 'I put it to you, Your Honour: if he has always helped himself to what he wanted from me for his pleasure, what was I to do—what *am* I to do—with that which is left over? Am I to throw it to the dogs?* Is it not far better to place it at the disposal of a gentleman who loves me beyond all telling, rather than to let it spoil or go to waste?'

Almost the whole of Prato had turned out to assist at the trial of a lady as eminent and well known as Philippa, and when they heard this delightful rebuttal they laughed heartily and at once shouted, almost with one voice, that the lady had spoken well and was absolutely right. So before they disbanded they altered the cruel law, with the Podestà's ready approval, so as to make it apply only to those women who betrayed their husbands for the sake of lucre. So Rinaldo left the seat of judgement balked of his insane proposal, while Philippa returned home in triumph, happy and free—a brand saved from the burning.

## VI. 8. *Uncle Fresco admonishes an over-fastidious niece, but her vanity proves impenetrable.*

Philostrato's story made the ladies feel a little embarrassed at first as they listened—this was evident by the honest blushes it called to their cheeks. But as they caught each other's eyes they could not keep a straight face, and they listened to it with broad grins. When he got to the end of it, the queen turned to Emilia and bade her go next. Emilia heaved a sigh, as if just roused from sleep, and began:

I'm afraid I've been miles away in a brown study, so to obey the queen I'll have to get by with a much briefer tale than I should have told had I had all my wits about me. I shall tell you about a pleasing quip a man came out with in order to teach his silly niece a lesson—though she may have been too stupid to grasp it.

A man called Fresco da Celatico had a niece nicknamed Cesca. A pretty face she had, and a shapely body, though she didn't look like one of those cherubs one used to see around. She had such a high opinion of herself, however, that she'd acquired the habit of disparaging whatever and whoever she laid eyes on, man and woman alike; she never stopped to consider what *she* was like, and she was so disagreeable, tiresome, and cross-grained, nobody could ever do anything right. And haughty? Her arrogance would have been excessive even if she'd been one of the French royals.* When she was out and about she wore such an expression of disgust she didn't know where to put her nose, as if a stench emanated from whoever she met or saw.

She had a whole lot of other off-putting and regrettable habits, but enough said. One day she came home and sat herself down beside Fresco, pouting and snorting. 'What's got into you, Cesca?' her uncle enquired. 'It's a holiday today—what brings you home so soon?'

'It's true I've come home early', she simpered. 'I don't believe there have ever been so many men and women as gross and unappetizing as there are in this town today. There isn't one I pass in the street who doesn't repel me like the plague. I don't believe there's another girl in the world who finds tiresome people so objectionable as I do, which is why I've come back so early—so as not to set eyes on them.'

To which Fresco, who was thoroughly fed up with his niece's susceptibilities, remarked: 'If you find tiresome people as objectionable as you say, just keep clear of mirrors if you want to stay cheerful.' However, being thick as two planks (though she fancied herself no less brainy than Solomon), she made as much sense out of her uncle's piece of wisdom as a sheep would have done. 'I'll look in the glass just like any other girl', said she, and continued as obtuse as ever. She still is.

### VI. 9. *Guido Cavalcanti discourages some importunate gentlemen with a nicely veiled insult.*

Realizing that Emilia had concluded her story, which left only herself to speak (aside from the one privileged to go last), the queen began her tale as follows:

Twice today you have deprived me of a story which I had been expecting to tell, but that still leaves me with one, which ends with a quip that for sheer acumen probably beats any of those hitherto recounted.

You will know that once upon a time our city boasted some very attractive and praiseworthy traditions that are no longer observed: they have all been displaced by the prevalent avarice that has accompanied the increase in wealth. One such tradition was for gentlemen living in one or another quarter of Florence to club together in sufficient numbers to spread the expense, and to take it in turns to give a banquet for their fellows. These were often an occasion to entertain visitors and fellow-Florentines alike. Once a year at least they would dress up in a uniform they had devised for themselves. And when the occasion deserved celebration, especially the major feast days and days when glad tidings of victory or whatever were brought to the city, they would ride through the streets and hold tournaments.

Among these clubs* was that of Betto Brunelleschi. Now he and his colleagues had tried every trick to recruit Guido Cavalcante de' Cavalcanti* into their membership, as well they might. Guido was, after all, one of the world's best philosophers and natural scientists—which left the club members fairly indifferent—but he was also a most elegant wit, and the most highly accomplished of gentlemen, added to which he was rich as Croesus and, if he chose to offer you entertainment, he did nothing by halves. Betto, however, had never succeeded in compassing his ambition. He and his colleagues blamed this on Guido's propensity to philosophical speculation which made him totally oblivious to those around him. Given his inclination towards Epicureanism, it was the common opinion of the unlettered that these speculations of his centred on an attempt to establish that God does not exist.

One day Guido set out from Orto San Michele and chanced to come to San Giovanni by way of Corso degli Adimari, a route he frequently took; the great marble tombs now in Santa Reparata used to be located around San Giovanni, along with many others, and he was standing there between these tombs and the porphyry columns flanking the church, and the church door itself, which was locked. Along came Betto and his friends, crossing Piazza Santa Reparata on horseback, and they spotted Guido among the tombs. 'Come on', they said, 'let's go and needle him!' They spurred their horses and mounted a playful charge upon him, catching him unawares. 'Guido', they cried, 'here are you, refusing to join our club. When you've found out that God does not exist, where will that have got you?'

Finding himself hemmed in, Guido promptly retorted: 'Seeing that here you are at home, my lords, you can say to me what you please.' With this he rested his hand on a tomb—they were not small—vaulted over it most athletically, and vanished from their sight.

They sat there gaping at each other. 'Why, the man must be wrong in the head', they remarked, 'talking a whole lot of nonsense like that.' After all, they pointed out, this particular place was no more home to them than it was to any other Florentine, or indeed to Guido himself. Betto, however, turned to them and said: 'If you've not worked out what he said, you're the numskulls, not he. He's just made a perfectly civil observation which is in fact deeply offensive. Look: these tombs are the houses of the dead—they are where the dead are laid, where they reside. Guido told us we are at home here, meaning that plain unlettered dunces like us are no better than dead men compared with men of learning like him, and so here we are where we belong—with the dead.'

Now they all grasped what Guido had meant and they were mortified; never again did they pester him, and thereafter they looked up to Betto as truly a deep one.

VI. 10. *Brother Cipolla promises his village congregation he will show them a feather of the angel Gabriel, but two pranksters steal it and substitute coals. How Brother Cipolla proves equal to the situation.*

Each one of the party had told a story, and Dioneo realized that it was his turn; so, without awaiting too formal a summons, he silenced those who were still applauding Guido's sharp rejoinder, and began:

For all that it's my privilege to speak on any topic I choose, today I'm not proposing to stray from the subject on which you charming ladies have all so pertinently discoursed. I shall follow in your footsteps and show you how discreetly one of Saint Antony's friars, thanks to a last-minute expedient, avoided a trap that two young men had set for him. To narrate the story in proper detail I'm going to have to run on a little, but this should not bother you if you look up at the sun—it's still but half-way across the sky.

As I expect you may have heard, Certaldo is a village in the Val d'Elsa, which is our own part of the world; while certainly small, it's had its share of men of rank and wealth. Now a friar who followed the rule of Saint Antony* used to come here every year to collect the alms given him by gullible folk, for this is where he found rich pickings. The friar's name was Brother Cipolla, and it may be that this Brother Onion was made welcome here as much for his name as for any piety of his, for his chosen resort produced onions that were the pride of Tuscany. He was a little fellow, was Brother Cipolla, with red hair and a smiling face, and as sociable as can be. He was totally unlettered, but such a good speaker and so quick-witted that anyone who did not know him might have taken him for a great orator, even the equal of Cicero himself or perhaps Quintilian.* There was scarcely a local inhabitant to whom he was not connected by ties of blood or friendship or mutual obligation.

Now on one occasion he paid the village his customary visit in the month of August, and one Sunday morning, while all the good folk, men and women, from the neighbouring estates had assembled for Mass in the parish church, he chose his moment to step forward and address them: 'Ladies and gentlemen, as you know, your custom is to make a yearly offering for the poor of Saint Antony from your harvest of wheat and oats; some of you give more, others less, according to the size of your fields and the measure of your piety, and this is to ensure that Saint Antony will protect your cattle and donkeys, your pigs and sheep. You also usually pay the little offering you make once a year—especially those of you who are enrolled in our Order. I have been sent to you by my superior, our Father Abbot, to receive your donations. So after nones, when you hear the bells ring, you're to be outside the church, with God's blessing, and I'll preach to you as I generally do, and you will kiss the cross. And as I know how devoted you all are to our holy father Saint Antony, I shall as a special favour show you a lovely and very holy relic, which I myself brought back from the Holy Land beyond the sea.

What it is is one of the angel Gabriel's feathers—it got dropped in the Virgin Mary's chamber in Nazareth when he went to her with the Annunciation.' He concluded with these words and returned to the Mass.

The large congregation present to hear these words of Brother Cipolla included two wily young men called Giovanni del Bragoniera and Biagio Pizzini. They were good friends and boon companions of the friar, but after enjoying a quiet chuckle over his relics, they took it into their heads to play a little joke on him with this feather of his. They discovered that Brother Cipolla was having lunch with a friend up at the castle and, as soon as they heard that he was at table, they went down into the street and made for the inn where the friar was staying. Their plan was for Biagio to engage the friar's servant in conversation while Giovanni was to search the friar's effects to find this feather, whatever it was, and remove it; then they would see what he would have to say to his congregation.

Brother Cipolla had a servant, Guccio by name, though some people called him The Whale and others Porky or else Mucky Pup. He was up to every trick and even Lippo Topo, that crafty dauber, could never have held a candle to him. Brother Cipolla often used to joke about him with his friends and say: 'This man of mine: there are nine things about him, and if only one of those things could be said about Solomon or Aristotle or Seneca,* that one thing would be enough to spoil every bit of good or of wisdom or of holiness they possessed. So just imagine what sort of man Guccio must be, with all nine of them, when he doesn't anyway have a scrap of virtue or wisdom or holiness about him!' If anyone asked him what these nine things were, he would answer them in doggerel:

'He's grubby, tells lies, and is seldom awake;
He's unruly and slack, with the tongue of a snake;
He's hare-brained, a bungler, and also a rake.

He has other little failings beside, but they're best passed over in silence. The funniest thing about him is that wherever he goes he needs must find himself a wife and rent a house. And what with that great sleek black beard of his, he thinks he's Adonis in person and imagines that every woman who sets eyes on him falls dizzily in love with him; given half a chance, he'd be chasing every last one of them—why, he'd outrun his own breeches. The fact is, though, he's a great help to me. No matter how much a person wants a word with me in private, he always manages to eavesdrop and if I'm ever asked a question, he's always so worried I won't have the answer that he answers for me, yes or no, whatever he thinks is right.'

When he had left the inn, Brother Cipolla had told his man to make sure nobody touched his things, least of all his saddle-bags, for these contained his holy objects. But Mucky Pup, who was as happy in the kitchens as a wasp is in a honey-pot, and especially if there was any sign of a kitchen-maid, had noticed one in the innkeeper's employment. She was a fat, dumpy little creature, utterly misshapen, with a pair of udders like a couple of overripe gourds, and a face like the back of a cart; she was sweaty, greasy, and grimy as well, but Mucky Pup swooped on her like a vulture on a carcase, leaving Brother Cipolla's door open and his things strewn all over the place. Though it was August, he sat down next to the stove and struck up a conversation with the girl, whose name was Nuta; he told her he was a gentleman by proxy, that his fortune was numbered in trillions plus what he owed other people (there were rather a lot of those), that there was nothing he didn't know how to do or say—why, he could even teach the Good Lord a thing or two! And, quite oblivious of his hood, which had enough grease deposited on it to fry fish for an entire monastery, and of his torn and patched doublet, and the spreading sweat-stains round his neck and beneath his arm-pits—a variegated and colourful patchwork of stains reminiscent of a Tartar or Indian quilt—and heedless, too, of his battered shoes and threadbare stockings, he addressed her as though he were the Grand Panjandrum himself. 'I mean to procure you some decent clothing', he told her, 'get you properly cleaned up, and take you away from this drudgery at another man's beck and call; penniless as you are, I shall hold before you the prospect of higher fortunes.' He said a good deal more beside, and he said it most affectionately; this initiative, however, like most of his initiatives, was quite lacking in substance and came to nothing.

So the two young men found Porky tied up with the kitchen-maid, which made them very happy because that took care of half of what they had to do. They entered Brother Cipolla's room with no one to prevent them, the door being open; and the first thing they laid their hands on to search was his saddle-bag with the feather in it. Opening the bag, they found a little casket wrapped up in a generous roll of silk, and inside that they discovered a parrot's tail-feather: this, they concluded, must be what he had undertaken to show the villagers. In those days he would have found it easy enough to hoodwink them, for the enervating luxuries of the Orient had not yet found their way into Tuscany except on a tiny scale—not like later on when they started flooding in, to the prejudice of all Italy. If such things were barely recognized elsewhere, in this part of the world they were virtually unknown to the inhabitants: here the rude integrity of their forbears still persisted and, far from having laid eyes on a parrot, the vast majority had never even heard of the creature. So the lads were very pleased to have found the feather; they took it and, in order not to leave the casket empty, they stuffed it with coals they'd noticed in a corner of the room. Then they shut the casket, put everything back the way thay had found it, and slipped away unobserved, to begin their happy anticipation of what Brother Cipolla would say when he found coals in place of the feather.

Those simple folk, men and women, who were in church to hear that they could see the angel Gabriel's feather after nones, went home when Mass was over. Then the word was spread from neighbour to neighbour and among the village gossips, and when everyone had had their lunch the men and women converged upon the village square, such a mob there was scarcely room for them all—they couldn't wait to see this feather. Brother Cipolla had enjoyed a good lunch followed by a little nap; he got up shortly after three o'clock and heard that a large crowd of peasants had assembled to see the feather, so he sent for Mucky Pup to come with his saddle-bags and bring up the handbells. So Mucky Pup, by dint of a stern effort, tore himself away from Nuta and the kitchen and trudged slowly up the hill with the items requested; he arrived quite out of breath, bloated as he was from all the water he had been drinking and, at Brother Cipolla's bidding, went to the church door to ring his bells loudly. Once the people were all assembled here, Brother Cipolla began his sermon, quite unaware that any of his things had been tampered with, and spoke at some length to lend credence to what he was about to show. When it was time to exhibit the angel Gabriel's feather, he first of all made a solemn recitation of the *Confiteor*, then had a pair of candles lit; he gently unwrapped the roll of silk, after first pulling up his hood, and drew out the casket; he spoke a few words in praise of and devotion to the angel Gabriel and his relic, then opened the casket. Seeing it stuffed with coals, he would not suspect Guccio the Whale of doing this to him, recognizing that the man would never have the wit for it; nor did he curse him for taking so little care to prevent someone else doing it; but he secretly cursed himself for entrusting to the fellow the custody of his affairs, knowing him, as he did, for a slack, unruly, hare-brained bungler. At all events he did not turn a hair but raised his eyes and hands heavenwards and cried out, to be heard by everyone: 'O Lord, praised be Your power forever!' Then he shut the casket, turned to the congregation and said:

'Be it known to you, ladies and gentlemen that, when I was still but a lad, I was sent by my superior to the lands of the rising sun, and I was expressly charged with a quest: to seek out the fiefs of Saint Porker's Hospice, and never mind that they were picked up for a song, they're still bringing money to others and not to us. Off I set, therefore, and I set off from Venetia and passed through Magnesia, and on I rode through Nemesia and past Freesia and came out at Lutetia, and after that—it was a thirsty journey—I landed on the Isle of Sardines. But why do I dwell on all these lands where I conducted my quest? I crossed the straits and came to a town in utter Rouen, so on I went as I had nothing Toulouse, though I had to go fast to escape from the Lyons. When I arrived in a town called Boloney I found plenty of our friars and other religious living there, all busy avoiding hardship for the love of God; they concerned themselves very little with other people's troubles, if they could see this attitude was more to their advantage, and in that whole part of the world the only money they would ever spend was counterfeit. On I went to Carpathia where the men and women walk up and down the mountains in clogs and make their pigs nice coats out of sausage skins. Not far beyond, I came across people who carried their bread in a barrel and their wine in a sack. On I went to the Basque Mountains, where all the water actually runs downhill. In a word, I travelled on and I travelled on until I'd gone all the way to the Cinnabar Coast (where cinnamon comes from); that's where I saw—it's true, I swear, by the habit I wear—I saw the peasants using hornbills for billhooks: you'd never believe it if you hadn't seen it. However, Maso del Saggio won't let me get away with a fib: I came upon him out there conducting a flourishing business, cracking walnuts and retailing the shells. But as I couldn't find what I was looking for, because there was nothing between there and there but water, I turned back and arrived in the Holy Land, where in summertime the loaves are half-baked and sell for twice nothing and straight from the oven they fetch four times nothing. Here I found His Most Reverend Worshipfulness, the Patriarch of Jerusalem, Blamoispas Sivouplay. Out of respect for the habit of Saint Antony it's been my habit to wear he insisted on showing me all the holy relics he had with him. There were so many, if I were to list them all for you the list would stretch from here to goodness knows where and back, but I'll tell you about some of them as I don't want to disappoint you.

'The first thing he showed me was the Holy Ghost's finger, as healthy and whole as ever it was; and the forelock of the seraph who appeared to Saint Francis; and one of the cherubim's fingernails; and a rib belonging to Hail-full-of-grapes; and Holy Mother Church's drawers; and a couple of rays from the star in the East which appeared to the Magi; and a vial containing Saint Michael's sweat when he fought with the devil; and the jawbone from Saint Lazarus's death's-head; and more beside. And as I shared with him a few choice pages from my *Sin of Sodom* which he'd been hankering after for ages (he kept Onan on about it), he gave me a share of his holy relics: a tooth from the Holy Cross, the sound of the bells of Solomon's temple in a wee bottle, and the angel Gabriel's feather (I've already mentioned), and a sandal thrown out by the first Discalced Carmelite—this I passed recently to a devout Florentine tertiary who does a brisk trade in such objects. He gave me, too, some of the coals on which the blessed martyr Saint Lawrence was roasted. All these objects I devoutly brought back with me, and I have them here today. Actually my superior never let me show them until he had satisfied himself that they were genuine; but now that he is sure, thanks to certain miracles performed with them and to letters he's received from the Patriarch, he has given me leave to show them. And as I wouldn't trust them to anyone else, I always carry them with me. Now in case the angel Gabriel's feather gets damaged, I do in fact keep it in a casket, and the coals on which Saint Lawrence was roasted I keep in another. But the two caskets look so alike, I often get them mixed up, and that's what's happened now: I thought I'd brought you the casket with the feather but what I've brought is the one with the coals. This, I believe, was not a mistake: indeed I am quite sure that it was the will of God, and that it was He Himself who put the casket of coals into my hands, for I remembered a short while ago that it's the feast of Saint Lawrence in two days' time. So as the Lord has wanted me to rekindle in your hearts the devotion you should have for this saint by showing you the coals on which he was roasted, what He has made me bring is not the feather, as I intended, but the blessed coals set a-sizzling by the juices of that most holy body. And so, my lucky children, draw up your hoods and approach devoutly to gaze upon them. But first, understand that whichever one of you is touched by these coals in the sign of the cross may rest assured that for the next twelve months he'll not be burnt by fire without feeling anything.'

After he had thus spoken, he intoned a Hymn to Saint Lawrence, opened the casket, and revealed the coals. The silly crowd gaped at them for a while in awe, then all surged forward to Brother Cipolla and pressed upon him bigger offerings than usual as they each begged him to touch them with the coals. So Brother Cipolla took out the coals and signed them on their white smocks and on their doublets and on the women's veils with the largest crosses that would fit; any coal used up in drawing those crosses, he told them, was made good once back in the casket, as he had found many a time. So, having drawn crosses on all the good folk of Certaldo, to his own not inconsiderable profit, he thus used his quick wits to turn the tables on those who, by taking the feather from him, had expected to make him look a fool. These had attended his sermon and listened to the neat subterfuge to which he had resorted, and at so little notice, and his speech had them laughing so hard they practically dislocated their jaws. When the crowd had dispersed they went up to him and told him amid gales of laughter what it was they had done. They returned his feather to him and this, the following year, he turned to as good an account as he had just turned the coals.

The entire party derived equal amusement from the story, which they found thoroughly entertaining; they laughed particularly over Brother Cipolla and his pilgrimage, and the relics, both those he had seen and those he had brought with him. Realizing, though, that the tale was now ended, and with it her reign, the queen stood up, removed her crown, and placed it on Dioneo's head with a smile. 'Here, Dioneo', she told him, 'it's high time you sampled the burden of exercising control and guidance over women. Be king, then, and so rule us that we'll be able to look back on your reign with approval.'

Dioneo took the crown and jovially replied: 'You'll have seen kings plenty of times who come a lot dearer than I do—I mean those ivory kings in the chess set. And mark my words, if you obeyed me the way a real king ought to be, I'd give you the sort of entertainment that no really successful party can be without. Ah well, enough said—I'll govern the way I know best.' He summoned the major-domo as usual and gave him precise orders for the duration of his reign, after which he said: 'In our story-telling we've covered the field of human activities and random chance fairly broadly, and I fear I'd have been hard put to think of a fresh topic, were it not for the recent intervention of our excellent Licisca, who's put me in mind of our theme for tomorrow. You heard her saying that there was not a girl in her neighbourhood who had gone to the altar a virgin; she added that she was well acquainted with the assortment of tricks married women played on their husbands behind their backs. Forgoing the first part, which is childish, I think it would be fun to talk about the second. So, as Licisca has given us the excuse, I want our topic for tomorrow to be the tricks women have played on their husbands, whether in pursuit of their amours or to protect themselves, and whether or not they've been found out.'

Now certain of the ladies felt that this topic was unseemly and asked him to choose another. But the king answered them: 'I'm as well acquainted as you are, ladies, with the order I have given, nor could your representations deter me from insisting upon it: bear in mind that at our present juncture we are taking every care to live irreproachable lives, men and women alike, which gives us licence to let ourselves go during our story sessions. Are you not aware that, the times being what they are, the magistrates have deserted their benches, the laws of God and man keep silence, and we are all accorded a generous licence to keep body and soul together? So if in your conversation you sail a little close to the wind, provided you have no intention to carry into practice any discreditable suggestion but air it simply to afford entertainment to yourselves and others, I cannot see what plausible reason anybody will have to criticize you for it later on. Furthermore, our company has trodden the most rigid path of virtue from the very first day, and I am not aware that we have compromised ourselves as a result of anything we have said—and God willing, we shan't. Besides, show me the man who fails to admit your probity. If it cannot be tainted by the fear of death itself, I cannot imagine it suffering prejudice on account of a little light-hearted talk. And let me tell you, if it ever came out that you avoided this kind of light chat, people might well suspect that your refusal to do so was tantamount to an admission of guilt. Besides which, I've been an obedient subject to you all, so what sort of dignity would you have conferred on me if you make me king and ordain me your lawgiver, then reject the topic I have appointed? This objection of yours would come more suitably from people with a bad conscience than from you ladies, so lay it aside and all of you give your minds to a good story to tell.' These arguments persuaded the ladies to do as he wished, so the king dismissed them all to pursue their own pleasures until supper-time.

As their story session had been so short, the sun was still high in the heavens. So, while Dioneo sat down to a game of backgammon with the other young men, Elissa drew the ladies aside and said: 'Ever since we arrived I've been wanting to show you a place close by that I don't think any of you will have visited; it's called Ladyglen, and today's the first occasion I've found to take you there, as the sun is still so high. If you'd like to come, I'm sure once you're there you'll be only too glad to have seen it.' The ladies pronounced themselves willing, so they sent for one of their maids and off they went without a word to the boys. They had gone barely more than a mile before they reached Ladyglen. They entered along a very narrow path beside which flowed the most limpid of brooks, and they saw that the place was as beautiful and delightful as one could imagine, not least during the dog-days. The valley-floor, as one of them later told me, was in the shape of a circle, for all the world as though described with a compass, even though it looked natural enough rather than man-made. Its circumference was a good half-mile and it was closed in by six knolls of modest elevation, each one crowned (they could see) with a small house built in the style of a pretty castle. The hillocks sloped down into the valley in the fashion of so many amphitheatres, forming terraces in arcs decreasing from top to bottom. As for the south-facing slopes, they were covered in vines, olive-trees, almond and cherry-trees, fig-trees, and all manner of other fruit-trees—there was not an inch of ground gone to waste. The slopes that looked towards the Great Bear were thickly wooded with oak and ash and other greenery, all growing as straight as could be. The valley-floor was accessible only by the path taken by the ladies, and was thickly planted with firs, cypresses, laurels, and pines which stood in such perfect order and harmony, it was as though a superlative artist had taken a hand in their disposition. Little or no sun penetrated these woods even at noontide; what rays did reach the ground would find a carpet of tenderest grass scattered with violets and other flowers. Another feature that afforded no little pleasure was a stream that cascaded down the living rock through a gully separating two of those hillocks; to hear the water falling was sheer delight, and from a distance it looked just like quicksilver forced out in a fine spray. On reaching the little valley-floor, the stream was channelled between narrow banks and flowed swiftly towards the middle of the valley where it collected in a little pool similar to those fish-ponds that townsfolk sometimes create in their gardens if they have the opportunity. This pool was nowhere more than chest-deep, and so limpid that its bottom, composed of the finest shingle, could be clearly seen—indeed someone with nothing better to do could have counted each little pebble. If you looked into the pool it was not only the bottom you would see but so many fishes darting hither and thither it was a pleasure, nay, a marvel, to behold. The pool had no banks but simply lapped the grass of the valley-floor, which deliciously retained its moisture therefrom. The excess water was drawn from the pool by a different stream which carried it out of the valley on its downward course.

So when the young women had made their way into this valley and taken in the whole scene and found it wholly to their liking, they looked at the limpid pool before them and decided, the day being exceedingly sultry, that they would enjoy a dip. They had no fear of being observed and, after ordering their maid to post herself on the path by which they had arrived and keep a look-out to warn them of anyone's approach, they all seven of them stripped off their clothes and entered the water, which offered as much concealment to their milk-white bodies as would a clear glass vase to a red rose. In the water they stirred up no sediment as they moved about in pursuit of the fish, who had little chance of hiding as the ladies made to catch them with their bare hands. They devoted a little time to this game and did catch a few; then they came out of the pool, dressed, and set off homewards at a leisurely pace, for they felt it must be time, and as they went they kept praising the little valley to the skies—they could not acclaim it enough.

It was still early when they reached the villa and found the young men at their game, just as they had left them. Pampinea laughed as she told them: 'Today we have in fact played you a turn!'

'What?' cried Dioneo. 'Are you getting up to tricks even before it's time for our words about them?'

'Yes, my lord', said Pampinea, who went on to give him an extended account of where they had come from and what the place was like and how far it was and what they had got up to there.

This description of the place and its attractions instilled in the king a desire to see it, so he promptly ordered supper and, when they all had dined with great relish, the three young men left the ladies and went off to this valley with their servants. None of them had ever laid eyes on it before and, when they had looked it over in detail, they spoke of it as one of the most beautiful places on earth. They had a bathe, got dressed, and returned to the house, for it was really getting late, and found the ladies treading a measure to the accompaniment of a song sung by Fiammetta. When this was over, they joined them in discussing Ladyglen in the warmest terms. Then the king sent for the major-domo and told him that that was where everything was to be laid out the next morning, including a few beds in case anybody felt inclined to lie down or take a midday siesta there. This done, he ordered lights, wine, and dainties to feast on, then set everybody to dancing. At the king's word, Pamphilo launched into a dance while Dioneo turned to Elissa and addressed her with a smile: 'Today, my beauty, you did me the honour of crowning me king; I mean this evening to give you the honour of singing: sing any song you please.'

'Willingly', said Elissa, and thus began in dulcet tones:

If from your talons, Love, if I can
  Be set free,
I may not conceive that ever a man
  Will catch me.

A tender maid, I entered your realm,
I unbuckled my sword and I laid down my helm
  And looked for peace and rest.
Ah why did I trust in my innocence?
You bore me down with your power immense,
  And dragged my heart from my breast.

A captive at once, bound fast in chains,
As I wept and lamented my heart's bitter pains,
  You gave me to the keeping
Of one who was born for my despair,
Whose spirit is cruel though his face is fair—
  See, I waste away with weeping!

My prayers and sighs are borne away
On the wind, and he hears not a word that I say,
  He is deaf and will not hear.
To live is a burden yet fear I the grave,
Ah pity me, Lord, and confer what I crave:
  Commit him, Love, to my care.

You will not, Love? Then grant me this grace:
The promise of Hope, I beg you, efface,
  Release me from her spell.
Delivered, you'll see, from the bondage of sighs,
Fresh bloom to my cheeks and new spark to my eyes—
  This truly can I foretell.

Elissa ended her song with a heart-wrenching sigh, and everyone puzzled over her words though nobody could make out the identity of the person who had occasioned them. The king, however, was in high good humour and called for Tindaro to come and play them his bagpipes, to which he had them all dancing and dancing until well into the night, when he sent them off to bed.

*Here ends the sixth day of the* Decameron *and the seventh begins; under the reign of Dioneo the stories show the tricks women have played on their husbands, whether in pursuit of their amours or to protect themselves, and whether or not they have been found out.*

There was not a star left in the eastern sky, other than the one known to us as Lucifer,* which remained bright in the gathering dawn, when the major-domo bestirred himself and left for Ladyglen with a substantial train of provisions; here he prepared everything in accordance with his master's instructions. Barely had he left than the king too was up, his sleep disturbed by the racket of the porters and pack-animals. Once up, he had the ladies and the young men called. The sun was only peeping over the horizon when they in turn set out; never before, it seemed to them, had the nightingales and other birds sung as merrily as they did this morning; their song accompanied them to Ladyglen, where they were greeted by a great many more songsters, as if their arrival occasioned an outburst of joy. As they took a turn around the valley and admired it once more in detail, it struck them as even more beautiful than on the previous day inasmuch as this particular time of day showed it at its best. They made their breakfast off assorted delicacies and good wine, after which they began to sing, for they would not be outdone by the birds, and the valley sang along with them, repeating each song as they sang it. The birds for their part, unwilling to admit defeat, chimed in with sweet new melodies of their own. When it was time for lunch the tables were laid beneath the flourishing laurels and other splendid trees, beside the pool, and they took their places at the king's bidding, and as they ate they could observe the fish swimming about in great shoals; they watched them and passed occasional comments about them. The meal finished and the tables cleared away, they burst into even lustier singing than before, then played their instruments and danced round-dances. Beds had been made ready here and there in the valley, each one complete with its cretonne coverlet thanks to the good offices of the major-domo; so anyone who felt like taking a nap received the king's leave to do so, while the rest, who preferred to stay up, were free to entertain themselves in their usual fashion. Finally it was time for everyone to be up and to assemble for their story-telling; not far from the spot where they had eaten lunch the king had rugs laid on the grass close to the pond; here they sat down and the king ordered Emilia to make a start. She was happy to do so and said with a smile:

VII. 1. *Tessa's lover knocks at her door while she is in bed with her husband, Gianni. She dreams up a way of seeing him off, aided by her unsuspecting spouse.*

Had it been your pleasure, my lord, I should have been only too happy for someone else to be given first call on a topic as enticing as the one we have for our stories today. But as it is your wish that I should inspire all these other ladies, I'll gladly make a start. And I'll do my best, dearest ladies, to tell you something that will stand you in good stead later on, because, if you're at all like me, we're all easily scared, and never more so than by a phantom: I haven't a notion what a phantom is, God knows, and I've never met a woman who did have, though we're all equally terrified of them. Now should one come to visit you, just pay close attention to my story and you'll be able to learn a good, holy prayer which is just what it takes to drive the thing away.

In the San Pancrazio district of Florence there once lived a man called Gianni Lotteringhi. He dealt in wool, and prospered in his calling, though in other respects he showed scantier abilities; artless fellow that he was, he frequently found himself in charge of the lay-singers of Santa Maria Novella, his job being to keep them in order—he often had similar little duties to perform, which made him feel he was really Somebody. (In fact these assignments came his way because he was well-to-do and often treated the friars to a good square meal.) The friars often got their clothing out of him—a scapular maybe, or a hood, or a pair of socks—so they would teach him a few handy prayers, like the Our Father in Tuscan, or the Song of Saint Alessio, Saint Bernard's Lament or Dame Matilda's Hymn,* and other such rigmaroles, all of which he treasured and stored away most scrupulously for the salvation of his soul.

Now Gianni had a pretty wife called Tessa (daughter of Mannuccio from San Frediano), a delightful woman and sharp-witted too. Well acquainted as she was with her husband's simple-mindedness, she took a handsome, fresh-faced lad called Federigo for a lover—and love her he did—and worked out a scheme with her maid whereby the lad would come to call on her at an enchanting villa her husband owned in Camerata, on the way to Fiesole, where she spent her summers. Gianni would sometimes join her there for supper and the night, returning to his shop (and occasionally to his singers) in the morning. As for Federigo, he could ask for nothing better, and chose his time to turn up one evening when he had received her summons, Gianni being absent. He dined and slept with the lady, all without haste and with great pleasure and, as she lay in his arms that night, she taught him a good six of her husband's tunes. However, Tessa had no intention of making this first visit his last, any more than he had, and to avoid her maid having to go each time to fetch him, this is what they arranged: he had a property of his own a little further up the road, and each time he passed on his way to or from it, he was to take a look at a vine that grew beside her house, and on one of the vine-poles he would see an ass's skull; when he saw its snout pointing towards Florence, he was to come to her without fail, that very night, with nothing to fear; if he didn't find the door open, he was to knock softly three times and she would open for him; but if ever he saw the snout pointing towards Fiesole, he was not to come, for Gianni would be there. Following this system, they kept many a tryst.

But on one occasion when Federigo was due to sup with Tessa and she had seen to cooking a couple of fat capons, Gianni turned up very late, though he was not expected. His wife was not a little put out; the pair of them dined off a little salted stew she had had cooked on the side, while she told her maid to take the two boiled capons, plenty of new-laid eggs, and a flask of good wine, wrap them in a white tablecloth, and carry them out into the orchard—which was accessible without passing through the house. She had supped here with Federigo on a number of occasions, and she told the maid to put everything down by a peach-tree that grew beside a little meadow. Tessa was so upset, though, that she quite forgot to tell the maid to wait up for Federigo, and give him the message that Gianni was here and he was to help himself to the things left in the orchard. So after she and Gianni retired to bed, and the maid likewise, it was not long before Federigo turned up and gave one soft knock on the front door, which did not go undetected by Gianni, their bedroom being right beside it. Tessa heard it too, but pretended to be asleep in order to avoid arousing Gianni's suspicions.

After a moment, Federigo knocked a second time. Gianni was startled and gave his wife a prod: 'Tessa', he said, 'do you hear what I hear? I think someone's knocking at our front door.'

Tessa, who had heard it a good deal more clearly than he had, pretended to wake up and murmured: 'What . . . what . . . what?'

'I said I think someone's knocking at our front door.'

'A knock? My God, Gianni, don't you know what that is? It's the phantom cat! It's given me such a scare these last nights, the moment I hear it I bury my head under the blanket and daren't poke it out again till it's broad daylight.'

Then Gianni told his wife: 'If that's what it is, don't let it trouble you: when we went to bed I recited the *Te lucis** and the *Intemerata* and a whole lot of other good prayers and, what's more, I made the sign of the cross at all four corners of the bed in the name of the Father and of the Son and of the Holy Ghost, so there's nothing to be afraid of—it can't do a thing to us, whatever its power.'

For fear that Federigo might become suspicious and have a row with her, Tessa decided she had better get up and ensure he could hear that Gianni was on hand, so she said to him: 'Well all right, you trot out your words, but the only thing that will make me feel really safe is if we put it under a spell, now that you're here.'

'How does one do that?'

'Well', said she, 'I know this spell from the other day when I went to church at Fiesole for the Pardon, and one of those anchoresses taught me a good, holy prayer, seeing how frightened I was—and she was as holy as could be, God knows, Gianni. She told me she'd tried it out many times before she retreated from the world and it had worked every time. But, Heaven knows, I'd never have had the courage to try it out all by myself; now you're here, though, let's go together and put this spell on the thing.'

Gianni declared himself willing, so they both got up and stole to the front door, outside which Federigo was still waiting, albeit with a lurking suspicion. When they got there, Tessa told her husband: 'When I give the word, spit.'

Gianni assented.

Tessa began her recitation thus: 'Phantom, phantom who prowl like a cat: you've come with tail erect. Now keep your tail up and off you go. Go into the orchard and see what you find at the foot of the big peach-tree: higgledy piggledy my fat hen, she lays eggs for gentlemen. Then bottoms up and drink your fill, and do no harm to my man and me . . . Spit, Gianni.' Gianni spat.

Outside the door, Federigo heard all of this; his jealousy subsided and, dejected though he was, he could barely contain his laughter. When Gianni spat, he simply muttered: 'Fangs very much.' This rigmarole the lady repeated three times and, with the spirit duly spellbound, she and her husband returned to bed. Federigo had been expecting to have supper with Tessa and had not eaten, but he grasped the meaning of the recital and went into the orchard, found the two fat capons at the foot of the big peach-tree, together with the wine and the eggs, and took them home to eat his supper in comfort. Subsequently, when he was with Tessa, they had a good chuckle over that incantation of hers.

There are some who say that the lady had in fact left the ass's skull facing towards Fiesole but that some labourer had thrust his stick into it as he passed the grapevine and set it spinning on its pole and it finished up facing towards Florence, which is why Federigo took it for a summons and came. So there's also this other version of Tessa's incantation which goes:

Phantom, phantom, by Heaven, get out.
It wasn't me who shifted the snout.
It was some God-blasted loitering lout.
Me, I'm at home with my Gianni.

And Federigo had gone away without supper and with no roof for the night. I have a neighbour, though, a very old woman, who tells me that both versions are true, from what she heard when she was a little girl; but that the second one had nothing to do with Gianni Lotteringhi but with a man called Gianni di Nello, who lived near Porta San Pietro and was as complete an imbecile as the other Gianni. So, my dear ladies, take your pick, or have 'em both if you prefer. They are the entire answer in such circumstances, as you've heard from experience. Learn them by heart: they may yet serve!

VII. 2. *When her husband returns home early, Peronella hides her lover in a barrel. The husband has brought a buyer for the barrel, but Peronella proves too quick for him.*

Emilia's tale was greeted with boisterous laughter, and the prayer won general approval as being good and holy. When she came to the end, the king ordered Philostrato to follow, and thus he began:

My dearest ladies, you are all too often the victims of male intrigue, and especially of married men's tricks; so on those occasions when a wife happens to turn the tables on her husband, you should not merely be delighted that this has come about or to know of it from another's report, but you should also spread word of it, so that the menfolk may grasp that if *they* know a few tricks, so does the fair sex. This can be only to your advantage because, when a man knows that it's a game at which two can play, he thinks twice before embarking on it. Will anybody doubt, therefore, that when the menfolk hear what we are going to relate on this topic today, they will have every reason to be inhibited from playing tricks on you, aware as they will be that you ladies are quite capable of doing the same to them if you're so inclined? So I intend to tell you what a young girl of humble condition did to her husband on the spur of the moment in order to retrieve an awkward situation.

Not long ago in Naples there was a poor man who married a pretty and engaging young girl called Peronella; they obtained a meagre living—he following the craft of bricklayer while she span yarn—and made ends meet as best they could. Now one day a young gallant set eyes on Peronella, found her much to his taste, and fell in love with her; he pursued her by one means and another until she made him welcome. Here is the arrangement they made for their trysts: as Peronella's husband got up early every morning in order to go to work, or to look for work, the lad was to post himself where he could see the husband leave the house; as their street, called Avorio, would be quite deserted, the lad could steal in the moment the husband was gone. This they did many a time.

There came a morning, however, when the bricklayer went out, Giannello Scrignario (to give the lad his name) stepped in to join Peronella, and the old fellow, who normally never returned home all day, was back shortly afterwards. Finding the door bolted, he knocked, then remarked to himself: 'O God, may You be forever praised: although You have created me poor, at least You have granted me the consolation of a good and virtuous young wife. See how she has bolted the door after me so that no one might come in and molest her.'

Peronella heard her husband, for she recognized his knock, and 'Help, my love!' she cried to Giannello. 'Now I'm for it: that's my husband, the devil take him! I don't know what's brought him back—he's never come back before at this time of day. Perhaps he spotted you coming in. But, whatever it is, for heaven's sake get into this barrel here,* and I'll go and let him in. Then we'll see what he's doing coming home so early.'

Giannello leapt into the cask and Peronella went to open the door to her husband. 'Now what's all this, coming home so early in the morning?' she demanded with a frown. 'It looks to me as if you're planning to take the day off—I see you've brought your tools back with you. If you do this, what are we going to live on? What shall we do for bread? D'you think I'll let you pawn my skirt and my one or two other bits of clothing when all *I* do all day and all night is work my fingers to the bone as I spin, spin, spin, so at least we'll have enough oil for our lamp? O husband! husband! There's not a woman in the street but eyes me askance and sniggers behind my back because I never stop working. And here you are coming home with idle hands when you ought to be out at work.' This said, she burst into tears and went on: 'O poor me! O my unlucky stars, what a bad sign I was born under! I might have had such a fine young man, but I refused him so I fetch up with this man who never spares a thought for the woman he's brought home! Other women have a merry time with their lovers; they all have two or three and enjoy themselves as they lead their husbands by the nose. And here's poor me, a good girl who doesn't go in for that sort of thing, and I have nothing but bad luck. I don't know why I don't get myself a lover as the others do. This you have to understand, husband: if I were minded to go astray I'd find a partner without a moment's trouble—there are some very fetching young fellows in love with me. They offer me money, lots of it, or else dresses or jewels, but I've never put up with them because I don't come from that sort of family. But here you are coming home when you ought to be working!'

'Come, wife', said her husband, 'please don't take on so. Believe me, I know what you're made of—I had some inkling of it just this morning. It is true that I went off to work but you seem not to know that today is the feast of St Galleone—I didn't know either—and it's not a working day; that's why I've come home again at this hour. But anyway I have provided for us and found a way to pay for our bread for a month and more: this man you see here with me, I've sold him the cask that's been cluttering up the house for so long, as you know. He's giving me five French silver crowns for it.'

'Why', said Peronella, 'that only makes it worse! Here you are, a man who goes out and about in the world, and you ought to know what's what: and you've sold a barrel for five French crowns when I, a mere slip of a girl who's scarcely set foot out of doors, I too have noticed that it's been taking up space and I've sold it to an honest fellow for seven. While you were on your way home he arrived and got inside it to see if it was sound.'

The husband was delighted to hear this and told the man who had come for it: 'Well, run along then, my friend: you've heard that my wife has sold it for seven, while five was all you were going to give me for it.'

The man shrugged his shoulders and left.

'As you're here', said Peronella to her husband, 'come up and see to it all with him.'

Giannello had been keeping an ear cocked in case anything transpired that he should worry about or guard against. On hearing what Peronella said, he promptly jumped out of the barrel and, as though he was unaware of her husband's return, he called: 'Lady, where are you?'

'Here I am', said the husband as he arrived; 'what can I do for you?'

'Who are you? It's the woman I want, the one I made a bargain with over this barrel.'

'Well, you can deal with me—I'm her husband.'

'The barrel looks to me sound enough', observed Giannello, 'but it would seem you've been letting the dregs settle in it, for it's entirely coated with goodness knows what—the stuff's dried on to it and I can't pick it off with my nails. Anyway, I shan't take it if I can't see it cleaned up first.'

'No', said Peronella. 'The sale won't fall through on that account: my husband will clean it all up.'

'Of course I will', said her husband, setting down his tools and stripping down to his shirt. He had a lantern lit, got himself a scraper, climbed into the barrel, and started scraping away. Peronella, meanwhile, stuck her head along with an arm right up to the shoulder in through the top, a fairly small aperture, as though she wanted to see him at work. 'Scrape here', she would say, 'and here . . . and here too . . . Look, here's a bit you missed.'

With Peronella in this posture as she gave her husband instructions and reminders, Giannello, who had not achieved total satisfaction this morning before her husband returned home, contrived to profit from the situation as he found it, for lack of other choice. So he approached her where she stood blocking off the mouth of the cask and, adopting the stance observed in the broad fields of Parthia during the rutting season as the unbridled stallions cover their mares, he gave rein to his youthful lust. And more or less simultaneously Giannello achieved his culmination, the barrel had its final scrape, he pulled back, Peronella withdrew her head, and her husband climbed out.

Then said Peronella to Giannello: 'Hold this lantern, my friend, and take a look to see if it's clean enough for you.' After peering inside, Giannello pronounced it satisfactory and himself content. He handed over seven French crowns and had the barrel removed to his house.

### VII. 3. *Brother Rinaldo is caught making love to his mistress. They both persuade her husband that he is much in the friar's debt.*

Philostrato could not disguise his allusion to Parthian mares well enough to get it past the ladies: they were too sharp, and could not but chuckle, while pretending it was something else that had amused them. Seeing that he had ended, the king bade Elissa tell her story, which she dutifully did, in these words:

Emilia's phantom cat and the spell put on it reminds me of another story to do with mumbo-jumbo. It is not as good as hers, but I'll tell it anyway as I can't think of anything else on today's theme.

You must know that once upon a time in Siena there lived a young gallant of good family called Rinaldo. He was madly in love with a most beautiful woman called Agnesa; she was a neighbour, the wife of a rich man. He hoped that if he could find some way of speaking to her without arousing suspicion, he might obtain from her his heart's desire. He couldn't think how to do it, though, until the woman became pregnant and he hit upon the idea of standing godfather to the baby. So he struck up a friendship with her husband and, by casting his intentions in the most unexceptionable light, gained acceptance. Once he was godfather to Agnesa's child, and was thus provided with a better excuse for having words with her, Rinaldo confidently put to her what he had on his mind—though in fact his eyes had conveyed the message to her clearly enough long ago. Little good did it do him, however, even though she was willing enough to hear him out.

Shortly after this Rinaldo became a friar for some reason or other, and, whatever joy he derived from this calling, he persevered in it. Even if on becoming a friar he had put aside the love he bore his lady, along with certain other wordly preoccupations, the fact is that, as time went by, he took them up again, without discarding his order's habit. He reverted to taking pleasure in his dress and appearance and to playing the gallant, trotting out ballads, songs, and sonnets, serenading and what have you.

Did I say Brother Rinaldo did these things? Name me a friar who doesn't!* O the ignominy of this corrupted world! They're not the least bit ashamed if they look plump and rosy-cheeked, dressed in softly textured habits redolent of their pampered state. Are they like doves? No, they strut about like the cock o' the walk, chest out, crest erect. But there's worse. Let's forget about their cells crammed with jars of ointments and salves, boxes with every kind of sweetmeat, phials and cruets of fragrant attars and other oils, flasks of malmsey and other exotic wines: friars' cells?—They look more like an apothecary's or a perfumer's shop! They're not even ashamed if people discover they're suffering from gout. They think no one's woken up to the fact that a regime of fasting, a simple and spare diet, and a habit of sober living are what keep a person lean and in the best of health. Besides, even if fasting did prove injurious to health, gout is one ailment it would not procure; the normal cure for that is chastity and everything else that marks the life of a simple friar. A life of poverty, with long vigils and much prayer and penance, should leave a man looking pale and drawn, but they imagine no one outside recognizes this. They forget that Saint Dominic and Saint Francis, far from having four cloaks apiece, wore what they needed to keep out the cold, not to look pretty in; their habits were not made out of rich men's fabrics, dyed in the wool, but out of coarse wool in its natural colour. As for our own needs, may God provide for them as He provides for the souls of the simple folk who minister to the friars.

Anyway, Brother Rinaldo reverted to his former cravings and became a frequent visitor to the mother of his godson, whose favours he started soliciting with ever-increasing boldness. The good lady found herself indeed hard pressed, but she also found her suitor more appealing than he used to be, and one day when he was proving unusually importunate, she resorted to the device employed by any woman disposed to accord what is requested of her: 'Come now, Brother Rinaldo', she cried, 'is this a way for a friar to behave?'

'Ah', replied Brother Rinaldo, 'just wait till I've pulled off my habit—and there's nothing easier—you'll be looking at a male like any other, and not at a friar.'

She grinned at this and said: 'Well dearie me! It simply can't be done—after all, I'm your godson's mother! It would be very wrong, therefore, indeed I've often heard it said that it's a grievous sin. Were it not for that, I'd be at your service.'

'Well you're very silly if you let *that* stand in your way. I don't say it's not a sin, but God forgives worse ones in a penitent soul. Anyway, tell me: which of us has the closer relationship to your child, I, who held him at the font, or your husband, who fathered him?'

'My husband is the closer.'

'Quite right. And doesn't your husband sleep with you?'

'Of course!'

'Well then', exclaimed the friar. 'I'm not as closely related to your son as your husband is, so it's as right for me to sleep with you as it is for your husband.'

Agnesa had little grounding in philosophy and, moreover, she didn't need much convincing, so she was persuaded by the friar's words (or pretended to be) and said: 'Who could resist wisdom such as yours?' and capitulated there and then, never mind the degree of kinship. This was only the first time:

the bond formed between them by the child afforded them any number of plausible opportunities to share each other's company.

On one occasion, though, Brother Rinaldo paid a visit to her and found no one at home apart from his mistress and a little maidservant of hers, the prettiest little thing, whom he sent upstairs to her garret with a fellow-friar who was to teach her the Our Father. Meanwhile he went into his beloved's bedroom—she had her child by the hand—locked the door, and set about making love to her on the divan. While they were thus engaged there was a knock on the door—the husband had come home unnoticed and was now at the bedroom door calling to her.

'Now I'm in for it', said Agnesa. 'That's my husband. This time he'll realize what all our meetings are really about.'

Brother Rinaldo was still in his cassock but had left off his hood and scapular. 'You're right. If I were properly dressed we might find some way out of this, but if you open the door and he finds me like this, we'll be caught red-handed.'

Suddenly Agnesa hit upon an idea. 'Get dressed', she said. 'Then take your godson in your arms and listen carefully to what I tell my husband. What you say must tally with what I say. Just leave it to me.'

The moment her husband left off knocking, Agnesa said: 'I'm just coming.' She got up, went to the door, and opened it to him, looking quite composed. 'Brother Rinaldo is here, husband', she said, 'and let me tell you, he's a pure godsend: had he not come, we should certainly have lost our child today.'

Her husband, an old bigot, almost fainted when he heard this. 'What?' he cried.

'Why, my dear', she said, 'our boy suddenly passed out just now, and I was convinced he was dead and I didn't know which way to turn; then who should turn up but his own godfather, Brother Rinaldo, who picked him up and said: "What he's got is worms. They're making for his heart and could be the death of him. But never fear—I'll kill them all off with a spell, and you'll find your lad as hale as ever before I leave." We needed you here to say certain prayers, but the maid couldn't find you, so he got his companion to say them up in the garret with the maid while he and I came in here. And as only the child's mother can assist at a thing like this and we hadn't to be disturbed, we locked the door. Brother Rinaldo is still holding him; I think all he's waiting for now is for his companion to finish saying his prayers, and then that should be it, for the boy is quite recovered.'

The simple fellow swallowed this all, for he was very concerned for his son; it never crossed his mind that his wife might be bamboozling him, so he heaved a deep sigh and said: 'I want to see him.'

'You can't', said his wife; 'you'd just undo the spell. Wait while I see if you can come in. I'll call you.'

Brother Rinaldo had had leisure to get dressed as he listened to all this. He took the child in his arms, set the scene properly, and called out: 'I say, is that the boy's father I hear out there?'

'Yes, it's me.'

'Well then, come in', said Brother Rinaldo. In he went, and Brother Rinaldo continued: 'Here, you can hold your son. He's cured, thanks be to God, though just now I was sure you wouldn't find him alive this evening. Now have a life-sized statue made in wax to the glory of God and place it before the image of Saint Ambrose, through whose merits the Lord has granted you this mercy.'

Seeing his father, the little mite ran to him and hugged him joyfully, the way young children do, and his father picked him up and wept over him as if he were back from the grave; he kissed him all over and thanked the friar profusely for having cured the lad. Brother Rinaldo's companion, meanwhile, had taught the maid her Our Father—indeed he'd taught it her a good four times—and he'd made her a present of a white linen purse given him by a nun, and had the girl eating out of his hand. When he heard the simpleton calling his wife at the bedroom door, he had slipped down quietly and placed himself where he could see and hear everything. Seeing that matters were turning out all right, he came all the way down, went into the room, and said: 'Brother Rinaldo, I've said all four of the prayers you told me to say.'

'Brother', said Rinaldo, 'well done. I'm glad you kept it up. I'd only got through two when our friend came along, but, thanks to your efforts and mine, the good Lord has granted us the grace of healing this boy.'

The simple husband sent for choice wines and refreshments to entertain his boy's godfather and the other friar, pressing them to restore themselves with whatever they felt most in need of. Then he left the house with them, bade them God-speed, and lost no time in arranging for a wax statue to be made and set up along with the other votive statues before the image of Saint Ambrose* (the Dominican one from Siena, not the Milanese one).

VII. 4. *Tofano, the lout, shuts his wife out of the house; she makes him wish he hadn't.*

When he heard the end of Elissa's story, the king at once turned to Lauretta and indicated his wish that she should follow, which she straight away did, in these words:

Oh what powers Love has at his disposal, what arts and wiles! What artist, what philosopher ever could, ever might, display half the subtleties that spring full-grown from the minds of Love's disciples! Certainly next to these, anyone else is slow-witted, as we have just been shown. Well, I have an instance to add, and it concerns a neat device employed by a simple woman—and who could have put the idea in her head if it was not Love?

Once upon a time in Arezzo there was a rich man called Tofano. He was allotted in marriage a most beautiful woman called Ghita, and in no time at all he was madly jealous of her for no good reason. She was quite put out to discover this and several times asked him what caused him to be jealous; Tofano's excuse, however, was never more than the usual lame commonplaces, and Ghita therefore decided that as he was so suspicious, she might as well give him cause.

She had noticed that quite a respectable young man, so it seemed to her, was rather smitten with her, and she tacitly began to accept his overtures. The affair proceeded apace until nothing remained but to pass from words to action, and the wife considered how this, too, might be done. Now she had noticed that one of her husband's failings was a weakness for the bottle, so she not only started viewing this trait with approval, but even contrived to encourage him to drink; when he was properly addicted, she could have him drink himself into a stupor virtually whenever she chose. When she saw that he was thoroughly tipsy she would put him to bed and go off safely to meet her lover—this became a regular habit. In fact she came to rely on her husband's inebriation to the point where she would risk bringing her lover home and occasionally go to spend a good part of the night at his place, which was close by.

While the wife thus pursued her amour, her luckless husband woke up to the fact that she kept encouraging him to drink, but never touched a drop herself. 'Something fishy here', he thought to himself; 'could she be getting me tiddly so she can go off and play little games while I'm sleeping it off?' If this was the case, he meant to find out, so one day he kept off the bottle but came home to all appearances rolling drunk at nightfall. His wife believed her eyes and reckoned that he did not need another drop—she put him straight to bed. Then off she went, as so often before, to pass the time till midnight at her lover's house.

Hearing no sound of his wife in the house, Tofano got up and went to lock the door, then he stood waiting at the window to espy her return and show her that he had tumbled to her tricks. Eventually she returned, and was far from pleased to find herself locked out; she tried her best to force the door open. Tofano bided his time then said: 'Don't exhaust yourself, my good woman—you're not coming in here. Go back where you've just come from, and make no mistake: you're not coming in here again till honour has been satisfied in front of your family and the neighbours.'

Ghita begged him for God's sake to let her in: she had not been where he thought she had, she'd been sitting up with a friend of hers down the street, a woman. 'The nights are so long', she said, 'I can't sleep right through or wait up at home all on my own.' But her prayers were in vain: the brute wanted to ensure that the whole city knew of their shame, a secret till now.

Seeing that entreaties were useless, Ghita tried a threat: 'If you don't open up, I swear I'll make you the sorriest man alive.'

'How will you do that?'

Said Ghita, her wits sharpened by Love: 'Rather than endure the shame you quite unjustly want me to suffer, I shall throw myself down our well. When they find me dead, no one will believe that you didn't throw me in during one of your drunken fits. You'll have to disappear and leave everything behind and be outlawed, or you'll have your head chopped off for murdering me, which is just what you will have done.'

These words left Tofano clinging just as oafishly to his opinion, so his wife said: 'Well, that's that! Enough is enough! I'm leaving my distaff right here—put it away for me, and may God forgive you!' With this, she went to the well—the night was so dark, you couldn't see your hand in front of your face—heaved up a great big stone lying beside the well, cried 'God forgive me!', and dropped it into the water with a mighty splash.

When Tofano heard the noise he was quite sure she had thrown herself in; he snatched up the bucket and rope and dashed out to rescue her. She, meanwhile, was hiding next to the door and slipped inside the moment he ran to the well; she locked herself in, posted herself at the window, and said: 'Water your wine when you drink it: that's the time, not later in the evening.'

At these words Tofano realized that he had been hoodwinked. He went back to the door, found it shut, and told her to open up.

'I'll be damned', she shouted, making no further attempt to keep her voice down, 'if you come in here tonight, you revolting drunken sot. I've had all I can stand from you. It's high time everyone found out what sort of a man you are and what time you come home at night.'

These words stung Tofano, who started hurling insults back at her. The neighbours heard the rumpus and came to their windows, men and women, and asked what was going on.

Ghita, sobbing, explained: 'It's this wretch of a husband: he comes home reeling at the end of the day, or passes out in the tavern and gets home at *this* time of night. I've put up with it for years and given him any number of talkings-to, but much good has it done me. So I've had no choice but to lock him out and make him look a fool—I hope this might help reform him.'

This drove Tofano wild: he kept saying what had really happened and uttered all manner of threats.

'There now', said Ghita to the neighbours. 'See what sort of man he is! What would you say if *I* was out in the street instead, and *he* in the house? I do believe in that case you'd accept his word—so I ask you, what sort of a fool is he? He accuses me of what he himself has done, it seems to me. He thought he could scare me by throwing something into the well. Would to God he really had thrown himself in and drowned—that way he'd certainly water all that wine he's been drinking!'

The neighbours and their wives all turned on Tofano and treated with contempt the accusations he levelled at his wife. Word spread and it was not long before it got back to Ghita's family. They turned up, heard what the neighbours had to say, laid hands on Tofano, and gave him a thorough pasting. Then they marched into the house, collected Ghita's things, and took her home with them, after threatening Tofano with worse.

Tofano saw what a sorry state he was now in, and that his jealousy was to blame for it. As his wife was still the apple of his eye, he managed, through the good offices of some friends, to persuade her to come back in peace, and promised her he would never be jealous again. Indeed he left her free to do just as she wished, only so long as she kept him in the dark. Acting like a silly goose, he got a basting, then made a truce. So three cheers for Love, and down with churls, skinflints, curmudgeons—and that goes for us too!

VII. 5. *A needlessly jealous husband disguises himself as a priest and confessor to catch out his wife. His stratagem rebounds on him.*

Lauretta ended her tale and everyone shared the opinion that the wife had done well and treated the wretch as he deserved. Then the king wasted no time but turned to Fiammetta and graciously summoned her to proceed with her story, and this is how she began:

The last story induces me to speak likewise about a jealous husband, for I think that what their wives practise on them, and not least when the men have no occasion for jealousy, is all to the good. And if those who frame the laws had taken everything into consideration, my view is that they should establish the same penalty for wives in this regard as they have done in the case of a man who injures another in self-defence: jealous men are a threat to young women's lives and seek their deaths all too diligently. Women are shut up in the house all week, taking care of the home and the family and they want, the same as anyone else, to have a good time on holy days; they want a little peace then, and the chance to go out and enjoy themselves, just as farm labourers do, and artisans in the towns, and magistrates in the courts, as the Good Lord appointed that He should rest from His labours on the seventh day, and as both canon and civil laws require, for they seek the honour of God and the good of the community by making a distinction between work-days and rest-days. But this is something that the jealous will not allow, far from it: those days which spell happiness for all other women, they will make them as dreary and miserable as possible for *their* womenfolk by keeping them even more shut away; only those poor creatures who've experienced it know how soul-destroying it is. So as I said, anything a wife does to a husband who is needlessly jealous ought not to be condemned but commended.

In Rimini there was once a merchant whose possessions and funds made him enormously rich. He had married a very beautiful woman and he became inordinately jealous of her. He had no cause to be, but as he loved her dearly and thought her exceedingly beautiful, and knew that she went to no end of trouble to keep him happy, he imagined that every other man loved her and found her ravishing and that she took equal pains to keep every other man contented—such an idea would only enter the mind of a heartless bounder. Such was his possessiveness, he guarded her and fenced her in so closely, it must have been worse than the guard put on convicts under sentence of death. His wife could not set a foot out of doors, let alone attend a wedding or a party or go to church; why, she dared not even show herself at a window or let anyone catch sight of her outside the house on any pretext. So her life was utterly miserable and she smarted all the more under these constraints inasmuch as she felt they were totally unmerited.

Seeing, then, that she was suffering unjustly at her husband's hands, it occurred to her, for her own satisfaction, to find some way, if at all possible, to justify what he was doing to her. She could not go near a window, and was therefore precluded from exhibiting her pleasure at the amorous advances of some passing swain. However, she was aware that an attractive and good-looking young man lived in the adjoining house, and considered the possibility of some chink in the party wall, which she might keep peeping through until she caught his eye and was able to engage him in conversation; thus she might offer him her love, if he wanted it, and look for some way to get together with him occasionally. In this way she might be able to abide her unfortunate existence until such time as her husband worked the suppurating jealousy out of his system. So when her husband was not around she explored the wall at every point until she chanced upon a fissure in a secret part of the house. She could not see through it at all clearly, but as she looked, she discerned that the chink gave on to a bedroom. 'If that's Filippo's room', she mused (Filippo being the youth's name), 'I'd be half-way there.' She had a maid who felt sorry for her, and she put her on to the task of cautiously prying at the chink; thus she discovered that the youth did sleep there and all on his own. So she paid frequent visits to the chink and, whenever she heard that Filippo was in, she would drop pebbles and twigs until she'd attracted his attention and he came over to investigate. She softly called out to him and he recognized her voice and answered; then she took the occasion to tell him briefly what she had in mind. Filippo was delighted and saw to enlarging the hole from his side, but not in any obvious way. Here they would often chat together and hold hands, though they could take matters no further than that because of the strict watch maintained by the jealous husband.

Now Christmas was coming and the wife asked her husband for permission to go to church on the morning of the feast, to go to confession and take communion as Christians do. 'Ah!' said the husband, 'and what sins might *you* have to confess?'

'What? D'you think I'm a saint because you keep me shut up? You know perfectly well I fall into sin just like any other living soul. But I'm not going to tell you—*you*'re not a priest.'

These words aroused the husband's suspicions, and he decided he'd like to discover what sins she had committed. He thought how this might be done, and told her that she was welcome to go but he insisted it must be to their chapel: she was to go there first thing in the morning, and she was to make her confession to their chaplain in person or to whichever priest the chaplain appointed, but to no one else. She was then to return home directly. The wife had an inkling of what lay behind these instructions, but she promised to obey them, without further comment.

On the morning of the holy day the wife got up at daybreak, made herself ready, and went to the chapel prescribed by her husband. He, meanwhile, also got up and went to the same chapel, arriving there before her; he had already made his arrangements with the priest, and he quickly dressed up in a cassock and a capacious hood, such as priests are normally seen wearing; this he pulled well down over his forehead, then retired into the choir-stalls. The lady appeared and asked for the priest. The priest came to her, and on hearing that she wished to go to confession, he told her that he could not attend to her himself but would send along a colleague of his. Off he went and despatched the jealous husband to his doom. He came up to her looking most dignified, but even though it was not yet fully daylight and he had pulled his hood well down over his eyes, she had no difficulty penetrating his disguise. 'Thank God!' she said to herself. 'This jealous fellow has become a priest. Very well, I'll see that he gets what he's looking for.' So she pretended not to recognize him and sat herself down at his feet. The jealous husband had slipped some pebbles into his mouth to affect his speech, the idea being that this would prevent his wife identifying him by his voice—he imagined that he'd so well disguised himself that there was no chance of her recognizing him otherwise. As she launched into her confession, she said among other things that she was a married woman but she was in love with a priest, and he came every night to sleep with her.

On hearing this, her husband felt a stab through the heart, and he would have forsaken the confessional and made off were he not so anxious to hear more. So he checked himself and said: 'What's this? Does your husband not sleep with you?'

'But of course.'

'Then how does the priest manage to sleep with you too?'

'How the priest does it I don't know', she said. 'But there's not a door in the house that's so tightly locked it won't open at his touch. He tells me that when he reaches my bedroom door, before he opens it he pronounces certain words which have the effect of sending my husband straight off to sleep; when he hears him sleeping, he opens the door and comes in and joins me. It never fails.'

'This, madam, is very wrong, and you must give it up completely.'

'I don't think I could ever do that, father. I do so love him.'

'Then I'll not be able to give you absolution.'

'I'm sorry', she said. 'I didn't come here to tell you lies. If I thought I could do it, I'd tell you.'

'Oh dear! I'm very sorry to hear that: at this rate I can see you going to perdition. But I tell you what I'm going to do to help you: I'm going to make a special intercession to God on your behalf—it'll be hard work but maybe it will be your salvation. And I'm going to send an altar-boy along to you now and then: tell him if my prayers are helping. If they are, we'll go on to the next step.'

'No, don't send anyone to my house, father. If my husband finds out, he's such a jealous man, nothing on earth will persuade him that the boy has not come on some mischievous errand, and I'll never hear the end of it.'

'Don't worry yourself. The way I'll go about it, you'll never hear a peep out of your husband.'

'Very well', said the wife, 'if you're sure you can manage it.' She finished her confession, was given a penance, stood up, and left to hear Mass.

The jealous husband went off, snorting over his bad luck, to strip off his cassock and return home; he wanted to find some way to catch the priest and his wife together, to give them something to think about. His wife got home from church and could see from his face that she'd given him a merry Christmas, though he did his level best to conceal what he had done and what he thought he knew.

He determined to wait up that night by the front door and stand ready for the priest's arrival. He told his wife: 'Tonight I'll have to be out for supper and overnight. Make sure the front door's locked, and the door on the landing, and the bedroom door. Go to bed when you feel like it.' His wife assented.

At the first opportunity she went to the chink in the wall and made the usual signal; Filippo heard it and came to the chink as well, whereupon she told him what she had done that morning and what her husband had said to her after lunch. 'I'm sure he won't leave the house', she added; 'he'll stand guard at the front door. So find some way to come here tonight over the roof and we can be together.'

Filippo was highly pleased. 'Lady,' he said, 'leave it to me.'

When it was night, the husband quietly concealed himself with his weapons in a ground-floor room. The wife chose her time to have every door locked, not least the one on the landing, so that her husband could not get upstairs, and the young man came to her by the most cautious route. They climbed into bed and gave each other a very good time indeed until daybreak, when the lad made his way home. The husband, meanwhile, waited up by the front door with his weapons practically the entire night expecting the priest's arrival. Freezing to death, supperless, and miserable, he could no longer keep awake as dawn approached, and he fell asleep in the ground-floor room. He got up about nine; the front door was now open and he climbed the stairs leading up from it as though he had come in from outside, and sat down to breakfast. Then he sent a little boy, in the guise of the altar-boy of the priest who had heard her confession, with a message to his wife asking whether that certain person had been round at all. The wife had no doubt who the messenger was, and told him that he'd not come that night; moreover, she added, were he to come, she would put him out of her mind, however reluctantly.

Well, what am I to say? The husband passed many a night at the front door hoping to catch the priest red-handed, and the wife enjoyed a succession of happy nights in her lover's arms. In the end the husband, now thoroughly fed up, angrily asked his wife what she had told the priest when she went to confession that morning. The wife replied that she wouldn't tell him: it was neither right nor proper to do so.

'You bitch', he cried, 'I know just the same what it is you told him, and you're going to tell me who this priest is you're so infatuated with, who uses his magic to sleep with you every night. Tell me or I'll slash your wrist.'

'It's not true, I'm not in love with any priest.'

'What? Didn't you say this to your confessor . . . and this too . . .?'

'Maybe he passed all this on to you—but from what you say you could have been there yourself in person! That is exactly what I said to him.'

'All right. Who's this priest? Out with it!'

The wife smiled and said: 'Oh I do like it when a simple woman can lead a wise man by the nose, as one leads a lamb by its horns to the slaughter! Not that you're wise—you stopped being so the moment you let the evil spirit of jealousy take possession of you without even knowing why you did it. The more like an idiot and a brute you behave, the more you dishonour me. D'you really think, dear man, that I don't have eyes in my head, just because you don't have eyes in your mind? Well you're wrong. I used my eyes and recognized the priest who heard my confession, and it was you. And I chose to give you the very thing you'd gone out looking for. Now if you'd had any sense, as you like to think you have, you wouldn't have tried to prise secrets out of your good wife that way, and instead of jumping to false conclusions you would have realized just how much truth there was in what she was confessing to you and that she had committed no sin at all. I told you I was in love with a priest: and hadn't you, whom I love quite without reason, turned yourself into a priest? I told you that no door in my house could remain closed to him when he wanted to sleep with me: and which door is there that you ever found shut in your house when you wanted to come and find me? I told you that the priest slept with me every night: and when did it happen that you didn't sleep with me? And that altar-boy you kept sending me: as often as you were not with me I sent him back to you with the message that the priest had not been with me. Any fool but you would have caught on, but you've let yourself be blinded by jealousy. So here you've been, spending the night standing guard at the front door, and imagining all the time I'd fallen for your story about being out for supper and overnight! Come now, mend your ways, be your old self again and don't make yourself a laughing-stock among people who know your little habits as well as I do. Just stop playing the sentry the way you do, for I swear to God, if I ever felt like making a cuckold of you I'd arrange to go my own sweet way without you're noticing a thing, not if you had a hundred eyes, let alone two!'

The deplorable fellow, who thought he'd been so clever at unmasking his wife, felt not a little foolish when he heard this, and found nothing to reply. He accepted that his wife was a good woman of impeccable morals, and now that he had cause to suspect her fidelity he set aside all suspicion, just as he had harboured endless suspicions when he'd had no reason to. As for the canny lady, she no longer made her lover slink to her across the rooftops like a cat but contrived to fetch him in discreetly through the front door, for all the world as if she'd been given leave to suit herself; and many a time after that was she to make merry with her lover.

VII. 6. *A husband catches his wife at home entertaining two lovers. She none the less succeeds in pulling the wool over his eyes.*

Everyone had enjoyed Fiammetta's tale enormously; they all agreed that the woman could not have done a better thing: it was exactly what the brute deserved. Her tale ended, the king told Pampinea to follow, and so she began:

Many people talk a lot of nonsense about Love turning people into fools; they virtually assert that a person in love simply loses his head. What a silly notion! say I: it's already clear enough from what we've been saying and I propose to demonstrate it myself.

In this well-endowed city of ours there was once a young lady of gentle birth and ravishing beauty; she was married to a knight, a gallant and worthy man. Now it is often the case that a person cannot keep to the same old diet but wants a little variety; thus the husband left the lady somewhat unsatisfied, and she fell in love with a youth called Leonetto, a charming, courtly lad, albeit not out of the top drawer. He fell equally in love with her, and more often than not, when both parties are after the same thing, they get it, as you know; it was not long, then, before the couple brought their love to fruition. Now being a woman of beauty and character, she chanced to attract the passionate attentions of a knight called Lambertuccio, a man she could on no account bring herself to love, he being (in her opinion) a boor and a bore. He pressed her with any number of solicitations but little good did it do him; so he issued a threat to expose her to public shame if she didn't fall in with his wishes—and he was a power in the land. Knowing what he was like and frightened of him, she bent herself, therefore, to his will.

The lady (her name was Isabella) had gone to stay in a lovely villa she had out in the country, as we tend to do in the summer, and one morning, when her husband had left on horseback for some place where he had to stay a few days, she sent for Leonetto, who turned up at once with the greatest of pleasure. Now Lambertuccio got wind of her husband's absence; he took horse, went alone to her villa, and knocked at the door. When the lady's maid saw him, she went straight up to her mistress, who was in her bedroom with Leonetto, and called her. 'Madam', she said, 'Master Lambertuccio is down below, all on his own.'

Isabella was the world's saddest woman when she heard this, but she was terrified of the man and therefore asked Leonetto if he wouldn't mind hiding for a moment inside the bed-curtains until Lambertuccio had left. Leonetto hid: he was as scared of him as Isabella was. Then she told the maid to open the gate to Master Lambertuccio. When the maid did so he dismounted in the courtyard, tethered his palfrey to a hook, and climbed the stairs. Isabella put on a brave face, came to meet him at the top of the stairs, and spoke to him as welcomingly as she could. 'What', she asked him, 'brings you here?' Lambertuccio gave her a hug and a kiss and told her: 'I heard your husband was away, my darling, so I've come to keep you company for a while.' This said, they went into the bedroom, locked the door, and Lambertuccio started having a good time with her.

While they were thus engaged, her husband happened to return, which was the last thing she had been expecting. When the maid saw him approaching the house she ran at once to her mistress's room and said: 'Madam, the master is back. I believe he is down in the courtyard.'

On hearing this, Isabella, conscious of having two men in the house, and aware too that there was no concealing Lambertuccio as his horse was down in the courtyard, thought she was as good as dead. However, she hit on a plan, leapt out of bed, and said to Lambertuccio: 'If you love me just a little bit and don't mind saving my life, then you'll do as I tell you. Draw your dagger and go downstairs holding it in your hand and looking angry and vicious and saying, "I swear to God I'll catch him somewhere else." If my husband makes to stop you or asks you anything, say nothing except what I've said, but get on your horse and don't linger with him on any account.'

Lambertuccio readily agreed. He unsheathed his dagger and did as Isabella had told him—his fiery look came from his latest exertions and from rage at her husband's return. The husband had already dismounted in the courtyard and was puzzled to see the other horse there. As he was on the point of climbing the stairs he saw Lambertuccio coming down and was struck by his words and the look on his face.

'What's all this, sir?' he asked.

Lambertuccio put a foot in the stirrup, swung himself up, but had nothing to say except: 'God's teeth! I'll catch him somewhere else.' And off he went.

The gentleman went on upstairs and at the top he found his wife in great distress and shaking with terror. 'What's happening?' he asked. 'Who's Lambertuccio threatening in that furious way?'

Isabella withdrew towards the bedroom so that Leonetto might overhear, then said: 'Never did I have such a fright as this. A young man I don't know came dashing in here followed by Lambertuccio brandishing a dagger. Finding my door open by chance, he stammered out: "For God's sake help me, lady, or I'll be killed in your very arms." I jumped up and was about to ask him who he was and what was the matter when up came Lambertuccio saying: "Where are you, traitor?" I stopped on the threshold of my bedroom and detained him when he made to come in. And he was gallant enough, seeing that I didn't want him in the room, to go away, after many words, just as you saw him.'

'You did well', said her husband. 'It would have been too bad if someone had been killed in the house. And Lambertuccio has absolutely no business to pursue anyone in here. Where is the young man?'

'I don't know where he's hiding.'

'Where are you?' shouted the husband. 'Come out without fear.'

Leonetto, who had heard all this, came out of his hiding-place quaking, and his fear had been genuine enough.

'What d'you have to do with Master Lambertuccio?' asked the husband.

'Absolutely nothing, sir', said the young man. 'I'm convinced he must have lost his wits, or that he mistook me for someone else. The moment he saw me on the road not far from this house, he reached for his dagger and cried: "Traitor, you're dead!" I didn't stop to ask why, but took to my heels as fast as I could and came in here where, thanks be to God and to this kind lady, I escaped.'

'That's good. No need to be frightened any more. I'll get you home safe and sound, and then you can find out what he was after you about.'

After lunch he lent the youth a horse, took him back to Florence, and left him at his own house. That same evening Leonetto had a word in secret with Lambertuccio, as Isabella had instructed him, and so arranged matters that, though the incident provoked a great deal of gossip, the husband never did realize how he had been duped by his wife.

VII. 7. *Beatrice takes her husband's servant Anichino for her lover, but succeeds in persuading her spouse that he is blessed with the most faithful of wives and most loyal of attendants.*

The entire company agreed that Isabella's astuteness, as described by Pampinea, was quite remarkable. Philomena, however, whom the king had bidden follow on, observed that, if she was not very much mistaken, she was sure she could tell them one every bit as good, and here it was:

Once upon a time in Paris there lived a Florentine of noble birth who, under pressure of want, had turned to commerce; and he so prospered as a merchant that he acquired an immense fortune. His wife had given him but one son, whom he had christened Lodovico. Now as Lodovico was, in his father's intention, to be brought up as scion of a nobleman rather than as a tradesman's son, he was not placed behind a counter but was found a position among other noblemen in the service of the King of France. Here he picked up the most elegant manners and a great refinement. This, then, is where he was when he happened to be involved in a discussion with other young men about pretty women in France, in England, and elsewhere, when they were joined by some knights freshly returned from the Holy Sepulchre. One of these stepped in to remark that he had knocked about the world quite a little and set eyes on a fair number of women, but for sheer beauty there was not one to match the wife of Egano de' Galluzzi in Bologna; her name was Beatrice. This assertion was borne out by all his companions who had been with him in Bologna and seen her. Lodovico had never yet been in love, but when he heard this he was so fired with the wish to set eyes on her, he could think of nothing else. Determined, therefore, to go to Bologna to see her, and to stop there if he liked the look of her, he told his father some story about wanting to visit the Holy Sepulchre and obtained his consent, albeit not without difficulty.

Assuming the name of Anichino, he arrived in Bologna and, as luck would have it, saw this lady the next day at a party and found her far more ravishing even than he had expected; as a result, he fell head over heels in love with her and decided he was not going to leave Bologna without having captured her heart. As he considered how he ought to proceed, he eventually discarded every possibility save one, and that was to take service with the lady's husband, who kept a large household, for he concluded that this stood a good chance of securing him what he was after. So he sold his horses and made all due provision for his own retinue, after instructing them to pretend not to know him. Then he struck up acquaintance with his innkeeper and told him that he would be glad to enter the service of a good master, if one might be found. 'Well, you're just the man to appeal to a nobleman of this city called Egano', said his host. 'He keeps a fair number, and requires them all to be more than presentable, as you are. I'll speak to him about it.' He was as good as his word, and by the time he left Egano he had placed Anichino with him—indeed, Egano could not have been more delighted. In Egano's household Anichino had ample occasion to see his beloved; meanwhile he gave Egano such excellent and satisfactory service that he earned a good place in his affections—Egano could not do a thing without involving his servant, who took complete charge of him and of all that belonged to him.

One day when Egano had gone out hawking and left Anichino at home, his wife Beatrice sat down to a game of chess with him. She was not yet aware that he was in love with her, although she had formed a very favourable impression of him and had often remarked on the excellence of his manners. Anichino, anxious to please, played a crafty hand to ensure that he was beaten,* which made Beatrice absolutely cock-a-hoop. After her ladies had given up watching the game and gone away, leaving them to continue on their own, Anichino heaved a tremendous sigh.

Beatrice looked at him. 'What's the matter, Anichino?' she asked. 'Is it my winning that bothers you?'

'Ah no. It's something far more important than that.'

'Go on then. If you care for me at all, tell me what it is.'

Hearing her qualify her request with the words 'if you care for me at all'—she whom he loved above all things—Anichino heaved another sigh that quite dwarfed the first, and Beatrice pressed him again to tell her what he was sighing about.

'I'm very much afraid you'll not be at all pleased if I tell you; and I'm worried lest you tell someone else about it.'

'Of course I shan't mind. And don't you worry: anything you tell me I shan't tell a soul except by your leave.'

'Since I have your promise', said Anichino, 'I'll tell you.' And, close to tears, he told her who he was, what he had heard about her and where, and how he had fallen in love with her, how he had come here, and why he had entered her husband's service. Then he meekly besought her to be good enough to take pity on him, if this were possible, and to satisfy his secret, burning wish. If she would not consent to do so, he begged she might permit him to continue in his present role and not object to his remaining in love with her.

O how mild the blood in Bolognese veins!* How admirable you have ever proved to be in cases like this! Never have you craved sighs and tears; nay, you have ever been touched by entreaties, moved by amorous yearnings. If I knew of praises fit for the purpose, I should sing them till kingdom come!

As Anichino spoke, the gentle lady looked at him and, fully convinced by what he told her, she too began to sigh, such was the impact his loving entreaties made upon her heart. She sighed a little, then, and answered him: 'Cheer up, Anichino my pet. I've been courted a great deal in my time, but presents, promises, melting looks never yet moved me to love any of my suitors, be they men of high or low degree. You, though, you've captivated me heart and soul in but a twinkling—in the time it has taken you to declare your love. I consider that you have exceedingly well deserved my love, so I am making you a gift of it; and before this night is out, I promise you, I'll give you joy of it. This is what we'll do: you'll come to my room at midnight; I'll leave the door unlocked, and you know which side of the bed I sleep in; go to that side; if I'm asleep, prod me awake, and I shall console you for the long fast you have endured. You don't believe me? Take this kiss, then, as a pledge.' And she threw her arms round his neck and gave him a tender kiss; he gave her one too.

These words exchanged, Anichino left Beatrice to go and see to his duties, while he waited, beside himself with happiness, for night to come. Egano came back from his hawking, had supper, and retired to bed, for he was tired; his wife followed him, and left the bedroom door unlocked as she had promised. At the appointed time Anichino arrived at her door, quietly entered the room, and locked the door behind him; he stole to the wife's side of the bed, laid a hand on her breast, and found she was not asleep. Sensing that Anichino had arrived, Beatrice took his hand in both of hers and held it tightly. As she turned in bed, however, she managed to awaken Egano, who had been asleep. She said to him: 'I didn't want to say anything to you after supper as you looked tired to me. Now tell me honestly, though, of all the servants in your household, which is the one whom you regard as your best one, your most trustworthy, the one you are fondest of?'

'What's this question all about? Don't you know who it is? I don't have and never have had a man I liked and trusted as much as I like and trust Anichino. But why do you ask?'

Hearing that Egano was awake and that they were talking about him, Anichino made several attempts to withdraw his hand and make off, for he had a strong apprehension that the wife was bent on cheating him; but she kept such a grip on his hand, he was unable to get away. She replied to Egano, saying: 'I'll tell you. I believed he was as you say, and that he is more loyal to you than any of the others. But he has opened my eyes: when you went hawking earlier today he stayed behind and chose a good moment to ask me, quite unblushingly, to grant him my favours. I wanted to avoid the need to convince you with a whole variety of evidence but to enable you to see and touch for yourself, so I told him I was perfectly willing and tonight after midnight I'd go out into the garden and wait for him by the pine-tree. Of course I'm not proposing to go; but if you want to acquaint yourself with the loyalty of this servant of yours, that's easy: put on one of my long cloaks, throw a veil over your head, and go down and wait to see if he turns up—I'm sure he will.'

'Well, of course I must see', said Egano. He got up and groped in the dark to put on a cloak of his wife's and a veil, then out he went into the garden to await Anichino by the pine.

The moment she heard him up and out of the room, Beatrice got out of bed and went to lock the door. Never had Anichino been so terrified in all his life; he'd been straining to pull free of the lady's grip as he called down a million curses on her, on his passion for her, and on himself for confiding in her. But when he realized what she had done in the end, he was in utter bliss. The lady got back into bed and, at her invitation, he undressed and they devoted themselves to their mutual pleasure and enjoyment for a good length of time. When she felt that Anichino ought not to stay any longer she bade him get up and dressed and told him: 'Listen, my honey; take a stout cudgel, go into the garden, and pretend that you'd only asked me out there to put me to the test. Give Egano a thorough dressing down, as if he were me, and give him a good hiding for me too—won't that be a lark!'

So Anichino got up and went into the garden clutching a length of white willow. As he approached the pine, Egano saw him coming and went to meet him, showing every sign of welcome—but Anichino said: 'Why you strumpet! So you've come, have you? Did you believe I really would serve my master such a turn? You make me sick to look at you!' He raised his stick and laid into him but these words and the sight of the cudgel sent Egano fleeing without a word, and Anichino dashed after him, crying: 'Be off with you, trollop! Believe me, I'll tell Egano in the morning.'

Egano made for the bedroom as fast as he could, well belaboured all over. His wife enquired whether Anichino had turned up in the garden. 'Unfortunately, yes', said Egano. 'He mistook me for you and laid about me with a stick—and the things he called me: a harlot never heard anything like it! The fact is, he certainly had surprised me when he'd said what he did say to you with a view to making a cuckold of me. But as he finds you so high-spirited and good-humoured he wanted to put you to the test.'

'Thank God he put me to the test with words and you with deeds. I think he can claim that I submitted more patiently to his speech than you to his action. Still, look at his fidelity: you must show him your appreciation.'

'You're absolutely right.'

From all of this Egano concluded that he had the most faithful wife and the most loyal servant a gentleman could wish for. And, while both he and his wife were constantly laughing with Anichino over this incident, Anichino and she had ample opportunity (which they might not otherwise have had) to procure their mutual pleasure and gratification for all the time Anichino chose to remain with Egano at Bologna.

VII. 8. *When Sismonda is caught with her lover by her husband, her quick-wittedness saves the situation, leaving a bruised but contented maidservant and a crestfallen, bewildered spouse.*

It was generally agreed that Beatrice had hit upon a quite original ploy to dupe her husband, and they all said that Anichino must indeed have been scared witless as the lady kept a tight hold on him while she confessed in his hearing that he had made advances to her. However, when the king saw that Philomena had finished, he looked at Neiphile and said: 'It's your turn.' A smile flitted across her face, then she began:

I feel quite daunted, my fair ones, at having to come up with a story that meets your satisfaction, as the ladies who have spoken before me have done. However, with God's help I trust I'll acquit myself perfectly well.

You have to know that there was once in our city a merchant of enormous wealth, called Arriguccio Berlinghieri, who had the absurd notion of stepping up in the world by marrying above his station*—even today it's a thing merchants are always doing. He made a wholly unsuitable match with a young gentlewoman called Sismonda. He was constantly out and about, though, as merchants tend to be, and spent very little time in her company, so she took up with a youth called Ruberto who had been courting her for ages. They became lovers, therefore, but once they had got carried away by their mutual passion they stopped taking simple precautions, and Arriguccio turned into the most jealous man in the world—possibly he had got wind of their affair, or something else had happened. So he stopped dashing off hither and yon and pursuing his business ventures, to devote himself almost entirely to keeping a close watch on her; he would never go to sleep until he had seen her getting into bed. Sismonda was quite heart-broken now that she could find no way to be with her Ruberto. She racked her brain to think of some way to meet him, while he kept on pressing her, and eventually she devised a plan: as her room overlooked the street, and as she had frequently noticed that Arriguccio took a long time getting to sleep but, once asleep, he slept like a log, she thought she might arrange for Ruberto to be at the front door at midnight and she would let him in and spend some time with him while her husband was sound asleep. Now to ensure that she would realize when he had come, but without letting anyone else notice, her plan was to drop a length of string out of her bedroom window so that one end would almost reach the ground while the other end she would lay along the floor and up into her bed, under the bedclothes. Then, when she was in bed, she would tie her end of the string to her big toe. She sent word to Ruberto to say that when he came he was to tug on the string; and if her husband was asleep she would let go her end, and come down and let him in; but if he was still awake, she would hang on to the string and draw it up, and then he was not to wait. This appealed to Ruberto and he paid frequent visits to her house, sometimes being admitted, other times not.

They carried on with this contrivance until eventually one night, while Sismonda was asleep, Arriguccio stretched out his foot in bed and came upon the string; so he took it in his hand and noticed that it was secured to his wife's toe. 'Something fishy going on here', said he to himself, an opinion only confirmed when he saw that the string led out of the window. He quietly cut the string from his wife's toe and tied it on to his own, then lay down, alert to see what would happen next. He had not long to wait before Ruberto arrived and gave the string a tug as usual, which Arriguccio felt; and as he had neglected to secure the string tightly to his toe, one vigorous tug of Ruberto's had pulled the string free in his hand, from which he concluded that he was to wait, which he duly did. Arriguccio leapt out of bed, seized his weapons, and ran to the front door to see who the fellow was and do him some injury. Now Arriguccio might have been a merchant, but he was a brawny, pugnacious man for all that; he got to the door and the way he opened it was not the gentle way his wife did; Ruberto noticed this as he waited outside and realized how matters stood—that the person opening the door was Arriguccio. So he was off like an arrow, with Arriguccio in hot pursuit. Ruberto had run a long way with the other hard on his heels when eventually he drew his sword, for he too was armed, and turned, and a battle of thrust and parry ensued.

As Arriguccio opened the bedroom door, Sismonda woke up, noticed that the string had been cut from her toe, and realized that her ruse had been discovered. She heard Arriguccio running after Ruberto and could see what was likely to happen, so she leapt out of bed and called her maid, who was in her confidence. By dint of much wheedling, Sismonda persuaded her to take her own place in bed and avoid giving herself away but put up with the smacks she would receive from Arriguccio: 'I'll make it up to you so well', she said, 'you'll have absolutely no cause for complaint.' She doused the bedroom lamp, left the room, and hid elsewhere in the house to await events. As Arriguccio and Ruberto were fighting, the neighbours heard the noise and got up and took to cursing them both, whereupon

Arriguccio, who didn't want to be recognized, broke away and made for home, albeit seething with rage and frustration, for he had been unable to discover the youth's identity or even leave a mark on him.

He entered the bedroom and: 'Where are you, you trollop?' he shouted. 'You've put out the light so I won't find you, have you? Much good will it do you!' And he went up to the bed and seized the maid, mistaking her for his wife, and laid into her for all he was worth with his fists and feet, giving her so many smacks and kicks that he beat her face to a pulp. He concluded by cutting her hair off, lambasting her all the while with insults of the kind heaped upon fallen women. The maid was crying her heart out, and not without reason. But although she occasionally shouted 'Oh please! Oh please!' or 'No more!', her voice was so choked with sobs and Arriguccio was so beside himself with rage that he was unable to tell that the voice belonged to another woman and not to his wife. So after he had beaten the living daylights out of her and cut off her hair, as we have said, he told her: 'You slut, that's all I'm going to do to you; but I'm off to fetch your brothers and tell them what a model of virtue you are. Then let them come along and take you away and deal with you as their honour dictates. One thing is certain: you'll not stay another moment in *this* house.' This said, he left the room, locking the door behind him, and went off by himself.

None of this had escaped Sismonda's ears and as soon as she heard her husband leave she unlocked the bedroom door, relit the lamp, and found her maid all battered, bruised, and howling. She consoled her as best she could, brought her back to her own room, and had her discreetly given every attention and comfort. Moreover, she repaid her so handsomely out of Arriguccio's money that she expressed herself contented. After leaving her maid back in her room, she straight away remade her bed and left it all smooth and tidy, as if no one had slept in it that night; with the lamp lit she dressed again and set herself to rights just as though she had not yet gone to bed. Then she lit another lamp, took her clothes, sat herself down at the top of the stairs, and settled in to some sewing as she waited to see how things would turn out.

Arriguccio left his house and went as fast as he could to his wife's brothers', where he hammered on the door till he was heard and admitted. Sismonda's brothers, who were there in number, and their mother all got up when they heard it was Arriguccio; they had lamps lit and came to ask him what he was doing out at that hour all on his own. He told them the whole story, from the string he had found tied to Sismonda's toe right up to his most recent actions and discoveries. As proof positive of what he had done he handed them the hair he had (so he believed) cut off his wife's head. They were, he added, to come and fetch her and do with her as they saw fit and consistent with their honour. He for his part had no intention of having her in his house ever again. Sismonda's brothers readily believed his report and were most incensed; they had torches lit and set out with Arriguccio for his house, quite furious with Sismonda and fully prepared to give her a rough passage. Their mother set out after them when she saw this, and with tears in her eyes begged them, first the one then the next, not to be so ready to believe the report when they had neither seen nor ascertained anything for themselves; the girl's husband could perfectly well have lost his temper with her for some other reason and laid into her, and might now be fastening this on her simply to clear himself. She was not a little surprised, she added, if this had taken place, for she knew her daughter well, having raised her from the cradle—and so on and so forth.

So they arrived at Arriguccio's, went in, and started up the stairs. When Sismonda heard them she asked: 'Who's there?'

'That you'll discover soon enough, you trollop', said her brothers.

'What on earth are you talking about? Heaven help us!' she replied as she stood up. 'Welcome, my brothers. What brings the three of you here at this time of night?'

After seeing her sitting there sewing, her face quite unmarked by any sign of blows—whereas Arriguccio had told them he'd beaten her black and blue—they were from the outset a little perplexed and held their wrath in check. They asked her to account for the complaints Arriguccio had laid against her, and told her she had better come clean or else . . .

'I don't know what I am supposed to tell you', replied Sismonda, 'or what Arriguccio is supposed to have complained about in my regard.'

Arriguccio looked at her and gaped like an idiot: he remembered having punched her and scratched her all over her face and made mincemeat of her—and here she was looking as if none of this had happened. Her brothers told her in a nutshell what Arriguccio had told them about the string and the thrashing and everything else.

She turned to her husband and said: 'Well my goodness, husband, what's all this I hear? Why are you making me out to be a fallen woman, to your own shame, when I am not? Why are you representing yourself for a cruel and spiteful man when you're not? When were you out of the house tonight, indeed when were you not in my company? When did you beat me? I can't say I remember any of it!'

'What, you slut!' Arriguccio burst out. 'Did we not go to bed together tonight? Did I not pursue your lover and then come back? Didn't I lay into you with my fists and cut your hair off?'

'You've not been to bed in *this* house tonight, but let's say no more of that as I can call on no witness but the truth of my own words. Let's come to what you're saying, that you beat me and cut off my hair. You certainly never beat me, and everyone here present, you included, can see for yourselves if there's any sign in me anywhere of having received a pummelling. Take my advice and don't you dare lay a finger on me or else by God, I'll make some changes to your anatomy! As for my hair, you never cut it off so far as I am aware—unless of course you did so and I failed to notice: come, let's take a look and see if I've been cropped.' She raised her veil from her head and showed that she had a full head of hair.

Having listened to and observed all of this, Sismonda's mother and brothers turned on Arriguccio: 'Now explain yourself, Arriguccio. This is all a long way from what you came to us claiming to have done—as for the rest of it, God knows how you're going to prove it.'

Arriguccio stood there in a stupor. He wanted to speak up but, as clearly the very thing he'd been confident of demonstrating was not so, he dared not say a word.

Sismonda now addressed her brothers. 'I see what he's after: he wants me to do what I've always refused to do up till now—speak to you about his pettiness and his nasty habits. All right, I will. I do honestly believe that he did do and did experience everything he's said he's done, and here's how: this excellent fellow, on whom you bestowed me in an unlucky moment, calls himself a merchant. He would like to be thought of as more temperate than a monk and more modest than a virgin, and so he ought to be. But there's scarcely an evening when he's not out at some tavern getting drunk, and consorting with some prostitute or other. As for me, he keeps me waiting up for him, as you have seen me, till midnight or sometimes even till daybreak. It's plain to me that when he was the worse for liquor he took one of his harlots to bed and woke up to find her with the string tied to her foot and performed all those splendid feats he's told you about, and ended up by going back and laying into her and cutting off her hair. And while he was still more or less in his cups he convinced himself that he had done it all to me—I do believe he's still under that impression. Take a good look at him: he's half tipsy even now. Anyway, he can say what he likes, you're not to give him any more credit than you would to a drunkard. I forgive him; you do so too.'

These words left her mother seething. 'By heaven, daughter', she cried, 'that's the last thing to do! He ought to be put down, the insufferable, vulgar brute. What ever made *him* deserve a proper young lady of your sort? Well, upon my word! Even if he'd picked you up out of the gutter he'd have no business treating you the way he has. May he rot in hell before you have to put up with verbal abuse from any paltry yokel of a tradesman who's been turned loose from some rabble militia. His type comes in prickly serge, with breeches no respectable man would be seen dead in, and wears his pen stuck in his backside. Give him three pennies to rub together and nothing less than a gentleman's daughter will do for *him*—he'll run up some coat-of-arms or other and say, "*I*'m the McTavish of that ilk", and go on about his ancestors. Would to God my sons had taken my advice: they might have made a Countess Guidi* out of you with only a farthing's dowry but they had to go and settle you on this priceless booby, a fellow who doesn't scruple to come out in the middle of the night and call you a slut, as if *I* didn't know you're the best girl in Florence and the most chaste. Mark my word, if you'd all paid attention to me, the man would get such a hiding he'd be smarting for a month.' She turned to her sons and added: 'I told you this should never have been allowed to happen. Didn't you hear the way your sister's been treated by this valiant brother-in-law of yours, scruffy little tradesman that he is? Now that he's said what he has about her and treated her the way he has, if I were in your shoes I shouldn't know a moment's peace till I'd got rid of him once and for all, and if I were a man instead of the woman I am, I wouldn't let anyone else see to it but me. Why, the shameless old soak, the devil take him!'

The young men took note of all this and turned on Arriguccio and called him every name under the sun. In conclusion they said: 'We'll let you off this time as you're under the influence . . . but if you value your life, take care we don't have any more of this ever again, for if we do hear any more of it, we shall most assuredly pay you out and collect the arrears.' This said, they left.

Arriguccio was left utterly dazed and quite unable to say whether what he had done had actually happened or had only been a dream. He left his wife in peace and did not say another word, and she, thanks to her presence of mind, not only avoided imminent disaster, but opened the way to giving herself a good time for the future, and her husband no longer caused her a moment's anxiety.

VII. 9. *To persuade a young man to become her lover, Lydia imposes on her elderly husband Nicostratos in a number of ways, the last of which leaves him wondering if he's seeing things.*

The ladies had so much enjoyed Neiphile's story that they could not stop laughing or chattering on about it, however much the king told them to be quiet. After he had bidden

Pamphilo to start his, though, they eventually fell silent, so Pamphilo began:

It's my belief that anyone who is passionately in love will be prepared to go to any lengths, no matter how serious the risks involved. And though this has been attested in a good number of stories, I think I can demonstrate it all the more clearly with one that I propose telling you, about a woman whose enterprise was attended by sheer good luck rather than by sensible conduct. I would not, therefore, advise any of you ladies to risk following in the footsteps of the woman I'm going to tell you about: luck is not something you can always count upon, nor are all men equally gullible.

In Argos, a very ancient Greek city of no great size but highly renowned for its kings of old, there lived once upon a time a nobleman called Nicostratos. On the threshold of old age Fortune allotted him a considerable lady for wife; she was as spirited as she was beautiful, and her name was Lydia.* Being a man of rank and wealth, he kept a large household, as well as hawks and hounds aplenty, and he took great delight in hunting. One of his servants was a graceful youth called Pyrrhus; he was well built and handsome, and could turn his hand to just about anything. He was Nicostratos's favourite, and he trusted him best of all. Now Lydia fell madly in love with him—couldn't focus her mind on anything else, night or day—but Pyrrhus showed not a flicker of interest in her love, either because he never noticed, or because he simply would not be drawn; this grieved the lady quite intolerably.

Determined that he should be acquainted with her sentiments, she sent for her maid Lusca, who was entirely in her confidence. 'Lusca', she said, 'the favours you have received from me should assure me of your obedience and fidelity. So take care that what I'm about to tell you comes to the ears of the person I intend and to nobody else's. I'm a girl, as you see, in the first bloom of youth, and I'm well endowed with everything a woman could wish for; in short, I really can't complain, except on one score: my husband's so well on in years, compared to my own, that I get little joy from him in the one thing that girls like best of all. It's something I want as much as any other woman, and I decided a good while ago that if Fate was unkind enough to saddle me with such an elderly husband, I at any rate would be kinder to myself and find a way to satisfy my desire and sustain my health. To enjoy the same advantages on this score as on all the others, I've decided that our Pyrrhus is to stand in for my husband with his embraces, for he seems to me the best suited of any to the role. I've devoted so much love to him that the only times I feel really myself are when I'm seeing him or he's in my thoughts. I'm absolutely sure I'm going to die if I don't get together with him at once, so, if you value my life, acquaint him with my love in whatever way you think best, and entreat him from me to come and join me the moment you go to fetch him.'

The maid readily consented and, drawing Pyrrhus aside at the first opportunity, pleaded her mistress's cause to the best of her ability. Pyrrhus was astonished at her words, for he'd been quite unaware of anything of the sort; he suspected that the lady had sent the message simply to test him out. So he promptly gave her a sharp retort. 'Lusca', he said, 'I can't believe my mistress sent you to tell me this, so just mind what you're saying. If this really is a message from her, I don't believe she was being serious. If she *is* being serious, my master treats me far better than I deserve, and I wouldn't serve him such a turn to save my life. So just take care I don't hear any more of such stuff out of you.'

This austere response left Lusca undismayed. 'Pyrrhus', she said, 'I'll speak to you about this or about anything else my mistress bids me as often as she tells me to, I don't care whether you like it or not. What an ass you are!'

Somewhat disgusted with Pyrrhus's remarks, Lusca returned to her mistress, who was ready to die when she was told of them. A few days later she had another word with her maid: 'The oak doesn't fall to the first axe-stroke, as you know. So it seems to me you should go back to the fellow, as he's discovered in himself this bizarre sense of loyalty at my expense; choose your moment and tell him fairly and squarely of my passion; do your utmost to bring him round. If we get no further than this, I should die of it and he'd think he'd been put to the test—so instead of securing his love we'd simply unleash his hatred.'

The maid told her mistress to take heart, then went off in search of Pyrrhus; she found him in a good mood and told him: 'A few days ago I mentioned to you how passionately in love with you is your mistress and mine. Now let me put it to you again: if you're going to remain as hard-hearted as you seemed to be the other day, you can be sure of one thing—she'll not survive it. So do please give her the consolation she's set her heart on—if you simply refuse to relent, then it'll be clear to me that you're a prize oaf, whereas I'd always thought you were rather brainy. Imagine being loved to distraction by such a lady—a beautiful lady of gentle birth, rich as she is—what a feather in your cap! Added to that, imagine how you should thank your lucky stars that she's offering you such a perfect answer to a young man's desires, such a refuge to meet your needs. Name me one of your peers who'll be in for a better time than you will, if you do the sensible thing. If you're ready to give her your love, tell me who else you know who'll be as well off as you'll be for weapons and horses, clothing and money in your pocket. Wake up, then, listen to what I'm telling you! And don't forget that Luck is a lady who comes your way only once in a cheerful, open-handed mood; the fellow who can't give her a welcome at such a moment will have only himself to blame, and not her, if he falls on hard times. Another thing: you don't expect the same fairness in dealings between servants and masters as between friends and equals. On the contrary, servants should repay their masters in the same coinage with which they're paid themselves, whenever possible. If you had a pretty wife or mother or daughter or sister who caught Nicostratos's fancy, do you expect he'd treat you with the same honesty you're inclined to treat him with in regard to his wife? You'd be an idiot to believe that. Mark my words, if he couldn't get his way with wheedling and blandishments, he'd use force, never mind what *you* thought about it. So let's treat them and theirs the way they treat us and ours. Take advantage of Lady Luck, then, don't drive her away, go out to meet her, give her a welcome: if you don't, make no mistake about it, your mistress will definitely die, but worse than that, you'll regret it so often you'll wish you were dead yourself.'

Pyrrhus had given a good deal of thought to what Lusca had earlier said to him, and decided that, if she did return to the question, his answer would be different and he would fall in completely with the lady's wishes provided he could be satisfied that she was not simply putting temptation in his way. So, 'Look', he replied, 'I realize how right you are in all you say; nevertheless I know my master for a very canny and shrewd man and the more I think of it the more I shouldn't be surprised if Lydia hasn't set this up on his advice and instigation to test me out. So if she's ready to do three things I'll ask of her in order to set my mind at rest, she can count on me to do with alacrity anything she bids me to. Now here are the three things: first, she's to kill Nicostratos's pet sparrow-hawk in front of his eyes; next, she's to send me a tuft of Nicostratos's beard; lastly, she's to send me one of his best teeth.'

These tasks struck Lusca as very awkward; they struck Lydia as too awkward for words. Still, Love, a great morale-booster and a great schemer, keyed her up to do these things, and she sent her maid to tell him that she would fulfil his requirements without delay. What is more, she added, as he had such a high opinion of Nicostratos's intelligence, she would make love with Pyrrhus in front of her husband's very eyes and then persuade him that it was all a figment. Pyrrhus, therefore, waited for her to act. A few days later, Nicostratos gave an important dinner, as he often did, for a number of gentlemen. When they left the table, Lydia came out of her room, dressed in green velvet brocade and lavishly bejewelled; she entered the room in which they all were and, in full view of Pyrrhus and the assembled company, she went up to the perch on which sat Nicostratos's favourite hawk, released it as though she was going to transfer it to her wrist, took it by the jesses secured to its legs, and smashed it against the wall, killing it.

'Heavens, wife, look what you've done!' cried Nicostratos. She made him no reply but turned to his guests and said: 'Gentlemen, what sort of revenge would I take on a king who insulted me if I didn't dare avenge myself on a hawk? This bird, let me tell you, has for ages been depriving me of all the time a man should be devoting to a woman's pleasure. The moment the sun is up, Nicostratos is up too, mounts horse, and is off to the open country with his hawk on his wrist to watch it fly. And I'm left alone, fuming in bed, as you see me now. So I've frequently wanted to do what I've just done, and the only thing that's stopped me has been that I've preferred to wait and do it in the presence of men who might be fair judges of my cause, as I believe you will be.'

As the gentlemen listened to her, they accepted that she had given a true account of her feelings in regard to Nicostratos; so they turned to the angry husband and banteringly remarked to him: 'Well, hasn't your wife done the right thing in taking her revenge on the hawk: its death makes up for the hurt she has suffered!' And after Lydia had returned to her room they embroidered the joke for a while, until the nettled victim found himself laughing too.

Seeing this, Pyrrhus mused: 'Here's a fine start she's made to my happiness in love. God grant she so continue!'

Now a few days after killing the hawk, Lydia was in her bedroom with Nicostratos having a kiss and a cuddle; they became rather frolicsome and he playfully gave her hair a little tug, which gave her the occasion to carry out Pyrrhus's second request. She quickly grasped a small tuft of his beard and beamed at him as she gave it a terrific jerk that quite pulled it off his chin. This made her husband cross, but she remarked: 'Oh don't be an old fusspot, just because I pulled a couple of hairs out of your beard! You didn't feel what I did when you tugged my hair just now!' So they continued with their teasing and love-play, while Lydia carefully held on to the tuft of beard she'd pulled out, and sent it that very day to her beloved.

The third thing took greater thought, but Lydia was nothing if not resourceful, and Love made her all the more so. She therefore hit upon a way to bring it off. There were two boys who had been entrusted to Nicostratos by their fathers in order to pick up the rudiments of courtly behaviour in his household, for they were of good family. At meals one of them had the task of carving Nicostratos's meat, while the other served him his drink. Lydia sent for them both and apprised them of the fact that they had bad breath; when they served Nicostratos, she told them, they were to hold their heads as far back as possible, and never mention the subject to anyone. The boys took her word for it and acted in accordance with her instructions. So she once asked Nicostratos: 'Have you noticed what those boys are doing when they wait on you at table?'

'Indeed I have; in fact I was on the point of asking them why they're behaving this way.'

'Well, don't. I can tell you why. I've kept it to myself awhile, not wanting to offend you but, now I see that others have noticed, I can't conceal it from you any longer. The reason for it is that your breath stinks—I don't know why, for it never used to. It's a nasty thing, as you move in genteel circles, so it would be a good idea to see how it might be cured.'

'Now what could it be?' asked Nicostratos. 'I wonder if I have a decayed tooth in my mouth.'

'Maybe', said Lydia, who led him to a window, made him open his mouth, and peered into it, first one side then the other. 'O Nicostratos!' she cried. 'How have you been able to stand it? You've got one on this side that, so far as I can see, is worse than decayed, it's rotten to the core. If you keep it much longer, I'm sure it'll corrupt the teeth next to it. My advice to you is to have it out, before matters go any further.'

'If that's how it looks to you, you have my consent. Let's send for a physician without wasting a minute and have the thing drawn.'

'Fetch a doctor? God forbid! The way it looks, I can extract it for you perfectly well—no need for a doctor. Besides, those people set about these things so ruthlessly, I couldn't bear to see, or hear you, in anyone else's hands. So I want to do it myself, absolutely; that way, if you find it too painful, I'll leave off at once, which is more than your physician would do.'

So, after fetching in the requisite implements, she sent everyone out of the room, keeping only Lusca. They locked the door, laid Nicostratos out on a table, put the forceps into his mouth, and grasped a tooth, then, scream though he might for the pain, one of them held him while the other wrenched the tooth out by main force. Keeping this tooth aside, they took another hideously decayed one that Lydia had been clutching in her hand, and they showed it to him, aching and more dead than alive as he was. 'Look', they said, 'what you've had in your mouth all this time!' He believed it and, however fierce a pain he had suffered, which caused him no little grief, still, now that the tooth was extracted he felt he was cured. They cheered him up in one way and another, and when the pain had died down he left the room. Lydia took the tooth and sent it straight off to her beloved who, convinced now of her love, announced that he was at her entire disposal.

Now, although Lydia felt that every hour separating her from Pyrrhus was like a year, she was none the less anxious to convince him even more and to make good the promise she had given him. So she feigned illness and after lunch one day Nicostratos paid her a visit. She noticed that there was no one with him but Pyrrhus, and asked them to help her out into the garden to alleviate her condition. So Nicostratos supported her on one side and Pyrrhus on the other, and they brought her into the garden and sat her down on the grass under a fine pear-tree. After they'd been sitting here awhile, Lydia, who had already concerted the plan with Pyrrhus, remarked: 'Pyrrhus, I have a craving for some of those pears. Do climb up and throw a few down.'

Pyrrhus climbed quickly into the tree and started throwing pears down. As he threw them he burst out: 'Goodness, sir, what *are* you up to? Why madam, aren't you ashamed to submit to this in my presence? D'you think I'm blind? You were so ill a moment ago—how come you've got well so quickly you can get up to this sort of thing? If you have to, don't you have enough perfectly good bedrooms to do it in? Why don't you go and do it in one of them? It would be more proper than doing it here in front of me!'

Lydia turned to her husband and said: 'What's Pyrrhus talking about? Has he lost his marbles?'

'No, madam', said Pyrrhus. 'I've not lost my marbles. D'you think I can't see you?'

Nicostratos was totally perplexed. 'Pyrrhus', he said, 'I do believe you're dreaming.'

'No, sir. I'm not dreaming at all. And neither are you, far from it, you're shaking it up so well, if this tree jerked half as much there wouldn't be a pear left on it.'

'Now what can this mean?' said Lydia. 'Can he really be seeing what he's claiming to see? If I were in my normal state of health, God knows, I'd be up that tree to see with my own eyes these wonders he says he can see.'

Up in the tree, however, Pyrrhus kept insisting on what he was seeing, until Nicostratos told him to come down, which he did. 'Now tell me', he said, 'what can you see?'

'I believe you must take me for a dolt and a dreamer: if you want the honest truth, I saw you mounted on your lady. Then, as I climbed down, I saw you get off her and sit down where you are now.'

'A dolt you certainly were', said Nicostratos. 'The whole time you were up in the tree we never moved from where you now see us sitting.'

'Well, let's not argue about it', said Pyrrhus. 'I saw you. And what's more, I saw you mounted.'

Nicostratos, finding this ever more mystifying, eventually said: 'Very well. I'm going to see if this pear-tree is enchanted. Let's find out what marvels are to be seen by people who climb into it.' And up he went. Once he was installed, Lydia and Pyrrhus set about making love, and Nicostratos shouted: 'Hey, you strumpet, what are you doing? And you Pyrrhus—I'd never have thought it of you!' As he spoke, he made his way down from the tree.

'Let's sit down', said Lydia and Pyrrhus, and as they saw him climb down from the tree they resumed the positions in which he had left them. When he was back on the ground and saw them as he had left them he rounded on them.

But Pyrrhus said: 'Now truly I confess, Nicostratos, that when I was up in the pear-tree my eyes deceived me, as you have just said. And I recognize this by one token if by no other: it's obvious to me that your eyes have deceived you. You need no other proof of the truth of what I'm saying, beyond considering whether your wife, who is a thoroughly sensible woman and the soul of virtue, would go out of her way to flout you thus—if she were so minded—before your very eyes. I'll say nothing on my own account: I'd sooner see myself cut into quarters than even entertain the thought of such a thing, let alone do it in your presence. So there's no doubt about it: the pear-tree must be responsible for bewitching us into seeing what isn't there. After all, nothing in the world would have persuaded me that you had not been making love with your wife, not, anyway, until I heard you say you thought I was doing something that assuredly never entered my head, far from actually doing it.'

After which Lydia stood up and in a pretence of indignation cried out: 'Well, the devil take you if you think I'd ever be so silly as to indulge in these filthy practices you say you've seen me do—assuming I even wanted to—right in front of your eyes! Mark my words, if I ever had a mind to do such a thing I'd not come out here; I'd do it in one of our bedrooms, of course, and I'd see to it that you never found out.'

What they both said seemed true enough to Nicostratos: they'd never permit themselves to do such a thing here in front of him. So he reproached them no further and dropped the subject, turning instead to the puzzling fact of the trick played on the eyes of anyone climbing into that tree.

His wife, however, continued to feign anger over the attitude he had taken towards her and said: 'Well really though! This pear-tree shan't play such a shabby trick on me or on any other woman ever again, not if I can help it! Run and fetch an axe, Pyrrhus, and vindicate yourself and me by chopping it down—though it would be far better to apply it to Nicostratos's head, as he was so thoughtless in the way he let his eyes get the better of his judgement. I mean, however much things looked the way you say they did to the eyes in your head, you had absolutely no business jumping to conclusions on the strength of their testimony.'

Pyrrhus hastened to fetch the axe and chopped down the tree. When she saw it fallen she turned to Nicostratos and said: 'Now that I see the enemy of my virtue laid low, my anger is gone', and she obligingly forgave her husband, who craved her pardon, and told him never again to suspect her of such a thing, for she loved him more than her own self.

So the poor dupe of a husband returned indoors with his wife and her lover; and many a time thereafter Pyrrhus and Lydia took their mutual pleasure at their greater leisure. God grant as much to us.

VII. 10. *Tingoccio makes love within a prohibited degree of kinship and dies a sudden death. He returns to visit his friend Meuccio and reports on how he has fared in the next world.*

Only the king was left to tell a tale and, once he saw that the ladies had quietened down—for they had been lamenting over the pear-tree that had fallen to the axe though it was quite blameless—he began:

It goes without saying that a just sovereign ought to be the first to obey his own laws; if he acts otherwise, he is to be considered not a king but a slave who deserves punishment. And I, who am your king, I'm virtually obliged to incur this fault, and this censure. It is true that yesterday I laid down the rules governing today's narration, and it had been my intention to deny myself the exercise of my privilege today and to join you in submitting to my law and speak on the theme on which you all have spoken. But not only has the story been told that I had been expecting to tell you, but also you have come out with so many stories and so much lovelier that I, for my part, cannot think of anything, however much I search my memory, that relates to our topic and could stand comparison with the stories already told. So, as I am going to infringe my own law, I am fully prepared here and now to submit myself to whatever penalty is required of me by way of a suitable punishment—and I shall revert to my usual privilege. Now Elissa's story about the pair who were related as godparents* and about the imbecility of the Sienese made such an impression on me that I shan't pursue the pranks played by clever wives on brainless husbands, for I'm tempted to tell you a little tale about the Sienese; it does contain some things that stretch belief, but even so it will on the whole amuse you, dearest ladies.

Well, in Siena there once lived two young plebeians; one of them was called Tingoccio Mini, the other, Meuccio di Tura, and they lived at Porta Salaria. They were scarcely ever apart and were, to all appearances, devoted to each other. As they went to church and listened to sermons, the way people tend to do, they had frequently heard accounts of the glory or tribulation accorded in the next world to the souls of the departed, in keeping with their deserts. Anxious as they were for more definite information on the matter, but finding no way to come by it, they promised each other that whichever of them was the first to die would return to the survivor, if he could, and answer whatever questions he asked. They shook hands on this.

Having made this pact, and continuing, as we have said, to keep each other's company, Tingoccio happened to become godfather to a son born to Ambrogio Anselmini (who lived over in Camporeggi) by his wife Mita. Now Tingoccio would sometimes pay calls with Meuccio on Mita, a very pretty and attractive woman and, in spite of the prohibited degree of kindred now that he was godfather to her child, he fell in love with her. Meuccio was also attracted by her—and besides, Tingoccio was constantly singing her praises to him—and he fell in love with her likewise. Where this love of theirs was concerned, however, each was guarded with the other, but not for the same reason: Tingoccio kept it to himself because, conscious of how sinful it was to be courting his godson's mother, he would have been ashamed to be found out. This is not why Meuccio kept it to himself, but because it had not escaped his notice that Tingoccio had his eye on her, and he took the view that if he let his friend into his secret, he'd only stir up jealousy. 'As Tingoccio, given their kinship, can talk to her whenever he feels like it', he brooded, 'he'll do all he can to turn her against me, so I'll never get anywhere with her.'

So the young men were both in love, as we have said, and Tingoccio, who was the better placed to press his suit, achieved so much success by what he said and did that he had his way with her. Meuccio was aware of this and it made him quite sick at heart; but as he still entertained the hope of eventually obtaining her favours too, he pretended not to have noticed, his object being to avoid giving Tingoccio any excuse to put a spoke in his wheel.

The two friends pursued their amour, then, the one more prosperously than the other. Tingoccio, however, had discovered in his kinswoman such fertile soil that he could not have enough of turning it over with his spade; the result of so much effort was to prostrate him with an infirmity which, in a matter of days, so undermined his health that he succumbed and died. Three days later* he appeared by night in Meuccio's room as he had promised—maybe he'd not been able to get there any sooner—and called out to his friend, who was fast asleep.

Meuccio woke up and asked: 'Who are you?'

'I'm Tingoccio. I promised I'd come back and tell you all about the next world.'

Meuccio was somewhat alarmed to see him, but composed himself enough to bid him welcome and enquire whether he was lost.

'Lost? Lost is what's never found again! What in heaven would I be doing here if I was lost?'

'That's not what I meant', replied Meuccio. 'What I was asking was whether you're one of the damned souls in the penal fires of hell.'

'I wouldn't put it that way, though I'm getting a fair old grilling for my sins, that's for sure.'

Meuccio questioned him particularly about the various punishments allotted in respect of each sin committed here below, and Tingoccio gave him the full list. Then Meuccio asked him if there was anything he could do for him here, and Tingoccio told him there was: he could have Masses and prayers said for him and alms given on his behalf, for this sort of thing was a great help to those who'd passed on. Meuccio said he would be glad to.

As Tingoccio was leaving, Meuccio remembered his friend's kinswoman; he looked up a little and asked: 'Oh, something I forgot: that woman you were sleeping with, the mother of your godson—what's your punishment for *that*?'

'When I got there, brother, there was this person who seemed to have learnt all my sins by heart. He told me to go to the place where I'm purging my sins very painfully. There I came across a great many friends who were condemned to the same punishment that I was. So I was put in with them and, as I thought back on what I'd been doing with my kinswoman, I expected to get a far worse punishment even than the one I'd been given—and there I was already in a great big fire, a real scorcher—and I trembled like a leaf. So the fellow next to me asked: "What have you got the rest of us haven't? You're quaking in the fire." "The thing is, my friend", I told him, "I'm dead scared of the judgement I'm expecting for a terrible sin I committed." He asked me what sin that was and I told him: "It was a bad, bad one: I was sleeping with my godson's mother. I ploughed her up so well I ploughed myself into the ground." At that he simply elbowed me in the ribs and said: "Get along with you, you ninny! Don't worry: godparents count for less than nothing round here!" Was I relieved to hear it!' Dawn was approaching so he just added: 'Goodbye, Meuccio, I can't stay any longer.' The next moment he was gone.

When he heard that godsons' mothers had no special status in the next life, Meuccio could have hit himself, for he had given all too many of them a wide berth. Anyway, now that he was set right on this point, he conducted himself with greater gumption thereafter where this was concerned. And had Brother Rinaldo known about it, he wouldn't have needed to go splitting hairs when he talked *his* godson's mother into submission.

Zephyr, the West Wind, got up as the afternoon drew to a close and the king removed his crown—for, his tale being ended, none remained to be told—and placed it on Lauretta's head. 'Here, Lauretta', said he, proferring her the laurel, 'I am crowning you with your namesake, queen of our company. It is now up to you as our mistress to command whatever you deem to be conducive to our pleasure and solace.' He resumed his seat.

Raised to the throne, Lauretta summoned the major-domo and instructed him to serve dinner here in the pleasant valley a little earlier than usual so that they might return to the villa at their leisure. She also gave him the rest of his instructions for the duration of her reign. Then she turned to the company and said: 'Yesterday Dioneo gave us for today's topic the tricks women play on their husbands; and I suppose I might set you tomorrow to telling stories of the tricks husbands play on their wives, except that I've no wish to appear catty and vindictive. So what you're each to think of instead is a story about the tricks men play on women day in day out, and women on men, and that people play on each other; I think we'll derive as much fun from this as we have enjoyed today.' This said, she stood up and dismissed them until supper-time.

So they all stood up, lads and lasses alike, and some of them went wading barefoot in the limpid water while others enjoyed a stroll across the green grass, amid the beautiful trees that grew so straight. Fiammetta and Dioneo spent a while singing a balled about Palemon and Arcites.* Entertaining themselves in these various ways, then, they thoroughly enjoyed the interval until supper was ready. The meal was served beside the pool, and they dined to the sound of a thousand singing birds, while they were refreshed by a gentle breeze coming off the surrounding hills; there was not so much as a fly to disturb them or mar their good spirits at table. As the tables were cleared they all took another turn round the valley, after which, the sun being close to setting, it was the queen's pleasure that they slowly retrace their steps to their usual night's lodging. On the way, they exchanged all manner of banter touching on the day's topic and other matters, and then reached their villa at nightfall. They restored themselves from the modest exertion of their walk with nice cool wine and little snacks, then launched straightaway into a round of dances beside the fountain, accompanied by Tindaro on his bagpipes, or by different instrumentalists. Eventually the queen called for a song from Philomena, who thus began:

Fain would I turn back to the day
Before you upped and went away!

So great the love, dear lord, so great
  The passion that consumes me,
I would to God I knew the road
That led me back to Love's abode;
My heart, ensnared, its master needs;
Show me the way, my spirit pleads,
  Before despair quite dooms me.
Preserve me for a happier fate.

I have no words that may express
  The radiance he sheds:
It haunts my eyes, my ears assails,
Upon my every sense prevails,
And lights new fires at every hour
And rings me with obsessive power
  That leaves my soul in shreds.
Come save me, Lord, in my distress.

Is it to be, are we again
  To find ourselves united?
Am I once more to kiss those eyes
Whose magic all my peace defies?
Will you return? Will it be soon
That I may hope for such a boon?
  My love must be requited.
Come, therefore, come, dispel my pain.

Now if the future keeps in store
  That I am yet to hold you,
I'll not again repeat my blunder
And let us two be torn asunder:
I'll feast, my treasure, on your lips
The way the bee a flower sips—
  Come, let my arms enfold you!
Such hope can make my spirits soar.

This song left them all convinced that Philomena was in the throes of a remarkable and delicious amour; indeed, the words of the song suggested that the affair had progressed beyond mere glances so, if they regarded her as all the happier for it, there was also more than one of them who felt a touch of envy.

When the song was ended, the queen remembered that the next day was Friday, so she observed amenably: 'Tomorrow, as you know, is the day consecrated to the Passion of Our Lord; when Neiphile was queen we observed it devoutly, if you recollect, by suspending our story-telling. And we did the same on the ensuing Saturday. Now as we wish to follow the good example given us by Neiphile, I think we'd do best to forgo our pleasant story sessions tomorrow and the day after as we did earlier, and consider instead what took place on these days for the salvation of our souls.'

Everyone approved the queen's devout words and, as the night was well advanced, she dismissed them and they all retired to their rest.

*Here ends the seventh day of the* Decameron *and the eighth day begins; under the reign of Lauretta, the stories show the tricks men play on women day in day out, and women on men, and that people play on each other.*

On Sunday morning, when the rays of the rising sun were bathing the mountain tops and, as the shadows scattered, every object found its recognizable form, the queen rose up and went out with her friends to take a turn on the dewy grass, after which they attended the divine office, a little after nine o'clock, in a small local church. On their return, they enjoyed a festive meal, sang songs, danced a little, then went—those who so wished—to take a nap by the queen's leave. But once the sun had passed the zenith they all took their seats, as the queen required, by the fountain for their accustomed story-telling, and Neiphile, at the queen's bidding, thus began:

VIII. 1. *Guasparruolo's wife consents to Gulfardo's advances on condition that he pay her in cash. He does so, but in such a way that she is left none the richer.*

If that's the way the Good Lord has arranged it, I'm perfectly happy to start the day with a tale of my own. Now, granted that a great deal has already been said about the tricks played by women on their menfolk, I'm inclined to tell you of one played by a man on a woman. It's not my concern to censure the man for what he did or to suggest that it was other than the woman deserved. On the contrary, my purpose is to commend the man and censure the woman, and to demonstrate that men too are perfectly capable of hoodwinking those who rely on their word, just as they are hoodwinked by those they trust, although if we want to call things by their proper names, what I am going to describe is not a prank so much as a just reward. The thing is, every woman has a duty to be the soul of virtue and to guard her chastity with her life; on no account ought she to allow it to be sullied. But while it is not possible to live up to this duty all the time, as we are supposed to do—for such is our frailty—I do declare that the woman who sets a price on her virtue deserves to go to the stake. The woman who is forced to sin out of love, on the other hand, recognizing as she does its overwhelming power, deserves pardon from a not-too-rigorous judge—this was demonstrated a day or two ago by Philostrato in the case of Philippa* at Prato.

Well, in Milan there once upon a time lived a German called Gulfardo, a mercenary. He was a well-built man and of scrupulous loyalty to his masters—an uncommon trait* in the Germans. And as he was so meticulous in paying back any money he borrowed, there was no shortage of merchants ready to advance him money, up to any amount, on the most reasonable terms. While he was living in Milan he conceived a passion for a great beauty called Ambrogia, the wife of a rich merchant called Guasparruolo Cagastraccio, a close friend of his. He courted her most discreetly, without attracting her husband's attention or anyone else's, and one day he sent word to her asking her to be kind enough to bestow her favours on him, for he was at her service to do her every bidding. The wife strung out the discussions but eventually arrived at the conclusion that she was ready to gratify Gulfardo on two conditions: the first, that he was never to divulge the affair to a soul, and the second, that as she needed two hundred gold florins for some purpose of her own and as he was a rich man, he was to give her this sum, whereupon she would be at his continued disposal.

Gulfardo had always reckoned her to be a pretty straightforward sort of woman, so to hear her coming out with this mercenary proposal made his blood boil—how sordid could she be! His passion turned to disgust and he conceived the notion of playing a trick on her: he sent back word to say that he would willingly do that and whatever else she wanted, if it lay in his power. She was to let him know, he added, when he was to attend upon her, and he would bring the money with him; moreover, nobody would get to hear of it, apart from a friend of his in whom he placed absolute trust, who always accompanied him on his ventures. The wife, trollop that she was, received this answer with joy and sent to him to say that her husband Guasparruolo was going to leave in a few days for Genoa on business; she would let him know and send for him then.

Choosing his moment, Gulfardo went to Guasparruolo and said to him: 'I'm on the point of needing two hundred gold florins for a venture of mine. I should like you to lend me this sum on the same terms as you have done before.' Guasparruolo readily acceded to his request and counted out the money to him there and then.

A few days later Guasparruolo left for Genoa as his wife had said, and she sent word to Gulfardo to come and bring the two hundred gold florins with him. So Gulfardo went to the woman's house, bringing his companion with him. He found her waiting for him and the first thing he did was to put the two hundred gold florins into her hands, as his friend looked on, and say to her: 'Here, take this money and give it to your husband on his return.'

As the woman took the money she did not grasp why Gulfardo had spoken as he had: she thought it must be to prevent his friend realizing that he was giving it to her as a payment. So her reply was: 'Of course I shall, but let's see how much it comes to.' She spread the money out on a table and then put it away very happily when she saw that it made two hundred florins. Then she came for Gulfardo and led him off into her bedroom and let him make free with her not only on that occasion but on many subsequent ones before her husband returned from Genoa.

Once Guasparruolo was back from Genoa, Gulfardo called on him after ensuring that his wife would also be there, and said to him in her presence: 'Those two hundred gold florins you lent me the other day, I didn't need them after all, as I couldn't bring off the business for which I borrowed them. So I brought them straight back here to your wife and handed them to her. So please write off the debt.'

Guasparruolo turned to his wife and asked her whether she had received it. As she could see the witness here present, she could not deny it but said: 'Yes I did, but till now I've forgotten to mention it to you.'

'Well, that's all right then, Gulfardo', said her husband. 'Go in peace—I'll see it credited to your account.'

After Gulfardo had left, the thwarted wife handed over to her husband the squalid price of her shameless conduct. So the canny lover took advantage of his greedy mistress at no cost to himself.

VIII. 2. *A priest seduces Belcolore, a comely young wench, on the strength of a pledged cloak. Belcolore is almost, but not quite, crafty enough to hold him to his part of the bargain.*

Everyone, lads and lasses alike, approved of what Gulfardo had done to the grasping Milanese woman. The queen then turned to Pamphilo with a smile and asked him to follow, so he began:

I feel like telling you a little tale against people who are forever besetting us without our being able to get back at them in like manner: priests. They have proclaimed a crusade against our wives, and whenever they succeed in getting on top of one of them, they imagine they've won pardon and remission for their sins just as though they had brought the sultan in chains from Alexandria to the Pope at Avignon. Now this is something we wretched layfolk can't do to them, even if we put as much zeal into avenging ourselves on the priests' mothers, sisters, girl-friends, and daughters as the priests do in assaulting our wives. So I mean to tell you a little tale of rustic lechery; it doesn't take long to tell and its ending will make you laugh; moreover, you'll be able to draw the moral, that priests are not always to be believed in every particular.

Well then, there was once a priest at Varlungo which, as you ladies know or will have been told, is a village only a step from here. He was a capable man and unflagging in his attentions to the ladies; and although his reading was not all that proficient, he did manage to edify his flock by the parish elm-tree of a Sunday with a good clutch of more or less well-chosen words. And he was better than any priest who had been there before him when it came to visiting the women in his parish while the menfolk were out of the way; he would bring them his Sunday trinkets—holy pictures and rosaries—and holy water and the odd candle-stub; he'd bring these things into their houses and impart to them his blessing.

Now among the parish womenfolk he'd taken to the soonest, his favourite was the wife of a labourer, Bentivegna del Mazzo, and her name was Belcolore. And the truth is she *was* a sturdy little body, she was your luscious, fresh-faced, olive-skinned country wench, and when it came to milling, why, she could grind your corn into flour with the best of them. What's more, there wasn't a village girl to touch her when it came to shaking a tambourine and singing the Song of the Mill-Race,* or leading the dance—the *branle*, the *farandole*—when the occasion arose, with a dainty handkerchief at her wrist. The effect of all this was that His Reverence quite lost his heart to her, indeed she sent delightful shivers up his spine, and he'd spend the entire day hanging about just to catch a glimpse of her. And if he heard her in church on a Sunday morning, he'd show off his musical skills as he entoned the Kyrie or Sanctus for all the world like a donkey braying; but if he couldn't see her there, he'd make no feature of his singing. At all events, he took care to avoid rousing Bentivegna's suspicions, or those of any of the neighbours. And, in order to win her good graces, he would make her a present from time to time: it might be a bunch of fresh garlic from his kitchen garden, for he himself grew the best garlic plants in the neighbourhood; or maybe a little basket of silkworms, or a string of onions or a pot of chives. And, choosing his moment, he would give her a reproving glance, and gently chide her, to which she would respond by keeping her distance and blithely walking past with her nose in the air—His Reverence made but little progress with her.

Once, as the priest was out and about under the noonday sun, he ran into Bentivegna walking behind a well-laden donkey. He gave the labourer a cheery greeting and asked him where he was going.

'I'll tell ye, father, I be going to the city for I do have summut needs doing, and I be bringing these here to Bona

Cory him what's going to help me with this 'ere summings afore they Proc'raters Ficscal or summut.'

'Well done, my son', said the priest, beaming. 'Go with my blessing and come back soon. And if you happen to see Lapuccio or Naldino, don't forget to tell them to bring me those thongs for my flails.'

Bentivegna said it would be done; and as the labourer pursued his way towards Florence, the priest thought it was time now to call on Belcolore and try his luck. So off he went and never stopped till he had reached her house. He stepped inside and called: 'God rest you. Anyone at home?'

Belcolore was up in the attic. When she heard him she said: 'Welcome, father. How comes it you're tramping about in this heat?'

'God willing, I'm going to keep you company for a little: I came upon your husband on his way into town.'

Belcolore came down, drew up a chair for herself, and set about sieving the Brussels sprout seeds her husband had just finished threshing. 'Well, Belcolore', the priest began, 'how long are you going to keep me on tenterhooks?'

Belcolore burst out laughing. 'Am I doing something wrong?'

'It's not what you're doing, it's what you're not letting me do, in defiance of the Lord's command.'

'Get away with you! Priests don't do that sort of thing.'

'Don't we just? We do it far better than other men! And why ever not? Let me tell you: we perform heaps better than the others, and you know why? It's because we hold our fire; and so much the better for you as you'll see if you just keep mum and let me get on with it.'

'What rubbish! There's nothing in it for me', said Belcolore. 'You're a bunch of dried-up old skinflints.'

'Well try me!' said the priest. 'How about a nice pair of shoes? A silk band for your forehead? A skein of fine wool? You only have to say.'

'Very good, sir, but those are all things I've got. If you really care for me so much, why not do me a service and then I'll do what you want me to.'

'Tell me what you want me to do, and I'll see to it with pleasure.'

'On Saturday I have to go to Florence to hand in the wool I have spun and get my spindle mended. Lend me 5 lire—I'm sure you have it—and I'll be able to get my dark blue gown back from the pawnbroker's, and my best leather belt, the one for feast-days, which I brought with my dowry. You see, I can't go to church or anywhere that takes some dressing up because I don't have them. Then I'll always do as you want me to.'

'I don't have it on me, and that's God's truth', said the priest. 'But take my word, I'll most willingly let you have it by Saturday.'

'You don't say! Why, you all talk big, but it doesn't add up to a row of beans. D'you think you'll get round me the way you got round Biliuzza—you surely took her for a ride! Not on your life, though that taught her a thing or two! As for you, if you haven't got it on you, off you go and get it.'

'Oh come', said the priest. 'Don't make me go all the way home *now* when there's no one about and you can see my luck's standing tall. There's no time like the present—if I came back later Goodness knows who might be hanging about getting in the way.'

'As you wish. If you want to leave, there's the door. If not, you'll have to do without.'

Seeing that she was not disposed to let him have his way unless he left her some pledge, while he wanted to go ahead on tick, the priest said: 'So you won't trust me to bring you the money? Very well, I'll leave you this deep-blue cloak of mine as a pledge—now will you trust me?'

'What, that cloak!' said she with a sniff. 'What's it worth?'

'What d'you mean, what's it worth? I'll have you know this is best Flanders cloth from Douai, you'll not find better in Troyes; why, people from here go all the way to Quatrebras for a mere scrap of it! It's not a fortnight ago I bought it off Lotto the rag-and-bone man for 150 cents and I have it on the authority of Buglietto d'Alberto—he knows a thing or two, remember, about these Flanders fabrics—that it's worth a whole 5 cents more than that.'

'Is that a fact? Well blow me, I'd never have thought it! Hand it over, then.'

His Reverence, all burdened as he was with a full quiver, pulled the cloak off and gave it to her. She put it away then said: 'Come, let's go into this hut; no one ever comes near it.'

In they went, and the priest nibbled her all over with the softest kisses and carried her into her seventh heaven as he made love to her for a very long time. When he left to go back to his church he was clad only in his cassock, as though he'd just been officiating at a wedding.

Once home, he realized that not even an entire year's harvest of candle-stubs would raise even half the value of 5 lire, so he felt he had made a bad bargain and regretted having left her his cloak; he turned his mind, therefore, to thinking how he might recover it scot free. Being a bit of a sly puss, he hit on the perfect plan to get it back, and next day, which was a feast-day, he sent a neighbour's little boy to Belcolore's with a message asking her as a favour to lend him her stone mortar: Binguccio del Poggio and Nuto Buglietti were having lunch with him and he wanted to make a sauce. She let him have it. As lunch-time approached, the priest watched to see when Bentivegna and Belcolore sat down to eat, then fetched his sacristan and said to him: 'Take this mortar and bring it back to Belcolore, and tell her, "Father says, thank you very much and can he have back the cloak the boy left you as a deposit?" '

The sacristan took the mortar to Belcolore's house and found her at table with Bentivegna having lunch. He put down the mortar and conveyed the priest's message.

Hearing him ask for the cloak, Belcolore was about to reply when Bentivegna chimed in gruffly: 'What? Be you taking pledges from Father? By Christ, I do have half a mind to box your ears. Give it him back this minute, blast you, and just you remember, anything he wants, anything, even if it's our ass, he gets it and that's that.'

Belcolore got up muttering to herself and went to fetch the cloak from the chest at the foot of the bed and handed it to the sacristan. 'Tell Father this from me', she said. 'Belcolore says, she prays God you'll never again pound up sauce in *her* mortar. It's made for a great deal better sauce than *you* can make.'

The sacristan left with the cloak and carried the message to the priest, who laughed and said: 'Next time you see her, tell her that if she won't lend me her mortar, I shan't lend her my pestle. Tit for tat.'

Bentivegna assumed that his wife had spoken as she had because he had scolded her, so he thought no more about it. Belcolore, however, who had been swindled, fell out with the priest and refused to speak to him till the grape-harvest. In view, however, of his threat to send her to the devil, she grew so alarmed that, come the season of roast chestnuts and bottling, she made her peace with him and they had several sessions of slap and tickle. And instead of giving her the 5 lire, the priest had new parchment put on her tambourine and another jingle added, which made her very happy.

VIII. 3. *Calandrino goes in search of the magic heliotrope. Bruno and Buffalmacco come to help. Calandrino's wife unfortunately spoils it all.*

The ladies laughed so much at Pamphilo's tale that there was no stopping them, and Elissa was still laughing when, at the queen's command, she began her own.

My little story is as true as it is fun, but I don't know whether it will make you laugh as much as Pamphilo's has done; still, I'll do my best.

Our city has always teemed with eccentric characters of one kind and another. Not all that long ago there used to be such a one, called Calandrino,* a painter by profession. He was a simple soul, with some funny ways, and he spent most of his time in the company of two fellow-painters, Bruno and Buffalmacco. These two were a cheerful pair, but they were nobody's fools, unlike Calandrino, whose company they kept because he was so gullible and they loved to take him for a ride. There was also then in Florence a young man called Maso del Saggio, a shrewd and able young fellow with a very winning way about him. He had heard what a simpleton Calandrino was, and he thought what fun it would be to play some prank on him or feed him some very tall story. One day he chanced upon Calandrino in the church of San Giovanni; the artist was scrutinizing the painting and carving on the tabernacle* recently installed above the altar. This, thought Maso, was just the time and place to fulfil his wish. He had a companion with him, whom he advised of his intention; they wandered over to where Calandrino was sitting on his own and, pretending not to have noticed him, started conversing about the properties of certain stones: Maso talked with all the authority of a veteran connoisseur of gems. Calandrino listened in for a while, then stood up and came to join them, for their conversation did not seem to him to be private. Maso was delighted, and continued his discourse until Calandrino asked where stones with the properties he described might be found.

'In Berlinzona,* where the Basques live', explained Maso, 'that's where most of them are found—more precisely in a region known as Bengodi, the happy valley. In Bengodi they use sausages to tie up their vines; they keep a goose that lays golden eggs and, come to that, a duck too; they have there a whole mountain of grated parmesan, and the people who live on it do nothing all day but make gnocchi and ravioli and cook it in capon broth, then whoosh it down the slope, and the people who collect the most collect the most. That's where the stream of *Vernaccia* flows—the best you'll ever drink and not a drop of water gets into it.'

'Oh my', said Calandrino. 'That's the place for me! But tell me, what do they do with the capons they cook?'

'The Basques? They eat them all.'

'Have you ever been there?' asked Calandrino.

'Have I ever? If I've been there once, I've been a thousand times.'

'How far is it?'

'Eighty-score leagues and four and then a whole little bit more.'

'Goodness', exclaimed Calandrino, 'it must be further than the Abruzzi.'

'You never said a truer word.'

Naïve as he was, Calandrino noticed what a straight face Maso kept as he spoke, and he accepted his account as the Gospel truth. 'If only it weren't so far', he sighed. 'Otherwise, believe me, I'd come with you once just to see those ravioli whooshing down the hill and I'd make a real pig of myself. But do me a favour and tell me: these stones with magic properties—are any of them to be found hereabouts?'

'Yes', Maso told him. 'We have two kinds of stone with miraculous properties. One is your Settignano sandstone—you get it, too, up the Montisci—which is reduced to millstones and goes to make flour, hence the local saying: "Grace comes from God, grist from Montisci." However, we produce the stuff in such profusion that we set no greater store by it than those Basques do by their emeralds—they have a mountain of the stuff higher than our Mount Morello, and at night the stones shine out and light your way. You know, anyone who took an uncut, unpierced stone and tied it into rings and brought it to the sultan could quite simply name his price. The other is a stone we lapidaries call the heliotrope, and now *that*'s a stone for you: anyone carrying this stone about his person, while he's actually got it by him, no one else can see him where he isn't.'

'Now that's really something! This second stone, where is it found?'

'You'll find it in the Mugnone.'*

'How big is it? What colour?'

'They come', said Maso, 'in all sizes, some bigger, some smaller, but all of them are more or less black.'

Calandrino took note of all this, then bid farewell to Maso on the pretext of some other engagement. He was quietly determined to look for this stone, but would not do so without the knowledge of his very dear friends, Bruno and Buffalmacco. He set off in search of them so that they might go together at once to find the stone before anyone else did. He spent the rest of the morning looking for them, then remembered—it was now already mid-afternoon—that they would be working for the nuns at their convent outside Porta di Faenza; so he dropped everything else and practically ran all the way there, regardless of the heat. He called them to him and said: 'Believe you me, friends, we can become the richest men in Florence: there's this stone and someone carrying it about his person can't be seen by anyone else, and it's found in the Mugnone,

I have it from someone who knows what he's talking about. It seems to me we shouldn't waste a minute but go and look for it now before anyone else does. I know we'll find it—I know what it looks like. Once we've found it, all we have to do is pop it in our pouch, nip over to the money-changers'—their tables are always overflowing with florins and crowns as you know—and just help ourselves. Nobody'll see us, so that way we'll get rich quick instead of having to daub paint on walls like a snail's trail.'

Bruno and Buffalmacco exchanged a secret smile as they listened to him even though, catching each other's eye, they pretended to be overcome with surprise. They totally approved his idea, and Buffalmacco asked what the stone was called.

Calandrino, who was rather dense, had already forgotten. 'What do we want its name for?' he remarked. 'We know what it *does*. It seems to me we should be looking for it without wasting any more time.'

'Very well', said Bruno. 'What does it look like?'

'They come in all shapes and sizes, but they're all more or less black. I think what we have to do is pick up every black stone we see till we come across it. So let's not waste time, come along!'

'Wait a minute', put in Bruno, and turned to Buffalmacco: 'Of course Calandrino's right, but I don't think this is the right time for it: with the sun overhead and beating down on the Mugnone, it will have dried all the stones, so that stones which look black in the morning before the sun has been on them will look bleached white at this hour. Another thing: today's a working day and there'll be plenty of people with business of one sort or another down by the Mugnone. When they see us they'll guess what we're about and maybe start copying us, so the stone may end up with them; so maybe it's a case for "more haste, less speed". Don't you think this is something we should be doing in the morning, when we can tell the black from the white, and on a holiday, when there won't be people watching us?'

Buffalmacco thought Bruno was quite right and Calandrino fell in with his idea, so the three agreed to meet the coming Sunday morning and look for the stone. But Calandrino begged them on no account to mention this to a living soul, for he had been told of it in confidence. After this discussion, he went on to tell them what he had learnt about the place called Bengodi, 'and you have my word for it', he said, 'it's the absolute truth'. Calandrino took his leave, and his two friends sorted out between them what needed doing.

Calandrino couldn't wait for Sunday morning. When it came he was up at crack of dawn and called for his friends. They left the city by Porta San Gallo, went down to the Mugnone, and set off downstream, looking for the stone. Calandrino, being the keenest, went on ahead, hopping from one spot to the next; he leapt on every black stone he saw, picked it up, and dropped it inside his shirt. His friends followed, picking up the odd stone here and there. Calandrino, however, had not gone far before his shirt was bulging, so he hauled up the hem of his tunic (which he wore as a loose-fitting garment), tucked it carefully into his belt all round, and thus fashioned himself an ample lap—which he had filled up in no time, so he turned his mantle into a further receptacle and filled *that* up with stones. Noticing what a load of stones Calandrino was carrying, and that lunch-time was approaching, Bruno said to Buffalmacco, as the two had arranged: 'Where's Calandrino?'

Buffalmacco could see him only a step away, but he looked about him in all directions and said: 'I don't know. He was certainly here in front of us a moment ago.'

'A moment ago's not *now*!' remarked Bruno. 'If you ask me, he's back home now having his lunch, leaving us down here in the Mugnone looking for black stones like a pair of ninnies.'

'Well, if he's left us here like a pair of ninnies', said Buffalmacco, 'we had it coming to us for being such nitwits as to fall for his story. I mean, listen: you have to be a prize ass to believe you're going to find a stone with such magic properties here in the Mugnone! Aren't we a right pair?'

When Calandrino overheard this, he imagined that the stone must have come into his possession, which was why they couldn't see him though he was right in front of their eyes. Thrilled at such a stroke of luck, he decided to say nothing to them and make for home; so he started retracing his steps.

On sight of this Buffalmacco asked Bruno: 'What shall we do? Why don't we quit?'

'All right', answered Bruno, 'let's go. But I swear to God, that's the last time Calandrino's going to make a monkey of *me.* If he were still with us, as he has been all morning, I'd fetch him such a smack on the heels with this stone, he'd not forget it for a month of Sundays.' As he spoke he swung his arm and hurled the stone straight at Calandrino's heel. Calandrino picked up his foot and blew on it when he felt the pain, but he kept quiet and hastened onward.

Buffalmacco was still holding one of the stones he'd picked up. 'See this stone?' he said to Bruno. 'I wish it had got Calandrino in the small of the back.' He swung his arm and fetched Calandrino a great wallop with it in the back. This way they proceeded from the Mugnone back to Porta San Gallo, pursuing Calandrino with stones and threats. At the city gate they threw down the stones they had collected and chatted for a while with the toll-collectors, whom they had tipped off—they let Calandrino through, pretending not to have seen him, and had a merry laugh over it. Calandrino reached home without stopping; it was close to Porta San Gallo, at the Canto della Macina. Luck was with the pranksters, because neither down by the river nor on his way through the streets did anyone address a word to him, not that he met many people, for most of them were having their lunch.

Thus laden, Calandrino went into his house. His wife happened to be standing at the top of the stairs—she was a good woman, and pretty too, and her name was Tessa. She was rather cross that he'd been gone so long, so when she saw him come in she started scolding him: 'Well, well! Look what the cat's brought in! Everyone else has had their lunch and now you're ready for yours!'

Realizing that he could be seen, Calandrino's heart sank and he yelled at her in a rage: 'Why you bitch, what are you doing here? Now look what you've done to me! By God, you'll pay for this!' He went up to his room, dropped his great burden of stones, and in a foul temper fell upon his wife. He seized her by the hair, threw her down at his feet and punched and kicked her for all he was worth, till he'd torn out all her hair and broken every bone in her body. She crossed her arms and begged for mercy, but little good did that do her.

After Buffalmacco and Bruno had stopped a while for a giggle with the gatekeepers, they strolled on after Calandrino and reached his front door. They heard him giving his wife a thorough thrashing, and they called up to him as if they had only that moment arrived. Calandrino came to the window red-faced, panting and perspiring; he asked them to come up. They went up, looking somewhat put out themselves, and found the room littered with stones, and Calandrino's wife in a corner, all battered and bruised and sobbing her heart out; across from her sat Calandrino with his belt off, chest heaving, a picture of exhaustion.

They stood there looking awhile, then said: 'What's this all about, Calandrino? What are you doing with all these stones—building walls? . . . And what's happened to your Tessa? It looks as if you've been beating her. Just what *is* going on?'

Calandrino was worn out, what with the weight of stones he'd been carrying and the fury he'd put into beating his wife, not to mention the weight of woe on discovering that his luck had evidently run out, so he couldn't find breath to make a coherent reply. Without waiting, therefore, Buffalmacco started again. 'Calandrino', he said, 'if you were out of temper on some other account, that was still no reason to have mocked us the way you've done. There we were, talked into looking for magic stones with you, and off you went without so much as a "See you later", leaving us there by the Mugnone like a pair of nincompoops and slipping away. That's not at all the way to behave, and believe me, it's the last time you'll get away with that one.'

At this, Calandrino pulled himself together and exclaimed: 'Now don't be cross—it's not at all as you think. I found the stone—worse luck!—so listen while I tell you what actually happened. When you first asked each other where I was, I was barely ten yards away. Seeing you struggling to find me, I set off ahead of you and stayed just ahead of you all the way back.' He told them the whole story from beginning to end, with everything they had said and done, and showed them what they'd done to his back and his heel with their stone-throwing. 'When I came in through the gate', he went on, 'I was carrying a whole lapful of stones, the ones you see here, but nobody said a word to me, and you know what a bore those gatekeepers usually are, wanting to look at every little thing. But that's not all: I ran into several of my cronies and acquaintances, and usually we bandy jokes and they ask me to stop for a drink, but this time not one of them said even half a word, just as though they hadn't seen me. And finally, when I got home, this blasted woman popped up and *saw* me, because of course women ruin the magic in everything. So here I'd been thinking myself the luckiest man in Florence, and now I was the unluckiest. That's why I've thrashed her as hard as I could, in fact I don't know what's keeping me from slashing her wrists. A curse on the hour I first set eyes on her, and when she came into my house!' He was so worked up he made to go and start beating her all over again.

Buffalmacco and Bruno made a great pretence of astonishment as they listened to Calandrino, and kept corroborating what he had just said, though they were practically bursting to laugh. When they saw him leap up in a fury to beat his wife again, though, they jumped in and restrained him, and told him that none of this was any fault of his wife—it was his own fault, as he knew that magic failed in the presence of women but he had never told her to keep out of his way today. Doubtless Providence had made him forget such a precaution, either because he was fated to be unlucky, or because he had been meaning to deceive his friends, when he ought to have shared his find with them. It took much effort and a great deal of talk to reconcile Calandrino to his aching wife, after which they left him in a gloomy state with his house full of stones.

VIII. 4. *How a pretty widow gets rid of a lecherous cleric and her hideous maid earns herself a new chemise in the process.*

When Elissa reached the end of her story, which the whole company found a most satisfying one, the queen turned to Emilia and indicated that she was to follow Elissa. She promptly began as follows:

Several stories, as I recall, have pointed up the role played by priests and friars and the clergy at large* in assailing the virtue of us women. But, however much one discussed this topic, there would still be plenty left to be said, and I'm going to tell you another tale, this time about a provost who didn't care what anyone thought, he was going to seduce a well-born widow, whether she liked it or not. She was a clever woman, though, and gave him the treatment he deserved.

Fiesole is a town of great antiquity and used to be very important, as you all know—look, we can see its hilltop from here. Today it has gone to rack and ruin, which doesn't stop it still having its own bishop. Once upon a time there was a widow called Piccarda, who owned a plot of land with a modest house on it, next door to the cathedral; she was well born but not all that well off, so this is where she spent most of the year, together with her two brothers, young men of excellent conduct and character. Piccarda was still a very pretty and attractive young woman, and as she regularly attended services in the cathedral, the provost (he was dean of the chapter) quite lost his heart to her—she filled his entire horizon. It was not long before he plucked up the courage to go to her and tell her what was on his mind; he asked her to accept his love and respond to it with equal passion.

This provost was well advanced in years but in spirit he was boyish, cheeky, and very full of himself; he imagined that everything and everyone was at his beck and call, and he'd make himself thoroughly unpopular as a pompous, ill-mannered bore. There was no one, however, who found him more repugnant than this widow—she couldn't stand him, she'd sooner have a hole in the head. Still, her answer to him was judicious enough: 'That you should love me, sir, is most gratifying, and it will be my duty and my pleasure to love you in return. But between your love and mine there must never be a trace of anything impure. You are my spiritual father, you are a priest, and you are well on the way to old age, all of which should make you pure and chaste. A young maiden could, of course, be the suitable object of a man's love but I am not a young maiden: I am a widow, and I don't have to tell you what standards of chastity are required of a widow.

Excuse me, therefore, if I will not love you in the way you want, nor do I wish to be loved by you in that way.'

The provost could get nothing else out of her on that occasion, but he didn't throw in his hand at this first set-back; relying on his brazen effrontery, he continued to press her, sending letters and messages and confronting her in person whenever he saw her in church. Piccarda eventually found these solicitations altogether too much, and considered how, for lack of other remedies, she might be rid of him in a way he deserved. However, she would take no steps until she had discussed the matter with her brothers. She told them what the provost was up to and what she planned to do and, with their full consent, went to church a few days later, as was her custom. The provost sidled up to her the moment he saw her and struck up a conversation in his usual familiar way.

As she saw him approach, Piccarda looked him in the eye and gave him a smile. They drew to one side and, after the provost had come out with his usual patter, she heaved a sigh and said: 'I have heard it said time and again, sir, that there isn't a castle, however strongly built, that won't eventually succumb if it is battered day after day. That seems to be what's happened to me: you've so hemmed me in on every side, what with the sweet things you keep saying and all your little attentions, that you've finally got the better of my determination. As you're so fond of me, I don't mind doing as you ask.'

The provost beamed. 'Madam', he said, 'thank you! To tell you the truth, I've been quite surprised you held out so long—it's never happened to me with any other woman. Far from it, as I've occasionally remarked: if women were made of silver they'd be useless for minting, as there's not one of them could stand up to the hammering. But that's by the by; when can we get together and where?'

'Well, my love, as to when—that can be any time you please: I don't have a husband to answer to for my nights. But where: I can't think.'

'How come? What's wrong with your house?'

'You know I have these two younger brothers who are in and out of the house at all hours with their friends, and the house is not all that large. So it wouldn't do, unless one didn't mind pretending to be dumb, without uttering so much as a whisper, and staying in the dark like blind people. If you didn't mind that, we could do it, for they keep out of my room. But their room is right next door to mine, they'd hear the slightest murmur.'

'Then let's put up with that for a night or two', said he, 'while I think where else we might meet more conveniently.'

'As you will. But one thing I do beg of you—keep it a secret, don't let a word of it get out.'

'Don't you worry. Just see if we can't get together tonight.'

'All right', said she. And she left for home, after telling him how and when to turn up.

Now Piccarda had a maid. She was no longer in her first youth, and you'd never have seen a more hideous, misshapen face: she had a squashed nose, her mouth was all aslant, with thick lips and big, uneven teeth; she was cross-eyed—her eyes were a constant irritant—and her complexion was quite sallow, as if she'd spent her summers not up at Fiesole but down in the marshes of Sinigaglia. As if that was not enough, she was a cripple with a stoop to her right side. Ciuta was her name but, with a complexion like hers, everyone called her Eggyolk. However ill favoured she was to look at, though, she was none the less something of a sly puss.

Piccarda sent for her maid and told her: 'If you want to do me a service tonight, I'll give you a nice new chemise.'

At the word 'chemise' the maid said: 'O madam, give me a new chemise and I'll throw myself in the fire for you, never mind what else!'

'All right, what I want you to do is to sleep in my bed tonight with a man and make love to him, but take care not to utter a word or my brothers will hear you as they sleep next door, remember? Then I'll give you that chemise.'

'Sleep with a man?' cried Eggyolk. 'Why, I'd sleep with six if I had to!'

That evening the provost arrived according to instructions and the two boys banged about noisily in their room, as agreed with their sister. Then the provost crept quietly into the darkness of Piccarda's bedroom and got into bed, as she had told him to, and so did Eggyolk, who had been told precisely what she was to do. Believing he had his mistress there beside him, the provost enfolded Eggyolk in his arms and started kissing her, never speaking a word, and she did likewise. Then the provost mounted her and took possession of the goods he had so long been hankering for.

When Piccarda had got to this point with her plan, she told her brothers to go ahead with the rest of it as agreed. So they stole quietly out of their room, made for the piazza, and luck took them several steps further than they had even hoped for: it was unspeakably hot and the bishop, feeling convivial, had sent for these two lads to ask if he might stop by at their house for a wee drop. Seeing them approaching, he made his request and set out in their company. Stepping into their deliciously cool courtyard, which was lit with plenty of lamps, with relish he partook of one of their excellent wines.

When they had drunk, the young men said: 'Your Lordship, as you've been so good as to deign to visit our little home, which we were on our way to invite you to do, we should be glad if it might be your pleasure to see a little sight we should like to show you.'

The bishop consented, so one of the lads took a flaming torch and led the way, the bishop and the others following, till he reached the room in which the provost was in bed with Eggyolk. Being in a hurry, he had been riding her hard, and was already past the third milepost when the crowd arrived, so he was just a bit tired and was drowsing with Eggyolk in his arms, despite the heat. The boy entered the bedroom, then, holding the torch, and he was followed by the bishop and then by all the others, and what they saw was the provost with Eggyolk in his arms. The provost came wide awake on seeing the light and everyone crowding round; acutely embarrassed and apprehensive as he was, he dived under the bedclothes, but the bishop gave him a piece of his mind and had him show his head; he wanted to see whom he had been sleeping with. And there was no sadder man than the provost when he discovered that Piccarda had played a trick on him and he'd landed himself in such a mess. The bishop told him to get dressed, then sent him under a strong guard back to the cathedral to endure a huge penance for the sin he had committed.

As the bishop wanted to know how the man came to be here in bed with Eggyolk, the boys gave him the full story, and the bishop expressed his strong approval of Piccarda, and of the young men too, as they had avoided sullying their hands with priestly gore but had served him according to his deserts.

For this sin the bishop kept him weeping for forty days, but in fact love and indignation made him weep for more than forty-nine, not to mention the fact that it was ages before he could go out in the street without all the urchins pointing at him and shouting: 'Look at the man who sleeps with Eggyolk!' This he found so intensely irritating it nearly drove him out of his mind. So that's how the brave woman got the shameless provost off her back, and Eggyolk earned herself a chemise.

## VIII. 5. *How a judge comes to lose his breeches while sitting on the seat of judgement.*

Emilia came to the end of her story and the widow was generally commended, after which the queen turned to Philostrato. 'Now it's your turn', she said. He was quick to pronounce himself ready and thus began:

Elissa's mention a short while ago of that young man Maso del Saggio prompts me to abandon the story I was proposing to relate, in order to tell you one about him and some friends of his. While it's not exactly naughty, it does mean using words that you charming ladies would blush to use, but still, it's so amusing that I'm going to tell it anyway.

As you will no doubt be aware, our city often brings in Podestàs from the Marche,* men who tend to be skinflints and lead such a crabbed, penny-pinching existence they're virtually beneath contempt. With their ingrained habits of miserliness, the men they bring with them as magistrates and notaries are fellows who might have come straight from the plough or the cobbler's bench rather than from a school of jurisprudence. Now one of these men who came from the Marche as Podestà brought with him a large number of judges, including one who went by the name of Niccola da Sant' Elpidio—a fellow whom, from the look of him, you would have taken for a blacksmith—and this Niccola was appointed one of the judges to hear criminal cases. Well, it often happens that a citizen will set foot in the lawcourts even if he has no particular business there, and Maso del Saggio chanced to step in there one morning as he was looking for a friend. He glanced across to where this Judge Niccola was sitting and stopped to give him a closer scrutiny, for he seemed to him a likely new pigeon for the plucking. He noticed that his squirrel's-fur bonnet had a charred look about it, a quill-pen and ink-horn dangled from a sheath at his belt, his gown was too short to cover his tunic, and altogether his dress assorted ill with the dignity of his office; but what most caught his attention was the man's breeches which could be observed as he was seated and his robes, being too tight, hung open in front: the crotch came barely half-way up his thighs.

Maso stopped and stared for but a moment, then abandoned his quest and went off on a new one till he found two of his friends, one of them called Ribi, the other Matteuzzo, both of them as ready for a lark as Maso was. 'Now listen', he told them. 'Come with me to the lawcourts: I want to show you the biggest dummy you've ever set eyes on.'

He went with them to the lawcourts and pointed out the judge and his breeches. Seeing him from a distance they had a good laugh, and made their way closer to the dais on which the judge sat. They noticed that it was easy enough to slip in beneath the dais, and moreover that there was a broken plank at the point where he was resting his feet, which made it simple to reach a hand and an arm through the gap.

'Let's get his breeches off', suggested Maso to his companions. 'It'll be child's play.'

The three of them hit upon a way to do it, so they worked out what each of them was to do and say, and returned the following morning. The courtroom was very crowded and Matteuzzo slipped underneath the dais unnoticed and took up station right beneath the point where the judge rested his feet. Maso approached the judge from one side and grasped the hem of his gown; Ribi approached from the other and did likewise.

Then Maso cried: 'Your Honour, for God's sake do make that thief there give me back my boots before he makes off; he's stolen them, though he denies it; I saw him with them not a month ago, getting them resoled.'

As for Ribi, he was yelling: 'Don't believe him, Your Honour, he's a dirty rascal. Just because he knows I've come to sue him over a valise he's stolen from me, he has to come along with his story about boots which I had in my house only a couple of days ago. And if you don't believe me, I have witnesses: the woman next door in the greengrocers', Mrs Butterball the tripe-seller, and the man who sweeps the streets between Santa Maria and Verzaia, who saw him coming back from the country.'

Maso kept interrupting and Ribi kept shouting him down. And as the judge stood up, straining towards them to catch what they were saying, Matteuzzo chose his moment to reach up through the broken plank, grasp the judge's breeches by the crotch, and give them a sharp tug; the breeches came down at once, for the judge was a skinny string-bean. He felt something had happened but did not quite know what, and as he tried to cover himself by pulling his gown together across the front and sit down, Maso and Ribi still clung to him, each on one side, and kept shouting: 'What do you mean, sir, by not giving judgement in my favour? Why, you're not even listening to me, you're trying to get away! Here in Florence there's no call for written judgements over so slight a matter.' As they spoke they clutched his robes so that everyone in the courtroom could see that he had lost his breeches. Matteuzzo let go of them after he had held on to them a while, and slipped away without being noticed.

'Honest to God', cried Ribi, feeling it had all gone far enough, 'just wait till you're called to account at the end of your term—that's when I'll have this matter sorted out!'

Maso, too, released hold of his gown and said: 'Not I. I'll keep coming back till I find you less preoccupied than you seem to be this morning.'

They made off, each from his own side, as fast as they could. His Honour pulled up his breeches in the presence of the entire company, as if he had only just got out of bed; when it dawned on him what had happened, he asked where those two men had got to who had been in dispute over the boots and the valise. As they were nowhere to be found, he swore by all that's holy, saying there was one thing he would dearly like to know, and that is whether it was a Florentine custom to pull down a judge's breeches as he sat dispensing justice. As for the Podestà, he was furious when he heard about it; he was advised, however, by his friends that nothing lay behind this prank beyond the Florentines' wish to demonstrate their awareness of the fact that, instead of bringing judges with him, he saved himself money by importing clowns. So he thought fit to say no more, and indeed he took the matter no further on that occasion.

VIII. 6. *Calandrino kills a pig to salt it, but Bruno and Buffalmacco creep in at night and steal it. How they help him find the culprit.*

No sooner was Philostrato's tale finished—it provoked much laughter—than the queen told Philomena to follow with hers, and so she began:

Just as mention of Maso's name prompted Philostrato to tell the story you've just heard, so am I impelled by the simple mention of Calandrino and his friends to tell you another one about them; I think you'll like it.

I don't have to tell you who Calandrino, Bruno, and Buffalmacco were: you've heard enough about them already. So, on with my story. Calandrino had a little property not far from Florence—it came to him in his wife's dowry—and along with the other produce he derived from it was a pig once a year. He had the habit of going there each December with his wife to slaughter the pig and salt it.

Now there was one occasion when Calandrino's wife was not well and so Calandrino went on his own to slaughter the pig. When Bruno and Buffalmacco got to hear of this and knew that his wife was not coming, they went to stay for a few days with a close friend of theirs, a priest who was a neighbour of Calandrino's in the country. Calandrino had killed the pig on the morning of their arrival. When he saw them with the priest he called them over, welcomed them, and said: 'I want you to see what a handy fellow I am.' He brought them indoors and showed them the pig.

They saw that it was a most excellent pig, and were told by Calandrino that he intended to salt it for his household. 'Don't be an ass', said Bruno. 'Sell it; let's make merry on the proceeds! You can always tell your missus somebody came and filched it off you.'

'No', said Calandrino. 'She'd never believe me; she'd throw me out of the house. Save your breath—I'm not going to do it.'

This led to much discussion, but all to no purpose. Calandrino asked them to stay for lunch, but with such ill grace that they declined and left him.

'Shall we steal his pig tonight?' said Bruno to Buffalmacco.

'How would we do that?'

'I can see how, if he doesn't shift it from where it was just now.'

'Then let's do it', said Buffalmacco. 'Indeed, why not? That way we can enjoy it here with the Reverend.'

The priest quite fancied the idea. So Bruno said: 'What we need here is a little cunning. You know, Buffalmacco, what a skinflint Calandrino is—he'll drink any amount if someone else is paying the round. Let's bring him to the tavern; the priest will pretend to play host to us and pick up the bill and not let him pay a penny. He'll get blind drunk: it will be child's play after that—he's all alone in the house.'

They did as Bruno suggested. Seeing that the priest would never let him pay, Calandrino did not stint himself and, though a little liquor went a long way with him, he tanked up with a will. The night was quite well advanced when he left the tavern and, eschewing his supper, went home and to bed, thinking he had locked his front door—only he hadn't. Buffalmacco and Bruno went to dine with the priest, after which they collected their implements in order to break in to Calandrino's house at the point Bruno had decided on. They made a silent approach but, finding the front door open, in they went, removed the pig, and carried it back to the priest's house, then turned in.

When Calandrino got up in the morning, his head no longer befuddled, he went downstairs and looked, but could not see his pig. He saw the door was open. So he asked around to see if anyone knew who'd taken the pig, but he got nowhere and started making a great fuss—poor him (he cried), poor wretched him, someone had made off with his pig! Bruno and Buffalmacco got up and approached Calandrino to hear what he had to say about the pig. When he saw them he was practically blubbering: 'Oh dear oh dear, my friends, my pig's been taken.'

Bruno edged up to him and whispered. 'Well blimey, you've used your loaf for once!'

'Oh dear no! I'm telling you the truth.'

'That's right', Bruno kept saying. 'Make a big noise, so people will think that's what's happened.'

Then Calandrino really raised his voice and yelled: 'God strewth! I'm telling you I've been robbed!'

'That's it, that's the spirit', said Bruno. 'Keep it up. Shout good and loud, make sure everyone hears you, make sure you make it *sound* true.'

'Well I'll be damned! I'll be hanged if I don't convince you my pig's been stolen!'

'Just a minute: how can it have been?' asked Bruno. 'I saw it here only yesterday. Do you expect me to believe it's flown away?'

'It's as I've been telling you.'

'No! It can't be', said Bruno.

'I'm telling you it is! And I'm plain flabbergasted, I don't know how I can go home, my missus won't believe me, and even if she does, she'll give me no peace in a month of Sundays.'

'Well blimey', said Bruno. 'If it's true, that's rotten luck. But mind you, Calandrino, I told you yesterday about this line of talk. I should not take it kindly if you're making fools of us and of your missus all at once.'

Calandrino started yelling again: 'Oh you're going to drive me crazy! I'm telling you somebody took away my pig in the night.'

'Well, if that's the case', put in Buffalmacco, 'we'll have to see if we can't find a way to get it back.'

'What way could we find?'

'Well', said Buffalmacco, 'whoever took your pig won't have come all the way from India to do so. It must have been one of your neighbours: if you can get them all together, I know how to carry out the trial by bread and cheese.* We'll see soon enough who's taken it.'

'Oh will you just?' put in Bruno. 'A fat lot of use your bread and cheese will be with some of the gentry you've got around here! I'll bet one of them's got it, but you'll never get the likes of them to walk into your little trap.'

'Then what's to be done?' asked Buffalmacco.

'It has to be done', explained Bruno, 'with some nice pills made out of ginger, and a drop of *Vernaccia* wine. Invite them for a drink, and they'll come without a second thought. The ginger pills can be blessed the same as the bread and cheese.'

'How right you are', said Buffalmacco. 'What d'you say, Calandrino? D'you want to do it?'

'You bet!—Let's get on with it for God's sake. If I knew who'd stolen it, I'd feel a lot better already.'

'Right', said Bruno. 'I don't mind going to Florence to pick up the things you'll need—if you give me the money.'

Calandrino had a handful of coppers which he passed to him.

Bruno went to Florence and called on a friend of his who was an apothecary. He bought a pound of nice pills, had a couple more made up out of fresh hepatic aloe on centres consisting of dog's turd, and had these sugar-coated the same as the rest, but with a little mark by which he would clearly recognize them and avoid confusing them with the others. He bought a flask of good *Vernaccia*, returned to Calandrino in the country, and told him: 'See to inviting all your suspects for a drink tomorrow morning. It's a holiday so they'll all be glad to come. Tonight Buffalmacco and I will place the spell on the pills and I'll bring them to your house in the morning. Seeing that it's you, I don't mind handing them out myself and doing and saying whatever needs to be said and done.'

Calandrino did as bidden, collecting a good crowd made up of young men who had come out here from Florence, along with local labourers, and gathering them the next morning round the elm-tree in front of the church. Bruno and Buffalmacco turned up with the pills in a box and the wine in a flask. They made them all form a circle, and Bruno said: 'Gentlemen, let me tell you why you're here; that way, if anything happens that you don't care for, you won't hold *me* to blame. Last night Calandrino here had a fine pig of his stolen, and he can't lay his hands on the culprit. As whoever took it can only be one of us here present, to find out who it is, he's going to give each of you one of these pills to eat, and some drink. What you have to realize straight away is that whoever's taken the pig will be unable to swallow his pill—he'll find it tastes more bitter than gall and he'll spit it out. So maybe it would be better, before the culprit is shown up in the presence of so many people, if he goes and makes his confession to the priest, and I'll stay my hand.'

All present insisted they were ready to eat one, so Bruno sorted them out into order and placed Calandrino among them, then started at one end handing each man his pill; when he came to Calandrino he took out one of the dog-turd pills and placed it in his hand. Calandrino promptly popped it into his mouth and started chewing—but the moment he tasted the aloe, the bitterness was more than he could stand and he spat it out. They were all looking at each others' faces to see who was going to spit out his pill; Bruno had not completed his round and pretended not to notice what Calandrino had done, but when he heard someone behind him cry: 'Hey, Calandrino, what does this mean?' he spun round, saw that Calandrino had spat his out, and said: 'Wait! It could be something else made him spit it out. Here, take another.' And he took out the second one, put it into Calandrino's mouth, and carried on handing out the remaining pills. Now if Calandrino had found the first pill bitter, this second one was far, far more so; ashamed as he was to spit it out, he kept it in his mouth and chewed a little, great tears welling up in his eyes, tears the size of cob-nuts, but eventually he could stand it no longer and spat it out as he had done with the first. Buffalmacco was passing the drink round, together with Bruno. When they and the rest saw this, they all said that of course Calandrino must have taken the pig himself—in fact some of them were quite tart with him.

But when Bruno and Buffalmacco were left alone with Calandrino after everyone else had gone: 'Well', exclaimed Buffalmacco to Calandrino, 'I knew all along that you took it yourself and wanted us to believe someone had stolen it, so you wouldn't have to stand us drinks on the proceeds of the sale.'

Calandrino, who had still not finished spitting out the bitterness of the aloe, swore that it wasn't he.

'Come on, pal', urged Buffalmacco. 'What did it fetch? Six florins?'

This drove Calandrino to despair. Then Bruno said to him: 'Now look here, Calandrino. I have it from one of the fellows in the crowd eating and drinking with us that you've been keeping a young lass up here for a little bit on the side, and you've been paying her with whatever you could scrape together. He's absolutely certain you sent that pig to her—clearly you've become a deep one, *you* have! There was the time you led us down to the Mugnone to pick up black stones and, once you had us running round in circles, you skipped off; then you tried to convince us you'd found the stone! Now it's just the same: you expect us to fall for your solemn oath that your pig has been lifted when you've actually sold it or passed it along. Well, we're no longer taken in—we know *you*, and you'll not catch us out again. The fact is, we went to a great deal of trouble putting a spell on those pills; so here's what you're going to have to do—you're to give us each a brace of capons, or else we'll spill the beans to your Tessa.'

Seeing that they refused to believe him, and feeling that he had had trouble enough without also bringing his wife down about his ears, Calandrino gave them their capons, a brace apiece. So Bruno and Buffalmacco salted the porker and took it with them back to Florence, leaving Calandrino out of pocket and out of countenance.

VIII. 7. *A woman keeps an unwanted suitor standing all night in the snow. Come summer, the suitor pays her back handsomely.*

Poor Calandrino, how the ladies laughed at him! They would have laughed even more had they not felt sorry for him, losing even his capons to the people who had taken his pig. But when the story was ended, the queen bade Pampinea to tell hers, which she promptly began as follows:

It often happens that one may be too clever for one's own good; so where's the sense in making fun of others for one's own amusement? We have had a good laugh over many stories concerning pranks, but none of the stories makes any mention of retribution. Now I propose to move you to pity with my tale of a just vengeance carried out against a lady of our city, who played a trick and nearly lost her life when the stratagem was turned against her. And you'll derive some advantage from listening to my story, for you'll take better care to avoid playing pranks— and how wise you will be!

Not many years ago there was a young woman living in Florence, called Elena. She was beautiful, proud, nobly born, and not short of money. When she became a widow, she had no wish to remarry, but chose a handsome and refined young man for her lover. They met frequently and had a marvellous time together, for she had not a care in the world and she enjoyed the services of a trustworthy maidservant who acted as go-between.

Now it was around about this time that a young Florentine nobleman called Rinieri returned home from Paris,* where he had for a long time been a student—he was not concerned to sell his knowledge for gain, as many do, but only to learn the origin of things and their cause, which sits well in a man of breeding. He settled down, then, to live stylishly in Florence, well respected both for his rank and his learning. But what often happens to people who are better acquainted with profound scholarship* than with the toils of Love also befell Rinieri: he went one day to enjoy himself at a party and this lady Elena surged up before his eyes, dressed in black as our widows are, and, in his view, so radiantly beautiful and alluring that he had never seen another like her. The man to whom the Good Lord conceded the favour of holding this woman, naked, in his arms could, he thought, truly call himself blessed. He gave her one or two discreet glances and, recognizing that the important and worthwhile things in life are not acquired without an effort, he determined to devote his every care and solicitude to pleasing her; this way he might secure her love and therefore have his fill of her. The young lady, who had a very good opinion of herself and was not accustomed to drop her gaze in company, contrived to turn round and have a look, and quickly spotted who it was who was gazing at her so ardently. Noticing Rinieri, she secretly exulted and remarked to herself: 'I shan't have come here for nothing today; if I'm not mistaken, I've hooked myself a proper Charlie.' And she started casting sidelong glances at him, and did her best to convey to him that she was not indifferent to him—her idea was that the more men she managed to attract, the greater value* would be set on her beauty, not least by the man to whom she had dedicated it together with her love.

The scholarly fellow, then, set aside his philosophical speculations and devoted his every thought to her. He discovered where she lived and, in the belief that it would please her, he started passing back and forth in front of her house on one pretext and another. Elena pretended to be delighted to see him, for the reason already mentioned—she was very conceited. Rinieri, therefore, found a way to scrape acquaintance with her maid and confided to her his love for her mistress; he asked her to work upon her mistress so that he might win her favours.

The maid was lavish with her promises and reported it all to her mistress, who was in fits of laughter as she listened to her, and said: 'The fellow's brought his wits back from Paris, and look where he's come to lose them! Well, let's give him what he's looking for. Tell him, next time he speaks to you, that I love him a great deal more than he loves me, but I have my reputation to consider, if I'm to hold my head up in the company of other women; this should make him cherish me all the more, if he's the wise man he claims to be.'

Oh dear oh dear, ladies! Little did she know what comes of tangling with intellectuals. The maid found him and carried out her mistress's bidding. Rinieri happily pressed on with more passionate entreaties; he wrote letters and sent gifts, every one of which was accepted but the replies that came back were always of the vaguest. This way Elena led him by the nose for ages.

Eventually she told her lover all about it, which made him really rather jealous and angry with her. So, to prove to him that his suspicions were groundless, she sent word by her maid to Rinieri, who kept pressing her, to say that she had never yet found a moment to grant him his desire, not since she had become convinced of his love. She did hope, however, to spend some time with him during the coming Christmas festivities. If he liked, he could come to her courtyard by night, on the day after Christmas, and she would come down to fetch him as soon as ever she could. The student was overjoyed at this, and went to Elena's house at the time she proposed and was left locked up in the courtyard by the maid. Here he began to wait for his lady.

That evening Elena sent for her lover and enjoyed a jolly supper with him, after which she told him what she planned to do that night. 'And you'll be able to see', she added, 'precisely how much I love the fellow you've grown so absurdly jealous over.' These words were balm to her lover's heart; he was anxious to see in practice what his mistress had assured him of in words.

There had, as it happened, been a heavy snowfall the day before, and everything was blanketed in snow. Rinieri, therefore, had not been waiting long in the courtyard before he began to feel colder than he would have wished; still, he endured it patiently as he waited for better entertainment.

After a while Elena said to her lover: 'Let's go into the bedroom, and look at him from a window, the man you've grown jealous of, and let's see what he's doing. Let's see how he answers my maid, as I've sent her to have a word with him.' So they went to a window where they could observe him without being seen, and listened as the maid spoke to Rinieri from another window. 'Rinieri', she said, 'my mistress is terribly sorry but one of her brothers has turned up this evening and kept her talking for ages and then had to have supper with her. He's not gone yet, though I think he'll be leaving soon. That's why she's not been able to come to you, but she'll be along at any moment; she asks you not to mind waiting a little longer.'

Rinieri took this for the truth and replied: 'Tell my lady not to worry about me at all till she's at liberty to come, but ask her to come as soon as possible.'

The maid pulled her head back in and went to bed.

'Well, tell me', said Elena to her lover. 'If I loved him as much as you fear I do, d'you really think I could bear to leave him standing out there freezing?' Her lover was largely satisfied, and on these words they went to bed and spent a good long time attending to their pleasure, while they had ever such a giggle over the poor old student.

Rinieri paced back and forth about the courtyard to keep warm; there was nowhere to sit down, no escape from the night-time damp, and he cursed the brother for staying so long. Every sound he heard he mistook for a door being opened for him by his beloved, but his hopes were in vain.

She and her lover were disporting themselves till about midnight, when she said: 'Tell me, darling, what d'you think about our student? What d'you think there's more of, his brains or my love for him? Won't the cold I'm exposing him to drive out of your heart whatever took hold of it the other day when I joked about him?'

'Yes indeed, my own sweet sugar-plum', said he. 'How well I know that just as you are my treasure, my repose, my delight, my only hope, so am I yours.'

'Good. Then give me a thousand kisses to show me you're telling the truth.' Her lover hugged her tightly and gave her not one thousand, but more like a hundred thousand kisses.

After indulging in such discussions for a while, Elena said: 'Listen. Let's get up a minute and go and see if the fire's yet gone out in that suitor of mine—he never stopped writing to tell me how he was burning for me.'

They got up and went to their usual window; looking into the courtyard, they saw the young man dancing a frantic quickstep in the snow, to the accompaniment of a rattle of teeth as they chattered for the cold; never had they seen a figure danced to such a measure. 'What d'you say, my precious?' asked Elena. 'Don't you think I'm good at making men dance without trumpets or bagpipes?'

'Yes yes, my treasure', agreed her lover with a laugh.

'Come, let's go down to the entrance', said Elena. 'You keep quiet, and I'll talk to him. Let's hear what he has to say—we should have even more of a lark than just watching him.' She softly opened the bedroom door and they went down to the entrance, where she called him in a muffled voice through a little crack, without opening the door.

Rinieri thanked God when he heard her call: he was quite convinced he was now to be let in. He approached the door and said: 'Here I am, my lady. Open the door for God's sake, I'm freezing to death.'

'Well of course', she said, 'I do know how you're apt to feel the cold, and cold it certainly is—there's a sprinkling of snow in the courtyard—though I'm sure you get far heavier snowfalls in Paris. I can't let you in yet because that wretched brother of mine, who came this evening for supper, hasn't gone yet. He will go soon, though, and I'll come straight away and let you in. I've just managed to slip away from him—my, it took some doing!—to come and console you, so you won't mind waiting a little longer.'

'Oh please, my lady, I beg you to let me in, so that I can be under cover. It's just come on to snow an absolute blizzard, and it's still coming down heavily. Then I'll go on waiting for you as long as you please.'

'Oh dear me, my love, that I cannot do: this door makes such a noise when it's opened, if I let you in my brother would hear me at once. But now I'm going to tell him he's got to leave, that way I can come back and let you in.'

'Do that quickly, then. And do please stoke up a good blazing fire so that when I come in I can warm myself; I'm so cold now I'm just about numb.'

'What nonsense', said Elena, 'if you've been telling me the truth in all those letters, that you're all ablaze for love of me! But I'm sure you've only been saying it in jest. Anyway, I'm going now. Just wait, and don't despair.'

Elena's lover heard all this with enormous pleasure, then they went back to bed, though they slept little, for they spent practically the rest of the night enjoying each other and thumbing their noses at the student.

The unhappy fellow had just about turned into a stork so hard were his teeth chattering. He realized now that he had been hoodwinked and he several times tried the door and looked about for some other way out. There was none to be seen, though, and as he paced up and down like a caged lion, he cursed the weather, the woman's spitefulness, the endless night, and his own naïvety. He was so angry with her, his long-standing and passionate love changed on the instant into fierce, bitter hatred, and he turned over in his mind any number of vast plans for revenge: if he had hitherto thirsted to be with the woman, he now thirsted far more to avenge himself on her.

After a long, long time the night gave place to day as dawn began to break. The maid, therefore, went downstairs and opened the gate to the courtyard, as instructed by her mistress, and put on an expression of pity. 'Well', she said, 'I hope he meets with bad luck, the fellow who came last night! Such trouble he put us to, madam and I, all night long—and he made you freeze. But I'll tell you what: don't give it another thought—what we couldn't manage last night we'll do another time. I know there's nothing could have made my mistress more upset.'

However angry he was, Rinieri was wise enough to see that threats are simply a weapon placed in the hands of the person threatened, so he kept to himself the passions that would otherwise have been given unfettered expression. Without showing the least irritation, he meekly observed: 'This has truly been the worst night I've ever spent, but I do realize that your mistress is in no way to blame; she came down herself to apologize and console me, because she was sorry for me. And as you say, what was not possible last night we'll keep for another time. Remember me to her and a good day to you.'

Home he went as best he could, quite numb with cold, and dropped straight into bed, dog-tired and dying to sleep. But he woke up to find he had lost virtually all sensation in his arms and legs. So he sent for the doctors and told them about being out in the cold, and ensured he received treatment. The doctors attended to him promptly and effectively, so by and by they managed to relax his muscles and cure his paralysis; his ordeal might have proved fatal were it not that he was young and had returned to the warmth in time. He made a full recovery, and feigned to be more than ever in love with his widow, while he nursed his hatred.

After a while the time came when Fate afforded Rinieri the opportunity to satisfy his wish. The young man with whom the widow was in love fell for another woman, heedless of the love the widow bore him. There was no longer a thing, be it never so trivial, that he was prepared to say or do for her pleasure, and she was consumed with grief and bitterness. The maidservant felt very sorry for her mistress, but could find no way to alleviate her misery over her lost love. Seeing the student passing down the street in his usual way, a foolish notion took hold of her, and that is that her mistress's lover might be restored to her by means of black magic, and that the scholarly young suitor might be well versed in such necromantic skills. She mentioned this to her mistress, and the silly creature took her maid's suggestion seriously, never stopping to think that if her student-suitor had been skilled in necromancy he would have used it to his own ends. She told her maid at once to find out from him whether he would be willing to do this, and to promise him faithfully that she would reward him by doing whatever he asked.

The maid performed her mission well and diligently. Rinieri rejoiced at her words. 'The Lord be praised!' he said to himself. 'The time has come when with His help I'll inflict punishment on that spiteful woman for what she did to thank me for the great love I bore her.' To the maid he said: 'Tell my lady not to worry: if her lover were in India I'd soon fetch him back to crave her pardon for causing her displeasure. What she'll have to do, however, is something I expect to tell her directly, when and where she pleases. Tell her this and comfort her for me.' The maid brought back the message, and a meeting was arranged at Santa Lucia del Prato.

Here the widow and Rinieri met to talk, just the two of them. Elena, quite oblivious of the fact that she had as good as killed her suitor, openly confided in him; she told him what she wanted and begged him to save the situation.

'It's true, my lady', said Rinieri, 'that one of the things I studied in Paris was black magic, and there's not much about it I don't know. As the practice is deeply offensive to God, though, I did take a vow never to make use of it either on my own or on anyone else's behalf. Still, the fact is I'm so coerced by my love for you, I simply don't know how to refuse you anything you ask me to do for you. So even if I had to go to the devil for this alone, I'm still ready to do it, as that's what you want. But I have to tell you that it's not as easy as maybe you think, least of all when it's a question of a woman recovering a man's love, or a man a woman's. You see, it can only be done by the interested party, in person, and he or she must be totally self-assured about it, because it has to be done at night in a remote place and without other company. I don't know whether you feel up to that.'

Elena was more lovesick than prudent. 'The way Love eggs me on', she said, 'there's nothing I wouldn't do to recover the man who's so unfairly forsaken me. Anyway, please tell me what I have to be self-assured about.'

Rinieri, who had some kinship with the devil, replied: 'I shall have to make an image out of tin in the name of the man you want to get back. When I send it to you, you will have to take it with you as you go to bathe naked seven times in a flowing river: do this all alone, not far into the night, and while the moon is in her last quarter. After this you must climb a tree or go up on to some uninhabited building, still naked. You're to face the north, hold the image in your hand, and pronounce certain words—I'll give you them in writing—seven times. When you've said them, two maidens will come to you, both as beautiful as you've ever seen, and they'll greet you kindly and ask what you'd like them to do for you. You'll tell them exactly what it is that you want; and take care that you don't go naming the wrong person. When you've told them, they will leave, and you can go back down to where you left your clothes and get dressed and return home. Before the next night's half-way through, your lover will come to you without fail, weeping and pleading for mercy. And I can assure you that from this moment he'll never desert you for another woman.'

Elena heard him out and believed every word he said; she felt that her lover was as good as back in her arms already, which went a long way towards restoring her spirits. 'Trust me', she said, 'it couldn't be easier for me to do all that, and I couldn't be better placed either, because I have a property up the Arno valley, right close to the river. Bathing will be a positive pleasure, now that we're in July. I remember, too, that not far from the river there's a little abandoned tower; occasionally shepherds go up to the platform on top, using a ladder kept there—it's made of chestnut wood—to look out for lost sheep. It's a very solitary place, quite out of the way. I'll climb up there and expect to carry out your instructions to the letter.'

Rinieri was well acquainted both with the widow's property and with the tower, and was highly pleased that his plan was assured of success. 'Madam', he told her, 'I've never visited those parts, so I don't know the place or the tower, but if what you say is indeed the case, why, nothing could be better. So when the time comes, I'll send you the image and the prayer. I do beg you, though, once you've obtained your wish and seen that I've served you well, please remember me and keep your promise.' 'Without fail', said she and, bidding him farewell, she returned home.

Seeing that his plan looked like coming to fruition, Rinieri was in high spirits; he botched up an image and wrote a bit of nonsense for a prayer, and when he thought the time was right, he sent them to the widow with a message to say that she was to carry out his instructions without further delay the following night. And, taking a servant, he went secretly to a friend's house—it stood quite close to the tower—so as to give effect to his plan.

Elena also set out with her maid, and went to her property. When it was night, she pretended to retire and sent her maid to bed. At the time when we generally fall asleep she slipped out of the house, went to the Arno river-bank near the tower, and after taking a good look around her and finding that the coast was clear, she undressed and hid her clothes under a bush. Then she took the image and bathed in the river seven times, after which she went, still naked, to the tower, holding the image in her hand. At nightfall Rinieri had gone with his servant and hidden among the willows and other trees near the tower, and had observed all these activities. When she passed almost close enough to brush him, naked as she was, and he saw her milky white body against the surrounding darkness, and when he observed her bosom and her other parts, he felt a twinge of pity for her, considering what was going to become of all this beauty in a little while. Moreover, he was assailed with sudden lust—indeed his recumbent appendage was prompted to stand up—and he felt the urge to leave his hiding-place and seize her and have his pleasure with her. These two promptings between them came close to getting the better of him, until he remembered who he was, what it was he had suffered and why, and at whose hands; this rekindled his anger, and banished both pity and lust, leaving him secure in his intention. He let her go her way. She climbed up on to the tower platform, faced north, and set about reciting the words given her by Rinieri. He entered the tower close behind her and quietly and very gradually removed the ladder which led up to the platform. Then he waited to see what she would say and do.

When Elena had recited her prayer seven times, she waited for the two maidens, and she had so long to wait (and it was a chillier wait than she could have wished) that she saw the arrival of dawn. Heartsick that the student's prediction had not taken effect, she mused: 'I fear that the man's been wanting to give me the sort of night I gave him. But if that's the case, his revenge doesn't amount to much, because this night hasn't been a third the length of his, and anyway, this hasn't been at all the same degree of cold.' Still, not wishing to be caught up here by daylight, she made to climb down from the platform but found the ladder was gone. It was as if the ground had vanished from beneath her feet: utterly crushed, she fell down on the platform in a faint. On coming to her senses, she began to grieve and cry miserably. It was all too clear to her that this must be the man's doing, and she regretted that she had crossed him in the first place, and been over-trusting in the second; she ought to have considered him an enemy. She remained thus absorbed for a very long time, then looked once more to see if there were any way to get down, but found none and burst out crying again. Bitterly she brooded: 'O poor me! What will my brothers say, and my family and the neighbours, alas what will the whole town say when they discover I've been found up here with nothing on? My solid reputation for virtue will be in shreds, and if I tried to bluff my way out, as maybe I could, that miserable student won't let me get away with it—he knows the truth. Poor, poor me, losing my young man (what a misplaced love that's been!) and my good name all at a stroke!' She came to such a pitch of despair, she was almost ready to throw herself off the tower.

After sunrise, Elena approached the wall at the edge of the platform and looked out to see if any boy were coming this way with his herd, whom she might send to fetch her maid. Rinieri, who had caught a little sleep in the shelter of a bush, now happened to wake up and see her, and she him. 'Good morning, madam', said he. 'Have the maidens come yet?'

Seeing him and hearing his voice started her crying again bitterly; she begged him to come into the tower so she might speak with him. This he did with alacrity. Elena lay down on her stomach, with only her head protruding over the opening in the floor, and tearfully said: 'Rinieri, if I gave you a bad night, you've well and truly taken your revenge: it may be July, but I thought I was going to freeze last night with nothing on. And I've cried so much over the trick I played you and my stupidity in believing you, it's a wonder my eyes are still in my head. So I beseech you, not for love of me, as you can't love me, but for love of your own self, being the gentleman you are, be satisfied with what you've done to me so far as your revenge for the way I treated you. Let me have my clothes back and let me get down: don't insist on taking from me the one thing you could never give me back if you wanted to—my good name. Look, if I deprived you of my company that night, I can make it up to you many times over and any time you please. Be satisfied, then. Be a gentleman and rest content to have taken your vengeance and made it clear to me that you've done so. Don't insist on pitting your strength against a woman; an eagle derives no glory from defeating a dove. So for love of God and for the sake of your own honour, take pity on me.'

The wrong she had done him still rankled very much in his mind, and the sight of her crying and pleading made him feel pleased, but also vexed: pleased that he now had his vengeance, by which he had set so much store, but vexed to find himself feeling sorry for the poor creature. His humane instincts could not, however, get the better of his wrath, so he replied:

'I, madam, did not have the art of watering *my* entreaties with tears, or making them as honeyed as you are making yours; but if, that night when I was dying of cold in that snow-filled courtyard of yours, if my entreaties had obtained from you a little shelter from the elements, how readily should I do as you ask. Since you're now so much more concerned, though, about your reputation than you have been in the past, and you're not happy to stay up there in the nude, address your entreaties to the man in whose arms you were quite happy to lie naked, the night you yourself have referred to, while you listened to me tramping the snow in your courtyard, my teeth chattering; get him to help you, have him fetch you your clothes, get him to replace the ladder so you can come down, try to make him feel some concern for your reputation on whose account you've not hesitated to jeopardize it now and a thousand times before. Why don't you call him to the rescue? Who better than he? You are his: what will he protect and help if he won't protect and help you? Call him, you fool, and see if the love you bear him and your combined wits can rescue you from my stupidity—when you were disporting yourself in his arms, you asked him which he thought the greater, my stupidity or your love for him. And don't you now be offering me what I don't want and what you couldn't anyway deny me if I did want it. Keep your nights for your lover, if it so happens that you leave this place alive. Let them be yours and his: I had one too many, and to have been spurned once should be sufficient for me. Another thing: you have a wily tongue. You're trying to win me round by flattery, calling me a gentleman, a good man;

you're tacitly attempting to play on my good nature so I'll think better of punishing you for your spite. But your wheedling shan't pull the wool over my eyes the way your deceitful promises once did. I know myself, I never learnt as much about myself all the time I lived in Paris as you taught me in a single night about your duplicity. Supposing, however, that I were magnanimous; you're the sort of woman on whom magnanimity would simply be lost. In wild beasts of your type, penitence, and vengeance too, must end in death; in human beings, what you proposed in this regard is sufficient. So though I may not measure up to being an eagle, what I see in you is certainly no dove but a poisonous snake, and I mean to persecute you with utter loathing and with all my strength as my age-old enemy. Not that what I'm doing to you may remotely be called vengeance, but rather punishment: vengeance has to exceed the offence, while this falls well short of it. If it were vengeance I was looking for, considering to what an extreme you reduced me, your life would not be sufficient compensation nor would the lives of a hundred women of your sort, for I should be killing a despicable, nasty, cruel minx of a woman. Aside from that face of yours with its fleeting beauty—in a few years it will have been marred with wrinkles—tell me, which particular devil is it that uses you for his paltry servant? You didn't hesitate to kill a good man—as you called me just now—but a single day of my life can still afford greater benefit to mankind than a hundred thousand lifetimes of your sort ever will so long as the world endures. What you're now suffering will be my lesson to teach you what it is to spurn men who have any feelings, and what it is to spurn men of learning; I'll give you reason never again to embrace such folly—if you survive. Now if you're so anxious to get down, why don't you jump? God willing, you'll break your neck and that way achieve two objects, escaping from the distress you're feeling, and making me the happiest of men. That's all I have to say. I've been clever enough to get you up where you are; it's up to you to be clever now and get yourself down, just as you were so clever at making a fool of me.'

While Rinieri was thus talking, the wretched woman never stopped weeping, and time passed, the sun gaining altitude.

When she had heard him out, she said: 'Oh, how cruel you are! If that cursed night bothered you as much as all that, and my offence seems to you so serious that you're untouched by my youthful beauty, my bitter tears, or my humble prayers, be moved a little at any rate by this one thing, the trust I have placed in you, and let it temper your rigour: I confided all my secrets to you and thus put you in a position to accomplish your wish and confront me with my wrongdoing. Had I not entrusted myself to you, you would have had no means to take your revenge on me, which seems to have been your most ardent wish. Ah, abate your anger and forgive me! If you forgive me and get me down from here, I'm ready to give up that faithless young man altogether, and make you my only lover and master, however ill you speak of my beauty, however fleeting and worthless you consider it. Whatever is to be said about my beauty, or any other woman's, the fact remains that you have one reason if no other to hold it dear and that is, it serves the desire, the pleasure and enjoyment, of men in their youth—and you are not old. And however cruelly you're treating me, I still cannot believe you'd want to see me die so disgracefully, throwing myself off here in sheer desperation before your very eyes—eyes that once took such pleasure in looking at me, if you were not yet a liar when you said so. Ah, be moved to pity, for God's sake. The sun is growing very hot, and as I suffered from the cold in the night, now the heat is beginning to torment me.'

Rinieri, who was enjoying this conversation, replied: 'It's not been out of love for me, madam, that you've placed yourself in my hands, but in order to recover possession of the love you have lost, so what do you deserve if not to suffer worse? And you must be mad if you imagine that this has been the one and only course available to me to get the revenge I have craved. I had a thousand others, I'd laid a thousand snares for your feet as I pretended to go on loving you, and it would not have been long before you were bound to stumble into one of them had this one not come to fruition: then you would have landed in even worse affliction and worse shame. However, I took this opportunity, not to spare you but to obtain my happiness all the sooner. Besides, even if all else had failed, I should still have had my pen, with which I should have written such things about you that when you came to hear of them—and you would have—you'd have wished every minute of the day that you had never been born. The power of the pen is vastly greater than people believe who've never experienced it, and I swear to God—and may He prosper this vengeance of mine right to the end as He has done the beginning of it—I'd have written things about you that would have made you so ashamed of yourself, never mind what others thought, you'd have plucked out your eyes to avoid looking at yourself. So don't go blaming the sea if the little brook has added to its waters. As for your love, I've already told you I don't give a hoot for it. Give it to the fellow who had it before, if you can. I loathed him earlier, but now I love him for the way he's treated you. You go around turning young men's heads, getting them to fall in love with you—it's fresh-faced youths with good black beards that you go after—and you like them to vie with each other in serenading you and entering the lists wearing your favours. Their elders have been through all that, they know what the youngsters still have to learn. Not only that; you fancy they ride their mounts harder and last the course better than older men. I agree with you, when they have a thrash they put more vigour into it, but it's the older, more experienced men who know at once where the flea tickles: you do far better to choose the short and sweet over the lengthy and insipid. Hard riding only tires everyone out, never mind how young they are: a gentle pace might bring you a little later to your inn, but at least you'll arrive rested. You brainless animals have no idea how much evil lies hidden beneath that thin veneer of beauty. Young lads are never satisfied with one woman: they want every one they set eyes on, and think they're entitled to them all, so their love's not to be relied on, as you can now witness all too well from your own experience. They think they have a right to be respected and cossetted by their women; their greatest boast is of the women they have had—how many women have ended up with the friars on this account, relying on their vow of secrecy! Though you tell me that nobody knows of your love-affairs apart from your maid and I, how wrong you are! If that's what you think, you must think again: where she comes from they speak of virtually nothing else, and the same goes for your district. But as a rule, the last person to hear is the one most directly involved. The young steal from you, then, while their elders are givers. You made a bad choice, madam. Remain with the fellow you gave yourself to. As for me, you spurned me; leave me to another—I have found a lady you could never measure up to, and she's got to know me far better than ever you did. What, then, is the apple of my eye? That you'll discover beyond any doubt in the next world (for clearly in this one you've taken little account of my words), if you throw yourself off the tower right now: I do believe that your soul will be able to see, as it is welcomed into the devil's arms, whether my eyes show any regret or not at watching you fall headlong. However, as I expect you won't wish to oblige me in this, let me suggest, if the sun starts to burn you, that you call to mind the cold you made me suffer; mix that with this heat, and you're bound to find the sun's fire tempered.'

Seeing that his drift tended entirely towards a cruel resolution, the unhappy lady burst into tears again. 'Very well', she said, 'as nothing about me moves you to pity, be moved by the love you feel for that other lady who is, you say, wiser than me in your opinion, and who loves you too; for love of her, pardon me, and let me have my clothes back so I can get dressed, and let me come down.'

Rinieri laughed, and as it was now a good hour beyond nine, he said: 'Hm, I don't know how to refuse, now you've invoked this other lady. Tell me where they are and I'll go and fetch them and let you come down.'

Elena believed him and took comfort. She told him where she had left her clothes. Rinieri came out of the tower, and instructed his servant not to leave but to stay close by and do his best to ensure that no one went in until he got back. This said, he went to his friend's house, breakfasted at leisure, and then, when he felt it was time, retired to bed.

Left on top of the tower, Elena was somewhat comforted by her idle hope, but still felt as wretched as could be. She changed to a sitting position, moved to the part of the wall still offering a little shade, and set about waiting, her mind full of bitter thoughts. She brooded, she wept, she hoped for, then despaired of, the man returning with her clothes, she hopped from one thought to the next, and finally, worn out with misery and a wakeful night, she fell asleep. The sun was baking hot and had climbed to the meridian whence it shot its rays unobstructed on to Elena's tender, delicate body and on to her unprotected head with such strength that it not only roasted every inch of flesh it saw, it cracked it all open minutely. Though she had been in a deep sleep, the burning forced her awake. She felt she was being roasted alive and, when she moved, she felt all her burnt skin split open and fragment, like a singed parchment that's being tugged at. She had a splitting headache, furthermore, which was no wonder. The tower platform, too, was so scorching that her feet could not stand it, nor could any other part, and she kept shifting about, tearfully, never still a minute. There was, moreover, not a breath of wind, so the place was swarming with blowflies and horse-flies which settled on her cracked skin and stung her so badly it felt like any number of spear-jabs; so she never stopped swiping at them, all the time cursing herself, her life, her lover, and the student.

And thus, as the unbelievable heat, the sun's rays, the blowflies and horse-flies, her hunger and, vastly more, her thirst—and a thousand noxious thoughts to boot—stabbed, stung, and tormented her, she stood up and looked to discover if she could see or hear anybody close by; she was fully prepared, come what may, to call for help. But even this was denied her by her adverse fate. Because of the heat the labourers had all left the fields, not that anyone had been to work in this neighbourhood—they were all at home threshing their corn. So all she could hear were the crickets, and she could see the Arno, with its inviting waters: the sight made her only the thirstier. Here and there she could see houses and woods and shade, which all filled her with painful longing. What else is there to say about the unfortunate widow? What with the sun above, the heat radiating from the platform beneath her, and the blowflies and horse-flies biting her from either side, she had been reduced to such a state that if the previous night the milk-white pallor of her skin defied the darkness, now she was crimson as madder and mottled with blood; anyone seeing her would have taken her for the world's most hideous creature.

This, then, was her condition, at her wits' end and dead to hope, indeed expecting death sooner than anything else. It was now past mid-afternoon and Rinieri got out of bed, remembered that woman of his, and went back to the tower to see what had become of her. His servant, who was still fasting, he sent off to eat. When Elena heard him, weak and suffering torments as she was, she came to the opening in the platform, sat down there, and cried, saying: 'Rinieri, you've certainly taken your revenge to extremes: if I made you freeze by night in my courtyard, you've made me roast, you've set me on fire, up on this tower by day, and you're making me die of hunger and thirst. So I beg you, for God's sake alone, to come up here and kill me off as I lack the courage to take my own life; such is my torment, there's nothing I want better than to die. If you won't do me this favour, let me at least have a glass of water so I can rinse my mouth, which is more than my tears can do, so parched am I.'

Her weakness was evident enough to him from her voice, besides which, what he saw of her body was all scorched by the sun, and this made him feel a little sorry for her, as did her meek request. None the less, his answer was: 'You'll not die at my hands, you spiteful woman; you'll die at your own, if you find in yourself such a wish. And you'll have as much water from me to relieve you of the heat as I had fire from you to make the cold endurable. I'm only sorry that while the remedy for my frost-bitten condition was reeking manure, your sunburn will be treated with cool, fragrant rose-water. And while I came close to the loss of all feeling and of my very life, you'll come out of your sunburn as beautiful as ever, like the snake that casts its old skin.'

'Oh poor me!' she cried. 'Any beauty I come by in that way, I would to God it were bestowed on those who hate me. But you, how have you found the stomach to torture me like this? You're more savage than any wild beast. What more could I have expected from you or from anyone else if I'd murdered your entire kin after the cruellest of tortures? I certainly don't know of any worse torment that might be inflicted on a traitor who had delivered up an entire city to slaughter than what you've subjected me to, leaving me to roast in the sun and get eaten alive by flies, and not even letting me have a glass of water, when even condemned murderers are often given a glass of wine before their execution—they have only to ask for it. Very well; I see that you're not to be moved from your implacable savagery, and my torment leaves you quite untouched. So I shall resign myself patiently to my death, that God may have mercy on my soul. And I pray He will look with eyes of justice on what it is you are doing.' This said, she dragged herself painfully to the middle of the platform, with no further hope of surviving such a blistering heat. Not once but a thousand times she felt herself at her last gasp for thirst, among her other torments, and ceaselessly she bewailed and lamented her misfortune.

But it was now evening and Rinieri felt he had done enough, so he had Elena's clothes fetched and wrapped in his servant's cloak, and proceeded to the wretched woman's house. He found her disconsolate maid sitting miserably on the doorstep, quite at her wits' end. 'Tell me, my good woman', he asked, 'how fares your mistress?'

'I don't know, sir. I expected to find her in bed this morning as I thought I saw her go to bed last night. But I didn't find her there, I couldn't find her anywhere, I don't know what's become of her, and I'm so worried I can't bear it. Is there anything you can tell me, sir?'

'If only I'd had you along with her where I've been keeping her!' said Rinieri. 'That way I might have punished you for your offence as I've punished her for hers. But rest assured, you shan't escape my clutches and I'll pay you back for what you did. Believe me, you'll never again play tricks on people without remembering me.' With this he told his servant to give her the clothes and bid her fetch her mistress if she wanted to.

The manservant did as bidden and, on receiving the clothes, the maid recognized them and barely stopped herself from crying out at his words, for she was terrified they might have killed her mistress. Rinieri having left, she straight away ran with the clothes to the tower, weeping.

Now one of Elena's labourers had unfortunately lost two of his pigs, and in his search for them he came to the tower a little after Rinieri had left. As he hunted about for some sign of his pigs he heard the unfortunate lady's sad weeping. So he climbed up as far as he could and shouted: 'Who's crying up there?'

Elena recognized her man's voice and called him by his name. 'Oh, go and fetch my maid and help her climb up here to me.'

The labourer recognized her and said: 'My goodness, Ma'am. Who got you up there? Your maid's been hunting for you all day long, but who'd ever have thought you'd be up here?' And he set to work re-erecting the ladder in its proper place, using cord to secure the rungs.

Now in came the maid and, once inside the tower, she could contain herself no longer but beat her hands together and cried out: 'Alas, my sweet madam, where are you?'

Elena heard her and answered as loudly as she could: 'O my sister, I'm up here. Don't cry but bring me my clothes quickly.'

The maid was considerably relieved to hear her speak. She climbed the ladder which the labourer had more or less secured and, with his help, reached the tower platform. When she saw her mistress looking more like a charred log than a human being, lying naked on the floor, more dead than alive, she scratched her cheeks and burst into tears over her, for all the world as if she were dead. Elena begged her maid for Heaven's sake to shut up and help her dress. Discovering from her that no one knew where she was other than those who had brought her clothes and the labourer here present, she took some comfort from this and besought them for God's sake never to breathe a word of it to a living soul. After a fair amount of talk the labourer heaved the lady up over his shoulder, for she was unable to walk, and brought her safely out of the tower. The maid, poor old thing, taking less care as she followed them down, lost her footing on the ladder and fell the rest of the way, breaking her thigh. Such was her pain she started roaring like a lion.

The labourer had set Elena down on a grassy patch and now went back to see what was the matter with the maid; finding she'd broken her thigh, he carried her out to the grass as well and laid her down beside her mistress who, seeing this misfortune added to the rest—for the person she had been most counting on to help her now had a fractured thigh—broke into such a woeful fit of weeping, for she was unbearably distressed, that the labourer, far from being able to console her, burst into tears as well. But as the sun was setting and they did not want to be caught out here by nightfall, he went home, at the unhappy lady's request, and returned with two of his brothers, his wife, and a plank; on this they laid the maidservant and carried her home. Elena was revived with a little fresh water and words of comfort, then the labourer lifted her on to his shoulder and carried her back to her own bedroom. The labourer's wife fed her a little bread soaked in broth then undressed her and put her to bed. They arranged for the lady and her maid to be conveyed back to Florence during the night, and this was indeed done.

Here Elena, who was nothing if not artful, put out a story bearing no resemblance to what had actually happened, and had her brothers and sisters and everyone else believe that what had befallen her and her maid was purely the result of demonic spells. The doctors were assiduous, and cured Elena of a high fever and her other ailments, a most painful and trying ordeal, for she several times left all her skin stuck to the sheets; similarly they healed the maid's thigh.

So Elena dismissed her lover from her mind, and was wise enough thereafter to avoid both jilting and loving. As for Rinieri, when he heard that the maid had broken her thigh, he felt himself amply avenged and was happy to put it all behind him without another word.

That, then, is what befell the silly girl for playing on a man's affections—and for imagining you could flirt as readily with a man of learning as with any other. Little did she realize that scholars—most of them, if not all—have a keen nose for the way the wind blows. Take care then, ladies: no jilting, and least of all, of scholars.

VIII. 8. *Two young Sienese are boon companions until one seduces the other's wife. The other repays him in the same coin, and repairs the friendship.*

The ladies found it painful to listen to the sad plight of Elena, even though their pity was somewhat tempered, as they listened, by their acceptance that she had to some extent brought her troubles on herself; however, they felt that the student was certainly inflexible and ruthless, indeed plain cruel. When Pampinea reached her conclusion, the queen told Fiammetta to follow, which she did with alacrity:

I expect that the offended student's rigorous attitude will have left you all rather excruciated, so I think I ought to soothe your feelings with something more cheerful. I'm going to tell you a little tale, then, about a young man who suffered a wrong, but endured it more meekly and got his own back without going the whole hog. It will show you that enough is as good as a feast, and you should be content to give as good as you get; if you have to get even with someone who's hurt you, there's no call to carry your vengeance to extremes.

In Siena, so they say, there once lived two young men of ample means and good citizen stock; one was called Spinelloccio Tavena, the other, Zeppa di Mino; they dwelt as neighbours in Cammollia. The two were quite inseparable and, to all outward appearances, they couldn't have been more devoted to each other had they been brothers. Each of them was married to a very beautiful woman.

Now Spinelloccio was often round at Zeppa's house, whether or not Zeppa himself was in, and he became so intimate with his friend's wife that he started sleeping with her; this went on for a good while before anybody noticed. However, came the day when Zeppa, unknown to his wife, was at home as Spinelloccio called by for him. 'He's not in', said Zeppa's wife, so Spinelloccio was up the stairs and into the sitting-room in no time, where he found the lady; seeing no one else about, he threw his arms round her and started kissing her, and she him. Zeppa saw this but kept quiet; he hid and watched to see the game develop. In a moment he saw his wife and Spinelloccio walk arm in arm into the bedroom and lock the door. This made him extremely cross. He realized that all he had to do was kick up a row and, far from improving the situation, he'd end up only the more humiliated. So he set to pondering what sort of revenge he should take that might restore his equanimity while keeping the matter secret. After much thought he felt he'd hit upon a solution, and he remained in concealment the whole time Spinelloccio was in with his wife.

When Spinelloccio had left, Zeppa went into the bedroom, where he found his wife still busy setting her veils to rights, for Spinelloccio had knocked them to the floor just for a lark. 'What are you doing?' he asked.

'Can't you see?'

'Indeed I can. I saw something else too I'd sooner not have done!' On which subject he gave her a piece of his mind. She was terrified. After much beating about the bush she made her confession, for she was scarcely able to deny her intimacy with Spinelloccio, and she tearfully begged his forgiveness.

'Now listen, woman', said Zeppa. 'What you've done is odious. If you want me to forgive you, take care you do exactly as I tell you, and it's this: tell Spinelloccio to find some excuse to leave me tomorrow morning about nine and come to you here; when he's here I'm going to come back; as soon as you hear me, you're to have him get into this chest; shut him inside, and when you've done that I'll tell you what else you have to do. Don't worry about it—you have my word I shan't lay a finger on him.' His wife, to make amends, promised to do as bidden.

Next morning Zeppa and Spinelloccio were out together and at nine o'clock Spinelloccio, who had promised to call on his friend's wife at that hour, said to Zeppa: 'A friend has invited me for a bite of lunch, and I don't want to keep him waiting. So long!'

'It's some way to lunch-time, isn't it?' observed Zeppa.

'No matter—I need to have a word with him about some business of mine, so I should be with him on the early side.'

So off went Spinelloccio, made a little detour, turned up at Zeppa's, and went into the bedroom with his friend's wife. A moment later Zeppa was back. Hearing his arrival, she feigned utter panic and made him hide in the chest her husband had pointed to, and shut him up inside it. Then she left the room.

When Zeppa got upstairs he asked her: 'Tell me, is it getting on for lunch?'

'Just about.'

'Spinelloccio's gone off to dine with a friend, leaving his wife all on her own. Go to the window and give her a shout: tell her to come and join us for lunch.'

His wife was on tenterhooks and therefore the soul of obedience; she did as bidden, and Spinelloccio's wife, after much entreaty by Zeppa's, did come over when she discovered that her husband would not be in for lunch. Zeppa greeted her more than cordially, took her by the hand without ceremony, and brought her into the bedroom after quietly bidding his wife go into the kitchen. Once in the bedroom he turned back and locked the door. When Spinelloccio's wife saw him locking the door: 'Good gracious, Zeppa!' she cried. 'What are you doing? Is this what you've brought me here for? Is this your way of loving Spinelloccio? Is this how you show yourself a true friend of his?'

Zeppa held her tight and ushered her over to the chest in which her husband was confined. 'Now before you start complaining', he said, 'just you listen to me. I love Spinelloccio like a brother, always have done. Yesterday, though he doesn't know it, I discovered where my trust in him led: it led to his sleeping with my wife the way he does with you. Now the fact is I'm devoted to him; so I don't propose to take any revenge on him other than to repeat his offence. He's had my wife; I'll take you. If you refuse, I'll have no choice but to catch him in the act—as I don't propose to leave this offence unpunished, I'll serve him a turn that will leave you both smarting.'

Spinelloccio's wife believed him after he had given her repeated assurances, and she said: 'Zeppa, my dear, as I'm the one your vengeance is to fall on, so be it, but on one condition: that after what we're going to have to do, you'll patch things up between me and your wife, because, in spite of what she's done to me, I want no quarrel with her.'

'Of course I shall', he replied. 'What's more, I'll give you a rich and beautiful jewel—you won't have another like it.' This said, he hugged and kissed her and laid her down on top of the chest inside which her husband was shut, and here he took his pleasure with her, and she with him, to his heart's content.

Inside the chest, Spinelloccio had heard every word spoken by Zeppa and his wife's answers; he had felt the jig-jig being danced on top of his head, and for ages he was so cut up about it he was ready to die. Were he not afraid of Zeppa, he would from his prison have addressed a very rude epithet to his wife. However, on second thoughts, he realized that it was he who had started it all and Zeppa was acting quite within his rights, indeed he was letting him off very lightly and behaving like a real pal. He determined to be an even better friend to Zeppa, if he was willing.

When Zeppa had had his fill he got off the chest, and the lady reminded him about the promised jewel. Zeppa opened the bedroom door and called his wife, who came in and ventured only to remark: 'Well, you've given me tit for tat!' This she said with a chuckle.

'Open this chest', Zeppa told his wife. She did so, and Zeppa showed the lady her Spinelloccio inside it. And it would take a while to describe which of the two was the more deeply mortified, Spinelloccio as he looked at Zeppa, knowing that his friend knew what he'd been up to, or Spinelloccio's wife, as she looked at her husband, knowing that he had heard and felt what she'd been doing to him just over his head.

Zeppa said to her: 'Here's the jewel: I'm making you a present of it.'

Spinelloccio climbed out of the chest and came to the point at once: 'All right, Zeppa: now we're quits, and just as well for, as you were saying to my wife a moment ago, we're still friends as before. As the only thing standing between us is our wives, why don't we pool them too!'

A good idea, agreed Zeppa—and the four of them sat down to lunch in total harmony. From that day on each wife had two husbands, each husband had two wives, and this common ownership never gave rise to a single blow or argument.

VIII. 9. *A doctor, Master Simone, seeks a short cut to the good life; Bruno and Buffalmacco zealously help him on his way.*

The pooling of wives, as practised by the two Sienese, kept the ladies prattling for a while. The queen was now the only one left with a tale to tell—she was not going to interfere with Dioneo's privilege—so she began:

Spinelloccio richly deserved the prank played on him by Zeppa, and I'm inclined to believe that if a person deserves to, or even goes out of his way to, have his leg pulled, the prankster—as Pampinea showed us—is scarcely to blame. Spinelloccio received his deserts. And I'm going to tell you about a man who went looking for trouble: those who played tricks on him are not to be censured, I should say, but positively commended. The victim was a doctor fresh back in Florence from Bologna,* tricked out in his new squirrel's-fur doctor's regalia, but no less of an idiot for that.

Not a day goes by but our fellow-Florentines come back to us from Bologna where they've turned into judges, physicians, notaries, and so on, with their great flowing cloaks, their splashes of scarlet, and their squirrel's-fur hats, dressed to beat the band—how they measure up to all this splendour is, alas, all too evident. One such Florentine was Simone da Villa, a man well endowed with inherited wealth but starved of brains. Not long ago he returned here in scarlet splendour, with the ceremonial hood attesting his doctorate in medicine (we have his word for it), and took up residence in the street now called Via del Cocomero. This new arrival had one noteworthy habit: he could not see a man pass in the street without having to turn to whoever he happened to be with and ask who the fellow was. He'd take careful note of what he was told, as if the medicines he concocted for his patients depended on his observation of people's behaviour.

Among the people who impinged especially upon his notice were two painters, Bruno and Buffalmacco—we've already met them twice today. The pair were inseparable and lodged nearby. He was quite struck by their remarkably happy, carefree disposition, and asked several people about them. They were, everyone told him, penniless painters. This the doctor could not swallow: they could not possibly be so cheerful if they were poor—they were no fools, he had been told, so they must have some secret source of funds. He decided, therefore, to try striking up a friendship with the pair of them, or with one at any rate. And with Bruno he succeeded. It didn't take Bruno long to size up the doctor as a prize ass and to start taking the mickey out of him. As for the doctor, he'd lie on his back and wave his paws in the air. He invited Bruno to dinner a number of times, till he felt the ice was sufficiently broken for a heart-to-heart talk, whereupon he confessed his wonder at the carefree life-style he and Buffalmacco adopted: given their penury, what, he asked, was their secret?

Bruno listened to the doctor and burst out laughing: another of the man's daft questions, he thought, and up he came with a suitably silly answer. 'What we do', he said, 'is not something I'd reveal to many people; but I don't mind telling *you* because you're a friend and won't give us away. You're quite right: my friend and I do indeed live like lords, and it's not on the proceeds of our painting or of landed rents—they wouldn't yield us enough to pay even for the water we use. And I wouldn't have you thinking that we go around robbing people. What we do is go hunting, after our fashion, and that, sir, provides us with everything we require for our pleasure and utility, all without harming a soul. This is how we live as happily as you've noticed.'

The doctor didn't know what Bruno was talking about but he believed every word. His mind boggled. He couldn't wait to find out about this 'hunting' of theirs—he promised not to breathe a word to anyone.

'Oh dear!' cried Bruno. 'If you only knew what you were asking! It's the biggest secret, and if it once got out, sir, I'd be right flummoxed, I'd be out on my ear, I'd be in the doghouse and no two ways about it. And yet . . . and yet I think you're just great, never known a man so marvellously big-headed, I'd trust you almost as far as I could throw you, so . . . well . . . I simply can't say no to you. So I'm going to tell you, but on one condition: you've got to swear on the Holy Whatsit you'll never never tell a soul—you did promise.'

The oath was sworn.

'I'll tell you, then, my simple Simon. We had a great necromancer living here not all that long ago, Michael Scotus* (he was a Scot) and he was entertained right royally by a number of gentlemen, most of them now departed. When he made to leave us, his hosts begged him to leave behind a couple of his abler disciples, and this he did, with the instruction that they were to be at the disposal of these gentlemen who had been so kind to him, and fulfil their every wish. So these disciples remained behind at the service of these gentlemen, readily seconding them in their amorous quests and whatever else. In the end they chose to settle here—they like us Florentines and our life-style, and they made a number of close friendships, taking no account of wealth or social class, but simply consulting their own tastes. Now as a favour to their friends they organized them into a club, some twenty-five of them, meeting not less than twice a month at a rendezvous of their choosing. At these gatherings each person was free to make his request to the disciples, who would make their wish come true for the night. As Buffalmacco and I were on the best of terms with them, they included us in the club, and we're still members.

'At these gatherings of ours you'd scarcely imagine the gorgeous hangings that bedeck the dining-hall, the place-settings fit for a king, the elegance of the attendants waiting on the tables, the beauty of the serving-maids, the pleasure of feasting off gold and silver plate, the salvers, ewers, goblets and flasks; and the dishes brought to the table as each guest desires—such abundance, such variety, each one served at its proper time. How can I describe to you the airs and melodies played on any number of instruments, the melodious concert of voices? Or the candles—you never saw so many candles burning as on these occasions; and the sweets of all kinds, and the rare vintage wines we drink. And don't you go imagining that we go there in the clothes we're wearing now: the least one of us sits there dressed to the nines—in our apparel no expense is spared.

'To cap it all there are the ladies, and when I say beautiful . . . and they're fetched in from all over the world just the moment you clap your hands. Why, you'd find there the Begum of Bombay, the Dame of Dymchurch, the Infanta of Ibiza, the Maharanee of Madhupur, the Margravine of Mühlhausen, the Princess of Palmyra, and the Sultana of Santiago. What more can I say? Talk of a bevy of queens!—you'll even find the Grand Panjandrina herself.'

'No!'

'Well, it's true! When we've all drunk our fill and finished our desserts we cut a few capers on the dance-floor, then each of us goes off into our room with our chosen mistress. Those bedrooms, they're sheer heaven: they're fragrant like your jars of aromatics when you've been crushing cumin seed, and the beds we go to sleep in would be the envy of the Doge of Venice. In the bedrooms there are all kinds of games to play together, you can imagine, like "Putting the bung in the barrel". Buffalmacco and I come off among the best, I should say, because more often than not he draws the Queen of France and I the Queen of England, and they are quite simply the world's two most beautiful women—and the way we treat them, they have eyes for us alone. So you see: we have to be the happiest of men, with the love of two such queens. Furthermore, if we want a couple of thousand florins off them, "Done!" they say, "here you are." This, then, is what we mean when we say we "go hunting"; in a sense we hunt our quarry like pirates going after plunder—though, unlike pirates, we give back what we take after we've had the use of it. So now you know what we mean by going hunting, and you can see how vital it is to keep this all to yourself, so I shan't ask you again.'

The doctor, whose medical knowledge extended doubtless no further than treating babies for milk-scab, placed as much reliance on Bruno's report as on any self-evident truth, and he conceived a burning desire to be admitted to the circle; it was the sum of his ambitions. He told Bruno it was no wonder they were such a happy pair, and it was all he could do to stop himself asking there and then to be put up for membership—the request would come more confidently once he had wormed his way further into Bruno's good graces. So he deferred his request and applied himself to ensuring an ever closer friendship: Bruno was his guest for meals morning, noon, and night—indeed the doctor fawned over him to the point where he seemed to be only half there when he was not in Bruno's company.

So as to repay the doctor's kind attentions Bruno thought he would do some paintings for him: in his living-room a starveling woman representing Lent; at the door to his bedroom a sheep to represent the Lamb of God; above his front door a chamber-pot, as a signboard to identify his services to his clients; on his terrace, too, he painted the Battle of the Cats and Mice, which enchanted the doctor. On occasions when he had not supped with the doctor Bruno would tell him: 'Our club met last night. The Queen of England? What a yawn! I called in the Chin Ying Yang of Cathay.'

'The Chin Ying Yang? Who she?'

'You don't know? I'm not surprised. I gather Hippo's Guts hasn't come across her, neither has Hava China.'

'Don't you mean Hippocrates and Avicenna?'*

'You may be right', said Bruno. 'Can't say I know much about your crowd, any more than you do about mine. The Chin Ying Yang, though, that's what the Cathayans call what we call an empress. And was there ever a finer figure of a woman! Take one look at her and you'd forget if you were swallowing a pill or a poultice.' Bruno dropped such remarks periodically to keep the doctor's appetite whetted.

One evening, when there were just the two of them up late, as Bruno was working on his Battle of the Cats and Mice, the doctor, who was holding the lamp for him, finally felt he had earned the painter's complete confidence and decided to make known his wish. 'Bruno', he said, 'God knows there's not a man alive whose wishes I should more readily honour than yours. Why, even if you asked me to run around the block for you, I do believe I'd do it! So don't be surprised if I'm absolutely open with you. You remember you recently spoke to me about your club and its happy gatherings, and frankly there's nothing in the world I'd like so much as to become a member. And if I do become a member, you'll see soon enough that it was not for nothing that I asked you. Look, you have my permission to pull my leg forever and a day if I don't put you in the way of the prettiest serving-girl you'll have seen in a month of Sundays. I saw her a year or two back in Red-Light Alley and my, how I dote on her—I offered her 10 fat silver crowns if she'd come with me but she refused. So I do earnestly beseech you, tell me how I join, help me to get in. Then I'll be your best friend, that's a promise. You have to admit I'm a fine, upstanding fellow, I know how to carry myself. Look at my face: a rose's envy! Add to this, I'm a physician—I'll wager there's none other in your club—and I'm bursting with stories and ditties; hold on, I'll sing you one'; and he burst into song.

By dint of enormous self-control Bruno kept a straight face. The doctor finished his song and asked: 'How did you like it?'

'What a voice!' sighed Bruno. 'Beautiful! I've only heard a crow sing better.'

'And yet you'd never have believed me if you hadn't heard me.'

'I can't argue with that.'

'I know a whole lot more', said the doctor, 'but that'll have to do for now. Come now to my father: he was a man of gentle birth, even if he did live on a farm; as for my mother, I'll have you know her people hail from Hicksville. There's not a doctor in Florence whose library or whose wardrobe can match mine, as you see. Some of my attire, I'll have you know, cost me upward of 100 pence, and we're talking about a good ten years ago! So do, do, do get me in and, if you do, I swear to you, I don't care what illness strikes you down, you'll have my services free and gratis.'

Bruno heard him out and was confirmed in his suspicion that the doctor must be the world's ripest moron. 'Let's have that light over here a bit', he said. 'Just bear with me while I get the tails on to these mice, then you'll have my answer.'

When the mice had their tails, and Bruno had shown every sign of serious reflection: 'You, sir', he said, 'would go to great lengths for me, I know; and what you ask of me may look small to a man of your vast attainments, but to me it's utterly enormous. Of course if I did it for anyone in the world I'd do it for you, because I'm as devoted to you as can be, and besides, you speak so convincingly you'd persuade a vegetarian to lay off cutlets, so how can I resist! The more I see of you, the more I'm struck by your sheer brain-power. Besides, if I took to you for no other reason, I'd like you for setting your heart on so fine an object. Now the point is, what you're after is not in my power to grant; there's nothing *I* can do to bring it about. But if you promise me on your honour (such as it is) to put your trust in me, I shall tell you how you are to go about obtaining your wish; and I'm confident, what with all those fine books and other things you have, as you've told me, that you'll succeed.'

'Speak freely: I see you still don't know me all that well, you don't know how good I am at keeping a secret. When Gasparruolo da Saliceto was chief magistrate at Forlimpopoli there were few secrets he didn't impart to me, he found me such a good private secretary. Why, when he was about to marry his Bergamina, I was the first person he told. Now what d'you think of that?'

'Well I must say', answered Bruno, 'if he trusted you, then so can I. Now this is what you have to do. Our club is run by a president assisted by two counsellors, who rotate every six months. Buffalmacco will be president from the first of next month and I one of the counsellors, that has been decided. The sitting president has considerable say in who gets elected. It seems to me, therefore, you should be cultivating Buffalmacco for all you're worth. Seeing how clever you are, he's bound to take to you, and when you've broken the ice with him with your sheer native wit and the gifts you can lay your hands on, then you can put your request to him, and he'll be unable to refuse. I've already spoken to him about you and he is very well disposed towards you. Do that, then leave it to me.'

'Now that's the way I like to hear you talk', said the doctor. 'If he's a man who appreciates intelligent company and enjoys their conversation, you can rely on it, he'll be seeking me out the whole time—I've got enough wit for an entire population, and more to spare.'

This was the point at which Bruno gave Buffalmacco a full account of where things stood, and the latter could not wait to give Dr Dogsbody his heart's desire. And the doctor, impelled by his urge to 'go hunting', spared no efforts to ingratiate himself with Buffalmacco, and readily won his friendship. Buffalmacco was entertained to lavish meals, and Bruno too; the pair of them became relentless browsers and sluicers at his expense—there was no way of keeping them apart from a fragrant wine or a plump capon, they required no second invitation, though (as they kept assuring the doctor) were it anyone else inviting them, they'd have refused.

Eventually, picking what seemed to him the right moment, the doctor put his request to Buffalmacco as he had earlier to Bruno. Buffalmacco affected outrage and lashed out angrily at Bruno: 'By thunder', he shouted, 'I don't know what keeps me from bashing your head into your ribs, you sneak! Who but you could have told the doctor about this?'

The doctor, however, pleaded for him, assuring Buffalmacco that he'd learnt of it from another party; with smooth words he eventually restored the peace, and Buffalmacco said to him: 'It seems clear enough, sir, that you've been to Bologna and have brought back the art of keeping your mouth shut. I know you for a clever man—I dare say you can talk rubbish in three languages and if I'm not mistaken you were born under the sign of Aries the mutton-head. Bruno tells me that you've qualified in medicine, so you must be clever at inventing diseases—a man only has to listen to your prattle for half a minute and he feels he needs a doctor.'

Here Buffalmacco was interrupted as the doctor turned to Bruno: 'What it is to converse with brainy people! Here's a man who understands me intimately from the word go. Compared with him you were, let's face it, jolly slow to grasp what I'm worth. But anyway, repeat what I said when you told me that Buffalmacco enjoyed intelligent company. Well, haven't I been as good as my word?'

'Better', said Bruno.

'You should have seen me at Bologna', the doctor continued, addressing Buffalmacco. 'How they all doted on me, young and old, masters and scholars, they got so much out of my wise sayings! What's more, I'd always keep them in stitches with my witty remarks. When I left, what a wail went up on all sides, they all begged me to stay, they went so far as to suggest that I alone tutored all the medical students. But I refused: I wanted to return here, as I had come into a huge family inheritance. So here I am.'

'Now how about that?' said Bruno to Buffalmacco. 'What did I tell you, and you wouldn't believe me! Damned if you'll find another doctor between here and Paris who's as steeped as he is in donkey's piss. Just try going against his wishes!'

'Bruno's right', put in the doctor. 'I'm simply not known here. Let's face it, you belong more or less with the plebs—you should see me among my fellow-physicians.'

'Dear me, sir', said Buffalmacco. 'You're even more of an egghead than I would have imagined, and I must address you as one speaks to brain-boxes of your order, in words of one syllable: I shall see to it that you join our club.'

After this promise the doctor couldn't do enough to entertain them, and they played on his gormlessness with a vengeance. The lady they promised to fix him up with was the gorgeous Gräfin von Scheisse, a woman so fragrant she took your breath away.

'Tell me about her', asked the doctor, and Buffalmacco explained: 'Very well, my little button-mushroom. The Gräfin is a Top Person and there are few households where her writ does not run; her title is Superintendent of the Throne. She commands respect from high and low—even the Friars Minor trumpet her praises (especially after beans have been on the menu). And did I say she was fragrant? You'll catch her perfume a mile off when she's out in the street, though you'll normally find her in the smallest room in the house. She passed our door one night recently on her way down to the Arno to get a breath of air and dabble her toes. Her principal residence, however, is in the town of Looe. Her pages are to be seen in her livery, carrying the emblems of her noble line, the Long Rod and the Brush of Looe. Her liegemen are so numerous you can scarcely avoid stepping on them in the street—they come in many shapes but all bear the honorific title of Stools.

So if we manage to bring it off we'll see to putting you into the soft arms of this paragon of a lady—you can forget about your girl from Red-Light Alley.'

The doctor, a Boloney born and bred, understood not a word of these Florentines' lingo, so expressed himself delighted with the lady chosen for him, and the painters were soon able to bring him news of his admission to the club.

The night before the next club meeting, the doctor invited them both to dinner; when they had eaten, he asked them how he should turn up at the meeting.

Said Buffalmacco: 'Intrepid, sir, that's what you shall have to be: if you're not intrepid you may not be admitted, and we'll stand to suffer too. And I tell you why you are to be intrepid. Round about bedtime you must arrange to be standing on one of those raised tombs recently built outside Santa Maria Novella. Wear one of your best gowns to make your first appearance before your fellow-members with suitable dignity. Furthermore, I'm told (though we weren't there at the time) that, as you're a man of breeding, the Gräfin means to anoint you with the chrism of knighthood at her own expense. Wait there till you are called for. Next, mark this, a black, horned beast of modest size will be despatched to you; it will charge around the piazza in front of you, leaping and snorting, all to scare you. When it sees that you're not scared, it will slowly approach you; once it's standing beside you, get down from the tomb and mount it quite fearlessly, without so much as a "God help me!"; when you're properly settled, fold your arms across your chest like a courtly mandarin, this way, and don't touch the creature again. The beast will then move off slowly and carry you to us. But if before that you even whisper "God help me!" or feel any fear, then it could well throw you off and spike you and the result would be one hell of a stink—you'll be in the shit and so will we if you're not sure of your courage.'

'Ah', said the doctor, 'you don't know me. All you can see, perhaps, is my scholar's gown and my smooth gloved hands. If you knew what I used to get up to at night at Bologna when a crowd of us went chasing skirts you'd be surprised. I'm telling you, one night there was this slip of a girl, knee-high to a grasshopper, dammit, and she didn't want to come with us; so who was the first of us to lay about her with his fists? Who picked her up bodily and carried her a good stone's throw? She came with us in the end: *I* saw to that! Then I remember the time I was passing the Franciscan cemetery a little after the angelus, and a woman had been buried there that very day; I was all on my own except for an attendant of mine, but I remained totally fearless. So don't you worry, I'm as brave as they make 'em. And don't fret, I'll give you a show: I'll turn up in the scarlet gown in which I received my doctorate—you'll see, the whole club will be thrilled. They'll make me president in a trice. Just watch how things go when I arrive: here's your Gräfin, who's never laid eyes on me, already so smitten she wants to anoint me her knight. Aren't I just cut out for a knighthood? Are you thinking I'll never live up to it? Just leave it to me!'

'Very well, then', said Buffalmacco. 'But take care you don't welsh on us and fail to turn up and be there when you're sent for. I know you doctors: if it's cold out you stay indoors.'

'Fear not. I don't need mollycoddling. The few times I have to get up in the night to answer the call of nature (who doesn't?), all I throw on is my fur cape over my jerkin. I'll be there.' So the painters left.

At nightfall the doctor made some excuse to his wife, furtively got out his best gown, and, in due time, put it on and went to the tombs. He climbed on to one, huddled down against the cold, and awaited the beast. Buffalmacco, a strong, well-built man, obtained one of those masks worn at a carnival (the one in question no longer takes place), and a black fur he put on back to front. He looked passably like a bear, except that the mask was horned and gave him the appearance of a devil. In this outfit he went to the new Piazza Santa Maria Novella, with Bruno tagging along to watch. The doctor was there, he saw, and so he set about prancing up and down the piazza; he stormed and ranted, snorted and bellowed like one possessed, and the doctor's hair stood on end at the sight, his teeth chattered, he was scared out of his wits. There were moments when he would have given a lot to be back at his own front-door, but, having come this far, he mastered his terror, so anxious was he to see the marvels that had been described to him.

After Buffalmacco had carried on this way for a while, he made a show of calming down, and approached the tomb where the doctor was and stood still. The doctor was still quaking and couldn't decide whether to mount the beast or stay put. In the end the fear of what the beast might do to him if he *didn't* mount overrode his earlier fear, so he got down from the tomb and gingerly mounted, muttering 'God help me!' the while, and settled himself carefully; still shaking, he folded his arms across his chest as he had been instructed. Then Buffalmacco set off slowly on all fours towards Santa Maria della Scala and brought him to the convent of S. Jacopo in Ripoli. In those days there were pits around there, into which the field-labourers tipped night-soil to the enrichment of their crops. Buffalmacco drew near to the edge of one, gave himself time to place a hand beneath one of the doctor's feet, and shot him clean off his back head-first into the pit, then started to snarl and leap about like mad before making off past Santa Maria della Scala towards Ognissanti, where he met up with Bruno—Bruno had fled there holding his sides for laughter. They pummelled each other in playful celebration and stood watching from a distance to see what the reeking doctor would do.

His nibs tried to pull himself out of this ghastly bog but kept falling back in; eventually he did manage to clamber out, leaving his hood behind; he was dripping muck from head to foot, aching, and not a little peevish, and had drunk more than his fill. He brushed himself off as best he could, then, thinking of nothing better to do, made for home and banged on the door till he was let in.

By the time the door had been closed behind the stinking fellow Bruno and Buffalmacco were there, listening to the reception he got from his lady wife. She gave the culprit a proper dressing-down. 'Well', she said, 'we do look a sight! Pretty ourself up in scarlet and all to go and call on another lady! Don't I satisfy you? Brother, I could satisfy a regiment, never mind you! They dumped you in right where you belonged—a pity you didn't drown. A fine doctor you are—a married man running after other women at night!' And so on. She didn't give over till midnight, then she sent him off to wash.

The next morning Bruno and Buffalmacco daubed 'bruises' on their skin beneath their clothes, and went to call on the doctor, who was already up. There was still a stench in the house: everything had been washed without quite getting rid of the smell. The doctor came to greet them and bid them good morning, but Bruno and Buffalmacco scowled at him, as they had agreed to do.

'Keep your good mornings', they said. 'Just lie down and die, damn you! Run yourself through! Never was there a blacker traitor! Here we were, sweating our guts out to do you a favour, and it's no thanks to you if they didn't kill us off like dogs. You let us down, and the result was we got such a thrashing last night, it would have taken fewer blows to drive a donkey all the way to Rome. We came within an ace of being thrown out of the club we'd contrived to get you into. If you don't believe us, take a look at this'—and they pulled open their shirts in the half-light to reveal their chests all daubed with bruises, and quickly covered them up again.

The doctor made his apologies and told them of his misadventures, and how he'd been thrown and where. 'If only he'd thrown you off the bridge into the Arno', said Buffalmacco. 'Why did you have to say "God help me!"? Weren't you warned?'

'Truth to say, I forgot.'

'What?' cried Buffalmacco. 'You forgot? Like hell you did! Our witness says you were trembling like a leaf and didn't know if you were coming or going. Well, it's done now—but no one's going to catch us out a second time: from now on we'll treat you no better than you deserve.'

The doctor craved their pardon and begged them not to castigate him any further; he strove with honeyed words to pacify them, and for fear that they might spread the news about his mortifying experience, he made even more of a fuss over them and plied them with more meals than he had done before. So you see, even if a man learns nothing at Bologna, he can still be taught a lesson.

VIII. 10. *A Sicilian woman dupes a Florentine merchant out of five hundred gold florins. Too late she learns that this is a game at which two can play.*

There is no need to ask how much laughter the queen provoked at various points in her story; there was not a dry eye among the ladies, who shed tears of merriment a good dozen times if they did so once. When she was finished Dioneo, realizing that it was his turn, spoke up:

There is no denying that we take all the more delight in a crafty trick when it is successfully practised on a deep-dyed trickster. So although you charming ladies have all told the most heavenly stories, you ought to enjoy this one all the more inasmuch as the woman who is duped was a greater trickster than any of the victims, men or women, mentioned in your tales.

A system used to subsist in every maritime community that has a port—and maybe it still does to this day—whereby all merchants who land their cargoes there discharge them into a warehouse (referred to in many places as the custom house) maintained by the prince or the city authorities. The merchant provides the authorities with a full register of his wares, including prices, and is accorded a store-room in which to deposit them under lock and key. The excise men enter the full tally of the merchant's wares in their ledgers as a credit to his account, and subsequently are entitled by law to levy dues from the merchant on the whole or part of his deposited goods, in measure as he withdraws them from bond. Now from these ledgers kept by Customs the brokers frequently discover what cargoes are in the warehouse, and their value, and the identity of the merchants who have landed them; thus they may, as the occasion arises, negotiate with the merchants over terms of trade, barter, or sale, and other such transactions. The system obtained in the Sicilian town of Palermo, as it did in many other places. Here, too, were to be found innumerable women of dazzling beauty but of easy virtue: they would (and do) pass, in the eyes of the unwary, for ladies of eminent virtue and breeding. And, dedicated as they are to fleecing the menfolk till they're shorn of their last hair, the moment they set eyes on a foreign merchant they ascertain from the Customs ledgers what cargo he has brought and what it should fetch. Then they deploy their lascivious charms and honeyed words to entice the merchant into the toils of their love. How many have they not enticed, relieving them of a good portion of their wares, if not indeed of the entire consignment! In truth, there are merchants who've been shorn so meticulously by these ladies' scissors that they've lost their cargo, their ship, everything down to the very marrow from their bones.

Well, not all that long ago, one of our young Florentines called Niccolò da Cignano, also known as Salabaetto, arrived in Palermo on his employers' business, bringing with him all the bales of woollen cloth left over from the fair at Salerno—a good 500 gold florins' worth. He paid duty on the consignment, unloaded it into the Customs warehouse, and, without being too pressed to dispose of it, set off into the town to have a good time. He was a fair-haired young gallant, fair-skinned and good-looking, and he caught the eye of one of these leeches, who went under the name of Jancofiore, after she had made some inquiries about him. He noticed this and, taking her for a lady of rank, he imagined that he had made a conquest thanks to his good looks, and determined to pursue the *affaire* with all due discretion. So without a word to a soul he took to parading back and forth outside her windows. She made a note of it, and once she had softened him up for a few days with passionate glances and given him to understand that she was head over heels in love with him, she sent a woman—a practised bawd—to him in secret. This woman addressed him with a semblance of tears in her eyes, and after a long rigmarole informed him that her lady was so smitten with his good looks and attractive manners that she was quite driven to distraction. So, if he didn't mind, there was nothing she would like better than to meet him in secret at one of the public baths.* This said, she drew a ring from her purse and presented it to him on her lady's behalf. At these words Salabaetto was over the moon; he took the ring and pressed it to his eyelids, then to his lips, after which he slipped it on his finger. He told the good woman that if Jancofiore loved him, the feeling was wholly mutual, for he loved her more than anything in the world and was ready to go wherever she said and at whatever hour she chose.

So the bawd returned to Jancofiore with this reply and the next thing was that Salabaetto was told at which public bath he was to meet her the following evening. He hastened there at the appointed hour, without saying a word about it to anyone, and found that his beloved had arranged an exclusive hire of the bath. A moment later two slave-girls made their appearance, both laden, the one with a large, well-padded mattress which she carried on her head, the other with a huge basket crammed with objects. They laid the mattress on a bedstead in a room of the bath-house and over it they spread a pair of the finest silk-trimmed sheets, followed by a Cypriot quilt of the snowiest white linen, and a pair of pillows sporting the most delicate embroidery. This done, they undressed and stepped into the bath with brushes and gave it the most thorough cleaning. Shortly after this Jancofiore herself arrived with another two slave-girls, and at the first opportunity gave Salabaetto the heartiest welcome; she fetched up the deepest sighs and said to him, after giving him hugs and kisses in abundance: 'I don't know of a single man who could have brought me to this except you! Look, you darling Tuscan firebrand; my heart is singed!'

After this, in accordance with her wish, they both stepped naked into the bath, with two of the slave-girls. Here she would not let any but herself touch him as she soaped him and gave him a good wash all over with a soap scented with musk and clove, after which she had her slave-girls wash and massage her. This done, the slaves brought two of the whitest, gauziest sheets that were so impregnated with attar of roses the whole place smelt of roses; one slave wrapped Salabaetto in one sheet while the other wrapped Jancofiore in the other, then they lifted them up and carried them over to the ready-made bed. When the pair had had enough of perspiring, the slaves pulled those sheets off them to leave them lying naked in the other set, while they took out from the basket the most exquisite silver flasks filled with various perfumes—rose-water, orange-flower water, scent of jasmine, orange oil—and sprinkled them all over with them. Next they unpacked boxes of sweetmeats and some of the choicest wines and they took some refreshment. Salabaetto was in his seventh heaven; he could not take his eyes off Jancofiore, who was undoubtedly a beauty, and he was counting the hour-long minutes until the slave-girls withdrew and left him in the arms of his beloved. Eventually the lady ordered them out, leaving a lighted candle in the room, whereupon she and Salabaetto embraced and enjoyed a good hour's dalliance, he in a state of utter bliss as she appeared to be completely devoured with love for him.

When Jancofiore felt it was time to get up, she summoned the slave-girls; they dressed, had a little more to eat and drink, and bathed their hands and faces with the perfumes. On the point of leaving, she said to Salabaetto: 'If it's all the same to you, I'd love you to come to me for supper and to spend the night.'

Salabaetto was quite bewitched by her beauty and her specious charm and fully convinced that she was heart and soul in love with him, so his answer was: 'Your every pleasure is my delight, so this evening and every other time I mean to do as you wish—your every command is my pleasure.'

So Jancofiore returned home, where she had her bedroom beautifully decked out with hangings and a splendid supper made ready. Then she waited for Salabaetto, who made his way to her as soon as it grew dark; she gave him a most cheerful welcome and they sat down to a festive and beautifully served meal. Then they repaired to the bedroom, where he inhaled a delicious aroma of aloe-wood and Cypriot incense; the bed, he saw, was magnificent, and over the bed's curtain-rails were draped any number of opulent dresses, all of which taken together—as well as severally—led him to the conclusion that the lady must be extremely wealthy and well connected. Whatever he had heard rumoured about her life-style that might have contradicted this appraisal, he refused to believe it; even if he was ready, up to a point, to accept that she had deceived other men, he was never going to believe that she would ever do so to *him*. He spent the night most pleasurably in her arms, growing more passionate by the minute, and in the morning she slipped an exquisite silver belt with a fine purse round his waist and said to him: 'Salabaetto my darling, you won't forget me, will you? My body is at your disposal, and so equally is all I have. Give me any command and I'll do it if it lies in my power.' Salabaetto hugged and kissed her and went happily out of her house and on his way to the neighbourhood where merchants tended to foregather.

He frequented her time and again, and all at no expense, as she cast an ever-stronger spell upon him. Meanwhile he sold his bales of cloth for cash at a good profit, a fact that the good lady at once discovered, not directly from him but from other sources. One evening when Salabaetto called on her, she was thoroughly frolicsome and at her most kittenish; she hugged and kissed him and made the most passionate love to him—he was left feeling that she was ready to die in his arms out of sheer desire. She insisted on giving him a pair of her most gorgeous silver bowls, even though Salabaetto was reluctant to accept them because the gifts she had given him from time to time amounted to a good thirty gold florins' worth, while he'd been unable to persuade her to accept a thing, not so much as a pennyworth. Eventually, once Jancofiore had fanned the flames with her demonstration of erotic passion and open-handed generosity, one of her slave-girls called her, as pre-arranged, and she left the room. After pausing for a few moments she returned in tears and threw herself prostrate on to the bed, crying her heart out.

This perplexed Salabaetto, who took her in his arms as the tears came to his eyes and he said: 'Come, joy of my heart, what's happened all of a sudden? What has made you cry? Tell me, my love.'

She let herself be pressed for a good while, then 'Oh dear!' she cried, 'I don't know what to do or what to say, kind sir! I've just received letters from Messina: my brother writes to say that I must send him a thousand gold florins in the next week without fail, even if it means selling or pawning everything I own: otherwise his head's for the block. I simply don't know what to do to let him have the money that soon—if I had even two weeks' grace I'd find a way of raising the sum from a source where I have a good deal more than that, or I'd sell off one or two of our properties. That can't be done, though, and I wish I'd died before receiving such horrible news!' This said, she laid the anguish on thick and carried on sobbing.

Now if the lad needed to keep his wits about him Love had blunted them to a great extent and he took her tears to be genuine and her words for Gospel truth. 'I can't help you to a thousand gold florins', he said, 'but I could certainly let you have five hundred if you think you'll be able to pay me back in two weeks. You're in luck, you see, because only yesterday I sold my bales of cloth—otherwise I'd not have been able to lend you so much as a bean.'

'Oh no!' she cried. 'Have you yourself been short of money? Why did you not ask me? I may not have a thousand to hand, I could certainly have given you a hundred or even two. Now you've gone and completely inhibited me from accepting your offer!'

This served to assure herself of him all the more. 'Now *that*', he said, 'must not stop you accepting: if I stood in the need you do, I'd certainly have asked your help.'

'Well, my goodness, darling, now I really know how truly, how perfectly you love me: without even waiting to be asked for such a huge sum you've come so generously to my rescue. I was yours heart and soul even without this, but now I'll be so all the more. I'll be eternally in your debt for my brother's life. God knows, though, how reluctant I am to accept it, for I realize that you're a merchant and merchants depend on ready money for their living. However, such is my need, and anyway I'm quite sure I'll be able to pay you back soon, so I'll accept it; as for the balance, I'll pawn everything I have here if I can't find some faster way to raise it.' This said, she dropped on to Salabaetto's face, weeping copiously, and he set about comforting her. He spent the night with her, and the next day, without awaiting a further request, he brought her the five hundred lovely gold florins to demonstrate what a generous lover he was. She took the money with a song in her heart and tears in her eyes, as Salabaetto relied on nothing but her simple word.

Once Jancofiore was in possession of the money Salabaetto found changes creeping into her calendar: whereas previously he had enjoyed unrestricted access to her whenever it took his fancy, now obstacles were cropping up nine times out of ten to prevent her being able to receive him; and when she did allow him in, it was no longer with the cheerful demonstrations of affection there had been before. The time came when he was supposed to have his money back, indeed a further month elapsed, then a second one, but his requests were met with nothing but words by way of repayment. So the lad woke up to realize what a wicked, scheming woman she had been and how irresponsibly he had behaved; but he realized, too, that it was a matter of his word against hers, for he had had nothing in writing from her and there had been no witnesses; he was ashamed to complain about it to anyone for he had, after all, been warned about her, and besides, he'd make himself a laughing-stock, and rightly so, silly ass that he was. So he wept bitterly over his stupidity. As he had received several letters from his principals requiring him to change the money and forward it to them, to avoid the shortfall being discovered when he failed to do so, he decided to leave, and embarked for Naples rather than for Pisa as he ought to have done.

At Naples in those days there lived our fellow-Florentine Pietro dello Canigiano, a man of high intellect and great shrewdness; he was 'Trésorier' to Madame the Empress of Constantinople, and a close friend of Salabaetto and his family. After a few days, Salabaetto took him into his confidence, for he was a man wholly to be trusted, and told him what he had done and what an unfortunate disaster had ensued; he asked for his help and advice to enable him to make a living in Naples, for never, he said, would he return to Florence.

Canigiano was sorry to hear his story. 'What a dreadful thing you've done!' he said. 'What a way to behave! That was a fine way to carry out your masters' orders! Look at all the money you've squandered in dalliance! However, what's done is done, the thing is to find a way out.' Now a mind as sharp as his took little time to come up with a solution; he imparted it to Salabaetto who was delighted with it and was ready to risk carrying it into effect.

With the little money he possessed and a small loan from Canigiano he made ready a good number of bales, each one well trussed up; he bought some twenty oil-casks and filled them, loaded them all on board ship, and returned to Palermo. He paid duty to the excise men on the bales and similarly the levy on the casks, and had the lot entered in the ledgers to his account; then he deposited everything in the warehouse, saying that he was not going to touch any of it until the arrival of a further consignment he was expecting. When Jancofiore got wind of this and heard that what Salabaetto had brought with him was valued at a good two thousand gold florins if not more, to say nothing of the goods he was still expecting which were worth above three thousand, she felt she had been playing only for pennies when the best part of five thousand gold florins was there for the taking. So she decided to hand him back his five hundred, and she sent for him.

Salabaetto went, but he had been taught cunning. Jancofiore welcomed him with open arms, pretending she was unaware of what he had brought with him. 'Look', she said, 'if you were cross with me for not paying your money back when it fell due . . .'

Salabaetto burst out laughing. 'Well, all right, I *was* a bit upset, for I would have torn my heart out to give to you if I'd thought it would make you happy. But let me tell you what my cross feelings really add up to: I love you so much, I've sold off most of what I own and have brought over a cargo worth two thousand florins and more; and I'm expecting delivery from the west of at least a further three thousand's worth. I'm going to set up a warehouse in this city and settle here, so that I can be with you for ever, because I do feel happier in your love than I think any lover ever felt.'

'Listen, Salabaetto', said she. 'What really makes me happy is whatever suits you best, because you're the one I love best in all the world. How pleased I am that you've come back here meaning to settle; I'm looking forward to the two of us having a rare old time together. But I do want to explain to you why, before you went away, you sometimes wanted to come here and it was not possible, and sometimes when you did come you didn't get as cheerful a welcome as before, and especially why I didn't pay you back your money when I'd promised to. You know of course that I was in the most desperate straits then and quite beside myself with worry; and a person in that state of mind can't be as responsive and cheerful as she would wish, however much she's in love. The other thing is that it's no easy matter for a woman to lay hands on a thousand gold florins: she is strung along every day of the week, promises are not kept, and she in her turn has to lie to other people. That's the reason why I didn't pay you back your money—nothing more sinister than that. Anyway, I got the money together a little after you'd left and, had I known where to send yours, you can be sure I should have sent it back to you. But as I didn't know, I've been keeping it for you.' She sent for a purse which contained the very coins he had brought her, handed it to him, and added: 'Count them to see they make five hundred.'

Salabaetto was as happy as could be. He counted the money, found that it came to five hundred, and put it back. 'I know that you're speaking the truth', he said, 'but now you've done more than enough. This—and my love for you as well—is why you have only to tell me what it is you need and I'll provide it if it's a sum I can raise. You'll see for yourself once I'm settled here.' Thus their love affair was patched up at the level of words, and Salabaetto reverted to his dalliance with her, or at any rate went through the motions, while she paid him all manner of attentions and made a pretence of boundless love.

Salabaetto, however, was meaning to requite her for her deception with a trick of his own, and the day she sent for him to come to supper and spend the night, he turned up looking so wretched and distraught, he might have been on the point of giving up the ghost. Jancofiore hugged and kissed him and asked him what was the matter and he, after letting himself be coaxed for a little, told her: 'I am ruined. The ship I was expecting with my goods on board has been captured by pirates from Monaco. They want a ransom of ten thousand gold florins and my share will be one thousand. But I do not have a penny because I took the five hundred you paid me back and sent it straight off to Naples to buy cloth to import. And if I were now to put on the market the goods I have here, they would fetch barely half their value, for this is not the time to sell them. And as I'm barely known here, I'd never find anyone to help me out, so I'm absolutely at my wits' end. And if I don't send the money soon, the cargo will be taken back to Monaco and that's the last I'll see of it.'

How infuriating! thought Jancofiore, who could see herself losing at every turn, as she brooded on what might be done to stop the goods going to Monaco. 'Heaven knows I'm sorry for your sake', she said, 'but there's no use crying over spilt milk. If I had the money, God knows I'd lend it to you here and now, but I don't have it. There is, in fact, the man who let me have the five hundred I was short of that other time, but he charges a huge rate of interest—thirty per cent, not less. If you wanted to borrow off him, you'd need to put up good collateral; as for me, I'm ready to pledge for you all these things of mine and myself into the bargain, for whatever you can raise on all of that, if it will be of any help—but how will you secure the rest of the loan?'

Salabaetto realized what her motive was for making him this offer, and that the loan would in fact be coming from her. Finding it quite satisfactory, however, he thanked her kindly and told her that although the rate of interest was exorbitant, he would accept the loan, given the straits he was in. He would secure the loan, he added, on the merchandise lodged in the Customs warehouse: he would make it over to the money-lender, though the keys to the storeroom he would hold on to himself—that way he would be able to show his wares on request, and could ensure that nothing was touched or tampered with or substituted. Jancofiore agreed that this was well spoken and that his collateral was ample. When it was day she sent for a broker whom she trusted completely and discussed the business with him. She gave him a thousand gold florins which the broker lent to Salabaetto; he had Salabaetto enter to his account the full tally of what he had in bond and, after drawing up an agreement for signature and counter-signing, they shook hands on it and went about their respective business.

Salabaetto boarded a small vessel at the first opportunity and returned to Pietro dello Canigiano at Naples with fifteen hundred gold florins. From here he remitted the full settlement due to his Florentine principals in respect of the cloth with which they had sent him out. He repaid Pietro and anyone else from whom he had borrowed and, after several days celebrating with Pietro over the trick he had played on the Sicilian woman, he left for Ferrara, not wishing to continue in trade.

In Salabaetto's absence from Palermo, Jancofiore was initially puzzled and eventually suspicious; after waiting two months for his return, seeing no sign of him, she had her broker force the storeroom door. He sampled the casks which were supposed to hold oil, and found them all filled with sea-water, all but an inch or two of oil at the top by the bung-hole; then he untied the bales of cloth and found that all but two were simply rolls of the lowest-grade flax; the entire consignment would fetch barely two hundred florins. So Jancofiore realized that she'd been cheated and for many a day she rued the return of those five hundred florins, though not half as much as she rued the loan of the thousand. Her constant refrain was:

> Florentine merchants* are dealers in lies,
> To bargain with them takes a sharp pair of eyes.

Plucked clean as she was, and left looking a proper ninny, she had to conclude that imposture is a game at which two can play.

When Dioneo concluded his tale, Lauretta praised Pietro Canigiano for his advice the soundness of which was proved by its result, and equally Salabaetto's cleverness in carrying it into effect. Then, realizing that she could be queen no longer, she took the laurel crown from her head and graciously placed it on Emilia's, observing: 'I don't know whether we'll find in you a kind ruler, but a beautiful one we shall have for sure; pray then, may your beauty be reflected in your actions.' This said, she returned to her place.

At this Emilia came over a little bashful, less on account of being made queen so much as from hearing herself praised in public for a quality by which her sex is inclined to set great store. She blushed like a new-budding rose at dawn, but after keeping her eyes lowered a while and allowing her crimson cheeks to resume their normal colour, she made the necessary arrangements with her major-domo for the company's needs, then spoke as follows:

'We notice that, after the oxen have been labouring under the yoke for a good part of the day, they are removed from the yoke and left quite free to browse at will among the trees; we also notice that gardens containing a good variety of leafy plants are no less beautiful than a wood comprising nothing but oaks—indeed such gardens are more beautiful. This is why, considering how many days we have confined our story-telling rigorously to a given theme, I hold the view that we should find it not merely helpful but indeed necessary, in our deprivation, to stray a little and, by according ourselves free rein, build up our strength to submit once more to the yoke. So I'm not proposing to limit you to any topic when you come to regale us tomorrow with a tale; you're all to tell whatever story you please,* for I have no doubt that the variety of topics will be not a whit less appealing than narratives on a single theme. This done, whoever succeeds me on the throne will all the more safely be able to confine us within the usual law, for we shall have recruited our strength.' With these words, she left them all free to go their ways until supper-time.

What the queen said was considered by one and all to be well spoken. They stood up, then, and went about their several pleasures: the ladies to making garlands and finding their own amusements while the young men played board-games and sang songs. Thus did they pass the time until supper. Supper was eaten by the pretty fountain, an enjoyable and festive occasion. Afterwards they amused themselves for a good while in their accustomed fashion, singing and dancing, until the queen, conforming to precedent, bade Pamphilo sing a song, regardless of all the songs many of them had been singing unbidden. Pamphilo was willing, and thus began:

Happiness, Love, in my spirit resides
Though I burn, Love, I burn.
Aye, Love, my heart in your friendship confides.
Bursting with joy and transported with rapture,
Such is my state now my heart is given
Over to one who is utterly peerless.

Leaping, my spirits, and far beyond capture,
Bliss lights my face and my eyes enliven;
Nothing can hurt me; my heart is quite fearless
Now that my love in th' empyrean abides.

I cannot teach my voice how to sing
Even a part, Love, of what I am feeling,
Not that I'd give any large demonstration
Wittingly—nay, to my secret I'd cling:
Whispered abroad, it my peace would be stealing.
Truly my love thrives without explanation:
Passion speaks out but mere words it derides.

Only consider: these very arms embraced her!
Who would have guessed or who believed,
Aye, that her cheek to my lips was pressed
Even as my hands joined together and encased her?
Thus was my burdened soul reprieved.
I am the one who her heart has possessed;
I too the one who this precious secret hides.

So Pamphilo ended his song. And while everybody joined in the refrains with a will, there was not one of them who neglected to attend to the words with maybe excessive concentration, striving to penetrate the identity whose secret lay concealed in the singer's utterance. Various ideas were floated but nobody arrived at the truth of the matter. Seeing that Pamphilo's song was finished and the ladies and gentlemen were ready for bed, the queen commanded them all to retire.

*Here ends the eighth day of the* Decameron *and the ninth begins; under the reign of Emilia, the stories are about whatever the narrator pleases.*

The light whose splendour the night seeks to avoid had washed the deep blue of the eighth heaven (the heaven of the fixed stars) with a blue far paler, and the meadow flowers were beginning to raise their heads when Emilia left her bed and had her companions, men and women, called. When they assembled, they left with the queen for a gentle stroll as far as a little wood adjacent to the villa; as they entered it they saw deer, roebucks, and other such animals who just stood and awaited their approach, for all the world as if they had quite lost their timidity or become domesticated—the ravages of the plague had given them a respite from the hunters. The companions would advance towards one of these creatures, then the next, as if on the point of reaching them, when they would go bounding away; this they found a pleasant distraction for a while, until they felt it was time to go back, the sun being higher in the sky. They all wore oak-leaf garlands* and carried fragrant herbs or flowers, and whoever had met them on the way could have reached only one conclusion: 'Death will never get the better of these folk, or if it does, they'll die happy.' Home, therefore, they came, setting foot before foot and singing and jesting every step of the way; at the mansion they found everything in a beautiful state of preparation and their domestics in high good humour. Here, after a pause for rest, they were ready to dine, but not before they had delivered themselves of six ditties, each one merrier than the last. Then they rinsed their hands and the major-domo, at the queen's behest, showed them to their places at table, where the dishes shortly appeared and they all dined to their hearts' content. On leaving the table, they enjoyed a round of singing and dancing and played tunes awhile until, at the queen's command, those so inclined withdrew for a siesta. At their usual hour and at the usual place they assembled for story-telling, and the queen fixed her eye on Philomena and told her to embark upon the day's opening story. Philomena smilingly obliged with this one:

### IX. 1. *How Francesca finds use for a corpse when she wishes to be rid of her two importunate suitors, Rinuccio and Alessandro.*

How pleased I am, my lady, that it is your own good pleasure to invite me to be the first to break a lance in this broad, open field you have so generously afforded us for our story-telling. If I acquit myself well, I've no doubt that those who follow me will do equally well, if not better.

Time and again our stories have rehearsed the many different ways in which love exerts its power, and I don't imagine we've covered them all, nor should we do so if we talked of nothing else for the next twelve months. As love not only incites its votaries to run all kinds of mortal risks,* but even provokes them into entering the charnel-houses as if they were already dead, the story I feel like telling you makes an addition to those already told: if it gives you some notion of love's power, it will also introduce you to a good woman who used her wits to evade the attentions of two unwanted suitors.

There was once in the city of Pistoia a most comely widow with whom two of our Florentines were deeply in love. Their names were Rinuccio Palermini and Alessandro Chiarmontesi; they had been exiled from Florence and were settled in Pistoia; each had fallen for the lady while remaining ignorant of the other's existence, and each strove with all due caution as best he might to acquire the lady's love. Well, this good lady, whose name was Francesca de' Lazzari, had received countless solicitations from each of them in the form of billets-doux and entreaties, and had been rather unwise in failing to turn a consistently deaf ear to them; so, now that she wanted to make a prudent withdrawal she found it impossible to do so, until she lit upon a way to rid herself of those nuisances once and for all. What she would do would be to require a service of them which was not impossible to fulfil, but which she thought they would be most unlikely to achieve; this way, when they failed to do as required, she would have a perfectly plausible excuse to reject all further advances on their part. Here is what she had in mind: the day on which she came by her inspiration, a man had died in Pistoia, a man who came from noble stock but was none the less reputed to be the vilest blackguard in town—indeed, in the whole world. What is more, he had been physically so misshapen and grotesque that, when he was still alive, anyone who did not know him got quite a nasty shock on seeing him for the first time. Now he had been buried in a tomb outside the Franciscan church, a factor, the lady recognized, which could serve her ends rather nicely.

So she said to her maid: 'You know what an irritating nuisance those two Florentines, Rinuccio and Alessandro, are as they pester me every day. Well, I've no mind to show *them* any of my favours. So, in order to be rid of them, as they keep making me lavish offers, I've decided to try them out with a request which I'm convinced they'll never fulfil*—that way I can get them to leave me in peace. So listen how I'll do it. You know that Devildog (that's what people called the reprobate just mentioned) was buried at St Francis's this morning; you know that when he was alive, never mind now that he's dead, even our bravest men quaked on sight of him. Well, you're to go in secret first of all to Alessandro and give him this message: "Madam bids me say the time has come to grant you her favours which you've so badly wanted, and for you to be with her if you would like, and this is how it's to be done: for a reason that you'll discover, a relative of hers is to bring to her house tonight the corpse of Devildog, who was buried this morning; but she doesn't want to have it in the house because she's frightened of him even now he's dead. So she would consider it a great favour on your part if you would go tonight a little before midnight and get into the tomb in which Devildog is buried, and dress up in his clothes and lie there as though you were he until someone comes to fetch you away; let yourself be taken out of the tomb without uttering a word or a sound, and you'll be brought to her house and she'll be there to welcome you and you'll be with her; then you can leave her any time you feel like it, and she'll take care of the rest." If he is willing to do it, well and good; if he refuses, tell him from me he's to avoid my sight and, if he values his life, take care to send me no further word in any form.

'Then go to Rinuccio Palermini and tell him this: "Madam says, she's ready to be at your entire disposal, but you're to do her a big favour first, and that is, you're to go about midnight tonight to the tomb in which Devildog was buried this morning, and you're to lift him out gently, without uttering a word, whatever it is you hear or see or feel, and you're to bring him to her house. There you'll see why it is she wants it, and you'll have your way with her. If you refuse to do this, she bids you send her not another word of any kind from now on." '

The maid went and delivered her message quite punctiliously to each of them, as she had been instructed. Each of them replied to the effect that if it were the lady's good pleasure, they'd go to hell, never mind going into a tomb. This answer the maid brought back to her mistress, who waited to see if they'd be mad enough to do it.

Night came and, shortly before midnight, Alessandro Chiarmontesi, clad in little more than a jerkin, left the house to take Devildog's place in the tomb. On his way, his heart was filled with the most dreadful presentiments and he brooded: 'Lord, what an idiot I am! Where am I off to? For all I know, her relatives may have realized that I'm in love with her and have jumped to false conclusions, and are making her do this in order to kill me in that tomb! If this happened, I'd be the one to suffer, and they'd all get off scot-free for lack of evidence. Or who knows? Some enemy of mine may have set this up, someone she loves perhaps, and she wants to make such a gift to him. But even supposing', he continued, 'that none of this is the case, and that her kinsmen do in fact take me to her house. I'm never going to believe that they want to lay hands on Devildog's corpse just to cradle it in their arms, or so that she may cradle it in hers. It's far more likely that they propose to vent their spleen on it, assuming that in some way they had suffered at his hands. She tells me not to make a sound, whatever I feel; what if they poked out my eyes, or ripped my teeth out, or cut off my hands or did something of that sort, what then? How could I keep silent? And if I speak, they'll recognize me and perhaps do me some injury. But even if they don't lay a finger on me, I'll still have got precisely nowhere, because they're not going to drop me off on the lady. And then she'll say I never did as she bade me and I'll get no favours out of her.' So saying, he had more than half a mind to turn back for home, but his great love urged him on so forcefully with arguments that contradicted these that he reached the tomb, opened it, climbed in, stripped Devildog of his clothes, dressed up in them, pulled the cover of the tomb shut over himself, and lay down in Devildog's place. Now he began to recollect who the man had been, and some of the things that had happened at night—so he had heard—not only in the graveyards but elsewhere. His hair stood on end and every now and then he imagined that Devildog was about to stand up and cut his throat. However, his ardent love helped him to overcome these and other terrifying thoughts, and he lay back as if he were the corpse, waiting for whatever was to happen to him.

As midnight approached, Rinuccio left the house to accomplish the task laid upon him by his beloved. On the way, he turned over in his mind all manner of thoughts of what might happen to him: he might be caught by the Signoria's watch with the body over his shoulder, and be condemned to the stake as a sorcerer; or, if it ever got out, he might incur the enmity of Devildog's family; with these and similar considerations in mind, he was on the point of turning back. But on second thoughts he said: 'Come now, I'm not going to refuse the lady this, the first favour she's ever asked of me, when I love her so dearly and especially when this would earn me her good graces. Even if I were certain to die for it, let me not go back on the promise I gave her that I would do it.' So on he went and reached the tomb and raised the cover without difficulty.

As he noticed the tomb being opened, Alessandro was terrified, but kept quiet. Rinuccio stepped inside, grasped Alessandro by the feet, under the impression that he was grasping Devildog's, and dragged him out of the tomb; he lifted him on to his shoulder and made off towards his beloved's house.

Treating the corpse without all that much consideration, he kept banging it into the corner of the occasional roadside bench as he went along—the night was pitch-dark and he could not see where he was going. When Rinuccio reached his beloved's door, she stood waiting with her maid at a window to see if he was going to bring Alessandro. She was all set to send the pair of them about their business when there was a cry of: 'Who goes there?' It happened that the Signoria's watch had quietly posted an ambush in that street in the hope of catching an outlaw; when they heard Rinuccio's feet shuffling along, they suddenly put up a lantern to see who it was and where he was going, then stood to with their lances and shields. Rinuccio recognized them at once and, with little time for mature reflection, dropped Alessandro and vanished as fast as his legs would carry him. Alessandro leapt to his feet and, though the dead man's clothes trailed about his ankles, cleared off too.

In the light of the watch's lantern Francesca had an excellent view of Rinuccio fleeing with Alessandro at his back, and she noticed that Alessandro was dressed in Devildog's clothes. She was greatly impressed by each of them for their bravery, but this did not stop her enjoying a good laugh at the sight of Alessandro being dropped in the street then both of them taking to their heels. Delighted with this happy accident, and thanking God for getting the pair of them off her back, she left the window and returned to her bedroom. Clearly, she and her maid agreed, those two really were smitten with her, for evidently they had done what she had bidden them to do.

Smarting as he was, and cursing his luck, Rinuccio was not going to make for home even so but, once the watch had left the street, went back to where he had dropped Alessandro and set to work groping about to find him again, so as to complete his task. However, he was unable to find him and concluded that the watch would have removed him, so he sadly made his way home. Alessandro, who had no idea what to do, nor any notion of who it was who had carried him, similarly returned home, sick at heart.

When Devildog's tomb was found open in the morning and there was no sign of the body (for it had fallen to the bottom when Alessandro rolled it aside), argument raged all over Pistoia, with the simpler brethren propounding the view that devils had come and taken him off. None the less, the two suitors each advised the lady of what they had done and what had befallen them, giving this as an excuse for not having fulfilled her command in every respect; so they each besought her love and her favour. She showed no inclination to believe them, however, and curtly gave them notice that she was at the disposal of neither of them, as neither had done as requested. With this, she was rid of them.

## IX. 2. *An abbess reprimands a young nun caught with her lover, but then is forced to be more lenient.*

Philomena fell silent. The woman in the story was deemed very clever for the way she had got rid of her unwanted lovers, while it was unanimously agreed that the lovers' brash presumption was not love at all but sheer lunacy. The queen now turned playfully to Elissa. 'Your turn', she said, and Elissa started straight in.

Francesca was indeed clever the way she eluded her suitors, as we have seen. There was a young nun, too, who avoided a threatening danger by dint of a quick tongue, and a little luck. As you know, there are plenty of daft idiots who set themselves up as teachers and censors to their fellows; occasionally, however, Fate trips them up, and rightly so, as you shall see in my tale about the abbess under whose tutelage our nun was placed.

You must know of a certain convent in Lombardy renowned for its piety and holiness. One of the nuns there was a young woman of noble birth and phenomenal beauty called Isabetta. One day she went to the grille to see a caller, a relative of hers, when she fell in love with a handsome youth accompanying her visitor. Seeing her beauty, he was equally smitten, but for ages there was very little they could do about it, which was hard on both of them. As they both remained alert for an opportunity, the young man eventually found a way to visit his nun on the sly, which suited her very well; and so he visited her not once but any number of times, to their mutual gratification.

This went on for a while, but then one night as he was leaving Isabetta he was spotted by one of the nuns, little though the lovers realized it, and she mentioned the matter to some of the others. Their first thought was to go and tell the abbess, a lady called Usimbalda, who was held by the nuns and indeed by all her acquaintance to be a good and holy woman. However, on second thoughts they decided they'd rather the abbess caught Isabetta in the act with her lover, to prevent her being able to deny the accusation. So they kept quiet and organized themselves into watches in order to entrap her.

It happened, therefore, one night that Isabetta let him in, quite unaware of what was going on behind her back, and the watchers spotted him at once. At what seemed to them the right moment, fairly well on into the night, they split into two groups, one to watch Isabetta's cell door, the other to run to the abbess's cell. They knocked on her door and when she answered they said: 'Quick, Reverend Mother, get up! We've caught Isabetta with a young man in her cell.'

That night the abbess had a priest for company—she regularly used a chest to smuggle him in. On hearing this, she was frightened that the nuns in their impatience and zeal might lean on her door and push it open, so she leapt out of bed and dressed in the dark as best she could. When she reached for her veil (they call it a psaltery because of its shape) what she grabbed hold of were the priest's breeches. Short of time, she flung the garment on her head in place of her veil, quite unawares, and out she strode, hastily closing her door behind her as she cried: 'Where is this miscreant?' And with the other nuns, who were so keyed up to catch Isabetta red-handed that they never even noticed what the abbess had on her head, she reached the cell door and, with the others' help, drove it crashing to the floor. In they surged and found the lovers hugging each other in bed and so stunned at this irruption they just didn't react. Isabetta was instantly seized by the nuns and, on the abbess's orders, taken to the chapter house. The young man stayed behind and got dressed, then waited to see how it was to end; if they laid a finger on his beloved he proposed to take his revenge on as many nuns as he could catch, then make off with her.

The abbess took her seat in the chapter house and in the presence of all the nuns, whose eyes were fastened upon the guilty party, she addressed her in the most opprobrious terms ever used against a woman: she was a woman, she said, whose disgusting and scandalous conduct would defile the good name, the holiness, and honour of the convent if it ever got out. And she accompanied her diatribe with the most solemn threats.

The culprit kept silent; she hung her head, shamefaced, quite lost for words, so that people began to feel a bit sorry for her. The abbess piled up her invective, until Isabetta looked up and noticed what the lady had on her head—the leggings with their ties were hanging down on either side of her face. Drawing the right inference, she recovered her composure at once and said: 'Reverend Mother, pray God help you tie your bonnet-strings, then do tell me what is on your mind.'

'What bonnet-strings, you whore?' snapped the abbess, who had failed to grasp her meaning. 'Do you have the impudence to bandy words with me? Do you think what you have done is a laughing matter?'

Isabetta, however, repeated what she had just said: 'Do please, Reverend Mother, tie your bonnet-strings, then say to me what you will.' At this, several of the nuns turned to look at the abbess and she herself raised her hands to her head. Now they all realized what Isabetta had been talking about.

The abbess, therefore, recognizing that she had committed the selfsame fault and that it was plain to everyone present, and that there was no way she could conceal it, quite changed her tune: she began speaking along very different lines, asserting how impossible it was to resist the lusts of the flesh. Each one, therefore, was to feel free to take her pleasure when it offered, just as they had been doing on the sly. So she released the young woman and went back to bed with her priest, while Isabetta returned to her lover's arms. Frequently thereafter she summoned him to her, regardless of the jealousy she aroused in the sisters—who, being without lovers, secretly attempted to remedy this lack as best they could.

IX. 3. *How Calandrino's friends, Bruno, Buffalmacco, and Nello, persuade him that he is pregnant, and how everyone ends up feeling pleased—except his wife.*

When Elissa had finished her tale, and the ladies all thanked God that the young nun was happily rescued from the clutches of her jealous sisters, the queen told Philostrato to proceed, and he set forth without awaiting a further summons.

That boorish judge* from the Marche I told you about yesterday interfered with a story about Calandrino I was on the point of telling you. A great deal has already been said about him and his friends, but as my story about him can only contribute to our mirth, I shall go ahead and tell you the one I was going to yesterday.

Who Calandrino was and the other characters I'll be mentioning in this story has already been made abundantly clear so, without describing them further, I shall go on and tell you that an aunt of Calandrino's died, leaving him two hundred lire in cash. So Calandrino started talking about buying a parcel of land, and off he went to negotiate with every agent in Florence, as if he had ten thousand gold florins to disburse. But the transaction fell through every time when they touched on the matter of the asking price.

Bruno and Buffalmacco knew all about it and had told him time and time again that he would do far better to go on a spree with them instead of running off to buy land as though he were in the business of manufacturing bolts for crossbows. But far from persuading him to such extravagance, they had never yet been able to induce him to stand them a meal.

One day as they were having a grumble over this, a painter friend of theirs called Nello joined them, and they all decided they were somehow or other going to get their heads in the trough, with Calandrino paying the bill. They lost no time in concocting a plan, and the following morning they lay in wait for Calandrino outside his house. He had barely stepped out when Nello went up to him. 'Good morning, Calandrino', he said.

'God grant you a good day and a good year', replied Calandrino.

At this point Nello stopped in his tracks and looked him closely in the face.

'What are you staring at?' enquired Calandrino.

'How did you feel last night? You don't look your normal self.'

This at once alarmed Calandrino. 'Good God! What's that you say? What d'you think I've got?'

'Heaven knows', remarked Nello; 'you look peculiar but let's hope it's nothing.' With this, he let him go.

There was nothing Calandrino could actually feel but he was thoroughly perturbed as he went on his way. Seeing him leave Nello, Buffalmacco, who was close by, went up and greeted him. 'How are you feeling?' he asked.

'I don't know', said Calandrino. 'Nello was telling me only a moment ago that I didn't look my usual self. I wonder if I've gone and caught something.'

'Something? Of course it's something—you're looking more dead than alive.'

Now Calandrino was already feeling a little feverish. Then who should come along but Bruno, and the first thing he said was: 'Calandrino! Just take a look at yourself! You look like a corpse—how are you feeling?'

Hearing them all speak like this, Calandrino was convinced he was ill. Thoroughly distressed: 'What shall I do?' he asked them.

'It seems to me', said Bruno, 'you should go home and get to bed and make sure you're well covered up; send a urine sample* to Master Simone—he's a good friend, as you know. He'll tell you straight away what you have to do, and we'll be along ourselves—if anything needs doing, we'll take care of it.'

So together with Nello they returned with Calandrino to his house. He looked quite drawn as he went into his bedroom and told his wife: 'Come on, you must get me plenty of covers: I'm not feeling at all well.'

So he retired to bed and sent a maid with a specimen of his urine to Master Simone, who at that time kept shop in the Mercato Vecchio, at the sign of the melon. And Bruno told his friends: 'You stay here with him; I'm going to see what the doctor has to say; if need be, I'll bring him back.'

'Oh do please, my friend', said Calandrino. 'Go and find out all about it—something odd's going on inside me.'

Bruno reached the doctor's ahead of Calandrino's maid with the specimen and told him what they were up to. So when the girl arrived and the doctor looked at the specimen, he said to her: 'Go and tell Calandrino to be sure to keep warm, and I'll be straight along to tell him what he's got and what he'll have to do.'

The maid told him as bidden, and shortly afterwards the doctor arrived with Bruno, sat down beside him, and took his pulse. After a little he said, in the presence of Calandrino's wife: 'Listen, Calandrino, I'm going to speak to you as a friend. There's nothing wrong with you but this: you're pregnant.'

On hearing this Calandrino let out a wail of anguish. 'Oh Tessa', he cried, 'now look what you've done, just because you always have to be on top. I told you this would happen!' Tessa, who was modesty personified, blushed crimson at her husband's remark and, bowing her head, left the room without a word. Calandrino kept up his moaning: 'Oh heaven help me, what shall I do? How am I to give birth to this child? Where will he come out from? It's obvious that wanton woman is to be the death of me, damn her eyes! If only I were well, I'd get up and give her a good hiding—indeed, even if I were fighting fit I'd break every bone in her body, because I should never have let her mount me. One thing's for sure, if I pull through, she can die of lust before she'll do that again!'

Bruno, Buffalmacco, and Nello managed to keep straight faces though they were all at bursting-point; their quack, however, had dissolved in helpless mirth, he was laughing to split his sides. Eventually though, as Calandrino implored his counsel and assistance, the doctor told him: 'Calandrino, you're not to be upset, because we have, thank goodness, caught it in time, and I'll have you cured without much trouble in a matter of days. The only thing is, there'll be a few expenses.'

'My heavens, sir—go ahead, for the love of God! I have two hundred lire by me; I was going to spend it on a plot of land, but if you need it all, take it all, just so long as I don't have to give birth. That's something I don't know how I'd manage: when women are about to give birth I hear them raising such a din, and what *they* have gives them plenty of space for it; so if *I* felt that sort of pain, I'm sure I'd be dead before I delivered.'

'Don't worry', said the doctor. 'I'm going to give you a quite delicious brew to drink; it'll sort you out in three days and you'll be as right as rain. Then take care to behave yourself in the future and not to do stupid things like that any more. Now for this infusion we'll need three brace of the best, plumpest capons. We'll need certain other things too, and you're to give one of these men five lire in small change so they can buy them. Have everything brought round to me at my shop, and tomorrow I'll send you that draught, which you're to start drinking straight away, a good mugful at a time.'

At this, 'I'm in your hands, sir', said Calandrino, and gave Bruno five lire along with money for three brace of capons, exhorting him to be a real friend and make a good job of it.

The doctor left to concoct some sort of medicinal draught and sent it to him. Bruno bought the capons and whatever else was needed for their feast and dined off them with his friends and the doctor. For three mornings running Calandrino drank the potion, after which the doctor visited him with the three friends. He felt his pulse and told him: 'Calandrino, there's no doubt about it, you're cured. Off you go about your business—no need to stay indoors a moment longer.'

Overjoyed, Calandrino got up and went out to see to his affairs; every time he ran into anyone he would lavish praise on Master Simone for his splendid cure, quite painlessly terminating his pregnancy in three days. Bruno, Buffalmacco, and Nello were pleased to have got the better of Calandrino's stinginess by dint of a little guile; Tessa, however, saw through their trick and gave her husband a good piece of her mind.

IX. 4. *After losing everything at the gaming table, Cecco Fortarrigo takes the purse of his master, Cecco Angiolieri, and loses its contents the same way. But the servant still has one card up his sleeve.*

The things Calandrino said about his wife sent the whole company into hoots of laughter. When Philostrato ended, Neiphile began her story, as the queen wished.

Were it not for the fact that we find it easier to display our stupidity and nastiness than our good sense and our virtues, there are certain people who would never guard their speech, try as they might. Calandrino is a case in point: the silly man had no need at all to divulge his wife's little secret propensities in order to be cured of the condition he had been naïve enough to think he'd contracted. This reminds me of a story pointing in the opposite direction, about an intelligent man who is hoodwinked by another's cunning, much to his shame and vexation. That's what I'd like to tell you about.

In Siena not so long ago there lived two young men, only recently arrived at maturity and both called Cecco Angiolieri and Fortarrigo* respectively. Although they were in most respects quite ill assorted, they did have one thing in common: neither of them could stand his father, and this had bonded them together in friendship, so they kept each other's company.

Now Angiolieri was a handsome man of good breeding and he felt that living in Siena on his father's allowance was not much of a life; so when he heard that a cardinal whose protégé he was had been appointed by the Pope as legate to the March of Ancona, he decided to go and join him, expecting thereby to improve his fortunes. He put this to his father and arranged with him to receive six months' allowance all in one payment, so that he could make a fitting appearance at court, with a suitable wardrobe and proper mounts. As he was looking out for a suitable attendant, word of it came to Fortarrigo, who went straight away to Angiolieri and implored him as eloquently as he could to engage him for the expedition: he would be his page, valet, and whatever else, and would require no wages, only his keep. Angiolieri told him that he would not take him on: he recognized that he was quite capable of performing the required duties, but he was a gambler and, furthermore, he was inclined towards the bottle. Fortarrigo replied that he would certainly guard against both these vices, indeed he promised faithfully to do so. Eventually his repeated entreaties got the better of Angiolieri, who gave his consent.

They set out together one morning and stopped for lunch at Buonconvento. After lunch, as it was a hot day, Angiolieri had a bed made ready for him at the inn, undressed with

Fortarrigo's help, and retired to rest, bidding his valet wake him on the stroke of three. While Angiolieri slept, Fortarrigo went into the tavern, had a drop to drink, then joined some gamblers who made short work of winning such money as he had about him. Then they went on to win all the clothes off his back. Anxious to recoup his fortunes, Fortarrigo left, clad in nothing but his shirt, to find the sleeping Angiolieri: seeing that he was in the soundest slumber, he helped himself to the entire contents of his purse, which he proceeded to lose at the gaming table just as he had lost the rest. When Angiolieri awoke, he got up and dressed and asked for Fortarrigo, but as he could not be found he assumed that the man was lying somewhere or other in a drunken stupor, as he used to do in the past; so he decided to leave him to his own devices and had his horse saddled and the valise loaded up, with a view to engaging another attendant at Corsignano. But as he was going to settle the bill with his host he found he had been cleaned out of his last farthing. So he raised a terrific rumpus and set the entire household by the ears, claiming that he had been robbed in this house and was going to have them all arrested and taken to Siena. At this point Fortarrigo turned up again in his shirt, with a view to stealing his master's clothes as he had taken his money. When he found Angiolieri on the point of setting off on horseback, he said: 'What are you doing, Angiolieri? We're not leaving already, are we? Do wait a minute: I'm expecting a man any moment to whom I've pawned my doublet for thirty-eight *soldi*; I'm sure that if we settle with him at once, he'll let me have it back for thirty-five.'

While the arguments still raged, someone came along to certify to Angiolieri that it was Fortarrigo himself who had purloined his money: he displayed to him the sum of Fortarrigo's losses. So Angiolieri turned furiously on Fortarrigo and called him every name under the sun and, were it not for his fear of the consequences (if not for his fear of the Lord), he would have suited his actions to his words. Still, he threatened to have him hanged or to have him banished from Siena under pain of being strung up. Then he mounted his horse.

Fortarrigo, however, speaking as if Angiolieri's words were addressed not to him but to someone else, said: 'Come on,

Angiolieri! Let's not keep on about it—what you're saying doesn't add up to a row of beans. Here's what matters: we'll get it back for thirty-five *soldi* if we pay him right away, otherwise, if we leave it till tomorrow, he won't take a *soldo* less than the thirty-eight he lent me on it. Come, do me this favour—I did leave it up to his discretion. Look, why don't we pick up this three-*soldi* profit?'

Hearing the man carry on this way drove Angiolieri to despair, the more so because he noticed that the onlookers appeared not to believe that Fortarrigo had lost all his master's money at the gaming table, but that Angiolieri still had funds. 'What's your doublet got to do with me?' he cried. 'I'll see you hanged first, man. You've stolen from me, you've gambled away my money, and now you've stopped me getting on my way, and what's more you're making a fool of me!'

As if these words were not addressed to him either, Fortarrigo didn't bat an eyelid, but 'Oh go on', he said, 'why won't you let me make those three *soldi*? Can you doubt that I'd make you a loan of them again? Come, do me a favour—what's all the hurry? We'll easily get to Torrenieri this evening. Try finding your purse. I could hunt all over Siena without finding a doublet that fitted me as well as that one did. Just imagine: I let the man have it for thirty-eight *soldi*! It's worth not a *soldo* less than forty, so you would have made me lose twice over.'

Thoroughly nettled as he saw the fellow delaying him with talk after robbing him, Angiolieri turned his horse's head and set out for Torrenieri without giving him an answer. Now Fortarrigo thought up a cunning stratagem. Still dressed as he was in nothing but his shirt, he set off after him at the double, and so they proceeded for a good two miles, Fortarrigo constantly begging for his doublet while Angiolieri pressed his pace in order to get out of earshot of the importunate fellow. Then Fortarrigo noticed some labourers in a field close to the road ahead of Angiolieri, and started shouting: 'Stop him! Stop him!' and the labourers blocked Angiolieri's approach, one man clutching a mattock, the next a spade, for they imagined that he had robbed the man running along behind him in his shirt, yelling. They stopped and grabbed Angiolieri, and it was little use his trying to explain to them who he was and how matters actually stood.

When Fortarrigo caught up, he looked daggers at Angiolieri and said: 'I don't know what keeps me from killing you, you sneaky thief, running off with my property! Look, gentlemen', he added, addressing the labourers, 'look what he left me to wear as he sneaked away from the inn after losing everything he owned at the gaming table! At least I'm able to say that, thanks to the Good Lord and to you, I've got this much back, for which I'm eternally grateful to you.'

Angiolieri put in his own word, but no one took any notice of him. With the labourers' help Fortarrigo dragged him off his horse, stripped him of his clothes, and dressed himself in them; then he mounted and rode back to Siena, leaving Angiolieri barefoot and in only his shirt, and put it about that he had won the palfrey and the clothes off Angiolieri.

Angiolieri, then, who had been expecting to look prosperous as he joined the cardinal in the March of Ancona, returned to Buonconvento a pauper dressed in a shirt. He was too shamefaced to reappear in Siena at that time, but borrowed some clothes, mounted the jade that Fortarrigo had been riding, and went to stay with relatives at Corsignano until his father made him a further allowance. So it was that Angiolieri's sound plan was upset by Fortarrigo's knavery—though it was not to go unpunished when the time and place allowed.

## IX. 5. *How Calandrino is induced to give his heart to a lady, and what his wife does about it.*

Neiphile finished her tale—it was not long—and the party afforded it only little discussion or laughter before the queen turned to Fiammetta and told her to follow. 'Gladly', she said with a twinkle, and thus began:

I think you're all aware that, whatever topic comes up frequently for discussion, it is always more fun to talk about it if the speaker has the wit to choose the right time and place to bring it up. So, considering what we're all here for, which is to have a good time, I shall say that anything that conduces to our pleasure will be seasonable; even if it's a topic raised any number of times already, it should still go on keeping us amused. That's why, for all that Calandrino's adventures have been cropping up in our stories rather frequently, seeing that they're all amusing—as Philostrato remarked a few moments ago—I'm going to risk adding my own to those already recounted. If I'd wanted to take leave of historical accuracy, I could only too easily have altered the names in the telling. However, it greatly diminishes the listeners' pleasure when the narrator tampers with the historical truth, so, emboldened as I am by what I've just explained, I'm going to tell it to you precisely as it happened.

Niccolò Cornacchini came from our city. He was a rich man, and one of his properties was a pretty place out on the Camerata, where he had a fine stately mansion built. He arranged for Bruno and Buffalmacco to decorate it, and as that would mean a great deal of work, they recruited Nello and Calandrino as well; then they set to. Though there was a room with a bed and other basic necessities in it, and an old woman living there to keep an eye on the place, there was no other staff in residence. So a son of Niccolò's called Filippo, a young bachelor, was in the habit of bringing a woman out here on occasion and taking his pleasure with her for a couple of days, then sending her back.

On one such occasion he brought a girl called Niccolosa—a ruffian known as the Guzzler kept her in a house on Via Camaldoli and hired her out. She was a presentable young woman and well turned out; for one of her sort she was remarkably poised, too, and well spoken. Once, she left her room at midday, dressed in a white linen dress and with her hair put up, to wash her hands and face at a well in the courtyard. Calandrino happened to come out to fetch some water and gave her a jovial greeting. She responded, and gave him a good look, not that she was drawn to him but she found him rather odd. Calandrino let his eyes dwell on her, too, finding her not bad looking; he invented some excuse to avoid returning with the water to his companions, but, as he did not know her, he was shy of starting a conversation. She noticed the way he goggled at her and, to lead him on, she threw a glance or two in his direction accompanied by a little sigh; this was enough to sweep Calandrino off his feet—he did not leave the courtyard till Filippo had called her back into the bedroom.

Back at work Calandrino did nothing but sigh, as Bruno could not fail to notice, for he kept an eye on his friend and derived endless amusement from his funny ways. 'What the devil's got into you, my friend?' he asked. 'All you can do is sigh.'

'I'd be all right', said Calandrino, 'if I had someone to help me.'

'What d'you mean?'

'Look, you're not to tell a soul. There's a girl here: talk of a beauty! I tell you she's a real siren. And she's fallen for me, hook, line, and sinker, you'd never believe it. I noticed just now when I went to fetch water.'

'Dear me!' cried Bruno. 'Just you take care she's not Filippo's wife.'

'I do believe she is; when he called her, she went to join him in the bedroom. But what does it matter? A bit of goods like that—I'd pinch her off Christ Himself, never mind Filippo! You know what, Bruno, I haven't half taken a fancy to her, believe you me!'

'Tell you what', said Bruno, 'I'll find out for you who she is. If she *is* Filippo's wife, I'll set things up for you with a word in her ear—I'm very well in with her. But how can we manage it without Buffalmacco cottoning on? I can never speak to her without him hanging about.'

'Who cares about Buffalmacco? Nello's the one to watch: he's related to my Tessa and could put a spanner in the works.'

'True enough.'

Now Bruno knew who the girl was: he had seen her arrive and, besides, Filippo had told him. So when Calandrino left the site where they were working and went off to take a peek at her, Bruno put Nello and Buffalmacco in the picture, and they quietly agreed on what they'd do with him over this infatuation of his.

When Calandrino came back, Bruno whispered to him: 'Did you see her?'

'Didn't I just! She's fair bowled me over!'

'I'm going to see if she's who I think she is. If she is, just you leave it to me.'

So Bruno went down and caught Filippo and her together, and told them all about Calandrino and what he had told them; he arranged with them what part each was to play if they were to enjoy a bit of a lark over their friend's lovesick state. Then he returned to Calandrino and said: 'It's her all right. So we'll have to handle this very skilfully because, if Filippo gets wind of it, we'll never hear the end of the matter. Anyway, what d'you want me to tell her if I get to talk to her?'

'Tell her? Humph! Give her my love . . . bushels of love . . . a whole thousand bushels of it . . . brimming up and running over and pressed into her bosom and so forth. And tell her . . . tell her I'm her beadsman, I mean her bondsman and I'm at her whatsit, her disposal any time—know what I mean?'

'Leave it to me', said Bruno.

When it was time for supper they stopped working and went down into the courtyard to join Filippo and Niccolosa; here Calandrino became rather the centre of attention, as he set himself to gaping at Niccolosa and going into a whole routine that would not have escaped the notice even of a blind man. Niccolosa, meanwhile, went out of her way to fan his flame, and, knowing what she knew from Bruno, enjoyed no end of a giggle at Calandrino's performance. Filippo, Buffalmacco, and the others made a show of chatting together and not noticing.

But after a little, to Calandrino's intense vexation, they left, and on their way back to Florence Bruno said to him: 'You're melting her, I tell you, like ice in the sun; believe me, you fetch your rebec* and sing her some of your love-songs, and you'll have her jumping out of the window to come to you.'

'D'you think so, partner? D'you really think I should fetch it?'

'Absolutely.'

'You didn't believe me today when I told you, did you?' said Calandrino. 'I'm a man who knows how to get his way. There's not another man could turn the head of a girl like her as fast as I could. God knows how long it would have taken your simpering young dandies flouncing about with their citherns*—why, those ninnies couldn't find their what-nots with a map and a compass! Just you watch me on my rebec—I'll show you a trick or two! I'm not as old as I look: see for yourself. Well, it's obvious enough to *her*! Besides, she'll realize soon enough once I get my hands on her; by Heavens, I'll keep her in play—I'll have her running after me like a bee to a honey-pot!'

'Oh', said Bruno, 'you'll make a meal of her. I can just see you nibbling away at her luscious red lips and those rosy cheeks of hers, and then finishing her off in two mouthfuls.'

Convinced by these words that he'd virtually arrived, Calandrino was in his seventh heaven. He went about singing and skipping for joy. The next day he brought his rebec and accompanied himself as he sang song after song to the delight of the company. Before long he'd worked himself up into such a state from seeing so much of her that he quite gave up working, but was forever dashing to the window or the door or right out into the courtyard to catch a glimpse of her, while she, cleverly putting Bruno's lessons into practice, gave him plenty to look at. Bruno, for his part, acted as his messenger and occasionally carried messages from her. When she was away, which was more often than not, he brought Calandrino letters from her in which he raised his hopes enormously; she would be—as he pointed out—staying with relatives and he could not get to see her. Thus Bruno and Buffalmacco, who kept the ball in play, enjoyed no end of a lark at Calandrino's expense; they'd make him hand over all manner of things, ostensibly at his beloved's request: one day it would be an ivory comb, another, a purse or a knife or suchlike trifles; they'd bring back to him cheap trumpery rings that would send him into ecstasies. Added to that, he'd offer them little treats and favours to keep them zealous in his interest.

They carried on this way for a good two months without making any further progress; but when Calandrino realized that their work was almost completed and that, if he didn't bring his love to consummation by the time the job was done, he never would bring it off at all, he put Bruno under redoubled pressure. So when Niccolosa was back, Bruno agreed with her and with Filippo how they were to proceed, then he told

Calandrino: 'The thing is, my friend, this woman of yours has promised me any number of times that she'd fall in with your wishes, but she's done absolutely nothing about it. I think she's leading us by the nose. As she won't stick to her promise, we're going to make her do it willy-nilly, that is, if you'd like us to.'

'Oh please do, and the sooner the better.'

'If I give you a letter with magic words', said Bruno, 'are you game to touch her with it?'

'Yes yes.'

'Very well. Bring me some parchment made from the skin of an unborn lamb; bring me also a live bat, three grains of incense, and a holy candle, and leave the rest to me.'

Calandrino spent the entire evening contriving to catch a bat, and when he had caught one he brought it to Bruno along with the other things. Bruno disappeared into a room, scribbled a little hocus-pocus and a doodle or two on the parchment, and gave it all back to him. 'Calandrino', he said, 'if you touch her with this document you can be sure she'll follow you at once and do whatever you want. So if Filippo goes off anywhere today, approach her somehow or other and touch her, then come into this straw hut over here: that's far and away the best place as no one ever goes into it. She'll follow you in, just you watch; when she's inside, well, you know what to do.'

Calandrino was over the moon; he took the parchment and said. 'Leave it to me, partner.'

Now Nello, of whom Calandrino remained wary, was in on the plot to fool him and was enjoying the joke as much as the others. He went back to Florence, as instructed by Bruno, and called on Calandrino's wife Tessa and said to her: 'Tessa, you know what a beating you got from Calandrino for no reason, the day he came back from the Mugnone loaded with stones. Now I want you to settle the score; if you don't, mark my words, I'm no longer your friend or relative. He's fallen in love with a woman up there, and she's such a hussy she's forever creeping off into corners with him. Just now they've arranged another tryst: what I want you to do is to come along and catch him in the act and give him a thorough spanking.'

Tessa did not take these words lightly; she jumped up and cried: 'Why, the arrant thief! Is that what he's doing to me? By Heaven he won't get away with it—see if I don't make him pay!'

She snatched up her cloak and set out at a brisk trot, accompanied by a maid and by Nello. When Bruno caught sight of her in the distance, he said to Filippo: 'Here's our friend.'

Filippo then went over to where Calandrino and the others were working and said: 'Fellows, I have to go into Florence. Keep up the good work.' He slipped away and found himself a hiding-place where he could see what Calandrino was up to without being seen himself.

When he thought that Filippo was well out of the way, Calandrino went down into the courtyard, where he found Niccolosa on her own. He struck up a conversation with her and she, knowing precisely what was expected of her, nestled up to him and showed herself a good deal friendlier than usual, whereupon he touched her with the parchment. After touching her, he turned away without a word and made for the straw hut. Niccolosa followed him. Inside the hut she shut the door, threw her arms round him, and shoved him down on to the straw that covered the floor. She then sat astride him, resting her hands on his shoulders, but never letting him reach up to her face, and she gazed at him with eyes full of desire (so it seemed) and said: 'O Calandrino my darling, my love, my own sweetie-pie, what a long wait it's been to have you, to hold you in my arms to my heart's content! Why, I've found you so irresistible, you can twist me round your little finger. You've seduced my heart out of my body with that rebec of yours. Can it really be true that I'm holding you in my arms?'

Calandrino, who could barely move, kept saying: 'Come, darling, let me kiss you.'

'My, you *are* in a hurry', replied Niccolosa. 'First let me drink you in, let me have my fill of gazing on that sweet face of yours!'

Bruno and Buffalmacco had gone to join Filippo, and the three were watching and listening to all this. Now while

Calandrino was still trying to snatch a kiss from Niccolosa, along came Nello with Calandrino's good wife Tessa. 'I swear to God', said Nello, 'the pair of them are together.' They reached the door of the hut and Tessa threw it open with a furious shove—in she went, and found Calandrino with Niccolosa sitting astride him. The moment the girl saw her, she leapt up and fled to Filippo.

Tessa ran at her husband, who had not yet got to his feet, and attacked his face with her fingernails; she seized him by the hair, tugging it this way and that as she said: 'You filthy dog, have you no shame? Just look what you're doing to me! The doddering oaf—I once loved the fellow, damn it! What? Do you reckon you don't have enough to do at home so you have to go chasing after other women? Just look at you, my beautiful lover-boy! As if you didn't know, you poor twit, I could squeeze you from top to bottom and not get out enough juice to fit in a jelly-spoon. God knows, it's not your Tessa who put you in the family way—whoever the woman was, blast her! She must be a proper cow if she gets an itch for a crumb like you.'

Seeing his wife turn up, Calandrino wished the earth would swallow him whole; he was too cowed to offer any resistance. Scratched, plucked, and dishevelled as he was, he retrieved his hood, stood up, and meekly entreated his wife to keep her voice down unless she wanted him to be cut to pieces, because the lady he'd been with was the wife of the master of the house.

'Is she now?' said his wife. 'Well, a plague on her!'

Bruno and Buffalmacco, who had enjoyed no end of a laugh with Filippo and Niccolosa, now came up as though alerted by the rumpus; after a great deal of talk they managed to calm Tessa, and they advised Calandrino to return to Florence and not to come back—that way, if Filippo ever found out about it, he wouldn't hurt him. So poor, wretched Calandrino returned to Florence, all scratched and minus some of his hair, and never dared go back up to the Camerata, while his wife gave him hell night and day. So he snuffed out his fervent love, which had afforded such merriment to his companions and to Niccolosa and Filippo.

IX. 6. *Two youths stop for a night's lodging, as a result of which the host's wife and daughter each finds a young man in her bed. The fault lies partly with a cat, partly with a cradle.*

The party had derived amusement before from Calandrino and so did they again this time. But when the ladies had finished discussing him, the queen bade Pamphilo tell his tale, which he did as follows:

The mention of Niccolosa as the name of the lady with whom Calandrino was in love reminds me of another Niccolosa whose story I should like to tell you: it will illustrate the way a good woman averted a shocking scandal by her quick-wittedness.

Not very long ago there lived in the plain of the Mugnone a worthy fellow who, for a fee, would afford travellers food and drink. Although he was far from rich and his house was but small, he would occasionally offer lodging, not to simply anyone but to certain acquaintances, if the need were pressing enough. He had a very pretty wife and two children; one was a lovely, graceful little creature of some sixteen summers, still unmarried; the other was a baby boy, not yet a year old, who still fed at his mother's breast. Now a charming, well-bred young gentleman from our city had formed an attachment to this girl; he was forever gadding about her part of the world and he loved her passionately. She, for her part, took no little pride in having aroused such strong feelings in a lad of his sort, and strove to secure him to herself by welcoming his advances—and in the course of so doing, she fell in love with him. Many a time would they have relished consummating their love, but Pinuccio (to give the young gentleman his name) was anxious to avoid putting either of them to the blush. However, as his love grew more fervent by the day, he felt he just had to get together with her, and it occurred to him that he would have to find some means to obtain lodging from her father: knowing the layout of her house, he felt he might contrive to be with her and escape discovery. Once this plan occurred to him, he lost no time in putting it into effect.

Late one evening, accompanied by his close friend Adriano, who was in the secret, he hired a pair of hacks, loaded them up with a couple of suitcases—maybe filled with straw—and they both left Florence. Turning off their road, they cut round towards the plain of the Mugnone. It was night by the time they reached it. Here they took another turning, so as to approach the good fellow's house as if on their way back from Romagna. They knocked at his door, which he promptly opened to them, for the pair were no strangers to him. 'Look', Pinuccio told him, 'we'll need you to put us up tonight. We'd expected to be able to reach Florence, but we've misjudged it so badly, as you see, that we've got only this far by this late hour.'

'Pinuccio', replied his host, 'you know how well placed I am to offer hospitality to men of your station. But since this is as far as you've got at this hour of night and there's not time enough to go elsewhere, I'll certainly put you up as best I may.'

So the two young men dismounted and entered the inn yard and, after attending to their mounts, sat down to supper with their host—they had brought their own provisions. Now the only bedroom their host possessed was a very little one, in which he had made up three small beds as best he could. With two beds against one wall and the third against the opposite one, there was barely room to squeeze between them. The host placed the least uncomfortable bed at the disposal of the two friends, and invited them to retire. In a while, when they showed signs of being asleep—though neither of them was—the host had his daughter get into one of the two remaining beds, and climbed into the third with his wife, who pulled alongside of it the cradle in which she had laid her baby. This, then, was the situation when Pinuccio, who had taken note of everything, stealthily got up after a while, as everyone seemed to him to have gone to sleep, and crept across to the bed in which his beloved lay, and slipped in beside her. She welcomed him gladly, albeit with some trepidation, and they now fulfilled their heart's desire and took their pleasure together. While Pinuccio was thus abed with the girl, the cat knocked something over. This woke up the host's wife, who got out of bed, fearing it might be something else, and groped in the dark to where she had heard the noise coming from. Of this Adriano was oblivious when he himself got up, as he needed to answer the call of nature; as he went to do so, he bumped into the baby's cradle where the mother had left it; as he could not get past without shifting it, he moved it from its place, leaving it standing alongside his own bed. Once he had completed his business he returned to the bedroom and, without giving a further thought to the cradle, got back into bed.

When the host's wife had gone to look and found that what had fallen down was not what she thought, she didn't bother to light a lamp to take a better look but returned to the bedroom after scolding the cat. She felt her way towards the bed in which her husband was sleeping but, not finding the cradle: 'Heavens!' she remarked to herself, 'naughty me, look what I was going to do, climbing straight into bed with my guests!' So she went on a few steps till she came upon the cradle and got into the bed next to which it stood, and lay down beside Adriano, thinking it was her husband. Adriano, who had not yet gone back to sleep, gave her a most cheerful welcome, without uttering a word, and luffed to bring his bowsprit into the wind, a manœuvre that was wholly to her liking.

At this point Pinuccio, who had taken the pleasure he had craved, was worrying lest he fell asleep in the arms of his beloved, so he got up to go back to sleep in his own bed. Arriving there, he found the cradle, so imagined he must have happened upon his host's bed. On he went, therefore, and got into bed with the host, waking him up in the process. Assuming that his bed-mate was Adriano, Pinuccio remarked: 'Take my word, there never was a sweeter bit of goods than Niccolosa! Believe me, she's given me the most delicious time a man ever had with a woman. Since I got out of this bed I've taken my bucket to the well six times.'

This observation left the host feeling far from happy. 'What the blazes is this fellow doing in here?' he asked himself and then, anger prevailing over common sense, he said to Pinuccio: 'Now that really was a shabby trick! How could you do such a thing to me? At all events, I'll make you pay for it.'

Pinuccio, who was not the world's brainiest youth, did not hasten to salvage the situation when he realized his error, but observed: 'Pay? What for? What can you do to me?'

The host's wife, who thought she was in bed with her husband, remarked to Adriano: 'Oh dear! Listen to our guests. They seem to have fallen out over something.'

'Let them be', said Adriano with a chuckle; 'they had too much to drink last night, curse them!'

The wife thought she heard her husband expostulating and certainly recognized Adriano's voice, which brought her at once to realize where she was and who with. Being a wise woman, however, she kept mum but got straight out of bed and, though the room was in pitch darkness, she grasped her baby's cradle and felt her way with it across to her daughter's bed and got in beside her. Then, pretending to have been awoken by the noise her husband was making, she called to him and asked him why he was bandying words with Pinuccio.

'Can't you hear what he's saying', replied her husband, 'about what he's been up to with our Niccolosa?'

'Well he's lying in his teeth', said the wife. 'He's not slept with Niccolosa. I got into bed with her and haven't slept a wink since. You, you're a plain ass for believing him. You drink so much in the evening, you fall to dreaming and you go sleepwalking—God knows what you get up to! More's the pity you don't break your neck! But what's Pinuccio doing over there? Why isn't he in his own bed?'

Adriano, for his part, noticing how cleverly his host's wife was concealing her shame and that of her daughter, said to Pinuccio: 'Come, I've told you a hundred times you must stop this roving about: this bad habit of yours of walking in your sleep and trotting out a lot of dream-nonsense as though it were the very truth—one day it's going to get you into big trouble. Now come back to bed, and God send you a rotten night!'

Hearing what his wife and Pinuccio were saying, the host was all too ready to believe that Pinuccio was having a dream. So he took him by the shoulder and shook him and shouted at him: 'Wake up, Pinuccio. Get back to your own bed.'

Pinuccio heard all this and, putting two and two together, set about rambling and muttering like someone having a dream, which sent the host into fits of laughter. Eventually, however, as he felt himself being shaken, he pretended to wake up and called out to Adriano: 'What? Is it day already? That why you're calling me?'

'Yes', said Adriano. 'Come here.'

Pinuccio continued his pretence of being half asleep but did finally get up from his host's bed and return to Adriano's. When they got up in the morning, the host enjoyed a good laugh about Pinuccio and his dreams. To the accompaniment of such merry banter the two youths saddled up their mounts, loaded on their luggage, had a glass with the host, set foot to stirrup, and returned to Florence, pleased with what they had accomplished and even more so with the way it had worked out. Subsequently Pinuccio found other ways to enjoy Niccolosa's company, and she would constantly assure her mother that the boy must have been dreaming. Her mother, therefore, who well remembered Adriano's embraces, continued to persuade herself that *she* had not.

## IX. 7. *Talano d'Imolese dreams a prophetic dream about his wife. Unfortunately she is too perverse to heed it.*

When Pamphilo's story was ended, and the lady's presence of mind had won general approval, the queen told Pampinea to tell her tale, and so she began:

We have already discussed the veracity of dreams, which many people pooh-pooh. But none the less, I shall tell you a very short tale about what happened to a neighbour of mine not all that long ago, for not taking heed of a dream her husband had about her.

I don't know whether you ever knew Talano d'Imolese, a man of the highest standing. He married a young woman called Margarita, an exceptionally pretty woman, but inordinately touchy, irritable, and cantankerous. She'd never fall in with what anyone else suggested and was totally intractable. Talano found this a real trial, but as there was nothing he could do about it, he endured it. He had gone with his Margarita to a place they had in the country and, one night while he was asleep, he dreamed that his wife went into a beautiful wood, one they in fact owned not far from their house. As he watched her go into the wood, he dreamed that a big, fierce wolf came out from some part of the wood and leapt at her throat and dragged her to the ground and tried pulling her off with him as she screamed for help. When she was free of his jaws her whole neck and face were, he dreamed, completely lacerated.

As he got up in the morning, Talano said to his wife: 'Though you're a woman with whom I've never yet enjoyed a day's happiness, because you have to contradict the whole time, even so, I'd be sorry if anything happened to you. So take my advice and stay indoors today.' She asked him why, and he told her his dream in every detail.

His wife shook her head. 'The man who wishes you ill', she said, 'dreams ill of you. You make yourself out to be all concerned about me, but you dream what you'd like to see happen to me. Mark my word, though, I'll take good care, today and always, to give you no chance to gloat over me for this or any other misfortune.'

'I knew that's what you'd say', answered Talano. 'Comb out a flea-ridden woman and she'll send you off with a flea in your ear. Think whatever you want, I've been quite straight with you, and I advise you, once again, stay at home today, or at any rate take care not to go into our woods.'

'Very well, I'll take care', she said, adding to herself: 'Now take a look at that for sheer cunning! He thinks he's scared me off going into our woods today! What he'll have gone and done is arrange a tryst with some hussy and he doesn't want me to catch him. Ha! Eat with the blind and you do yourself proud. If I didn't know him, if I took him at his word, I'd be a real cuckoo! That, however, is not what's going to happen. I'm going to see, if I have to stand there all day, just what it is he's planning to get up to.'

This said, she left by one side of the house just after her husband had gone out by the other. She didn't waste a moment but slipped away as furtively as possible to the wood, and hid where it was thickest, watching alertly in all directions to see if anyone was coming. While she was thus engaged, with no thought of wolves, what should emerge from a thicket right next to her but a frightful great wolf, and when she saw him she could barely exclaim 'Lord help me!' before he leapt at her throat, took her in a powerful grip, and started dragging her off as if she had been a baby lamb. With her throat clamped she could not shout or help herself in any way, so she would undoubtedly have been throttled as the wolf dragged her along, were it not that he ran across some shepherds; they shouted at him and forced him to let go of her. In her sorry state she was recognized by the shepherds, who took her home, where the doctors cured her after a lengthy treatment. She was left, though, with her entire throat and part of her face so disfigured that, whereas she had been a beauty before, she was to look a horrible fright forever after. She was ashamed now to show her face in public, and time and again she rued her contentiousness and her refusal to take the option, scot-free, of trusting to her husband's truthful dream.

## IX. 8. *Biondello plays a trick on Ciacco the glutton. Ciacco gets his own back.*

It was the general opinion of the happy gathering that what Talano had seen in his sleep was not a dream but a vision, for it had all meticulously come to pass. As soon as they fell silent, the queen bade Lauretta follow, and this was her story:

Nearly all those who have already spoken today have taken their inspiration from what has just gone before. I am taking mine from the tale Pampinea told us yesterday about the ruthless vengeance exacted by the student. The vengeance I'll speak of was painful enough to the one who suffered it, though not so savage.

There once lived in Florence a greedy glutton called Ciacco.* He lacked the means to pamper his stomach as much as he would have wished, but as he was well mannered and had a fund of amusing table-talk, he found a role, not maybe as a fully blown courtier, but anyway as a sedulous gadfly at courtly tables. He could generally find a place at the table of any rich man who kept a good cook and a good cellar—indeed he would often enjoy a meal with him even when he had not been invited.

There also lived in Florence at that time a dapper little man called Biondello, sleek as though he'd stepped out of a bandbox; he affected a hat and wore a neat page-boy cut with never a blonde hair out of place. He followed the same trade as Ciacco.

One morning in Lent Biondello went to the fish-market to buy two enormous lampreys for that power in the land, Vieri de' Cerchi. Ciacco spotted him, sidled up to him, and asked: 'Hey, what's this in aid of?'

'Yesterday afternoon they sent up three of these fellows—you should have seen, they make these two look pathetic—and a sturgeon, too, to Corso Donati*—'

'Corso Donati himself? Wow!'

'—and he sent me down to buy another two as he's got gentlemen for dinner and not enough to feed them. Won't you be there?'

'You can bet on it', said Ciacco.

After a suitable interval, Ciacco presented himself at Corso Donati's residence; the great man was in the company of neighbours and had not yet sat down to lunch.

'What brings you here, Ciacco?' asked Corso.

'I've come to join you and your friends for lunch, sir.'

'Welcome—you've timed it nicely, we're just going to eat.'

They sat down to a first course of tuna and chick-peas, followed by a plate of fried fish from the Arno. That was all. Ciacco realized that Biondello had made a fool of him and was not best pleased. He proposed to get his own back. Biondello had been dining out on the joke for quite a few days before he bumped into Ciacco. 'Tell me', he asked with a smirk, 'how did you enjoy Corso's lampreys?'

'Ask me again in a week—you'll know better than I do.'

Not a moment did he waste. After leaving Biondello he struck a deal with a plausible villain. Handing the man a bottle, and taking him to the Loggia de' Cavicciuli where there was a crowd of people, he pointed out one of them, Filippo

Argenti,* a tall, well-built gentleman, solid muscle, and with a very short temper. 'See that man? Now run along to him with this bottle and say: "Excuse me, sir. Biondello sent me. He asks if you'd be kind enough to replenish this bottle for him with some of that good red wine you have there: he wants to wet his wooden whistle with his chums." Take care to stand well back: if he grabs you he'll give you a hiding and that will spoil my plan.'

'Is that all I have to say?'

'Yes. Off you go, and when you've passed the message, bring me back the bottle and I'll pay you off.'

So the tout went and delivered his message. Filippo listened to him and turned puce in the face—patience was never his strong point. He knew Biondello and realized his leg was being pulled. 'What's all this "replenishing" and "wooden whistle"? I'll give you a wooden whistle!' he shouted as he leapt up and made a grab for him. But the tout knew what was coming and didn't hang about—he made off back to Ciacco (who had watched the encounter), and reported Filippo's words.

Ciacco gladly settled up with his go-between and hastened off to find Biondello. 'Have you just been in the Loggia de' Cavicciuli?' he asked him.

'No. Why d'you ask?'

'I gather that Filippo Argenti's looking for you', explained Ciacco. 'I don't know what about.'

'I'm going that way', said Biondello. 'I'll stop by and have a word with him.'

Biondello left and Ciacco followed to observe. As Filippo had not been able to lay hands on the tout he was still fuming: he didn't know what the man had been on about but suspected that Biondello, or someone who'd put him up to it, was taking the mickey out of him. Then, while he was still fretting, who should turn up but Biondello himself. Filippo went straight up to him and punched him on the nose.

'Ouch!' cried Biondello. 'What's got into you, sir?'

Filippo seized him by the hair, tore his hat to pieces, hurled his hood on to the floor, and laid into him. 'You rat', he shouted. 'I'll show you what's got into me! I'll "replenish" you! I'll wet your wooden whistle! What d'you take me for—a fool?'

And he attacked him again with his fists, which seemed made of iron, and smashed his face in and didn't leave two of his hairs on speaking terms and sent him rolling in the mud and tore his clothes to shreds. This all happened so fast, Biondello couldn't get a word in or find out why he was being so treated. He had caught the words 'replenish' and 'wooden whistle' but didn't know how they fitted in.

Eventually, after Filippo had given him a sound drubbing, the people with him made a concerted effort and managed to drag Biondello out of his clutches—he was in sorry shape and less than dapper. And they explained to him why he had been so treated, and chided him for the message he had sent. 'Now you know what sort of man our Filippo is—he's not a man to bandy words with', they said. Biondello tearfully made his apologies and assured them he had never sent anyone to Filippo Argenti for wine. Once he was somewhat recovered he made his aching, doleful way home, and realized that Ciacco must be the culprit.

Several days later, once the bruises no longer showed on his face and he could go out again, he ran into Ciacco, who inquired with a grin: 'How did you like Argenti's wine, Biondello?'

'I wish Corso's lampreys had struck you the same way!'

'Well, it's up to you. You treat me to another meal like that and I'll treat you to another bottle of the same vintage.'

As Biondello realized that he could do little more than dream about getting back at Ciacco, he wished him a very good day and took care not to tease him again.

## IX. 9. *Two young men go to Solomon for advice, and come away, so they think, empty-handed. Very soon, though, it serves their turn.*

It remained only for the queen to tell a story, if Dioneo was to retain his privilege; so she cheerfully embarked on hers (once the ladies had finished chuckling over Biondello's *contretemps*) in these words:

If we take an objective look at the natural order of things, amiable ladies, it will be readily apparent that nature, custom, and the law subject our entire female tribe to the males, to be commanded and directed as they see fit. Therefore the woman who is looking for a life of peace, tranquillity, and comfort with the men to whom she belongs needs to practise meekness, patience, and obedience, to say nothing of fidelity, which is the prudent woman's sovereign gift. And even if we were not schooled to this by the law, which has an eye to the common good in every respect, or by custom or habit (call it what you will)—a hallowed force that exerts no end of pressure—Nature herself makes it all too obvious: has she not endowed us with soft, tender bodies, timid, diffident souls, kind, compassionate hearts, only modest physical strength, mellifluous voices and supple grace in our movements, all of which point to our need to be ruled by others? Now it stands to reason that anyone who needs to be helped and given orders should obey such a helping and commanding person with due submission and respect; and who represent assistance and authority to us women if it is not the menfolk? So we are bound to submit to men and treat them with every respect and, in my view, any woman who fails to do so richly deserves a solemn rebuke, indeed a thorough hiding. Although we've been over this before, I was reminded of it just now by Pampinea's story of Talano's recalcitrant wife,* who got her deserts from the Good Lord when her husband proved unable to punish her. To my mind, all those women who fail to make themselves agreeable, charming, and tractable, as nature, custom, and the law require, deserve—as I said—to be punished most severely.

So I should like to pass on to you a piece of advice from Solomon, which may serve as a cure for women afflicted by such an inclination. Of course those of you who are not asking for such medicine must not imagine that the advice applies to you, for all that men have a saying: 'Be she a jade or a good filly, a touch of the crop doesn't come amiss.' Make light of the proverb if you will, but any woman will admit that it's the truth—and I'd say it's certainly to be conceded by those of us who are ready to take it seriously. All women are by nature fickle and inconstant, so there's a call for the rod of chastisement to mend the wickedness of those who step too far outside the limits; as for the rest, to assist their virtue they need the rod as an encouragement and dire warning not to go astray. Anyway, enough of this preaching, here is the story I'm minded to tell you.

At a time when word of Solomon's prodigious wisdom had reached practically every corner of the world, and it was known that he bestowed it quite freely upon anyone who wished to be acquainted with it at first hand, people came in droves from all over the place to seek his advice on all manner of pressing or intractable problems. One of these seekers was a very rich young nobleman called Melissus, who set out from his native city of Laiazzo in Armenia.* On his way from Antioch as he was riding towards Jerusalem he fell in with another young man, called Joseph, who was making the same journey; and, as travellers will, he struck up a conversation with him. Melissus discovered from Joseph what his background was and where he was from, then asked him whither he was bound and wherefore. Joseph told him that he was on his way to see Solomon, to obtain his advice as to how to deal with his wife, the most perverse and wayward woman in the world: he had entreated and wheedled her, he had done everything he could, but there was no curing her of her fractious disposition. This said, Joseph asked him, in turn, where he was from, whither bound, and to what end.

'I'm from Laiazzo', Melissus told him, 'and if you have a problem, I have one too, of a different sort. I'm a wealthy young man and I lavish my money on entertaining my fellows to meals, but it's the oddest thing—I do all this and yet can't find so much as one person who really cares for me. So I'm going your way, to obtain advice as to how to make myself loved.'

So they continued their journey together and, on reaching Jerusalem, obtained an audience with Solomon on the introduction of a courtier. Melissus briefly told him his problem, and Solomon's answer was: 'Love.'

This said, Melissus was promptly bundled out and Joseph explained the object of his visit. For all answer, Solomon said: 'Go to Goose Bridge.' With this, Joseph was similarly hustled out of the royal presence without futher ado, and found Melissus waiting for him. He told him what answer he had received.

As they pondered these words without being able to derive any sense, let alone profit, from them for their purposes, they ruefully started on their journey home and, in a few days, arrived at a river spanned by a fine bridge. A great caravan of laden mules and horses was crossing it, so the travellers had to wait till the bridge was clear. When nearly all the caravan had crossed, it happened that a mule baulked, as one often sees them do, and was totally unwilling to continue, so the muleteer took a stick and tapped the beast lightly enough to begin with, in order to budge it. But as the mule would just stand crosswise to the bridge, facing one way then the other, or turn back the way it had come, but stolidly refused to advance, the muleteer flew into a rage and lay about the beast with his stick, whacking it on the head, on its flanks, on its rump, but all to no avail.

Melissus and Joseph were watching, and kept saying to the muleteer: 'Hey, you brute, what are you doing? D'you want to kill him? Why don't you try just leading him gently? He'll come more readily that way than if you whack him the way you're doing.'

'You know your horses', answered the mule-driver, 'and I know my mule. Just leave me to it.' And he went back to beating it, raining blows on it from one side and the other until the beast moved forward, which left its driver vindicated.

As the young men were about to continue their way, Joseph asked a fellow sitting by the bridgehead what the place was called. 'This, sir, is Goose Bridge', he was told.

This reminded Joseph of what Solomon had said. He turned to his friend and remarked: 'D'you know what? It could be that Solomon's advice is true and sound: it's quite obvious to me that I had no idea how to thrash my wife, and this mule-driver has shown me what I have to do.'

Some days later they reached Antioch, where Joseph detained his friend for a few days' rest. Joseph's wife extended him an indifferent welcome, but he told her to prepare supper the way Melissus would like it. As this was Joseph's wish, Melissus described in a few words what he would like. The lady, however, followed her usual habit and supper came not as Melissus asked for it but the very opposite in just about every respect.

This irritated Joseph, who said to her: 'Were you not told precisely how this meal was to be prepared?'

His wife drew herself up and remarked with a sniff: 'What are you going on about? Get on and eat if you want to eat. Maybe I was told differently but this is the meal I've chosen. Like it or lump it!'

Melissus was surprised by the wife's retort and roundly told her so, while Joseph, on hearing it, said: 'You're still no different from before, woman, but I'm going to alter your manner, believe you me.' Then he turned to Melissus. 'We'll soon see what Solomon's advice is worth, my friend. Pray don't mind witnessing this; imagine that what I'm going to do is mere playfulness. Before you try to stop me, just remember what the muleteer said to us when we took him to task over his mule.'

'I'm in your home, and have no intention of crossing you.'

Joseph found himself a round stick cut from an oak sapling; he went into the bedroom, whither his wife had withdrawn, muttering, after leaving the table in a huff. He grabbed her by the hair, threw her down at his feet, and started belabouring her with this stick. She yelled to begin with, and uttered threats, but when she saw that none of this stopped him, she quite crumpled and begged for mercy, pleaded with him for God's sake not to murder her, for she would never again disregard his wishes. Joseph never laid off all this while, but thrashed her with ever increasing ferocity, getting her in the ribs one moment, on the hips the next, then across the shoulders, hammering her into shape and never letting up until he was dog-tired. In fact the good woman was not left with a single bone, not an inch of her back, that was not reduced to pulp.

When he was done, he went over to Melissus and observed: 'We shall see tomorrow how effective has been the advice to go to Goose Bridge.' He took a few moments' rest, washed his hands, sat down to supper with Melissus, and in due course they went to bed.

The wretched woman struggled to her feet, threw herself into bed, and got such rest as she could. The next morning she was up very early and sent to ask Joseph what he would like for lunch. He placed his order as he and Melissus had a good laugh. They came back at lunchtime to find everything prepared to perfection and exactly as he had instructed. So they had only praise for the advice that at first they had failed to grasp.

A few days later, Melissus left Joseph and returned home, and told somebody who had a little sense what Solomon had said to him. The man's comment was: 'He could not have given you a truer or better piece of advice. You know that you don't care for anybody, and that everything you lay on for other people is done not because you like them but because you like showing off. So do as Solomon said: Love, and you'll be loved.'

Thus the awkward wife was punished and the young man earned love by giving it.

IX. 10. *At Pietro's request, his friend Don Gianni sets about transforming his wife into a mare; but when Don Gianni comes to the hard part, Pietro ruins the spell.*

The tale of the queen's had the ladies muttering somewhat, and the young men chuckling. When they had simmered down Dioneo spoke up:

A bevy of white doves will see its beauty heightened by the presence of a black crow far better than by that of a white swan; similarly an assemblage of learned men will find that an oaf in their midst does not merely add lustre to their mature intellects but even supplies a little mirth and entertainment. So whereas you ladies are every onc of you as judicious and temperate as could be, I regard myself as *not* the brightest of intellects, which is why you should find me all the more to your liking in that my lunacy enhances your superb intelligences: if I possessed enormous brain-power I'd put you all in the shade. I should therefore enjoy all the broader discretion in revealing myself to you for what I am, and you should afford me all the greater tolerance than you would if I were a man of wiser judgement, as I tell you the story I am about to relate. Very well, my tale is on the short side, and will teach you that when people practise magic on you, you have to obey their instructions to the letter: it takes only the most trivial mistake to abort the entire spell.

Some years ago there was a priest at Barletta called Don Gianni. He had a poor parish and, to make ends meet, he had to load up his mare with merchandise and go round the fairs in Apulia, buying and selling. In the course of these peregrinations he formed a close friendship with a man from Tresanti called Pietro, who followed a similar trade with his donkey. In token of his friendship and affection, Don Gianni called him (in the Apulian fashion) his old mate Pietro, and would bring him to his presbytery every time he turned up at Barletta, and offer him a night's lodging and such hospitality as he could muster. As for his old mate Pietro, he was poor as poor could be and lived in a wee hovel at Tresanti with barely room for his pretty young wife and his donkey. Still, every time Don Gianni passed through Tresanti, Pietro would bring him home and extend him such hospitality as he could, to requite him for the hospitality his friend afforded him at Barletta. Where the night's lodging was concerned, however, as Pietro possessed nothing but one narrow bed in which he slept with his lovely wife, he could not accommodate him as he would have wished, but had to leave his guest to bed down on a little straw alongside his mare, who shared a stable with the donkey. Aware of the hospitality Pietro received from the priest at Barletta, his wife had several times wanted to go and sleep at a neighbour's, a woman called Zita Carapresa, when the priest was visiting; that way the priest could share her husband's bed. She had frequently suggested this to Don Gianni but he had always refused.

On one occasion he said to her: 'Don't worry about me, Gemmata my dear: I'm fine. When I want to, I turn my mare into a pretty lass and enjoy her company. Then I turn her back into a mare when I feel like it. I wouldn't part with her on any account.'

'How marvellous!' thought Gemmata, who fully believed him. She repeated it to her husband and added: 'If he's really your old mate as you say he is, why don't you have him teach you the spell? Then you can turn me into a mare and go about your business with the donkey *and* your mare—that way we'll earn twice as much. Once we're back home, you can turn me back into the girl I am.'

Now Pietro was thick as two short planks and believed what he was told. He accepted her suggestion and set about badgering the priest for all he was worth to teach him how to do it. Don Gianni did his best to deter him from this nonsense, but as he was unable to, he told him: 'All right, then, if you insist, we'll get up tomorrow before sunrise, as usual, and I'll show you how it's done. To tell you the truth, the hardest part, as you'll see, is sticking the tail on.'

Pietro and Gemmata barely slept a wink that night, they were so eager for what was to come, and when it was almost day they got up and woke Don Gianni, who came into Pietro's bedroom in nothing but his shirt. 'I don't know of a single person in the whole world I'd do this for', he said, 'apart from you. I'll do it for you as you want me to. The thing is, if you want it to work, you must do just as I say.'

They promised to do as he told them, so Don Gianni took a lantern and handed it to Pietro. 'Watch closely what I do', he told him, 'and bear well in mind whatever I say. You'll ruin everything if you don't take care to keep absolutely quiet—not a word, whatever you see or hear. And pray God the tail sticks on all right.'

Pietro took the lamp and promised he'd certainly do so.

Don Gianni then had Gemmata strip down mother-naked and drop on all fours, in equine posture. He warned her, too, not to utter a syllable, whatever happened. Then he touched her face and head with his hands and said: 'Let this be a fine mare's head.' He touched her hair and said: 'Let this be a fine mare's mane.' He touched her arms and said: 'And let these be fine mare's legs and feet.' He touched her breasts and felt they were firm and round, which aroused him to a state that was alien to his calling, and he said: 'And let this be a fine mare's breast.' He did the same with her back, her belly, her posterior, her thighs and legs. Last of all, with nothing left to be done but the tail, he pulled up his shirt, grasped the peg used in his seedsmanship, and, as he promptly stuck it into the furrow made for the purpose, he cried: 'And let this be a fine mare's tail!'

Pietro had been following the proceedings closely up to this point, but when he saw this last item, he took it amiss and cried: 'No no, Don Gianni, no tail! I don't want any tail!'

The seminal fluid that promotes new growth was already a-coursing when Don Gianni pulled it back and said: 'Now look what you've done, Pietro my old mate! Didn't I tell you to keep mum, never mind what you saw? The mare was almost ready but you've ruined it all with your talking, and now there's not a chance of ever starting it again.'

'Never mind, I wasn't having that tail, not me! Why didn't you tell me, "Do the tail yourself"? Anyway, you were sticking it on too low.'

'Well', said Don Gianni, 'you wouldn't have been able to get it right first time, the way I could.'

Hearing this, the girl stood up and said to her husband in all innocence: 'Why have you gone and spoiled it all for yourself and for me, you daft idiot! When did you ever see a mare without a tail? So help me God, poor though you are, you're not half as poor as you deserve to be.'

She glumly got dressed as there was no further chance of her turning into a filly after all, thanks to what Pietro had blurted out. And he carried on his business in the same old way, with a donkey; he went with Don Gianni to the fair at Bitonto, but never again asked this particular favour of him.

Dioneo wished that the ladies in his audience were not quite so sharp—the laughter his story provoked in them will be clear enough to any woman who is yet to be amused by the recollection of it. But as the stories were now all told and the sun was beginning to lose its heat, the queen, realizing that her reign was at an end, stood up and removed her crown to place it on Pamphilo's head, he being the only one to whom this honour had not yet been accorded. She smiled and said: 'I leave you, sir, with a great responsibility: since you are the last, it is up to you to make good my deficiencies and those of the rest who have held your present office. May God's favour rest upon you, as it has done on me in making you king.'

Pamphilo was glad to accept the dignity and replied: 'I shall afford satisfaction, just as my predecessors have done, relying as I shall on your qualities and those of all my subjects.' He conferred, according to the custom of his predecessors, with the major-domo about the dispositions to be taken, then turned to address the expectant ladies: 'Today's queen, Emilia, decided in her wisdom to give you susceptible ladies a little respite to your ingenuity and left you free to speak on whatever subject took your fancy. Now that we are rested, I think we might revert to our normal procedure, and for tomorrow I shall want you to tell a story on the following topic: about people who acted in a generous and open-handed manner, whether in an affair of the heart or otherwise. Recounting such tales, and listening to them, is bound to kindle your latent ambition towards acts of generosity. Life, after all, can endure for but a short span in mortal bodies, but your lives will thus be extended in a commendable reputation. Now is this not something that everyone should wish for, indeed sedulously strive for and achieve—unless they are like brute beasts who serve only their bellies?'

The happy group found this to its liking; they all got up, then, and the new king dismissed them to employ their leisure as each of them preferred, in the customary manner, until supper-time. They came gladly to table and the meal was served with stylish diligence. When it was finished they got up to engage in their usual round of dances, and sang scores of songs—the melodies may have lacked finesse but the words, at all events, were rollicking. Then the king required Neiphile to sing one of her own, and she was happy to oblige at once, singing in a blithe, clear voice:

Young maiden that I am, mine's a merry disposition;
Ah, blissful thoughts of love come in springtime to fruition!
My steps lie through the meadows where the grass is lush
  and green;
 I mark the yellow blooms and white

The crimson roses—sheer delight!—
And lilies in their silken dress, as proud as any queen.
In each of them I recognize the face of my own dearest,
The lord and keeper of my heart
(His soul of mine is but a part),
I live now but to worship him with love that is sincerest.

Now when I come upon a flower that wears my love's expression
I cull it, kiss it, then address it,
Disclose my mind and there express it,
Admitting that my one desire's to be his sole possession.
Then, once to him my dearest wish I've candidly disclosed,
And all my speech is said and done,
I garland these my flowers in one,
And bind them with a tress of mine and hold them thus enclosed.

What gladness 'tis to rest the eye upon a pretty flower!
For me the joy indeed is stronger:
It helps me for to gaze the longer
Upon the one who keeps my heart, who is my rock and tower.
Aye, colour graces every bloom but, more, the scent bewitches,
It snares me so and leaves me weak
My sighs betray what I cannot speak
For that which leaves me lost for words my passion but enriches.

Ah true it is, my sighs well out from my impassioned breast;
But grim they're not, nor full of woe,
'Tis gentle fervour that they show,
They fly, winged messengers, to seek him out whom I love best.
And when they come before him, he gives ear to their entreating:
'Oh come', they plead, 'come soon, be near,
Your absence drives me to despair!'
Then to my side he promptly runs, towards my welcome greeting.

The king and all the ladies thoroughly applauded Neiphile's song. The night being well advanced, he now bade them all retire to rest until the morrow.

*Here ends the ninth day of the* Decameron *and the tenth and last day begins; under the reign of Pamphilo, the stories are about people who have acted in a generous and open-handed manner, whether in an affair of the heart or otherwise.*

A few small clouds still lay crimson in the west while those in the east were now edged with brightest gold, touched as they were by the rays of the advancing sun. So Pamphilo got up and had the ladies and his comrades called. When they all assembled, he discussed with them what pleasant destination their steps might lead them to, then he set out at a gentle pace, accompanied by Philomena and Fiammetta, the rest following. As they went they chatted about what the future held for them, and spent a good while in desultory conversation, each having observations to make; this took them on an extended ramble, until the sun's heat grew oppressive, when they returned to the villa. They gathered round the limpid fountain, had the glasses rinsed in the water, and those who were thirsty took a drink, after which they sought the welcome shade of the garden to enjoy their leisure until lunch-time. After they had eaten and taken a nap, as usual, they reassembled at the king's behest, and Neiphile it was who, by royal command, was the first to speak. Thus she merrily began:

X. I. *Fortune proves a poor friend to a valiant Tuscan knight in the King of Spain's service; the king proves to be kinder.*

I must account it a signal favour that our king has put me first to so great a task as this, to tell a story about generous dealings: for generosity is the splendour and light of all other qualities, just as the sun is the fairest ornament of the heavens. So I'm going to tell what seems to me a charming little tale, and one that is surely useful to bear in mind.

You must know, then, that of all the gallant knights who have resided in our city, not one of them has for a long time achieved the excellence of Ruggieri de' Figiovanni. He was a man of wealth and high enterprise who felt that living in Tuscany offered little scope to give the best of himself, and so he decided to move for a while to the court of King Alfonso* of Spain, whose reputation for gallantry surpassed that of any other prince of his day. So he went to him in Spain, with a highly respectable retinue of men-at-arms and horses. The king gave him a gracious welcome, and while he stayed here, leading a splendid existence and performing magnificent feats of arms, he soon established a reputation for valour. After he had been there for some time, however, closely observing the king's behaviour, he fancied that he was giving away a castle or town here, an earldom there, with very little concern as to the merits of his recipients, whereas he, Ruggieri, who had a shrewd idea of his own worth, was left empty-handed, which reflected badly on himself. So he decided to be on his way, and went to take leave of the king. The king gave him leave to depart, and presented him with as fine, handsome a mule as a man ever rode; this was much to the liking of Ruggieri, who had a long journey ahead of him. The king then entrusted a tactful courtier of his with the task of endeavouring, in whatever way he thought best, to ride with Ruggieri on his first day's journey, but avoiding any suspicion of having been sent by the king; he was to report back to him anything Ruggieri said about him, and he was to instruct Ruggieri the following morning to return to the king. The courtier kept watch, and as Ruggieri rode out of the town he deftly contrived to join him, giving him to understand that he was on his way to Italy.

So Ruggieri rode on, mounted on the mule the king had given him, while his companion talked of this and that. Towards mid-morning he said: 'It seems to me it would be a good idea to rest up our mounts awhile.' They rode them into a stable where every horse, except for the mule, relieved its bowels. Then they rode on some more, the courtier ever attentive to what Ruggieri was saying, and they came to a river where they watered their steeds: here the mule loosed her droppings into the water. On sight of this, Ruggieri observed:

'Well, you are a damnable brute, you're just like the master who gave you to me!'

The courtier made a note of this sally, and though he had noted a great deal more in the course of a day's ride with him, this was the only thing he picked up that was unfavourable to the king. So the next morning when they mounted and made to continue towards Tuscany, the courtier produced the king's instruction, whereupon Ruggieri turned back at once. The king was already informed of what he had said about the mule, and sent for Ruggieri. He received him cheerfully and asked him why he had compared him to his mule or the mule to him.

Ruggieri answered him quite candidly: 'I suggested the resemblance, my liege, because you tend to bestow your gifts in the wrong quarter and to hold back when a gift would be suitable; similarly the mule neglected to deposit her droppings in the right place and deposited them in the wrong place.'

'If I did not make a gift to you as I have to many another who is not to be compared with you', replied the king, 'it was not because I failed to recognize you for a knight of outstanding valour and one deserving of the most lavish of presents; it was your own fortune that prevented me from doing so, and that is where the blame lies, not with me. Furthermore I will give you clear proof that I'm speaking the truth.'

'My liege, it's not your failing to give me a present that upset me, for I had no wish to increase my wealth; what upset me was your not bearing any material witness to my qualities. However, I accept your excuse as a good, sound one and am quite ready to see what you wish to show me, for all that I believe you without further proof.'

So the king brought him into a great hall in which two enormous coffers stood, both locked, as he had arranged. A crowd was present as he said: 'Ruggieri, in one of these coffers there is my crown, along with my orb and sceptre, plenty of my best belts and buckles, rings and every one of my precious jewels; the other is full of earth. Help yourself to one of them; the one you choose is yours to keep. Then you'll be able to see who it is who has failed to take account of your merits, me or your luck.'

As he saw that this is what the king wanted, Ruggieri made his choice; the king ordered the selected coffer to be opened, and it proved to be the one filled with earth. So the king said with a smile: 'You can see for yourself how right I was in what I said to you about Fortune. However, your merits certainly oblige me to throw my weight against her. I know that you have no intention of becoming a Spaniard, so I won't give you a castle or a town here; I'll give you the coffer denied you by Fortune—I want you to have it in spite of her, and I want you to take it home to your own country and glory among your fellows in the witness to your virtues that my gift deservedly affords you.'

Ruggieri took it, gave thanks to the king such as befitted so great a gift, and returned with it happily to Tuscany.

X. 2. *Ghino di Tacco, a brigand, captures the Abbot of Cluny. He treats his prisoner better than might be expected, and the abbot returns the favour.*

Everyone applauded the generosity with which King Alfonso treated the Florentine knight. The king, too, thought very well of it. Now he bade Elissa follow, which she promptly did:

There is no denying that the king's bounty towards his servant is a fine, praiseworthy thing. But what shall we say about a churchman's remarkable bounty shown towards a man whom he could have treated as an enemy, without incurring the smallest reproach? What else can be said, but that the king's bounty attested his virtue while the churchman's smacked of the miraculous? Churchmen are, every one of them, the soul of stinginess compared with women and will resist any form of liberality to their dying breath. Moreover, while every man naturally thirsts for vengeance when he has been wronged, it is noticeable that the clergy preach patience and forgiveness of sins with a will, but turn to vengeance with greater passion than any. At all events, my tale will make plain to you how magnanimity was displayed by a cleric.

Ghino di Tacco* was widely known as a savage highwayman, after he'd antagonized the counts of Santafiore and been banished from Siena; he made Radicofani rebel against the Church of Rome and set up his quarters there, sending out his bandits to rob anyone passing that way. Now when Boniface VIII was Pope in Rome, the Abbot of Cluny came to his court, reputedly one of the richest prelates in the world. In Rome he developed a stomach complaint, and the doctors advised him that the baths at Siena would be the place for a cure, without a doubt. So with the Pope's leave, and heedless of Ghino's reputation, the abbot set forth in splendid array, with a whole baggage train and a great retinue of horses and servants. Getting wind of his arrival, Ghino di Tacco laid a trap in a narrow defile and secured the abbot with his entire household, bag and baggage—not even the smallest of the pages got away. This done, he sent the most smooth-tongued of his men, with a suitable train, as ambassador to the abbot, to present his compliments and invite him in all courtesy to partake of Ghino's hospitality at the castle. The outraged abbot answered that he would do no such thing: he wanted nothing whatsoever to do with Ghino, but proposed to continue on his way, 'and I'd like to see anyone try to stop me!' he added.

To which the envoy politely replied: 'This place you've come to, my lord abbot, is our realm, where we fear nothing beyond the power of God; here interdicts and excommunications* are of no effect. May it please you, therefore, to fall in with Ghino's wishes.'

As he was speaking, the bandits threw a cordon round the place and the abbot saw that he and his suite were caught in a trap, so he very angrily set out for the castle with the envoy, together with his retinue and baggage. Once arrived, he was lodged in a dark, cramped, and comfortless room of a house, as Ghino had instructed, while his suite was all accommodated in the castle, each man according to his station but all most comfortably; the horses and baggage were safely bestowed and everything was left untouched.

This done, Ghino went to the abbot and said: 'My lord abbot, I am sent by your host Ghino with the request that you kindly inform him whither you were bound and for what purpose.'

The abbot was wise enough to abate his temper and tell him his destination and purpose. Hearing this, Ghino left with the intention of curing the abbot without recourse to the baths. He had a big fire lit in the abbot's room and constantly tended, and returned to visit him only the following morning, when he brought him two slices of toast in a sparkling white napkin and a large glass of *Vernaccia* from Corniglia, drawn from the abbot's own supplies. He said to the abbot: 'When Ghino was younger, sir, he studied medicine, and he says that he never discovered any treatment for an ailing stomach that was so effective as the one he will administer to you; these things I have brought you are the start of the treatment: take them to restore yourself.'

The abbot was too hungry to bandy words with anyone, so with ill grace he ate the toast and drank the wine, then delivered himself of some cutting remarks assorted with a list of demands and a good deal of advice. In particular he requested a meeting with Ghino. Ghino listened to his remarks, let some of them ride, gave a perfectly civil reply to others, and assured him that Ghino would wait upon him just as soon as he could. With this he left, to return only the following day with another two slices of toast and large glass of *Vernaccia*. He maintained this regime for several days, until he noticed that the abbot had eaten some dried beans he had carefully left concealed for him.

He therefore enquired on Ghino's behalf how his stomach was feeling, and the abbot said: 'I'd be feeling quite well if I were out of his clutches. Aside from that, my greatest wish is to eat, so successfully has his treatment cured me.'

Ghino therefore had the abbot's servants make a room ready for a great banquet; it was an elegant room, and the abbot's own things were brought into use. The guests were the abbot's entire household and many of Ghino's men. Ghino went to the abbot the next day and said: 'Since you are now feeling well, my lord abbot, it is time for you to leave your sick-room.' Thus saying, he took him by the hand and brought him to the banqueting room where he left him with his retinue while he went off to ensure that the banquet would be truly magnificent. The abbot somewhat recovered his spirits in the company of his own people; he described to them the conditions in which he had been living, and they all told him how they, on the contrary, had been given right royal entertainment by Ghino. When the dinner was ready they all sat down with the abbot and were served course after course of the choicest dishes and the best of wines. Ghino, however, still concealed his identity from his guest.

The abbot spent some further days in this fashion, after which Ghino had all his possessions assembled in one room, and all his horses, down to the most knock-kneed jade, assembled in a courtyard below, then went to the abbot and asked him how he was and whether he felt up to riding again. The abbot told him he was now in fine fettle and his stomach was perfectly recovered—if only he were free of Ghino he'd be as right as rain.

So Ghino took the abbot into the room where his possessions and his retinue all awaited him; then led him to a window from which he could look down into the courtyard and survey all his horses. 'My lord abbot', he said, 'if Ghino di Tacco has been forced to become a highwayman and an enemy to the court of Rome in order to safeguard his life and his prestige, he should have you know that it is not an evil disposition that has led him to it but his being a man of high birth and few means, driven from his home and faced with many powerful enemies. I, sir, am Ghino di Tacco. However, as you appear to me to be an upright man, and as I have cured you of your stomach complaint, I do not propose to treat you as I should treat anyone else falling into my hands, plundering his possessions at will. What I propose is that you consider my needs and appoint to me that part of your possessions that you yourself see fit to. Everything of yours stands here before you and you can see your horses down in the courtyard from this window. Take the part or the whole as you wish; from this moment you are free to go or stay as you please.'

The abbot was amazed to hear such a generous speech from the mouth of a brigand and he was deeply touched. His anger and indignation were transmuted into affection and he ran to embrace Ghino as a friend. 'I swear to God', he said, 'I'd be ready to suffer far worse injury than you seem to have done to me hitherto, if that secured me the friendship of a man such as I now see that you are. What ill luck it is that you should be obliged to pursue such a nefarious calling!' Then, out of his great abundance he selected just a handful of necessities, and selected likewise from among his mounts; everything else he left behind, and made his return to Rome.

The Pope had learnt of the abbot's capture, and was greatly upset by it. When he saw him, he asked if he had derived any benefit from the baths. 'Your Holiness', the abbot answered with a smile, 'before I reached the baths I came across an excellent physician who has quite cured me.' He told his story to the Pope, who was much amused by it, then, feeling in a generous mood, he went on to request a favour from His Holiness.

The Pope readily offered to grant his request, little imagining what it was the abbot would ask. 'Your Holiness', pursued the abbot, 'what I should like to ask of you is to grant pardon to Ghino di Tacco, my healer, because he is one of the best and most commendable of men I know; I think that Fate is far more to blame than he is for his wicked ways. If you could mend his fortunes by making some gift that will enable him to live as befits his rank, I've no doubt at all that you will come to see him in the same light that I do.'

There was nothing petty-minded about the Pope*—indeed he could never resist a good man. So on hearing this he willingly agreed to the request: if the man was as admirable as the abbot maintained, let him come in all security. Ghino therefore came to the Roman court under safe conduct, in accordance with the abbot's wishes, and the Pope soon accepted him for a man of virtue and they were reconciled. The Pope made him a Knight Hospitaller* of St John of Jerusalem and accorded him the benefice of a great priory within the order; this office he held for the rest of his days, during which time he remained a devoted friend to Holy Mother Church and to the Abbot of Cluny.

X. 3. *Unable to outdo Nathan in open-handed generosity, Mithridanes takes umbrage and goes to murder him. Nathan, however, disarms him.*

That a member of the clergy should have acted with generosity struck all the listeners as something verging on the miraculous. However, when the ladies finished commenting on it, the king told Philostrato to proceed, and thus he promptly began:

Great, indeed, was the liberality of the King of Spain and, as for that of the Abbot of Cluny, why, who ever heard of such a thing? But I expect you excellent ladies will be no less astonished to hear of one who used all his tact in order to present another man with what that man wanted of him, namely his blood, his very life! Indeed, the gift would have been given, had the beneficiary been inclined to take it, as I propose to show you in my little tale.

If we may rely on the evidence of certain Genoese and others who have visited those parts, it is an undoubted fact that in Cathay* there was once upon a time a man of noble stock and incomparable wealth called Nathan. His residence stood by a road almost inevitably travelled by anyone going from the West to the Orient or returning to the West. He was of a generous, lavish disposition and was anxious that nobody should be in any doubt about this, so he had himself built in the shortest possible time one of the most beautiful, vast, and luxurious palaces ever seen—there being no shortage of skilled craftsmen in the area—and had it sumptuously furnished with everything required for the proper entertainment of gentlemen. He maintained an ample household in excellent array and would offer hospitality and entertainment and the most festive of welcomes to whoever passed his way; and so assiduously did he pursue this commendable practice that he acquired a reputation not merely in the East but throughout most of the West. He reached a ripe old age, never wearying in his lavish hospitality, and eventually his fame reached the ears of a young man called Mithridanes.

Now Mithridanes, who lived no great distance away, recognized that he was quite as wealthy as Nathan and became jealous of Nathan's reputation and sheer goodness; he determined to obliterate or at any rate overshadow such munificence by outdoing it. He built himself a palace similar to Nathan's and stopped at nothing in the generosity he lavished upon those who came his way. Assuredly he achieved a great reputation in no time at all.

Now one day, as the young man happened to be on his own in his palace courtyard, a little old woman came in through one of the gates and asked for alms and received them. Then she returned to him, coming through the second gate, and received more alms. So she proceeded until she had entered by twelve of the gates. When she came back to him through the thirteenth gate, Mithridanes said to her: 'How importunate you are, my good woman!' though he still gave her alms.

On hearing this, the little old woman exclaimed: 'Ah for Nathan, such a wonderfully generous man *he* is! His palace, like this one, has thirty-two gates, and I went in through each one and asked him for alms; he never took note of me, or gave any sign of doing so, and always made me a gift. Here I come in by only thirteen of the gates when I'm picked on and taken to task.' This said, she left and never returned.

These words of the old woman sent Mithridanes into a towering rage: this endorsement of Nathan's reputation was, he felt, a slight upon his own. 'Oh what a curse this is!' said he. 'How am I ever to equal Nathan, let alone achieve my aim to surpass him in the greatest acts of generosity when even in the most trifling ones he leaves me miles behind? The fact is it's all a waste of effort if I don't remove him from this earth. And as old age is not carrying him off, I'll simply have to see to it myself with my own hands.'

Stung to this decision, he leapt up and, keeping his proposal to himself, took horse with but a small escort and reached Nathan's domain after a three-days' journey. He instructed his company to pretend that they were not associated with him and did not know him; they were to find their own accommodation and await his further orders. It was towards sundown that he had arrived and was left on his own; not far from the gorgeous palace he came across Nathan all by himself; he was simply dressed and out for a stroll, and Mithridanes did not recognize him. 'Can you tell me', he asked him, 'where Nathan lives?'

'My boy, there's not a man in these parts who is better able to tell you this than I am', said Nathan good-humouredly. 'If you like, I'll show you the way.'

The young man said there was nothing he would like better but he would prefer, if possible, not to be seen or recognized by Nathan. 'Leave it to me', said Nathan, 'if that's what you would like.'

So Mithridanes dismounted and accompanied Nathan to his fine palace, Nathan making the most agreeable conversation on the way. Once arrived, Nathan ordered one of his attendants to take charge of the young man's mount, and as he did so he had a word in his ear, telling him, 'Don't you or anyone else in my household tell the young man that I am Nathan.' And this was done. They entered the palace and he brought Mithridanes into a splendid room where he would be seen by no one but those he had placed at his service. He paid him every attention and himself kept him company.

While Mithridanes treated him with filial respect as they consorted together, he did make bold to ask him who he was. 'I'm a humble servant of Nathan', the other replied. 'I'm an old man now but I've been with him since I was a boy, and never received any preferment from him. So although the whole world speaks highly of him, I personally cannot bring myself to do so.'

These words encouraged Mithridanes in the hope of being able to give effect to his evil purpose with somewhat greater deliberation and security. Nathan asked him most politely who he was and what brought him here; he offered to be of service to him in any way he might with his help and advice. Mithridanes hesitated at first to reply, but eventually decided to take him into his confidence; after beating about the bush for a good while he asked him to keep his secret, and to give him the benefit of his aid and counsel; then he told him all about himself and what motive and purpose it was that had brought him here.

What the young man told him of his brutal resolution left the older man profoundly shaken, but after only the shortest pause he answered steadfastly: 'Your father possessed true nobility and you wish to live up to his standards, Mithridanes, for you have set yourself a lofty goal, to treat everyone with generosity. As for the jealousy you feel towards Nathan and his qualities, I find it highly praiseworthy; if there were only more jealousy of this sort, the world would cease to be so beggarly a place and would change for the better in no time. The plan you have divulged to me will of course be kept secret; I can't offer you much help towards its fulfilment, but I have some useful advice: here it is. You see that little copse over there, about half a mile off: Nathan goes there practically every morning all by himself for a good leisurely stroll. What can be easier for you than to meet him there and dispose of him as you will? If you kill him, you should leave the wood by the path you can see there to the left, not by the one you took coming here, if you want to avoid any obstacle on your way home. It's a slightly more tangled path but it brings you out closer to home and is safer for you.'

Equipped with this information, after Nathan had left and his companions had joined him, Mithridanes surreptitiously advised them where they were to meet him on the morrow. Now when the new day dawned, Nathan, still being of the same mind in which he had offered his advice to Mithridanes, made his way alone to the copse where he was to die.

Mithridanes remained as resolute as ever. He got up, took his bow and his sword, the only weapons he had by him, mounted his horse, and made for the wood; from a distance he espied Nathan walking there all on his own. As he had decided, before attacking him, that he would like to have a good look at him and hear him speak, he galloped up to him, seized him by his turban, and cried: 'Old man, you're dead!'

To which Nathan's only response was: 'Well, I've deserved it.'

Once he had heard his voice and looked him in the face, Mithridanes recognized him for the very man who had welcomed him so kindly, offered him such easy companionship, and given him such trustworthy advice. His passion subsided, his anger turned to shame, and he threw down the sword he had drawn in order to run him through. He dismounted and fell, weeping, at Nathan's feet: 'Your kindness to me, dearest father, is too inescapably obvious', he cried; 'I can see just what tact you employed in coming here to yield me up your life, on which I had no just claim though I apprised you myself of my designs upon it. But God has shown greater concern than I have for where my duty lay and has opened my eyes just when I stood most in need of it, for they have been blinded by despicable envy. So I acknowledge that I'm fit to be punished for my wickedness, and all the more so in view of your readiness to satisfy my wish. Take your revenge on me, then, in whatever way you deem suitable.'

Nathan raised Mithridanes to his feet, then hugged and kissed him tenderly. 'No matter how you describe your enterprise, my son—call it evil or not as you will—there is no case for either seeking or granting pardon: you did not undertake it out of hatred but in order to be held in greater esteem. So have no fear of me; let me assure you that there is no man alive who loves you half as much as I do, for I appreciate the nobility of your spirit—baser mortals are concerned only to amass wealth while your wish is to spread it around. Don't be ashamed of your decision to kill me in order to enhance your fame: believe me, I am not surprised. How have the greatest emperors, the mightiest monarchs increased their dominions and thus their renown? By pursuing virtually one policy, and one alone: slaughter. They have killed men by the score, not merely one man as you aimed to do, and they have spread fire across the land, razed cities to the ground. So if you meant to murder only me in order to enhance your reputation, you have done nothing all that remarkable—it happens every day.'

Mithridanes did not seek to excuse his ill-conceived purpose but spoke highly of Nathan's well-meaning extenuation; in the course of their conversation he remarked on his astonishment at the way Nathan had fallen in with his design and given him advice as to its execution.

'Well', said Nathan, 'you're not to be surprised at my decision or at my advice: ever since I became master of my own will and determined to do precisely what it has been your ambition to achieve, nobody has ever come to my house and failed to be satisfied in that which he requested of me, to the limits of my power. You came, hankering for my life. When I heard you asking for it, I promptly decided to make you a gift of it so that you should not be the one and only person to leave here with your wish unfulfilled; to ensure that you obtained it, I gave you such advice as seemed to me serviceable if you were to have my life without forfeiting your own. I do urge you once more, then, take my life if you would like it, give yourself this satisfaction; I cannot think of a better way to expend it. I've had the use of it for eighty years, for my pleasure and comfort. In the normal course of nature I know that it will be left to me only a little while longer, as is the situation for other men and generally for all things. And it is far better, in my view, to give it away, as I have always given away and lavished what I treasure, rather than clinging on to it until Nature robs me of it against my will. A hundred years is a small enough gift to make; how much less is the gift of the six or eight years remaining to me? Do take it, therefore, if such is your pleasure; in all my years I've never yet come across anyone who has required it and I don't know when I ever shall if you don't take it, you who have sought it. Besides, even if I did find someone else who was after my life, I know that the longer I hold on to it, the smaller will be its value. So before it becomes any more worthless, take it, I beseech you.'

Mithridanes was utterly shamefaced. 'Your life is so precious, God forbid that I should even covet it, as I have been doing, let alone wrest it from you! Far from shortening the number of your years, I would gladly add some of mine to them if I could.'

'You'd like to add to mine?' put in Nathan at once. 'You'd be making me do to you what I've never done yet to a soul, taking something that belongs to you—I've never taken anything from anyone.'

'Oh but yes!' cried Mithridanes.

'Very well, then. Here's what you must do; you're to stay here in my house, young man that you are, and be called Nathan. I shall go to your house and will always be known as Mithridanes.'

'I shouldn't think twice about taking up your offer', said Mithridanes, 'if I had your capabilities; but I have not the smallest doubt that whatever I did would only diminish your reputation as Nathan, and it is not my intention to spoil for another that which I cannot make a success of myself. So I'll not accept it.'

After much agreeable discussion of this kind the two of them, at Nathan's invitation, returned to the palace, where the old man entertained the younger one with every attention for several days; he devoted all his shrewdness and wisdom to encouraging Mithridanes in his lofty ideal. When Mithridanes was ready to return home with his company, Nathan, having made it abundantly clear to him that he was never to be outdone in generosity, gave him leave to go.

X. 4. *Gentile de' Carisendi covets Niccoluccio Caccianimico's wife; but by the end of the story he has put Niccoluccio in his debt.*

To be generous with one's own blood was a wonderful thing, they all agreed, and Nathan's magnanimity outdid that of the King of Spain and the Abbot of Cluny. They talked this over for a while, then the king turned to Lauretta and indicated his wish that she speak next. So she at once began:

What splendid things we've been hearing about! There doesn't seem much left for the rest of us to add on the subject of high and magnanimous deeds that will make a story to entertain you with; so we shall have to resort again to the topic of love, which does remain an inexhaustible source for the story-teller. This is why I'm going to tell you about a dazzling deed performed by a lover—besides, I offer it as a mark one should be striving for at our age. What he did will seem to you no less remarkable, when you come to think of it, than any of the instances hitherto narrated. I take it to be a fact that people will make rich presents, forget enmities, stake their own life, and, what is more, their reputation in order to possess the object of their love.

There once lived in Bologna, one of the Lombards' noblest cities,* a gentleman called Gentile de' Carisendi.* He was highly regarded for his innate excellence and high birth, and as a young man he fell in love with a lady called Caterina, the wife of Niccoluccio Caccianimico. She rejected his advances, however, and, fairly resigned to failure, he accepted the post of Podestà at Modena. Niccoluccio was away from Bologna and his wife went to stay on a property she owned some three miles outside the city, as she was pregnant. Now it so happened that here she suffered a sudden stroke which left her to all appearances lifeless. Even the doctor pronounced her dead, so, as her nearest relatives claimed to have it from her own lips that her pregnancy was too recent for the baby to be anywhere close to term, they took her as they found her and placed her in a tomb in the local church, and tearfully buried her.

Gentile was brought the news at once by a friend of his and he was heartbroken, for all that she had afforded him no solace whatsoever. He said to himself, however: 'Well look, Caterina, you're dead now. I couldn't so much as catch your eye while you were still alive. Now that you're dead and no longer in a position to hold me off, I shall certainly help myself to a kiss or two.'

It was already night, and he slipped out furtively with a servant for escort and rode off without a second thought to the burial place. Here he opened the tomb, carefully climbed in, lay down beside Caterina, and wept as he covered her face in kisses. But as we know, men are never content to say 'Enough'—they always want more, and especially if they are in love: Gentile determined not to limit himself to kissing her face. 'While I'm here', he told himself, 'why don't I just fondle her breast a little? I've never touched her before and shall never do so again.' Yielding to the temptation, he placed a hand on her breast; after a while he fancied he felt a slight heartbeat. When he'd got over the shock, he felt more carefully and concluded that she was definitely not dead, even though she was only barely alive. So with the help of his servant he eased her out of the tomb as gently as possible, laid her across his horse, mounted behind her, and secretly brought her home with him to Bologna.

He lived with his mother, a woman of great strength and wisdom. Her son told her exactly what had happened and, moved to pity, she quietly went about lighting a good fire and heating up a bath, and she coaxed the dying woman back to life. When Caterina came round, she heaved a great sigh and asked: 'Heavens, where am I!'

'Cheer up', said the mother, 'you're in good hands.'

More fully awake, the sick woman looked about her in bewilderment, not knowing where she was. She stared in surprise at Gentile and asked his mother to tell her how she came to be there. Gentile told her, but his explanation left her quite dismayed; she thanked him but went straight on to pray him, in virtue of the love he nurtured for her and his gentlemanly breeding, to do nothing while she was his guest that might compromise her honour or that of her husband. She asked, too, to be allowed to return to her own home in the morning.

'However it was that I desired you in the past', Gentile replied, 'I have no intention now or indeed ever to treat you here or anywhere else as anything but a dear sister. God has already granted me the boon of restoring you to me a living person, thanks to the love I have borne you. The favour I have done to you tonight does, though, deserve some reward, so I'd ask you to grant me the one request I make of you.'

'If it is honourable, and lies within my power', said Caterina gently, 'I am willing.'

'Every one of your relatives, my lady, and indeed the whole of Bologna, is convinced that you are dead; not a soul expects you back home any more. What I want you to do, if you please, is to stay here in secret with my mother till I get back from Modena, which won't be long. The reason for my asking this is that I intend to make a much-cherished present of you to your husband, solemnly, in the presence of the most select group of our citizens.'

Caterina recognized that she was under an obligation to the gentleman and that his request was virtuous, so she agreed to do as he asked, however anxious she was to rejoice her relatives at seeing her alive. She gave him her binding promise.

Scarcely had she finished speaking than she went into labour and, tenderly assisted by Gentile's mother, shortly afterwards gave birth to a fine baby boy. Gentile was doubly delighted, and made all the necessary arrangements for her comfort as if she had been his own wife. After this he slipped away back to Modena.

For the morning of his return to Bologna, once he had seen out his period of office at Modena, he arranged a great banquet at his house, to which he invited many Bolognese gentlemen, including Niccoluccio Caccianimico. He reached home, dismounted, and joined his guests, after noticing that Caterina was looking a picture of health and beauty and her baby likewise; then he sat down at table with his guests in the happiest frame of mind and served them a magnificent repast.

When the meal was almost over, Gentile addressed his friends, having first disclosed his plan to Caterina and agreed with her on how they were to proceed. 'My friends, I remember having once been told of a pleasing custom, so it seems to me, that they practise in Persia: when a person wants to do a signal honour to his friend, he invites him home and produces for him whomsoever he holds dearest, his wife maybe or lady-friend or daughter; and he says to his friend: "As I bring this person forth to you, so much more willingly would I offer you my heart if I could." This custom I should like to observe here in Bologna. You have favoured me with your presence at my banquet, and I propose to return the compliment in the Persian manner, by showing you that which I hold most dear in all the world, now or ever. But first of all I should like your opinion on a question that has been perplexing me. Suppose a person has a good, loyal servant in his house, and the servant falls seriously ill, and the master has him put out in the street without waiting for him to die, and takes no further care of him. And supposing a stranger comes along and takes pity on him and brings him home and goes to the trouble and expense to nurse him back to health. Now tell me: if the stranger keeps the servant for himself, has the original master just cause to complain to the new master if he requests the return of his servant and is refused?'

After a little discussion the gentlemen all reached the same conclusion, and entrusted their reply to Niccoluccio Caccianimico, for he was an elegant speaker. Niccoluccio first of all commended the Persian custom, then affirmed that they all of them shared the view that the first master had no further claim upon his servant, once he had not simply abandoned him but had actually thrown him out; the kindness shown him by the stranger made him justifiably the servant of the stranger. If the stranger kept him, he was doing no injury whatsoever to the original master. At that table there were good men and true, and not one of them dissented from the opinion recorded by Niccoluccio.

Gentile was gratified by this reply and the fact that it was Niccoluccio himself who had propounded it; this, he said, was his own opinion exactly, and he continued: 'Now it's time for me to honour you as I promised.' He summoned two servants and sent them to the lady, whom he had decked out in fine array, with the request that she would please come and rejoice the gentlemen with her presence.'

She took her pretty baby in her arms and came into the dining-hall, accompanied by the two servants, and took her seat near to a gentleman, as Gentile had proposed. 'Gentlemen', he said, 'here is the fondest object of my desires, and I shall never have another such. Look at her and tell me if I'm not right.'

The guests paid her their respects and spoke highly of her to their host. How right he was, they said, to hold her dear. But as they looked more closely at her, several of them would have sworn they knew who she was, were it not that she was believed to be dead. Niccoluccio scrutinized her most closely of all; their host had stepped a little away from the table, and he, bursting to know who the lady was, asked her whether by chance she was from Bologna. Caterina heard her husband put the question and could scarcely forbear from answering, but she kept silent, as agreed. Others asked her if the baby was hers, or if she was Gentile's wife or some relation, but she held her peace.

Gentile returned to his place and one of his guests said: 'She's beautiful, this lady of yours, but she appears to be dumb. Is she really so?'

'If she has not yet spoken, that is merely some indication of her worth.'

'Well, tell us who she is', pursued the same guest.

'I shall gladly do so, but you must first promise me not to leave your places, whatever I say, until I've told you my story.'

They all promised, and when the tables had been cleared Gentile sat down beside the lady and said: 'This lady is the faithful servant about whom I have just consulted you, gentlemen. Her own relations took no account of her and tossed her into the street as an object of little worth or utility, but I picked her up and cared for her on my own and restored her to health. And God repaid my kindness and turned her from a repulsive corpse into this beauty. Let me briefly explain how this came to pass.' He started with his falling in love with her and went on to describe all that had happened up to this point. His hearers were amazed. 'So unless you—and Niccoluccio in particular—have gone and changed your minds', he added, 'this lady is deservedly mine and no one is entitled to claim her back.'

To this there was no reply: they all waited to hear what more he had to say. Niccoluccio was moved to tears, as were other guests, and as was Caterina herself. Now Gentile rose from the table, picked up the baby in his arms, took the lady by the hand, and led her to Niccoluccio. 'Stand up, my friend', he said. 'I'm not returning your wife to you—your relatives and hers got rid of her—but I mean to make you a present of this friend of mine and her little son, who I am sure is of your begetting; I stood godfather to him and had him christened Gentile. She has indeed been under my roof for close on three months, but do cherish her not a jot less for that: you have my word for it that she never lived more virtuously with her father and mother or with you than she has done in my house with my mother—God knows, who maybe providentially had me fall in love with her in order to restore her to health by my devotion.' This said, he turned to Caterina. 'Now let me release you from your every promise: I leave you freely to Niccoluccio.' He gave the woman and child into Niccoluccio's hands and returned to his place.

Niccoluccio accepted his wife and child eagerly, all the happier for having entertained so little hope before. He thanked Gentile as best he could. There was not a dry eye in the place, and everyone applauded him most warmly, as indeed did whoever came to hear of it. Caterina was welcomed home with great celebrations, and for ages afterwards the local people would stare at her as someone back from the dead. Gentile remained on excellent terms with Niccoluccio and his relatives as with those of Caterina.

So what shall we say, ladies? We've had a king giving away his sceptre and crown; an abbot, at no expense to himself, reconciling a miscreant to the Pope; and an old man offering his throat to his enemy's blade: do you think that any of these match up to Gentile's good deed? He was young and love-struck, and felt justified in taking what others had carelessly tossed aside and he had the good fortune to pick up; and yet he not only virtuously tempered his ardour but handed back what he actually possessed after he had sought to steal her with such passionate longing. Certainly none of the previous instances seems to me to compare with this one.

## X. 5. *To dismiss an unwanted suitor Dianora, a married lady, promises herself on an impossible condition, but by sorcery her suitor, Ansaldo, achieves it. Her husband requires her to honour her promise, therefore, but his magnanimity calls forth an equal response in the suitor.*

The entire merry throng, one and all, praised Gentile to the skies. Then the king bade Emilia follow, and she, nothing loath, plunged into her story as follows:

Nobody could reasonably deny that Gentile had acted magnificently; and yet it is perhaps not all that difficult to show that there's no limit to what a person can do when he sets his mind to it—aye, there's nothing like a real challenge, as I propose to tell you in my little tale.

Friuli is a chilly part of the world but delightful, none the less, for its beautiful mountains, abundant rivers, and limpid springs. In Friuli there is a town called Udine, and here once lived a beautiful woman of high birth called Dianora, an admirable and delightful lady married to a man of great wealth and station called Gilberto. A woman of her character deservedly attracted the devotion of a leading baron called Ansaldo of Grado, a nobleman of the first rank with a considerable reputation for gallantry and military prowess. But however fervently he loved her, whatever he did—and he did all he could—to win her love in return, his efforts and his repeated solicitations proved to be all in vain. Now as the lady was distressed by the baron's importunity and saw that, even if she refused him every single thing he asked of her, he still would persist in courting and pestering her, she hit upon a novel and, to her mind, impossible request as a way to be rid of him.

There was a woman who often came on these errands for him, and one day Dianora said to her: 'You've told me often enough that Ansaldo loves me more than anything, and you've offered fabulous presents on his behalf. Let him keep them, I say, for they will never induce me to love him or make myself agreeable to him. However, if I could be sure that he really loved me as much as you say he does, then I would most assuredly respond to his love with my own and comply with his wishes. So if he were willing to prove his love to my satisfaction by doing as I ask, I should be straight away at his disposal.'

'What do you want him to do?'

'Here's what I want: this coming January I want a garden* right here with green grass and loads of flowers and trees in leaf, the sort of garden you'd find in May. If he won't do that for me, he's not to send you or anyone else to me again, because until now I've kept it a secret from my husband and my relations but, if he bothers me any more, I'll go and complain to them and try to get him off my back that way.'

When the baron heard what his beloved was requesting and offering, he realized that it was a difficult, a wellnigh impossible thing to accomplish, and that she had had only one purpose in mind in making the request, and that was to put an end to his hopes; none the less, he determined to try his utmost to achieve it. He sent people all over the world to discover whether there were anyone who might be able to afford him help or advice in this matter; and one man came forward who offered to do it for him by sorcery if he were adequately remunerated. Ansaldo came to terms with him for a large sum of money, then happily waited for the appointed time. It came when there was a tremendous frost, with snow and ice everywhere, and the resourceful fellow exercised his art in a fair meadow outside the town: on New Year's Eve he did it, and the following morning, according to the eye-witnesses, the meadow had turned into one of the loveliest gardens anyone had ever seen, with grass and all manner of trees and fruit. Ansaldo was in raptures when he saw it; he had some of the choicest fruits and flowers picked and secretly presented to his lady, with an invitation to come and see the garden she had asked for, thus enabling her to be satisfied that he really did love her; thus, too, she would be reminded of the promise she had made to him under oath and which, being a woman of honour, she would keep.

Dianora, who had already heard many people exclaiming over the wonders of the garden, looked at the flowers and fruits and began to regret her promise, in spite of which she could not resist going to peek at strange sights, and off she went with a crowd of fellow townswomen to see the garden. She too exclaimed over it in wonderment, but went home the saddest of ladies, as she considered what this garden committed her to. She felt so wretched that she could not keep her misery to herself, it could not but show on her face, and her husband noticed it and insisted on knowing what was the matter. For a time Dianora was too ashamed to say anything, but eventually she was forced to tell him the whole story.

At first the story made Gilberto unspeakably angry, but wiser counsel prevailed as he reflected on his wife's intention, which was so innocent, and he mastered his anger. 'Dianora', he said, 'a wise and virtuous woman does not listen to people who turn up with that kind of message, and she doesn't pledge her chastity to anyone for *any* consideration. A word transmitted to the heart by the ears has a greater impact than many people think, and virtually nothing is impossible to a lover. You were wrong to pay any attention and you were wrong to strike a bargain; but I know the purity of your heart, so I shall let you discharge your obligation, though there's scarcely another man who would: I'm driven to it also out of fear of the sorcerer—if you welshed on Ansaldo, he might get the man to play us a bad turn. What I want you to do is to go to him and see if you can't find a way to save your virtue and be absolved from your promise. But if this cannot be done, let him just this once have your body, but not your heart.'

Dianora listened to him with tears in her eyes and insisted that she desired no such favour from him, but despite her repeated refusals, that is what her husband wanted. So the next morning at sunrise she went to Ansaldo's house, accompanied by two men of her household and her maid. She took little care over her appearance.

Being advised that his lady had come to him, Ansaldo was quite surprised; he got out of bed, sent for the sorcerer, and told him: 'I want you to witness the benefit I have obtained thanks to your skills.' Together they went to Dianora and the lover welcomed her with becoming respect and no show of lecherous appetite; they all went into a pretty room with a great big fire burning, and here he invited her to sit down, and asked her: 'Do tell me, madam, if the love I have so long borne you deserves any reward: confess to me the true reason for your coming here at such an hour as this and with the company you have brought.'

Shamefaced and on the point of tears, Dianora replied: 'It is not any love I bear you, sir, nor any promise that brings me here; I've come at my husband's bidding, for he is more concerned for the efforts you have expended in your unwholesome love than he is for his honour or my own. It is at his bidding that I am placing myself this once at your disposal.'

After listening to her words Ansaldo's amazement was all the greater. He was touched by Gilberto's magnanimity and this made him more sensitive, less ruled by passion. 'If the matter stands as you say it does, madam, God forbid that I should prove destructive to the honour of the man who has shown such consideration for my love. Therefore, so long as it is your pleasure, your presence here will be simply as though you were my sister; you're free to go the moment you choose to, provided you render your husband such thanks as seem to you fitting for the great chivalry he has demonstrated—from now on he is to consider me his brother and his servant.'

This rejoiced Dianora's heart. 'Bearing in mind what manner of man you are', she said, 'nothing could ever have induced me to believe that my coming here should have ended otherwise than as you have appointed. For this I shall be eternally grateful to you.' And, taking her leave, she returned to Gilberto with her honourable escort and told him what had happened, as a result of which he and Ansaldo become the closest and most faithful of friends.

Ansaldo now prepared to pay the stipulated fee to the sorcerer, who had witnessed Gilberto's magnanimity towards Ansaldo and Ansaldo's towards the lady. 'God forbid', said the sorcerer, 'now that I've seen Gilberto behaving so selflessly over his honour and you over your love, that I should not be equally selfless when it comes to my payment. I realize that it lies just as well in your own hands and that is where I propose that it remain.' This embarrassed Ansaldo, who did his utmost to persuade him to take the payment or at least a part of it, but all in vain. On the third day the sorcerer removed his garden and, as he wished to leave, Ansaldo bade him godspeed. And his love for Dianora was transmuted from concupiscence into a virtuous affection.

What, then, shall we conclude, my loving ladies? Which are we to prefer: the lady almost ready to die and the suitor's love cooling off in the failure of hope? Or this generosity of Ansaldo, as his love remained more fervent than ever and his hope if anything increased now that he held in his grasp the prey he had so long been stalking? It would seem to me absurd to imagine that there is any comparison.

X. 6. *King Charles of Anjou falls in love with the two young daughters of a knight who has sought refuge with him, but he gains a famous victory over himself.*

Who could give a full account of the debate which the ladies engaged upon to determine which of the three observed the greatest liberality in their dealings with Dianora, whether it was Gilberto, Ansaldo, or the sorcerer? It would take too long.

But when the king had left them arguing awhile, he looked at Fiammetta and told her to put an end to the discussion by starting her story, which she straightway did, as follows:

I've always held the view that when groups such as ours engage in discussions they should adopt a broad approach to the topic in question and avoid splitting hairs over too fine shades of meaning: that's something better left to the erudite schoolmen than to us women—we can barely hold our own with the distaff and spindle. So, even though I may have had some debatable topic in mind, seeing that the last story's set you at sixes and sevens I'll leave it to one side and tell you instead a tale about a man of no little consequence, indeed about a gallant king, and the chivalrous deed he did, which was wholly in keeping with his honour.

You ladies will often have heard mention of King Charles the Elder, or First, the same Charles of Anjou* whose splendid expedition and glorious victory over King Manfred resulted in the Ghibellines being driven out of Florence and the Guelphs returning. Thus one Ghibelline knight, Neri degli Uberti, left Florence with all his household and a great deal of money and went to place himself under the exclusive protection of King Charles. Choosing a remote spot where he might live out his days in peace, he went to Castellammare di Stabia. Here, about as far from the neighbouring houses as a crossbow might carry, he bought a piece of land planted with olive, chestnut, and walnut, with which the region abounded, and on it he built himself a fine, commodious residence. Beside the house he laid out a nice garden, and in the middle of the garden he created—after our Florentine fashion—a beautiful, limpid fish-pond, there being spring-water in abundance, and he had no trouble stocking it with fish aplenty.

Now while Neri devoted all his attention to making his garden more beautiful by the day, King Charles happened to visit Castellammare to enjoy a little repose during the hot weather. Here he heard about the splendours of Neri's garden and conceived a desire to see it. On discovering who its owner was, the king decided that, as the knight belonged to the party opposed to him, he should not stand too much on ceremony but sent word to say that he proposed to come with four companions to dine with him informally in his garden the following evening. Neri was overjoyed at this; after making the most sumptuous preparations and running through the proceedings in detail with his servants, he received the king in his lovely garden as merrily as possible. When the king had seen over the whole garden and the house, and spoken highly of both, he washed his hands and sat down at one of the tables which had been placed beside the fish-pond; he bade one of his companions, Count Guy de Montfort, to sit on one side of him and Neri on the other, while the king's other companions were to be seated as Neri had disposed. The fare was exquisite, the wines of the choicest, and everything proceeded with the most commendable ease and decorum, which the king found wholly to his liking.

While he was enjoying his meal and relishing the seclusion of the place, two girls came into the garden; they were each some 15 years of age, with blonde hair like spun gold falling in ringlets and crowned each with a dainty garland of periwinkle; their faces were so exquisitely pretty they looked like nothing less than angels. They were both wearing the finest snowy-white linen dresses which clung tightly to their figures from the waist up, while below the waist they billowed out capaciously to sweep the ground. The one in front was carrying a pair of fishing-nets over her shoulder; she held them in her left hand while in her right she held a long pole. The second girl carried a frying-pan over her left shoulder, a bundle of sticks under her arm, and a tripod in her left hand; in her right hand she carried a cruse of oil and a small flaming sconce. The king gazed at them in wonder, and couldn't wait to see what it all meant.

The two young girls came forward modestly and dropped a bashful curtsy to the king, after which they approached the point giving access to the fish-pond. Here the girl with the frying-pan set it down along with the rest of the things she was carrying and took the pole from the other girl; then they both stepped down into the pond, whose water came up to their chests. One of Neri's servants promptly lit the fire, set the pan on the tripod, poured in oil, and waited for the girls to start tossing him some fish. One girl stirred the water where she knew that the fish were to be found while the other held her nets poised and in no time had caught a great number of fish, much to the delight of the king, who was looking on closely. Some of their catch they threw to the servant, who dropped them still practically alive into the pan; they also, as instructed, started picking out the best fish and tossing these on to the table in front of the king, Guy de Montfort, and their father. These fish flipped about on the table-top, which greatly amused the king, who would pick them up and throw them politely back to the girls—they carried on with this game for the time it took the servant to cook what was in the pan. When it was cooked, it was placed before the king, not as any *pièce de résistance* but as a simple *entremets*, for thus had Neri ordered it. Seeing that the fish were now cooked and they had caught plenty, the girls climbed out of the pond, their thin white dresses clinging to them all over and leaving virtually no part of their dainty figures unexposed. They each picked up the implements they had brought with them, passed bashfully in front of the king, and withdrew indoors.

The king, together with the count and his other henchmen, had taken a close look at the two girls, and they had nurtured a high opinion of them, finding them pretty and shapely; furthermore they were agreeable and of good bearing. The king was taken with them most of all; as they came out of the water he had been devouring every part of their anatomies so intently with his eyes that if anyone had pricked him then he would not have felt a thing. On reflection, he discovered in himself a passionate desire to earn their good opinion, for all that he had no idea as to who they were or anything about them; in fact he realized he was close to falling in love with them if he didn't take care, though he himself could not have said which of the two he liked the better, so alike were they in every respect.

After brooding a little on the question, he turned to Neri and asked him who the two maidens were. 'They are my daughters, my lord; they were born both at once, and their names are Ginevra the Fair and Isotta the Blonde.'* The king spoke highly of them and encouraged him to marry them off, but Neri made his excuses, as he had not the wherewithal.

Nothing now remained to serve but the fruit, and the two girls appeared, dressed in gorgeous silk tunics, each bearing an enormous silver salver laden with a choice of whatever fruit was in season; these they placed on a table before the king. Then they stepped back and sang a song whose opening words are:

Here, Love, am I come
Where I could not long narrate . . .

They sang with such sweet, pleasant voices that the king, looking and listening in utter enchantment, felt as if the complete hierarchy of angels had come down here to sing. Their song ended, they knelt down and respectfully begged the king's leave to withdraw, which, however reluctant he was to see them go, he accorded with evident goodwill. When dinner was over, the king and his companions mounted their horses, left Neri's, and, conversing about this and that, returned to the royal palace.

Here the king concealed his passion, but not even affairs of state could cause him to forget Ginevra the Fair, her beauty and charm, on whose account he also loved her twin sister. Love so ensnared him that he could think of almost nothing else, and kept finding excuses to cultivate a close relationship with Neri, paying countless visits to his lovely garden to set eyes on Ginevra. When he could no longer endure the situation, it occurred to him, for lack of any other expedients, that he'd have to remove not merely one but both girls from their father's keeping. He confided his love and his proposal to Guy de Montfort who, being the good man he was, said to the king:

'My lord, I am utterly astonished at what you are telling me, and all the more so inasmuch as I have been better acquainted than any with your manner of life since you were a small boy. I never saw any evidence of your experiencing such a passion when you were a young man—an era during which you should have been the more prone to fall into Love's clutches. To hear that now, when you are on the verge of old age, you have actually fallen in love, why, it seems to me so odd, so remarkable, it strikes me as nothing short of miraculous! If it were up to me to take you to task, I know precisely what I should have to say to you about it, bearing in mind that here you stand fully armed in a realm only recently acquired, amid an alien people, and surrounded by plots and treachery; here you are, utterly preoccupied with enormous anxieties and crucial problems and you've not for one moment been able to drop your guard—yet in spite of all that you've allowed yourself to be coaxed by Love. This is not the behaviour of a mighty king; it is the behaviour of a lily-livered boy.

'What is more—and what is far worse—you say you've decided to take the two girls away from the poor gentleman, who has had to stretch his means in order to afford you entertainment in his home, and for your better entertainment has shown his daughters off to you practically naked: is that not evidence of the trust he places in you, of his solid belief that you are a king, not a ravening wolf? Have you so soon forgotten that if you gained a ready access to this kingdom it was because Manfred had violated the women here? Was ever a betrayal more worthy of eternal punishment than this: to rob a man of his honour, of his hope and comfort when that man has honoured *you*? What would be said of you if you acted in this way? Maybe you feel you have sufficient justification in saying, "I did it because he is a Ghibelline"? Is it perhaps consistent with a king's justice if those who cast themselves into his arms in this manner, whoever they may be, are to be treated this way? Let me remind you, Your Majesty, that great though your glory was in defeating Manfred* and routing Corradino, there is far greater glory in overcoming your own self. You, therefore, as you rule over others, must conquer yourself and rein in this appetite of yours; forbear to spoil with such a stain what you have acquired so gloriously.'

These words pierced the king to the heart, the more so because he recognized the truth in them. So he heaved one or two impassioned sighs, then said to the count: 'There's no doubt that a well-trained warrior will find that any foe, however mighty, is utterly weak and unresisting in comparison with his own passions. And yet, however much it hurts, however superhuman the effort needed, I've been so stung by your words that, before too many days have passed, I'll have to show you in very deed that I can get the better of myself just as I can defeat others.'

Not many days after this conversation the king returned to Naples, both in order to avoid the opportunity of turning his hand to evil, and so as to prepare a reward for the knight who had been his host. It was no easy thing for him to make another man the possessor of what he desired above all things for himself, but he none the less determined to give the two girls away in marriage, and moreover not as Neri's daughters but as his own. Much to that gentleman's delight, the king lost no time in settling upon each girl a magnificent dowry, and in bestowing Ginevra the Fair on Maffeo da Palizzi and Isotta the Blonde on the German knight Wilhelm, both noblemen of high degree. This done, he left for Puglia in a state of unspeakable sorrow and there he undertook a round of labours and so crushed his overweening passion that he snapped the chains of Love and remained free of them for the rest of his days.

Some will perhaps say that it was but a small thing for a king to marry off two girls, and I shan't deny it; but I shall maintain that it was far from a small matter for a king to have done this when he was in love, giving his beloved away in marriage without having first deprived her of her flower, not even the tiniest bud. That is what this magnificent king did, bestowing a high reward on the knight, paying the highest compliment to the young ladies he loved, and stoutly overcoming his own nature.

## X. 7. *Lisa, a grocer's daughter, almost dies of love for the King of Sicily. A minstrel and a song save her.*

Fiammetta came to the end of her story, and King Charles's robust liberality won marked approval—except among one lady whose Ghibelline sympathies prevented her from commending him. Thereupon Pampinea, at the king's command, began as follows:

Any reasonable person would speak of good King Charles in the terms you ladies have used, unless such a person had some other reason to dislike him. But I've been reminded of something maybe no less admirable than this, which an enemy of his accorded to one of our Florentine girls, and that's the story I want to tell.

In the days when the French were driven out of Sicily* there lived in Palermo a Florentine grocer, Bernardo Puccini by name. He was immensely rich and his wife had given him a single daughter. She was a great beauty and now of marriageable age. Now when King Pietro of Aragon* had established himself as overlord in the island he ordained a magnificent festival with his barons, in the course of which he was seen in the lists by Bernardo's daughter—her name was Lisa—watching from a window along with some other women. She found him so marvellously attractive as he jousted (in the Catalan fashion)* that after looking at him once or twice she was head over heels in love with him. The festival came to an end, and as she dwelt in her father's house all she could think about was this splendid, exalted love of hers; what afflicted her most of all was the recognition of her lowly condition, which offered virtually not a grain of hope for a happy outcome. She was unwilling, even so, to withdraw her love for the king, and dared not divulge it to anyone for fear of worse. The king had no inkling of this; it concerned him not at all. Lisa's anguish, therefore, was intolerable, worse than anyone could have imagined, with the result that, as her love increased and her despair with it, the pretty young woman could stand it no longer and fell sick; from day to day her health was visibly failing, as snow melts in the sun. This greatly distressed her father and mother, who helped her as best they could, constantly ministering to her and getting in doctors and medicines; but it was no good—she saw no prospects for her love and had determined she no longer wished to continue in this life.

As her father conceded her every whim, it occurred to her that, if there were a suitable way to do so, she would like her love, her determination, to be brought to the king's knowledge before she died. So one day she asked her father to send for Minuccio d'Arezzo. In those days Minuccio was highly regarded as a singer and instrumentalist and enjoyed the favour of King Pietro. Bernardo told him that Lisa wanted to hear him play and sing a little, and Minuccio, a kindly man, sent back word that he would come, and did so very promptly. He encouraged her with kind words, then softly played her some Provençal *estampidas* on his viol and sang her a few songs. His intention was to soothe her, but the songs only added fuel to the fire of her love.

After this, Lisa said there was something she wanted to speak about to him alone, so the others withdrew and she said: 'Minuccio, I've chosen you as the most faithful guardian of a secret of mine. I hope first of all that you'll reveal it to nobody, apart from the person I shall tell you; and secondly, that you'll help me as much as you can. This is my prayer, so listen, Minuccio: the day His Majesty King Pietro held his great coronation festival, my eyes fell upon him as he jousted, at such a particular conjunction that love took fire within me to a degree that's brought me to my present pass. I know how unsuitable my love would appear to a king, but I can't damp it down, let alone get rid of it, and as it's become past all bearing, I've chosen to let myself die as the lesser evil. That's what I'm going to do. The point is, though, that I'd die in the blackest despair if he did not first get to know of it, and I could think of no one better placed to tell him of my situation than you, so I'm laying the charge on you. Please don't refuse to do it; and when you've done it, let me know—that way I'll die comforted and be delivered of my heartache.' She had been in tears as she spoke, and now she fell silent.

Minuccio marvelled at the loftiness of her sentiments and at her stark decision, which he was very sorry to hear. A way suddenly occurred to him, however, to serve her purpose honourably. 'Lisa', he said, 'you have my word of honour, rest assured, I'll never let you down. I have to applaud this noble undertaking, this devotion of yours to so great a king, and I offer you my help. I hope, if you're ready to take courage, that the result of my efforts will be to bring news to delight you before three days have passed. I should like to make a start and lose no time.' After repeating her plea and promising to take heart, Lisa bade him farewell.

Minuccio went off to find a man called Mico da Siena, then a writer of excellent ballads, and prevailed upon him to compose a song. Here it is:

Pray speak, Love, go speak to my Lord;
Tell him of one who lives in sorrow,
Of one who'll never see tomorrow—
She trembles, and will utter ne'er a word.

In pity go, Love, and my heart
Take with you to my Master's hall.
God, how desire holds me in thrall!
And yet this craving dare I not impart
For shame and fear: thus to my death I go.
How hard, alas, if he should never know.

He has my heart, Love, but I dare
Not make my passion clear to him.
And yet I might be dear to him
If he could only see my love laid bare
And watch the pain and anguish in me grow
Till death's your only blessing to bestow.

Speak to my Lord, Love, be my voice;
Go tell him how I watched him prance,
Great warrior, with bright shield and lance
In festive tourney, and I had no choice:
My heart, Love, craved my Lord, to him did flow.
How bitter 'tis to die and he not know.

These words Minuccio soon set to the soft, sad melody they called for, and two days later he went to court while King Pietro was still at table. The king told him to sing something to his viol, and Minuccio set about singing this song to such a sweet accompaniment that the entire assembly in the royal hall seemed to fall into a trance as they listened in breathless silence—and the king perhaps more than the rest. When Minuccio ended his song the king asked him where it came from, for he could not remember having ever heard it before.

'The words and the music were composed not three days ago, my lord.'

The king asked him why they were composed.

'I dare not tell anyone but Your Majesty.'

The king wanted to hear about it, so they all rose from their meal and he brought Minuccio into a private room, where the minstrel could tell him the whole story just as he had heard it. The story overjoyed the king, who spoke very highly of the young woman and said that he wanted to take pity on a girl as constant as she was. Minuccio was to go and convey to her the king's encouragement, and tell her that he would come this very evening without fail to visit her.

Minuccio was delighted to be the bearer of such good news, and went to Lisa's straight away with his viol; he spoke with her in private, told her all that had happened, then sang her the song to his viol. This made Lisa so happy and contented that her health improved on the instant, as was clear to see. And without any of her household knowing or at all suspecting what was afoot, she longingly waited for evening, when she was to see her lord.

The king was a big-hearted and kindly ruler, and he had given much thought to what Minuccio had told him. He was very well acquainted with the young woman and her beauty, and felt increasingly sorry for her. When evening came he took horse and under pretext of going off for a jaunt, he came to the grocer's house. The grocer had the loveliest of gardens and the king asked that it be opened to him; he dismounted and went into it, and after a while asked Bernardo how his daughter was and whether he had yet married her off.

'She is not married, my lord', replied Bernardo. 'Indeed she has been very ill—she still is. However she has in truth made an enormous improvement since mid-afternoon.'

The king knew at once what this improvement betokened. 'Well I do declare', said he, 'it would be lamentable if a creature so beautiful were yet taken from this earth. We wish to visit her.' And, with two retainers and Bernardo for all company, he shortly afterwards went into her room and, once inside, approached the bed in which Lisa lay slightly propped up waiting for him. He took her by the hand. 'What does this mean, my lady?' he said. 'You are young, you should be the solace of others: how is it you succumb to sickness? We wish to beg you, for our love's sake, to take heart and recover your health quickly.'

Feeling her hand touched by the one she loved above all else, Lisa was a little bashful but felt such utter bliss, she could have been in heaven. She replied as best she could: 'My lord, it was wanting to shoulder the heaviest burden with my very puny strength which brought my sickness upon me; but with your gracious kindness you will soon see me cured of it.'

The king was the only one to understand Lisa's veiled words, and she grew hourly in his esteem, so that he kept secretly cursing Fate for making her the daughter of such a man. After he had lingered with her a little and spoken further words of encouragement, he left. The king was held in the highest regard for his humanity, and the grocer and his daughter felt it did him all honour. She remained as happy as any woman ever was with her lover, and, buoyed by rising hope, she recovered her health in a few days and grew more beautiful than she had ever been.

The king had discussed with the queen what reward to make to Lisa for so great a love, and when the girl was quite better, he rode to the grocer's house with several of his barons and went into the garden, where he sent for the grocer and his daughter. The queen now appeared with several of her ladies; they welcomed Lisa into their company and made a great fuss of her. After a while the king and queen called Lisa to them and the king said to her: 'You're a valiant young woman, and the great love you have borne towards us has prevailed with us to grant you a great honour, with which we want you for our sake to be happy. And the honour is this: you, being of marriageable age, we wish you to take for your husband the man we shall give to you, it being understood that we shall nevertheless forever call ourselves your knight. All we shall require of you for this love is but a single kiss.'

Lisa, blushing crimson with embarrassment, made the king's pleasure her own and, speaking in a low voice, replied: 'My lord, I have no doubt that, if it were known that I was in love with you, most people would think I was mad, assuming perhaps that I'd taken leave of my senses and was unaware of my station, and unaware of Your Majesty's. But as God knows, who alone sees into the human heart, at the moment I was first smitten I recognized that Your Majesty was king and I the daughter of Bernardo the grocer, and that it ill behoved me to set my heart on so lofty an object. But as my lord knows far better than I do, no one falls in love by deliberate choice but by virtue of instinct and desire, against whose rule I fought my battle but, my strength failing, I loved you, I love you, I shall always love you. In truth, when I felt that you had captured my heart, I determined forever to make your will my own. So not merely will I readily accept a husband and cherish the man you are pleased to bestow upon me, as will befit my honour and my condition, but even if you told me to stand in fire, it would be my pleasure to do so in the assurance of pleasing you. To have a king for my gallant—well, you know how appropriate that is, so I'll make no answer on that! And the single kiss you demand as love-token, I should not concede it to you without Her Majesty's permission. But for Your Majesty's great kindness to me, and that of Her Majesty who is here as well, may God reward you, for there is nothing I can give.' Here Lisa fell silent, and the queen was very much taken with the girl's answer, finding her every whit as sagacious as the king had told her.

The king sent for her father and mother and discovered from them that they were happy with his proposal. So he sent for a young man called Perdicone, not rich but well born, and put some rings into his hand and gave Lisa to him in marriage—to this he had no objection.

The king and queen at once gave Lisa a great quantity of costly jewels and, in addition, Ceffalu and Calatabellotta, two excellent and productive territories. 'These we give you', said the king to Perdicone, 'as your bride's dowry. What our plans are for you, you shall discover in the course of time.' Turning to Lisa, he said: 'Now we should like to take the fruit we are to receive from your love.' He took her head between his hands and kissed her on the forehead.

Perdicone, and Lisa's father and mother, and Lisa too, were all delighted and held a great wedding feast. And many people say that the king kept his word scrupulously and continued as long as he lived to call himself Lisa's knight and never to engage in a feat of arms wearing any colours but those she bestowed on him.

It is in deeds like this that a ruler secures the hearts of his subjects, provides a framework for reciprocal kindness, and earns an enduring reputation for good. Today few if any rulers take such notions into consideration: most of them have turned into cruel tyrants.

X. 8. *Titus is dying for love of his friend Gisippus's betrothed. Gisippus gives her to his friend to be his wife, in order to save him from death. Later, Titus will be able to do as much for his benefactor.*

When Pampinea finished, and everyone (particularly the Ghibelline lady) had spoken well of King Pietro, Philomena, at the king's behest, began her story:

We all know that a king can do pretty well anything he chooses, so it is most especially incumbent on him to act with generosity. The man who does something which it behooves him to do and which lies within his capabilities does well; but his action should not attract the admiration nor the plaudits due to the man who does as much but of whom less would be expected, owing to his more limited means. So if you are going to be so voluble in your praise of kings and their works and find them marvellous, I'm sure you'll be all the happier with and all the readier to praise deeds performed by our peers, when they match or even surpass those of kings. This is why I've decided to tell you a story about two ordinary citizens who were friends and treated each other with commendable generosity.

In the days when Rome was governed by Caesar Octavian,* who was not yet known as Augustus but held the office of triumvir, there lived in Rome a patrician called Publius Quintus Fulvus. He had a son, Titus Quintus Fulvus, whom he sent to Athens to study philosophy, for he was of no mean intelligence, and recommended him with all his heart to an old friend of his there, of the local nobility, called Kremetes. So Kremetes gave Titus lodging in his house, to share the company of his own son Gisippus, and the two were set to study under the same philosopher, one Aristippus. Now as they shared each other's lives, the two young men found they had so much in common that they became the firmest friends and brothers—a bond that was to endure till their dying day. Neither of them could feel happy or relaxed except in the other's company. Together they embarked upon their studies and together they made equal progress in scaling the glorious heights of philosophy—for they both possessed keen intellects—and they each won golden opinions. Thus did they live, perseveringly, for the next three years, to the ineffable satisfaction of Kremetes, who scarcely made a distinction between his son and his son's friend. After this lapse of time Kremetes, now an old man, passed from this life, for this is the lot of all things. The two lads were equally distressed over this, as at the passing of their common father—indeed, Kremetes's friends and the rest of his family were at a loss to know which of the two was in the greater need of comforting.

A few months later Gisippus was visited by his friends and relations and urged to take a wife—a suggestion to which Titus also subscribed—and they found him a very pretty young woman, an Athenian girl from one of the best families; her name was Sophronia, and she was about 15 years old. As the period of their engagement drew to an end, Gisippus one day asked Titus to come with him to pay her a visit, for he had not yet seen her. They arrived at her house and, as she sat between the two of them, Titus ran his eye over her most attentively, as though appraising the beauty of his friend's intended. There was no feature of her body that did not leave him in raptures and overwhelm him with admiration, and he fell head over heels in love with her, though he contrived to avoid showing it; never was a man more smitten by a woman. They spent a little time with her, then left for home.

Here, Titus went into his room and settled down to think about the ravishing girl, and the more he thought about her, the more passionate became his feelings for her. As he realized this, he gave vent to many a hot sigh, and brooded: 'Oh Titus, what a wretched life is yours! Look where you've placed your heart, your love, your hope! Can't you understand that you ought to be holding this girl in the same respect in which you hold a sister? After all, think of all the hospitality you've received from Kremetes and his family, think of the flawless friendship that binds you to Gisippus, to whom she is betrothed. Think whom you've fallen for. Look where you're letting deceitful love carry you. Look where your hopes are luring you. Open your eyes, you poor wretch, take a good look at yourself. Give reason its place, bridle your lust, temper your unwholesome desires, and fix your thoughts on some other object. Nip it in the bud, this incipient lechery, conquer yourself before it's too late. This desire of yours is quite wrong, it's shameful. Even if you were certain of obtaining what you're after, which you're not, you ought to be avoiding the very object you've set yourself to pursue, if you stopped to consider what true friendship demands of you. So, what will you do, Titus? Will you abandon this reprehensible love, if you're to do as you ought?' Then he would remember Sophronia and dismiss everything he'd told himself. Making a complete turnabout, he would say: 'The laws of love take precedence over all others: they infringe the divine laws, let alone those of friendship. How often has it happened that a father has fallen in love with his daughter, a brother with his sister, a stepmother with her stepson? Isn't that far more heinous than a man falling in love with his friend's wife—that's happened any number of times. Anyway, I'm a young man, and youth is totally subservient to the laws of love: if love commands, I needs must obey. Virtuous living is all very proper for older people—I can only will that which love wills. The girl's beauty deserves to attract everyone's love, so if I, who am young, fall in love with her, who can justly blame me? It's not because she's Gisippus's that I love her, I'd love her whose-ever she was. It's just hard luck that she's been allotted to my friend Gisippus rather than to somebody else. And if she's bound to attract love—and she *is* bound to on account of her beauty—Gisippus should be all the happier, if he gets to know of it, that she's attracted mine rather than another's.' After coming up with these arguments, however, he turned round and sneered at them, espousing the opposite view, then shifted ground, then shifted back yet again: this went on all that day and the following night, and many days and nights to follow so that, for lack of sleep and appetite, his strength failed him and he had to take to his bed.

Gisippus was extremely concerned to see his friend lost in thought for so many days and now fallen ill; he never left his side but concentrated all his efforts and skills on trying to cheer him up. He never stopped questioning him about what was on his mind and what had made him ill, but Titus kept putting him off with untruths. However, as Gisippus saw through them and Titus felt under pressure, he finally answered him, with sighs and tears, in these words: 'Had the gods so willed it, Gisippus, I should have found death far preferable to life, considering that I've been fated to see my moral character put to the test only, to my utter shame, to fail it. Of course I expect shortly to receive the reward I deserve—death, that is—and it would appeal to me a good deal better than going on living with the memory of my baseness: this I shall now confess to you, though I'll blush to do so, because I cannot and ought not to conceal anything from you.' And, starting at the beginning, he disclosed to his friend the reason for all his brooding and the battle he had fought with himself and where victory had ultimately lain and how he was dying for love of Sophronia. Recognizing how reprehensible this was, he had, by way of penance, chosen to die, he said, and did not expect to survive much longer.

This tearful admission set Gisippus pondering for a while: he was not indifferent himself to the fair young girl's charms, albeit to a lesser degree, but he decided on the spot that he set greater store by his friend's life than by Sophronia; so, moved as he was by Titus's tears, he broke down weeping as he said: 'If it were not for the fact that you need your spirits raising, Titus, I should be taking you to task for disparaging our friendship by keeping me so long in the dark about this intolerable attachment of yours. Maybe it did strike you as a reprehensible passion, but what is base is no more to be concealed from a friend than what is good, because, just as a man takes pleasure in the good things about his friend, so he will strive to redeem his friend from whatever makes him guilty. But for the moment I'll not hold this against you; let me concentrate on what is clearly at present your most pressing need. That you have quite fallen for my betrothed Sophronia does not surprise me in the least: I'd have been surprised had you not done so, for she is a considerable beauty and you a man of spirit and with a taste for excellence. However understandable it is that you should be in love with Sophronia, you have no reason to complain of your luck—as you're doing implicitly—because she has fetched up with me while, had she fallen to anyone else, there might have been less shame attaching to your feelings for her. Now if you'd just revert to using your head, tell me this: to whom might Fate have allotted her, rather than to me, in order to earn your thanks? It doesn't matter how pure your love for her, if she had been accorded to anybody else, that man would have cherished her for himself alone, not for your sake, while you're not to expect such an attitude from me, not if you regard me as a friend in the way I regard you. After all, I can't remember a time, since we became friends, when I possessed something that was not yours as much as my own. Now if the matter had gone so far that there was no turning back, I'd have to take it as I found it. But things are still at a point where it's possible for me to make her over to you, and that is what I will do. After all, I can't imagine what my friendship would be worth to you if I could at will and without taint of dishonour put you in possession of an object, but denied it to you. It's true that Sophronia is engaged to me, and that I've loved her very dearly and have been looking forward with great joy to our wedding. But as you are far more deeply in love with her than I am and yearn for the dear creature far more passionately, take my word for it—she'll enter my bedroom not as my wife, but as yours. So stop fretting, shake off your gloom, recover your lost health, take comfort, cheer up: look forward now with gladness to reaping the reward of your love, which has so much better deserved it than mine has done.'

As he heard these words of Gisippus, Titus was certainly elated by the enticing hope they offered, but equally did he blush to recall where his duty lay, for it was clear to him that the nobler was his friend's generosity, the more unthinkable it was for him to accept it. So he continued to weep as he laboured to reply: 'Your friendship, Gisippus, is so genuine, so open-handed, it shows me all too clearly what duty my own friendship owes you. May the gods forbid that I should ever accept from your hands a woman whom they have bestowed upon you as the worthier of us two: had they seen that *I* was the one due to receive her, neither you nor anyone else should believe that they would ever have conceded her to *you*. So make the most of their wise dispensation, their gift to you, your election, and leave me to waste away in tears, for this is the part they have reserved for me as a person unworthy of so great a good. Either I shall master my tears, which is what you would wish, or I shall succumb to them and will be out of my misery.'

'Titus, if our friendship affords me licence enough to compel you to do as I wish, if it may prevail upon you to humour me, this is the one thing above all else in which I'm determined to employ it. And if you're not ready to concede my wish of your own free will, I shall resort to such compulsion as is necessary in a friend's interest in order to make Sophronia your wife. I know well enough what a powerful force love can be; I know it has driven lovers to a tragic death on more than one occasion. I can see you so close to it yourself that you might not be able to conquer your sorrow and turn back—another step and you'd be overwhelmed and succumb. And if you went, I'd be bound to follow you soon enough. So if I had no other reason to cherish you, I hold to your life to be sure of my own survival. Therefore Sophronia shall be yours: you would not easily find another girl so much to your liking. As for me, I can dispose of my heart elsewhere readily enough, and the result is I'll have made both of us happy. Perhaps I should not be such a ready giver if wives were as scarce or as hard to find as a good friend is. So, as I can find myself another wife at the drop of a hat, but not another friend, I'd sooner make her over to you than be deprived of you; it's not as if I'd lose her, for in passing her over to you I'd not be losing her—I'd simply be enhancing her value in the eyes of my other self. So if you are not proof against my entreaties, I do beg you to cure yourself of your sickness of heart and bring good cheer to me and yourself at one go; recover your hope and be disposed to take the pleasure you seek in the object of your desires.'

Though Titus was embarrassed to accept Sophronia for his wife and continued therefore to resist his friend's blandishments, as love kept tugging him on, while Gisippus pressed him with his solicitude: 'Very well, Gisippus', he finally said, 'if I'm to do what you insist means so much to you, I can't say it's clear to me whether it's my wishes or yours I'm obeying; but as your generosity is of a breadth to sweep aside my due sense of delicacy, I'll do as you ask. Do bear this in mind, though: I do it in the full recognition that you have not only given me the woman I love, but that you have thus saved my life. May the gods grant that I'll be able to serve your own honour and interest if I'm given the chance to show you my gratitude for what you are doing, for you have shown me greater pity than I have afforded myself.'

'Here, then, is what I think we should do', said Gisippus, 'to achieve our aim. As you know, Sophronia was betrothed to me after extensive negotiations between my family and hers. So if I went along to them now and told them I didn't after all want to marry her, there'd be the devil to pay: her people and mine would be outraged. That wouldn't bother me in the least if I could see the girl becoming yours at the end of the day; but I fear that if I let her down this way, her family would quickly bestow her on somebody else, and that person might not be you, in which case you'll have lost what I'll have failed to secure. So, if you don't mind, I think I should carry on with what I've started, and bring her home as my bride and go through with the wedding. After that we'll arrange for you to take her to bed secretly as your wife. Later, at the right time and place, we'll bring it out in the open. Then, if they're agreeable, so much the better; if they make a fuss, well, the damage will be done and, as there'll be no going back, they'll just have to put up with it.'

Titus thought this was a sound idea so, once he had recovered his health and was back in good form, Gisippus brought Sophronia home as his bride. A splendid wedding-feast was laid on and, when it was night, the women left the bride in her husband's bed and withdrew. Titus and Gisippus had adjoining bedrooms with a connecting door, so, after putting all the lamps out, Gisippus stealthily crept from his room into Titus's and bade him go in and slip into bed with his wife. This left Titus thoroughly abashed and he made to change his mind and refuse the invitation. Gisippus, however, had meant every word he said, being scrupulously honest and, after much discussion, succeeded in coaxing him to her bed. So Titus got into bed with her, took her in his arms, and playfully asked her in a whisper if she was ready to be his wife. She, taking him to be Gisippus, said yes; so he placed a fine, expensive ring on her finger and said: 'Then I'm ready to be your husband.' After which he consummated the marriage, taking his pleasure with her for a good while, and neither she nor anyone else ever realized that the man sleeping with her was anyone but Gisippus.

This, then, was the marital situation in which Sophronia and Titus found themselves when the lad's father, Publius, passed away and a letter arrived summoning him back to Rome at once to take charge of his affairs. What he decided, therefore, with Gisippus was that he would have to leave and take Sophronia with him—a course which would not be suitable, nor indeed practicable, until she had been advised how matters stood. So they invited her one day into the bedroom, where they gave her a complete account of the situation, and Titus explained to her the meaning of a good number of incidents to which they had both been party. She rested a pained look on each of them in turn, then burst into tears, complaining bitterly of Gisippus's deceit. And before any word of it could get out in Gisippus's household, she returned to her father's house, where she told her father and mother of the trick Gisippus had played on the pair of them, for she was married to Titus, she said, and not (as they supposed) to Gisippus. Sophronia's father took this very much amiss; his kinsmen and those of Gisippus became embroiled in his bitter complaints—words grew heated and they almost came to blows. Both families were utterly disgusted with Gisippus, who was considered to be due for a good dressing down, nay, for a thorough thrashing. His answer was that he had done nothing underhand, indeed Sophronia's family ought to be profoundly grateful, for he had procured for her a far better husband than he was.

As for Titus, he missed nothing of all this and found it all extremely distasteful. Knowing the Greek propensity to rant and rage* until they came upon someone who stood up to them (whereupon they would back down very meekly, the cowards), he decided he was not going to stand for their nonsense another minute. Gifted as he was with a Roman spirit allied to an Athenian intelligence, he assembled the two families, Gisippus's and Sophronia's, in a temple in due and proper form, and went in accompanied only by Gisippus. Thus he addressed them: 'Many philosophers hold the view that what we mortals do is the direct outcome of divine providence and therefore, in their opinion, all that we do now or in the future is done of necessity. Others maintain, however, that this law of constraint applies only to the *fait accompli*. An attentive consideration of this view will reveal clearly enough that to take issue with the inevitable is nothing less than pretending to a greater wisdom than the gods who, we are supposed to believe, govern us and what pertains to us in accordance with immutable laws, immune to error. That's why it should not be difficult for you to see the utter folly, the dumb arrogance of criticizing the operation of Providence: anyone so brazen deserves to be thrown into chains—and I'll leave you to judge their weight. Now that, in my view, is where you all belong, if there's any truth in what I hear you've been saying, and indeed keep saying, on the grounds that Sophronia has become my wife whereas you accorded her to Gisippus; you've simply ignored the fact that it was decided *ab aeterno* that she was to belong not to Gisippus but to me, as indeed you're all aware that in effect she now does. But as many people find any reference to the hidden providence and intentions of the gods a difficult concept to grasp if they take the view that the gods are sublimely indifferent to our concerns, I'm quite willing to set the matter on a simple human footing. To this end I shall have to do two things that I find quite out of character: blow my own trumpet, and make disparaging remarks about other people. Still, that is what I shall do, for I don't intend to palter with the truth in either respect, and it is necessary to our purpose.

'Your complaints against Gisippus partake of blind anger far more than of common sense; you castigate, damn, and abuse the fellow, you grumble and make a great fuss—why? Because he has thought it suitable to give Sophronia to me for my wife, just as you had thought it suitable to present her to him—and I think what he has done is thoroughly commendable, and I'll tell you why. First, he has fulfilled the function of a friend, and secondly, he's shown a good deal more sense than you have. It's not my intention at present to explain to you the requirements of the sacred laws of friendship, the mutual obligations they impose; let me remind you only of this, that the bond of friendship is immeasurably tighter than those of blood or kinship, inasmuch as our friends are of our own choosing while our kinsmen are but the gift of fortune. So if Gisippus was more concerned for my life than for your goodwill, given that I reckon myself to be his friend, this should be no surprise. Let's come now to the second point: he has acted more wisely than you have, as I shall be at some pains to prove to you. The fact is, you don't give me the impression of possessing the first idea of the workings of Providence, and still less have you any notion of how friendship operates. The outcome of your carefully weighed deliberations was to bestow Sophronia upon Gisippus, a young philosopher, and whom did Gisippus bestow her upon? A young philosopher. You elected to bestow her upon an Athenian, Gisippus to bestow her upon a Roman; you proposed giving her to a young man of good family, Gisippus to one of even better family; you thought to hand her to a rich young man, Gisippus to a man of vast wealth; your judgement assigned her to a young man who not only did not love her, he barely knew her, while Gisippus assigned her to a young man who loved her to the limits of his own life and happiness. You have only to take a close look to see that what I'm saying is the truth and is more commendable than what you have done. That I'm a young man and a philosopher just like Gisippus is obvious enough from my face and my studies—no need to waste a lot of words on that. We're the same age and we've kept pace with each other in our studies. True, he's an Athenian, I a Roman. If we're going to argue about the relative standing of our cities, I shall say that I come from a free city, he from a subject city; I shall say that I'm from a city that holds sway over the whole world, he from a city that obeys mine; I shall claim to be from a city in which military prowess, *imperium*, and learning flourish, whereas all he can advance for his is its learning. Besides, you may see in me only a very humble student, but I'm not born from the dregs of the populace; our residences and the public places in Rome are full of all manner of representations of my ancestors going back for aeons, and the Roman annals are stuffed with the countless triumphs awarded to Quintii on the Capitol; what's more, our name may be ancient but it is not decayed—it's flourishing now more than ever. I'll not be so lacking in good taste as to mention my wealth: I take the view that a dignified poverty is the traditional, bounteous heredity of the Roman nobility. The common throng may frown on poverty and hold wealth in high consideration, but if I am prosperous it is not owing to cupidity but merely to Fortune's favour. I'm fully aware that there have been and still ought to be people here who are glad to own Gisippus for their kinsman; but there is no reason for my not being equally dear to you in Rome, considering that there you shall find in me an excellent host and a powerful patron, an effective and sedulous promoter of your private and public interests.

'And so, looking at the matter reasonably and dispassionately, which one of you will maintain that your counsels are preferable to those of my Gisippus? None of you, surely. Sophronia has therefore contracted a good marriage to Titus Quintus Fulvus, a Roman citizen and wealthy member of the old nobility, and friend of Gisippus; so anyone who wants to complain of this is acting improperly and has no idea what he's doing. Again, some of you may observe that it's not her becoming Titus's wife that bothers them, but the way in which it was done—in an underhand, furtive manner, keeping friends and family in ignorance. Yet there is no prodigy about it, it's far from being without precedent. I'm quite happy to overlook all those brides who've taken a husband against their father's wishes, and those women who have eloped with their lovers, those who started as mistresses then became wives, and those who made no mention of being married until pregnancy and childbirth provided the evidence, and a virtue had to be made out of necessity. None of this applies to Sophronia; on the contrary, she was accorded by Gisippus to Titus in an orderly, discreet, and honest fashion. Others will say that the man who gave her away in marriage had no title to do so; well, what a silly, childish little grumble that is! How ill-considered! In order to compass a predetermined object, doesn't Fortune make use of a variety of novel means and instruments? What difference does it make to me whether it's a cobbler rather than a philosopher who uses his judgement in pursuing my interest, and whether he does it openly or on the sly, if the final result is satisfactory? If the cobbler bungled it, I must take good care that he should not do it again, and just thank him for what he has done. If Gisippus has arranged a good marriage for Sophronia, it's absurd and pointless to be fussing about him and the way he went about it; if you have no faith in his judgement, take care he doesn't contract any more marriages, and thank him for just this one.

'Anyway, believe me, I never had the slightest intention of resorting to deceit or trickery to tarnish the good name of your family in the person of Sophronia. And for all that I wedded her in secret, I did not come as a seducer to steal her virginity; I did not come as an enemy to have her by dishonourable means, spurning your kinship. I was passionately in love with her enticing beauty and attracted by her qualities of spirit, but I recognized that, had I sought her hand in the way perhaps you would have proposed, I might have failed in my quest, for, devoted as you are to her, you could have feared lest I took her away with me to Rome. I went about it secretly though now it is plain to you, and made Gisippus consent in my name to what he himself was not disposed to do. After which, for all the fervour of my love, I sought to sleep with her not as a lover but as husband. She herself can bear truthful witness that I did not approach her until I had wedded her with the proper form of words and with the ring: I asked her if she desired me for her husband and her answer was "yes". If she feels she was tricked, I'm not the one to blame; she is, for she never asked me who I was. This then is the great evil, the heinous crime perpetrated by her friend Gisippus and by me her suitor: Sophronia has become the wife of Titus Quintus. It's on account of this that you revile and threaten him. What more would you do had he bestowed her upon a peasant, an outlaw, a serf? What chains, what dungeon, what crucifixion would suffice?

'But enough of that. The time has come—I was not yet expecting it—when my father has died and I have to return to Rome. As I want to bring Sophronia with me, I've revealed to you what I might perhaps otherwise have continued to conceal. And your sensible course will be to take it cheerfully, for if I'd been minded to deceive or flout you, I could as well have left her high and dry. Heaven forbid, though, that such an abject spirit should ever inhabit a Roman! Sophronia, then, by the consent of the gods, by virtue of our human laws and that of my Gisippus's admirable good sense, as also by virtue of my lover's guile, is mine. You, meanwhile, evidently fancying that your wisdom is superior to that of gods and men alike, are behaving like idiots and condemning this match in two ways, each of which I find not a little exasperating: first, you're holding Sophronia, on whom you now have no more claim than I am prepared to allow; and secondly, you're showing hostility to Gisippus, whereas you are rightly in his debt. You're behaving like dolts, then, but I'm not proposing to go on about it now; instead, take a word of friendly advice: lay aside your anger, stop fretting and fuming, give me back Sophronia—that way I'll be able to leave happily as your kinsman and live in your friendship. And make no mistake about this: whether you like it or not, should you have anything different in mind, I'll take Gisippus away from you and if I get to Rome I shall most assuredly recover the woman who is rightly mine, and you'll just have to put up with it. If you persist in crossing me, I'll give you firsthand experience of what can happen when you rouse a Roman to anger.'

This said, Titus stood up looking like thunder and, grasping Gisippus by the hand, strode out of the temple uttering threats and shaking his head, evidently quite indifferent to the crowd within. These stayed behind and, whether persuaded by Titus's arguments in favour of kindred and friendship, or whether alarmed at his final words, they all agreed that it would be preferable to have Titus for kinsman, as Gisippus had declined to become one, than to lose the kinship of Gisippus only to acquire the enmity of Titus. So they went after Titus and told him that they had no objection to his keeping Sophronia and would regard him as a dear relation and Gisippus as a good friend. Then as kinsmen and friends they held a celebration together, after which they left and despatched Sophronia to him. She was wise enough to make a virtue of necessity and readily transferred to Titus the love she had felt for Gisippus. She left with Titus for Rome, where she received a most honourable welcome.

Gisippus stayed in Athens and was held in scanty consideration by most people. It was not long before certain intrigues within the city resulted in his being condemned to perpetual banishment, together with all his house, and he was driven out in a state of abject poverty. In this condition of penury, indeed of beggary, Gisippus made his way to Rome with such conveyance as his means allowed, to see whether Titus remembered him. He ascertained that Titus was still alive and still in general favour, then discovered where he lived and took up his station outside until Titus should appear. Given his beggarly condition, he dared not address a word to him but strove to catch his eye so that he would be summoned by him. But Titus swept past and Gisippus imagined that the Roman had noticed but avoided him—so the Athenian went his way in rage and despair, remembering what he had done for his friend.

Night had fallen. He was starving and penniless and wished for nothing so much as to be dead but, with little idea where he was going, he came to a very inhospitable part of the city where he noticed a large cave; in he went to bed down for the night on the bare earth, wrapped in his rags, and cried himself to sleep. Now two men who had been out that night on a robbery came into the cave towards dawn with their booty and fell to quarrelling; the stronger of the two killed the other and left. Gisippus had seen and heard it all and it occurred to him that here was a way to compass the death he now so craved without actually doing violence to himself. So instead of leaving, he waited there until the minions of the law, who had come to hear of the incident, turned up and led him away, not very gently. Under questioning he confessed to the murder and said he had not been able to make his escape; so the praetor, Marcus Varro by name, gave orders for him to be crucified, as was then the custom.

Titus happened, though, to be visiting the praetor at that moment and, as he scrutinized the wretched convict's face and heard what the charge was, he suddenly recognized him for Gisippus and was quite bewildered that he was so down on his luck and had contrived to fetch up here. He was burning to come to his assistance but could think of no way to save him unless he accused himself of the crime and exculpated Gisippus. So he promptly stepped forward and cried: 'Marcus Varro, call back the poor fellow you've just condemned: he's innocent. I've committed a bad enough offence against the gods, murdering the fellow your men found dead this morning, and don't want to offend them further with the death of another innocent.'

Varro was perplexed; he was sorry that this had been said in the hearing of the entire praetorium; he could not honourably evade the requirements of the law, so he recalled Gisippus and said to him, in Titus's presence: 'What made you so mad as to confess to a crime you never committed, when your life was at stake and no one had applied torture to you? You said you were the man who committed the murder last night, and now this person comes along and says it was not you but he who did it.'

Gisippus looked and saw that it was Titus; he realized well enough that his friend was doing this to save him, in gratitude for the favour done to him previously. So he wept for compassion and said: 'Varro, it really was I who did it, and Titus's concern for my safety is now too late.'

Titus, for his part, said to the praetor: 'This man is a foreigner, as you see, and he was found without any weapon next to the murdered man. You can see that his wretchedness gives him a motive for wanting to die. So let him go and punish me as I've deserved.'

Varro found the constancy of these two quite amazing, and had reached the conclusion that neither of them was the culprit. As he pondered over some means to discharge them, who should arrive but a young man called Publius Ambustus, a notorious thief and totally beyond redemption. He was the one who had actually committed the murder. Recognizing that neither of the two was guilty of the crime of which each accused himself, he was so touched at the thought of their innocence that a great impulse of compassion moved him to appear before Varro and say: 'Praetor, my fates are urging me to resolve the difficult problem raised by these two; some god within me is pricking me, prompting me to confess my fault to you: neither of them is guilty of what each charges himself with. It was actually I who killed the man at daybreak today; this poor wretch here, I saw him asleep there while I was sharing out the loot with the fellow I killed. I don't need to exculpate Titus: a man of his reputation would never stoop so low. Set them free, therefore, and condemn me to the penalty the laws require.'

The affair came to the ears of Octavian, who sent for the three of them and had them tell him what prompted each of them to claim the penalty. Each one explained, and Octavian absolved the first two as they were guiltless and the third for their sakes.

So Titus fetched away his friend Gisippus and straight away chided him for being so diffident and irresolute; this said, he greeted him rapturously and brought him home, where Sophronia welcomed him as a brother, with tears of pity. They revived him a little and dressed him once more in attire consistent with his qualities and station in life. Then the first thing Titus did was to institute with him a common ownership of all his wealth and possessions, after which he gave him a younger sister of his, called Fulvia, as his bride. Then he told him: 'It's up to you, Gisippus, whether you want to stay here with me or go back to Achaea with everything I've given you.' Banished as he was from his city, and constrained in addition by the love he rightly bore Titus for his welcome friendship, he agreed to become a Roman. Here they lived happily for many a year, Gisippus with his Fulvia, Titus with his Sophronia, all sharing the same house, and growing closer each day, if that were possible, in friendship.

Friendship, then, is a sacred thing. She deserves singular respect, indeed she deserves to be commended with eternal praise, for she is the most prudent of mothers, whose children are generosity and propriety; her sisters are gratitude and kindness; she is hostile to antipathy and greed, and is always ready, without waiting to be asked, to do as she would be done by. All too rarely nowadays are the sacred effects of friendship to be observed in two people—this is the fault, this is the shame of human kind's mean selfishness which looks only to its own advantage and has relegated friendship to the outer limits of our world, a perpetual exile. What love, what wealth, what kinship would ever have proved so effective in impressing Titus's ardour, his sighs and tears on the heart of Gisippus, to the point that he made over to Titus the beautiful, sweet bride he loved? Only friendship. What laws, what sanctions, what terrors would have served to restrain the arms of young Gisippus from embracing the attractive girl wherever he could count on solitude, darkness, in his own bed maybe—possibly in face of her own enticing? Only friendship. What advancement, what rewards, what benefits would have made Gisippus reckless of alienating his family and Sophronia's, heedless of the disgusting rumours spread by the mob, indifferent to the leering and the mockery, in order to gratify his friend? Only friendship. And on the other hand, when Titus could quite properly have feigned not to notice him, who would have made him quite spontaneously jump to procure his own death in order to save Gisippus from the crucifixion he was striving to bring upon himself? Only friendship. Who would have made Titus so open-handed in sharing his ample inheritance with Gisippus, not losing a moment to do so, when Gisippus had suffered the ill luck to lose his? Only friendship. Who would have made Titus so keen to bestow his own sister on Gisippus, without a second thought, seeing him in the direst penury? Only friendship.

Let mankind, therefore, crave a host of spouses, a horde of brothers, children by the score; let it lavish its fortune on ever more servants. And let it overlook the fact that there's not one of these people who will forbear to put his own little problems ahead of any concern for the far greater problems affecting his father, his brother, or his master—whereas a friend does exactly the opposite.

X. 9. *Torello, a citizen of Pavia, shows kindness to a foreigner, falls on hard times in the Orient, but chances once more upon the stranger, who will not let his kindness go unrewarded.*

At the conclusion of Philomena's narrative, everyone thoroughly commended Titus for the magnificence of his gratitude. Then the king, reserving Dioneo for the last, spoke up in these terms:

What Philomena says about friendship is undoubtedly true, and she was quite right to deplore, in her closing remarks, how little room people have for it nowadays. And if we were here in order to set the world's evils to rights or to castigate them I should follow her with a lengthy sermon. But as our aim is different, it has occurred to me to tell you a story, maybe on the long side but thoroughly enjoyable, about a generous action of Saladin's. My object is that, in listening to my tale, even if our defects may prevent us fully meriting a person's friendship, we may take pleasure in being of service, hoping that in due course we shall not go without thanks.

In the days of Emperor Frederic I,* we are told, the Christians launched a crusade to recover the Holy Land, but an early notice of this came to the ears of Saladin,* a most remarkable man who was Sultan of Babylon. He decided to make his own reconnaissance of the Christian princes' warlike preparations, the better to counter them. Making every necessary provision for this in Egypt, he gave it out that he was off on a pilgrimage, and left in the guise of a merchant, accompanied by two of his wisest senior retainers and only three servants. He had travelled the length and breadth of many a Christian land, and was riding through Lombardy to cross the mountains when, one evening on their way from Milan to Pavia, they met a gentleman from Pavia called Torello di Stra. This man was on his way with his retinue, his hawks and hounds, to stay on a fine estate he possessed on the Ticino.

One glance told Torello that these men were gentlemen and foreigners, and he wished to offer them hospitality. So when Saladin asked one of Torello's attendants how far they were from Pavia and whether they would arrive in time to gain admittance, Torello did not let his servant reply but spoke up in his place: 'You'll not reach Pavia in time to pass within, gentlemen.'

'Then pray advise us', asked Saladin, 'where we might best find a night's accommodation, for we are foreigners.'

'With pleasure', said Torello. 'I was just on the point of sending a servant on the road back towards Pavia to run an errand. I shall send him with you and he'll escort you to a most suitable place for you to spend the night.'

He approached the most discreet of his attendants, gave him his instructions, and sent him off with them, while he himself hastened to his villa and organized the best supper he could, with the tables set out in the garden. This done, he went to the gate to meet them. The servant engaged the foreign gentlemen in conversation on one topic and another as he took them by a roundabout route before leading them, without their realizing it, to his master's house.

When Torello saw them, he came out on foot to meet them and, smiling broadly, cried: 'Welcome, gentlemen, welcome!' Saladin, who was nobody's fool, realized that this gentleman evidently doubted whether his invitation would have been accepted, had he proferred it on first meeting them; so he had employed a little ruse in bringing them to his house to prevent their refusing to accept a night's hospitality. Saladin replied to his greeting: 'Sir', he said, 'were it possible to find fault with a display of courtesy, we should have to deprecate yours: you have somewhat obstructed our journey—never mind that—but you have virtually obliged us to accept your quite singular kindness though we have done nothing to deserve it beyond a single greeting.'

Torello, a man of shrewd, well-chosen words, replied: 'Gentlemen, such kindness as you are receiving from me is quite negligible, bearing in mind the sort of hospitality appropriate to gentlemen of what I judge to be your condition. The truth is, however, that you would have found no adequate accommodation outside Pavia, so you must not take it unkindly if I've brought you a little out of your way in order somewhat to limit your discomfort.'

After these words, the travellers found themselves surrounded by their host's servants, who stabled their horses once they had dismounted. Torello conducted the three gentlemen to the bedrooms made ready for them. Here their shoes were removed and they were served refreshingly cool wine to drink and entertained with pleasant conversation until it was time for dinner. Saladin, his retainers, and attendants could all speak the local tongue and so could easily understand what was said and be understood; they were all of the opinion that this gentleman was the most agreeable, well-bred man they'd ever met, and the one whom it was the greatest pleasure to listen to. Torello, for his part, felt that these were splendid men, and that there was much more to them than he had first thought, so he was sorry that he could not entertain them this evening with a fuller company and more lavish meal. He decided, therefore, to make up for this the following morning: he told one of his servants what he was minded to do, and despatched him to his wife, a woman of high spirit and intelligence—she was at Pavia, no distance from here, and at this hour no gate would be shut.

After this he led the gentlemen out into the garden and politely enquired where they hailed from and what was their destination. 'We are Cypriot merchants', was Saladin's answer. 'We've come from Cyprus and our business takes us to Paris.'

'Would to God', remarked Torello, 'that our country produced gentlemen who could assort with the merchants evidently raised in Cyprus!'

They conversed on one topic and another until it was time for dinner, when he invited them to do him the honour of joining him at table and served them an excellent, well-presented meal within the limits of such last-minute resources. Not long after leaving the table, it was clear to their host that they were tired, so he invited them to take their rest in the most elegant beds, and shortly afterwards retired himself to sleep.

The servant despatched to Pavia carried the message to Torello's wife, and she, being no frail woman but of truly regal spirit, promptly summoned Torello's friends and attendants in profusion and organized a lavish banquet; accompanied by torches, she invited many of the city's nobility to attend, and she got out all manner of silks and furs and other attire. In a word, she made all the preparations in accordance with her husband's instructions.

When it was day, the gentlemen got up, and Torello, sending for his falcons, took horse with his guests and brought them to a nearby fen to show off the birds in flight. When Saladin requested that someone might accompany them to Pavia and show them to the best inn, Torello said he would be the man, as he had to go there anyway. They were glad to take him at his word, and all set out together, arriving in the city at about nine in the morning. Imagining that they were being conducted to the best inn, they came to Torello's house, where a good fifty of the leading citizens had assembled to welcome the gentlemen. At once they advanced to hold the guests' bridles and stirrups.

Seeing this, Saladin and his companions grasped well enough what had happened and, 'Torello, sir', they said, 'this is not what we requested of you. You've already done so much for us this last night, far more than we deserve, and you could quite suitably have left us to continue on our journey.'

'I have Fortune rather than you, gentlemen, to thank', replied Torello, 'for such service as could be offered you last night. You chanced to be on the road at an hour that made it incumbent on you to come to my small villa. This morning, however, I shall be in your debt, and so will all these gentlemen here assembled around you, unless you feel that courtesy requires you to decline to join them for dinner—which you are free to do if you so wish.'

Saladin and his company had to concede. They dismounted and the gentlemen there to receive them were delighted to bring them to their rooms, which had been made ready for them most sumptuously. They laid aside their travelling clothes, rested a little, then proceeded to the great hall where the tables were laid quite magnificently. They were offered water with which to wash their hands, then shown to their places at table with the most elaborate ceremony. Here they were served dish after dish, all with such pomp and splendour that if the emperor himself had arrived he could not have been more royally entertained. Saladin and his companions, for all that they were themselves great lords and accustomed to the sight of opulence, could not help marvelling at the splendour of their entertainment, all the more so considering that their host was not a man of high rank—this they knew—but a simple burgess. When the meal was over and they left the table, they pursued their elevated conversation awhile, after which, at Torello's behest, the Pavian gentlemen all withdrew to rest, for the day was hot. Torello remained behind with his three guests, and brought them into a room to which he had his good wife summoned, for not one of his treasures was to remain concealed from them. She was a great beauty, tall and splendidly attired; she came into their presence accompanied by her two little sons, who looked like a pair of cherubs, and greeted them cordially. The guests stood up when they saw her and welcomed her most politely; they had her sit down with them and made a great fuss of her pretty children. After she had engaged them in a little light chat, Torello drew aside and she questioned them very charmingly as to whence they came and whither they were bound; to which the guests answered in the same terms as they had replied to Torello.

'Good', said she cheerfully, 'I see that my woman's insight will be of service to you, so pray do me the favour of not declining or neglecting the very modest present I'm going to give you. Bear in mind that women make trifling gifts in keeping with their modesty, and do accept it in recognition of the donor's good intentions rather than of the size of the gift.' She sent for a couple of gowns apiece, one of which was lined in silk, the other in squirrel's fur, not the sort of attire worn by a simple burgher or merchant but rather by a lord; she also gave them each three gowns for special occasions, made of the finest silk, and three pairs of breeches. 'Take these things. I have clothed my husband in garments similar to yours. The other things are of little value but they may be welcome to you considering that you are far from your wives, that you have travelled a great distance and still have a long way to go, and that merchants tend to be neat and well turned out.'

The gentlemen were astounded and had to concede that Torello would never let himself be outdone in kindness—indeed, given the high quality of these clothes, which were not at all merchant's attire, they wondered whether Torello may not have discovered their identity. One of them, however, replied to Torello's wife: 'These things are most extravagant, madam, and we should hesitate to accept them were we not bound by your entreaty, which we cannot refuse.'

This done, Torello rejoined their group and his wife took her leave of them, going to oversee the provision to their guests' servants of similar gifts, suitable to their condition. Torello pressed his guests to spend the rest of the day with him so, after they'd taken a nap, they dressed in their new clothes and joined him for a ride about the city. At supper-time they dined splendidly in a large but select company.

In due course they retired to bed, and the next day they got up to find their exhausted hacks replaced by three sturdy great saddle-horses, with similarly fresh, robust mounts for their attendants. On seeing them, Saladin turned to his companions and said: 'I swear to God, there never was a more perfect, more kind, more considerate gentleman than this! And if the Christian kings measure up to their standard the way this gentleman does to his, the Sultan of Babylon must expect such excellence not merely in one man but in as many as are evidently preparing to set forth against him.' Realizing that to refuse the horses was out of the question, they thanked him most graciously, and got into the saddle.

Accompanied by many of his friends, Torello escorted his guests for a good stretch of the way out of the city; and, however reluctant Saladin was to part from his host, such was the affection he felt for him, still, he had to press on, so he asked Torello to turn back. Torello also found the parting painful and said: 'I shall, gentlemen, if you so wish, but this I have to say: I do not know who you are, nor do I ask you to tell me more than you're inclined to. But, whoever you are, you'll never persuade me that you are merchants. Now God go with you.'

To which Saladin, taking leave of all Torello's friends, replied: 'It may yet happen, sir, that we shall display to you our merchandise, and this will effectively convince you. Farewell.'

Thus Saladin set off with his companions, utterly determined, if he lived and the forthcoming war did not make an end of him, that he would afford Torello no less hospitality than he had received from him. He spoke a great deal to his companions about the gentleman and his wife, and all the gifts and courtesies showered upon them, applauding each one ever-more warmly. Now once he had scoured the entire West most laboriously, he took ship and returned to Alexandria with his company, and made ready his defences on the basis of a complete intelligence. Torello returned to Pavia and mused for ages about the three men's identities without ever arriving anywhere close to the truth.

The time for the expedition arrived, preparations were set in train on a huge scale, and Torello, in spite of the tears and entreaties of his wife, determined to go. When all his own preparations were complete and he was about to ride away, he said to his wife, whom he loved above all things: 'I'm going on this crusade, as you see, both to acquire reputation by my physical presence and in order to assure the salvation of my soul. To you I entrust our possessions and our good name. And as I am certain about my setting out but, what with one thing and another, far from assured of my return, I want you to do me a favour: whatever happens to me, if you receive no certain tidings of my still being alive, wait a year, a month, and a day for me before you remarry, starting from now, the day of my departure.'

His wife sobbed as she said: 'I don't know how I shall bear the sorrow in which you leave me with your departure. But if I do survive it, and anything happened to you, live and die assured that I shall live and die wedded to Torello and to his memory.'

'I've no doubt at all that what you have promised you will observe, so far as it lies with you to do so. But you are a beautiful young woman of very good family, and you are known far and wide for your exceptional qualities. I therefore have no doubt that, in the absence of reliable news of my survival, a great number of prominent citizens will approach your brothers and others of your family to seek your hand. Under pressure from such men as they, you will be unable to defend yourself however much you wanted to, and you will be obliged to fall in with their wishes. This is the reason why I'm asking you to observe this interval and not a longer one.'

'I'll do all I can to stand by what I've said to you. But if I'm obliged to do otherwise, I shall certainly fulfil this condition you have laid upon me. I pray God that neither you nor I be brought to such a pass.'

With these words his wife embraced him tearfully, then drew a ring* off her finger and gave it to him, saying: 'Should I die before I see you again, this will be a memento of me.'

He took it, mounted, bade everyone farewell, and rode off to Genoa with his company. Here they boarded a galley and soon reached Acre to join the rest of the Christian host. Now almost at once a great epidemic* brought death throughout the army, and in the course of it practically all the survivors were rounded up by Saladin, whether it was a matter of luck or skill on his part. He divided his prisoners among a number of cities, and Torello was brought captive to Alexandria. Nobody knew him here, and he was afraid to make himself known, so under pressure of necessity he set up as a bird-trainer, in which he had no little skill. It was on this account that he came to Saladin's attention, who released him from captivity and appointed him his Master of Falcons. Torello was known to Saladin merely as 'the Christian'; he did not recognize the sultan any more than the sultan recognized him. At all events, Torello could think only of Pavia, and he had made several attempts to escape but all in vain. So when certain Genoese ambassadors, who had visited Saladin to negotiate the ransom of some of their fellow-citizens, were about to leave, he decided to write to his wife to say that he was alive and would return to her as soon as he could, so she was to expect him. He wrote his letter and fondly requested one of the ambassadors, whom he knew, to see that it came into the hands of the Abbot of San Pietro in Ciel d'Oro,* an uncle of his.

This, then, was Torello's situation when, one day, as Saladin was talking to him about his birds, Torello broke into a smile—and there was something about his smile that had struck Saladin when he had been his guest at Pavia. This peculiarity reminded the sultan of Torello; he looked at him closely and thought this must be the very man. 'Tell me, Christian', he said, abandoning the thread of their discussion, 'where are you from in the West?'

'I'm a Lombard, my lord, from a city called Pavia. I'm a poor man of humble station.'

His suspicion practically confirmed by what he'd heard, Saladin rejoiced. 'God has given me occasion', he reflected, 'to show this man how much I appreciated his kindness.' He said no more, but had his entire wardrobe laid out in one room and brought in Torello. 'Look, Christian', he said, 'and tell me if you've seen any of these clothes before.'

Torello looked over them, and noticed those which his wife had given to Saladin, but he never imagined that these could be the same ones. 'My lord, I don't recognize any of them', he said, 'though it's true that those two look like garments in which I attired three merchants who chanced to be my guests.'

At this Saladin could no longer contain himself but embraced him tenderly and said: 'You are Torello of Stra, and I am one of the three merchants to whom your wife gave these garments. And now the time has come to apprise you beyond doubt of what it is I trade in, as I said might happen when I took my leave of you.'

Torello was over the moon when he heard this, but he was also mortified—delighted to have entertained a man such as he, mortified at what seemed to him the poverty of his entertainment. Saladin, however, told him: 'As God has sent you to me, sir, pray regard yourself, rather than me, as lord and master here.'

So they fell into each other's arms rejoicing, and Saladin had Torello dressed in princely fashion, then brought him into the presence of all his leading barons. He spoke to them at length of Torello's virtues and bade them all, if they were concerned to retain his favour, to treat his friend with the same deference with which they treated himself. This they all did from that very moment, and none of them more diligently than the two barons who had been Saladin's companions under Torello's roof. The heights to which he had suddenly been raised somewhat distracted Torello from his concerns in Lombardy, particularly in view of his confidence that his letter would have been delivered to his uncle.

Now the day on which the Christian army was taken captive by Saladin, a knight from Provence called Torello of Dignes, a man of modest attainments, had died and received burial. As Torello of Stra was well known throughout the army, however, anyone hearing the news that Torello had died assumed that the knight in question was the Torello from Stra, not the one from Dignes; moreover, the circumstances of the army's capture precluded those who had the story incorrectly from being undeceived. Many crusaders from Italy, therefore, took this report home with them, and there were even some who dared to assert that they had seen his corpse and attended his funeral. The news caused unspeakable grief to Torello's wife and family, and not only to them but to everyone who had known him. It would take too long to describe the sorrow and agony endured by his wife. For several months she never stopped grieving over him, but when her sorrow was somewhat abated, her brothers and other kinsfolk started pressing her to remarry, for her hand was being sought by some of Lombardy's greatest men. Time after time she refused and simply wept and wept; but eventually she was obliged to do as her family wished and she consented, on condition that she remained single for the term she had promised to Torello.

This is how matters stood in Pavia, Torello's wife being only a week or so short of the time set for her remarriage, when in Alexandria Torello chanced to see a man he had noticed boarding the galley bound for Genoa with the Genoese ambassadors. He called him, therefore, and asked him about their journey and when would they have reached Genoa. 'The galley, sir, made a disastrous passage', he was told. 'This I learned in Crete, where I stopped off. As it approached Sicily a dangerous northerly got up and drove it on to the reefs of the Barbary coast. Not a soul survived. I had two brothers on board who perished.'

The man had spoken the simple truth and Torello believed him. Mindful that the interval he had requested of his wife came to an end in but a few more days, and that in Pavia they knew nothing of his present situation, he was convinced that his wife must have undergone a fresh betrothal. This plunged him into such a state of despair that he quite lost his appetite and took to his bed, determined to die. Saladin was devoted to him and came to him the moment he heard of this; by dint of pressing him a great deal he discovered the reason for his grief and infirmity, and chided him sternly for not having told him sooner; then he begged him to take heart. 'Do so', he said, 'and I will ensure that you are back in Pavia by the agreed date.' And he told him how this would be done. Torello trusted Saladin; he had often heard that what was proposed was feasible and had been effected many a time, so he did take heart and urged his friend to set the plan in motion. Saladin gave orders to a sorcerer of his, a man whose skills he had already assayed, to find a means to transport Torello to Pavia in a single night on a bed. 'That shall be done', said the sorcerer, 'but I'll put him to sleep for his own sake.'

The matter thus arranged, Saladin returned to Torello and found his mind made up either to be back in Pavia by the requisite date, if this proved possible, or, if it were not, to die. 'If you dote upon your wife', Saladin told him, 'and are concerned lest she pass into another's hands, God knows I cannot possibly hold this against you: never did I meet a woman whose bearing, manner, and conduct—never mind her beauty, which blooms for so short a season—so impressed and enchanted me. As Fortune sent you my way, how happy I should have been had we been able to live out our lives together, sharing the government of my dominions. And if God were not to grant me this, as your mind is made up either to die or to be back in Pavia before the term expires, how I should have wished to know of it in time, so that I might have returned you to your home in the style and with the company that your qualities deserve. As this is not to be, and you do wish to be home straight away, I shall send you there in the way I can, as I have explained it to you.'

'All you have done for me, my lord, never mind the things you have said, have afforded me ample proof of your kindness, which I never deserved to anything like this degree; and I shall live and die utterly confident in what you have told me, even had you left it unsaid. But as I have determined on my course, I beg you to put your promise into immediate effect, for tomorrow is the last day that they will wait for me.'

'It shall be seen to without fail', said Saladin. And the next day, in the expectation of sending him away that very night, Saladin had the most gorgeous and sumptuous bed made ready in one of his great halls. It consisted of mattresses, according to their custom, fashioned out of velvet and silk embroidered with gold thread; on it was laid a quilt whose hems were worked in a circular pattern of the fattest pearls and the costliest jewels—this alone was considered beyond price here in the West—and two pillows fit to be placed on such a bed. This done, he had Torello (now quite recovered) dressed up in a traditional Saracen robe, the most beautiful and expensive one anybody had ever seen, and a huge great turban wound about his head. As it was getting late, Saladin, accompanied by many of his barons, went into the room in which Torello waited, sat down beside him, and, barely repressing his tears, said: 'The hour is approaching, sir, when I have to be parted from you. I cannot come with you or send anyone to accompany you, as the method of your transport does not permit it, so I'm obliged to take my leave of you here in this room, and that is what I'm here for. But before I bid you goodbye, I pray, for the sake of the love and friendship that subsists between us, that you will keep me in mind. And before our lives reach their end, and once you have settled your affairs in Lombardy, do please come to visit me at least once if you can; that way I shall rejoice at having seen you once more, and be able to make up for the deficiencies of hospitality forced upon me by your hurried departure. Until this may come about, I hope you will not mind remaining in touch with me by letter, and requesting of me whatever conduces to your pleasure—I should, of course, fulfil such requests more willingly for you than for any man alive.'

Torello could not hold back his tears, so he spoke but haltingly as he answered in a few words that he could never possibly forget his kindness and his merits; he would unquestionably do as he was asked, if he were spared to do so. Then Saladin hugged and kissed him tenderly and wept copiously as he said goodbye. He left the room, the other barons all took their leave, then joined Saladin in the great hall where the bed had been prepared. It was now late and, as the sorcerer waited impatiently to perform his role, a physician entered with a draught; he explained that he was administering it to him as a fortifying cordial and had him drink it; a moment later Torello was sound asleep. Thus sleeping, Torello was at Saladin's command lifted on to the handsome bed. Saladin himself placed upon it a beautiful big crown of enormous value, and set his stamp on it, so it was recognized thereafter as a gift from Saladin to Torello's lady. Then he slipped on to Torello's finger a ring set with a carbuncle which glowed like a flaming torch—it would scarcely have been possible to estimate its value. Then he had a sword slung from his belt, and its decorations were also beyond price. Added to this, he fastened on his breast a brooch studded with pearls the like of which was never seen, and quantities of other gems. Then he had two enormous golden bowls set down on either side of him, crammed with golden doubloons, and strewn all about him were any number of hair-fillets threaded with pearls, and rings and belts and all sorts of things, far too many to describe. This done, he gave Torello another kiss, then told the sorcerer to be quick. Thus, in the presence of Saladin, the bed with Torello in it was suddenly whisked away, leaving the sultan and his barons behind, talking about him.

In accordance with his request Torello was set down, together with all the jewels and finery already described, in the church of San Piero in Ciel d'Oro at Pavia. He was still sleeping when the bell for Matins sounded and the sacristan entered the church holding a light. He at once caught sight of the sumptuous bed, which surprised, indeed scared him out of his wits; he turned and fled. The abbot and community were puzzled to see him thus fleeing and asked him why he had done so. He told them.

'Come, you're no longer a child', said the abbot, 'and you know this church well enough—you shouldn't take fright so easily. Let's go and see what it is that's startled you.'

So they lit plenty of lamps, then the abbot and all the monks entered the church and saw the bed in all its splendour, with the knight asleep on it. And while they were gazing in awe and alarm at these princely jewels, keeping well back from the bed, the effect of Torello's potion wore off and he awoke with a great sigh, which sent the abbot and monks all scuttling off in a panic, crying 'God help us!' Torello opened his eyes, looked about him, and easily recognized that he was right where he had asked Saladin to leave him, which was a great relief. So he sat up and made a detailed scrutiny of all the objects beside him on the bed; and though he had already experienced the measure of Saladin's generosity, he realized that till this moment he had not known the half of it. None the less, as he heard the monks running away and realized why, he stayed as he was and called the abbot by name, entreating him not to be frightened, because he was Torello, his nephew. This only alarmed the abbot the more, for he believed his nephew had died months ago. Eventually, however, he was reassured by the soundness of Torello's arguments and, on being summoned yet again, crossed himself and approached.

'Father', said Torello, 'why so anxious? I am alive, thank God, and here I am back from across the sea.'

Though Torello wore a bushy beard and Saracen dress, the abbot recognized him after a while. Quite reassured now, he took his hand and told him: 'Welcome back, my son. You should not be surprised', he added, 'if we were afraid: there's not a soul here but is convinced that you're dead, to the point that your wife Adalieta has finally given way to the entreaties and threats of her kinsfolk and is, much against her will, engaged to be married again. It's this morning that she is to be united to her new husband—the wedding ceremony and the feast are all prepared.'

Torello rose from his opulent bed and extended the heartiest greeting to the abbot and his monks, but asked them all to say not a word to anybody about his return until he had attended to something that needed doing. He had the precious stones put away in a safe place, then gave the abbot an account of his adventures up to this point. The abbot rejoiced at Torello's good fortune and they both gave thanks to God. Torello then asked the abbot who it was who was to marry his wife, and the abbot told him.

'Before news of my homecoming gets out', said Torello to the abbot, 'I mean to see how my wife is taking this new celebration. I know it is not customary for the clergy to attend such functions but do please for my sake arrange admittance for the two of us.'

'Willingly', replied the abbot and, when it was fully day, he sent to the bridegroom to say that he should like to attend the celebration with a friend of his. The groom pronounced himself delighted. So when it was time for the wedding breakfast, Torello, dressed as he was, proceeded with the abbot to the bridegroom's house, where everyone goggled at him but no one recognized him. The abbot explained to everyone that he was a saracen on an embassy from the sultan to the King of France. So Torello was given a seat at table right opposite his wife. He gazed upon her with enormous pleasure, and it seemed to him that she was not looking all that happy about this wedding. She too glanced at him from time to time, not because she recognized him at all—his bushy beard and foreign attire and her firm conviction that he was dead quite precluded that—but because his dress was so exotic.

When Torello felt the moment had come to test his wife's recognition, he took in his hand the ring she had given him on his departure, and summoned a page who was waiting on her. 'Give the bride this message', he instructed him, 'that in my part of the world we have a custom whereby should a foreigner, such as I am, eat at the table of a bride, as she is, she takes the goblet from which she has been drinking and sends it to him filled with wine, as a token of her appreciation that he has come to partake of her meal. And when the stranger has drunk his fill from the goblet, he puts its lid back and the bride drinks what is left.'

The boy carried the message to the lady who, being a woman of tact and breeding, and taking the gentleman for a man of some consequence, showed her appreciation of his visit by picking up a large gold cup set before her and having it washed and brought to the gentleman after being filled with wine. Torello slipped her ring into his mouth and transferred it into the cup as he drank; nobody noticed him doing so. Then he put the lid back on and sent the cup back to the lady with a little wine still left in it. She took it and, in order to fulfil his custom, lifted off the lid, set the cup to her lips, and noticed the ring. Without a word she looked it over and recognized it for the one she had given to her husband on his departure; so she took it in her hand and stared at the man she imagined to be a foreigner, and she recognized him. Then, as if she had gone berserk, she pushed over the table at which she sat and shouted: 'There's my husband, there's Torello, that's him!' So she dashed to the table at which he sat and threw herself across it with no thought for the tablecloth or anything placed on it, and hugged him tightly, nor could any of them, do or say what they might, prise her off his neck until Torello himself told her to take a grip on herself, for they would yet have ample leisure to embrace.

The wedding was now in total disarray, though for a good proportion of the participants it was all the merrier now that such a knight as Torello was restored to them. Anyway, his wife stood back and he asked everybody to be silent, then related all that had befallen him from the day he had left up to the present moment; he ended by saying that the gentleman who had engaged to marry his wife in the belief that he was dead should not take it amiss if, as he was still alive, he reclaimed her. The bridegroom, albeit somewhat put out of countenance, answered magnanimously and as a friend that Torello was at perfect liberty to do what he liked with what belonged to him. Torello's wife left behind the ring and the crown presented to her by the bridegroom, and put on the ring she had found in the cup, and also the crown sent to her by the sultan. They left the bridegroom's house and returned in the full pomp of the wedding to their own home, where they held a long and happy celebration to lift the hearts of their friends who had been grieving, and their relatives and the whole city, all of whom looked at Torello as if a miracle had befallen him. Torello gave a share of his precious gems to the man who had borne the expense of the wedding, and a share to the abbot and to many others. He conveyed news of his happy homecoming by more than one messenger to Saladin, whose friend and servant he considered himself to be. And for years afterwards he lived with his excellent spouse, growing ever more open-handed in his hospitality.

Thus it was that the misadventures of Torello and his dear wife came to an end, and they were rewarded for their open-hearted and ready kindness. Many folk seek to do as much, but although such munificence lies within their power, they set about it so clumsily that they first effectively extort a price out of all proportion to their gift—little wonder if they receive a scant reward!

X. 10. *The Marquis of Saluzzo, who has no time for women, marries a poor peasant girl, Griselda, and abuses her atrociously to prove that his prejudice is well founded. How Griselda's patience proves more than a match for him.*

When the king had told his lengthy tale, to the evident enjoyment of all present, Dioneo observed with a chuckle: 'The honest fellow who was looking forward to meeting the phantom cat that next night and putting its perky tail down for it,* *he* wouldn't have given a brass farthing for the praises you've been heaping on Torello!' Realizing that only he was left to narrate, he continued:

It seems to me, my gentle ladies, that today has been given over to kings and sultans and others of that ilk; consequently, as I don't mean to stray too far from you, my tale will be about a marquis. His was not an act of liberality, it was the work of an utter brute, even though it came out all right in the end. And I'm not suggesting that anyone should do as he did: it ended happily enough for him, and more's the pity.

A long time ago the eldest son of the Saluzzo family was the Marquis Gualtieri, a young bachelor without issue of his own, who devoted his time entirely to his hawking and hunting; it never crossed his mind to marry and have children—the wise man! His subjects, however, did not care for this, and frequently pressed him to take a wife to ensure that he was not left without an heir nor they without a master. They offered to find him one whose qualities and pedigree offered good prospects and would wholly satisfy him.

Gualtieri's reply to them was: 'My friends, you would force me to do what I had quite made up my mind never to do, considering how hard it is to find a woman whose character makes her a suitable match and, conversely, what a crowd of women there are who wouldn't do at all; besides, what a hideous life a man endures if he's saddled with an unsuitable wife! And it's utterly absurd for you to tell me you feel you can weigh a girl up by reference to her father and mother, and thus expect to give me one to my liking. How are you supposed to know the father? How will you discover the mother's secrets? And what if you could?—daughters are often quite different to their fathers and mothers. However, if you really must fasten these chains on me, so be it; but to avoid my having anyone but myself to blame if it goes wrong, I myself will find her—and, whoever it is I choose, take care to respect her as your sovereign lady or you'll learn very much to your cost what my feelings are about marrying against my own inclination but only to satisfy yours.' So long as he married, said his honest subjects, they would ask for nothing better.

Now Gualtieri had long been taken with a penniless young girl from a neighbouring village; she was a real beauty, he thought, and with her he could expect a trouble-free life. So he looked no further but settled upon her and, sending for her father, arranged with him—a quite destitute man—to take his daughter to wife.

This done, Gualtieri assembled all his friends in the locality and said to them: 'It has been, and remains, your pleasure that I consent to marry and I have so consented, more as a favour to you than out of any personal wish to be possessed of a wife. You know the promise you made to me, to be satisfied with whomever I took to wife, and to respect her accordingly as your liege lady. Now as the time has come for me to honour my word to you, you must keep yours to me. I have found a girl after my own heart; she is a close neighbour and I propose to marry her and bring her home a few days hence. So you're to see to preparing a splendid wedding feast and to welcoming her with befitting dignity: that way I shall be satisfied that you have observed your word as you may be that I've kept mine.'

The good folk all expressed themselves delighted; whoever he chose, she would in all things be accepted and honoured as their lady. They then set about preparing a truly grand, beautiful, and festive wedding, and Gualtieri did likewise. He had the finest nuptial celebrations set in train and invited many of his friends, relations, and persons of consequence and others in the neighbourhood. He had several fine, rich dresses made up to the measurements of a young woman who was, he thought, of the same build as the girl he was to marry. Furthermore he made ready plenty of girdles, rings, and a beautiful coronet and whatever else a bride needed.

When the day he had appointed for the wedding arrived, Gualtieri, along with everyone who had come to attend the function, mounted horse a little past nine o'clock. Everything now being prepared, he said: 'Gentlemen, it's time to go and fetch the bride.' And off he rode with all his company to the village. They came to the house of the girl's father and found her hastening back with water from the spring: she wanted to join a crowd of women going to watch the arrival of Gualtieri's bride. When Gualtieri saw her he called her by name—it was Griselda—and asked her where her father was. 'He's at home, sir', she bashfully replied.

So Gualtieri dismounted, told everyone to wait there, and went alone into the hovel, where he found her father, whose name was Giannucolo. 'I've come to wed Griselda', he said. 'But first I want to find something out from her in your presence.' He asked her whether, if he took her for his wife, she would always strive to please him and never object to anything he did or said, and whether she would be obedient, and a whole lot of other things; to each one of which she answered yes. So Gualtieri took her by the hand, led her outside, and had her stripped naked in the presence of all his retinue and the entire crowd; he sent for the clothes he had had made for her and had her quickly dressed and shod, and a coronet placed upon her tousled head. This done, to the bewilderment of all present, he said: 'This, gentlemen, is the woman I propose to make my wife, if she wishes me for her husband.' He turned to her then, as she stood there blushing, her heart in her mouth, and asked: 'Griselda, would you like me for your husband?'

'Yes, sir', said she.

'And I should like you for my wife.' And in the presence of all the company he plighted his troth, then had her mount a palfrey and brought her home under honourable escort. Here the wedding celebrations and the feast were as sumptuous and elaborate as though he had given his hand to the daughter of the French king.

With her change of clothing the young bride appeared to change inwardly, too, and to alter her comportment. She was, as we said, a shapely lass with a pretty face; and just as she was pretty, she became so capable, so engaging and attractive in her manner, she looked far less like the daughter of Giannucolo, a girl who looked after the sheep, than like the scion of some noble house. Anybody who had known her before was most surprised. She was, moreover, so obedient and attentive to her husband that he considered himself the most satisfied, most contented of men. Towards her husband's subjects, too, she was so gracious and kind that she acquired the devotion of one and all and their unstinting respect. Everyone called down blessings on her and prayed for her prosperity. If earlier they had decried Gualtieri for an ill-considered choice of bride, now they were all applauding him as the wisest, shrewdest man in the world, as none but he could ever have suspected the abounding merits concealed beneath her poor peasant's garb. In a word, it was not long before she had effectively inspired the whole world—and not merely the neighbourhood under her husband's rule—to speak of her qualities and her exemplary conduct; she also confuted any who might have criticized her husband at the time he married her. They had not been long together when she became pregnant and in the course of time gave birth to a little girl, much to Gualtieri's delight.

But, a little while later, he took it into his head to test her patience by an experiment to be carried out over a long term; he meant to try her to the limit of endurance, and began by carping at her querulously and feigning displeasure on the grounds that his subjects were thoroughly discontented with her: she was, after all, a plebeian, and seeing that she was giving him children only made matters worse. They were deeply upset over the daughter she had borne and could do nothing but grumble.

As kindly disposed and unruffled as ever, Griselda replied: 'Pray, sir, do with me whatever you think best for your honour and peace of mind; I shall be quite content, for I know I am of lower birth than they and that I'm not worthy of this honour to which, out of your kindness, you have called me.' Gualtieri found this answer most satisfactory, for he could see that the respect he or anyone else had paid her had not turned her head.

Shortly after that, he intimated to his wife that his people could not abide the daughter she had produced for him; then he instructed a retainer of his and despatched him to her. 'Madam', he said to her with a very long face, 'if I'm not to die, I have to do as my lord bids me. He has ordered me to take this daughter of yours and . . .' He did not go on.

Hearing this, and seeing the look on the man's face, and remembering, too, what Gualtieri had said to her, she understood that the man had been ordered to kill the child. So she promptly took the baby out of her cradle, kissed her and blessed her, and placed her in the man's arms without turning a hair, for all that she was sick at heart. 'Here', she said, 'do exactly what your master and mine has commanded. But don't leave her to be devoured by the birds and beasts, unless he commands you to do so.' The retainer took the child and reported to Gualtieri what Griselda had said. He was amazed at her constancy, and sent the man with the baby to a kinswoman of his in Bologna with the request that she would take care to raise and educate the child without ever divulging whose daughter she was.

Griselda conceived a second time, and when she came to term she gave birth to a boy, which made Gualtieri very happy. And yet, not content with what he had already done, he inveighed even more ferociously against her and, feigning utter fury, said to her one day: 'Ever since you produced this boy I've not had a moment's peace from my subjects: they're complaining most bitterly at having to have a grandson of Giannucolo ruling in my place after I'm gone. If I'm not to be driven out, I fear that I'll have to deal with him as I dealt with the girl last time, and eventually be rid of you and take another wife.'

She listened to him with great forbearance and all she said was: 'Just think of your own needs, sir, and your own satisfaction, and don't bother yourself at all about me: there's only one thing that I care about and that is your happiness.'

Not many days later Gualtieri sent for the boy just as he had sent for the girl and similarly pretended to have him killed, while actually sending the baby to be raised in Bologna as he had done with the girl. Griselda showed no more emotion than she had done in the case of the girl, and spoke in the same fashion. This left Gualtieri not a little astonished, and he concluded that there was not another woman who could have taken it as she was doing; indeed, were it not that he had observed the affection she had lavished on her children while he had tolerated them, he would have assumed that her behaviour stemmed from indifference. He recognized, however, that her motives were sublime. His subjects believed that he had indeed had the children murdered and considered him a cruel man; they reproached him bitterly, while feeling profoundly sorry for his wife. And all she would ever say in answer to the womenfolk who condoled with her over the death of her children was that whatever pleased the man who begot them pleased her too.

Several years had elapsed since the birth of the little girl when it seemed to Gualtieri that the time had come to set Griselda's long-sufferance to a final test. So he put it about that he could no longer tolerate the woman for his wife and admitted that in marrying her he had acted with the recklessness of youth. He was going to see, if possible, to obtaining a dispensation from the Pope to relinquish Griselda and take another wife. This brought down upon him strong recriminations from many a good man, but he was content to reply that that was the way it had to be. When this came to Griselda's ears she could see herself having to return to her father's house and perhaps revert to minding the sheep as she had done before; she could anticipate seeing another woman possessed of the man to whom she had devoted all her love, and she wept inwardly. But still, just as she had endured the previous blows of Fortune, so did she put on a brave face to confront this latest one.

A little while later Gualtieri arranged for dummy letters to reach him from Rome and passed these off to his subjects as a papal dispensation to repudiate Griselda and take another wife. So he summoned her to him in the presence of a crowd of people and told her: 'The Pope has given me a dispensation to be rid of you and marry another wife. And as my ancestors have all been gentlemen of good breeding and high estate in these parts, whereas yours have never been anything but labourers, I don't intend to retain you any longer as my spouse. You're to return to Giannucolo's with whatever dowry you brought me, and I shall replace you here with another woman I've found who is more suitable.'

It took her a supreme effort, generally beyond the capacity of her sex, to check her tears when she heard this. 'I have always been aware, sir', she said, 'that my humble condition was not at all suited to your nobility. And I have always known that the position I have held with you has been entirely due to the Good Lord and to you. I never did regard it as my possession, as something given to me, but always as something lent to me. May it please you to take it back, as I must be content, and am content, to return it to you. Here is your ring, with which you wedded me. Take it. Bid me take away with me the dowry I brought to you. To do this you'll not need any treasurer, and I'll need no purse to put it in, no animal on which to load it, because I have not forgotten that when you received me I was naked. And if you think it is suitable for everyone to see me naked, though mine is the body which carried the children you begot, then I shall leave naked; but I do beseech you, in reward for the virginity which I brought to you and leave behind, let me keep but one chemise over and above my dowry, to take away with me.'

Gualtieri, whose strongest urge at this moment was to cry, remained stony-faced, but said: 'Very well. Keep one chemise.'

The bystanders all begged him to let her keep a dress: the woman who had been his wife for more than thirteen years should not have to leave the house in the squalid, humiliating manner implied by going away in nothing but her chemise. As their pleas fell on deaf ears, Griselda bade them goodbye and left the house barefoot, bareheaded, and clad in only a chemise, to return to her father while all the onlookers wept. Giannucolo never had been able to believe that Gualtieri really would keep his daughter as wife, and was in daily expectation of this eventuality, so he had kept the clothes stripped off her the morning of her wedding to Gualtieri. He brought them to her, therefore, and she put them on and set about the little household tasks just as she had formerly done for her father, stoically enduring the brutal assault of hostile Fortune.

This done, Gualtieri intimated to his people that he had betrothed himself to a daughter of one of the counts of Panago. He set in hand elaborate preparations for the wedding, and sent for Griselda. When she arrived he told her: 'I'm about to bring home my newly affianced lady and propose to receive her with proper ceremony. As you're aware, I have no women in this house who are capable of getting the rooms ready for me or doing the thousand and one things that such occasions require. Now as you are better than anyone else at these domestic duties, see to having these preparations made, and draw up the women's guest-list as you see fit. Then welcome them here as if you were still mistress of the household. When the wedding is over, you can go home.'

These words were so many daggers in the heart of Griselda, who had never been able to get over her love for him the way she had succeeded in sloughing off her good fortune. Nevertheless, 'I'm ready and willing, sir', she said. In she came in her coarse peasant attire, into the house she had but recently left wearing nothing but a chemise, and set to work. She swept out and tidied the bedrooms, prepared the arrases for hanging, and the drapes to go over the chairs in the public rooms; she had everything made ready in the kitchens and busied herself all over the place as though she were a little parlourmaid, never stopping for breath until all was absolutely the way it had to be.

After this, she invited all the local ladies on Gualtieri's behalf, then waited for the celebration. The wedding-day arrived and, dressed though she was in the plainest, most rustic attire, she offered a cheerful welcome to the ladies as they came, and conducted herself as a person of true breeding. Gualtieri had taken the greatest care to have the children brought up by his kinswoman in Bologna—she herself was a countess married into the house of the Panagos—and by now the girl would be 12 and the prettiest thing you ever saw, while the boy was 6. He sent word to his kinsman, the foster-father, requesting him to come to Saluzzo bringing this daughter and son of his with him, and arranging for a splendid, dignified retinue to accompany him. He was to put it about that he was bringing the girl to be Gualtieri's bride, and not drop the slightest hint to anyone as to her true identity. The gentleman did as requested by the marquis and set out with the girl and her brother and a noble escort. At dinner-time a few days later he reached Saluzzo where he found the townsfolk and any number of people from the neighbourhood all waiting to receive Gualtieri's bride. The bride was welcomed by the ladies and led into the hall where the tables were laid; here Griselda came forward, just as she was, and warmly greeted her: 'A hearty welcome, my lady!' The womenfolk had persistently urged Gualtieri to allow Griselda to remain in a room outside, or else to lend her one of the dresses she used to possess, to avoid her having to appear before his guests attired as she was; but it was all in vain. Now they were invited to take their seats at table and the meal was served. The men all gazed at the girl and said that Gualtieri had made a good exchange; but Griselda, too, heaped praises on her, as also on her little brother.

Gualtieri felt that he had now seen all he wanted of his wife's constancy. This latest turn of affairs made no difference, he saw, to her attitude—a fact which, as he very well knew, could not be ascribed to feeble-mindedness, for he recognized that she was no fool. So he felt the time had come to deliver her from her grief which he imagined she must be concealing behind a brave face. He sent for her, therefore, and asked her with a smile in the presence of the whole company: 'Well? What d'you think of our bride?'

'I find her ever so nice, sir, and if she's as good as she's pretty—and I expect she is—I'm sure you'll not have a single thing to complain about in her. But one thing I do beg of you: don't hurt her the way you hurt the wife you had before. I scarcely think she'd be able to stand it, because she is younger and has been gently nurtured, while your last wife was brought up in hardship ever since she was a little girl.'

Seeing that Griselda was convinced the girl was to be his wife and yet had nothing but good to say of her, Gualtieri sat her down beside him. 'The time has come, Griselda', he said, 'for you to enjoy the fruits of your endurance, and for the people who've considered me a cruel and wicked ogre to realize that all I've done I've done with a particular end in view. I meant to teach you to be a wife and to teach them to accept you loyally. I wanted to assure myself of perpetual tranquillity so long as I lived with you. When I came to marry, I very much feared I should enjoy no peace, which is why I tested you out with all the various afflictions you'll recollect. Now as I've never known an occasion when you went against my wishes, either in word or deed, it seems to me I'll be as comfortable with you as I could ever have wanted, and I propose to restore to you at a stroke all that I've wrenched from you over the years, and to apply the gentlest balm to the wounds I inflicted upon you. So cheer up and accept this girl, whom you imagine to be my bride, and her brother: they are our children, whom you and many others have long assumed to have been butchered at my hands. And I am your husband and love you above all else: I believe I can boast that there is not another man who can be so satisfied with his wife as I am.'

Saying this, he hugged and kissed her, then drew her to her feet and went with her, as she wept for joy, over to where their daughter was sitting—the girl could scarcely believe her ears. They gave her a tender embrace, and her brother as well. Thus was she finally undeceived, as were many others here present. The ladies were overjoyed. They left the table and took Griselda into a room, where they stripped off her beggarly wear—under happier auspices than they had done on that earlier occasion—and dressed her in one of her more sumptuous gowns; then they led her back to the company attired as lady of the house, not that she seemed anything less even in her old rags. Here she celebrated her wonderful reunion with her children; everyone was overjoyed at this turn of events and they all prolonged the celebrations for days afterwards. They considered that Gualtieri had been remarkably astute, even if they felt the way he had put his wife to the test had been excessive and wellnigh intolerable. Above all, they agreed that Griselda had shown herself a paragon of goodness. The Count of Panago returned a few days later to Bologna. And Gualtieri relieved Giannucolo of his peasant labours and set him up in a condition suitable to a gentleman's father-in-law; he lived out the rest of his declining years in dignity and comfort. He made a noble match for his daughter, and lived a long and happy life with Griselda, to whom he paid every possible regard.

What are we to say, then, if not that heaven rains forth sublime souls even on to the hovels of the poor, just as it showers the palaces of the mighty with spirits better suited to herding swine than to ruling men? Who but Griselda would have been capable of enduring the cruelties, the utterly incredible ordeals imposed by Gualtieri, with never a tear shed, nay, with a cheerful face? As for him, it would maybe have served him right if he'd saddled himself with a wife who, the moment he turned her out of the house in her chemise, went off and insinuated herself into a nice new dress provided by a lover who could ride her better.

Dioneo's story was ended and occasioned considerable discussion among the ladies—some taking one line, others the opposite, as they found one element or another that earned their censure or approval. Then the king looked up and noticed that the sun was setting and evening was upon them. Without leaving his seat he addressed them as follows: 'I believe you comely ladies are well enough aware that human wisdom does not reside simply in the recollection of things past or an acquaintance with the present: men of the highest intellect believe that it makes the greatest sense to base upon such knowledge a prediction of the future. Tomorrow, as you know, will be the fifteenth day since we left Florence in search of a little recreation, the better to preserve our health and our lives, turning our backs on all the affliction, the pain and misery that was constantly before our eyes from the first moment the plague possessed the city. We have, in my judgement, pursued our entertainment virtuously for, unless my eyes have deceived me, I have not once noticed either on you ladies' part or on ours one single action or word that might attract censure, for all that we told high-spirited tales that might have been an invitation to lechery, and we always ate and drank to our hearts' content, and we played music and sang songs—all activities that might have led the weaker brethren to compromise their virtue. What I seemed to observe was constant modesty, constant harmony, unfailing goodwill—and on this I cannot set too high a value, for it does you honour and stands you and me in good stead. Now, in case our present life should go stale with repetition and give rise to something noxious, and to allay criticism over our extended absence, and as we now have all shared for a day in the eminence that is still vested in me, it would seem to me, subject to your approval, that we should do well to return whence we came. Besides, if you take a look around you, you'll notice that our party is the talk of the neighbourhood and might start giving rise to imitators who would quite spoil our fun. So if you like my idea, I shall retain the crown allotted to me until we leave, which I propose should be tomorrow morning. Should you decide otherwise, I have my candidate ready on whom the crown will devolve.'

After considerable discussion, the ladies and the young men finally concluded that what the king proposed made good sense and they decided to act upon his suggestion. So he summoned the major-domo and gave him his instructions for the following morning; then he dismissed the company until supper-time and stood up. The ladies and gentlemen followed their usual practice when they too got up, and set off in pursuit of their various amusements. Came supper-time and, after a most enjoyable meal, they embarked on a round of singing and music-making and country-dancing, until Lauretta was leading a dance and the king bade Fiammetta sing a song to it. So she began her song, quite enchantingly:

If I might love possess
With jealousy untainted,
There'd be no woman born
With bliss like mine acquainted.

If any woman's heart
To buoyant youth responded,
To manly valour, pluck,
And strength with prowess bonded;

If wisdom earned my grace
And gallantry and verve,
Then let me be the one
These riches to deserve.

But I am not alone
In aiming at perfection,
For other women too
Aspire to his affection.
I tremble with alarm,
For that which makes my joy
May, slipping from my grasp,
My comfort quite destroy.

If I could but perceive
In my beloved's soul
A loyalty to match
His virtues as a whole . . .
But with so many ladies
For him to pick and choose
I'm heartsick with mistrust
For fear my love I'll lose.

So, sisters, pray forbear
To catch my loved one's eye,
For should I come to know of it
You'll rue your smallest sigh.
I'd sooner lose my radiance
And chill my heart to ice
Than let you steal my gallant
And not exact the price.

As Fiammetta ended her song, Dioneo, who sat beside her, remarked to her with a chuckle: 'You would do a considerable kindness if you revealed your beloved's identity to all your sisters, in case he were stolen from you unwittingly, which would surely infuriate you.' They sang many more songs after that, and when night had run wellnigh half its course, they all retired to sleep, at the king's pleasure.

As the new day dawned they arose; the major-domo had sent all their baggage on ahead, and the party returned to Florence under the leadership of their capable king. The three young men left the seven young women at Santa Maria Novella, their starting-point, bade them farewell, and continued about their business, while those ladies returned home at their leisure.

## AUTHOR'S AFTERWORD

I do believe that I have wholly accomplished the task I undertook, at the opening of this book, to fulfil; this have I done with the help of divine grace, so it seems to me, and thanks to the encouragement of your prayers, most noble young ladies to whose solace I have devoted myself by engaging in so extensive a labour, rather than owing to any merits of my own. I therefore give thanks first to the Good Lord and then to you ladies, now that the time has come to lay down my pen and put my exhausted hand to rest. But I cannot allow them to rest before I have replied briefly to certain small matters—unspoken questions, as it were—that some of you ladies, or others, might raise, not that I am by any means of the opinion that such questions deserve special prominence, though I do recall not having addressed them at all in the opening to the fourth day.

Conceivably some of you ladies will observe that in writing these stories I have made a little too free, occasionally putting into my ladies' mouths, and frequently having them listen to, things that no reputable woman should say or hear. This I deny: nothing is too unseemly for utterance in polite company if it is delivered in polite language—and it seems to me I found the proper tone. But let us suppose it is as you say, I have no intention of getting into an argument with you—you would be sure to win. I can readily summon up any number of reasons to explain what I have done. To begin with, supposing there *were* anything off-colour in any of the stories; the nature of those stories required it, and any reasonable person considering the matter objectively would readily grant that there was no other way in which I could have told them without distorting them out of their proper form. And what if there were some tiny hint of ribaldry, the odd little word that perhaps might ill become your dyed-in-the-wool prude?—for that sort of woman sets greater store by words than by deeds and takes greater pains to appear virtuous than to be so. I still maintain that there was nothing improper in my writing such things, any more than there is in men and women coming out all day long with words like 'hole', 'peg', 'pestle and mortar', and so forth.

Besides, my pen should be accorded no smaller licence than is granted to the brush of the painter who attracts no criticism—at any rate, no justified criticism—if he shows Saint Michael piercing the serpent with a sword or lance, and Saint George striking the dragon here, there, and everywhere, and, what is more, if he portrays Christ as a male and Eve as a female; why, he will stick sometimes a single nail, sometimes two, through the feet of the One who was ready to die for the salvation of human kind, to fasten Him to the cross.

It is perfectly obvious, furthermore, that these discussions were not held in church, where all speech has to conform to purity of heart and chastity of language—for all that, within those hallowed precincts you will come across plenty of stories considerably more scurrilous than mine. Nor were they held in the Philosophy Schools, in which virtue is no less requisite than elsewhere; nor were the participants clergymen or philosophers. The discourses were held in gardens, places devoted to pleasure, and the participants were young people, though not immature nor readily influenced by stories; and the times were such that no offence was given by people—highly respectable folk—who went about with a pair of breeches wrapped about their heads as a precaution. Now whether those stories, for what they are worth (indeed whether anything of any description) prove wholesome or noxious depends entirely on the hearer. We know that wine is highly beneficial to sound constitutions—we have it on the authority of Messrs Bacchus and Silenus, to name only two—but it is harmful to those with fever. Are we going to condemn it because it injures the ague-ridden? And fire, fire is undeniably an asset, indeed vital to human life. Are we going to condemn it because it burns down houses and villages and entire cities? Again, weapons safeguard those who wish to live in peace, but they also slay people all too often, and not because those weapons are evil—the evil resides in those setting hand to them. To the corrupt mind nothing is pure: and just as the corrupt derive no profit from virtuous conversation, so the virtuous cannot be corrupted by a touch of wantonness, any more than the sun's rays or the beauties of heaven may be contaminated by mud or earthy squalor. What books, what words, what letters are vested with greater holiness, excellence, and dignity than those of Holy Scripture? And yet plenty of people have put a false construction on them and procured their own and others' damnation. There is nothing but will not possess an innate value within a given framework, and yet it may prove in many ways injurious if it is abused—and the same goes for my stories. If a person is determined upon perverted thoughts or evil deeds and derives them from my stories, they will not prevent him from doing so if that is what he can see in them and he distorts and misconstrues them to his ends; and should a person look for a solid benefit from them, they will not deny it him, nor will they be considered or said to be other than beneficial and innocuous provided they are read on those occasions and by those persons for whom they have been narrated. Anyone who needs to attend to her rosary or prepare a black pudding or bake a cake for her confessor—well, she does not have to read them: they do not go running after people insisting on being read, for all that even your prudes will occasionally come out with or get up to some funny things!

Some ladies will also say that certain stories have been included that would have been far better omitted. I'll not deny it: but how was I, indeed how could I, set down any story but those narrated? It was up to those who told them to make them unexceptionable, and I should have written them down unexceptionably. But even supposing that it was I who invented those stories and was their author (which I was not), I still would not apologize if not every one of them was unimpeachable: after all, there's not a craftsman, leaving God aside, who has made every last thing quite flawlessly. Take Charlemagne, who created the paladins: he was unable to make enough of them to constitute an army on their own. Numbers will necessarily give rise to diversity. There never was a plot so well tilled that not a single nettle, thorn, or bramble could be found growing amid the good crop. Anyway, my audience were unsophisticated young lasses, as most of you ladies are, and it would have been rather silly for me to have gone rooting about in search of all sorts of refinements and gone to great lengths in choosing my words. At all events, anybody dipping into these tales is invited to skip the bothersome ones and read those that are enjoyable; to avoid leading anyone astray, each story is introduced by a description of what lies hidden within it.†

I fancy, moreover, I shall be told that some of the stories go on too long. My answer to that is that if people have better things to do, there would be little sense in their reading these stories even if they were only short. A great deal of time has elapsed between my starting on my narrative and this moment that brings me close to the end of my labours, but even so, never have I overlooked the fact that I have devoted my toil to ladies of leisure, not to the others; the person who reads as a pastime will not deem anything to be of excessive length so long as it achieves what the reader requires of it. Brevity is far better suited to students, whose efforts are directed not to filling their leisure but to using their time to the best advantage, than it is to you ladies, for whom any time is spare that you are not devoting to your amours. Besides, as none of you are pursuing your studies at Athens, Bologna, or Paris, there is a case for spelling things out for you at greater length than is necessary for those whose minds have been sharpened in the schools.

I have no doubt, either, that some of you will be telling me that the thing is too facetious and loaded with quips to have come suitably from the pen of a mature, responsible man. To such ladies I owe a vote of thanks, and indeed I am grateful to them, for they are moved by a tender concern for my reputation. Here's how I should answer their objections: I shan't deny that I'm a mature man and have often acted maturely in my day. So let me address myself to those ladies who find me immature and assure them that solemn I am not—I'm no more weighty than a bobbing cork. Now if you consider that friars, in their sermons castigating men's iniquities, are forever resorting to quips and jokes and tomfoolery, it seemed to me that such things would not come amiss in my

† Well, more or less—but please refer to the Note on page xxxiii. (Trans.)

stories which were, after all, written to raise the spirits of women who were down in the dumps. Still, should these jokes give rise to too much mirth, the remedy is ready to hand—in the Lamentations of Jeremiah, the narratives of Our Lord's Passion, and the Complaint of Mary Magdalen.

And who is going to be anxious to discover some ladies to proclaim that I keep a wicked, poisonous tongue in my head, because there are places where I come out with home-truths about the friars? We must be indulgent with those who speak in this manner, for they are undoubtedly inspired by the fairest motives: the friars are, after all, good people; they avoid hardship for the love of God, and where women are concerned they hold their fire and keep mum about it; their conversation would be a positive pleasure were it not for the faint odour of billy-goat* they give off. However I do admit that the things of this world are wholly lacking in stability and are in a constant state of flux—and this is precisely what may have happened with my tongue. I place little reliance on my own judgement—indeed, so far as I am concerned, I take care to steer clear of it; but a lady who lives in my neighbourhood remarked to me only the other day that, when it comes to tongues, I have one of the best and most endearing in the world. And the fact is, when she said this, I had not many of these stories left to write. Now as the women who take this line speak out of animus, I should like to limit my reply to what I have just said.

And so it is time for me to write my last word, leaving you ladies free to say and think whatever you wish; and I humbly thank the Lord for His help in bringing me to the end I have sought after so lengthy a labour. And you, most amiable ladies, may peace be with you by God's grace, and may you bear me in your thoughts if any of you have derived the smallest profit from reading what I have written.

*Here ends the tenth and last day of the book called* Decameron, *known also as the* Book of Prince Galehaut.

# EXPLANATORY NOTES

3 *Prince Galehaut*: 'Lord of the Far Isles' in the prose *Lancelot*, who helped Lancelot woo Guinevere: Boccaccio is referring here to the passage in Dante, *Inferno* V, where Francesca brands the *Lancelot* romance as a an erotic go-between.

14 *Galen, Hippocrates, and Aesculapius*: two Greek doctors of antiquity, proverbial for their skill by the Middle Ages, and the Greek god of medicine.

14 *Santa Maria Novella*: major Florentine church, famous at the time for its preachers.

15 *Pampinea . . . Elissa*: *Pampinea*: 'sprouting' or 'lively' (also found in *Comedia delle ninfe*); *Fiammetta*: 'little flame' (also found in several of his earlier works, and heroine of the *Elegia di madonna Fiammetta*); *Philomena*: 'songstress' or perhaps 'beloved' (also found in *Filostrato*); *Emilia*: 'flatterer' (also found in *Teseida*); *Lauretta*: 'little laurel' (Petrarch's *senhal*, or symbolic beloved, in the *Canzoniere*); *Neiphile*: 'new love' (generic reference to *stilnovismo*—see Introduction); *Elissa*: other name for Dido in Virgil's *Aeneid*.

18 *Pamphilo . . . Dioneo*: *Pamphilo*: 'all love' or 'love all' (the fickle lover in the *Elegia di madonna Fiammetta*); *Philostrato*: 'love-stricken' (the unlucky protagonist of the *Filostrato*); Dioneo: 'venereal' (reference to the erotic allegories of the *Comedia delle ninfe fiorentine*).

21 *Parmeno*: this and the other servants' names are traditionally 'literary' names for plebeian characters in Roman comedy and satire.

24 *Charles Sansterre*: Charles of Valois, brother of Philip the Fair (1268–1314).

24 *Boniface VIII*: pope from 1294 to 1303, whose relations with the French monarchy were frequently difficult.

39 *Saladin*: Salah al-Din al-Ayyubi (1138–93), sultan of Syria and Egypt who defended Islam against the crusaders: a byword, even in the West, for chivalry (see also X. 9).

39 *Babylon*: common medieval appellation for Cairo.

46 *Gonfalonier*: 'standard-bearer', often a high official.

46 *Philip Augustus*: Philip II of France (1165–1223), one of the leaders of the Third Crusade (1189–92).

48 *with swords and staves*': Matthew 26: 47.

49 *St John Moneypenny*: golden florins featured a portrait of a bearded John the Baptist.

49 *Epicurus*: Greek philosopher (341–270 BC), regarded in the Middle Ages as an atheistic promoter of unrestrained sensualism; see Dante, *Inferno* X.

49 *yellow cross*: traditionally sewn to clothes as a sign of penance.

49 *Santa Croce*: Franciscan convent in Florence, seat of the Inquisition.

49 *Ye shall receive a hundredfold . . . everlasting life*: Matthew 19: 29.

51 *Cangrande della Scala*: lord of Verona (1291–1329), celebrated by Dante (*Paradiso* XVII).

51 *Frederick II*: Holy Roman Emperor (1194–1250), renowned for his liberality, though much libelled by Guelph apologists.

52 *Primasso*: legendary composer of goliardic songs.

52 *Cluny*: French Benedictine abbey, renowned for its fabulous wealth.

55 *Guglielmo Borsiere*: Boccaccio was probably inspired by Dante, who names Guglielmo as an example of vanished chivalric values in *Inferno* XVI.

57 *first King of Cyprus*: Guy of Lusignan, whose reign (1192–4) was synonymous with appeasement and vacillation.

57 *Godfrey of Bouillon's conquest*: famous for his capture of Jerusalem (1099) during the First Crusade.

62 *pleasure . . . profit*: see Horace, *Ars poetica*, 333 ff. ('Poets wish either to profit or to delight . . .').

65 *Arrigo*: Blessed Henry of Treviso (d. 1315), reputedly the author of many miracles (including the bell-ringing mentioned here).

67 *Podestà*: governor of the town.

69 *Saint Julian*: Julian the Hospitaller, traditionally invoked for safe journeys and 'room at the inn'.

69 *Marquis Azzo*: probably Azzo VIII (d. 1308).

70 *Dirupisti . . . De Profundis*: slightly garbled versions of genuine Latin prayers: they are probably used here as criminal slang for beatings, threats, and murder respectively.

70 *Castel Guglielmo*: small town between Ferrara and Este.

77 *between the king and his son*: possibly an echo of the revolts by the sons of Henry II, who reigned from 1154 to 1189.

77 *white Benedictine*: here probably Cistercian, given the English context.

80 *King of Scotland*: the monarch of the time would have been William the Lion (1143–1214), but he would not have been 'very elderly'.

87 *good horse fair*: as part of his defence policy, Charles I had promoted notable improvements in horse-breeding.

89 *Malpertugio ... name implied*: literally 'evil hole' (with vulgar overtones).

90 *Guelph*: supporter of the papal party, and therefore allied to the Angevins who were expelled from Sicily during the Sicilian Vespers (1282).

90 *King Charles*: Charles the Lame, who reigned from 1285 to 1309. He was the father of Robert of Anjou.

90–1 *King Frederick*: Frederick II of Aragon, proclaimed king of Sicily in 1296, and hostile to the Angevins.

96 *Filippo Minutolo*: the archbishop died in the autumn of 1301, not the summer as Boccaccio implies.

100 *Manfred*: son of Frederick II, he was crowned in 1258, eight years after the death of his father.

100 *Benevento*: decisive battle (1266) which sealed Guelph ascendancy and put the Angevins on the throne of Naples.

105 *Pietro of Aragon*: Pedro III, who seized the opportunity of the Sicilian Vespers (1282) to become ruler of Sicily. See also X. 7.

105 *Ghibelline*: supporter of the Imperial claim to rule Italy (as opposed to the Guelphs, who supported the Papal faction).

111 *expulsion of the French*: the rallying cry of the Sicilian rebels was 'Death to the French'.

113 *Babylon*: see note to p. 39 above.

132 *from French to German hands*: the Holy Roman Empire passed to Otto of Saxony in 962.

151 *ring ... belt*: often employed as love tokens (see III. 3).

159 *lizards*: traditional rivalry between Florence and Pisa extended to insults about each other's womenfolk.

159 *Vernaccia*: powerful white wine with reputedly restorative properties (wine was frequently prescribed by doctors as a medicine).

177 *Agilulf... Teudelinga*: Theodolinda was the wife of Autari, king of the Lombards from 584–90. Agilulf succeded to the throne by marrying Theodolinda, and reigned from 591 to 615. Boccaccio's source is probably Paulus Diaconus, whose plague description was the model for the *Decameron* Introduction.

190 *slubs*: implements used to draw out wool before spinning.

190 *tertiary*: lay brother, not vowed to celibacy or poverty.

191 *Brother Nastagio*: imaginary figure, a byword for over-zealous piety.

192 *Compline*: the religious day was divided into twelve hours, from sunrise to sunset. The hours were grouped in threes, from Tierce (the first three hours after sunrise) to Sexts (six hours), Nones (nine hours), Vespers (the last three hours before sunset). Compline was the last service at sunset.

200 *Minutolo*: same family as the dead archbishop in II. 5.

201 *Catella*: one of the beauties named in the *Caccia di Diana*, but not the real wife of Sighinolfo.

201 *another lady*: traditional smoke-screen; see Dante, *Vita nuova*, V.

214 *cast them before swine*: Matthew 7: 6.

214 *Christ began to do and to teach*: see Matthew 4: 23; Mark 1: 21; Luke 4: 18.

217 *ring*: traditional love-token: see II. 9.

219 *Signoria*: Magistracy.

221 *green silk costume*: the colour symbolized the triumph of hope.

226 *Old Man of the Mountain*: Hasan-ben-Sabbah, fabled leader of the 'Assassins', who was reputed to drug his followers to make them carry out terrorist missions. Boccaccio's information probably derives from Marco Polo's *Milione*.

230 *... you shall call him Benedict*: the abbot's words parody the angel's address to Zacharias, father of John the Baptist (Luke 1: 13).

246 *Chastelaine de Vergi*: thirteenth-century French poem about a love-intrigue, very popular in Italy.

249 *lack even a title*: indicating that the novellas circulated before the compilation of the *Decameron*.

254 *Apostle's words*: in the Epistle to the Philippians 4: 12.

266 *sink of all iniquity*: traditional rivalry meant that the Florentines had few kind words for Venice.

272 *a man dressed as a savage*: genuine folk ritual in medieval Venice.

279 *Guglielmo II*: William the Good, king of Sicily from 1166 to 1189. Roger (Ruggieri) and Constance (Costanza) were, however, his uncle and aunt.

279 *Barbary*: the Maghreb region of North Africa.

280 *Granada*: an anachronism, as the Moorish kingdom wasn't founded for another century.

280 *gauntlet*: chivalric symbol of an unbreakable pledge.

285 *in a dream*: revelatory dreams were a frequent narrative device in medieval fiction. Boccaccio's *Amorosa visione* and *Corbaccio* take the form of extended dream sequences, but nearly all his work contains such episodes.

286 *song we still sing today*: complete versions of the song still survive in Neapolitan popular culture: it tells of a woman lamenting the theft, by a man, of her pot of basil—the sexual innuendo is very clear.

288 *roses, white and red*: traditional symbols of resurrection, and therefore employed at funerals: Boccaccio is hinting at the outcome of the novella.

289 *golden collar . . . chain*: traditional poetic imagery for amorous devotion.

294 *the church of San Gallo*: site of monthly pardon, mainly frequented for fleshly rather than spiritual indulgences.

302 *Roussillon . . . Cabestaing*: Boccaccio's account embroiders on Provençal tales of the late twelfth-century troubadour Guillem de Cabestaing's love for his lord's wife.

306 *Salerno*: seat of the most famous medical school of the early Middle Ages.

306 *Chinzica*: see II. 10.

317 *estampidas*: lively dances of Provençal origin.

317 *pro tribunali*: Latin for 'before the court'.

318 *Galeso*: Greek, as Boccaccio imagined, for 'milksop'.

330 *Carapresa*: 'kindly taken', a name that augurs well for Costanza.

331 *Muli Abd Allah*: two Tunisian monarchs bore this name, the first (1249–77) and the second (1295–1309).

334 *only the rump*: the seat of the papacy had been moved to Avignon in 1309.

334 *Anagni*: town south of Rome. The highways around Rome were notorious for banditry.

338 *Orsini*: powerful and ruthless Roman clan, one of whose members became Pope Nicholas III (1277–80).

342 *nightingale*: traditional motif for nocturnal passion.

348 *Emperor Frederick*: Frederick II laid siege to Faenza in 1240/1.

349 *scar*: traditional recognition motif, like the wife's mole in II. 9.

351 *Marin Bolgaro*: famous shipping magnate still alive in Boccaccio's youth.

351 *Federigo, King of Sicily*: Frederick II of Aragon, who ruled Sicily from 1296 to 1337.

351 *La Cuba*: Norman-Arab building, still standing in Palermo.

354 *Ruggero di Lauria*: Frederick's admiral from 1296–7.

356 *good King William*: William the Good, who ruled from 1166 to 1189.

356 *Armenian coast*: Boccaccio is clearly referring to 'lesser' Armenia, the vulnerable enclave centred round Adana in present-day Turkey. At the time it had active trading links with Italy.

357 *storm*: the pretext is modelled on the cave episode in *Aeneid* IV, where Dido and Aeneas profit from more than shelter.

363 *Friday . . . May*: Friday was traditionally the day of penitence (which receives an unorthodox interpretation in this novella), and May was the canonical month for love and visions.

363 *mastiffs*: Boccaccio is probably thinking of the punishment of the wastrels in *Inferno* XIII, who are pursued by dogs through the wood of suicides.

372 *man who's in need of money . . . lacking a man*: echoes a famous saying of Themistocles, which Boccaccio probably got from Cicero, *De officiis*, II. 20, or from Valerius Maximus, VII. 2.

374 *Saint Verdiana*: medieval Italian saint, reputed to have fed the two serpents sent to her cell to tempt her.

381 *to sing a song*: Dioneo suggests several popular and highly suggestive ditties, quite genuine, and certainly not of the kind to be sung in respectable company.

383 *Troilus and Cressida*: reference to Boccaccio's own *Filostrato* (composed *c.*1335).

385 *Geri Spina*: real-life character—see following note.

387 *Geri Spina . . . Pope Boniface*: Spina was head of the Guelph faction in Florence, and therefore an ally of the Pope, Boniface VIII whose reign (1294–1303) coincided with active intervention in Florentine politics.

387 *certain important matters*: probably the unsuccessful peace negotiations between Blacks and Whites in June, 1300, in which Dante participated. The Blacks and Whites were originally factions of a clan dispute in Pistoia, but the names came to replace the terms Guelph (Black) and Ghibelline (White) when the Ghibellines were defeated (1266) and the Guelphs split into two camps. Dante, for instance, was a White Guelph, and therefore an imperialist.

390 *Dego della Ratta*: Diego de la Rath, Robert of Anjou's vicar (lieutenant) in Florence in 1305, 1310, and 1317/18. Given the references to other characters, the action of the novella must take place either in 1310 or 1317/18.

390 *Palio*: Famous race, originally for a prize of cloth (*palio*).

394 *Baronci*: see VI. 6.

394 *Giotto*: the celebrated painter (1266–1337) whom Boccaccio may have met whilst in Naples (1329–33).

394 *the Mugello*: country district north-east of Florence.

399 *to the dogs*: Matthew 7: 6.

400 *French royals*: proverbial expression for haughtiness.

402 *clubs*: the ten young narrators of the *Decameron* are effectively reconstituting one of these *brigate* when they head for the country together.

402 *Guido Cavalcante de' Cavalcanti*: famous poet and mentor of Dante, who places Guido's father in the part of Hell reserved for Epicureans (atheists), *Inferno* X. The punishment was to be incarcerated in burning sarcophagi.

404 *Saint Antony*: third-century founder of monasticism, patron saint of diseased animals: the Antonian friars, however, had a very bad reputation for 'door-to-door salesmanship', concentrating their efforts on the gullible.

404 *Cicero . . . Quintilian*: classical rhetoricians, personifications of eloquence for the Middle Ages.

405 *Solomon or Aristotle or Seneca*: here ironically paraded as examples of wisdom.

417 *Lucifer*: here, Venus.

419 . . . *Dame Matilda's Hymn*: popular prayers designed for the laity.

420 *Te lucis*: the hymn contains the line, 'may the spirits of the night retreat'. For the *Intemerata*, see also II. 2.

423 *get into this barrel here*: Boccaccio takes Peronella's stratagem straight out of Apuleius, *Golden Ass*, IX. 5.

427 *Name me a friar who doesn't!*: another instance of conventional friar-bashing, like Tedaldo's outburst in III. 7.

431 *Saint Ambrose*: not the Church Father and author of hymns, but the local medieval Saint Ambrose Sansedoni (1220–86).

447 *to ensure that he was beaten*: losing at chess as a seductive gambit was a topos already present in Arthurian literature: Boccaccio had previously employed it in *Filocolo*, IV.

447 *Bolognese veins*: the carnality and sensuality of the Bolognese was proverbial.

451 *marrying above his station*: social climbing by marriage was common: see also III. 3.

456 *Countess Guidi*: a byword for aristocratic status.

458 *Lydia*: Boccaccio's story is a rewriting of the medieval French *Comoedia Lydiae*, possibly by Matthew of Vendôme.

467 *godparents*: see VII. 3.

469 *Three days later*: ironic reference to Christ's resurrection; see Luke 24: 7.

471 *Palemon and Arcites*: reference to Boccaccio's own *Teseida* (composed 1340/1).

475 *Philippa*: see VI. 7.

475 *uncommon trait*: Boccaccio echoes anti-German sentiment shared by Petrarch, *Canzoniere* CXXVIII.

478 *Song of the Mill-Race*: the song, sexually highly suggestive, was very popular at the time.

482 *Calandrino*: this minor fresco painter, historically documented, is one of the few characters to appear in more than one novella (see also VIII. 6, 9; IX. 3, 5). He forms part of a distinctly 'Florentine' sub-text of practical jokes and urban humour.

483 *tabernacle*: the work was contracted to Lippo di Benivieni in 1313, which gives an approximate date for the action of the novella.

483 *Berlinzona* . . .: Maso's verbal pyrotechnics are worth comparing with those of Cipolla in VI. 10.

484 *the Mugnone*: tributary of the Arno.

490 *priests* . . . *friars* . . . *clergy at large*: see e.g. I. 4; III. 4, 7, 8, 10; IV. 2; VII. 3; VIII. 2.

494 *from the Marche*: it really was the case that many of the governors came from 'wild and woolly' regions, and resentful 'city-slickers' like the Florentines used to look on these provincials as unsophisticated boors, hopelessly out of their depth.

500 *trial by bread and cheese*: a parodic recreation of the judicial process called 'ordeal', effectively a kind of selective torture.

503 *Paris*: renowned, even in Italy, for its faculty of theology, and for philosophical studies generally.

503 *better acquainted with profound scholarship*: Boccaccio is echoing a widespread maxim that the wise were especially vulnerable to being rendered foolish by love.

504 *the greater value*: this jealousy ploy is analogous to the one adopted by Ricciardo III. 6.

528 *Bologna*: there being, at the time of the story, no university in Florence (the university's much-heralded foundation-date of 1321 is purely notional), Florentines searching for professional qualifications were forced to go to Bologna. Popular sentiment held that Bolognese graduates were not quite as clever as they thought they were; see Bonagiunta Orbicciani's barbed comments in the last lines of the sonnet 'Voi c'avete mutata la mainera'.

530 *Michael Scotus*: philosopher and Frederick II's astrologer (d. *c.* 1236), who translated and commented on Arabic Aristotelian treatises. His popular reputation was, however, that of a magician and geomancer.

532 *Hippocrates and Avicenna*: celebrated medical writers, one Greek, one Arab, whose works were part of the standard curriculum for physicians.

542 *public baths*: notorious in the south as places of assignation: see also III. 6.

551 *Florentine merchants*: the sly intelligence of the Tuscans was, and is, proverbial in Italy.

552 *whatever story you please*: thus returning to the pattern of Day One.

554 *oak-leaf garlands*: symbol of Jupiter, here standing for balance and self-control.

555 *mortal risks*: Boccaccio is here poking fun at the conceits of love poetry that overstressed the links between *eros* and *thanatos*.

556 *they'll never fulfil*: a common device in medieval literature; see also X. 5.

563 *boorish judge*: see VIII. 5.

564 *urine sample*: along with the pulse, the most common diagnostic technique for a range of illnesses, not specifically for pregnancy. Machiavelli makes full comic use of it in his play the *Mandragola*.

567 *Cecco Angiolieri and Fortarrigo*: the former a robust poet (*c.*1258–1313) of some renown, who had a reputation as a bit of a rake. One of his surviving sonnets is addressed to Fortarrigo.

573 *rebec*: a medieval forerunner of the fiddle, held on the lap and played with a bow.

574 *citherns*: a plucked instrument, forerunner of the guitar.

584 *Ciacco*: Dante refers to him as a celebrated glutton in *Inferno* VI.

585 *Corso Donati*: celebrated and terrifying leader of the Black Guelphs, who was murdered in 1308—just in time, according to some.

585–6 *Filippo Argenti*: another violent Florentine potentate of the Black faction, and a deadly enemy of Corso. Boccaccio's placing of Ciacco, Corso, and Filippo in the same novella reflects their mention together in the *Inferno* VI episode of the gluttons.

588 *Talano's recalcitrant wife*: see IX. 7.

589 *Laiazzo in Armenia*: already referred to in V. 7.

599 *King Alfonso*: Alfonso VIII of Castille (1155–1214) whose fame for fighting the Moors was only eclipsed by his reputation for generosity.

602 *Ghino di Tacco*: outlaw (d. sometime in the decade 1303–13), mentioned by Dante in *Purgatory* VI as having murdered one of his enemies during an open court session. He was in open rebellion against Boniface VIII.

602 *interdicts and excommunications*: an interdict was a blanket territorial ban on religious activity, designed to put popular pressure on recalcitrant rulers; excommunications were individual bans on receiving the sacraments, effectively rendering the excommunicate 'non-persons'.

605 *nothing petty-minded about the Pope*: Boccaccio's attitude is markedly different from Dante's visceral hostility (see *Inferno* XIX and XXVII).

605 *Knight Hospitaller*: ironic reference to Ghino's therapeutic skills, and his performance as 'host' to the abbot.

606 *Cathay*: Northern China, fabled in the West for its fantastic wealth. Boccaccio was probably inspired by accounts of Kublai Khan in Marco Polo's *Milione*.

612 *Lombards' noblest cities*: 'Lombard' here not in the modern, restrictive sense, but as a term for the whole of Northern Italy: Bologna is of course the capital of the Romagna.

612 *Gentile de' Carisendi*: from a celebrated Bolognese family whose name still graces one of the 'leaning towers' of the city. Boccaccio had already written a version of this story in Book IV of the *Filocolo*.

619 *I want a garden*: traditional impossibility topos, or *adynaton*. As in the previous novella, Boccaccio had already exercised himself with this story in Book IV of the *Filocolo*.

623 *Charles of Anjou*: the victor of Benevento (1266), founder of the Angevin line in Naples, and one of Boccaccio's 'heroes'.

625 *Ginevra the Fair and Isotta the Blonde*: romantically literary names, both of queens loved by feudal inferiors: Guinevere, King Arthur's wife, and Isolde, lover of Tristan.

627 *Manfred*: Manfred was defeated at Benevento (1266).

629 *the French were driven out of Sicily*: during the Sicilian Vespers (1282).

629 *Pietro of Aragon*: see note to p. 105 above.

629 *Catalan fashion*: jousting was an imported sport in Italy, arriving in the wake of a foreign nobility.

635 *Caesar Octavian*: Octavian's appointment as triumvir dates from 43 BC; the title Augustus was conferred by the Senate in 27 BC.

642–3 *the Greek propensity to rant and rage*: Greeks generally had a very bad press in the medieval West—see also Dante, *Inferno* XXVI.

652 *Emperor Frederic I*: Frederic Barbarossa, Holy Roman Emperor from 1152 to 1190. The Third Crusade, in which Barbarossa lost his life, was launched in 1189.

652 *Saladin*: see note to p. 39 above.

659 *ring*: conventional symbol of faith, but also a recognition device; see III. 7.

659 *a great epidemic*: no mention of such an episode is made in the chronicles of the Third Crusade, though later writers like Giovanni Villani mention sickness.

659 *San Pietro in Ciel d'Oro*: celebrated church in Pavia.

668 *phantom cat . . . tail down for it*: a not-so-veiled allusion to male erection; see VII. 1.

686 *billy-goat*: an oblique reference to homosexuality.

# THE WORLD'S CLASSICS

*A Select List*

HANS ANDERSEN: Fairy Tales
*Translated by L. W. Kingsland*
*Introduction by Naomi Lewis*
*Illustrated by Vilhelm Pedersen and Lorenz Frølich*

ARTHUR J. ARBERRY (Transl.): The Koran

LUDOVICO ARIOSTO: Orlando Furioso
*Translated by Guido Waldman*

ARISTOTLE: The Nicomachean Ethics
*Translated by David Ross*

JANE AUSTEN: Emma
*Edited by James Kinsley and David Lodge*

Mansfield Park
*Edited by James Kinsley and John Lucas*

Northanger Abbey, Lady Susan, The Watsons, *and* Sanditon
*Edited by John Davie*

HONORÉ DE BALZAC: Père Goriot
*Translated and Edited by A. J. Krailsheimer*

CHARLES BAUDELAIRE: The Flowers of Evil
*Translated by James McGowan*
*Introduction by Jonathan Culler*

WILLIAM BECKFORD: Vathek
*Edited by Roger Lonsdale*

R. D. BLACKMORE: Lorna Doone
*Edited by Sally Shuttleworth*

KEITH BOSLEY (Transl.): The Kalevala

JAMES BOSWELL: Life of Johnson
*The Hill/Powell edition, revised by David Fleeman*
*Introduction by Pat Rogers*

MARY ELIZABETH BRADDON: Lady Audley's Secret
*Edited by David Skilton*

ANNE BRONTË: The Tenant of Wildfell Hall
*Edited by Herbert Rosengarten and Margaret Smith*

CHARLOTTE BRONTË: Jane Eyre
*Edited by Margaret Smith*

Shirley
*Edited by Margaret Smith and Herbert Rosengarten*

EMILY BRONTË: Wuthering Heights
*Edited by Ian Jack*

GEORG BÜCHNER:
Danton's Death, Leonce and Lena, Woyzeck
*Translated by Victor Price*

JOHN BUNYAN: The Pilgrim's Progress
*Edited by N. H. Keeble*

EDMUND BURKE: A Philosophical Enquiry into the Origin of our Ideas of the Sublime and Beautiful
*Edited by Adam Phillips*

FANNY BURNEY: Camilla
*Edited by Edward A. Bloom and Lilian D. Bloom*

THOMAS CARLYLE: The French Revolution
*Edited by K. J. Fielding and David Sorensen*

LEWIS CARROLL: Alice's Adventures in Wonderland *and* Through the Looking Glass
*Edited by Roger Lancelyn Green*
*Illustrated by John Tenniel*

CATULLUS: The Poems of Catullus
*Edited by Guy Lee*

MIGUEL DE CERVANTES: Don Quixote
*Translated by Charles Jarvis*
*Edited by E. C. Riley*

GEOFFREY CHAUCER: The Canterbury Tales
*Translated by David Wright*

ANTON CHEKHOV: The Russian Master and Other Stories
*Translated by Ronald Hingley*

Ward Number Six and Other Stories
*Translated by Ronald Hingley*

JOHN CLELAND:
Memoirs of a Woman of Pleasure (Fanny Hill)
*Edited by Peter Sabor*

WILKIE COLLINS: Armadale
*Edited by Catherine Peters*

The Moonstone
*Edited by Anthea Trodd*

JOSEPH CONRAD: Chance
*Edited by Martin Ray*

Typhoon and Other Tales
*Edited by Cedric Watts*

Youth, Heart of Darkness, The End of the Tether
*Edited by Robert Kimbrough*

JAMES FENIMORE COOPER: The Last of the Mohicans
*Edited by John McWilliams*

DANTE ALIGHIERI: The Divine Comedy
*Translated by C. H. Sisson*
*Edited by David Higgins*

DANIEL DEFOE: Robinson Crusoe
*Edited by J. Donald Crowley*

THOMAS DE QUINCEY:
The Confessions of an English Opium-Eater
*Edited by Grevel Lindop*

CHARLES DICKENS: Christmas Books
*Edited by Ruth Glancy*

David Copperfield
*Edited by Nina Burgis*

The Pickwick Papers
*Edited by James Kinsley*

FEDOR DOSTOEVSKY: Crime and Punishment
*Translated by Jessie Coulson*
*Introduction by John Jones*

The Idiot
*Translated by Alan Myers*
*Introduction by W. J. Leatherbarrow*

Memoirs from the House of the Dead
*Translated by Jessie Coulson*
*Introduction by Ronald Hingley*

ARTHUR CONAN DOYLE:
Sherlock Holmes: Selected Stories
*Introduction by S. C. Roberts*

ALEXANDRE DUMAS *père*:
The Three Musketeers
*Edited by David Coward*

ALEXANDRE DUMAS *fils*:
La Dame aux Camélias
*Translated by David Coward*

MARIA EDGEWORTH: Castle Rackrent
*Edited by George Watson*

GEORGE ELIOT: Daniel Deronda
*Edited by Graham Handley*

Felix Holt, The Radical
*Edited by Fred C. Thompson*

Middlemarch
*Edited by David Carroll*

HENRY FIELDING: Joseph Andrews *and* Shamela
*Edited by Douglas Brooks-Davies*

GUSTAVE FLAUBERT: Madame Bovary
*Translated by Gerard Hopkins*
*Introduction by Terence Cave*

A Sentimental Education
*Translated by Douglas Parmée*

FORD MADOX FORD: The Good Soldier
*Edited by Thomas C. Moser*

BENJAMIN FRANKLIN:
Autobiography and Other Writings
*Edited by Ormond Seavey*

ELIZABETH GASKELL: Cousin Phillis and Other Tales
*Edited by Angus Easson*

North and South
*Edited by Angus Easson*

GEORGE GISSING: The Private Papers of Henry Ryecroft
*Edited by Mark Storey*

WILLIAM GODWIN: Caleb Williams
*Edited by David McCracken*

J. W. VON GOETHE: Faust, Part One
*Translated by David Luke*

KENNETH GRAHAME: The Wind in the Willows
*Edited by Peter Green*

H. RIDER HAGGARD: King Solomon's Mines
*Edited by Dennis Butts*

THOMAS HARDY: A Pair of Blue Eyes
*Edited by Alan Manford*

Jude the Obscure
*Edited by Patricia Ingham*

Tess of the D'Urbervilles
*Edited by Juliet Grindle and Simon Gatrell*

NATHANIEL HAWTHORNE:
Young Goodman Brown and Other Tales
*Edited by Brian Harding*

HESIOD: Theogony *and* Works and Days
*Translated by M. L. West*

E. T. A. HOFFMANN:
The Golden Pot and Other Tales
*Translated and Edited by Ritchie Robertson*

HOMER: The Iliad
*Translated by Robert Fitzgerald*
*Introduction by G. S. Kirk*

The Odyssey
*Translated by Walter Shewring*
*Introduction by G. S. Kirk*

THOMAS HUGHES: Tom Brown's Schooldays
*Edited by Andrew Sanders*

HENRIK IBSEN: An Enemy of the People, The Wild Duck, Rosmersholm
*Edited and Translated by James McFarlane*

Peer Gynt
*Translated by Christopher Fry and Johan Fillinger*
*Introduction by James McFarlane*

HENRY JAMES: The Ambassadors
*Edited by Christopher Butler*

A London Life *and* The Reverberator
*Edited by Philip Horne*

The Spoils of Poynton
*Edited by Bernard Richards*

RUDYARD KIPLING: The Jungle Books
*Edited by W. W. Robson*

Stalky & Co.
*Edited by Isobel Quigly*

MADAME DE LAFAYETTE: The Princesse de Clèves
*Translated and Edited by Terence Cave*

WILLIAM LANGLAND: Piers Plowman
*Translated and Edited by A. V. C. Schmidt*

J. SHERIDAN LE FANU: Uncle Silas
*Edited by W. J. McCormack*

CHARLOTTE LENNOX: The Female Quixote
*Edited by Margaret Dalziel*
*Introduction by Margaret Anne Doody*

LEONARDO DA VINCI: Notebooks
*Edited by Irma A. Richter*

MIKHAIL LERMONTOV: A Hero of our Time
*Translated by Vladimir Nabokov with Dmitri Nabokov*

MATTHEW LEWIS: The Monk
*Edited by Howard Anderson*

JACK LONDON:
The Call of the Wild, White Fang, and Other Stories
*Edited by Earle Labor and Robert C. Leitz III*

NICCOLÒ MACHIAVELLI: The Prince
*Edited by Peter Bondanella and Mark Musa*
*Introduction by Peter Bondanella*

KATHERINE MANSFIELD: Selected Stories
*Edited by D. M. Davin*

MARCUS AURELIUS:
The Meditations of Marcus Aurelius
*Translated by A. S. L. Farquharson*
*Edited by R. B. Rutherford*

KARL MARX AND FRIEDRICH ENGELS:
The Communist Manifesto
*Edited by David McLellan*

CHARLES MATURIN: Melmoth the Wanderer
*Edited by Douglas Grant*
*Introduction by Chris Baldick*

HERMAN MELVILLE: The Confidence-Man
*Edited by Tony Tanner*

Moby Dick
*Edited by Tony Tanner*

PROSPER MÉRIMÉE: Carmen and Other Stories
*Translated by Nicholas Jotcham*

MICHELANGELO: Life, Letters, and Poetry
*Translated by George Bull with Peter Porter*

JOHN STUART MILL: On Liberty and Other Essays
*Edited by John Gray*

MOLIÈRE: Don Juan and Other Plays
*Translated by George Graveley and Ian Maclean*

GEORGE MOORE: Esther Waters
*Edited by David Skilton*

MYTHS FROM MESOPOTAMIA
*Translated and Edited by Stephanie Dalley*

E. NESBIT: The Railway Children
*Edited by Dennis Butts*

ORIENTAL TALES
*Edited by Robert L. Mack*

OVID: Metamorphoses
*Translated by A. D. Melville*
*Introduction and Notes by E. J. Kenney*

FRANCESCO PETRARCH:
Selections from the Canzoniere and Other Works
*Translated by Mark Musa*

EDGAR ALLAN POE: Selected Tales
*Edited by Julian Symons*

JEAN RACINE: Britannicus, Phaedra, Athaliah
*Translated by C. H. Sisson*

ANN RADCLIFFE: The Italian
*Edited by Frederick Garber*

The Mysteries of Udolpho
*Edited by Bonamy Dobrée*

The Romance of the Forest
*Edited by Chloe Chard*

THE MARQUIS DE SADE:
The Misfortune of Virtue and Other Early Tales
*Translated and Edited by David Coward*

PAUL SALZMAN (Ed.):
An Anthology of Elizabethan Prose Fiction

OLIVE SCHREINER: The Story of an African Farm
*Edited by Joseph Bristow*

SIR WALTER SCOTT: The Heart of Midlothian
*Edited by Claire Lamont*

Waverley
*Edited by Claire Lamont*

ANNA SEWELL: Black Beauty
*Edited by Peter Hollindale*

MARY SHELLEY: Frankenstein
*Edited by M. K. Joseph*

TOBIAS SMOLLETT: The Expedition of Humphry Clinker
*Edited by Lewis M. Knapp*
*Revised by Paul-Gabriel Boucé*

STENDHAL: The Red and the Black
*Translated by Catherine Slater*

LAURENCE STERNE: A Sentimental Journey
*Edited by Ian Jack*

Tristram Shandy
*Edited by Ian Campbell Ross*

ROBERT LOUIS STEVENSON: Kidnapped and Catriona
*Edited by Emma Letley*

The Strange Case of Dr. Jekyll and Mr. Hyde
*and* Weir of Hermiston
*Edited by Emma Letley*

BRAM STOKER: Dracula
*Edited by A. N. Wilson*

JONATHAN SWIFT: Gulliver's Travels
*Edited by Paul Turner*

A Tale of a Tub and Other Works
*Edited by Angus Ross and David Woolley*

WILLIAM MAKEPEACE THACKERAY: Barry Lyndon
*Edited by Andrew Sanders*

Vanity Fair
*Edited by John Sutherland*

LEO TOLSTOY: Anna Karenina
*Translated by Louise and Aylmer Maude*
*Introduction by John Bayley*

War and Peace
*Translated by Louise and Aylmer Maude*
*Edited by Henry Gifford*

ANTHONY TROLLOPE: The American Senator
*Edited by John Halperin*

The Belton Estate
*Edited by John Halperin*

Cousin Henry
*Edited by Julian Thompson*

The Eustace Diamonds
*Edited by W. J. McCormack*

The Kellys and the O'Kellys
*Edited by W. J. McCormack*
*Introduction by William Trevor*

Orley Farm
*Edited by David Skilton*

Rachel Ray
*Edited by P. D. Edwards*

The Warden
*Edited by David Skilton*

IVAN TURGENEV: First Love and Other Stories
*Translated by Richard Freeborn*

MARK TWAIN: Pudd'nhead Wilson and Other Tales
*Edited by R. D. Gooder*

GIORGIO VASARI: The Lives of the Artists
*Translated and Edited by Julia Conaway Bondanella and Peter Bondanella*

JULES VERNE: Journey to the Centre of the Earth
*Translated and Edited by William Butcher*

VIRGIL: The Aeneid
*Translated by C. Day Lewis*
*Edited by Jasper Griffin*

The Eclogues and The Georgics
*Translated by C. Day Lewis*
*Edited by R. O. A. M. Lyne*

HORACE WALPOLE : The Castle of Otranto
*Edited by W. S. Lewis*

IZAAK WALTON and CHARLES COTTON:
The Compleat Angler
*Edited by John Buxton*
*Introduction by John Buchan*

OSCAR WILDE: Complete Shorter Fiction
*Edited by Isobel Murray*

The Picture of Dorian Gray
*Edited by Isobel Murray*

MARY WOLLSTONECRAFT:
Mary *and* The Wrongs of Woman
*Edited by Gary Kelly*

VIRGINIA WOOLF: Mrs Dalloway
*Edited by Claire Tomalin*

Orlando
*Edited by Rachel Bowlby*

ÉMILE ZOLA:
The Attack on the Mill and Other Stories
*Translated by Douglas Parmée*

Nana
*Translated and Edited by Douglas Parmée*